AFTERBLIGHT CHRONICLES
AMERICA

WWW.ABADDONBOOKS.COM

An Abaddon Books™ Publication
www.abaddonbooks.com
abaddon@rebellion.co.uk

This omnibus published in 2011 by Abaddon Books™,
Rebellion Intellectual Property Limited,
Riverside House, Osney Mead, Oxford, OX2 0ES, UK.

10 9 8 7 6 5 4 3 2 1

Editor-in Chief: Jonathan Oliver
Desk Editor: David Moore
Junior Editor: Jenni Hill
Cover Art: Mark Harrison
Design: Simon Parr & Luke Preece
Marketing and PR: Keith Richardson
Creative Director and CEO: Jason Kingsley
Chief Technical Officer: Chris Kingsley

ISBN (UK): 978-1-907992-13-1
ISBN (US): 978-1-907992-14-8

Printed in the US

INTRODUCTION

WELCOME TO THE END OF THE WORLD

So VIRTUALLY EVERYBODY is dead, all the major cities are either on fire, being looted, or home to roving gangs of blood-thirsty criminals, or all three, and the world has gone to hell. Reasons not to be cheerful? Well, not really, because that's not the approach we ever intended to take with *The Afterblight Chronicles*. This series of post-apocalypse science-fiction is more *Mad Max 2* than *The Road*: while the end of the world is certainly a daunting and terrifying prospect, for the survivors it provides a brave new world of adventure and opportunity. This, then, is the approach that the three authors presented here have taken.

Simon Spurrier was the very first *Afterblight* author. Mainly known for his comic work on *2000 AD*, Simon's approach to prose mixes his eye for grand visuals with a talent for snappy dialogue. The hero of *The Culled* (who is never named) is a mean son-of-a-bitch who will happily shoot first and ask questions later. His quest takes him deep into a broken America to confront the lunatic leader of the sinister religious organisation, The Apostolic Church of the Rediscovered Dawn. When I requested a novel packed full of crazy gangs, Spurrier more than delivered the goods, with a bad guy who is perhaps one of the most vile creations in post-apocalyptic fiction.

Rebecca Levene's *Kill or Cure* features the partner of our hero from *The Culled.* What gives Rebecca's novel an interesting edge is the fact that her protagonist, Jasmine, is schizophrenic; haunted by a corrupting Voice, born of the gene therapy that saved her life. Rebecca builds on the world described by Spurrier to produce a novel that is every bit as gutsy and entertaining, with yet more crazy gangs and tinpot dictators.

Finally we come to Al Ewing's *Death Got No Mercy.* Al's original pitch for this novel was 'A man goes to San Francisco and kills everybody.' Basically Al set out to write the most violent novel he could. This being a work by Ewing, though, what you can expect is a crazy adventure written with wit and a borderline-insane sense of invention. When I asked Al what he wanted on the cover of his novel his response was 'a man punching a bear in the face.' God bless him, that's exactly what artist Mark Harrison delivered (on page 439 of this volume). *Death Got No Mercy* is a suitably disturbed closer for this collection of fiction from the end of the world.

So, although the world as you know it may be over, there's no need to sulk or channel your inner emo. Simply strap on your shotgun and head out into the wastes, for out there is where true heroes are made.

Jonathan Oliver
Editor-in-Chief, Abaddon Books
March 2010

THE CULLED

SIMON SPURRIER

CHAPTER ONE

Somewhere over the Atlantic, with a canyon of heavy clouds spilling open below like a hungry gullet, I decided enough was enough.

"Fuck it," I said.

I'd moved three times already. Like a trail of cheap Pollock imitations I'd converted the aisle-seats of rows one and two into sticky red monuments to my own mortality, and already First Class Reclining Lounger 2B was streaked with enough congealing blood to saturate the upholstery. I felt a lot like I was dying, and if not for that boring old voice spitting from the back of my mind – *don't you fucking give up, soldier* – the idea might even have seemed alluring. The pain killers we'd lifted from the storage lockers at Heathrow appeared to have achieved exactly squat – except maybe to enhance the growing desire to puke – and try as I might to sit still, the ugly little 'O' of puckered gore just below my left shoulder was refusing to clot. It dripped and oozed, and soaked through everything I wore, and got into places I'd rather it didn't. Last time I took a piss in the cubicle behind the cockpit – door missing, safety lights plundered years ago – I looked down and for one horrible second thought I'd caught a stray in my undercarriage. Even the relief at disproving *that* theory hadn't occluded the pain.

So. The decision crept up slowly enough, but lacking for any idea of what sort of reception committee we'd get at LaGuardia, I couldn't put it off indefinitely. I chewed my lip for a while, munched philosophically on a thought-displacing can of dog food from my pack and decided to have a dig.

They teach you self-triage in the first year of training, but it's rudimentary stuff. The basic attitude is that if you get wounded on a mission you've already fucked up the whole 'covert' gig, so what happens to you afterwards is entirely *your* problem. I remember the staff medic they sent over from the MOD squinting thoughtfully at the roomful of grunts ranged out in front of him, with an expression that said: *Oh, you poor bastards.* He spent two weeks lecturing us on sterilisation and euthanasia policy, and when he got to the part about bullet-removal simply sighed over his clipboard and said:

"Just make sure you're dosed to the *gills.*"

Sir, yes sir, etc, etc.

I stood up, refusing to concede to the shakes in my legs, and made my way forwards. The pack we'd loaded with tranqs and stimms – and every other bloody thing we could find – sat in the co-pilot's chair next to Bella. From the glassy eyes, and beads of sweat tangled in her hair, I guessed she'd been staying awake care of amphetamine pick-me-ups, and she barely looked around as I rummaged for a cocktail of my own. She'd come through the firefight at Heathrow unscathed – mostly by hiding behind me – and looked like she was taking the piloting pretty seriously. Knuckles white on the control stick, breath laboured, lower lip creased where she'd bitten too hard. The amount of empty vials scattered on the floor, I hoped she didn't give herself a heart attack before we hit the tarmac at the other end.

Hit. Bad choice of word.

I found a stack of hypoderms marked 'Bliss' – stylishly bound with an elastic band – and shrugged. Since the whole 'End of the World' shtick a veritable smorgasbord of crazy narcotics had bubbled to the surface – repressed military Perf-Es, street drug mixtures and DIY chembrews – and who the hell was left to say what they all did? But 'Bliss' sounded better than 'infected screaming agony,' so I told myself *side-effects be damned* and yanked one out of the bundle.

The elastic band snapped and stung me on the cheek. Very fucking macho.

"Might be out for a bit," I grunted, hoping Bella hadn't noticed, unwrapping a hypo and ambling back to the cabin. If she heard me at all, she didn't answer.

I took time setting myself up. Despite the engine's growl and the unsettling *bong-bong*s of warning instruments from the cockpit, the empty plane was an eerie sort of place. Like a dried-up river, or a morgue without a corpse, you take away the thing that makes something what it is – in this case the passengers required to make this thing more than just a big flying cigar-tube – and all that's left is a hollow promise.

Oh, and a wounded man getting shitfaced on 'Unknown Drug X,' with an unsterilised pair of tweezers and a roll of nylon twine set aside.

I took it easy with the dosage. No telling what's normal, what's an OD, what's instant death. The candyfloss comfort came up like a warm bath, sliding along each limb in turn, and for a second I worried I'd spiked myself with some barbiturate crap that'd put me to sleep before I'd even poked into the wound. But then it hit my brain like a slap, airburst an embarrassingly orgasmic sensation into my crotch and told me – over and over, like a scratched vinyl playing in my ear – that everything was going to be okay.

Seriously good shit.

I was already jabbing about in the exposed muscular layers of my upper arm before it even occurred to me I should be in agony. I guess that in some abstract sense I *was*, but like watching a bad film through the wire-caged windows of the TV shops they used to have on Tottenham Court Road, it was a distant and silent sensation; and it didn't take much to turn around and focus elsewhere.

Don't you fucking give up, soldier.

Sir, no sir, etc, etc.

When it came out, grinding against something I'm pretty sure was bone, trailing strands of half-congealed blood like cobweb threads, the bullet was an unimpressive little thing. For the amount of pain it'd caused, I was half-expecting an AMRAAM sidewinder with barbed fins, so the amorphous blob of iridescent snot that emerged was curiously disappointing. I *plinked* it down on my foldout meal tray, squirted a thick loop of military-issue antiseptic into the crater and got to work with the twine. The whole thing was a botched job – I knew that – already oozing pus and still refusing to stop bleeding, but in the absence of an emergency unit, doctor, nurse, or person with the slightest clue what they were doing, it was a work of fucking *art*.

I tied the last knot, broke the cord with my teeth, slapped an antiseptic dermal pad over the top and wound a thick strip of torn cloth around it several times.

Then I stopped, felt smug, allowed myself a moment or two of self-satisfaction and passed out.

Maybe the 'Bliss' was mildly hallucinogenic. Maybe I was delusional from loss of blood and suppressed pain. Maybe the sleep deprivation was getting to me and screwing with my thought process.

Or maybe I've just got a lot of nasty shit clogging up my imagination.

Whatever the reason, slumped there in my seat aboard an empty 737, thirty-five thousand feet above the Sargasso Sea, my unconscious brain shat a kaleidoscope of blurred irrelevance: contradictory and clashing symphonies of half-remembered experience. I felt sick.

It felt a lot like rewinding through my own life. It felt a lot like viewing my history in cinematoscope vibrancy, except with DVD extra features and a meaningless musical track, on a TV screen with the colour mixers fritzed to shit.

It took a while to stabilise (whatever meaning *time* had) and when the psychedelia surrendered and the ugly memories came into uglier focus, I would have done anything to wake myself up – except that when you're asleep you don't *know* it. The human brain's annoying like that.

It all went in reverse. It jumped about and skipped important stuff and generally confused the hell out of me. I don't know for sure, and Bella wasn't much good for paying attention right then, but I'm guessing I scrabbled about inside the cabin like an epileptic sleepwalker. Should have remembered to buckle up.

In my head, I was back in London, running and panicking, and –

Chattering rifles, out in the darkness. Muzzle flash behind the slats of scripture-daubed blast-shields and swabs of knackered concrete cracking open as strays struck the earth.

Heathrow. It'd gone downhill since the Culling Year. Planes stood like dead sentries; plundered for glass or metal, listing at strange angles where tyres had punctured or wheel columns had snapped: all marks of whatever violence had first swept through the compound five years before.

Back in the centre of the city, the random aggregate of survivors and raggedymen I ever actually spoke to had dismissed such scars – everywhere you looked – with a shrug and a philosophical grunt.

"Cullin' Year," they'd say. As if that covered – and excused – every anarchic sin, every thoughtless act of destruction that went along with a city entering self-destructive free-fall. All the looting. The thieving. Murdering. Raping. Burning the shop fronts, clogging the river with car wrecks, hoarding tinned foods, slaughtering police horses, coughing and stumbling and spitting blood from lungs on the verge of liquefaction.

Waiting for the nukes that never came.

The Culling Year. It was a crazy time.

Here and now in the airport, the devastation was all that much harder to ignore. The precision of the planes, the carefully mapped elegance of the compound: all distorted, broken, salvaged and left to withdraw behind bristly weeds and the slow creep of rust. The violence had ended years ago, but its effects stood untouched, like alabaster monuments to the insanity of an entire population.

Over my shoulder, the gunfire faded out. I kept running, dragging Bella along by either her coat or her hair – I hadn't stopped to check – and headed for the one aircraft that was patently undamaged: repainted in the garish blue of the Apostolic Church of the Rediscovered Dawn.

Neo-Clergy. Currently trying to kill me.

Somewhere, out between the hungry darkness of the airstrip and the humming lights strung up around the tower, someone shouted. A rasping burst of biblical condemnations, to cover the clattering of clumsy hands reloading rusted hardware. Even further away, booted feet raced towards the racket with the sort of haste one learns to associate with hardcore well-trained military types, and I reminded myself with a groan that most of the barracks emptied their survivors into the Church during the year, with the casual abandon of men swapping one institution for another. I wished the shouting voice would shut the fuck up.

I was a heretic, apparently. A defiler, a philistine, a walking abomination, a devil fit only for immediate destruction and above all else a sneaky motherfucker. I recognised the dulcet tones of the same fat monk I'd 'befriended' earlier that day – playing unscrupulously on the hints of his sexuality he'd betrayed in coy glances and coquettish gestures – then unceremoniously clubbing him over the head with the stock of a rifle when he turned to fetch me some water.

It was a way in, anyway.

And then Bella was shrieking something behind me – "the bag! the bag!" – and as I turned to assess what was going on, the Kalash' opened up again. Something dull and hard happened to my left arm, and I was pirouetting in my place without meaning to.

"Oh," I said, wondering why cracked concrete was pressed against my cheek. "Oh."

And Bella screaming, and the engines of the aircraft powering up with a whine, and the throb of more guns, and pain and confusion and drugs and more blood than I've ever seen before, and –

Bong-bong.

The aircraft, flying itself, chiming out warnings about who-knew-what.

I half-opened my eyes; a fissure of light strong enough to spot the curved steel struts of underchair braces, the lifejackets stowed in wire compartments beneath each one, and an ancient packet of dry roasted peanuts. Empty, of course.

Back in the present.

You're on the floor, soldier.

Addled thoughts turned over lazily, wondering how long I had before the hostess came and told me to get up, whether I'd barfed on anyone's hand luggage, whether I could ask someone to get me a coffee. I think reality would have asserted itself pretty soon after that, if the Bliss hadn't flexed in my veins again.

Another proto-climax, building in my groin. Another rush of shivering oddity, and the most distant reports of pain in my left arm, before –

The signal.

This was before Heathrow. Shit - this was the reason for Heathrow. This was before the Neo-Clergy and Bella and all that.

This was lying alone on my palette, stretched out in the corner of Comms Room 221A, in the eastern wing of the Vauxhall Cross SIS building. Dozing, staring out at the river and wondering at all the other raggedy survivors, curled up in tube stations and mall stockrooms, clustered round oil drum fires and squabbling over rats and pigeons.

I wasn't smug at my own warm little womb of safety – not exactly – but it came close.

London was ugly before *the Year. Afterwards, it was...*

Different.

Let me tell you: a city looks strange without lights. At night, the sky is black and star-pebbled, just like anywhere else, and if you've lived in London any length of time you know that's wrong. *The sky should be yellow-green. Blazing with light pollution, oozing out of the constant clouds. It was like the Cull had stolen the very colour from the sky; flattening all that was civil, all that was advanced. Look at the world now, it said:*

Eco-friendly, yeah. But not much fucking fun.

Curled there in my room, mind empty, chin resting on a heap of stolen pillows, it was a well-practiced thought process. Five years into this dismal new reality, and there was nothing much left to say about it.

Nothing new to get excited abo...

The signal sparked the consoles to life with a neon-storm and a chatter of code, and I jumped like I'd been electrocuted. Down to reserve power, the building wouldn't even let you switch the bloody dimmers on, let alone the systems. There must be some kind of automated kicker, powering-up for the duration of an incoming signal. Clever.

Five years, they'd stood silent. Consoles growing dusty, covered in tinned-soup spillages and stolen porn, or whatever other luxuries I'd plundered on any given day. For five years the antennae on the roof – concealed ingeniously within blocky, deco architecture – had stood inert, listening to a silent spectrum.

Five years I'd slept in the same room, getting by, scavenging up and down the riverbanks by sunlight, creeping back at night like a bear to its den. I'd always ignored the others who'd adopted the same routine.

Old administrators or low-level secretaries, I guess, lucky enough to remember the entry codes to let them in, but never getting past the divisional checkpoints inside the central lobby. All automated. All closed.

But not to me. Not to senior personnel.

Up here there was still the ghost of power. Low-level illuminators at night, self-sealing doors. Solar panels on the roof, I think, though I'd never found them. There was even a functioning vending machine down in the armoury, although the coffee tasted like plastic and the tea frothed with mouse shit. Still, here was safety. Here were sealed doors built to shrug-off a missile-strike, a tunnel beneath the river to the heart of bleak, deserted Whitehall and all the accoutrements of my old life.

Files. Computers. Weapons.

And now a signal.

I thought it was a joke first of all, but that was daft. Who amongst my friends – and there were never many of them to start with – had the means, let alone the diseased sense of humour?

Nobody. Nobody was left. Nobody senior enough to know the codes, nobody who knew how to tap in up here. Not since the Chief choked on the mushy debris of his own lungs and the two surviving directors were mobbed en route *to a COBRA meeting. Since then, camaraderie amongst ex-employees had been pretty low on the agenda.*

The code chattered away like a chorus of angry crickets, transferring to the flickering screen in unbroken columns; flashing green as each security clearance was challenged, negotiated, allowed.

And then a word, immersed in the stream of data.

It scrolled by so quickly I almost missed it. Eyes wide, I convinced myself I was mistaken, and ignored the prickles of sweat wriggling out of my forehead as I hunted it down again.

There.

++PANDORA++

My stomach lurched. Something happened to my heart that felt a lot like a black hole opening in my rib cage. I staggered, I think, because suddenly I was sitting down with my hands out, pressed on the edge of the desk like a safety-bar holding me into the carriage of a rollercoaster.

The word raced past again, bottom to top, a pixellated burst of... of what?

Choirs of angels, rays of light, divine intervention. Who the bastarding hell knows? It wasn't possible, *but there it was.*

And then the final security clearance was offered, the linkage was established, the vocal channel opened with a greasy pop, and I was listening to static.

And someone breathing.

And a voice that said: "Are... are you there?"

I recognised it.

"Oh," I said. It was all I could manage. It came from the one deep-buried part of me that – alone – was able to function in the face of this revelation. The rest of my brain was a stunned fish, flapping on a pier, waiting for a rock to pound it to paste.

"Oh..."

And then the reserve power died, the channel closed, the screens winked to blackness one by one, the lowlights perished and the great black silence rolled in to gobble the building like never before.

I remember losing it. Just a little.

I remember storming and breaking things and snarling. I remember the blood so thick on my mangled knuckles, from beating on the walls and the consoles, that they dripped across the carpet. But most of all I remember the feeling swelling up inside me; the feeling I'd forgotten, cast off like a dead skin all those years ago. The feeling that said, loud and clear in the base of my skull, wrapping iron knuckles around me, straightening my posture and giving me no room to argue:

Don't you fucking give up, sold –

Something touching my face.

I came out of the delusion/flashback far quicker this time, and with the scream of engines abusing the edge of my consciousness I remembered where I was without much preamble. It felt like I'd managed to pull myself up into another of the plane's chairs – still as groggy as fuck – and, nylon be praised, the blood had stopped trickling down the inner edge of my arm. I wondered how long had passed.

Somewhere an alarm was whooping quietly, a polite emergency. I almost laughed at the idea, and decided, with a half-hysterical chuckle, the drug was still in me.

Concentrate.

I felt another light touch, a gentle *something* brushing against my lips and, with sluggish realisation, tried to form words.

"No, Bella..." I mumbled, struggling to open my eyes. "S'not... s'not *likethat...*"

The plane seemed to shiver. She touched my lips again.

"*Toldyou...*" I slurred, aware of the spittle hanging off my chin and the cotton wool dampening every movement. "I'm not... not *innarstd* inthatshit..."

Then my ears accustomed themselves to the whine of the plane (higher pitched than before?), filtered it out like layers being peeled clear, and picked up the mantra of garbled words hammering out of the distance, lurking beneath.

"...fuck..." it hissed. "Fuck fuck fuck... oh God, fuck no... what's... what's... oh, fuck..."

Bella. Still in the cockpit. In trouble.

So who's – ?

I rammed my eyes open, combat conditioning superheating every instinct, muscles tensing from head to toe... and wished I hadn't. My senses shortfired, adrenalised my fragile waking mind, and kicked the last vestiges of the Bliss into action. It came on like a storm of white noise, wrapped under and over everything I could see and hear and touch, and my last impressions before I slid under for a third time were of a tangled, tentacled *thing* stretching down towards me from above, brushing sensually against my lips.

Air mask. Emergency procedure. The plane's in trouble.

Shit.

Alarms and swearing and airquakes, adjustments to fickle impermanent gravity –

A siren raced past outside. Two, maybe three weeks ago I would have bothered to get up and check what it was. Police, fire, ambulance, mountain-sodding-rescue?

Now there wasn't much point. They were all *ambulances.*

This was... before. At the start. This was before The Thing went airborne, before the mass graves and gasmasks, before they firebombed St Mary's and sent out the A-Vee body carts with the speakers and the flamethrower turrets ("...deposit all corpses upon the pavement... do not approach this vehicle... deposit all corpses upon the..."). This was at the very beginning, when the hysteria hadn't had time to get going, when people clung to their fragile little hopes of stability, when no one had quite figured out how bad things were going to get and the brass were playing it cool. No need for alarm, blah-fucking-blah.

This was five years before I got the signal.

I slumped into an armchair, alone in my flat, listening to the alarm dopplering its way into the distance, and swirled the ice in my drink. For some reason the tinkling of cube against glass put me in mind of the street café in Kabul – tanbur and sarinda music, heavy scent of melon-molasses in shisha pipes – where two months before I'd broken two of my fingers.

I winced at the memory. Getting old, maybe. The mark's guards had soaked up both clips of hollow point .22, and in the end I had to choke the poor bastard to death as he did his best to prise my fingers off his windpipe.

Krak, krak, gurgle.

Don't you fucking give up, soldier.

Sir, no sir, *etc, etc.*

I took a sip of scotch. Glanced around, gloomy.

The flat wasn't up to much, if I'm honest. A smattering of CDs on shelves, expensive and unnecessary gadgets to sharpen kitchen knives and open wine bottles, an aquarium with no fish (who'd feed them?) and a double bed that was rarely double booked.

I believe "unlived-in" is the phrase.

Sometimes I'd feel inclined to pluck shirts and socks – fresh – out of the drawers in the bedroom, and drape them artfully about the place, like they'd been thrown off or forgotten about. Designer slobbery, for Christ's sake. How tragic was that?

Well it was all going to change, and there was no avoiding that. I glanced at my watch and took another sip, wondering why the removal van was so late, and fidgeted.

Another ambulance, another streetside-dirge for the slumbering city. I think even the throb of a helicopter (air ambulance, sure as eggs are eggs) passing somewhere in the background hum of London.

On the TV a BBC anchorman was busily disseminating the day's developments.

"...and was joined by the health secretary in re-issuing his assurances that all possible efforts are being made to contain and counter the epidemic. When challenged by protestors on the alleged withholding of public inoculations, the prime minister appeared visibly shaken; assuring members of the press that viable treatments could not be issued until scientists understood more about the nature of the disease.

"In a parallel incident, the Pentagon was today sealed off as protestors converged upon Washington, DC demanding action against soaring cases of infect –"

I hit the 'standby' stud like it had offended me.

Another ambulance, outside. Sounds of people arguing in the next flat along.

Someone coughing in the room above. Not *a good sign.*

I was woken up an hour later – unaware I'd even fallen asleep – by a shrill double-bleep from my mobile phone. A text message. I flipped the oyster-lid open, spotted the name in the 'Sender' register and hurried to open the message, feeling a vague sense of unease that I could neither shake nor explain.

SOZ. *It read.* CHANGE F PLAN.

BIN CALLED IN.

MAYBE 2 WKS?

U WAIT?

I stared at it for about an hour. Like watching a football replay, hoping against hope you'll spot something you missed last time, hoping it'll all turn out differently.

"Oh," I said. To myself. To the invisible fish in the tank, maybe. Maybe just to the phone, which kept switching off its illuminated display every time I left it alone. "Oh."

Another ambulance went past.

AND I WOKE up for absolutely the last time in the blood-streaked shuddering cabin of a hijacked Boeing 737, feeling like a volcano had taken a shit in my skull, wondering why everything was rushing backwards and forwards.

This time, it really *was* Bella. Gripping me by the moist rags that passed for my clothing. Shaking me back and forth, so the base of my skull rebounded over and over off the plasticated upholstery of the seat.

"...know you can *hear* me, you *fuck*, you *wake up*, you *wake up*, you..."

I mumbled something inarticulate. Her vocal barrage didn't stop, just shifted gear like a machine heading straight for burnout.

"...we're going to *die*, you prick, we're going to *crash*! The *gear*, okay? It didn't *deploy*! Bloody autopilot's taking us *down* and, fuck, we're going to *die*..."

I wondered if I had enough time to take more 'Bliss.'

CHAPTER TWO

I'VE ALWAYS HAD a thing about landings.

Before the Cull, before the streets filled with dead/dying/hoping-for-death bodies, before the survivors realised what was going on, before the public accusations and riots and whirlwinds of violence and lynchings and general bad shit, I was a frequent flyer.

Under less sinister circumstances I would have built up enough air-miles to take me as far as Jupiter, but when every flight is accompanied by a new passport, new name and new identity, it's difficult to keep track. In my line of work, there wasn't much by the way of perks. Not that it mattered much. Not any more.

The point is, I'd been on enough journeys to know the routine. The sudden gees of the take-off run, the misery of getting a seat next to the toilet, the Sod's Law ratio of passengers in the neighbouring seat (normal people to weirdoes, 1 to 3).

And every time, at the culmination of every tedious stint, after hours and hours of staring glumly at the inner surfaces of a brightly lit tube, when the captain's voice crackled in hidden speakers to announce the imminent touchdown, *every time* my stomach took a little lurch.

I know all the arguments. I've *had* them all. Usually with the weirdo next to me.

"...still statistically the safest way to travel..."

"...more likely to get hit by a bus than..."

Blah-blah-*blah*.

Call me a pessimist, but there's something about the image of 40,000kg of tightly compacted metal and plastic descending at catastrophic speed towards a strip of rock, which is not – let us be quite clear about this – renowned for its *softness*, that does my head in. There's something about 200-plus people strapped together in a cylinder with fins, undertaking a controlled stall in mid-air, that gets my palms a little sweaty.

Paint me irrational.

Five days before I woke up from the Blissout in the cabin of a doomed 737, with Bella shaking my head and telling me we were going to *die*, she and I had been making plans.

Talking it through, sat in a burnt-out pub in a burnt-out street on the outskirts of Heathrow, eating feral rabbit and an optimistic harvest of wild berries. Bella had told me about autopilots. I'd only found her the week before and we were still getting used to each other. To me she was someone with piloting experience, too dosed out of her head to care about the hazards, with her own private reasons for wanting to get Stateside. I didn't waste any energy caring what they were. Not then. It meant she'd help me without needing payment, cajolement or threats. Bonus.

To her, I was just the gun-toting psycho that'd get her aboard.

"Thing is," she'd said, picking blackberry pips out of her teeth, "an autopilot can do pretty much everything."

"You what?"

"S'right." She waved a dismissive hand. "I mean... obviously you need a *real* pilot too. Keep an eye, re-plot, react to shit. But basically the auto's doing the tough stuff. Following the course, regulating height and speed, all of that. If it weren't for the takeoff thing I figure they would've got rid of the crew altogether, given a year or ten." She scowled, adding the silent:

If not for the Cull, I mean...

Still a common thing, in conversation, talking about the future like there still *was* one.

"The takeoff thing?" I repeated, confused.

"Yeah. Don't ask me why. Trainers never explained it, and I was only on the course three weeks. Needs a human touch, I guess. Too many variables, too much down to chance."

I nodded, faintly relieved. The idea that each time I'd taken off in the past my life had been in the hands of a glorified calculator hadn't sat well.

Until:

"Hang on. *Only* takeoff?"

Bella had smiled at that. She'd cadged a cigarette off me earlier (I don't smoke, but currency's currency) and now she lit it carefully, tar drawling lazily past her teeth.

"Only takeoff."

"Then... the landing's... ah..."

"Yep." Another evil little grin, blowing out smoke like a squid venting ink, then a shrug. "Not *always*. Most pilots'll do it themselves. Matter of faith, I guess. But say it's raining, or there's mist on the runway. Hit some buttons, sit back, Bob's your uncle."

"Fuck."

"Yep."

"So when we, ah..."

"Heh, heh."

She had a pretty laugh, all things considered. She was far more prone to sniggering nastily, which got on my nerves, but still. It's not like there was much to laugh about.

"When we fly," she said, "you can bet your last soggy Marlboro I'll be using the auto as much as I can. Trust me, it's the more reliable option."

Needless to say, this conversation had not filled me with confidence.

At around a thousand feet, with the alarms hitting an unbearable crescendo and a visible gash of smoke rising past the starboard windows, the full stinking reality of the situation leeched its way past the Bliss hangover and punched me between the eyes.

I was flying aboard a plane belonging to a notoriously unforgiving sectarian movement, which hadn't been properly maintained or serviced in five years, which had an unknown quantity of fuel in its reserves, a terrified junkie at the controls who'd never progressed in her training beyond a computerised flight simulator, and a catastrophic amount of damage to part or parts unknown of its undercarriage.

And it was being landed, single-handed, by a geriatric computer.

"Oh fuck," I said. "We're going to die."

Bella stopped shaking me.

"S'what I've been trying to SAY!" she screamed, eyes bulging.

For a moment or two we stared at each other, with nothing but the irregular whine of the engines and the spasmodic whooping of alarms between us. Then we burst into laughter.

Adrenaline does funny things.

Bella's laugh didn't sound all that pretty just then.

As NEAR AS I can tell, the auto brought us in on target.

I wasn't watching closely – the seat I'd buckled myself into was set some way back from the cockpit on the grounds that if things *did* get ugly the further forwards one sat the uglier they'd be – but in snatched glimpses through the open doorway I could make out the distant scar of what might be an airstrip, burnished in the bronze light of the afternoon, bordered on one side by a blurry haze of outbuildings and on the other by a bright mirror of water. To me it seemed to be directly ahead and low on the horizon, which I can only assume is the best place for an airstrip to be.

Bella sat next to me, singing freaky little nursery rhymes, refusing to talk.

Listing vaguely to the right, even through the muddy soup of my senses (ironically the pain from my arm had returned to full strength long before my instincts had), I sat grimly prepared for the wingtip to clip the tarmac, shearing off the entire thing and sending us cartwheeling – trailing fuel and smoke – like a colossal Catherine Wheel.

Or maybe the tail would dip, and we'd ricochet up like a throwing knife on the backspin, somersaulting up and over until the cockpit nosed into the rock like a blunt javelin, shattering every surface and filling the cabin with atomised glass.

Or maybe the starboard engine would blow on impact. Maybe we'd know nothing about the crash at all except an exquisite burst of fire; a supernova to shred every window, every seat, and every fragile little bone in our bodies.

Maybe we'd hit a building.

Maybe we'd over-fly the runway and bury ourselves, full tilt, into the mass of service yards and hangars cluttering the distant reaches of LaGuardia. Maybe we'd topple down into the mid-island water, venting bubbles as the dark swarmed up around us.

Maybe we'd...

Oh, fuck.

Having an imagination is never a good thing in a desperate situation.

"– in the tree top... when the wind blows, the cradle will –"

"Bella?"

Distant bushes through the windows at the edge of my vision.

"– when the bough breaks, the cradle will fall –"

"Bella – shut the *fuck up*..."

The horizon bobbed into view on both sides. The tarmac came up.

"– down will come ba –"

Kroom.

Sparks. Alarms screaming like abandoned babies.

Everything shuddered. A backblast of air funnelled down the cabin from ahead, peppered with glass and stone, and my neck twisted so hard I yelped in shock. Grass and distant buildings snickered past outside the window, but not in a straight line. We were curling on the runway, half-deployed landing gear screaming and twisting in protest beneath us, rolling us sideways, careening in a cloud of molten metal and whirligig embers. Spinning off the tarmac.

A sudden moment of weightlessness, and pain all across my midriff as the seatbelt bit. From the corner of my eye I saw Bella rise into the air, pancake-spreadeagle on the ceiling with a cockroach *crunch*, and then back down, nutting a headrest and flipping, upside down, onto her side.

No seatbelt.

Shit.

A bone jarring shudder, and crippled metal twisting with an operatic screech. Through the window beside me, lost behind a grid of contradictory smoke-trails and fluttering debris, I could make out the arrowhead of the wing tilting backwards and up, shearing itself off as the plane barrel-rolled into its slow skid. It ripped clear with a terrifying lurch, sprayed fuel which ignited immediately, and shattered itself magnificently across the tarmac like a neon waterfall. The metal of the fuselage – four seats in front of me – buckled with a shriek, shattering all the glass down the left side and vomiting smoke into the cabin. Everything went black and toxic, and even through the acrid fog and my own desperate coughing I could hear the battered impacts of the plane's death throes. It snarled and groaned its way across the last of the runway, ripping gouges of rock with an angle-grinder roar, then dipped with another lurch onto the grassy rough. Bella groaned somewhere in the murk.

Time started to return, piece by piece. Sparks drooled.

And – slowly at first, but gathering speed as inertia surrendered to the shifting weight – we rolled. Landing gear comprehensively AWOL, single remaining wing arcing up and over the fuselage like a shark's dorsal, ceiling bowing and sagging then snapping straight as it took the strain. My seat swapped verticality for an abrupt horizontal, lifting the whole cabin like a theme-park ride, sharp-edged seatbelt constricting me again.

The second wing slapped at the ground with a bowlike shudder and snapped off. Like some cylindrical juggernaut the fuselage rolled across it, breaking apart at the seams as it went.

Inside: tumbling chaos.

Debris dropping then lifting, blood rushing to and from eyeballs, hands swapping between lap and forehead.

Bella flapped like a dying fish, *thud, thud, thud*, off ceiling and floor with each new rotation. If she was still alive, she didn't look it. Nothing much I could do to help.

We seemed to be slowing down.

Then something detonated behind us. The all pervading jet-whine of a long-lost engine maxed out with a painful hiss and – *oh fuck oh fuck* –

striated everything, inside and out, with shrapnel. Metal was punctured. The craft rocked and shunted forwards, heat-blast roiling back from the mangled tail, and hacked at the rags of my bloody clothes. Something stung my knee. My face bled. What few windows remained exploded like froth on a wave, and I had the fleeting impression of singed grass surfing past the shattered porthole as we rolled again. Something sharp and long punched itself through the metal beside me, coming to rest a scant foot from my side: a shattered stanchion from the rough beside the runway, picked up like a thorn.

And finally, like a great engine throbbing itself into dormancy, the airplane came to an appalled halt; listing on its back like a clapped-out whore, waiting for another bout. Smoke plumed on every side, and the quiet crackle of flames tugged at my punch-drunk consciousness.

"Shit." I said.

And Bella's inert body – half resting on the back of a chair directly above my head – surrendered to gravity, flopped in mid-air with a boneless kick, and impaled itself on the jagged spike in the wall.

I don't think I'll ever forget the sound it made.

THE FIRST INSTINCT was to get out.

All that Hollywood bullshit about fuel tanks spontaneously going up like Krakatoa – long after the crash – could be safely ignored. The second engine had fallen silent shortly after the mad tumbling stopped, killing with it any obvious danger of explosion. But the irrational panic remained like an ember in my guts, and the fires already lit were plentiful enough to be scary. With the smoke gradually thickening and the slippery cut across my forehead leaking into my eyes, I thrashed about to get to the seatbelt buckle, finding a sudden unshakeable *need* to be away from this bastarding plane.

Away from Bella's limp little body. Staring straight at me.

Don't you fucking give up, soldier.

Sir, no sir, etc, etc.

It was stealing over me by degrees that I'd *done* it. I'd got to the States. I'd fucking *done it.*

And yeah, there had been sacrifices and hardships. Yeah, there had been pain and chaos and untidy scrambling. Yeah, there had been death.

But you don't do what I used to do, for fifteen years, without seeing some or all of that at some point. You don't get to slink like a shadow between the raindrops, killing and cutting behind the scenes of a hundred and one foreign powers, without learning how to bottle it all away. Screw it up into a venomous little ball and dump it, derelict and forgotten, somewhere in the poisonous wastes of the unvisited mind.

Anything it took to get-on-with-it. Mental conditioning. Emotional disconnection. Whatever.

I'd got to America. Nothing else mattered.

Though, to be fair, the victory was soured somewhat by the attendant uncertainty of what I'd find out there. Five years ago, before the news-shows stopped broadcasting and the emergency radio fell silent, before the Internet became an unchanging frieze – dying piece by piece as humming servers across the world sputtered out – it had looked like the US had not fared well.

Certainly they'd caught a nuke or two.

Listen: it turns out nothing brings out the aggression in a population like a shared disaster. If you believed the projections they made back at the start – and I did – the AB-virus took out 93% of the world's population. That's five-point-nine billion people, for the record, bent-double with the pain, spitting mangled clusters of alveoli out of their lungs and into their mouths, bleeding from eyes and ears and arse, dying by fractions.

You hear that?

Five. Point. Nine. Billion.

It's a bigger number than I can imagine – and that wasn't even the end of it.

There was a time – perhaps a month or two – when the governments and networks and lines of communication were still nominally functional. Stripped down, understaffed, kept afloat by the efforts of men and women who'd watched nine out of ten of their colleagues drop dead, who'd been left blinking in the glare of responsibility with no clue, no hope and no idea.

I guess it was inevitable some stupid fuckwit would start throwing accusations.

The AB-virus was manufactured, they said.

Biological weaponry, they said.

State-sponsored terrorism hiding behind pandemic disaster, they said, and they pointed fingers and found 'proof,' and let the tension escalate. The news was all but dead by the time the missiles dusted off, but we heard about it. Even in London.

I like to think nobody targeted Britain because our diplomatic status was untarnished, our potential involvement in any biological assault was laughable, and our impartiality prevented any accusations being aimed at us.

Yeah. And pork-chops come with wings.

No, we were spared because there were no wankers left in Whitehall to stick their heads over the parapet and join the row. No one left to contribute to the growing worldwide squabble. No one left to press Big Red Buttons.

After the Cull, any poor fucker left in charge was either lynched by the mob or ran and hid. It was a very British way of dealing with disaster.

It was also, now, half a world away.

I drew myself painfully through the interior of the destroyed plane and tried to assess. From the heat and glare ebbing through the largest of the ragged rents in the fuselage it looked like a pleasant day, which was something of a novelty after five years of acid rain and London skies.

I threw a last look back at Bella – hating myself for not having the energy to lift her off that spike; for not pausing a moment longer to at least close her eyes. But no... that same feeling of being bottled-up; trapped in a cage. Waiting for *something* to come and get me.

It's a cliché, but you don't get any good at what I used to do without letting your instincts guide you. That and the fact that, in my line of work, there was *always* something coming to get me.

Logic suggested the Neo-Clergy would be nearby. This was, after all, their plane. It was also *their* route, plotted ahead of time into *their* autopilot, landing us (for want of a better word) at *their* chosen destination. They could be relied upon to take exception to the way I'd treated their property.

I probed a hand into the pocket of my coat, seeking reassurance.

Still there.

Good.

But what else to expect? A nuclear desert? A radioactive wasteland haunted by the insane and the dying? Cancerous wildlife staggering on tumourous legs, lurching up to feast on the new arrival?

Probably too much to hope New York had changed that little.

I'd stowed the supplies pack in a luggage locker near the cockpit. Working my way forwards, past twisted seats and dangling airmasks, it was easy enough to retrieve. But as I tried to heft it onto my shoulders, grunting under my breath, it occurred to me exactly how weak I was. My head rushed for a split second – the legacy of the Bliss – and I staggered, overbalancing awkwardly.

"Bollocks!" I hissed, falling onto my arse.

It saved my life.

A stuttering burst of semi-auto rang out from somewhere behind me, clawing a neat geyser of shattered plastic and fibrous insulation from the ceiling/wall above my head.

Exactly where I would have been.

I dropped and rolled, textbook fast, before my brain even caught up. A chatter of gunfire followed – I guessed from the same source – shaking the air like a giant fan and tugging on my raggedy coat as it ripped a hole in the trailing edge. I swatted out the singed fabric before it caught light, finding myself hidden by the padded shield of a sideways seat, and let the adrenaline take over.

Identify the enemy.

"Where the *fuck*," a voice shouted, New York accent thicker than a sergeant's skull, "are the *kids*?"

Ah.

The kids.

"I can explain!" I shouted, keeping the terror thick in my voice. "Just... just don't shoot me! *Oh God, oh God.* It wasn't me! They sent me to tell you!"

"Who sent you?"

"T-the..." *Think fast.* "The Bishop! There was a problem! W-with the kids, I mean. They wanted me to explain, s-so they..."

"What problem? Where the *fuck* are they?"

Get a direction. Zero in.

"*Answer* me! Where *are* they?"

Further along the cabin. Standing in the aisle. Must have climbed in through the missing tail.

Alone?

"Please, I... I just... *oh God...*" I knocked out my best sob. I hammed it up like a true thesp. I poured every false fear into that gurgling pitiful little voice, and when the figure appeared slowly on the edge of my vision, creeping forwards with his lips pursed, it was set in a posture of laughable unwariness. His gun was lowered.

He rolled his eyes when he saw me, cowering and shivering in bloody rags with snot pouring off my nose.

And the Oscar goes to...

"Pull yourself together," he said, a fraction softer. "Now tell me who the fuck you are or it's..."

I moved faster than my own senses could register. Mental conditioning. Third year training. Biological reactions: without thought or judgement. Zen disciplines with chemical catalysts: reaching down into the subconscious, switching off your abstractions and *dis*tractions, becoming something less and more than rational.

Letting the body take over.

"Hng," he said.

I took out his jugular and carotid with a single sweep of the hunting knife I'd been carrying since Heathrow. More blood, soaking through my coat.

Doesn't matter.

I pirouetted downwards whilst the poor bastard was still wondering where I'd gone, wondering why his voice had stopped working, wondering why only gurgles arrived in his mouth where there should be angry, demanding words.

Three stabs to the ribs. Two directly between intercostals, the third glancing sideways off the breastbone, snapping something with a greasy *pop*, then sliding in as soft as you like.

Stepped back.

Considered a fourth stab upwards from solar plexus, decided it wasn't needed.

Retreated to my cover behind the chair and waited with animal patience for the human parts of my brain to come back on line.

Start to finish, it took about six seconds.

The man stayed upright for another five as his body worked out it was already dead.

He hit the puddle of his own blood like a belly-flopping pig, jerked once or twice, and went still.

I wiped the knife clean on a sleeve and cleared my throat.

There didn't seem to be anyone else around.

CHAPTER THREE

INTERLUDE

THE MAN HAD opted to change his name for the duration of his mission – not that he'd had a lot of choice. It was that or put up with the Sachems nagging him for the rest of eternity.

A week ago he was Rick. Today he was Hiawatha. Go figure.

He gunned the Honda along the main street of a picturesque everytown, enjoying the growl of the old engine – still a perfect melody, despite its hiccups and occasional coughs – and selected a sidestreet at random. Nobody on the sidewalks. No curtains twitching or faces peering over tumbledown walls. Nobody here to see the Mighty Hiawatha passing through.

He supposed he ought to be honoured. It was, after all, a name dredged from the deepest troughs of tribal heroism – belonging first to the great warrior/prophet who reconciled the squabbling nations. Hiawatha – the original – had been friend and brother to the deific Great Peacemaker; a glorious ancestor-totem in his own right and the illustrious architect of the first Great Confederacy. Four hundred years later and the white men still insisted on calling the Union of Five Nations by its insulting handle – the Iroquois – and never gave it another thought.

Ignorance and arrogance. So said the sachems, anyway.

(Cue dull lectures about the Confederacy's 'invention' of democracy, its influence on the US's own constitution, and a hundred-and-one other details, hopelessly out of date, that the clan mothers and their chieftain pets meme-repeated every time anyone was dumb enough to ask a vaguely cultural question.)

Iroquois meant 'Rattlesnakes.' The clan mothers hated it.

Rick (née Hiawatha) rather enjoyed the description. It appealed to the youngster inside him, a sinister sort of moniker to match the leathers and war paints the Tadodaho had given him. Certainly it had more character than the title the Confederacy gave itself *– 'Haudenosaunee': the people of the long houses. Not exactly a name to strike terror into the hearts of one's enemies, particularly when most of the 'long houses' these days were Winnebagos.*

Rick let the bike drift to a halt before an imposing building at a crossroads. It looked like maybe it'd been a courthouse or something grand and prestigious – long ago – but a glistening plastic sign announced its more recent owners to be RAY N' JAKE*, this being their* GENERAL STORE.

Bless.

Rick listened to the engine rumble itself away into silence, wondering if anything was left inside the boarded-up building. His stomach gurgled. He'd have to start worrying about fuel soon too. Either that or stay stranded out here in ghost-town suburbia forever – and a more hellish prospect he could not imagine. He pocketed the keys, and swung himself down onto the sidewalk, flicking his long double-braid out of his eyes. Everything seemed quiet. An overgrown sign – hanging off its rusted pole on the far side of the street – let him know he'd strayed into the curiously-named town of Snow Hand (this on a day of glorious sun and only minor quicksmog), and asked him to drive carefully.

He smirked.

On the subject of misinformative names, he also found it tricky these days to refer to the ubiquitous enemy (i.e.: assholes who persisted in calling the Haudenosaunee the 'Iroquois') by such a simple term as 'The White Man.' It seemed ridiculous. Some of his best friends inside the tribe were white, genetically speaking, and the council had supposedly granted them just as many rights, freedoms and opportunities as its trueblood members. It never ceased to amaze Rick that the 'new' tribesmen – who had eagerly joined the Confederacy since the Cull and were mostly paler than an anaemic goth – seemed utterly untroubled by the constant bitching about the goddamn 'white man.'

It was like they'd resigned from their own race.

Lucky bastards.

His silent perplexity brought a little smile, unbidden, to his face. He was remembering the last night before he left his home village to embark on this ridiculous trip, and his good pal Leicester (formerly a whitebread bank clerk, now a hunter-scavenger with the Kanien'kéhaka lodge), smoking an enormous hash pipe. The dumbass had actually started griping, perfectly serious as only a raging pothead could be, about the 'Pale-Skinned Devils.'

Rick still found himself sniggering at that *one, a week later.*

Snow Hand's unremarkable environs looked unlikely to yield much by the way of food or fuel. Small white and green houses, clad in sycamore and aluminium, nestled into the wooded hills on every side. Pretty much all the trees were dead, Rick noticed, which didn't help the sense of cloying not-quite-rightness. He'd stopped in enough places up and down the I-80 in the last few days to know this was hardly a rarity. Maybe some weird effect of the fallout had taken its toll along the eastern face of the Appalachians. Maybe a lack of rain, or just too much fucking sun, or something in the quicksmog or... or whatever. The forests around here were dead. Not his problem.

Rick squared up to the door of the general store, not letting the little gang of crows squatting on its roof startle him. They – or others like them – had been keeping pace with him for a good fifty miles now, perhaps hoping he'd spontaneously drop dead. It didn't bode well for his hopes of finding food.

The wide window outside the shop had been comprehensively boarded up: first with planks (long since desiccated and crumpled), thereafter with an increasingly desperate array of corrugated iron, chicken wire and a long lost car door.

Impregnable. Ish.

"Hello?" Rick called out, casually drawing a feather-pocked crowbar from his saddlebag, not entirely sure if he wanted to be heard. A fat cat, long since gone feral, glared impudently at him from a weed-choked driveway across the street. He shrugged. At least if there was nothing in the store he might find some lucky tins of pet food somewhere. Or...

He wondered how easy it was to skin a cat...

He had a half-hearted attempt at prising open the door – fat chance – then quickly and efficiently scrambled up the boarded window like a squirrel up a tree, coming to rest on the ledge of an upstairs window, scaring the choir of nosey crows from their holier-than-thou vantage. Iron bars, of all the luck, bisected the window, but the wood was so ancient and the plaster sealing the cavity so rotten that a few hefty swats with the crowbar and some hot-faced brute force was all it took to gain entry.

The way Rick saw it, the harder it was to get into one of these dismal places, the more likely it was there'd be something worthwhile inside. He slipped in, silent as death, gripping the crowbar like a samurai sword.

Whoever had occupied Snow Hand five years ago – Pale Skinned Devils no doubt, ha! – had either died or moved on. Same as most places. Uprooted families, the dead going unburied. Back at the start, when people began to die and the Government said conspicuously less and less about it every day, people had clued-up quicker than the suits had expected. Something big, going down, being kept quiet.

Maybe the townsfolk had even seen the flare-flashes in the night, out across the southeast horizon, as the Sovs or the Saudis or whoever-it-was took out Washington like bleach on a stain. That's the sort of thing that'll kill your community spirit, deader than disco.

Snow Hand. Some of them went east to New York, probably, and no doubt died there. Some went west, over the hills. Probably died too.

Some of the lucky ones maybe fell in with the Haudenosaunee, to stay alive and count their blessings and get on by.

*(*Yeah, *the uncharitable voice of rebellion grumbled inside,* just so long as they respected the goddamn old ways and didn't rock the fucking boat.*)*

Rick checked the rooms of the first floor on automatic, adrenaline burning away like a barely-noticed light. Nothing. Not unless you could eat a child's rat-nibbled dollies, or run a Honda on the contents of a cologne drawer. Taking it as read that the place had been looted before, it was still no surprise to find jewels and gold stashed away, untouched in makeup cases and bedside drawers. Who was going to steal something so useless, after all?

He shouldered the crowbar and made his way downstairs, into the store, sighing as his thoughts turned back to the tribe, wondering what would happen if he just turned around right now and headed home. Fuck the mission. Fuck the Sacred Duty.

Back in the Haudenosaunee, the sachems – forever peering cautiously over their shoulders to check the matriarchs approved – had told him all the 'Nationalistic Crapola' (his phrase, not theirs), all the white man/red man dogma, all the 'Them-and-Us' bullshit: it was a state of mind. The Confederacy had found its place and its path in this topsy-turvy post-Cull world, and anyone who made the effort to stand in their way or interfere was designated 'The White Man' – whatever their skin tone. Simple as that.

Rick would have gone on to point out the flaws in this terminological morass – mainly that it was fucking stupid – except at this point in the conversation the sachems generally parroted the same trite platitude that inevitably cropped-up in the answer to any challenge to the status-quo:

"If it was good enough for the ancestors..."

At the bottom of the stairs he could see the interior of the front door. A heavy-duty lock – well oiled, well tended – had prevented his entry from outside. Hmm.

Actual skin colour, *the Confederacy maintained, didn't matter in the equation any more. How could it, when at least half the modern Haudenosaunee were as Caucasian as they came? They'd been welcomed into the tribes with open arms (altruism or smugness? Rick secretly wondered) and taught the interminable lessons of the past. What mattered, the matriarchs croaked, was not the identity of those practicing the Old Ways, simply that* they were being practiced.

Pushing open a connecting door into the service area, Rick reflected gloomily on how eagerly the new white Iroquois had embraced the lifestyle, the ceremony, the trappings of something culturally genuine. He'd been hearing the same old stories all his life – born and bred on a cockroach-infested reservation – and couldn't remember it ever filling him with the same sense of childlike glee and religious satisfaction as Leicester and the others. Smearing their snowy skins with ash and paint, eschewing modern clothing – and there was plenty of that *about, since the Cull – for old style jerkins and deerskin rags.*

Somehow, deep down in the (plentiful) ocean of his immaturity, Rick had felt betrayed. Jealous, even. How dare they, these interlopers? How dare they show up out of nowhere, join the tribe, and get twice as fucking much out of it as he did?

The problem was this:

He'd spent all his childhood, all his years of education, all his earliest years of adulthood, trying so hard *to be white. How dare the world roll on its head? How dare every bastard suddenly want to be Iroquois!*

The shop smelt of dust and cigarettes, with the faintest tang of ancient alcohol. He pushed through a mildewed bead curtain into the storeroom out the back, and paused to yank cobwebs out of his hair.

Whenever he was in a really *bad mood, Rick tended to call the white Iroquois 'Tourists.' He'd call the quaint little village-lodge a theme park, and loudly offer to take photos of fat Yankees wearing branded ethnic costumes for a mere $5. Then he'd caper about trying to sell make-believe hotdogs, or guided tours of the casino complex cunningly disguised as a wooden longhouse.*

Last time he pulled this routine, one of the Sachems had beaten him so hard he'd had to sleep sitting up for a week... but it had been worth it, just for the look on everyone's face.

The point was... the point was, it was all such a joke! The Confederacy existed – thrived! – because its way of life worked. *In this twisted, devolving excuse for a world, it worked. It worked because its infrastructure remained when everything else collapsed. It worked because it created ties that didn't rely on material benefits or familial ancestry. It worked because it was a shared egalitarian society that would only –* could *only – function when everyone was progressing together.*

Rick was confident about this. He'd been studying social sciences when the Cull began.

That put a stop to that.

The point, the point, the point. The point was there were reasons *for the good old Injuns to swap places with the Pale Skinned Devils as the most stable and viable community, and none of them had anything to do with the old stories and religions and myths. Running and dancing around fires, throwing clods of earth, chanting and smoking and yadda-yadda-yadda.*

Theme park stuff.

Worse still, despite their voluble claims to the contrary, the council simply weren't playing it as fair as they said. Otherwise how in the hell did he, *Rick, a so-called 'pureblood' Onundagaono – who had never given a shrivelled racoon's cock for the history or religion of the Haudenosaunee – been chosen for a sacred role any number of the white tribesmen would have happily killed to fulfil?*

It was, in a word, bullshit.

They'd given him three gifts before they sent him out. That was a headache, too. Sort of mythic: three fabulous tools for a bold knight to take on his quest. Scant goddamn consolation for being thrown to the wolves, in his opinion. It wasn't like any of the gear was even worth much.

From the matriarchs who ran the Confederacy from the sidelines, the bike. XR650L Honda street bike with mismatched tyres, scavenged engine parts and highly unreliable homemade saddlebags. A clapped out piece of shit, by any other name, but they'd been so proud as they wheeled it over. Rick remembered being mystified. The lodges had access to much *better gear than that, but the womenfolk had stared at him so earnestly, puckered faces intense, and warned him of dire misfortune should he desert the vehicle.*

Don't you lose it, *they'd said.* Don't you leave it behind.

Great.

From the sachem council, smiling toothlessly, nodding and gurning, he'd received a packet of the sickly weed the old bastards smoked relentlessly in their shanty lodges. Rick would've appreciated that *one, at least, if the stuff in question wasn't notorious amongst the Haudenosaunee as having some... strange properties. No one knew where the old men grew it (certainly not in the same carefully-cultivated beds as the dope the youngsters raised), or what they added to it, or how it worked. But it did... things.*

Given that they'd sent him on a holy mission, Rick had been quietly astonished that they'd thought it was a clever idea to give him two ounces of dried Brain Death for the ride.

And finally, from the Tadodaho, a tiny bundle of fabric, with something hard at its centre. Rick had been a little more positive about this. He and the Tadodaho had always got along; the old man was alone in all the tribe in being prepared to listen to Rick's gripes and answer them – patiently, infuriatingly, correctly. *Rick had fumbled open the fabric wrapping with excited hands to find...*

A needle. *A silver sliver of metal, like a sewing-pin.*

"Should come in useful, that," the Tadodaho had said, nodding sagely. Rick had felt like the victim of an awful joke.

And now, days later, he could feel the same package, bundled-up in his back pocket. He gripped it vaguely through his leathers, blinking in the low lighting of the dusty store and glancing around himself with the trailing vestiges of his mental tantrum retreating.

He let his jaw hang open.

He'd never seen so many guns in his life.

AN HOUR OR so later – or so it seemed – in the upstairs bedroom full of mouldering dollies and toys, Rick awoke to someone shouting.

Footsteps on the stairs.

Not a good start.

Ungumming his eyelids carefully, the afternoon sun did its meagre best to piss a few half-hearted rays through the quicksmog, between the mouldering frames of the upstairs window, and onto his face.

"Fuck..." Rick mumbled, wiping dribble off his chin. He hadn't meant to fall asleep.

Looking back over the tail-end of the dream he'd been woken from, he supposed he must have been vaguely aware of something coming; the grumbling tone of an engine, the creak of the General Store's front door: all incorporated into some rapidly-diminishing abstraction involving tomahawks painted white, flocks of shrieking crows with heads like hash pipes and a fat cat telling him, in the Tadodaho's whispery voice:

"If it was good enough for the ancestors..."

Well, thanks. Thanks very much, oh glorious old ones. Now *he was good and fucked.*

"Ram?" the voice snarled from halfway up the stairs, chain-smoker-deep and alcohol slurred. "Ram? That you? Where'd you get that pieceashit fucking bike, *man? Looks like it got squirt straight outta the junkyard's prick!"*

Rick visualised his battered ride. The voice had made a pretty fair assessment.

The footsteps on the stairs sounded, now that he thought about it, heavy.

He lifted himself upright as quickly and quietly as he could, still half asleep, and considered his options. None of them looked good.

After finding the cache of guns – pistols, rifles, Uzis, grenade launchers, shotguns, two dusty old mortars and a gargantuan shoulder-rocket hanging off the wall – he'd put two and two together and come up with a single word:

Collectors.

Out here, outside the major cities, in the great field-strewn swathes of American Nowhere bisected and fed by cracked freeways, the Collectors were everywhere. Rick knew only too well who the mercenary bastards worked for, gathering up supplies, weapons, drugs, and...

– he thought of the tribe, whittled away little-by-little –

...and other *things.*

But Collectors were just collectors. That was the point. *As long as you had nothing they wanted, as long as they weren't on some big-assed spree, they'd ignore you.*

As long as you were over eighteen.

As long as you weren't red-skinned.

Shit.

Back in Fort Wayne, and across all the lands of the Haudenosaunee, every day *was a spree. But out here things were quieter. Right? Out here, surely, the Collectors wouldn't* know *about the Blood Anomaly...*

On the other hand, if some psychotic biker got home to his secret stash of hardware to trip over a sleeping injun, it'd be fair to expect he's gonna be pissed.

Rick had therefore placed himself in the upstairs room at the front of the General Store, exactly where he'd climbed in, stolen shotgun in hand. Just a short rest, he'd promised himself. There'd been no food or drink anywhere inside, and whilst an armoury groaning with enough hardware to take out a war party could only be considered an exciting *find, it didn't go far to re-enlivening the flesh. He'd sagged like a nosebag to the floor beside the window, eyes already heavy.*

He'd see anyone coming a mile off, he'd told himself. He had an easy exit if some asshole tried sneaking up, and he'd always been a light sleeper. If something woke him, he'd have plenty of time to react.

Yeah, right. And in the meantime some vicious sounding colossus had pulled up outside, come in through the front door (which meant he came here frequently, which meant he knew about the guns, which meant he almost certainly had *one), and come stamp-stamp-stamping up the stairs to find Goldilocks eating his porridge.*

Metaphorically speaking.

"Ram! Fucksakes, man! You bin shootin' my shit again I'll kick your a *–"*

The door burst open. Something vaguely bear-like – but somehow smart at the same time – reared in the entrance, a silvery covering shimmering. Rick barely had time to see it, let alone react intelligently, but somehow the shotgun was levelled and his finger was on the trigger while sleep was still fogging his thoughts.

In the split second or two before the muzzle roared, he realised the behemoth was human. Facial hair like a dead orang-utan pasted to his head, narcotically unfocused beetle-eyes peering out beneath red-weed eyebrows; a ridiculous bowler-hat perched jauntily atop the thatch. The creature's frame was encased inside an enormous silver puffer-jacket, covered in bright strips of cloth and fluttering pendants; pinstriped office-pants that looked utterly out of place but glaringly showcased tiger striped shin guards and gym socks; goth-spec boots like they'd been dragged off an astronaut in mourning, and – ironically the last thing his eyes fell upon – an outrageously fucking massive machete.

The man looked like a Vietnam vet who'd got a job as a taxman, then gone cuckoo one day in a camping gear shop. It was a lot to take in. Rick didn't even bother.

"Hey!" the man grunted, eyes briefly finding focus.

The shotgun took his right hand off.

Rick was no stranger to firearms, but he yelped quietly at the shotgun's kick and staggered backwards, fighting to line up the second barrel. The grizzled creature barely slowed: fist reduced to a frothing stub of congealing paste and dangling tendons, machete shattered and bent out of shape, hurled away in an expanding cloud of meaty lumps and bony shards. From somewhere inside the crippled mess an artery squirted feebly.

"You're not Raaam!" was the freak's only concession to shock or pain. Even with half his knuckles popping greasily beneath his booted feet, he kept coming.

Totally and completely, Rick decided, out of his skull.

A paw wrapped around the barrel of the gun and yanked it, hard. A wad of sparks and smoke roared somewhere underneath the giant's armpit, knocking a head-sized hole in the plaster behind him and sending Rick jerking backwards again. The gun was wrenched out of his hand, swivelled expertly in the man's remaining fist like a baseball bat, and swatted him across his cheek. Despite the flashes of light and building pain – getting sharp quickly, now – Rick felt that this was somehow unfair.

"I... I shot your fucking hand off..." he muttered, as if trying to remind the roaring monolith above him. Somehow, at some point, his face had got itself stuck to the floor.

Above his head the shadow of the shotgun moved backwards and up; wooden stock brandished like the head of some arcane mace, ready to pulverise his skull. It almost seemed like too much bother to try and roll *aside, but with a sort of half-hearted fatigue he flopped onto his back, curled his head downwards, and held his breath.*

The stock bounced off the floor, above his scalp, with a thud.

Rick stared groggily upwards, peering through the misty haze of arterial ejecta, and kicked the bear as hard as he could right between the legs. This was all happening to someone else, of course: as disassociated from reality as the dream with the tomahawks and crows. Rick fought the urge to laugh.

Real or not, sheer overwhelming damage seemed to be slowly catching up with the giant. The groin trauma had done what no amount of shock or blood loss had managed: making him stagger, retch, and topple to his knees with a sharp crack. The shotgun – empty – skittered away into the corner, and Rick felt himself, as if from a whole world away, pick himself up and dust himself down.

"Raaam...?" the stranger warbled, flopping onto his side like a greasy mudslide, squeezing at the pulsing abortion that had once been his fist, trying to stop the bleeding. Rick stared down at him – at his froth-flecked lips and buzzing eyeballs – and decided that whatever the guy was on, he wanted some.

In fact, an unpleasantly guilty sensation was stealing over Rick like a fart in reverse: he'd broken into someone's home, wrecked their window, stolen their gun...

...and then shot them when they caught him red handed. Not exactly the type of criminal ignobility you'd expect from someone carrying the name of the Mighty Hiawatha.

"A-are... are you okay?" He mumbled, feeling ridiculous, to the sobbing colossus.

The creature focused on him on the third attempt – spasmodic eyeball rotations calming for an instant or two – and scowled, sweat and grease dappling his scarlet forehead.

"You're not Ram," he said, surprisingly softly.

"Uh. No. No, I'm not. Look, I'm really s..."

"Where's Raaam?"

"I don't know. Who's Ram?"

"Raaaymond."

"Oh. I see. I..." A vision bobbed into Rick's mind: the glittering plastic sign dangling just outside the window. "S-so, uh... So you'd be Jake?"

The fat man's eyes became suddenly still, brows bunching together. "Jake?" he said.

"Yeah."

"Jake's dead. I'm Slip."

Rick coughed, wondering if he should perhaps offer some sort of medical care but wishing he could be a million miles away. Instead, scrabbling about for something to say – anything! – he blurted:

"What, um. What happened to him?"

"Dead."

"Yeah, you sa..."

"Screwed-uppa mission. Let the kiddies getta wayaway. Bosses inna Ay-pos-tol-ic-Church got pissy. Blamed him, see? So I fucked him inna eyes."

"Um." Rick cleared his throat. "What?"

"Pulled 'em out. Best bits. Juicy. Likealikealikea lychee, *Ram says."*

Oh yeah. That was the other thing.

Collectors.

Weren't too fussy where the next meal came from...

"You... uh..."

"Sucked 'em out. Et 'em. Fucked the holes. Fucking catamite Jake asshole. Fucked him good, *heh-heh-heh."*

The weird thing, Rick discovered, was that it was a relief. Accidentally blowing off someone's hand who'd just been trying to protect their property would've tested even his *powers of conscious amorality. Discovering said mutilatee was a cannibalistic psychopath took the edge off the guilt, and the confirmation that his unintentional victim had been dealing with the Neo-Clergy was enough to leave Rick positively* elated. *It was all he could do not to spit on the guy's bristly jowls as the blood pumped out of him and his life rustled away.*

He went downstairs, feeling a little dazed, and helped himself to as many guns and as much ammo as he could carry.

He went outside.

He went back inside and dumped the shoulder-launched rocket, cursing under his breath. It turned out 'as much as he could carry' wasn't as much as he thought.

He went outside again, and stared at his bike. The clan mothers had been quite specific.

Don't you lose it, *they'd said.* Don't you leave it behind. It'll only bring you grief.

The cat was still glaring at him from across the street, reminding him of his dream and the withered-faced old Tadodaho whispering about the Ancestors.

"Fuck that." Rick said, out loud.

Then he threw a stone at the cat, slung a leg over the monstrous Harley Davidson trike his would-be murderer had kindly left parked beside the Honda, and gunned his way back towards the I-80 with the purr of a zombie tiger.

He had an appointment in New York, and he intended to meet it in style.

CHAPTER FOUR

BACK IN LONDON, every Sunday, if you had the time and the inclination and something to barter your way inside, you could watch a little entertainment. Of sorts.

John-Paul Rohare Baptiste, basking in directed light: a beacon of divine purity in white robes and towering mitre, marked with the simple scarlet 'O' of his order.

Offering prayers. (Ranting, if you ask me, but then I'm not the target audience.)

Performing miracles. (Staged, if you ask me.)

Evangelising, enthusing, speaking in tongues, convulsing in communion with angels, dribbling and shrieking. Reading snippets from the bible, sometimes. Sometimes from other books, as the whim took him. Standing stock-still, like a rabbit in the headlights, as his underlings snuck into frame and proclaimed, accents Noo-Yoik thick, that the "Holy Spirit has come upon him..."

Nobody else seemed to find that as funny as I did.

The man was as mad as a stoat, in my professional opinion, not that anyone ever asked. This, after all, was entertainment. This was, in some dimly understood part of the survivors' 'society,' one last link with the past. Media. Broadcast signals. Something civilised...

This was back in London. All over the UK as far as I could work out. Christ, all over the whole world, for all I knew.

They called it The Tomorrow Show.

The luckiest people – scratching out a survival in the suburbs, or holed-up in automated offices like me – had the remnants of electricity. Enough to plug-in for the requisite one-hour session every week, entranced like a spectator at the advent of the moving image. It felt like that, sometimes. Like something that had become mundane – the broadcast of sounds and shapes – had rediscovered the awe of its inception.

No one expected there to be TV in the aftermath of the Cull. It was almost magnetic.

Other people pilfered rusting generators from abandoned worksites and derelict studios, summoning the juice required to bring their equipment to life, be it knackered B&W antique or plasma screen treasure. They'd set up in debris-covered squares and graffiti-pocked warehouses, charging the great crowds who gathered to gawp in food or fags or favours, to squint up at the fuzzy image and await the broadcast.

Every Sunday, at four o'clock in the afternoon (that's eleven EST), it came on. Since the Cull, London had become a silent city anyway, but never more so than in that crystalline moment before the show began. Breaths held, fists clenched. I guess not many of them had been overly spiritual before it all happened, but having the word of God disseminated directly into your eyeballs still beat hunting pigeons and scavenging in the underground. No contest.

"Abbot!" they'd shout, as the crowds gathered. "Abbot's on! Trade tickets! Tins, meat, fresh water, fags! Abbot Baptiste on soon!"

I'd been to a few, down through the years. Just out of interest. Just to see what all the fuss was about, maybe even (whisper it) just to be around other people.

It was always the same routine. They'd flick the switches one minute before four. Hush fell, and eyes focused on that bright oblong of swarming white noise, like a blizzard in zero-gee. Time dragged, and before you knew it people were muttering, trading worried glances, adrenaline overflowing. Is he coming? Have we missed it? Has something gone wrong? Oh, Jesus, pray for him! Pray for him to come! Don't let him desert us!

Idiots.

Bang on four: the signal. A test card marked with a spectrum colour-check, enclosed in the same scarlet circle that decorated everything the Neo-Clergy ever touched, and that included the clothes of their audience.

A ragged cheer from the crowd, a tinny burst of recorded organ music, and there he was.

Smiling. Serene. Wrinkled like a geriatric prune. Wobbling mitre slipping down over a frail brow, nose classically aquiline, chin jutting proudly from the abyssal folds of a robed collar. I always thought he looked like an albino vulture. Like a friendly old granddad with a secret perversion. Like a war criminal, trying to fit in.

Saying so out loud probably wouldn't have gone down well.

The sermons always began the same way. Push hard into a close-up – friendly eyes and soft smile filling the screen – slip into a vague soft focus that could have been intentional or technical inefficiency, and let the old goat speak, deep-south drawl sincere and stupid, all at once.

"Blessed," he said, "are the children."

"*Where*," the voice roared, loudspeaker whining with painful distortion, "*are the children?*"

"Please!" I shouted, bracing myself against the ragged tear where the plane's tail had parted company with the fuselage. "I... I'm hurt! I'm bleeding! I need help!"

"The fucking *children!*"

Too much to hope the despairing nobody routine would work twice in a row. This was going to get messy.

In snatched glances, staying low against the tortured edges of the fuselage, I figured there were ten men out there, give or take. Wafting through haze-coated patches of burning fuel and smoking debris, creeping forwards like sodding commandos assaulting a hostage siege. The tail was the obvious way in, but there were others. Smaller rents in the metal walls, the shattered panes of the cockpit, up through the sagging crater halfway down the cabin, leading into the gloomy luggage hold; now resting on the horizontal.

I was, to put it bluntly, screwed.

"You come out!" the loudhailer squealed, changing tack; the speaker's voice gratingly high and delivered in uncomfortable bursts. "You get your ass *out*, mister! Arms *high*!"

Diversionary tactics. Keep me standing here at the rear, trying to buy time, whilst the kamikaze crew popped in somewhere else. *Subtle.*

I hefted the dead man's rifle and checked the setting. The wasteful idiot had it on a three-round burst. Quickest way to empty your clip.

He'd been sent in on point, I guessed. He and his mates stationed at the airport, waiting for flights from who-knew-where-else to disgorge their cargo and head back home for more. London, Paris, Madrid... Where else had the Neo-Clergy set up base?

"You got ten seconds! Ten, asshole! You hear?"

Oh yeah, the cargo...

No wonder they were pissed off with me. Not only had I fucked their plane, I didn't stop to load-up with the usual freight.

Blessed are the children...

I caught an ugly mental image of the same spinning, whirligig plane crash – sparks and metal storms spiralling in every direction, smoke venting like haemorrhaging blood – albeit packed to the gills with terrified youngsters. Crying out for parents they'd left in London, screaming and sobbing as windows shattered and shrapnel spun. Never quite making it to the 'rediscovered dawn' they'd been promised.

"That's seven, fucko!"

Yeah, yeah.

The man I'd killed lay at my feet, a deflated skinbag oozing congealing fluids. I'd dragged him all the way down from near the cockpit, and with a raging narcotic hangover and some major blood-loss issues, it hadn't been much fun. From what little I could see of his gung-ho colleagues, through the murk and smoke of the crash site, they were dressed the same: grey robes, black army-boots, heads shaved with military precision and M16A2 semi-automatic rifles clutched lovingly to their chests. I guessed the Apostolic Church of the Rediscovered Dawn got its fingers into the military on *this* side of the Atlantic as easily as the other.

The dead man had a scarlet ring tattooed around his left eye. It made him look lopsided. Sinister and ridiculous, all in one.

The loudmouth on the speaker got down to 'five.' It was a fair bet they'd punch in through the front and sides of the wreck shortly before the countdown finished. *Take the sucker by surprise.*

That's what I'd do.

Time to go to work.

I picked up the dead man, arms looped under his shoulders, and pressed my head into the small of his back. His lungs wheezed somewhere deep inside, more bloodpaste gathering on his lips. I folded myself carefully onto the floor (formerly the plane's left flank) and arranged the stiff so his cloak covered the more obvious extremities of my body. Something warm and damp dripped onto my chin.

Lurking in the lee of a battered service area, where hostesses had at one time heated their plastic meals and bitched about unruly passengers, I was nothing but a shadow beneath a corpse. I rested the gun against the guy's hip, flopped his sleeve across its stock, and curled a finger beneath the trigger guard, waiting.

The combat conditioning folded in again, running it all in slowtime, making an abstraction of everything, highlighting details. I was getting sick and tired of the insides of this fucking plane.

A whisper of cobwebbed aggression moved deep down in the calluses of my old brain. I was a caveman with an Armalite semi-automatic rifle, and a shield made of meat.

The grin came up unbidden.

"Two!" the loudspeaker snarled, voice dripping impatience and (the conditioning told me, senses tuned to a level far subtler than any I could detect alone) genuine fear.

They're not used to this.

Too fucking bad. *I* am.

Somewhere in the shell of the plane, noises dampened by the corpse's weight, glass shattered and booted feet struck the felt floor. In fuzzy half-vision, glimpsed in the acute angles of the robe, I could make out figures crawling sideways from the breached hold, slipping down from fissures in the fuselage further up the aisle, creeping forwards from the cockpit.

They had their weapons held ready, but too low, too macho, too seen-it-all-in-movies. They kept stopping and starting, listening for threats, fighting to keep the shakes out of gloved hands. They poked into every corner. They paused when they got to Bella and talked in a low whisper-murmur that no self-respecting covert op would touch with a bargepole.

A pair of booted feet stopped near me.

"Fucker got Garson..." he said.

Moron.

I relieved him of his face with shot number one. Not easy to aim from underneath a dead guy, but it did okay. Caught him broadside of the ear, flipped him back, shouting. Skull-flecks and a popped eyeball. I put another one in his chest somewhere, just for good measure.

Let the grin widen a notch.

Pushed poor old Garson out the way.

Sighted down the aisle. With care. No rush.

The others were panicking. Reacting to the gunshots, looking for targets. Shouting, arguing, crouching in that idiot combat-posture that looks like constipation. Narrow space, men standing one behind the other. No room for covering fire.

Begging to be killed.

One shot at a time. Nothing flashy. Aim, fire, aim, fire, aim, fire.

Muzzle flash, serpentine smoke. Quiet clods of blood and flesh, knocked astray from pale robes, like melons beneath sledge hammers. One guy got off a shot in return, but desperate, off-target. A convulsive squeeze, like pre-emptive rigor mortis.

There were eight in all. Four down already; dead or disarmed. Three more diving for cover (I caught a fourth as he fell, once in the ribs, again in the leg) and shuffled myself upright. Let Garson tumble to the floor, slippery.

Kept firing. Kept the other arseholes ducked down. Got lucky and caught one on the foot. He hadn't hidden from sight. Watched the boot fragment like a leather mine, his gun tumble away.

I was shouting, I realised. An unintelligible rush of animal sounds and half-formed words. *Speaking in tongues*. Heh.

Behold the Holy Spirit, coming upon him...

I kicked Garson through the mangled tail, letting him spoon outwards onto the tarmac like a man tripping on the edge of a cliff. Kept firing. Started shuffling back into the fuselage.

Outside the plane, whatever was left of Garson was ripped to shreds, silenced munitions plucking frayed tatters off his robes like feathers from a pillow. A trigger-happy sniper, then, somewhere out on the airport side of the strip; getting overzealous. Probably the same guy with the loudspeaker.

Moron.

Two guys left inside. I kept firing. Deliberately off-target. Let them think I didn't know where they were. Let them sweat. Let them pluck up the courage to –

"Asshole!"

The first one came up like a gopher from a hole. Pistol in each hand – fucking cowboy – shouting and cursing like a trooper.

Which, let's be quite clear, he obviously was not.

He got off a couple – misses, obviously – and went back down with an expression of ultimate bewilderment. The top half of his head was missing.

Good shooting, soldier.

I stopped firing. Stayed ready. Knew exactly where number eight was.

I could hear him crying.

"Oh, God..." he kept saying. "Oh God, oh God, oh God..."

I wondered, distantly, if he was playing the same trick I'd played. Get me off guard, then turn with a savage smile and a slicing edge.

No.

The subconscious analysis came online. Bone-deep, beyond thought or effort. Animal instincts peeling back layers of information with scary accuracy.

No, he's terrified. It's in his voice. He knows he's going to die.

I considered letting him live. Just a kid, probably. Some speccy troll inducted into the Clergy sometime since the Cull. Looking for strength in numbers. Never imagining he'd wind up huddled against an economy-class aeroplane seat, on its side, with a psychopath who'd just gone through his hardass pals like a flaming sword.

Poor little bastard. I almost felt sorry for him.

Then I remembered why I was here, remembered the signal and the five long years, and the pain and the mourning, and the deep dark voice –

Don't you fucking give up, soldier!

– and I stepped forwards and shot the little rat through the top of his skull, so his brains slapped out of his jawline like snot into a hanky.

Sir, no sir, etc, etc.

Outside the plane, beyond the sputtering of tiny fires up and down the runway, everything was still. Somewhere distant a couple of seabirds cawed, reminding me – with an ignorable spurt of melancholy – of London. But otherwise, *nothing.*

I lurked, vaguely combat poised, and stared out across the landing strip; torn and pocked by the plane's passage. It shivered here and there with a faint luminosity where fuel had spilled and ignited, like a fiery reflection of the calm waters stretching away beyond. The idea of sprinting across the tarmac – strafing to confuse the bastard sniper who may or may not still be out there somewhere – and diving into the swampy morass held a sudden and unshakeable appeal. I imagined the water washing away the filth and blood that had soaked my coat; all the congealing gore that had spattered me moments before, as I moved up and down the plane with one of the cowboy's pistols, putting an end to the moans and pleas from the monk-soldiers I'd wounded.

No time for last words, no gloating, no fucking power trips. Just step-up, barrel-between-eyes, look away, squeeze trigger.

The lecturers used to call this ruthless mercy.

Second year of training. Major Farnham Dow presiding.

"It's easy – piss-easy," he'd said, *"to feel sorry for someone you've clipped. He's lost everything. He knows he's for it. He's going to... to blub and piss himself. He's going to ask for mercy, if he can. Talk about his family, maybe. Whatever.*

"The point is, the only reason he's not dead is because you missed with the first shot. It's your *mistake, soldier, not his. And it doesn't change anything. Does it?*

"You think he wasn't trying to kill you too? You think he'll renounce a lifetime of violence if you spare his life? Dedicate himself to charitable-bastard-causes? You think he won't shoot you in the back, if he still can, when you walk away?

"No. Don't be so fucking stupid! A wounded enemy is just a dead enemy who doesn't know it yet..."

Rationalising it and doing it were worlds apart.

I'd exited through the luggage hold, scampering across perpendicular support-struts and cargo-webbing, heading for the chasm of shattered steel and twisted, solidified slag where the forward landing-gear had been rammed upwards into the guts of the plane, tearing a long scar in the fuselage. The exit opened onto the sea side of the strip, away from the airport buildings and – I hoped – the sniper. I spent a good five minutes at the opening, darting glances left and right, sneaking out to check the roof of the wreck and retreating once again. Nothing. Either he didn't have a bead on me at all, or he was waiting for me to come out to play.

I fucking *hate* snipers.

I stepped out and stayed out. The air smelt of salt and ash; an acrid cocktail that seemed to ride on the light breeze rippling over the waters. The feel of sunlight caught me unprepared, a warmth I'd forgotten in the perpetual greyness of London. Ever since the Cull – ever since the bombs fell, half a world away – England's Pastures Green had become 'Mires Grey.' I once spent half an hour with another survivor – I forget his name, but he was a talented rat catcher – rambling informatively about skyburst radiation and the fucking Gulf Stream. Used to work for the Met, he said.

I tuned out thirty seconds in.

Quite how all this enabled LaGuardia airport, squatting on the watery edge of New York like a growing patch of mildew, to enjoy unbroken sunlight and cloudless skies was quite beyond me. I felt like I'd just arrived at Disneyland.

I let the desire for a dip in the water ebb away; put off by the kaleidoscopic blobs of oil smearing the surface, and the brown tint to the shoreline. With more scratches and open wounds than I cared to think about, it would be less a bath and more a proactive infection.

Enough time wasting.

I edged my way along the length of the fuselage, pressed against the sagging underside in the shadow of the plane's girth. At the cockpit I paused and shouldered the fully-loaded rifle I'd liberated from another of the Clergy goons, and clambered up onto the pitted slope, wincing as I put a little too much weight on the wounded arm. It had started bleeding softly again; one or two of the messy stitches popping open. I swore under my breath and tried to ignore it.

Dangling there like meat on a hook, staying low, I could peer through the shattered panes of the cockpit and take careful stock of the flat killing-ground beyond, spread out on the left side of the wreck.

Wide, regular, empty. No cover.

Shit.

Halfway between the edge of the still-flaming debris field and the distant airport buildings – clustered like toys around the distinctive inverted-lampshade of the control tower – a series of ramshackle sheds and lean-tos had been erected, improbably sturdy, in a rough semicircle. Cables and joists held them in place, stretched out like a high-tension big top built of plastic and wood. A railed gantry ran along their tops, marked at each end with a conning tower plated with corrugated iron. I squinted through the haze coming off the fuel-fires and made out a big sign, graffiti-texted inexpertly and tacked to each end of the rail, hanging down across the front of it all.

I felt an eyebrow ruck upwards.

The sign read:

WELCOME TO THE NEW DAWN

...along with all the usual scarlet circles, colourful highlights and other assorted Neo-Clergy bollocks. The whole compound set up looked like it'd been made out of pipe-cleaners and bogrolls at the local school, then scaled up a couple of hundred times.

It was painted bright blue.

It was all a bit pathetic.

I could see the sniper now, through the chinks of shattered glass and mangled instrumentation of the cockpit, standing in full sight on the gantry. He had a loudspeaker slung on a cord across his shoulders and a seriously sexy scope-rifle cradled in his hands, at a guess an M82. I'd only even seen them in pictures.

Shit.

Above a pair of wide sunglasses – tinted ruby-red – a stupid sort of flat-cap was set jauntily on his scalp, somewhere between a beret and a devotional *kippah*, and his robes were several shades whiter than those of his dead colleagues. So:

The boss.

I tried to get a bead on him, squinting along the barrel of the M16, but at this range I might as well blow snot. He had his back to me, leaning down over the rear of the railing to point and shout at someone below, hidden behind the sign. There seemed to be an argument going on, and in his apoplexy the twat-in-the-hat was stamping and waving his fists in a full-on tantrum.

A violent growl picked up from out of nowhere – an engine, gunning hungrily – and a blocky shape emerged from behind the compound. Fat and square, grinding along slowly. For one awful moment I thought it must be a tank. Some ultra-rare military surplus these insane God-botherers had maintained for years. But no, it was far weirder than that.

It was a school bus, thick flanges of corrugated iron hanging down to protect its tyres, painted the same lurid blue as the buildings and marked with the same great scarlet 'O's on either side. The windows were blocked-up – padded by what looked like dozens of Kevlar jackets marked 'NYPD' – and the front windshield protected by a heavy-duty wire mesh. I couldn't see the driver. I couldn't see who or what was inside. All I could see was this surreal shape lumbering towards the plane, towards me and my complete lack of preparation, and the fucking stupid 'destination' inside the little window above the front:

SALVATION (ONE WAY)

I felt like shooting at it on general principle.

The vehicle took a wide arc around the plane's tail, circling behind the wreckage, shunting its way through lumps of flaming debris with the impunity of something big, impatient and impervious. I dropped quickly down from my shaky vantage and squirreled into the recess beneath the drooping camber of the cockpit, the first vestiges of panic rising inside. When it drew alongside, the driver would have to be blind not to see me. What precisely was I supposed to do *then*?

It didn't take a genius to work out what they were up to. A lazy recon around the perimeter to get a good look at the side they couldn't see from their hickledy conning towers. To flush me out into the open, if I turned out to still be alive.

With the sniper on one side and an armoured vehicle on the other, it wouldn't be hard work to catch me out, pick me off like a flaky scab.

I BREATHED DEEP, letting the conditioning guide me. Thinking like a machine.

Only viable place to hide now was back in the bloody plane, which I'd just spent half an hour trying to get *out* of. I considered crawling back. I even tensed, ready to hoist myself out from my pitiful cover and up through the shattered cockpit windows, probably lacerating myself all to hell in the process, but still... It was better than noth –

The bus stopped.

Its brakes squeaked quietly as it drew to a halt beside the knotted cavity of the missing tail segment, far off to my right. I could hear voices arguing inside. A hatch flapped-open near the rear and a robed figure leaned out. I froze.

The man tossed something, underarm, into the plane's tail.

"Go!" He shouted, presumably to the driver.

The hatch slammed shut and the bus moved on.

"Oh fuck..." I whispered.

The tail bulged. The whole wreck shuddered, scraping deeper into the dry grass. Round the corner of my cover, too far out in the open for me to see clearly, flames and tumbling lumps of metal arced high overhead, shattered fragments of blue-painted hull spiralling in orbital contrails of sparks and smoke, to bounce and break on the tarmac.

A few bits and bobs *pinged* cutely off the bus. It didn't seem to mind.

THEY THOUGHT I was still inside. It didn't much matter much, either way. Inside or out of the wreck, with the 'Cult Of Unfair Destructive Hi-Tech Gadgetry' around, I was as good as mince.

Think, think...

The bus cruised gently forwards, cornering the rear of the plane and pausing beside the next gaping rent in its fuselage, a third of the way along its flank. Again, the hatch flipped open, and like some surreally casual picture – a guy in a park pitching a ball to an overeager dog – the goon flipped another grenade into the wreck.

The bus moved on.

This time the detonation blew off an emergency exit door, straight upwards like a rocket, to tumble over and under back down again. More spilled fuel caught fire as the debris mushroomed out, and for the second time I felt a wave of weakness and nausea passing over me. Everything seemed to go grey.

Fuzzy.

Meaningless.

Not now!

Blood loss. Hollow prickles of heat up and down empty veins...

I –

Don't you fucking give up, soldier!

I brought the rifle up to my shoulder. This time the bus driver would see me. This time they'd be too close. The grenade would blow out the front of the plane, erupt through the cockpit like a great pulsing embolism, crushing and breaking and burning me all at once.

The brakes squealed.

The hatch flipped open.

The goon wasn't looking out, bending back inside to shout at the driver, hands curled snugly around the baseball bomb, ready to throw.

I heard:

"...fucking opinions to your*self*, grandpa, and let the *real* men do the..."

He pulled the pin.

I shot him.

The hatch flipped closed, bloodhaze wafting down and out. The grenade sill inside.

The unseen driver shouted.

I pushed myself deep into the recess and curled into a ball.

The bus's arse blew off like an overfilled balloon, smoke swallowed the sky, pulsing waves of weirdness sent me flopping like a boneless doll with vomit on my chin, and everything faded to white.

CHAPTER FIVE

My first worry was that my eyes weren't working properly.

Okay, so I'd just woken up. No need to panic yet, maybe, but the training and conditioning went *deep*, and the first thing you learn is *be aware.*

Know everything.

Cover the angles.

Right.

I had the vague idea I'd passed out from loss of blood. There was something about a... a bus? A plane? What the fuck? Maybe I was still hallucinating.

Maybe this hazy curtain obstructing everything I was seeing was just an effect of my traumatised mind, or something cloudy dripping in my eyes, or... or whatever.

Assume a worst-case scenario.

Sir, yes sir, etc, etc.

So: Major damage following oxygen starvation to the brain, leading to sensory corruption and an inability to effectively continue.

Solution: Abort mission.

I remembered where I was. I remembered the plane crash and the gunfight and was even starting to piece together the thing with the bus when the biggest puzzle-piece of all dropped into place: I remembered why I'd come here.

The Signal.

'Inability to effectively continue' wasn't an option. 'Abort Mission' could, pardon my French, fuck off.

I mentally nutted the worst-case scenario and tried out a little optimism for a change. When I twisted my head to glance at the floor beneath me – I was lying on my right shoulder, aching from my own weight – the cracked tarmac of the airstrip came into perfect and unobstructed focus. It was only when I looked further afield that my vision became obscured, as if the horizon was playing hard-to-get.

"Stay still," someone croaked. "Nearly done. Can't finish-up if you keep moving."

My skin prickled, and it took a moment or two to realise why. I was half naked. Lying on a mangled runway surrounded by debris and fuel, unable to see anything past a few dozen feet, in nothing but my underwear.

"H-hey..."

"Dammit! Stay *still*." A wrinkled hand – dark brown knuckles and a pale palm – dipped briefly into my field of view and gave me a chastising flick on the forehead, not doing much for my sense of security. I felt my whole body rocking a little, as if a dog had got hold of my left sleeve and was tugging it from side to side, though I wasn't wearing anything and consequently had no sleeves.

It was all very odd. There was no pain.

I poked my tongue around my mouth, half testing for the taste of blood, half summoning the strength to speak, and eventually tried: "What are you... uh...?"

"Sorting you out," the speaker said. His voice was hard-accented – African-American, New York sharp – with an inbuilt semi cackle that turned every statement into a grandfatherly demonstration of humouring the kiddies. I felt vaguely patronised, and couldn't work out why.

"And how," I said, failing to focus yet again on the murky distance, "are you doing that?"

"Minor transfusion, first up." The voice sounded matter-of-fact about this, despite the subject. "About the only good damn thing about the Cull. Everyone's a donor, see?"

"Blood?"

"He's a quick one!" I got the impression the guy, whoever he was, was squatting behind me. "Yeah, blood. Which is to say: you were seriously lacking for the stuff, pal."

"A-and you gave m... From where?"

"No need to worry 'bout *that.*"

I silently begged to differ, but the same tugging sensation from my left shoulder was distracting my attention and the voice – an old man, I'd decided – wasn't finished.

"Then it was tidying up, see? I mean... who made this damn *mess* of your arm here?" There was a quiet *tap-tap-tap*, and I imagined a finger poking the skin next to the bullet hole – though again I felt nothing. "Might as well have poured a quart of mud in the hole and closed it down with knitting needles."

"I... I did it."

"Done it yourself?" The voice went quiet for a moment, then whistled softly. "Well... maybe that's different. Still a fuckin' mess, mind."

"You've... You've sorted it?"

"Yep. Antisep, new stitches, new dressing." He paused, considering my voice. "Limey, huh?"

"But I can't feel it. My arm."

"Lived over there myself, for a time. Nice place. But for the weather."

"I said I can't fee..."

"Yeah. That'd be the anaesthetic."

I started to blurt: *Anaesthetic? Where the fuck did you get tha* – but my thought-process shifted rails with an inelegant *clang* and ran up against a far more obvious quandary.

"Why?" I said.

"Why what?"

"Why are you doing all this? What's going on?"

"*Ah.*"

The syllable was pronounced with the sort of enigmatic significance that said:

More to follow.

There was a heavier tug on my left side, executed with a certain amount of rough finality and a breathless grunt – "There!" – and then a coarse hand rolled me onto my back. I felt a little like a turtle inverted in the sun, unable to lift myself upright. Not that I'd tried yet. I was far too busy staring up at my benefactor, wondering if I was still asleep and hadn't realised.

"Evening," the shadow said. "Name's Nate."

He was an older man. I think. Five years since the Cull it was already difficult to say, hard living took its toll on some worse than others; youngsters quickly hardened, faces became taught, lines (not *laughter*, obviously) gathered at corners of eyes and mouths. Plus fallout, starvation, exposure, injury. Who could say? My best guess put this guy at sixty, but he looked older and acted younger. His skin was a uniform teak that gave his face an unreal quality every time he smiled. Perfectly white eyes and teeth lighting up like bulbs set into a dark sculpture.

"Nate," I repeated. He grinned.

He wore a strange getup, like he'd spent all his life pilfering clothes of a vaguely uniform bent. Tan and khaki camo combat trousers (sorry, *pants*), a pale blue shirt with an NYPD insignia stitched into the lapel and an outrageous jacket – dark blue, festooned with gold pips and double-buttons – which it took me a moment to recognise as an Union Army antique. I figured he'd looted it from some re-enactment society or fancy dress store, though admittedly – thanks to the scuffs, stains and frays – it did *have* a century-and-a-half-old look about it. Its effect was simply to add to the overall impression of a uniformed nutter, driven to steal anything vaguely official-looking like a magpie hording shinies.

I resisted the urge to salute.

This curious attempt to look authoritative was undermined somewhat by the accessories he'd chosen: bright red sneakers, a white New York Mets baseball cap and a vivid yellow belt with the most enormous buckle engraved with the legend:

POP BITCH

There was a dead guy sitting next to him.

Nate followed my glance and his grin faltered a touch. "Ah," he said again.

The corpse was one of the Clergy-soldiers, though I didn't recognise him from inside the plane. He didn't have a hole through his face, for a start.

His grey robes were blackened and singed, spattered with blood and dirty water, and the patches of his skin I could see were just as soiled: peeled back in moist red welts or incised totally by razor-like fragments of shrapnel. One of his arms was hanging off at the shoulder by a few threads of gristle and a notched bony core, and his head was so tattered the scarlet tattoo around his eye was barely visible at all. He sat slumped, semi-upright, against the tangled remains of the same armoured school bus that prowled my recent memories. It reminded me, surreally, of a novelty firework: its front-end all but untouched; the remnants of its length blown-to-shit so totally that their remains barely made any physical sense at all.

The dead Clergyman had been the guy inside. The grenade chucker.

Nate coughed, embarrassed.

A thin rubber tube meandered from a grimy cannula thrust into the corpse's wrist, out onto the floor where it coiled once or twice towards me, then vanished beneath the edge of my exhausted peripheral vision. I didn't want to turn my head to confirm it, but I had a pretty good idea where it led.

It was full of blood.

"Not like he needed it..." Nate said, a little surly. "And I disconnected *plenty* of time before he died."

Well that's okay then.

Nate fussed beside me – lifting up the other end of the transfusion tube and waggling it like a glove puppet – and then started tidying away the various equipment he'd scattered on a mostly clean blanket beside me. Stitching needles, bloody rags, sealed packs of military-issue sterilisers and antiseptic pads, and a roll of off-white bandaging that'd come partly unrolled and scampered off along the oil-spattered tarmac.

The horizon still hadn't come into focus. I was starting to worry.

"Why can't I see properly?" I asked, finding that I could control my body – just – but was so exhausted it hurt even to think about moving.

Nate scowled for a minute, confused, and peered around us. If I'd had to guess, his expression was one of someone who'd just spent hours saving a stranger from bleeding to death, only to discover they were already vegetative in the brain department.

"Can't *see*?" he said.

"It's... it's like a... a blur. Like... near-to things are okay, but the further away stuff gets..."

He looked at me like I was a retard.

"Well *that*," he said, "is what's sometimes called *fog*."

Even despite the panicky relief, I still had some headroom for feeling like a fuckwit.

"B-but... but it was perfectly clear when the plane... when it..."

"Well, that's New York for ya." He waved a dismissive hand, gazing out into the wall of soupy white. "It's called the quicksmog, eff-why-eye."

"Eff... what?"

"Eff-why-eye. For Your Info. Sorry... Guy gets sorta used to talking in letters, hanging around with the grunts, you know." He hooked a thumb towards the slumped body and shook his head. "Soldiers and monks, Jeez-us! Nary the twain should meet."

I struggled to hang on to a single thread. Nate was the sort of guy who could hold three schizophrenic conversations at once, leaping from tangent to tangent like a monkey on speed. There was a shielded intelligence simmering away in those eyes, too, hiding behind the accent and the daft clothes, but watching everything. Paying attention.

"Quicksmog," I repeated, bringing him back.

"Yeah, yeah. Guy I knew one time told me it started right after the camel-jocks zapped out dee-see. 'Cause, you know, I wasn't stateside back then. Never saw the lightshow. But yeah, quicksmog... Comes in quick, goes out quick. Just like that. No rhyme or reason. Doesn't seem to do much harm, though if you ask me right now it's a good thing."

"How come?"

"You kidding? Fucking great plane wreck, burning to shit... sending up a pillar of smoke higher'n a pothead's prick." He grinned. "And with your robe-wearin' pals here gone away, nothing to stop the scavs from coming to take a look."

Scavs. Robe-wearin' pals. Camel-jocks zapping DC.

One fucking detail at a time.

Know everything.

Cover the angles.

"There was a sniper... a-and a driver. Guy in the bus. He dead too?" The effort of talking was becoming appalling now; even as the sensations started to return to my numbed arm, the rest of me was screaming for rest.

Nate sniffed, wiping a dewdrop off his nose.

"Well now," he said. "Your sniper up there, that's a mean pieceashit Cardinal name of Cy. Near as I can tell he wasn't milit'ry before the Cull, so I guess something pretty damn nasty musta happened... Man's fucked in the head but good. Gen-you-ine psycho. *Heh.*" Nate spat on the ground. "High-up too. Maybe take over from the Abbot some day. See, Cy's in charge of bringing the freight from the airstrip back to the city. When the bird comes down all wrecked-up like that, and all the kids missin', he knows straight away his neck's on the line. That's how come the Choirboys went in so hard. Cy wanted to have a... a body, whatever. Like: 'yeah, the airport's fucked and we didn't get the Brit tithe, but I caught the guy who did it...'"

"Me?"

"Right. Only he didn't. And then you come out killin' every motherfucker left and right, and Cy starts to figure maybe he should stop worryin' what his boss gonna say, and start saving his ass. So he sends out the bus, all packed-up with grenades and shit, to keep you busy. Maybe even kill you, if he's lucky." He nodded towards the shattered school bus. "Soon as old Bertha went kablooie you can bet your ass Cy was hightailing back for the city in the Outrider."

"Just a diversion?"

"Right. Couple of... sacrificial lambs, you might say. Told to go *die* so Mister-Hat-Wearin' *fuck* gets to breathe another day. I figure he'll spend the whole journey wondering what to tell the boss. Ask for reinforcements – my guess. Be back here... maybe a day and half? Suggest you get yourself gone by then, huh?"

"And the driver?"

Nate grinned again, and leaned further over. Deep in the shadows of his left eye, all but indiscernible against the blackness of his skin, I could make out the long curve of a scarlet tattoo.

A half circle.

I stiffened.

He waved a set of keys playfully above me, then tossed them over his shoulder.

"Not much left to drive now."

"You're... you're Clergy too?"

He chuckled to himself, lifting up a bundle of something ragged and stinking which I first assumed was a dead dog, and then realised were my clothes.

"Not really," he said. "Not any more."

AN HOUR LATER, Nate and I sat in the alcove beneath the front wall of the shanty-compound, hiding from the wind, listening to the great Welcome sign flapping above us. The quicksmog had surrendered to a sudden squall that darted up with no obvious warning, phasing away into the dark.

Out across the waters encircling the airport, the distant smudge that was the northern reaches of the city faded by degrees into darkness. I'd expected – stupidly – the same neon jungle I'd seen in every film, the same speckled star field of glowing tower blocks printed in every guidebook. The same scene of candle-like serenity glossily reproduced on the cover of the city map I'd plundered from a bookshop in Covent Garden, and sat studying for days and days back in Heathrow, as Bella and I planned the journey. It was still in my pack, that much-thumbed map; not that I needed to look at it any more. I knew all its lines, all its labels, all the red blotches marked on its surface...

But no. From a distance the post-Cull city, just like London, was a haunted place; an inky nothingness flecked here and there by the fragile, sputtering lights of nestled survivors, and the brazen fumes of miniature industry.

Nate had moved me into the shadow of the blue compound's corrugated walls, across the grass and away from the wreck, as soon as I'd been strong enough to make the journey, bracing me with one arm and lugging my pack with the other. He said it would be best to get away from the plane before true darkness fell. The local scavengers would be slinking in to take a look at what had caused all the commotion, and it was all too easy to get caught up in the scraps and squabbles as they fought over the spoils.

I got the impression he wasn't talking about coyotes and wild dogs.

Now, on the cusp of night, the air was getting cold and the view growing grim.

The plane still flickered. *Things* moved in the smoke.

Nate said he was a 'trustee.' He said this meant the Clergy sort of employed him, but didn't expect him to do any of the shit stuff. No evangelising, no indoctrinating, and definitely no acting self-important about the Church's self-assumed manifest destiny in ushering in the New Dawn of Civilisation.

Actually, what Nate said was, "Those dress-wearing assholes couldn't get me down with that bullshit even when they *were* poking guns in my back," but he meant pretty much the same thing. "Eventually," he said, "they figured I was worth more alive, tried asking *nice* instead of just *demanding*. We've all been getting by just fine ever since."

Until I showed up and slaughtered your mates.

Until your boss ran off like a robe-wearing pussy, and left you behind.

Until you decided to keep me alive rather than kill me whilst you had the chance.

Hmm.

The whole issue of *why* he'd helped hadn't been entirely covered yet. I'd taken a bottle of supermarket vodka out of my pack to share with the guy – I figured it was the least I could do – and he was sinking it like a fish. I ought to have felt more grateful, I suppose.

Instead...

Those old instincts. Those old voices.

Know everything.

Don't you let yourself owe anyone anything.

Sir, yes sir, etc, etc.

Nate said he'd been a little... *uncooperative* when Cardinal Cy told him to drive out onto the killing-strip just to keep me busy. He said he'd kicked up a fuss at the idea that he should go throw himself into the jaws of the wolf, whilst said Clergyman ran like a custard-coated cockerel. Nate said he'd protested vehemently at the treatment, that he hadn't signed up as a trustee just to forfeit himself to let some vicious little prick live, and that he'd entered into a considerable argument with his fellow sacrificial lamb when ordered to play kamikaze.

He said eventually the guy chucking grenades out the back had to hold a gun to his head just to get the engine started.

That explained why he wasn't in any hurry to rejoin the Clergy. Traitor to the cause. Coward. Deserter. Blah-blah-blah.

Fine.

It *didn't* explain why he'd gone to so much trouble to keep me alive afterwards.

I asked him.

"More rat?" he said, ignoring me with a bright grin, hacking away at something small and furry with a skinning knife.

I nodded and lifted an empty skewer off the makeshift fire, and jabbed at the slimy morsel he held out. Second only to pigeon.

Over by the plane dark shapes crossed in front of the dancing fires, like inky puddles of moving shadow.

"Still a lot of guns aboard." I said, tense.

And Bella's body.

Nate said the scavs wouldn't be doing any shooting. "Relax," he said, and passed me the vodka with only the tiniest reluctance. He said that whatever the scavs found, they'd present immediately – with all due ceremony and cringing deference – to their bosses in the Klans. He said that if any of the poor fuckers dared waste a single bullet, and word got back to their bosses, they'd be in the hunt pens or skewered on territory poles before they knew it.

I asked him what the Klans were.

He smiled and bit into his rat.

The wind got colder.

Nate said he'd been a doctor, once.

"Kind of," he said.

He said he'd been born in the Bronx and miseducated in Harlem, and but for a lucky seduction in a downstate disco would've wound up still there, scrabbling for cash and crack. He said that twenty years ago – or so – he got lucky with a rich white chick who fell for his unmistakable charms and took him along to England when her company reassigned her. He said she paid through the nose to set him up. He said she enrolled him in night school to finish his basic, then community college, then – pushing harder – medical training. He said every step of the way he worked his balls off, because it turned out he could handle failure and addiction and crime and poverty, but the one thing he couldn't handle was seeing her disappointed.

It was all a bit 'soap opera,' but I didn't like to break the flow.

Nate said he flunked the final exams so bad he would've done better to leave the question papers blank.

"Morphine addiction," he explained, staring off into space.

And that, he said, was that.

"Couldn't you resit?" I asked, picking out rat bones from between my teeth. "Get cleaned up, try again? Seems a bit late in the day to go throwing it all away."

"Yeah," he said, and his voice was quiet. "Yeah, you're right there. Except Sandra – that's the lady, the... the one who took me over there – she sorta caught me with my pants down."

"Ah."

"Yeah. With her secretary."

I looked away, unsure whether to cringe or snigger. "Ah."

When I looked back, Nate's expression was... well, sad – obviously – but something else too. Like the face an exec gets when the deal falters at the last meeting. Like the face I used to see on missions, when the grunts and agents round me realised it'd all gone to tits, and people were probably going to die, and it just *wasn't fair.* Like... frustration, maybe. A sense of annoyance at circumstances beyond one's control.

Which is sort of weird, given that it was all his fault.

Something dark flitted through the shadows outside the circle of light cast by the fire. Nate stared at it for a moment, utterly untroubled, and spat into the flaming logs.

He said – the story rumbling on as if uninterrupted – that the money dried up pretty quick after that. He said he only realised how much he'd appreciated her (and/or her cash, depending on how you wanted to interpret it) when it was too late. Sandra cleared off, heartbroken. He let things slide. His visa hiccupped and lit up alarms on a Home Office computer, and before he knew it he was Nathaniel C. Waterstone of no fixed abode, with a deportation warrant next to his name and a brand new shiny heroin addiction to support.

I coughed as politely as I could, aware that this man had just sewed me up. "So when you said you'd been a doctor..."

"Yeah." He shrugged. "Kind of."

He looked away and sighed, as if he could see all the way across the Atlantic from where he sat. "*London,* man. Docklands, Tower Hamlets, the East End. Plenty of places they pay good money for a guy knows what he's doing with needles. Someone... *unofficial.* You know?"

Nate said he'd been a backstreet sawbones. Mob cutter. Bullets removed, knife wounds cleaned, bodies disposed: no questions asked. I guess I believed him, mostly.

He had an honest face.

Out across the roughage bordering the airstrip, somebody yelped. There were voices out there too – masked by the crackling of our little fire, muttering and arguing. More shapes darting in the dark.

"Scavs." Nate shrugged.

I kept a hand on the M16 and asked what would happen to the bodies of the men aboard the plane. I didn't mention Bella. I wasn't sure why, at the time, but I know now. Even then, sitting with Nate in the cold, the scratching at the back of my head was gearing up...

Something about him.

"Depends," he said.

"On what?"

"On what Klans they're with. Mostly they'll just... steal clothes, leave the bodies. Coupla tinpot tribes up west got a thing for fresh meat, way I heard, but no way we'll get that shit down here. Guy I knew once – you'll like this – said you go through ess-eye these days – that's Staten Island, you know? – you're a... *heh*... a goddamn moveable feast. They got crossbows and *arrows*, man, he says. They got fuckin' *spit roasts*, and I don't mean like in no porno.

"Up here, nah. Nah. Civilised, man. Welcome to Queens."

His grin lit up his face. With Nate, you never knew how serious he was being.

I asked him again to tell me about the Klans. He chuckled and lit a cigarette.

When the Cull started, he said, and folks started dying in the streets of London, he was holed-up with a gang of Albanians. He said up 'til then he'd been passing from group to group – Triads, Afghans, Jamaicans, even the old-school suit-wearing Pie and Chips brigade. He said these Kalashnikov-waving psychos took him on as a kind of examiner: checking the girls they ferried-in from the continent, making sure they'd last in the massage parlours and interactive peep-booths. Nate said he'd never stared at so much pussy in his life, and there came a point where it sort of stopped having any attraction.

He said at around the same time, he decided to go cold turkey.

He looked away again.

I got the impression there was more to it than that. But sitting out there in the cold with a fresh bandage on my arm and a half-digested rat inside me, listening to human filth arguing in the dark over guns and knives and all the other shit I'd left behind on the plane, I didn't have the heart to probe.

The thing was, someone almost certainly made Nate give up the skag. Maybe someone helped him, nursed him through it, whatever. I don't know. But the thing about Nate was, the thing I could tell within seconds of meeting the guy; he wasn't the kind who made decisions. Not on his own. He wasn't the kind to lead the way.

"Was eight days into the detox when the... the virus, you know? When it got as bad as it got. I had me a... a TV, little one, in the room. News shows, back to back. Bodies on the streets, hospitals over flowing. Pretty much all the Albanians dropped right there. Spat blood, hit the deck. I'm telling you, man, the *stink*... Rest of them upped and gone. Tried to get home, maybe. Everyone's got a family, huh?"

He sighed.

"I tell you, man... I was scared. There's me, pissing outta my ass, shivering, puking, all that shit, immune system *fucked* to hell, and the end-of-goddamn-times *plague* outside my door. Just about gave up."

I remembered too. London. Chaos. Panic. It was weeks before they could tell why some people survived. Why most didn't. Revealed little by little on garbled TV shows and home-printed leaflets, in that spasmodic time before the media gave up the ghost.

"But I survived," Nate said. "Fuck, yeah. Came out clean."

And so did I.

What I remember most is, the *unfairness.*

I suppose I always felt I was lucky. Due a fall, surely, but there I was, winning a lottery I never even bought a ticket for. Outside there's priests and nurses and charitable souls rotting on the pavement, and here's me – he's a fucking *killer* – breathing clear.

It didn't seem right.

It's a weird thing, feeling guilty for being alive.

"Anyways," said Nate, flicking a chunk of wood onto the fire from a stack beside the corrugated wall, "that put the cap on doctoring."

He said he'd wandered in London for a year or two. He hinted he'd done his best to help where he could – triage, treatment, tidying – but I guess there was always a price.

Nate didn't exactly radiate selflessness.

After two years the Apostolic Church of the Rediscovered Dawn was up and running. I remember that too. The Abbot broadcasting his miraculous sermon every Sunday, the crowds gathering, the scarlet tattoos and chanted prayers.

The robe-wearing creeps strolled straight out onto the charred remains of the world stage, and declared that they alone – as an entity embracing values of community, integrity, intelligence and of course *faith* – could sweep aside the horrors of the Cull and work towards a new, restored civilisation.

They said that they alone could overcome the 'inertia gripping humanity' and rebuild, recreate, re*start*!

Those.

Arrogant.

Fucks.

They came to London and spread the word. I ignored them.

They said for most people it was too late. The world they'd known was long gone. They said the people could console themselves with living as best they could, embracing Jesus, making the most of their lives in the rubble. They said devoting oneself to the Neo-Clergy was the only expression of purity and hope for the average man.

But for the children... for the children, there was so much more. Innocent, unsullied by the calamities of the past, not responsible for the sins that had visited the Cull upon the world. For them the future was clear. So said the Clergy.

They must build a new dawn.

So the priests came and got them.

At gunpoint, sometimes. But mostly they didn't even need to threaten, mostly it was parents waving goodbye, smiling, proud of their contribution to the world, and that was the worst thing of all.

The church ferried the kids off in blue-painted planes, and ignored the tears and shrieks, and told everyone, *everyone* involved:

Be grateful.

They were going somewhere better, the Clergy said.

Sitting there in the cold, listening to Nate's story, my eyes plucked at the huge banner above me. I shivered.

"They brought them here," I grunted, shaking my head. "The kids. Didn't they?"

Nate nodded.

"Why? What do they *do* with them? Where's this... this fucking *new tomorrow*?"

Nate shrugged, took a slurp of water from a screw cap cantina, and carried on with his story like he'd barely stopped to breathe.

Nate said the Clergy found him on the streets of London. They'd heard he was a doctor. They said they might have a need for someone like that. They might even raise him up to a state of grace. Besides, they said, he was already American.

They had two conditions:

"Number one," he said, "they told me I got to have faith. I told them if they gimme a job and food and somewhere warm to sleep, I'll believe whatever the hell they want.

"And number two, they said I gotta go back to New York."

He stopped, and looked for a second or two like he wasn't going to continue. It was strange to see. Nate's natural state was 'droning,' and every time he stopped to stare off into the darkness with those spotlight eyes it was... disconcerting. "So you came back," I said. "And did what?"

He looked at me for a second – proper eye contact, for the first time – then away again. Someone screamed playfully out by the wreck.

"Same as before, more or less. Ironic, huh? Just like the Albanians. Checking over the produce when it arrives. Making sure it's fit to travel. No sickness, no frailty. Clergy only wants the best."

"You inspected the kids?"

"Right. Shit, I was in *charge* of them. Clumsy old guy with a friendly face and a dumb costume. Made jokes. Patched up cuts and scrapes. Told 'em all everything would be just fine. Drove the bus into the city, came right back for the next batch. London, Paris, Moscow. Planes comin' in from all *over*."

"So you're the ferryman to the New Dawn?" I said, trying out a little sarcasm; seeing how the old man would react.

Know everything.

Check the angles.

He smiled, a little too slowly, then nodded. "I like that," he said. "Yeah, I like that."

Something rustled nearby. A spreading whisper of cloth and feet. My hand tightened on the M16, eyes scanning the shadows, but Nate waved a laconic hand in my direction and grinned.

"No need, man."

Not reassuring.

Something oozed out of the dark. Something hesitant and filthy, matted and feathered down each flank of its raggedy form. Something that broke-up as the firelight caught it; separated down by degrees into an aggregate. A crowd of people.

Staring, all as one, at the meat roasting over the flame.

They came into the light like a single entity, scuttling on far too many legs. They looked – *random thought here* – like extras from the set of a war film: recognisably human but coated in the makeup department's finest emulations of soot, dirt and dried blood, scampering with that expression of people who don't know what they're doing or why they're doing it. Several had fresh wounds – nicks and cuts from knives and teeth – and eyed each other warily.

The ones at the front carried themselves with a seniority based on whatever Byzantine pecking order was at work, clutching in their dirty hands stolen guns, scraps of clothing, bundles of chemical ephemera and all types of other salvage taken from the plane. One was holding a seatbelt buckle, smiling with the smug expression of someone who'd outperformed herself. Another one – a young man – had Bella's jeans slung over his shoulder.

The M16 felt good in my hand.

Let it go, soldier.

Sir, yes sir, etc, etc.

"Well, then..." said Nate, reclining back against the compound wall with as much disinterested ease as he'd shown before the darkness disgorged them. "What can we do for you?"

I think I half expected them to speak in grunts and moans, if at all. They looked so devolved, so fucking *prehistoric*, that at that point it wouldn't have surprised me if they'd dropped down and worshipped the 'Great Fire Makers.'

It sounds arrogant, now I come to say it. I mean... why should they be any less coherent than me? Why should their five years of hardship and filth be any less dignified than mine?

"We smelt the rat," a tall woman said, near the front. She reminded me of someone, and a shiver worked its way along my spine.

Shut that shit down, soldier. Job to do.

Nate shrugged. "And?"

"And we thought maybe you'd trade."

Nate shook his head. "No trades."

"But... *see?*" The woman plucked a plastic drinking beaker out of a raggedy pack, brandishing it like a jewel. "Good, see? Perfect for trading, that is. See what I've g..."

Nate's voice hardened a little. His face stayed the same. "No. *Trades.*"

The scavs flitted a few awkward glances back and forth, then the tall woman's eyes went sneaky. Heavy-lidded and intense, like a child conspiring to do mischief.

"We could *take...*" she said, quietly, acting nonchalant.

Nate chuckled to himself.

"You could," he said. "Yep."

The scavs shuffled, shifted their weight from foot to foot. Here and there a blade twinkled in the firelight, and my heart twisted in my chest: speeding up, blurring time.

Endorphins washed down me.

Muscles tensed.

An old man shuffled to the front, dark blue sweater decorated with stripes of white paint, and I watched him with the targeted eye of a predator.

"What Klan?" he wheezed. "Mm?"

"I'll show you mine if you show me yours." Nate ginned. The M16's grip was warm now, heated by my own palm.

All at once the scavs twitched; a great roiling ball of motion, and without a single conscious thought I was lifting the gun and reaching for the arming bolt and...

Nate's hand sat on the barrel, holding it down. He gave me a look, shook his head, and grunted towards the scavs. They hadn't been attacking at all.

They stood brandishing themselves, like a medical examination taking place *en masse*. In each case the proffered elbow, shoulder, arm, stomach, neck or ankle was decorated by a small mark. A burnt branding-scar in the shape of a smiling face, eyes like double-arches above a mountainous nose, with a pair of satellite ears protruding on each side.

"Mickeys," said Nate. He gave me a doting smile, like an old man discussing the merits of different chess pieces, and said: "Respectable Klan, that."

"Trade now?" the woman said. "Or we'll help ourselves."

"What Klan?" the old man whispered, hopping from foot to foot. "What-Klan-what-Klan-what-Klan?"

Nate tilted his head back, letting the fire chase away the shadows beneath the brim of his cap. The scarlet semicircle seemed to *blaze* on his cheek.

"*Clergy...*" went the whisper. A fearful susurration rushing around the crowd. "*Godshits...* Choirboys... Fuckin' *Clergy...*"

And then they were gone.

Nate and I sat in silence. Eventually I coughed under my breath and asked him, third time lucky, if he'd tell me about the Klans.

He gave me a funny look, smirked quietly, and said:

"Shit, man. What you think I bin *doing*?"

CHAPTER SIX

The Consolidated Edison Power Plant facility, directly off Astoria's Twentieth Avenue, was a continental wedge of pipes, cables, depots, spinal chimneys, blocky storage tanks and stark structures like geometric skeletons made from girders. All of it pressed up against the same polluted, watery banks as the airport. There was something undeniably sepulchral about it. A knotted tangle of hip-like joists, vertebral chains linking moving assemblies, and skull-like containers that had long since lost their sheen.

Nate had brought me here at first light, when I'd told him I needed transport.

He hadn't asked me why. He hadn't asked me what I was here to achieve.

Hadn't told me why he was tagging along.

Hmm.

Standing outside the power plant, it was plain to see the whole place was inactive. Rusted to fuck; plundered for raw materials, stripped apart in a million acts of petty vandalism and selfish salvage.

There was red bunting dangling above the concourse as we stepped off the street – giving the whole thing an air of ludicrousness – and the corrosion-melted gates slumped awkwardly, reminding me of reclining figures watching the world go by. The health and safety signs above their heads had been neatly crossed through with red spray paint, and someone had erected a billboard above the entrance, which read simply:

WHEELS

I felt someone staring, that same old prehistoric instinct, and glanced around, with hairs prickling, for the culprit. Only when I looked directly up did I find him: a dead head, sockets empty, skin tattered, lipless jaws set in a timeless grin. This grisly voyeur sat mounted on a telegraph pole; cables stripped away and its solid girth painted in stripes of tar and red paint.

"The fuck does *that* mean?" I asked, nodding up at it.

"Territory marker," Nate mumbled, smoking a straw-like cigarette. One of mine. "Black and red means this is en-tee."

I gave him a blank look. The acronym thing was starting to piss me off.

"Neutral Territory," he grinned, pointing further into the plant's network of alleys and avenues, all festooned with the same black and red flags and bunting. "No Klan business."

"So the dead guy...?"

Nate shrugged, drooling smoke. "Maybe picked a fight. Got outbid, tried to pull pecking rank. Who knows? Maybe just an unlucky schmo inna wrong place when someone wanted to make a point. Folks that run the en-tees don't take kindly to rule-breakers. They can afford to enforce, y'see?"

Like so much that poured from his mouth, Nate's casual explanations mixed the common sense with the bewildering. Pecking ranks, territory markers... it was all the stuff of just another drug-dream. A revisit to the malleable memories and landscapes of the Bliss trip. But still, I wasn't *entirely* in the dark. I'd spent much of the morning at the airport dozing and thinking, listening to the old man snore, picking his brains about the Klan-system whenever he deigned to wake.

If I understood one tenth of what he'd said, during the Culling year, New York – not to put too fine a point on it – had gone straight to hell. He'd painted a picture of streets clogged up with empty cars, skeletons tangled along sidewalks. Of the military running out of control with water cannons and teargas. Of riots like full scale wars and whole blocks burning to ash on the grounds of a single suspected infection. He hadn't been there – he was still in London at that point – but, leaving aside the narrator's propensity for hyperbole, it still wasn't easy listening.

What *was* certain was the Klan system. In a weird sort of way, despite everything, I was impressed by it. It was easy to see how it must have started, and at the back of my mind – beyond the doubts and disapprovals – it seemed like the most natural thing in the world. Like some new species released onto the savannah, frightened herds running together; accreting like shit flowing into a bowl.

Strength in numbers.

Pack mentality.

The oldest instincts in the book.

The way Nate told it, the Klans all had their origins in different places. Maybe some grew up around whichever politicians survived the Cull and got lucky, outside of Washington when the nuke skyburst. You can imagine that happening, maybe. Little guys in suits, standing on stone steps, kicking up a fuss. Like you used to get in Hyde Park, like Speakers' Corner every Sunday. Angry men and women on stools and ladders, spouting fire and brimstone. Since the Cull, they would have been *kings*.

Still... it's a big step from there to gang colours, to skin brandings, to closed territories and aggressive expansion and nightly raids and sallying-forth and midnight skirmishes and blood in the gutters...

The night before, as Nate explained this stuff, as I told him I just didn't *see* rational people acting so dumb, sinking so low, he stopped with a grin and said:

"Desperate times, man."

The main driveway along the interior of the power plant took a sharp corner, every inch of the way draped in swatches of fabric and makeshift adverts. Most carried the names of food stalls and barter points (promising FARE TRADE, WIDE SELECSION, ALL SCAV CONSIDERD), branded in each case with iconic images of bygone snacks; hotdogs, burgers, bagels. I found my mouth watering at the memory of such extravagant-seeming meals, and asked Nate what the stalls *really* traded.

"Rat," he said, not looking around. "It's all rat."

Some of the Klans, maybe, came up from less obvious sources. Lantern-jawed drill sergeants discovering they had no country left to fight for, nobody left to shriek at, no way of draining off the dynamo-level testosterone. Civic leaders, celebrities, lawyers. The local bloody postman. It didn't take much, back at the start, to be the centre of a pack; to let something comfortable and secure grow around you. Maybe some of those putative mobs – coalescing and running together – could even claim they'd formed their miniature little states for all the right reasons. Nate told me one of the Klans, back at the start, was called the 'Thin Blues.' Bunch of NYPD grunts, he said, banding together, facing down the chaos. He said that to start with they even had a decent stab at maintaining the peace; driving about, making arrests, shooting looters. He used the word 'altruistic,' which sounded weird when he said it, and tricky to take seriously.

He said it didn't last long.

He said ever since then, the Thin Blues had been one of the *smaller* Klans.

Inside the industrial sprawl of the Con Ed facility we reached a checkpoint, where two enormous blokes in black clothes and red bandanas stood divesting everyone of weapons. A small queue of raggedy scavs had formed, and beyond the canvas-draped checkpoint I could see the peristaltic movement of large crowds, deeper inside the facility. It made me nervous. In London, the only time you saw that many people gathered together was for the Abbot's sermons, and just *thinking* about those left a bad taste in my mouth.

I watched the guards frisking and checking, allocating each person a number to be used in recollecting their guns and knives, and tilted my head towards Nate.

"What Klan are they?" I asked, nodding towards the muscular goons.

"Right now," he said, "no Klan at all. Neutral Territory, remember? They're being paid to keep it that way."

As if to reinforce this point, the guards commanded each entrant to display his or her Klan marking. Elbows and shoulders were silently brandished, knees held out, necks craned, and I caught a few fleeting glimpses of the squiggles and meaningless icons depicting each different group. In every case the guard quickly tied a black rag, plucked from a filthy basket, around the scar; hiding the brand from sight.

"Neutral," was all that Nate said.

We reached the front of the queue and caused something of a commotion. For a start, Nate's branding could hardly be covered with a simple piece of rag – unless he was prepared to submit to blindfolding, which he wasn't – but it was the nature of the mark itself that really got them riled. They kept exchanging looks, clenching their jaws, wondering out loud if they should fetch the 'em-bee.'

More fucking acronyms. Nate seemed to be enjoying all the consternation.

He'd explained it to me last night, the instant that the scavs he'd called 'Mickeys' scuttled off into the dark.

"The Neo-Clergy," he said, "the mighty New Church, the holier-than-thou warrior priests of the New Dawn, were really just another Klan."

Oh, a *big* one, to be sure. The biggest. The de-facto rulers of New York, whose powerbase gave them an administrative control over all the others, but still...

It hadn't seemed possible, somehow. How could something so mundane, so *seedy*, as this feudal mob have spread across the devastated world to make its claims of ushering-in a new future? From angry thugs to architects of tomorrow.

According to Nate, the Apostolic Church of the Rediscovered Dawn started out as a band of raggedy-arsed bastards calling themselves The Choirboys. They had no particular defining features – besides a reputation for being twisted little shits – and would have languished in obscurity had they not encountered the man named John-Paul Rohare Baptiste.

No one knew much about him. No one knew where he'd come from or who he'd been. All they knew was that he shouldn't be alive, and he proved it to them over and over again, with tests and samples and nothing-up-his-sleeves, just as he had continued to do every week on his detestable fucking TV show.

The Blight should have *got* him. He should have been Culled.

But he lived anyway.

Under his guidance, and the fluttering banner of his self-declared divinity, the Klan swelled like a tumour. It came to the point they could have challenged and annihilated any other group they chose, but they *didn't.* They simply tuned out from the power struggle, announced that their intentions had transcended the merely territorial, and elected themselves into a position of magisterial arbitration.

Nowadays they monitored the others, like proud parents adjudicating the play-fighting of toddlers. They formalised the squabbles and scuffles, they leant their backing to whichever Klans they favoured, they provided weapons and drugs (their most valuable currencies), and in return they demanded The Tithe.

Oh yeah...

The Tithe.

"Every child above age five," Nate had said the night before, like reading from a scripture written inside his eyelids, "and below age eighteen, to be inducted into the ay-see-arr-dee."

That's Apostolic Church of the etc, etc.

They'd spread the good news across the oceans. They'd conquered the airwaves when all other frequencies had fallen silent. They'd taken responsibility for the future when all the starving, dribbling politicians and leaders and generals left behind could not, and then they'd made it their business to take charge of the children.

They'd made the people *want* to give up their own kids. And they were just another New York *gang.*

I found myself wishing I'd taken a little longer with the fuckers inside the plane.

Eventually, loving every minute of the guards' continuing bewilderment, Nate dug from his pocket a tattered eye patch and covered over his half-tattoo. He looked like he'd done this sort of thing before. The goons all but fainted in relief; apologising with twenty shades of uncharacteristic pomposity and explaining that members of

'The Great Klan' so rarely visited the Mart, they were unprepared. It's one of those sights that sticks in the mind: two seven-foot yetis fawning and scraping over a scrawny old git dressed like a tramp with a uniform fetish. Nate clucked and swaggered along the concourse.

The guards turned to me and let the panicky hysteria fade from their grizzled faces. They took my gun, glancing at it with suspicious eyes that said *how inna hell did* you *come by* this, *little man?* and told me to show them my Klan marking.

"Ah," I said.

The way it worked, Nate had told me, was that you had your Klansmen, and then you had your scavs. The scavs were like livestock. Their loyalties determined by whichever mob happened to rule the territory in which they'd chosen to eke out their lives. Some went wherever their Klans went, or chose the most profitable or benevolent of regimes to nuzzle up to. Others were just spoils, like land taken in territorial scuffles; unceremoniously re-branded as the occasion required.

It sounded feudal. It sounded fucking *stupid.*

"Why don't they just *leave*?" I'd said, in the airport, as Nate explained. "Why don't they just *rebel*? There must be thousands of them."

"They do." Nate shrugged. "All the time. Not a day goes by there ain't a little... revolution, uprising, whatever. Chaos on the streets, every fucking night. But here's the thing: you want a way to share out scavenged shit, or food, or whatever you got? Klans're the only way."

"Bullshit."

"Not bullshit. Good sense. And if not good sense then natural-fucking-order." He'd licked his lips, waving a hand as he hunted down an example. "Let's say you're a... a young girl, right? Only just escaped the tithe. No parents. No weapons. No friends or food. Who's gonna stick up for you? Who's gonna make sure that shitty squat you found to sleep in don't get raided, or burnt down, or torn-up by some crackhead rapist? Huh?"

I'd shaken my head, unable to bring myself to agree, but I could see what he was getting at. Just.

"And what if you're *not* helpless?" I'd said. "You've still got to... toe the fucking line. Join up, act like a piece of *property*, get branded like a sodding *cow*."

"Yes, you do. Yes, you do. But the only way is up. And what happens when you impress one of the hotshots, huh? Or maybe cosy-up to the Klanboss? Or kill someone in the communal bad-books?"

I'd shaken my head again.

"Promotion." He grinned. "Become a Klansman. Free to carry weapons. Free to roam. Work your way up. Maybe one day challenge for the top spot."

"And if you fuck up?"

His voice had gone quiet, all but lost behind the crackling fire.

"Then you out on your ear. And you better hope you can take care of yourself, or else find someone who can."

Talking about himself, again. Just like always.

Nate said the Klansmen wore gang colours, and let their brands heal over. They got to carry weapons and administer internal justice and expand territories and all the other bullshit war games you can imagine. They played at being generals, gladiators, law enforcers and conquistadors. They got all the best gear. They had first choice of any scav, ate the best pickings, collected on debts, upheld the Klan's integrity and generally acted big.

I told Nate I was shaking in my boots. I'm not sure if he knew I was joking.

Back to the power plant.

"I don't have a brand," I told the guards.

"You ain't a scav?" One of them ran his eyes up and down my pitiful clothing. "*Look* like a scav."

"Fully paid-up Klansman," I said, smiling, knocking-out my best US accent and still managing to sound (in my head, at least) like I was taking the piss.

I was.

"Yeah?" The guard said, looking like he'd already had a bad day and couldn't be arsed with it getting any worse. "What Klan?"

I thought for a moment, smiled sweetly and said:

"The Culled."

They let me through, eventually, and as I passed him by the biggest goon grumbled, half-hearted.

"No Klan business inside."

I grinned and told him to perish the thought.

As we passed the checkpoint and wound our way further into the facility, I caught Nate staring at me, like some freakish version of a pirate, uncovered eye twinkling.

He'd been carrying my pack since the airport – to spare my shoulder, he said – and now he unslung it carefully onto the floor, staring at me with a curious smile.

I wondered for the fiftieth time what he was hoping to get out of all this. Out of helping me. Out of saving my life and bringing me here.

Call me cynical, but Nate didn't strike me as the sort of guy to do something for nothing.

"Take another cigarette?" he asked.

He'd earned it. Of course he had.

Currency's currency.

"Go ahead."

But as he dipped his hands inside the pack they moved with a speed and confidence that betrayed all kinds of stuff, if you're a paranoid bastard like me. If you know what you're looking for.

Familiarity.

Confidence.

Avarice.

When he saved my life, when he made the choice to attach himself to me rather than kill me, as I lay with a dying man's blood pulsing into my veins, he'd had hours and hours to go through the bag. Was that it? Was that all there was to him staying with me?

He'd seen the goods and wanted to earn his share?

No. No that made no sense. He could have just let me bleed out, let me die there on the runway, then taken it all for himself.

What then?

That same scratching. That same itching *something* at the back of my mind.

Something not quite right.

Something not adding up.

"Nate."

"Mm?" he said, sparking the cigarette.

Just ask, dammit...

"Why are you helping me?"

The air smelt of salt and car fumes. For a long time, there was silence. He watched me. Eyes unmoving.

"Thought we'd established that," he said, slowly, as if I was being ungrateful. As if I'd told him I didn't *need* him.

"Try again," I said, gently.

He sighed. Pursed his lips.

"I walked out on the Clergy, pal. Saved my own skin when I shoulda... shoulda died like a martyr. That's what they expect. *Thoughtless obedience*, you understand?"

"So?"

"So if they catch up with me, it's... It'll be..." He looked away, face fearful, and coughed awkwardly. Another long suck on the cigarette, calming his nerves.

"Anyway," he said. "I seen you in action."

"And?"

"I kept you alive, raggedy-man. Now all you got to do is return the favour."

And it was an explanation, I suppose. It made sense. It all added up.

And underneath it all the dark voice in my mind, shouting:

Don't you fucking give up, soldier.

Don't you get distracted, boy.

Don't you let things slip.

Sir, no sir, etc, etc.

Nate was helping me. Because of him I was healthy enough to carry on; to get the job done; to go after it like a flaming fucking sword. Everything else was just dross. Everything else was just peripheral shit that didn't matter. Who *cared* why Nate was helping me? He'd given his explanation. Now *move on.*

Except, except, except.

Except that as Nate dropped the cigarettes back into the bag his hand paused – a split second, no more – next to the battered city map with its New York scrawl and red ink notes, and his lips twitched. A fraction. Just a fraction.

Then he caught me staring, and closed up the pack with a friendly smile, and led me further inside the power plant.

I took the pack and shouldered it myself.

"How you feeling?" he said, as we walked. "Got your strength back? Lot of blood you lost, back there."

Reminding me. Keeping me indebted.

Not subtle, Nate.

"I'm peachy," I told him, a little colder than I'd meant.

Basic training, year two:

Call in favours. Get people good and beholden. Make friends. Make the fuckers owe you *one.*

But don't you let yourself owe anyone anything. *You hear me, soldier? Don't you get yourself in arrears. Don't you feel obliged to take* care *of anyone.*

People are parasites, boy. They see something strong, they clamp on.

They slow you down.

They complicate shit.

"Just peachy," I mumble-repeated, morose.

CHAPTER SEVEN

By then, the TV broadcasts were getting random.

The signal itself was okay. Would continue to be for another year or two, up until the power died and the generators sucked dry on fuel and all the diehards up at White City gave up. By which time barely anyone had a TV left working anyway.

But at the start, loud and clear, picture-perfect, 100% dross.

Mostly it was repeats. A computer governed the scheduling, I guessed, to cover holes and overruns. Endless episodes of Only Fools and Horses, *long-gone seasons of* Porridge *and* The Good Life, *a smattering of game shows whose contestants won or lost years before.* Friends *reruns, over and over and over and over, and anyone who gave a shit waited in vain for an episode called* 'The One Where Everyone Dies of an Unknown Flesh-Digesting Virus.'

No one was making anything new. No documentaries about the present emergency. No one had the time or energy to programme the channels.

Everyone was too busy staying alive.

This was at the beginning. This was during the Cull itself, as The Blight swept the country, as the infrastructure gave way like a dam made of salt and all the comfortable little certainties – advertising, street-sweepers, hotdog stalls, the Metro *newspaper on the underground,* discount sales, pirated DVDs, free samples in supermarkets, full vending machines – all the little frills you never fucking noticed, just slowly...

...went away.

Except the news. Sometimes, anyway. "God Bless the BBC!" people would say, as they passed in the street, tripping on bloody bodies and dead riot cops. Sometimes days would piss past with nothing – no bulletins at the top of the hour, no "we-interrupt-this-antique-comedy-to-bring-you-breaking-news" – and out in the rain all the uncertain crowds who couldn't work out why they weren't coughing and dying like everyone else were all anxiety and confusion, waiting beside the screens. But once in a while... once in a while.

I imagined a skeleton crew, struggling on bravely at Television Centre; sleeping and living in its ugly bulges just to get the word out. I imagined them feeling pretty good about themselves, like the fireman who goes above and beyond to save a crying kid, like an artist who doesn't sleep for a week to get the right tones, the right shades, the right effects. Like the soldier who keeps going, who never gives up, no matter what.

In a civilised – and I use the word with the appropriate levels of irony – world, news is just another commodity. It so rarely affects you. It so rarely intersects with the sheltered, blinkered universe of your real world. It's just another entertainment. Another distant work of fiction (or as good as) to be picked apart and discussed in the local boozer, over tea or coffee, sat on the train, wherever.

The Cull changed all that. The Cull made it so everyone was *living* the news, all the time. Suddenly all the people – the quiet little nobodies who called themselves 'normal' and never made a fuss – knew what it was like to be a native of Baghdad, or an earthquake widow, or a disgraced politician. Suddenly they all knew what it was like to switch on the box and hear all about themselves, their own world, their own shitty lives, discussed in the same autocue-serious tone as every other dismal slice of bad news.

It must have been a weird sensation.

(Not for me, though. I'd been making the news for years, one way or another. And I mean 'making.' Some weeks it felt like foreign affairs correspondents would've been out of a job but for me and mine, though they didn't know it. And no one ever said my name.)

On this particular day, the eagerness to receive fresh information was stronger than ever. All throughout the blistered wastes of London, little knots of people had formed – their clothes not yet raggedy, but getting there; their faces not yet malnourished and gaunt, but getting there – to crowd around flickering sets in front rooms and electronics shops, tolerating the dismal repeats on the off-chance of a new bulletin.

Two days ago, they'd mentioned the bombs falling in America. Rumours of atomic strikes, attacks all across the world, missiles going up and tumbling back down, EM pulses like technological plagues and supertech 'Star Wars' defences misfiring; farting useless interceptors into lightning storms and spitting heat seekers into the sea.

When they'd made that *announcement – a couple of days before – it had been tricky to know how much was confirmed and how much was fabrication. Concocted, one suspected, by the dishevelled creature sat behind the news-desk, staring in terror at the trembling camera. It was difficult to imagine the usual BBC specimens – bolt upright, faces slack, Queen's English spoken with a crisp enunciation that bordered on the ridiculous – stammering and coughing quite so much as the nervous girl huddled behind her sheaf of papers, as she told an entranced London that nuclear Armageddon was right around the corner, then sipped carefully at her water.*

It had been a tense couple of days, since.

I sat it all out in the flat. It had changed since that gloomy day when I got the text, when the removal guys failed to show up, when the ambulances streaked past one after another. Now the fish tank lay smashed on the floor, the CDs were all off the shelf in a heap, a couple of pot plants were turning slowly brown with their stalks broken and roots unearthed, and the front door sported a few splintered little holes where I'd shot it – for no reason other than to let the neighbours know I was armed.

I'd had a tantrum or two, that's all.

The phone hadn't rung. There were no more text messages. Nothing.

Oh, and, PS: nuclear bombs may be about to fall.

Not the best week of my life.

The point was, on this day, when the catchphrase comedy was blissfully interrupted and the serious little Newsflash *screen cut-in without announcement or music, pretty-much every poor beleaguered fucker in the entire city leaned a little closer to the set, and held their breath.*

It was a new face behind the news desk – even younger than the last one, with an untidy mop of hair and a thick pair of glasses that reflected the shimmering blue of the autocue off-puttingly – and he cleared his throat agonisingly before beginning.

What he said had nothing whatsoever to do with bombs.

"Good afternoon," he said. I almost laughed. "A UN-sponsored team of researchers based in the United States have today released a statement regarding the unknown sickness that is now estimated to have struck two thirds of the countries of the world, and shows no sign of abating. Despite the poor quality of the signal, agencies still in contact with the BBC across the Atlantic have confirmed it to be genuine, though its source is as-yet unknown.

"According to the report, the disease targets particular biological conditions with a precision formerly unknown in medical science. Referred to by the unnamed author of the report as the 'AB-virus,' the infection – which is airborne and requires no physical contact to transmit – attacks red blood cells at an unprecedented rate; causing muscular, respiratory and cardiac failure within days."

A cut-rate graphic appeared on the screen: a crude image of eight identical human silhouettes, in two rows of four columns. Headers across the top of the table read A, B, AB and O, whilst the rows were marked with simple mathematical symbols for positive and negative.

"Oh shit..." I whispered. The penny was beginning to drop.

"Each person," the voice continued, settling into a sort of cod-documentary narration, "possesses one of four distinct types of blood – known as phenotypes. These are characterised by the various protein markers, or 'antigens,' upon the surface of each red blood cell. So, people of phenotype 'A' have A-antigens" – here the first column of the table lit-up in lurid yellow – "and people of phenotype 'B' have B-antigens. Those whose blood-type is 'AB' have antigens of both varieties, whilst those with no antigens at all belong to phenotype 'O.'"

In each case the strip of yellow highlighting clunked its way along the table. I felt like I was watching one of those godawful educational videos they used to crack out in biology lessons at school, with the unconvincing sexual metaphors and the pulpy innards of rats and frogs.

"The practical effect of this system is to determine what blood-types are safely viable for transfusion into medical patients. Patients of blood type 'A,' for example, cannot be safely given blood of any phenotype containing 'B' antigens and vice-versa."

The voice drew a breath. It was hardly compelling viewing, but I didn't envy the poor bastard delivering it. It was like 'Doomsday-By-Boring-Science.'

I guess even then, at the back of my mind, knowing as I did that I hadn't felt a twinge of sickness, and being all too familiar with my own medical stats, I knew what was coming.

"The categorisation is further complicated," the voice droned, "by the presence in most people's blood of a further protein marker: the so-called 'rhesus' antigen." Here the entire upper row illuminated, like a bad version of a Connect-Four game show. "Any person with Rhesus-positive blood cannot viably donate to those with Rhesus negative blood, whose bodies contain natural antibodies to defend against the antigen."

I caught a sudden mental picture of filthy people all across London, clustered into makeshift bomb-shelters, trading bewildered glances and muttering *"Wassefucken'* talkin' *baht?"*

The newsman continued, a little shakily.

"The UN report makes it clear that the virus, once contagion has occurred, will specifically target red blood cells bearing antigens of any type. So any person of phenotypes A, B, or AB; or of Rhesus-positive blood, is susceptible to infection."

On the screen, the little graphic changed, a crude red 'X' appearing upon each and every cell within the table, except for the last one.

"Subtle," I said, to nobody.

The camera cut back to the guy behind the desk. He looked tired, and someone had nipped-in to yank off his glasses during the off-screen monologue, so now he was squinting comically at the autocue.

"If the report is correct," he said, "less than seven percent of the population of the United Kingdom – those of phenotype O-Negative – are safe from infection."

He coughed quietly, glanced off-camera for a moment, and then licked his lips. He knew what was coming.

"The report ends... the report ends with a summary of the research team's attempts to develop a treatment for the 'AB-virus.' Viewers... uh. Some viewers may find the following audio file disturbing."

I laughed again, bitter.

"Yeah..." I said. "Yeah. Because telling nine-out-of-fucking-ten people they're going to die isn't at all disturbing, mate, is it?"

The poor kid was up out of his chair – face crumpled in disgust – before the image even blurred away into a bland red screen with the title 'UN Research Report.'

A man's voice – American – came out of nowhere:

"As to our findings regarding the – ugh – the – hnh..." A thick bout of coughing broke through the signal; ugly sounds of spittle flying and phlegm being swallowed, which lapsed by degrees into silence. Machinery and murmuring voices sounded quietly in the background. The voice started again, dry and uncomfortable. "– the treatment of the virus. We've... we've found nothing. No way to stop it. It obeys all these... these rules we don't understand, but even so... every division is a... a new strain. You treat one – kill it, even – the next one's different. It – hnnk – it can't be sto –"

The voice broke off again, the coughing far uglier this time, interrupted with staccato grunts of pain and short curses. It softened slightly – the speaker moving away from the microphone – but the obvious pain of the fit was hardly diminished, and I found myself wincing in sympathy.

And then everything changed.

It was only quiet, but I heard it. There's no doubt. No fraction of uncertainty in my mind.

It was barely audible. It rose out of the background hubbub and the storm of coughing and wheezing dominating the signal, but oh God, I heard it. I know *I did.*

"Lie him down!" a new voice said. Tinny with distortion and distance, but somehow resonant and deep nonetheless. "Get him down! And switch off that fucking micropho..."

The signal died.

The news programme stopped.

The repeat episode of Only Fools and Horses *picked up where it'd left off, with canned laughter roaring out of the box.*

Out on the streets of London, a low moaning, building through sobs and cries of horror, was growing all across the steepled skyline.

In my flat, I shot the door six more times, drank half a bottle of vintage single malt, and went out to start a fight.

That night – the night that London tore itself apart – I could take my pick.

SOMEONE TRIED TO rob me. Emphasis on the *tried.*

Give the little punks their credit: they had a system. Probably been pulling this shit every day for months, and if it weren't for the fact I clocked them as soon as I saw them, it might even have worked.

Somewhere inside the heart of the Con Ed power plant facility, a broad plaza had been cleared. Intestinal pipes and tanks dragged aside, buildings burned and shattered, the whole roughly-square patch razed to a cracked-concrete wilderness.

It *heaved.*

The weirdest thing was – and I didn't realise this until later – there were no kids. It seemed natural enough to expect them, somewhere amongst it all. At the heart of the colourful crowds, at the source of the excited shouts and squeals, amidst all the bodies squashed together or dashing through scant open spaces as they blossomed and filled. It was pandemonium. It was human convection in a tattered blend of colours and sizes, pushing and jostling and grunting, haggling out loud, or simply standing tall to yell offers at top volume.

But no kids. In all of New York, just like London: no kids.

"Wheels Mart," Nate said, leaning idly against a rusted pipe and lighting another of my cigarettes. "You want transport, you find it here." His eyes narrowed, almost imperceptibly. "Where we going anyways?"

I ignored him and let the sensory overload knock me about, letting my instincts adjust, taking stock.

A hundred and one aromas gusted past – not just the usual filth and stink of too many unhygienic people – but the smoky promise of meat and stew, served diligently by a long row of low stalls, to the colossal queues of hungry customers. Prices were written in arcane barter-notes: weighing cigarettes, ammunition, items of clothing, canisters of fuel and recreational narcotics against the value of ratburgers, dog food gumbo, home-grown potatoes and (*fuck me, the smell!*) freshly baked bread. My senses kept trying to tell me I'd died and gone to heaven.

All around the outer perimeter of this bustling plaza other stalls were erected, bartering all manner of curious products and scraps of salvage. So wide was the square – and so thick with people – that I couldn't even make out what the distant stock *was*, though a tent near me held nothing but live chickens and shrieking budgerigars in small wicker cages, and something that looked troublingly like a parrot was turning on a spit over a barbecue. There were no weapons visible anywhere, except those clutched by the small groups of black-clad guards lounging about on walls and turrets around the enclosure, keeping half an eye. The distinctive shriek-scream-grunt of pigs rose from a muddy morass behind another section of the crowd, and most audible of all – over the top of everything else – was the growl of engines. Dozens of them. From all quarters of the mart, fumes coiled upwards like greasy fingers, and at regular intervals a fresh cavalcade of bikes throttling, cars backfiring and heavier vehicles rumbling to life sounded above the mêlée.

The crowd was thickest at the centre, where a tall man in a wide-brimmed Stetson dangled uncomfortably from a series of cables and harnesses above their heads, waving arms and shouting out what I first mistook for unintelligible nonsense. The crowd seemed to be responding in kind – hands raised, necks craned, roaring out and waving bits and pieces of tatty scav every time the pendulous showman wobbled overhead.

It took me a while to realise he was running an auction.

"Four an' five!" He was wittering, almost too fast to catch, "four-and-five, pack of burns, pack of burns? Pack of burns! Anna piglet! Raise me? Best scoot inna house, here! Vespa, onlythabest! Raise me? Raise me?"

The crowd hollered – everyone shouting all at once – and the MB ("Master'f bids," Nate grunted) dangled about like a string puppet, pointing fingers, taking offers, and promising new barters. A shiny chrome moped sat on a plinth beside the crowd, guarded by four serious-looking guards.

"Pack of burns?" I asked, flicking Nate a look.

He shrugged and brandished his cigarette, then scowled and looked me up and down.

"You wanna try lookin' any *more* like a goddamn *tourist*?"

I realised I'd been blocking the causeway. Sticking out like a sore thumb with my bulging backpack invitingly obvious, bolt-upright and fascinated where everyone else was either rushing about like their arseholes were on fire or leaning, just like Nate, against whatever item of sturdy ephemera they found. There were two correct states of being inside the Wheels-Mart: involved or not involved, and neither one involved any sense of wonderment.

Paying attention; taking an interest; having a bag full of unknown goodies. These were one-way-tickets to getting noticed by someone.

My 'someones' emerged from the crowd to my left, and I knew what was coming immediately. Two young men – early twenties at a guess, maybe even tithe-dodgers – scrapping and squabbling, rolling in muck, dirtied fingernails clutching at torn rags. They sprang and locked again, snarling like ferrets, tripping each other in their clumsy aggression then scrambling upright for a renewed attack.

It was all very convincing.

Except for the glances.

The tiny sideways squints in my direction.

The subtle eyes that told me everything I needed to know.

One of them drew a knife, circling in suddenly to thrust inwards towards the other, who rolled aside theatrically and yanked his own shimmering little shiv out of the hem of his boot. The pair closed again, their angry wrestles and desperate stabs bringing them – as if by magic – stumbling towards me. Choreographed to perfection. Messy and fast and unpredictable, and as authentic as it gets, but *I* knew.

The body language.

The stance.

Nate was watching them with some interest, I noticed, completely taken-in; face a slack mixture of disapproval and distance. Even some of the crowd – studiously nonchalant of all other things – were twisting to watch the brewing carnage. Everyone was ignoring me, never considering it might all be for my benefit. One or two punters even started calling out encouragement to the fighters, making wagers and shouting advice, whilst others scanned the crowd for the nearest guards.

"No Klan business!" a woman hissed, trying to break them up. The young men shoved her away and kept circling around each other, knives hooking hilt-to-hilt, then twisting back and forth inside one another's guard. Vicious. Personal.

Always heading right for me.

By the time they dropped the pretence and pounced – both at the same time, unlocking from their fake pugilism like a bear trap in reverse, knives outstretched on each side like scissor blades – I was already moving. Diving beneath the double-stab, rolling awkwardly across the backpack and flicking out one orbital leg: roundhousing the first punk – a freckled beanpole with bright purple hair – off his feet. The other darted-in with a snarl, catching a straight-handed chop to the side of his tattooed neck and – as I vaulted upright from the ground – an angry, unsubtle head butt on the bridge of his much-pierced nose. To be blunt I think he was dead from the neck wound already – he bloody should have been, the way I hit him – but I was angry. Sue me.

He went down without a word.

The purple-haired geek got up slowly, shaking his head to clear the fuzz, and backhanded his knife into a downward slicer. I picked up his mate's shiv – dropped from one spasming hand – and grinned at him; letting my body tell him how calm I was, how much I wanted him to rush me, how much I was *urging* him to come take me on –

His eyes flickered, just a millimetre, to one side.

Cold sweat. That sinking feeling.

Third guy behind me.

Two for the diversion, one for the strike.

Clever.

I sidestepped a fraction early. I figured the attack was imminent, but I left the fucker with too much time to angle his swing. Still, if it's a choice between denting my skull with a heavy tyre-iron or missing by inches and instead swiping the fabric along the top of my pack – tipping me over like a sleeping cow – I'll take the latter every time. I slash-stabbed blindly with the shiv as I stumbled, snarling from somewhere deep inside me that wasn't entirely rational; feeling a tug and a tear and a spatter of warmth, rewarded with a scream. The breath exploded out of me as I thumped to the tarmac on my back, crushing the kid with the pierced face for a second time and sending something sharp punching through the top of my pack; digging me in the nape of my neck.

This Johnny-come-lately sneak-up-behind-a-guy arsehole – an enormous man with a braided beard and a pair of lensless glasses – staggered and moaned, squirting blood from an arterial gash on his thigh. He'd dropped the tyre iron at some stage, but as the purple-haired youth closed in on me with the knife, the giant swatted him on the shoulder, held out a bony paw for the blade, and dropped down to finish me himself.

Something small and red appeared between his eyes.

The back of his head came off, and for a second or two he looked startled; as if his brain was still feeding him waves of shock and uncertainty, despite being scattered in a semicircle across the mud. A gunshot echoed across the crowd – like a guest arriving late for a party – and everyone jumped.

"Fffff..." he managed.

The kid with the purple-hair took off.

Without being entirely conscious of it, sitting upright in one long fluid movement, I felt my arm extend, left eye closed, fingers releasing. The shiv – a curled tooth of flat steel, easily palmed beneath gloved fingers – spun off into space; a shuriken that caught the weak light as it whispered.

It hit the punk at the base of his skull, just beside his left ear. It looked like it went deep, and when he sagged to the floor – arms quivering, legs bending back on themselves – he wasn't in any rush to get back up.

There's a lot of blood in a scalp. It clashed with his hair.

It dawned on me slowly that a lot of people were staring. Several of them were wearing black clothes and red bandanas, and were going to great lengths to elbow their way through the crowd in my direction.

A shadow fell across me.

"Stay the fuck there," it said, poking the two dead punks near me with a smoking rifle.

My guardian angel, I guessed. The one who blew off the giant's head.

From below, it looked a lot like a tattered, hunchbacked ogre.

Its voice was actually kind of sexy.

CHAPTER EIGHT

HER NAME WAS Malice. I figure she was probably 'Alice' – maybe 'Melissa' – at one time, but the whole gung-ho nickname thing worked pretty well for the mercenaries the Wheels-Mart paid to keep the peace, and they were never happier than when striding about, calling out each other's ridiculous handles across the braying crowds.

Spuggsy.

Moto.

Tora.

Nike.

And so on. I pretended to be impressed as they introduced themselves. Pumped up and black-clad in every case, moving with that familiar 'I'm-a-hard-bastard' confidence you see in mercenaries the world over.

They'd propped me up in a canvas shelter off to one side of the auction (still noisily ongoing through the tent's doorway) and now Malice was staring at me, more-or-less-alone, with her arms folded. Nate stood behind me, dabbing at the cut on my neck. I think he was enjoying being part of the attention. Light through the tattered canvas ceiling dappled the interior of the room, making it seem busy and claustrophobic, and it was almost an effort – in amongst the extremes of brightness and shadow – to focus on Malice's eyes.

She was the blackest person I'd ever seen in my life, and she was so beautiful it hurt.

"So," she said, voice guarded. "Guess we owe you one."

"Why's that?"

"Took out the three Goddamn amigos back there. They been causing trouble few weeks now. Coming in off the water, we figured."

"Happy to oblige."

She smirked unconvincingly.

Malice wore the same black threads as all the other guards (though it would be unfair not to mention how the baggier parts of the ensemble crinkled as she moved, hinting at what was going on underneath) and the same red bandana – in her case folded into a bright sweat-band around her crown. Her hair was shaven away to that not-quite-stubble length – like the velvety patch on the tip of a horse's nose – which so few women can pull off, but makes the ones who can look so ball-rupturingly sensational.

Malice looked like she had a hunch on her back. A big one.

Once in a while the hunch – hidden away beneath black veils – gurgled to itself.

The kid, she told me, was a fraction over a year old. Malice never mentioned the father, so I figured he was long gone or dead. It (I never found out a name, or a gender) stayed quieter than any baby I've ever known, and seemed perfectly untroubled by its mother lugging about a high-powered air-rifle and a sweet assortment of other popguns. Once in a while Malice jiggled in a strange sort of way, rocking the wicker harness the baby was huddled inside, as if she knew when the sleepy sprog was on the verge of waking up without even having to look.

Every time she jiggled like that it looked like she was giving me the come-on.

"Who are you?" she blurted, just as the silence was getting uncomfortable.

I shrugged. "Just a customer. Just passing through."

She shook her head. "Uh-uh. I saw the way you took out them rats. You're ex-mil, pal. Showed in every move. Special forces, maybe. SEALs. Whatever it is you Brits got..."

Not even close, honey.

"Does it matter if I am?"

Her eyes narrowed. "Yeah, it fuckin' *matters.* Some psycho stalking 'bout in my Mart."

"I didn't start tha –"

"And the only ex-mils round these parts're with the Choirboys."

Aha...

I frowned. "Clergy, right?"

She spat on the floor, as if disgusted by the very name. I started to like her even more, and wondered just how highly the universally loved Neo-Clergy were *actually* regarded...

I held my palms out – like showing her I had nothing to hide – and pointed to the distinct lack of scarlet tattoos on my eye.

"I'm not with the Clergy."

Her eyes darted to Nate. In the cover of the tent he'd flipped-up the pirate eye patch like a pedal-bin lid, making him look like a astonished panda. "But your pet here?"

Nate 'tsk'd through his teeth and waggled a finger. "Ex," he said. "Ex, sugar."

She just glared.

"He's officially retired," I said, flipping Nate's eye patch back down with a quiet slap.

Malice spat again. "No such thing."

The silence stretched out. Malice started pacing a little, left then right, keeping her eyes fixed on us all the time.

I drummed my fingers on the arms of the chair, creating every impression of disdainful boredom, and whistled quietly. My neck felt tight, like Nate had stuck a monstrous plaster across it, and I hadn't had a chance to find out what had caused the wound yet. I was sort of glad I couldn't see.

Outside, the fast-talking MB sold a battered BMW to a man with three piglets of his very own, who'd outbid a guy with a portable power drill and a book of jokes.

Mostly the vehicles were cheap, in 'who-gives-a-shit' money terms, but I guess I shouldn't have been surprised. When 93% of the world shuffles off the mortal slinky there are a lot of jalopies left rusting in empty driveways. The way they saw it, the black-clad personnel of the Wheels-Mart were just agents. Middlemen to cut out the tedious business of finding, breaking into, hot-wiring and maintaining vehicles. The Klans sent their scavs along to buy the best of the pick, and as long as everyone kept themselves polite, self-serving, and oh-so-very-neutral, the whole system worked.

Until someone who stands out shows up. No one likes a guy who rocks the boat.

I got the impression Malice and the other guards were mighty twitchy. Ready to snap. Ready to kill.

And they didn't like the Clergy.

Hmm.

After long, boring minutes had passed, I cracked my knuckles nastily and said:

"So. You going to let us get on with it, or what?"

Malice made a show of ignoring me, pulling off that same weird rolling motion, hip-twitching as she soothed the baby.

I stood up.

"Or do you guys make a habit of pulling this shit on anyone who does your job for you?"

She smiled, and this time I think there was at least a glimmer of genuine humour in there, no matter how guarded it was.

"You want a *job*, limey? That it?"

"Fuck no."

"What, then?"

"Want a set of wheels."

"Going somewhere?"

"Yep."

"Want to tell me where?"

"Not really." I shrugged my tattered coat back on over the top of Nate's bandage, and threw Malice an impatient stare. "We able to do business here or not? 'Cos if it's less of a timewaster I'm quite happy to go stand in the crowd and shout at the wanker on the wire."

Her nose wrinkled thoughtfully. "You got currency?"

"Apprehending known villains not good enough?"

"Covers fuel costs, maybe. World don't turn on good deeds, pal."

"Too fucking right."

I picked up the pack the thieves had been after and brandished it for Malice's inspection, oozing all the business-like cool in the world.

"Ten cans Pedigree Chum," I said, letting the bag spin on its straps. "Six packs of cigarettes. Two bottles Jack Daniels, one bottle supermarket-brand vodka. One tin powdered milk. Three cashmere blankets, only the best will doodle-do. Two packs condoms." (Malice's eye met mine, lightning-speed) "Three vials amphetamine, six sachets barbiturate tablets, eyedropper full of acid, an eighth of Moroccan woodbine – if you believe the dealer – and five hypos of some weird mil-shit called 'Bliss.'" I smiled sweetly. "Take your pick."

Nate coughed, awkwardly. Malice was staring at me with an ironic eyebrow, like she was trying not to laugh. I became distantly aware of a quiet noise, like:

Spitaspataspitaspata

The pack was leaking. A few jagged shards of glass – half a vodka bottle and the angular rim of a JD litre – had torn their way through the fabric in several places, and their wasted contents were puddling on the floor. It looked like a lot of other shit had fallen out too. Somewhere outside, in the thick of the crowd.

"Ah," I said. "Bugger."

This minor calamity seemed to adjust the atmosphere somehow, as if by demonstrating that I wasn't *quite* as cool as I'd made out, I'd taken the sting out of Malice's suspicion. I'd like to say I'd planned it that way. The woman even smiled openly once or twice – her posture relaxing for a beat – as we rescued what we could from the doomed offerings.

The alcohol was all gone and the cigarettes reduced to a soggy mess, stinking of whisky. Nate (self-elected expert) declared them to be utterly worthless, then pocketed them quietly when he thought I wasn't watching. The blankets were stained but useable, the dog food and rubbers untroubled by their liquor soaking, and the drugs – which I'd hoped would be my most valuable bargaining chip – had alternately dissolved, shattered, fallen out of the pack, or dribbled away. Two of the Bliss hypos remained, along with a single vial of 'phets and the baggie of skunk. Nate kept moaning quietly under his breath every time we found something else ruined or missing, like he'd had it in his mind that the longer he stuck with me, the more of my stash he was liable to inherit.

I wondered vaguely if the drastic losses were enough to make him stop following me around. To break the debt.

I let the thought go, for now – content to let things carry me, trusting my instincts – and poked about in the miserly little stash we'd rescued. Five years of misery and starvation since the Cull, and the 'drugs problem' had mutated mysteriously from 'There's Too Much,' to 'There's Not Enough.' It's hard to take the moral high ground when you've watched your friends die, when you've spent all day chasing ornamental ducks along stagnant canals, when you're freezing to death and when someone's offering you a quick and easy way to escape.

'Just say no?' Fuck *that.*

Just say *gimme.*

If fuel was gold in this mean-arsed new world, then hardcore narcotic stimulation was platinum.

"Not going to get you much." Malice shrugged. "How far you gotta go?"

"How about you show me what you've got?"

She shrugged again – the baby hiccupped – and gestured towards the rear door of the tent.

I stepped outside and felt my neck prickling. This is the same feeling all men get, when they step into a room full of gadgets, or fast cars, or big guns.

Set back from the main square, on an adjacent street between black painted walls of corrugated iron and criss-crossed walkways manned by gun-toting guards, Malice led me through rows of cars, vans, pickups, SUVs, motorbikes, bicycles and – shuffling nervously against the rope walls of a makeshift paddock – a trio of horses. Amidst the dozens of wheeled contraptions the whinnying livestock was about the only means of transport in the place that hadn't been radically altered in some way, and even they'd been daubed with crazy patterns in black and red branding paint. On everything else clashing colours and crudities were smeared along every chassis, windows were shattered or missing, innards had been comprehensively plundered. It would have been faintly depressing – like a scrap yard refusing to give up the ghost – had it not been for the special area, roped-off with its own guards. Inside its boundaries everything had been augmented, streamlined, *changed.* I gazed lovingly at steel roll-bars, wheel-covers in three types of mesh, hulking nitro canisters wedged inside passenger seats and ten different variations on the theme of 'heavily armed.'

Pintle mounts poked like miniature SAM-sites from the roofs of jeeps and spot-welded AVs. Swinging hatches – just like on Nate's old school bus – replaced side-doors and load containers, whilst several cars sported a sneaky set of exhausts below the rims of the front doors, to blast flames at the touch of a button at anyone dumb enough to try getting inside.

I wanted to *play.*

All of them were painted black and red.

"What're these?" I asked Malice, barely able to control the drooling.

She smirked. "Rentals."

"And how do you make sure the customer brings them back?"

"Oh, that's easy."

"Oh, yeah?"

"Yeah. We go with them."

At the far corner of the section my eye fell on something. Something big and angry-looking. Something spiky.

I nearly fell in love.

"The *Inferno*," said Malice, following my eye. "Cute, huh?"

It had been a fire truck once, although to be fair it bore about as much similarity to its previous incarnation as a shark to a diving bell. It was... *sleek*, which was an adjective I'd never have picked to describe a fire engine before. 'Like a speeding brick,' maybe, but never *dangerous.* Never *predatory.*

Progressive layers of sheet-iron had been built-up from a sort of conical crest along the truck's nose, like the scales of a dagger-like fish. Below its new snout a shallow dozer-scoop clamoured with spikes and barbed wire, whilst wide flanges protected the windshield above.

All four tyres wore heavy swaddles of chains, canvas padding, rubber coils and thick iron rims, and a set of spares were lashed carefully beneath a wire and sheet gurney on the left flank. Halfway down the truck's thirty-foot length, an angle-poised turret reclined its muzzles towards the sky, its firing position enclosed on all sides by a low balustrade of welded plate steel. At one time it'd been a water cannon, easily hitched to a tanker truck and fired in great arcing loops. Now it had been modified. Converted in ways I couldn't easily see, so the central cannon stood surrounded in a clutch of cables, secondary devices and dangling controls. I think I picked out a Mk19 grenade launcher amongst the oily barrels, which told me everything I needed to know.

You did not fuck with the *Inferno*.

Secondary and rear-angle tertiary gunmounts were placed further along the vehicle's spine, each one protected by small forests of steel jags and corrugated shields. The whole thing was painted as black as sin, except the rims of the wheels and the hood above the windshield, which stood out in vibrant red like the belly of a Black Widow.

It was something of an effort to form words. "How many... does...?"

"Four crew. Five if you want the big guns out, but that's extra. Room for as many passengers as can hold on."

"And how much... ah. How much would it cost to...?"

She stared at me. She wasn't smiling.

"A lot more," she said, "than you've got."

So that squished *that* one.

Long story short: I ended up embarking on my perilous quest on the back of a fucking quadbike, which sputtered and farted every time I throttled it, and it cost me everything I had except a single can of dog food, a sodding cashmere blanket and a packet of condoms. Malice said I'd got myself a bargain, and filled the whiny little vehicle up for free.

I settled into the driver's seat – feeling pretty good, letting the engine tick over – and turned to thank her for her help. She was already walking away, disappearing into the tent, and the last I saw of her was her baby staring at me owlishly from her shoulders, dribbling with a smile. I sighed, wondering what I felt.

Attraction? Loss?

Guilt?

Nate was staring at the quad with a sort of disgusted fascination. I sat back in the seat and folded my arms. *Let him choose*, I thought, feeling nasty. *Let him ask*.

"So, *ah*..." He shifted from foot to foot.

Then *tsk*ed.

Then started clambering on.

"Whoa, whoa... hang on..." I waved him off. "You're coming just like that?"

"Too damn right."

"But, you're... I mean..." I gaped, earnestly astonished. It felt a little like a limpet had attached itself to me, and no matter how long I held it over the fire it wasn't going to let go. "You don't even know where I'm headed!"

I watched his face.

There. There it was again.

The hesitation.

The eyes flicking to the pack on my back, then away again.

"Don't matter." He said, forcing a smile. "I'm game."

"And if I wanna go on alone?"

"Then I remind you how I saved your life."

"But..."

"And I *add* – seeing as how you're bein' so hardass about it – that my price just went up. I get bodily protection, plus one blanket, one can dog food."

"You want all my shit *too*? For *what*?"

He smirked, white teeth electric beside me.

"Travelling medic," he said. "Keep you outta trouble."

And then it was too late, and he was perched on the pillion and pointing ahead like a general giving the order to advance, and that was that.

Good, I tried to tell myself. *He's a resource. He can help. He knows the area.*

But always the itching. Always the uncertainty. Always the suspicion.

What's your ulterior motive, doc?

And even deeper than that, drummed in at a genetic level, the angry lectures splitting open my head; a tac-command feed direct into my skull.

Don't you let yourself owe anyone anything. *You hear me, soldier? Don't you get yourself in arrears. Don't you feel obliged to take* care *of anyone.*

"Oh, hey," he grinned. "And throw in them rubbers, too."

My train of thought derailed itself in a blur of disbelief. "*You* want condoms?" I gaped.

He seemed vaguely affronted. "Damn straight! You think I wanna be a daddy aga..."

He stopped himself, mouth open, then blinked once or twice and started over; coughing his way through the hesitation. "You think I wanna be a daddy, *my* time of life?"

I stared at him for a moment, wondering what to say, how to react, then shrugged and tossed him the rubbers.

"Fine," I grinned. "Clean me out."

He scrambled onto the saddle's pillion like a scarecrow mounting a horse, and I gunned the bike along the Mart's central promenade with a fierce sensation of freedom, letting the customers still pouring in take responsibility for not getting run down. Even so, as I stopped to retrieve the rifle and pistols I'd lodged with the goons at the check-in, there was something grinding in my mind. Cogs interlocking, memories grinding. Something about Nate. Something he'd said, maybe.

Something not quite right...

We churned through the Mart's main gates, bobbing uncomfortably over untended tarmac and roadside debris, and took a sharp right. Nate leaned down and shouted over the roar of the wind.

"What I said!" he called, voice hoarse. "Earlier on! About the Clergy!"

"What about them?"

"About... About what if they catch up to me! They... they got these... what's it called, man! Jesus-cross!"

"Crucifix?"

"Yeah! Right! They got a shitload! All ready for any motherfucker pisses them *off*!"

Visions of medieval tortures and Inquisitorial nastiness slipped through my head. I kept seeing that scene from *Spartacus*; the main road flanked on both sides by crucified rebels, and saw me and Nate swinging in the breeze. "Oh yeah?" I shouted. "Where's that?"

"Midtown, man! Manhattan! Biggest territory there is! Centre of the fucking universe!"

I let the quadbike bring itself to a trundling halt, feeling the engine die-down, forming words carefully.

"What you doing?" Nate blurted, prodding the quadbike. "Is it busted?"

"No, no, it's... *ah*."

"What?"

I tried to grin. Failed.

"Well, it's just... you'll never guess where we're headed."

CHAPTER NINE

INTERLUDE

Raymond – or Ram – caught up with Rick somewhere in the city suburbs. The first he knew about it was a speck in his single remaining wing mirror, gathering size as it tore toward him at top speed.

At first he thought nothing of it. He'd seen little of anyone during this last leg of the journey, but the few people he'd spotted were enough to relax his nerves, where before he would have fled from anyone. Out here, beneath the ever-changing sky (one hour burning bright, the next choked with fog, the next boiling with turbulent clouds; but always on a scale that seemed somehow too big, defying the eye) his only company were the occasional figures distantly glimpsed across the hills, tending fields or felling dead trees. Once or twice he'd even passed vehicles, always heading west. Mostly monstrous pickups and HGVs crammed to the gills with filthy-looking people, who stared at him with dead eyes as the trike gunned by, manoeuvring awkwardly around the abyssal potholes and gaping cracks that striated the roads. Some of these travelling groups were surrounded by little clusters of motorbike outriders, who glared suspiciously as they hurried all other traffic off the road. Each time he saw them Rick stiffened, expecting more silver-jacketed Collectors, imagining Slip's bloodless body stretched-out in the hardware store back in Snow Hand.

None of the bikers so much as looked at him.

Other trucks bristled with quills like porcupines: men with rifles and swivelling arms-mounts, suspicious of everything that moved. He wondered who they all were, where they were all going, what they did all day long – then promptly forgot them as soon as he reached the next corner.

He was in a slightly fragile state of mind.

The I-80 was an endless grey snake, cracked and mud-drenched, pocked with deep wells and unexpected fissures that crept-up on the unprepared traveller, wending its way through hills and fields of green and brown. Here and there old heaps stood and rusted – breakdowns that no one ever bothered to tow clear – and only the twittering of unseen birds, and rabbits scampering for cover, disturbed the hypnotic progress of the tarmac serpent.

Rick was beginning to relax about the Harley too. At first it had seemed an unnecessarily flashy addition to his equipment: a mid-life-crisis on three tyres. It roared like the end of the world every time he gave it some throttle, and along with its dayglo paintjob in yellow and red, it conspired to be the absolute opposite of 'inconspicuous.'

The clan mothers would not *have approved.*

On the other hand, it was fast. It was far sturdier than the Yamaha, and in odd moments between small towns he'd begun to fancy he was riding an armchair; hovering across forests and lakes. With the stolen shotgun strapped across his back and a veritable cornucopia of other weapons stashed in the saddlebags, he kept seeing himself in some tacky Schwarzenegger moment. Crashing through flaming debris with a pithy one-liner and a minigun blazing.

In fact, Hiawatha – née Rick – kept imagining himself and his environment in all sorts of outrageous new ways. This had something to do with the boredom of cross-country travel, something to do with his natural imaginativeness, and a lot to do with the enormous quantities of the sachems' weed he'd been smoking since his run-in with the colossal bear-like sodomite who attempted to kill and eat him the night before.

He figured he owed it to himself.

He'd spent the night in a mid-sized town called White Deer, two hours or so down the interstate from his fateful encounter with Slip in Snow Hand. The place had been mostly deserted, but a pocket-sized population had set up a sort of commune around the central square, and Rick was too exhausted and too nervy to risk breaking in somewhere else. He traded one of the 9mms and a box of ammo for a comfy bed and two pouches of dried rabbit, and even got a bowl of vegetable soup into the bargain. The people were polite, eager to please, but ultimately empty. He could see the terror in their eyes; the way they kept looking back and forth from him to the Harley, to the bulging saddlebags.

At one point a little girl appeared – precociously smiley – and asked him if he was a Collector come to take her away to the bad men in dresses. He was about to tell her "no" – to tell the whole goddamn town he was nothing to do with the fucking Clergy, or any other troublemaking scum they might be afraid of – when her mother swept her away with a dozen fearful glances over her shoulder and a muttered warning for him to "stay the hell away from her!"

Point taken, he kept himself to himself after that: got as stoned as is it physically possible to get, sat staring at a fire with all the usual bullshit thoughts of spirits and voices that he only ever got when he 'wasn't himself,' and cleared off in the morning before the sun was fully up.

Two hours down the road, he passed a place called Kidder. There were three bodies strung-up on builder's scaffolding beside the turnoff; old and dried-out, almost skeletal now, dangling by their wrists on sharp cords of barbed wire. A spray-painted plaque below each one declared their crimes to the passing world.

THIEF

MUSLIM

INJUN

Each Tag had a scarlet circle sprayed below.

Rick decided against visiting Kidder.

He paused only once during the morning – another narcotic stop, to top-up the fuzziness that had insulated him from the terrors and confusions of the night – and now as he flew along the ridged spine of the grey snake road, sweeping in lazy arcs from left to right, his mind wandered in all the beautiful, empty places the Sachems would have been proud to lead him.

Endless valleys of sound.

Broken wildernesses, with great gnarled trees standing lonely on ancient barrows.

Horizon-spanning herds of buffalo (or at least, great shaggy monstrosities with horns like scimitars, which is how – never having seen one – he imagined buffalo must look), oozing across grassy plains and lowing, deep down where sound stops and feeling begins, to each other.

Ghost-dancers, capering from side to side, seething and hissing as the chalk-dust coating their dusky skin dripped away with their sweat.

They were singing a song, he could tell. All of them. The landscapes, the buffalo, the trees, the dancers. He'd never learned the language of his people – too busy playing the white kid, turning his back, ignoring the Tadodaho's patient sermons – but somehow he understood. Deep in his bones, it made a sort of sense. In his back pocket, the silver needle wrapped-up in its rags became a tuning-fork: humming a single note of crystal beauty that shivered all through him, connecting him to the world, to the sky, to the Song.

It was a hate-hymn, he understood, to drive the bad ghosts away; shrouded and tattooed, with their dusty god and their scarlet demagogue.

The sky was talking to him. The grass was tugging at his leather legs, whispering in great wind-driven susurration, and the boughs of an ancient vine – sagging over the Interstate as he drifted by on the back of the magnificent thunderbird – told him to "watch out, boy... watch out..."

It was a heavy-ass dream-vision, and the matriarchs would have been proud – it just wasn't very good timing.

Something slapped him in the face; waking him from the foggy dreamsleep to find grasses and leaves fap-fap-fapping against his chest and head, and the trike scrambling – almost on its side – along the verge at the edge of the interstate.

"Fuck!" he yelped, waking up in a hurry. "Fuck!"

He wound his way back into the centre of the road, negotiating more potholes, gulping for air and promising himself to stay awake – even considered getting rid of the remaining pot – when the black speck appeared in the mirror.

It got big quick.

And yeah; at first it didn't worry him. The relaxing tendrils of the smoke soothed away all his tension and he even found himself giggling, without quite knowing why, at the swiftly growing reflection. Just another biker, he figured – travelling even faster and more recklessly than him – soon to sweep past on his way to the smoking blot on the horizon that would, eventually, become New York. Descending from the hills, the city was a spillage of brown and grey paint, washed-through with quicksmog graffiti and chalk dust scribbles.

"Ha-ha!" It was hard not to laugh. Not just at the other biker, oh no: at everything.

Everything was good. Everything was funny.

"Ha-ha!"

In fact, so vast and smudge-like was the endless plain of industry and smutty air on the eastern horizon, that Rick's narcotically liberated consciousness completely forgot about the pursuing rider and went flashing off down a million new tangents, to get wrapped up in wonder at the patterns a smoking chimney made against the sky; the curious sweep of a green park amidst the urban sprawl; the flight of a bird overhead; the –

The roar of another Harley.

The flash of a silver jacket in his mirror.

Deep inside, at some cold rational level untouched by the cloying comfort of the drug, Rick was screaming and shouting in half-grasped terror. But outside, on the surface of the chilled-out shell containing him, he did nothing but giggle and make lion roaring sounds under his breath, trying to out-growl the approaching bike, trying inwardly to wrestle himself into some semblance of conscious control.

Swearing over and over that he'd never smoke dope again.

He watched a tiny flash-flicker in the mirror, like a speed camera shuttering open in his wake, and shouted "Say Cheeeeeese!"

At this distance, squinting carefully into the fly-spattered mirror, he could just make out something long and cumbersome poking at odd angles off the rider of the other chopper, and a corkscrewing contrail snarling-up the air between them.

The rocket launcher.

Fuck.

"Ha-ha!"

He would have died, but for his sluggish reactions. The idea of swerving furiously to his left gripped him by lazy degrees, so that when finally he twisted the forks of the trike's front wheel a whole second had already passed. A vicious grey blur – venting heat and smoke – squealed past him like a localised earthquake, directly beside his left ear. Right where he would've been if he'd managed to get his act together sooner and swerve.

"Whup!" he shouted, half drooling in bowel-voiding terror, half whooping with stoned elation.

The rocket dipped down a second or two ahead of Rick, then nothing but smoke and fire-flash and a bilious black-red-grey dome bulging up and out, and tentacles of soot and shrapnel curling down like the branches of a willow, and he was heading straight into the dark heart of the fireball and –

– and this time he swerved with a little more presence of mind, banking the trike through the blind heat and soot on the rim of a seething crater, gunning his way forwards with his eyes closed, his hair singeing, and no goddamn idea where he was going. The Schwarzenegger stunt shit suddenly looked pretty fucking ridiculous in his mind's eye.

By the time the smoke was out of his face and pouring off the bike's tyres, the other guy was almost on him; tearing an unconcerned hole in the wall of black smog and shouting something, deep and vicious, that Rick couldn't understand. In momentary glimpses at the speckled reflection he could see the rocket launcher was gone – hurled casually onto the verge the instant it was empty – and now the slumped character was crouched low over the handlebars of his reptile-green chopper like a ghost riding a lizard, free hand filled with a compact, matte-black machine gun, long silver jacket flapping in his wake.

Rick yanked the shotgun off his back and hoped he looked like he knew what he was doing. Riding one handed was all very well, and maybe he'd even be capable of firing a loaded weapon with the other, *but doing both simultaneously whilst harried from directly behind by an indistinct psycho was quite another matter. He struggled for a second or two to twist and aim, almost hit an abyssal pot-hole, and swerved once again with a shriek.*

The world blurred past.

The machine gun chattered somewhere over his shoulder, driving him low against the saddle, and for the second time he found himself driving blind. Miniature craters blossomed all across the tarmac below and before him, and something whined angrily as it ricocheted off some hidden part of the trike. Rick hoped it wasn't anything important, then remembered he wouldn't have known one way or the other anyway.

He was still finding it sort of tricky not to laugh.

The other bike drew level. Glancing to his side, Rick could see his attacker clearly for the first time – and wished he hadn't looked.

Ram wasn't a big guy. He was wiry and pale, with greasy red hair that hung in bedraggled knots over the front of his sweaty, pointed little face. He put Rick in mind of a rat. A compact and bundled package of lank fur and corded muscles. Not the fastest or the strongest critter out there, maybe, but corner the little bastard in the wrong place and it'll turn and fight and won't ever give up.

Ram had a look like he always *felt cornered.*

Rick shouted "Rraaabies!" Because it seemed sort of appropriate.

"Killed... fucking... Slip!" the gangly creature snarled, eyes blazing, tweaking his bike's course to be perfectly parallel to Rick's own, then raising the machine gun with theatrical slowness, yellowing teeth bared.

He wore a head guard, of sorts. A football helmet with its visor removed and a pair of rotten, curled horns – ripped from the head of a ram – affixed on each side. And a bowler hat glued to the top.

To Rick, despite the whole 'impending death' thing, the dribbling psychopath looked for all the world just like Princess Leia, complete with currant-bun haircoils on the sides of her head. Rick found this screamingly funny, and started laughing.

Then he stopped, and started to whimper.

That made him laugh too.

It was all pretty pathetic, but at the very least it made Ram pause in tightening a finger over the machine gun's trigger, fascinated by a piece of prey manifestly even more insane than he was.

Rick closed his eyes and waited.

And waited.

And then there was music, and voices, and rustling.

Abruptly he seemed to be half-asleep again; like a sudden wave crashing against his mind, prising open his eyes and altering everything in the subtlest ways. The world was still just as it had been, Ram was still riding there beside him, gun pivoting upright... but somehow everything was different. Everything was fluid and glacial, shimmering with a sort of hard-edged light that came from nowhere, and went to nowhere. Maybe it was the shadows, or the shape of the sky, or –

The music, again. The chanting voices with their hymn of hatred. The grass rustling and the buffalo lowing. The Tadodaho surrounded by the oldest Sachems, and the clan mothers – the true leaders – huddled in cloaks beyond the light of the tribal fire.

Another dream-vision, nuclear-bomb-bursting open in his pot-fuelled preconceptions.

The great spirit, the Earth-Initiate; the trickster coyote and the turtle-man.

Thunderbirds circled overhead, every wing beat a new calamity, every eye-flash a splinter of lightning to stab at the ground.

"We told you," one of the matriarchs hissed, peevish, "to stick with the fucking Yamaha."

Rick giggled. In his limited experience, dream-visions rarely cussed.

"No time for that," the Tadodaho croaked, folded-up in a bat-like shroud of leathery cloaks and feathered cords, hard-lined face bisected by sharp slashes of black paint. "Look."

He nodded out of the dream, and Rick stared past the hazy walls of his own subconscious back out into the real world, like a drive-in movie for his own skull. The lowing of the endless buffalo herds changed tone discreetly – modulated downwards into a synthetic blare, and became the panicky blast of a truck's horn.

Further along the freeway, a mile or so ahead of Rick and Ram's helter-skelter rush, there was an HGV oncoming. It had ducked through a splintered section of the central reservation to avoid a black mass of rusted debris on its own carriageway, and was now occupying two thirds of the road directly ahead of Rick. Just like all the others; crammed with stained workers and glaring guards, horn screaming over and over.

There was room to get past; but not much. And Ram's bike, tearing along solidly at Rick's side, wasn't budging an inch.

Rick flicked a glance across at the horned freak. His face had changed. He was smiling, twitchy and vicious, and victorious, gun raised but not fired. He'd spotted the juggernaut. He knew fun when he saw it.

"You hold!" he shouted, eyes watering. "Killed Slip, *you fuck! You hold your line! You chicken that motherfucker out, or I shoot!"*

Rick giggled, despite himself. At least the psycho was giving him the choice.

A blast in the brain or a head-on collision. Tough call.

The people in the truck's container were waving arms, roaring at him to move, to shift out the way, to fucking clear the ro –

The walls went back up, and the music carried him away again.

In the dream, the Tadodaho wasn't troubled. He eyed Rick – no, not Rick; Hiawatha – warmly, and said something that no one else could hear. The birds in the sky laughed and sang and rushed together. The trees bent down and doubled-over, chuckling so hard their trunks creaked and the ends of their branches snapped. The Thunderbirds roared their amusement and the grass... the grass just rustled its quiet titters into nothingness.

It was all a big goddamn joke. Hiawatha smirked, then started to giggle. It had never been like this, before. Oh, shit, he'd been stoned a million times. He'd tried to... to commune with the fucking spirits as often as any of the Haudenosaunee. But always he'd felt like a fraud; like peering-in on something from the outside, like he was trying to be serious and spiritual about something deeply stupid.

"That's just it," one of the Sachems said, head inflating like a balloon. "Who told you to be so damned serious?"

They all started laughing too.

The road ahead glowed.

A patch – nothing more – of purple fire and green smoke, with a knot of make-believe birds circling above it, igniting on the tarmac ahead. It wasn't real. It shifted and shimmered, changing directions and breaking form. It was on the far right of the highway, pressed up against the verge, like a patch of spilt oil, set alight by a passing rainbow.

Hiawatha laughed, and the world laughed too.

He understood.

The walls dropped down, the dream passed, and he was awake again. The world still streaked-by. Ram was still shouting at him to hold his line, to smear himself against the truck, to do himself in, to get dead, to make up for Slip, to just – fucking – die!

Slowly, without even looking, Rick angled the trike towards Ram. Ten seconds or so, maybe, before he hit the truck. A gradual drift, tectonically slow, towards the psycho, closing the gap between the choppers.

The machine gun poked against his cheek.

He smirked, imagining himself. Racing at top speed, bike-to-bike, with a gun to his head.

"Arnie," he whispered to himself, "eat your heart out."

"You get back over there!" Ram snarled, so close that even the wind couldn't diminish the force of his voice. "You get back or I'll shoot, I swear to Jesus, and when you're roadkill I'll fucking do *you in every goddamn hole you* got, *boy!"*

The distance to the truck was swallowed up. The massive vehicle was slowing, braking hard, but it didn't matter. He'd still hit it. There wasn't room for both bikes to pass.

The glowing mirage passed at the edge of the road. The birds shrieked. The trees groaned. The buffaloes snorted and rutted and screamed in the night, and –

Rick jerked the trike, hard, to the right. The gun-barrel dug in to the meat of his cheek, the choppers locked briefly then parted, sparks spat, Ram shouted, and then they were separating out, jerking outwards: Rick straight back into the path of the truck, Ram slinking outwards towards the verge of the road, smirking and laughing at Rick's dismal attempt to push him aside.

He was too busy laughing to notice the enormous pothole at the edge of the interstate.

The dream cleared totally. The coloured smoke and fire that had marked the cavity vanished, and the birds dissolved into the air.

Ram's bike nosedived, and made a noise a lot like:

Klut.

The front wheel dipped against the edge of the pothole. The forks crumpled. The rear segment flipped upright – a green horse bucking – and Ram sailed, asshole upright, out of the saddle and onto the tarmac, to scream and grind his filthy leathers away, tumbling and skidding.

Rick swerved perfectly into the vacated space, and braked hard.

The truck rumbled past, horn moaning into the distance.

Silence descended bit by bit, and the last thing to shut the fuck up was the roaring in Rick's ears.

Ram lay on his back, breathing shallowly, a bloody trail of skidmarks marking his slide across the floor. His face was half gone. His bike was a crippled mess, lodged and broken in the pothole's leading edge, and Rick took his time – feeling strangely dispassionate about everything – to siphon off the remains of its fuel into his own chopper's tank.

He felt like he'd seen the 'real' world, and this bland reflection of it was trivial by comparison. He gazed out to the east, and for the first time noticed that same purple-green haze, like an echo of the bright fire inside his dream, hanging above the endless city. Showing him where to go.

"...get you..." Ram whispered. "F-fucking... fucking get *you..."*

"You don't even know who I am."

"Tell me," the rat-like freak snarled. "Tell me who. Find you." There was blood trickling out of his mouth where he'd bitten his tongue.

"I'm Hiawatha," said Hiawatha.

Then he drove into New York, and stopped only once en route *for a smoke, just to keep the dream fixed in his mind.*

Five hundred miles *west, in a place that was once called Fort Wayne, the Tadodaho glanced around the circle of assembled Sachems – faces masked in the smoke-thick air of the Dreaming Lodge – and the shrewd-eyed women-folk standing behind each one, and nodded. The communal pipe at the centre (it looked like it had been carved out of a single piece of wood in the shape of an impressive bear totem, but in fact was a resin cast of a completely meaningless sculpture made in Taiwan in 1998) gave out the last few sputters of smoke and died, its usefulness complete.*

"He's through," the Tadodaho said, leathery skin crumpling as he smiled sagely. "Be in the city in a hour or two. Get the war party together. We need to get to the meeting place."

"Now?" one of the others said, peevishly.

The Tadodaho pursed his lips, then shrugged.

"Weeell... Soon, then. Who's for a beer?"

CHAPTER TEN

THE AIR IN the tunnel was almost tropical. Damp too, musty, like you'd get in a cave whose only visitors were incontinent foxes and a less hygienic class of beetle. Indistinct *stuff* – unexpectedly cold in the muggy darkness – dripped on my head, and in the gloom I had to force down the shivers and keep telling myself *it's just water, it's just water.*

The lights had died long ago – shattered lamp heads good now only for rat holes and bat-roosts – so Nate and I revved along the barren tube slowly; relying on the quadbike's stammering headlights and the fluttering flames of tiny hammock-dwellings, strung up in odd corners and service-nooks. The clapped-out engine sounded painfully loud, and more than once I saw pale faces eyeing us from the shadows, squinting at the sudden brightness before burying themselves back beneath nest/beds of rags and cardboard.

"More scavs?" I asked Nate, unnerved by the feral look of these troglodytes.

He shook his head. "Flips. Worse'n scavs." Their eyes caught at the light as we streaked by. "No Klans, no homes. Mostly they're... outcasts. Crackheads, maybe. Some loonytoons. Lot of folks went nuts, straight after the Cull. Happens, you know? Happens when you see your whole family puke up their lungs."

I shivered and shut the thought away.

Passing us by with their pale faces streaked by moisture, slack jaws mumbling, they put me in mind of salamanders. Fat, grub-like, nocturnal.

"The Clergy don't mind them being here?" I asked, eyeing yet another scarlet 'O' marked on the outer wall of a corner ahead. Someone had even formed a crude crucifix out of bicycle reflectors, which sat in the centre of the circle and *blazed* in the onrushing light. I felt like a dart, arcing towards a target.

Behind me Nate shrugged, as if to say the Clergy had far more pressing things to be *minding* than a few reprobate squatters.

Signs of the ownership of the Queens Midtown Tunnel were all around us. Even before we'd entered it, back on the other side of the East River, the territory markers had stood in long rows down either side of the approach-road; brittle white and topped in each case by a wide scarlet ring.

Three heavily-armed goons had stood on the outer perimeter of the abstract border. Two men and a woman, each wearing nothing but arctic camo trousers and braces, jointly conducting a heated discussion with a shambling host of raggedy scavs. Some of them were pointing at us.

"Mickeys," Nate had grunted, voice muffled. I noted with narrowed eyes how the tallest of the men – a swarthy giant with arctic white hair and livid red rank-stripes scarred onto his shoulders – broke off from the argument to glare as we rumbled by. It wasn't until we'd passed beneath the tunnel's arch that I realised Nate was hiding his face.

As the tunnel roof had closed over us, our last sight was of a carefully hand-painted sign, hanging above the on-ramp, which read:

AND HE SHALL FIND THE KINGDOM OF HEAVEN

"Yeah," Nate had spat. "One way or the other."

Back in the dark, a quarter hour or so later, I swerved to avoid a lump of congealing debris – a much-rusted car wreck, probably – and considered the tunnel roof above us. Back in London, a year or so after the Cull, I ventured down into the underground, just to see. Back there the place had been busy; thronging with communities trying to stick together, trying to stay warm. But the effect was the same. In the lightless depths you started to think...

About all those thousands of tons of rock and soil and water pressing down above your head. About ant colonies in zoos – with walls made of glass – and thousands of thoughtless creatures going about their business in the arteries of the earth.

The Queens Tunnel was kind of the same, except this wasn't an artery.

It was a vein; sluggish, deoxygenated, blue with worthless blood. Nate pointed ahead to another sharp turn and we cruised towards the faintest glimmerings of light – an illusion of day, always lurking beyond the next corner. Nate said this was the route he took whenever he was bringing kids from the airport. He said he knew the way like the back of his hand.

I asked him how many people *really* knew what the backs of their hands looked like.

He ignored me.

I was glad of his knowledge anyway. The number of rusting obstacles and dangling patches of ruined tunnel were prodigious, and without his instructions we would have collided with something straight away.

I asked him again what happened to the kids when they'd been delivered. Did they grow up to become priests? Did they go off to some secret place to begin building the future?

I couldn't see his face, but it took him longer than usual to answer.

"I told you," he said. "I don't know."

The tunnel cornered and re-cornered in defiance of all obvious directional architecture. I'd been under the impression it joined Queens to Manhattan with the minimum of fuss, directly across the strait, but evidently its sinuous course took us deeper into the island, below the knot of blocks and stores of Murray Hill, before curving back on itself to spit us out into the daylight up a debris-strewn ramp shadowed by overarching blocks. The muggy humidity retreated, and it would almost have been a relief to enter the sunlight had the quicksmog not slunk back during our time underground, covering the blunt buildings of Midtown in an unsettling, gloomy whitewash. Over my shoulder the distant peaks of the financial district were masked – just the ghostly suggestion of needles penetrating the earth – and every street corner had become a cheap special effect.

Just as before, the Clergy markings were everywhere. Territory poles, graffiti-tags of scarlet and red, banners strung across empty streets. An enormous mural showing a smiling John-Paul Rohare Baptiste regarded us from the gable-end of an apartment block. For some reason I couldn't have found it any more menacing, even had the grinning Abbot been clutching at an AK47 or wearing a balaclava like the terrace-markers in Belfast. He just radiated... *wrongness.*

The whole place was *still.* Static. No distant movement, no scavs, no dogs, no rats. Even the birds hadn't bothered to hang around, and from the empty horizon to the north – Central Park, I guessed, beneath the level of the rooftops – to the haze-choked shadow of the Empire State that rose above us over our left shoulders, the whole uncomfortable place more than deserved its epithet: *Hell's Kitchen.*

After the communal degradation of London, and the noise of the Wheels Mart, it felt a lot like the surface of the moon. Silent as a graveyard, with its own vacant atmosphere and a sort of giddying gravity; like nothing was real and would all spin away into the universal haze at any moment. I let the quad trundle to a stop at an intersection, and morosely scanned the skyline.

"There," Nate said. "Manhattan."

I'd expected something busier. Some sectarian commune, perhaps, filling the entirety of the midtown district, swarming with children abducted from across the ravaged world. I imagined a glowing paradise. An industrious enclave of forward-thinking radicals, blocks wide, staffed with the young and the enthused, building and *re*building, working hard on the civilisation of tomorrow.

What a load of old bollocks.

There were cars, frozen in time, bumper-to-bumper. Dead tyres and shattered windows. Skeletons slumped in front seats, or curled in skinless patterns on the sidewalk. Here and there fire-damage had blackened a rusty hulk, or scoured a section of street of its rough surface. Flamewagons, I guessed; burning the bodies of Blight victims, trundling by five long years ago.

Newspapers flapped. Colourful litter sat like bright decorations speckling the rusting, filthy morass.

The sun was sinking to the west. It even made the whole thing sort of beautiful.

I asked Nate where everyone was, and caught myself whispering. He glanced around at the rooftops, sniffed noisily, then shrugged.

"Two answers to that."

"Oh yeah?"

"Yeah. First one is: all holed up. Central office. See, your Clergyman, he's not a regular Klanner. No scavs and Klansmen, like that, no no no. This crew, they got the clerics, the soldiers, the pilgrims, the trustees." He tapped the tattoo on his face, eyes grim. "Whole different hierarchy. Besides, these fucks got more on the mind than the usual. Territory. Drugs. Guns. Whatever. These assholes got faith. Whole worlda complications."

I glanced around again, unnerved by the quiet. I slipped off the quadbike and rummaged in my increasingly empty pack, producing the battered city map and unfolding it carefully. "So... they don't mind strangers strolling about up here?"

"Ah, well... there's that *mind* again. Do they *mind*? Yeah, yeah, I figure they do. But they ain't gonna do anything about it until someone raises a hand. Then you better believe they'll go Krakatoa on your hairy white ass."

I looked up from the map, trying to get my bearings.

"My arse isn't hai..."

"Not the *point*. Point is, depending on whatever the fuck it is you're *doing* here, as long as it ain't to do with pissing off the Clergy, we'll be fine."

There was something strange in his eye. I pretended not to notice and rotated the map, staring off into the east.

Nate cleared his throat.

"So?" he said.

"So what?"

"So *are* you?"

"Planning on going up against his nibs there?" I nodded at the smirking mural on the wall. "Nope. None of my business. Couldn't give a rat's tit, mate. I'm just here for some information."

Nate looked relieved. I glanced down at the heavy red ring marked on the map's surface, then back at the eastern horizon, feeling an unexpected shiver of anticipation. Then I folded the booklet away and clambered back onto the quad, suddenly remembering something.

"You said there were *two* answers."

"Yeah. Yeah, I did. Answer number two is: they're all around us."

And he was right. I could feel it. Eyes peering out of the shadows, regarding me from half-boarded windows on either side, squinting from rooftops. I couldn't see anyone.

That just made it worse.

I gunned the quad towards Forty-Second Street and turned a sharp right, winding my way north-east in a series of step-like diagonals, working hard to create the impression I knew what I was doing. Nate had gone quiet. On the horizon, a shape swarmed slowly out of the haze. A blank slab of stone – vast and wide but skinny along its third dimension – like a cereal packet built to colossal proportions.

Nate seemed to be fidgeting, suddenly, throwing looks in all directions. I still hadn't told him where I was headed, and certainly not *why* I was headed there, but as the brooding shadow of the building loomed ever nearer, I guessed it was pretty obvious.

I should say something to him, I guessed. Ask him if it was safe. Ask him his opinion.

But:

Something not right...

Something not right about him...

Something to do with his story, with his name, with London...

It was the same old confusion. The same old contradiction between the information supplied by my senses – that Nate was easy to trust, a fun guy, a diamond in the rough – and my instincts; which grated against some tiny snippet of subconscious knowledge and made me wary.

But then, I'd been wrong before.

Eventually he leaned forwards on the saddle and called out over the noise of the quad's angry little engine, voice thick with trepidation despite the volume.

"You remember I told you how come none of the robe-wearin' fucks're on the street?" he called. "All in the... the central office, right?"

"Yeah?"

He pointed at the black building.

The quad roared. The buildings blurred-past, the black monolith got bigger.

"Oh," I said. "Fuck."

"And now, his holiness Abbot John-Paul shall demonstrate yet again the miracle of his bein', that those who do not believe may be enlightened, and those sons and daughters who cleave already to the bosom of our great community may be strengthened further by his diviniteh!"

Deep-south accent. Nothing better for delivering a bit of sermonising showmanship.

The tragic thing is, when the robe-wearing bastard said the word "bosom" I glanced round the fringes of the crowd to make eye-contact with some likely-looking kid, to titter conspiratorially at the naughty word.

But there weren't any kids. Obviously.

That was the point.

This was back in London. This was maybe two, maybe three years ago. This was one of the few times I let curiosity get the better of me, and went to see The Tomorrow Show.

Standing in a knackered old warehouse somewhere in Docklands, with a crowd gathered round a snazzy plasma screen TV, I couldn't help remembering midnight mass at Christmas, as a kid. Standing there with the family, heads bowed, singing carols...

Even then, I was old enough to know what I believed and what I didn't. Even then, that same sense of awkwardness, of hypocrisy, of toeing the line of something you don't believe in. That same half-formed urge to leap up and slap the vicar, and start shouting at everyone to think, *to open their fucking* eyes, *to stop being so* stupid*!*

I was young. What can I say?

But yeah, the same sensation. Huddled with the TV crowd on a Sunday, zombie-like expressions fixated on that square of flickering light, drinking every word the announcer said. That same sense of not belonging, *as everyone around me listened with an alien devotion to the words of John 'look-at-the-size-of-my-bloody-hat' Paul Rohare Baptiste, and his crew of evangelising loudmouths.*

That day the broadcast was stronger than usual – the signal more pronounced, the flickering of the screen less intrusive – and the gathering was determined to eke every last iota of information and holiness out of it that they could get.

"The miracle," they wittered around me. "He's going to do it! He's going to do it!"

Oh yeah...

The Miracle.

He performed 'The Miracle' maybe once a month. We'd all seen it before. Even so a little thrill went through the crowd; the fortifying knowledge that their faith was not only being reaffirmed, but positively vindicated. *They saw this shit as proof of the Abbot's divinity, and despite all my carefully-polished cynicism I couldn't help but be a little impressed. Oh, yeah, the routine was full of holes, any number of cheats and camera-tricks to muddle the results, but still... It was something about the faces of all the people on-screen, marvelling and gasping in astonishment. You could fool the camera, maybe, but it was a hell of a lot harder to fool the geeks in the studio.*

"Hallelujah!" shouted one of the guys in the crowd. Probably a Clergy plant.

It began like it always began, with the announcer bringing two smiling young acolytes into frame. Both were under 18 – a girl and a boy – either so utterly indoctrinated into the church that their beaming smiles were natural symbols of their contentment, or so doped out of their skulls that they didn't care at all. They wore the same dull grey cassocks as everyone around them, with one notable exception; they each lacked a left sleeve, exposing their bare arms to the shoulder.

"Brother James, Brother Tilda." The announcer introduced them with a smile and a swagger, leading them to a white desk inside the same old dusky studio. Three Petri dishes sat waiting, empty, next to a sophisticated microscope with a cable-drenched camera affixed to its viewing column.

The announcer smiled at the camera, mumbled a prayer with his eyes closed, then pulled a trio of sealed hypodermic needles out of a recess in his cloak.

The crowd shivered again.

"Both these fine young acolytes of the Rediscovered Dawn – bless their souls, Lord-ah! – got 'emselves blood type 'O-negative.' Same as us all, brothers and sisters! Same as everyone alive on this good green earth, created and Culled by Him Above!"

He jabbed a needle into the girl's arm, drawing out a puddle of blood with practiced speed. He then thanked the girl, made the sign of the cross between her and himself, and waved her out of the camera's frame.

The syringe was emptied into the first Petri dish, and the whole process was repeated with "Brother James."

"Now," said the preacher, placing a tiny swab of Tilda's blood on a glass slide beneath the microscope and brandishing the syringe containing James's like an old West sharpshooter. "Since both these wonderful sons and daughters of Jee-sus have the same blood types, it's no trouble at all to mix 'em together." He smiled ironically. "All you doubters out there – that ain't faith, people, that's science*!"*

The crowd laughed on cue.

The image shifted to a microscope view. A uniform expanse of red blobs, so tightly-packed together on a field of bright light that they could almost be mistaken for a solid block. Red blood cells.

The tip of the needle shunted into view like a clumsy freight-train, skimming layers of Tilda's blood aside in its haste. I wondered abstractly if there was some deliberate rationale behind choosing acolytes of different genders; some discreetly sexual overtone in the public mixing of their blood.

Maybe I just had sex on the brain. It'd been a while.

James's blood streamed down the needle and oozed into the patch of cells already cramping the screen. Without a pulse to meld them together there was little natural movement, but again the needle whisked back and forth, blending like an artist on a palette.

"Same as before," the preacher said. "No change, y'see? No reaction. No rejection. Both the same kinda blood."

Cut back to the smirking preacher, only now he had a guest. Seated and frail in a chair beside him, looking even less healthy – more zombified – than usual, was John-Paul Rohare Baptiste, filled with quiet serenity or incontinent senility, depending on your view.

The crowd around me – predictably – went nuts.

The preacher bent down, fussed, muttered prayers, kissed the old git's robes, and eventually got the hell on with it and stuck a needle in the withered skin of the human prune's arm. There were a few artfully displayed bruises clustered in the same area where the poor dear soul had undergone previous tests, making the audience cluck and sigh in sympathy at his selfless suffering. They all looked like makeup to me.

Whatever the truth, the preacher was eventually successful in drawing-off a spoonful or two of the holy man's divine fluids, and quickly returned to the microscope, syringe in hand.

The needle slid into the silent mixture of the acolytes' blood and immediately disgorged its own cargo, a slick of ruby covering over the rest.

The effect was almost immediate.

The cells intermixed. Knots formed. Colours darkened. Like some glue-smeared retraction, the whole bloody morass shrunk-down together, accreting and clinging, separating into dark nodules. It was like watching something perfectly transparent, held over a flame, warp and ruck into sharp new angles, forming nodes.

"What y'all are seeing," the preacher said, "is called clumpin'. It's what happens when you put the wrong kinda blood into someone. Now, all us O-negs, back before the Holy Wrath of Him On High – Hallelujah! – delivered the Cull upon our miserable sinner's world, you coulda' given our blood to just about any Tom, Dick or Harry. You do it slow enough, you get no reaction at all. Universal donor, brothers and sisters! Amen!

"But you try introducing something else *into an O-neg system, it's gonna react. It's gonna get to clumpin'."*

Cut back to the preacher. Face serious, now, all fire and brimstone, sweat prickling on his brow.

"'And I heard a great voice*,'" he hissed, "'out of the temple, saying to the Seven Angels, "go your ways, and pour out the vials of the wrath of God upon the earth!"*

"'And the first went, and poured out his vial upon the earth; and there fell a noisome and grievous sore upon the men which had the mark of the beast; and upon them which worshipped his image!'"

The preacher wiped his brow, as if he'd been overcome and then released from some powerful trance. I stifled a yawn.

"Revelations!" he yelled. "Revelations Sixteen, One and Two! The prophet foresees the wrath of God, claiming to death and damnation all them miserable sinners and heathens he's marked! Marked on the inside, *brothers and sisters! Marked in their very blood!"*

He took a deep breath, and in the pause I glanced across the crowd beside me. None of them could stand still; quivering, hopping from foot to foot, shivering in elation.

"Brothers and sisters," the preacher said, "the righteous Cull swept across creation and took from us the means to pursue our iniquities, our selfish agendas, our unholy wars. It took away our great numbers, our great technologies, our great civilisations – ha! Amen! – and left us only with our spirit and our faith. He spared only those without the mark – the O-negs – and all others have perished! Science tells it! The Lord-*ah explains it!"*

Extreme close-up.

"All were Culled - except one! One great man, whose purity was so great, whose vision so intense, whose strength was so indomitable, that he withstood the mark placed upon his vile family of sinners, that he bore the pain of his ancestry with cheek turned, and was spared, *alone in all the world, by the Lord on high!"*

A crash-zoom, crude and old-fashioned, but just right for the intensity of the moment; slinking away from the preacher and straight onto John-Paul's face.

Smiling. Beaming.

Crowd goes wild!

I let myself out at the back of the warehouse whilst the cheers were still echoing about.

He should be dead, the old shit. He should have choked and died.

Oh, fuck, I know, it could easily be a fake. Who's to say they're cutting to the same microscope as the one in the studio? Who's to say it's not someone else's blood in the syringe? But I've seen the cockups, when the blood of the acolytes react weirdly because of this or that blood disease, or some other unusual condition. I've seen the episodes where they have to fetch replacements, or the preacher's used his own blood, or the microscope-camera fucks up and they have to mix such massive quantities – live in Petri dishes – that the Abbot ends up looking whiter than a sheet.

Always the same. Always the clotting and the clumping.

I've seen episodes where they've held up his birth certificate for the camera, focused hard on the 'A(Rh+)' box. His name was John P. Miller, for the record, before the Cull.

I've seen episodes where they've filmed his blood – exposed to the air – shrivelling and dying as the Culling virus withers it away.

It could all be a stunt. It could, *but it wasn't. My instincts told me.*

So how the fuck had the old shithead managed it?

Either way, it was great TV.

CHAPTER ELEVEN

WE STARTED SEEING people – real ones, out in the open, slinking out of our way – as we approached our destination.

Evening came down like a curtain – sudden and soft – and the egg-yolk sun sat on the encrusted skyline and punctured the milky haze just enough to blaze along every angle of that great slab of rock, that great blue-black monolith, that towered over the East River like a gravestone.

Once, it had been the Secretariat building; the administrative heart of the United Nations HQ, with the library and the General Assembly (a shallow curl of white concrete with a colossal bowling ball embedded in its roof) cowering in its sunless shadow; the whole complex pressed-up against the river like it was trying to swim to freedom.

As we swept nearer, I couldn't help noticing how many of the windows were broken; how vividly the great satellite-dish squatting beside the river had been painted.

Scarlet. A great scarlet 'O.'

Clergy territory.

I've always been a tad conflicted, as far as the UN went.

On the one hand, it's a pretty bloody obvious idea, isn't it? An organisation to get all the contrary fucks in the world *talking*, cooperating. It's what an American would call a 'No-Brainer.' And yeah, you could whinge at length about how, at the end, it had no power to speak of, how its hands were tied up in red tape and corruption, how its goals were too vague or too elitist, how its unity didn't extend quite as far as everyone made out... but at least it was *there*. At least people could look at it and say:

"Check it out. There's *hope*."

On the other hand, I spent my entire professional life doing nasty secret things the UN had made illegal decades before, so chalk another one up to national disharmony.

Besides, there was a steaming crater where the White House once stood – along with everything else inside a ten mile radius – serving as cancerous testament to the UN's ability to mediate in a crisis.

I'm being uncharitable again. These poor fuckers must've been hit just as hard as everyone else when The Blight struck. It's not like you can calm someone down when their finger's on the Button, when the whole world's dying around you, when a mystery virus is in the middle of slaughtering nearly six billion people, just by appealing to their bloody humanity. These are *politicians* we're talking about!

But still. It was hard to reconcile the dismal uselessness of the whole bloody organisation with the magnificence of its home.

On the approach, the people on the road were moving slowly; barely looking-up as we passed. One or two vehicles shunted along cracked streets, full of people with dead eyes and no words. I got that quiet chill in the base of my spine, like with the combat conditioning except colder, more logical, and let my senses fill in the blanks.

Tear-streaked faces, eyeing-up the brooding edifice with fear and disgust curling their lips. Knuckles white.

Anger, resentment, terror.

Heads lowered, bodies resigned. Dejection and despair.

They had the look of people who'd come to see something; who'd travelled expressly for a sight, a vision, and were now wending their way home having seen it, heartbroken.

They had the look of pilgrims whose journey had been wasted. Misery tourists.

None of them were Clergy. None even sported the same brand as Nate. They wore Klan colours of a dozen different kinds, avoiding one another but united in the uniformity of their expressions.

And the vast majority were women.

"What's got *them* so pissed?" I asked Nate, as we took the last corner onto First Avenue. "I thought people *loved* the Cler..."

My voice just... stopped.

In the guidebooks, it was flags. A great arc of them, fluttering and proud, lining the approach along United Nations Plaza, one for each member-state. I used to wonder what happened every time someone new signed-up. Did they have to stick up a new flag? Re-space the others? Who determined the order?

It wasn't flags anymore.

Nate had warned me about this. The *Spartacus* moment. The forest of crucifixes.

The warning hadn't worked.

At one edge of the road there stood a tall truck with a cherry-picker, painted blue and scarlet in the Clergy's colours, and at the peaks of each immense flagpole, T-squared with crudely welded crossbeams, its grisly works hung down and moaned.

And bled.

And pissed.

And crapped on the heads of the crowd below.

Distraught lovers, I started to understand. Friends. Family. Unable to reach up to cut them down, eyed warily by the robed *fucks* with guns and vehicles and all the toys in the world, from the other side of the great razor-wire fence. Spike-tipped stanchions, scaffolds with heavy machine-gun positions, looping ribbons of barbed wire and more guns than I could count.

The United Nations had become a fortress, and it displayed its captured enemies with all the medieval subtlety of heads on gateposts.

"What did they do?" I whispered, as the quad chugged away to silence. One of the dangling men was screaming down at a face in the crowd, telling her to get away, to not see him like this, to go back home, forget him. Eventually the Choirboys took turns pelting him with stones until he shut up, then glared and sneered at the woman in the crowd, daring her to stop them.

They had a basket of rounded pebbles standing-by. I guess this sort of thing happened a lot.

Nate clambered off the quad and sighed. He looked jumpier than I'd ever seen him, hopping from foot to foot, nervous energy renewed, chewing his nails.

"Mostly rule breakers," he said. "Fight starters, thieves. Maybe tried to settle shit without appealing to the Adjudicators. Skipped-out on a Tag. Who the fuck knows?"

Staring up at those men and women – stripped naked, black and blue, lashed to their poles with barbed cables, necks sagging, shoulders aching – I found myself too exhausted, too disgusted, to even bother asking Nate what the fuck he was talking about.

The crux of it had come through loud and clear.

"Anyone who pisses them off," I said.

Nate nodded, expression wary, and pulled his cap lower over his face.

An even larger crowd was gathered directly outside the gates. They had the look of a picket or protest, but stood in silent rows with arms lowered, a bulging semicircle of quiet indignation, staring in with eyes smouldering. Their gazes were lifted past the bored guards, past the barricades and silent vehicles, past the shanty-buildings clustered like barnacles around the base of the Secretariat. Here an even greater proportion were women, and when I let my senses slip into that subconscious state of information ravening – drinking in every tiny indicator around me, letting my old brain piece it together – I could almost taste their hunger, their sorrow, their desperation. They'd come here to reclaim something they'd lost.

"Moms," Nate said, fussing with the quadbike. "Come to see their kids."

"They get to visit them?"

Nate gave a grim little laugh and shook his head. "Hell, no. Mostly they just... stand here. A week, maybe two. Hoping for a glimpse, some sort of sign, I dunno. Something to show 'em their kids really *are* building that... 'New Tomorrow.' Make them feel better, maybe. Not so guilty."

"They ever get their wish?"

"Uh-uh. Whatever happens in there, it *stays* in there."

"But you used to bring them here. You must have seen the inside."

Nate shrugged. "Parts. Reception garage, fuelling pump. But I tell you this... the New Tomorrow looks kinda the same as the Old Today, and there ain't no hordes of happy kids rushin' about in *there*, either."

I stared across the scene for a long time, letting the misery infuse. Nate lit a cigarette and sat smoking, turning away with overblown discretion every time one of the guards happened to glance our way.

If I'd stopped, if I'd thought about it right then and there, I might have been surprised. For all his posturing, for all his fear and anguish at the Clergy getting their hands on him, here he was. Hadn't raised a word of protest, coming to this place. He'd walked right up to the outskirts of the dragon's den, and sat down outside with his new-found protector and his knightly armour lowered to his ankles.

But I wasn't thinking of that, right then. Call me dumb. I was thinking of the groans from the crucifixes, and the sobs from the mothers, and the silence from inside the compound.

And Bella, briefly. Thinking about Bella, when I should have been focusing on the mission. When I should have been concentrating on –

Don't you fucking give up, soldier.

Sir, no sir, etc, etc.

"In London," I said, eventually, "they used to send out Catcher squads. Clergy goons. All armed. Lot of them were women... maybe the bigwigs thought it'd make things easier. Woman's touch, that sort of thing.

"A lot of the people who survived the Cull ended up well into the Church anyway. All those broadcasts, every Sunday. Never ceased to amaze me, but I saw it happen all the time. People giving up their own kids, *shit*. Treated it like a fucking ceremony."

Nate blew a smoke ring. "I was there too. Remember? I seen it."

"Yeah. But did you ever see them with the people who didn't give in so easy? The ones who... wouldn't let go. Hid their kids. Kept them safe. You ever see that? The Clergy used to call them 'selfish.' You believe that?"

He sighed.

"You ever see the Catcher squads?" I said, feeling strangely angry with him, wanting to press until he snapped. I couldn't work out why.

He shook his head.

"You ever see them kicking down a door, or shooting a screaming woman in the street, or dragging off kids to the fucking airport and telling the parents they were *dead* if they tried to follow them? You ever see that, Nate? You ever see that shit, before they brought you over here to ferry the sprogs back and forth?"

He looked away.

The sun dipped below the horizon. A few fires were being built by the more enterprising segments of the crowd. The silence stretched on.

"It's different here," Nate said, after long minutes had eked away. There was... *something* in his voice. Bitterness? Guilt? "All the Klan shit, you know? It's what's *expected*."

"I don't follow."

"Choirboys keep the Klans in order. Oversee disputes. S'what the Adjudies are for. And they... they parcel out guns, sometimes food, sometimes water. And the drugs. They got so much of that shit in there" – he nodded to the Secretariat, and again that *something* in his voice – "it's coming out their fucking asses."

"So they dish it out to all the Klans? Why? Just for... for loyalty?"

"Cos in return they get the *tithe*."

I glanced around the crowd, the tattered clothes, the dirt-smeared tags. "But these are just scavs. These aren't Klansmen."

"Right again. But they gotta do what the bosses say. They want to eat? They want to stay alive? They don't wanna get skewered on no territory-pole like a fucking shish kebab? Then it's easier to go with the flow. Hand over the youngsters. Believe they going someplace better." He sighed again, staring at the crowd. "You act like a good little scav, you give up your own flesh and blood; you maybe get an extra ration, maybe a better sleepin' pitch. Maybe you get promoted to Klansman earlier than otherwise. And if you're smart, if you figure out that's the way to the top, then the only way to do it is to... to make yourself *believe*. You understand? Make yourself believe it's *right*.

"Self-sacrifice, man. That's what the Klans *do*."

"Can you get inside there?" I said, suddenly tired of it all, hungry to press on.

He chewed on the smouldering dogend of his cigarette for a long time, closed his eyes, reopened them, and said:

"Snowman's chance in Hell. Sorry."

We camped out on the plaza in front of the crucifixes overnight, warming ourselves at an oil drum fire some of the desolate women had built, and ate dog food. We discussed getting inside.

Nate kept asking me why. Why the hell was I doing this? Why the hell would I go up against the Clergy?

I didn't answer. It wasn't his business. Nobody's but my own.

Nothing to do with anyone but me. Not Nate, not the Clergy, not these scavs with their dead eyes.

Just me.

Good soldier. Good soldier.

Except that every time I looked at the building, or at Nate, or at the sobbing mothers, I ended up thinking of Bella; sat in that burnt-out pub in Heathrow, with her bitter glances and don't-fuck-with-me face. Then hunched over the controls of the plane, shivering and sweating. Then dead.

Impaled in the middle of a mashed-up plane.

By midnight, when Nate's voice was getting croaky from explaining the ins-and-outs to me, when my eyes were starting to droop and the stink of his endless cigarettes was all over me, I had a plan.

At two in the morning – give or take – a convoy of AVs entered the compound. Seven in total. Old military models, repainted in sky-blue with scarlet circles, covered from tracked wheels to pintle-mount roofs in ablative shields and home-made deflectors.

In the lead vehicle, a tall man with a long face, a pale robe, and a strange cap stood with his arms folded, gesturing angrily in heated conversation with someone out of sight beside him. He wore scarlet sunglasses.

Nate almost popped.

"That's Cy," he hissed, shivering. "That's fucking *Cy*..."

The old man covered his face, lurking in my shadow like a terrified child, peering between his fingers.

As the lumbering machines took the final corner I caught a glimpse of Cy's companion, the unlucky receiver of his displeasure. I felt the skin prickle on my forehead, recognising the muscular man with perfectly white hair – bare chested – whose shoulders were criss-crossed with rank scars like a sergeant's stripes.

"The Mickey." I muttered. "That's the guy who saw us take the tunnel."

Nate moaned quietly, hopping from foot to foot.

The Klansman had a black eye, a foul expression, and a hateful glare reserved just for Cy. They appeared to be arguing, though if I know body language at all – and I *do* – the Mickey wasn't getting anywhere fast.

The Clergy've been tracking me.

Asking questions.

Plotting my movements.

It felt vaguely exhilarating. Almost a *pleasure*, to be hunted, to be second-guessed, to be looked-for but never found. Just like the old days; sneaking and scuttling in the shadows. Staying covert, staying secret. Doing what I'd been sent to do, then melting away.

Don't you fucking give up, soldier!

Sir, no sir! etc, etc.

It was an effort to push down the shivery desire for action. I flipped the remaining blanket over the quadbike's body; trusting to the darkness to hide the confused shape. I needn't have bothered. Cy was barely conscious of his surroundings; so busy grilling his unhappy witness that he didn't so much as glance at the crowd.

When he'd calmed down, Nate hazarded that the convoy had returned from the airport. He said that coming home empty-handed wasn't going to help Cy's standing in the Clergy *at all*, and it stood to reason he'd bring a witness back with him. Evidence that he'd been doing his job.

Nate said the Church wasn't exactly renowned for being forgiving. Not towards guys who'd slaughtered entire companies of Choirboys, trashed functioning aeroplanes and rendered one of the three Clergy airports useless.

I told Nate: thanks for the good news.

He didn't mention how the angry-looking Cardinal would certainly also have noticed that *he* hadn't been amongst the dead. He didn't mention that the white-haired Mickey would certainly have reported an elderly black man clinging to a stranger, on the back of a clapped-out quadbike, entering the Queens Midtown tunnel.

He didn't mention that he'd just become an official enemy of the Church, right up there beside me, with the added epithet of 'traitor.'

But it was all over his face and heavy in his voice.

Somewhere deep inside me – somewhere petty-minded and sadistic, which didn't really understand its own motivations – I *liked* that he was worried.

Something about him.

Oh yeah, one other thing:

As the last vehicle in the convoy growled its way through the razor wire fences, just before the guards slid the tracked walls back into place, a group of the women in the crowd broke free from the shadows and rushed the guards, sobbing as they ran.

The guards shot a few – almost perfunctorily, just to prove they *could* – but did their best to keep the others alive; clubbing at them with rifle-stocks and batons. I almost mistook it for mercy.

But at first light, as the sun broke over the sooty limits of the river, there were six new bodies dangling and shrieking at the tops of the flagpoles, and three more turning black on a pyre inside the gates.

THEY WERE CALLED the Red Gulls, though in defiance of all naming-logic their headquarters were black. *Very* black. Black in the same way the ocean is damp.

The whole thing was built of wood, laid down over shattered concrete. Cut and fixed lumber, crudely planed and inexpertly joined, sealed with sinuous rivulets of tar and vomit-patterns of wax, draped in layers of black bin-liners. Ultimately the whole thing looked not so much constructed as congealed; spreading out in a great glossy puddle like a drying cowpat.

Just as Nate had warned, the far perimeters were a tangled morass of razor wire, crude trip-alarms and grotesque territory-markers with picked-clean skeletons skewered at their peaks. It was almost embarrassingly easy to slink past.

The whole wretched thing stood near the heart of Central Park, set to one side of what had once been the great lawn, and where the twisted trees loomed out of the dappled sunlight they seemed to tangle and grow *into* the weird construction, as if its boundaries had little meaning. As if it intended to spread as far as it could, without human aid.

I worked my way towards a knotted entrance on the quietest face, using the shadows of the tree trunks and my own raggedy camouflage to avoid the traffic heading in and out in all other directions. To the south of the park the Clergy ruled absolute, so it didn't surprise me in the slightest that of all the scavs and muscular Klansmen striding out on their business – red feathers rising like spines from their scalps – hardly any did so in this direction. The guard at the door looked positively catatonic.

I opened his neck from the side – punching in and cutting forwards – oozing from the shadows before he could even call a challenge. I dumped the body on a natural shelf above the doorway, formed by a crook in a mouldy tree, and oozed inside like a ghost.

I *love* this shit.

Prowling. Slinking like an ethereal fucking tiger. Corridor by corridor, beaver-like nest chambers crossed in a doubtful blur, shadows adhered to, every passing footstep used to mask my own.

It was beautiful.

The Red Gulls were the biggest Klan in the city, besides the Clergy itself. This was important to my plan.

Years ago they'd put down a concerted coup by some long-gone uptown gang calling itself the NeverNevers, who thought they could take a crack at the Choirboys' power-base. Ever since, the Gulls had been John-Paul's most favoured underlings. Permitted to spread through territories on the Clergy's own doorstep, they were gifted with all the best weapons, all the choicest scav and all the craziest narcotics.

Maybe the boost made them sloppy. Like a spider invading a rabbit-warren, I was deep inside the labyrinth of sleeping chambers, food-stores, scav-holds and moonshine stills before the so-called 'guards' even became a problem. At a thickset corridor intersection Gulls stood posted at regular intervals (they might as well have pinned-up a sign saying '*you're near something important*'), and for all the adrenal shivers and subconscious hunger for violence I was forced to consider something a little more subtle.

So I put my head down and walked past them, confident as you like.

Just another scav.

For the record, this sort of scam works more often than you'd think. Trust me on this. Afghanistan, Peru, even once in North Korea... You put you head down and walk like you're *supposed* to be there. Doesn't matter what you look like, where you're going.

Note that it doesn't work *all the time.*

Like for example when you're just passing the last red-feather-wearing wanker in the row, stepping out into the sweaty cavern at the heart of the rickety palace, and some despicable little piece of *shit* somewhere starts shouting about the south entrance being unguarded.

And then, a beat later, about poor old Crocksy lying with his windpipe torn all to shit.

Situation like that, suddenly *everyone's* hefting a gun. Suddenly everyone's wondering who the guy that just walked past actually *was.* Suddenly everyone's on edge, and shouting, and running up and down, and the whole fucking place is *shaking* from the noise.

The shutters came down in my head.

The old brain took over.

I stepped into the cavern and cut a hole in the face of the guy shouting at me.

Didn't stop. Heard him screaming on the floor. Moved on.

Another guy running my way, pistol gripped tight, calling for help. Stabbed him in the stomach, lifted upwards under the ribs.

The way to a man's heart...

His pistol-arm stuck out under my shoulder, already going limp, so I hooked a finger under the trigger-guard, beside his own, and took out the next suicidal motherfucker in line. Forehead splatter. Red froth on the air. Singed gull-feathers.

Something inside me, howling in joy.

I helped myself to the gun, letting its owner empty out his guts on my shoes. Echoes still flapping in the air. Shocked faces and sprinting legs. Stop for a situation recon.

Know everything.

Cover the angles.

It was an audience chamber, like a medieval throne-room. Hordes of scavs and favoured women rushing out by other exits, hooting and spronking. Up the steps of a raised dais stood a succession of lieutenants and ranking Klansmen, each one in colours more gaudy than the next. Feathers, beads, bare skin with crimson tattoos, gull-feet headdresses and hands heavy with Uzis, AKs, machetes.

At the top sat a big fucking guy in a chair. He looked sort of startled.

I smiled at him.

First step. Ducked under a messy punch intended to slow me down whilst the other goons got themselves loaded up. Used the numbers against them; kept the greasy little shit with the knuckleduster between us.

Told him: "Scuse me." Put a knife through his ribs (felt the blade notch – *shit*) and spat pistol fire over his collarbone, taking out the obese sod with a Kalash' two steps up. Then turned and kicked – boot to the throat of the punk behind. Scamper three steps higher in the muddle of limbs and shouts. No one wants to risk a shot. Too many bodies packed together.

No one but me.

Shot a lanky youngster holding a .44. Probably would have broken his wrist anyway.

The ranking Klanners moved in, boxing me off from the honcho on the throne, shoving and snarling, letting space open-up for weapons to bear.

I let the knife play random patterns, spun behind the guard of a dog-faced woman with a fucking *sword* in her hand (amateur!) and hit step number five.

Shot out the knees of the biggest feather-wearing arsehole of the lot. Wasted another two rounds on his ham-hands when he smirked at the pain in his legs and tried to open up with his cute machine pistols anyway.

Time ticking by.

Ammo all gone. Bitch with a sword hacking at air.

Space blurring.

I shifted tack, rushing the downed giant and using my momentum; stamping on his shoulder to vault up (bloody Hollywood antics –

amateurish! Pathetic!), and pushed him down the slope on the rebound, toppling like a bowling ball towards the indignant youngsters at my back.

Satisfying shouts of alarm and pain as the steps cleared behind me.

I came down on top of the last goon, the last guard, the right hand man. Small but fast, wiry as shit. My landing was messy; knocking us both down, tangling and tussling on the floor with knives pressed together. I felt a blade-tip kiss my cheek and angle up towards my eye. Ignored it. Pressed in towards his sides; a slow squeeze against the resistance of his arm, forcing him back, knife entering like a slow-mo javelin.

I stamped on him as I stood, and blinked the blood out of my eye.

And there was the boss. Seated. Eyeing me.

Impassive, the cool motherfucker.

"Who," he said, and everyone else had gone still, and nobody wanted to shoot me because they'd hit *him*, and everything stopped, and the silence was thicker than the noise had ever been. "The *fuck*. Do you *think*. You *are*?"

So I slapped him playfully on his big forehead, and shouted: "Tag!"

Fun for the whole family, and all part of the plan.

CHAPTER TWELVE

THE TAG WENT back a year or four.

The Tag was one of those little things the Clergy put in place as soon as it was obvious no other motherfucker was ever going to get big enough to kick them off the top spot. The Tag was... a tradition. A ritual, if you want. A way for the robe-wearing arseholes to take charge of every dispute, every promotion, every powerplay.

Above and beyond all other things, The Tag was *entertainment.*

The way Nate had explained it to me, sitting in the dark outside the United Nations, was:

"You're a chicken. You spent your whole goddamn life afraid of the wolves. What you want right now is freedom. Get away from the meat-eating shitheads. Spend some quality time without carnivore assholes watching your back.

"But you know what? What you want *so much more* than that, is to have a go at being a wolf *too.*

"Tag's how you do it."

The Tag was a pretty simple concept, all things considered. A tough sort of justice: survival of the fittest with a lopsided twist to favour the overdog. I guess when you're living in a pit, the rules *need* to be as nasty as everything else, which is scant comfort for the underdog.

That'd be me.

In a nutshell:

One man, or woman, challenged another. Rules varied from here to there on the nature of the challenge, but generally you're looking at punching, slapping, kicking, hair-pulling, whatever. Something publicly humiliating; an affront to the challengee's dignity. He or she was permitted to defend themselves by any means – as if in self-defence – up to and including muscle-bound lieutenants with machetes, machineguns and magnums.

Heh. For all the good it did.

But as soon as the challenge was *made*, everything stopped. No more violence allowed. Break the rules and the Clergy Adjudicators would be down like a ton of bricks.

The challenger was escorted away, told a place and time, and left to prepare whilst the disgruntled VIP who'd been tagged set about assembling a hunting party.

Five people. Any weapons, vehicles or gadgets they wanted, which amounted to whatever stuff they could get their hands on.

Five people, drugged to the gills, with territorial knowledge on *their* side and not a scruple in sight.

At the alotted time the challenger and the hunting party were placed in position, normally beneath the gaze of a thunderous crowd. In a world without TV, *this* was the Superbowl.

The challenger was stripped of all guns, tools and blades. An electrical tag was pinned beneath his skin (joyously provided by the friendly neighbourhood Clergy), and with all due ceremony, gravity and cheer, he was told to fuck off and get running.

The hunters were released five minutes later.

When you initiated a Tag, there was only one rule worth knowing:

Stay alive for two hours; you've won. Everything that belonged to the loser now belongs to you. Power. Privileges. Property. Rank.

I got the impression it didn't happen often.

And just for the record, just to make the whole shitty thing even more wonderful, it was overseen from start to finish by representatives of – take a wild guess – the Apostolic Church of the Rediscovered Dawn.

The cleverest thing *I'd* done – and if I'm honest it wasn't until afterwards that Nate explained why it was such a smart move – was to wade in heavy and cause some serious collateral along the way. At the time I'd done it as a path-of-least-resistance thing: I wanted to get to the boss, his goons were in the way – *QED.*

But no. I'd got lucky. It turned out that killing a Klansman in the normal course of life carried an immediate penalty of 'Oh-God-Make-The-Pain-Stop-Please-Please-Please' death. It was supposed to prevent gloryhunters from killing their way up to the top without effort, to stop disgruntled scavs getting mutinous around their overlords, and to deter internal arguments from spilling-over. It worked too – most of the time – and the only ones exempt were the Klanbosses themselves.

Which meant I'd accidentally carried-off a neat spot of playing the odds. If I *won* the Tag I'd *be* the new Boss, and they couldn't hold me accountable for all the chop-socky I'd caused *en route*. And if, Nate said, I *lost*, then it didn't matter then either.

I scowled. "How come?"

"'Cos you'll be dead anyway."

I'd crippled, killed or incapacitated more of my potential hunters than seemed fair or decent. I'd wiped out the Klanboss's top dogs in one fell swoop. I'd left him with an untested rabble to try and catch me, and put the fear of God up them at the same time. They'd seen what I could do. They'd hesitate, I hoped, to corner me alone.

And, frankly, I needed every advantage I could get.

All this just to get into the UN building. It had better be fucking worth it.

THEY KEPT US waiting until ten o'clock. It meant that when things kicked off, the two hour limit would expire at midnight. I guess they thought it was more dramatic.

I wasn't about to complain. It gave me the rest of the day to sleep and prepare, whilst *they* – the Gulls – scuttled about like headless chickens, conspiring and scheming, treating the wounded and carting-off the dead.

All through the day, Nate kept a nonchalant sort of 'watch' while I kipped, nestled up in a bed of dry leaves beneath a footbridge, on an out-of-the-way path in the park. He shuffled off once or twice to chat to the little knots of Red Gull scavs living in bivouacs in other parts of the greenery, keeping himself out of sight of any Clergy passing through, and seemed to be warming to the role of information gatherer. I like to think he saw himself as a duellist's second, preparing for his benefactor's moment of pistol-waving tribulation... but frankly behind his open face and warming smile it was fucking impossible to work out *what* he was thinking, let alone what historical-romantic notions he was dreaming up.

He mumbled a lot, just under his breath, and had started to sweat too much.

All very weird.

As I slept, I dreamed of the signal on the computer in the Vauxhall Cross building – the glowing word PANDORA, beaming bright. I dreamed of Bella impaled on her spike, shouting at me to stop being so selfish and *think*, dammit, about what she'd told me. I dreamed of Nate, laughing, and John-Paul Rohare Baptise, dancing through it all like a daddy-long-legs, battering himself against polished glass to reach the shining light outside.

The light was red, and *sticky.*

I dreamed of somebody else too, but the face I'd memorised years before had become a fuzzy collection of features in my mind, and the figure dissolved the instant I reached out to grab it.

Nate woke me at eight. He'd caught a couple of rats off the banks of the stagnant Turtle Pond and sat cooking them, not once complaining at doing all the hard work, rambling away blithely on the events of the day, apparently not troubled by whether I was listening or not.

I was.

He said the whole territory was in uproar. He said the scavs were all but hysterical at the news of what I'd got up to that morning, and it was a toss-up as to whether said hysteria was based on delight or disgust.

He said no one had ever heard of a Klanboss getting himself Tagged before. He said already the other tribes in the area – the StripLims to the east and the Globies up on the edges of Harlem – were choked with gossip and book-running. Already barter-wagers were hot business all across the Island, he said, and scavs from Klans he'd never even *heard* of had been showing up in the NTs all around the edges of the Red Gull patch, to stand about and murmur in low voices about the 'Big Tag,' hoping to catch a glimpse of the action.

He said it was big news.

"You, *ah...*" He coughed awkwardly, and twitched. He looked unwell. "You sure you wanna do this?"

I told him, of course I did. How the hell else was I going to get into the UN building?

"Yeah, yeah... Yeah." He coughed again. "Only, *ah...* That Cardinal asshole, Cy. He was up here 'round noon." His voice shook.

"Did he see you?"

"You think I'd be talking to you if he did? Shit, no! Stayed well outta his way. You live in en-why any lengtha time, you get good at making sure folks ignore your ass. Like... There was this one time I got stuck with..."

"Nate." I interrupted the tangent before it got started, troubled by his uncomfortable manner. Even in the midst of his most enthused ramblings, he'd never seemed quite so twitchy. "You were saying. About Cy."

"Yeah. Sure. H-had himself a little chat to Scrim, that's all. In-depth, man. *Intense.*"

"Who's Scrim?"

Nate looked at me like I was stupid. "Motherfucker you tagged. Top dog."

"Fair enough." I poked the rat in the fire. "Stupid name, but fair enough. So what did our friend Cy have to say for himself?"

Nate shook his head, eyes rolling weirdly. "Pass. No way was I getting close enough to hear. But you want me take a wild stab, I'd say he's keeping an eye. Knows it's you. I mean, shit, it don't take a genius! Raggedy-assed stranger shows up at LaGuardia, goes through a pack of Choirboys like a razor. Next day you got witnesses see the same guy heading through Queens on a quad. And *next* day, Mister Nobody-Knows-Who-The-Hell-He-Is not only gets himself balls-deep in the Red goddamn Gulls, but slaps a challenge on Big Scrim.

"You think Cy ain't gonna make the connection? C'mon! He *knows.* He knows it's gonna be *you* out there tonight."

"But you said this shit is sacred, right? You said nobody else gets to interfere."

"And that's the truth. But that don't stop our pal the Cardinal from helping the odds. Clergy got themselves every killing toy in the world holed up over there." He nodded east, towards the unseen slab of the Secretariat. His hands were shaking. "They got every brand of... of *chem* with a name, and twice as many without.

"I hate to say it, *most* guys, running a Tag, they got less hope than a snowball in Hell. But *you...*? Up against the Gulls? And them tooled-up by the Choir?

"Shee-it!"

I let this sink in.

"I see," I said.

Ten o'clock. I stood and waited, tensed, beneath a canopy of spindle-fingered trees. Beside me the stagnant water sucked at the south bank of the Turtle Pond, on the fringe of what had once been Seventy-Ninth Street and was now a crippled lane of rubble, its tarmac long since plundered for the construction of the Gulls' shanty nest.

I'd filtered out the noise of the crowd by now, but the force of it was still there at the back of my head, nudging against my concentration. I'd spent an hour flicking through my tattered map, and a series of notes Nate had gathered from the scavs nearby; all of them covered in spidery descriptions that didn't help at all (*'gud rats!'* and *'watr mostly clean'*). I had a vague idea where I'd go. I wasn't stupid enough to let myself believe I had a plan; that I was *ready.* In situations like this, there's no such thing as 'ready.' There's just people who can wing it, and people who can't.

I let the instincts take over, like shrugging on an old coat; patched and frayed and stinking, but so comfortable you can't imagine ever taking it off.

Vehicles rumbling nearby. The five Gulls glared at me, weapons bristling in every direction. Four blokes, one woman. That same crazy chick who had the sword before, but the others were just faces. Muscular, armoured-up, ready to play. All except Big Scrim. *He* stood out; encased in flashy sports gear and rubber body-armour, holding the Clergy's tracker-device like a novelty TV aerial in the back of an open-top jeep.

Everywhere I looked, Clergy.

Clergy guns. Clergy AVs. Cardinal Cy whispering to Scrim, his four goons cross-armed behind him, pointing and directing, throwing glances my way beneath hooded eyelids. Silent communication between us, crackling like static.

Twat.

The crowd gets noisier. Arms slap against my shoulders, people shout and laugh, something painful digs beneath the skin of my neck.

The tracer.

Stay calm.

Breathe.

Are you ready, soldier?

Sir, no sir!

Well done, son. Right answer. Now get goi –

A flare went up.

I ran.

TREES WHIPPING PAST. Branches scraping cheeks already sliced and puffy from last night's mêlée. Legs pounding like pneumatics.

It's almost a joy to open-up. All cylinders. Let go. Feel the burn.

Know everything.

Cover the angles.

Their advantages: speed, local knowledge, the tracker in my neck, more guns than a survivalist all-comers WorldCon and enough drugs to make a pharmaceutical multinational look like a primary school chemistry kit.

So. One thing at a time.

Get off the track. Confound the vehicles.

I took the verge beside the street at a vault, darted through more trees; heading for the dark blot of stone ahead. Heading west, I think, over slimy husks of rotting trunks. Something man-made looming between the boles. An escape from the preternatural chaos of the park with its forested wilderness. Too many shadows here. Too many unknowns.

I paused for a second, shaking my muscles down, taking the time to stretch whilst I caught my breath, then onwards. Up steps greasy with lichen and mould, past knots of scavs hoping for a good view, clamouring in the shadow of a colossal building. The poor buggers recoiled and ran when they saw they'd got their wish, terrified I'd bring down the Gulls on their viewing spot.

A second flare went up behind me – blood red and baleful – and I stumbled without pausing through a shattered doorframe into a great emptiness.

It took my eyes a while to adjust, and as I groped, the echoes of my clumsy movements suggested a vast void all around me; the tinkling of broken glass and crunch of rubble underfoot. Shapes swam into focus. Button-like eyeballs regarded me. Brass signs and red ropes.

A fucking great elephant, staring down. Someone had snapped off its trunk.

AKELEY HALL OF AFRICAN MAMMALS

...a banner read; plucked out of the shadows in my peripheral vision by the overstretched blur of the instinctive training.

Trust your perceptions.

Don't think. Just react.

Trust yourself.

Go!

Reality swam and reformed, and I'd barely noticed myself rushing up stairs that folded back and forth in concertina ribbons, up the sides of a great hallway, passing glass cabinets crammed with taxidermy's greatest trophies and fossilised impressions screwed to walls beside plastic plaques.

Engines growled in the distance, rushing nearer, audible through crack-holed windows, arched and medieval. Raised voices.

Fuckers.

On the fourth floor a frieze of limp connections and cable-like structures swam together in my mind to form great prehistoric beasts: fleshless and comical in their gawky poses, tangled amidst steel supports and gaudily-coloured waxwork models.

In my state of mind, adrenalised to hell and incapable of rationalising through the tsunami of reactions, finding dinosaurs on the fourth floor of a vast building did not seem worthy of remark. Just another bunch of dumb bastards, wiped out before their time.

Up here, scav kit was everywhere. Blankets and cushions concealed lazily between titanic ribs, small piles of combustible rubbish pulled off the displays, heaped in odd corners for tinder and late-night fires. Beside me a glass cabinet containing rows of fossilised teeth had been partially shattered; torn away from the wall, left jagged. On the other side of the room someone had used the Apatosaurus as a toilet, and the whole chamber was thick with flies and dust.

Voices spiralled up from the great hall far below, shouts and curses followed by the conspicuous silence of people being quiet. I peered cautiously over the rim of the balcony, hoping the radio marker didn't provide a vertical reading. Sure enough, ghostly shapes moved in the light-dappled lobby; oozing from cover to cover with the exaggerated care of those who think their enemies are close.

Cat and Mouse. Rule number one:

Don't be the mouse.

Sir, yes sir, etc, etc.

So I picked up the remains of the cabinet with all the care I could muster, winced at every tinkle of fragmented glass, and pitched it with a roar over the balcony's edge.

The snarl took on a violent life of its own in the acoustic void of the stairwell, modulating musically with the xylophonic traumas of the cabinet.

Someone below reacted fast. The poor sod.

Automatic gunfire stitched the open stairwell with muzzlefire and noise, and then nothing but glass. Like champagne. Like watery froth, dazzling.

Shattering.

Tumbling.

Slicing.

The sound was shocking. A calamitous crash that resounded in every dimension and shook the air.

Then nothing but silence.

Then screams that bubbled away into gasps, as whoever was underneath the cabinet rustled off their jagged little coil. Then more silence.

Then just the moans of shocked survivors, cut to shreds.

And the soft sound of me, running like hell.

I'D STOPPED TWICE on the way down from the dinosaur exhibits. The few fractured shards of rationality still spinning inside my head had decided I was inside a museum, and the one thing museums *always* have is an enormous floor plan in every corner.

That was Stop Number One.

In a display of the Woodlands Indians, in the far western wing of the third floor (within easy sprinting distance of a stairwell which – I was reliably assured – led down to the side exit on West Seventy-Seventh Street), I crouched and bled.

This was the result of Stop Number Two.

Thick rivulets down my spine, oozing under the hem of my trousers and down the backs of my legs. Didn't matter. I was in control.

Taking my time. Calm. Breathing well.

The sensible savage.

I think somehow, somewhere inside, I felt *indignant*, too. Like: *how dare these fuckers chase me? How* dare *they? How* dare *they outnumber me?*

Me!

It was a useful emotion.

This was *home*, in a way. Worming through the darkened corridors of an embassy in some exotic place, waiting for the moment to strike. Lurking, stalking, closing in.

Or letting *them* come to me.

This time the arseholes came mob-handed. They'd closed on the tracker beacon with admirable speed, slinking along open corridor corners to avoid ambushes, sidestep-by-sidestep. I could hear their progress with practiced acuity: three together on point, and another (a softer tread, probably the woman) taking rearguard.

Only four. The other one was staked out in the lobby, crushed and sliced up by the glass cabinet. Twenty minutes into this nasty little game, and one fucker down already.

It would be dishonest to pretend I wasn't enjoying myself.

I could hear them beyond the last corner of the twisting hall.

"Strong signal," one grunted, voice terse. "Directly ahead. Other end of the room."

An arm blurred in the shadows.

Something small flying, bouncing, rolling, then –

Light and smoke and noise, and three heavy figures springing-out to let rip into the phosphor distraction. I couldn't even see the weapons; only feel the drumming of the air, the epileptic nightmare of endless automatic muzzleflare, and the quiet smugness on the bright faces of the attackers.

They were standing so close I could almost have touched them and, for the record, they were shooting in completely the wrong direction.

I waited until they'd walked further into the room. The one with the tracker grunted in satisfaction, claiming the marker was stationary and they *must* have hit me. They took up swaggering stances before the darkened 'Iroquois' display – now reduced to shattered plastic and crumbled wax – and took a few more potshots into the rubble, just to be sure.

Behind them, I ducked out from beneath the cosy chickenwire-supported wigwam of the Ojibwa tribe (never heard of them) and ghosted back along the empty corridor.

Divide and conquer.

The woman stood with her back to me, pressed into a pool of darkness, nervous at the cacophony her comrades were throwing up from around the corner. She had a mini-Uzi in each hand – compact little toys with folded stocks and extra-long mags – and the pale curve of her neck was perfectly caught by the dim moonlight of the arched windows, like a ski slope. Waiting for an avalanche.

Carefully, using swaddled fabrics I'd stolen from my pals in the Ojibwa, I palmed the long shard of glass I'd used to slice the electric tag out from the skin of my shoulder (stop two, remember?). I'd hidden it carefully amongst the dummy-display of the Iroquois, letting the morons walk right past me.

Some people might call that 'cheating.'

Don't you fucking give up, soldier!

Sir, no sir, etc, etc.

Cat and Mouse. Rule number two:

Even the biggest cat picks off mice one by one.

The woman had the good grace to die quietly, and she'd even warmed up the grips of my two brand new Uzis. That's consideration for you.

HALF AN HOUR later, the others were getting frustrated.

I'd left the museum and headed south, careful not to double back on the park. This whole lightless neighbourhood was their turf, and the more advantages I could give myself, the better. Right now that meant staying out from the moon-dappled weirdness of the trees, hugging the right-angles and solidity of the West Side.

I turned off down Seventy-Fourth and found a tenement block; took the fire escape up to the top floor and bust my way inside as quietly as I could. Still no sounds of pursuit – and after all, why *should* there be? The marker pressed under my skin was their only ace; and now that was nothing but a bloody shard of circuitry in the pocket of a mannequin. It was almost tempting to sit out the two hours here, reclining on the unscavved sofa in some long-dead New Yorker's grotty little apartment.

But.

Think. Cover the angles.

But other people had surely cut out the trackers before.

The fuckos must have a Plan B.

But.

But if they have the marker, couldn't they just claim victory anyway? 'Proof of kill'?

But, but, but.

And the biggest shitter of them all:

The End.

By midnight I had to present myself to a member of the Clergy. That's how it finished. That's how they knew who'd won or lost.

They'd given me a perfunctory description of places I could look: slums on the NT border zones, territory markers down to the south,

Clergy-run checkpoints. With each item on the list, spoken through softly clenched teeth by the pale-faced Cardinal Cy, I'd cast a quick glance at Nate – hiding in the crowd, face shadowed inside a hood. He'd simply shaken his head, over and over.

The Clergy weren't going to make this easy for me. They wouldn't be waiting to shake my hand, tell me well done. If they *were* waiting at all, it was with a bullet.

Think it through.

Cover the angles.

Which just left the park. Right back to the start. Presenting myself to the crowd and the bastard Cardinal himself, standing up there on the podium beside the turtle-pond with his four hulking Choirboy guards and his stupid ruby-red glasses, to *show* I'd done it.

Easy as that.

Big Scrim and his two remaining goons, they knew it as well as I did. They knew I'd be scurrying out from the undergrowth, back in the park, at five minutes before midnight. And that meant all they had to do was wait.

Shit.

Cat and mouse. Rule one.

So I plundered anything useful from the apartment – an out-of-date band-aid for my shoulder, a vac-sealed packet of salami on a shelf, a couple of rusty kitchen knives in plastic sheaths, and went out to find them. Followed the sounds of engines rumbling. I took the rooftops where I could; a raggedy tabby going arm-over-arm, pouncing across alleyways and ghosting up empty fire escapes, leaving a trail of terrified scavs, their sleep disturbed by a prowling monster.

I found the Gulls hunched in the back of the biggest AV, far below the roof ledge of a fire station. Voices rose from below the closed hood, and I worked my way down with the utmost care; letting go of everything, letting something unevolved and primitive – but so much *better* at this shit – swim to the forefront of my mind.

I climbed down to meet them. An ape with Uzis.

At the foot of the building, an alleyway cut out onto the main street, and there I nestled myself into the bricks, unfolding the stock of one of the tiny guns to give myself at least a fighting chance of hitting something.

I could see them clearly, shadowed by the moonlight like patches of cut-out card.

I could hear them.

Both of them. Two guys.

So where's Number Three?

Scrim was busy, bent down over the scrawnier of his two warriors. Jacking a hypodermic needle into the other man's neck, holding him tight in a vicious headlock as he grunted and pleaded. I found myself entranced, all but forgetting to poise myself for that critical moment, that perfect shot.

"You fuck! You stay *still*. You *fuck*!" Scrim kept up a volley of abuse, squeezing the plunger with a sly grin. "You gonna *help* us, boy. You gonna *find* that limey shit. You gonna track his *ass*."

The little man jerked his head and finally pulled away with a howl. Scrim watched him, smiling quietly, clambering down to the driver's seat.

The man shivered for a moment, sweat prickling along his forehead. I held my breath, wondering what weird shit Doctor Scrim had prescribed, what narcotic treats the all-conquering Clergy had handed over to help their pet Gulls finish me off.

The little man grunted. Frowned.

Then...

Changed.

He sat up. His head moved a little too quickly. Darting, like a bird's: from position to position with no intermediary movement. He drooled. He closed his eyes.

The thing inside me, the primitive 'self' in control, gave a little grunt of recognition.

The little man *sniffed*.

And licked his lips.

Scrim plucked something silvery-red from his pocket and dangled it above the man's nose. He tilted his head to taste it like a wolf on a scent, lapping at it, smearing it across his cheeks, then closed his eyes.

Scrim re-pocketed the tiny shape. Didn't take a genius to figure what it was.

The tracker. The tracker covered in my blood.

I shivered, despite myself.

The little man smiled. Sniffed again. Pointed his finger.

Opened his eyes.

Moaned.

Stared right at me.

Fuck.

I was already running, I think, although I didn't realise it. Engines growling to life behind me, a voice shouting "There! There!" Radios crackling in some distant world.

I heard someone say, through thick static:

"Yeah. Roj that. Got him."

And then the sniper *shitbag* on the roof above, the third Gull, who'd been waiting like an angler poised over bait, waiting for the dumb psycho to try and turn the tables, opened fire and blew my fucking ear off.

* * *

THINGS RUSHED PAST without shape. Everything seemed to throb; the whole world bulging in time to the pain inside my head.

It hurt like a bitch, and I hadn't even had the time to poke and prod at it yet; to see how bad it was. In the mean time I was letting myself get good and freaked, imagining the worst.

I think I could still hear okay, though frankly nothing much came through except the throbbing and the engines. *Always* the engines. It felt like they'd been chasing me forever, although I guess it was more like an hour. Maybe more. I'd stop and look at my watch, if stopping wasn't tantamount to getting dead quickly.

The *me* doing the thinking – the instinctive snarling primate bastard I was taught to *let out* in situations like this – howled and yelped at the pain, fighting to scratch at the torrent pouring down my neck.

The *me* inside – rational, detached, cold, keeping the monkey-man in control... he *loved* it.

Such focus!

Such *sensation*!

Don't you fucking give up, soldier!

I ran like a steam train. Like a bloody Duracell bunny, with an amphetamine volcano up its furry arse. Like an animator's run-cycle stuck on a fast-forward loop. The same movements over and over, with a background cyclorama tumbling by and nothing but the *throb, throb, throb* to accompany the slapping of my feet. Puddles. Cracked tarmac. Weed-strewn sidewalks.

What I'm getting at is, I ran like a *robot*. Never tiring, never *feeling*. I ran until I was sure my heart would pop, and smiled through frothing teeth and kept going.

Fuck it, I kept thinking. *Fuck it all.*

Down tight alleyways. Over dumpsters, through drifts of shitty litter. Sharp corners. Over wire fences and down labyrinthine passages. The vehicle-roar came and went, bashing and smashing at intersections, voices raised in curses.

Hot breath, burning my lungs.

The AV couldn't keep up. It kept trying to double round, to sneak ahead; headlights blazing then jerking off on some random course. They might have had some luck, if I hadn't been a contrary bastard. If I hadn't been changing my mind about what direction to run every five minutes.

The third man had a bike. Some superd-up Japanese travesty, whining like a prepubescent dragonfly, and *he* had no trouble sticking to me; negotiating alleys too tight for the four-wheeler. I took him down circuitous switchbacks and wide avenues, letting the skittish scavs confuse him, hiding behind dark corners and doubling back every time he scorched past. Earning ten minute respites here and there, curled-up in dark rooms with terrified squatters moaning beneath soiled sleeping-bags. But he was good. Give him his due; he turned on a penny and came straight back the instant the sniffer-freak on the AV caught the scent, headlight tracking like a laser-sight, rubber squealing.

It would be fair to say – in fact it would be a royal bloody understatement – that I got fed up with him. The bike was enclosed like a sleek little turtle with riot-shields and bullet-proof plex; caroming off angled walls that should have unseated him, slipping through the oil drum fires I pulled down in my wake like a galleon through fog. And yeah, maybe he couldn't shoot me through the balustrades of shielding; but it worked both ways, and every time I found some perilous vantage point – dangling from a low-hanging escape ladder, peering like Oscar the Grouch out of a scav-nest dumpster – to open up with the Uzis and riddle him with lead, all it achieved was to let him know where I was.

He was trying to make road kill. Exhaust me, flush me out in the open. Curved scythe-blades on the bike's front mudguard, ankle-breakers poking like twisted spokes from both wheels.

He was running me down, and he was fucking *good* at it.

So eventually what I did was: I stopped running.

Stood in full view.

Waited.

(Took a moment to glance at my watch. 23:13hrs, yank-time. *Not out of the woods yet, boyo.*)

He came round the corner like a flaming bullet, and pulled-up with unnecessary flashiness, propping himself on the far leg so I couldn't even blast open his knees.

Cautious little cocksucker.

I willed him to get on with it before the AV caught us up.

He laughed behind his dusty shield and shouted:

"Getting *tired*, little limey?"

I opened fire. For all the good it did.

He gunned the whiny engine like every mosquito in the universe shouting in unison, blurring tyres snagging at the floor with a smoky blast of inertia, and came for me.

Bullets punching worthless craters in the glass.

Laughing.

Closing the gap.

Scythe-blades looming.

It was all deeply melodramatic. I rolled my eyes, took three steps backwards – down the flight of stairs lurking in the moonless shadows directly behind me – and lay down.

He didn't see *that* one coming.

"The fu – ?"

The stupid little prick went hurtling over my head, angled in mid-air, hit the wall of the subway stairwell, and just sort of...

Came apart.

No flashy fireballs or smoke-drenched detonations. Just a noise like a big cockroach cracking, and a *lot* of debris.

He was gurgling nastily when I walked away – like he'd broken his back or something – and I should probably have put him out of his misery.

Paint me bothered.

THE AV FOUND me fifteen minutes later. The scrawny little freak – doped up on whatever military-grade tracking drugs Scrim had dished out – clung to the roof like a surfer, rapping on the glass and snarling inarticulately, directing the Klan boss's crazed steering. Again with the sodding circling-round, slipping along too-tight alleyways. It felt good to begin with. Rushing past their clumsy attempts to get ahead, disappearing into the shadows to clamber up on this or that fire-escape, pausing to catch my bearings, trying to head back towards the park. It was time to begin the home-run.

It took me a fair old while to realise they were herding me. They were smarter than I thought.

I came upon an office block – nothing special; redbrick and shattered windows – with a door hanging open on a narrow stairwell. Sick and tired of the growl of engines, I rabbitted up the first few flights without any trouble, pausing to vomit discreetly before pushing myself onwards. Somewhere near floor five – or maybe six – a particularly large scav wearing Gull colours tried to axe me in the head, yelling for me to get the hell away from his wife.

There was an inflatable sex-doll on the floor next to him, but it didn't seem like the right time to point this out. I shoved the Uzi up his nostril until he got the message and backed off, then carried on upwards towards the roof whilst he noisily comforted his 'wife' below.

On the roof, I puked again. The throbbing in my ear was jacking about with my sense of direction, and it didn't help when the moonlit city put itself together bit-by-bit inside my topsy-turvy bearings.

I was so far west of the park I could see the tiny fishing punts on the Hudson, beyond the tangle of docks and quays spread out below me. Taller buildings rose to my left and right – faint lights glimmering inside where innocent scavs struggled to get by with some semblance of a life.

It was actually sort of beautiful. If it hadn't been about a mile in the wrong direction I might have paused to appreciate it.

There were no roofs to leap across to here. No secondary stairways to scamper back down.

And, if I'm honest, no energy to go on. The thing inside me curled up and went to sleep, exhausted, and left me alone. Only human. Outnumbered and outgunned.

Trapped.

"Fuck," I said. "Fuck, fuck, fuck."

From the open door I heard the huge scav shouting again – "My wife! Tha's my fucking *wife*!" – then a sharp little gunshot to shut him up.

Footsteps up the stairwell.

Time for the endgame.

CHAPTER THIRTEEN

INTERLUDE

If he was honest, Hiawatha wasn't nearly as bemused as he felt he should be.

Or rather, as he felt Rick *should be.*

The name change had only been cosmetic at the beginning. Just a... a symbol of his willingness to embrace all the weirdness, to get stuck-in, to do as the Sachems asked. To drop all the moping angry-native-kid-trying-to-be-white crapola and cuddle up to the Old Ways, like a brand on his soul that said 'On A Mission.'

But it was purely temporary – always had been – and that was the point. When he got home he'd still be 'Rick.'

If. If *he got home.*

But then again, Rick wouldn't have sailed through the peculiarities of the last couple of days without feeling at least uncomfortable, whereas he – Hiawatha, whoever-the-fuck-he'd become – was taking it all in his stride. The sights and sounds, the little excursions into foggy dreamworlds, the blending of reality and legend.

At the back of his mind Rick ranted and raved about cod-mystical tribal bullshit, whilst at the forefront – in the driving seat – Hiawatha shrugged, listened carefully to the messages on the wind, passed a critical eye over the runic algebra decorating the stars, trailed a finger in bubbling brooks and paid close attention to the splinters of light – and the codes they inferred – on the surface of the water. He didn't even need to keep stopping to smoke dope any more. It was like he'd prised his brain through a sideways gap and – now that it was there – it could stay as long as it wanted.

The cynical part of Rick's mind told him he'd turned into a big dumb stoner expressing the classic idiocy of a drugged-up moron who suddenly decides everything is significant and the whole world resonates on some profound metaphysical level. If he'd been fully in charge, rather than just a morose little echo of a former voice, he would have rolled his eyes.

Hiawatha didn't give a rat's ass.

Hiawatha had suddenly decided everything was significant and the whole world was resonating on a profound metaphysical level.

Overall, Rick/Hiawatha was kind of messed up in the head.

Out on the road the dream-visions were at least straightforward. Talking trees, rumbling skies, fluttering crows, yadda-yadda; the sort of stuff the tribal myths were packed full of. But here in the city things were different. None of the Haudenosaunee legends spoke of buildings that shuddered like horses dislodging flies; of smog-palls becoming faces and hands; of rats seething from clogged sewers to become corkscrewing whirls of smoke; of tenements making love by starlight – balconies locked together like slippery tongues – and skyscrapers cutting great intestinal scars across the belly of the clouds, where blood and shit oozed into the rain, and huge thunderbirds pecked at the wounds like vultures.

It was kind of cool.

The silver needle in his back pocket hummed to him.

The coloured smoke had brought him here. Just like out on the road; revealing the pothole that wiped out Ram. All across the suburbs, through spaghetti-like turnpikes and graffiti-plastered tunnels, across the George Washington Bridge and down through the eerily silent West Side, it had hung above the city like an electric net; green and purple, narrowing itself down to a single column of hallucinogenic smoke. He discovered he could see it twice as well when he looked away, concentrating on the corners of his vision; like an optical illusion his brain tried to conceal whenever he stared directly at it.

It took him down Broadway, through Harlem and Morningside, places he'd heard of but never visited. A small part of him felt like he'd missed a chance; like the bustling human ratraces he used to see on bygone TV shows were lost forever, and when finally he'd got his dream and escaped his small-town roots to do what every youngster always claimed they would – leave for the big city – he'd arrived five years too late.

In the middle of a goddamn ghost town.

And now here he was, cross-legged on the roof of a colossal parking lot, in an unfamiliar part of an unfamiliar town, with the dark sky rippling like an inverted ocean, the moonlit streets pulsing with curious colours and stranger sounds; and the twisting column of smoke focusing down to a sliver of light above his head, before winking out.

Making him wait.

As ever.

As midnight approached, engines growled below him, and he looked down with a sort of foggy indifference. He'd been hearing the distant chatter of gunfire on and off, but given the ungentle look of the city he'd dismissed it as 'not my problem,' and even then hadn't been entirely sure whether it was a true sound or just another backflip of his brain. But now, glancing over the street-side canyon, he could see a bulky armoured vehicle slipping to a hurried halt outside a low office block, and knew not only that it was real and solid, but that it made him shiver and his blood turn sluggish.

The car had been painted half-heartedly – a smear of messy red along both flanks – but from Hiawatha's vantage the redecoration couldn't hope to disguise the undercoat. The glossy skyblue sheen marked on the thick roof with a wide scarlet 'O.'

Clergy.

Here.

Hiawatha rushed to his bike to snatch-up an appropriate weapon, acting on auto-pilot, scrabbling through pistols and automatics like a chef tossing salad. Finally his hand closed on a rifle – some crow-blasting farmer's friend, no doubt, stolen from a deserted homestead somewhere by Ram and his cronies – and raced back to the edge: just in time to see the AV's two occupants disappear into the office block.

He swore out loud.

And then he saw the man.

The man with green and purple fire tangled above him. With a great bird hovering over his head and wolves slinking past his legs. With rivers and grasses flowing in unreal ripples from his booted feet.

With one ear a tattered mess, with blood all down him, with rags on his back and an Uzi in each hand.

"You'll know him," the Tadodaho had told Rick. "You'll know him when you see him."

Everything stopped.

The man stood on the roof of the office block, opposite and below Hiawatha's own vantage point. He looked like he was breathing heavily, sweating buckets, bleeding from a dozen cuts; but even as Hiawatha watched, the man seemed to force-down the exhaustion, eyes closed, face calm. When he reopened his eyes he was almost a different person, moving with predatory grace, stepping to the shadows on one side of the door.

*A little part of the old Rick muttered: "*Jedi, *man..."*

In his swirling dream-vision, Hiawatha watched the man change. Become something different. *A puma-king of lank fur and subreal shadows; a primitive shade; a Walking Instinct. Reality kept adjusting around him; slowing down, jarring, highlighting its dangers and hazards, blazing along the edge of anything that could be used as a weapon, streaming into dark corners that offered cover, snaking in silvery beads along potential escape-routes, ambush points, blindspots...*

Hiawatha realised with a start he was seeing the world as the stranger saw it, and shook his head in annoyance, wanting to watch the spectacle unclouded by the druggish haze.

Out on the rooftop, the two goons from the AV bundled through the stairwell door together, hands full of blades and barrels, and everything went crazy.

The stranger sort of... blurred. Maybe he kicked the door, or slunk around in front before it was fully open. Maybe he duck-sneaked across the open hatch, below the aim of their guns, and darted-in towards them before they could react. Maybe he took them on the full, twisting sideways between outstretched gun arms with fingers locked and lunging.

Hiawatha couldn't say for sure.

An arm jerked, a leg flicked out. The scrawny goon shrieked and fell, the bigger man raised his gun –

Hiawatha gasped and struggled with the rifle. He'd save the stranger. He'd keep him alive! He'd –

Except the goon was already disarmed. Bleeding from his nose. A kitchen-knife up to its hilt in the soft meat of his leg.

He looked more pissed than hurt.

The stranger turned. Ducked. Flexed. Impacts raining on the swarthy thug, boots lashing out in balletic patterns. The smaller goon was back up now, pistol firing twice in the wrong direction, the stranger twist-turn-kick-duck-pouncing, then the little guy was back down again, all but launched off the roof; gun tumbling out into space.

Hiawatha sighted the rifle back on the big guy, adrenaline roaring, desperate to do something, to take part... *But the stranger was too fast.*

Didn't need any help.

He took the two shitheads apart like a surgeon, and when they both rocked back on the floor – disarmed, disoriented, slow like glaciers fighting fire – he scooped a single tiny Uzi out of his pocket, aimed it with the minimum concentration, and blew their surprised expressions right open.

The whole fight, from start to finish, took about five seconds. Hiawatha discovered he was still aiming at the dead goons and let his shaking arms relax by degrees.

"Fuuuck," he hissed.

Which is when an enormous naked freak, bleeding from a hole in his chest, tore through the remains of the door with a meat cleaver in one hand and a limp sex-doll in the other, screaming for revenge upon the murderer of his wife.

The stranger had his back to the colossus. Taken by surprise. Unprepared.

Even he *couldn't move that fast.*

Hiawatha blew two new holes through the fat man's ribs, smiled a secret smile, and melted away into the shadows of the parking lot before the stranger even knew what had happened.

He wondered if he should go over. Tell the poor guy who he was.

What he was doing here.

What he wanted with him.

"Not time yet," the sky told him. The needle sang in his back pocket. "Not time yet."

HIAWATHA FOLLOWED THE *stranger at a discreet distance. He seemed to be in a hurry; vaulting into the thugs' AV and tearing off into the east. Hiawatha stayed out of his sight, letting the signs and portents – the roiling purple fire – guide the throb of the Harley's progress; grumbling internally about relying on hippy bullshit to guide him.*

It felt a lot like cheating.

Half an hour after the rooftop struggle, at the edge of a great blocked-in wilderness, encircled by dead trees and stagnant swamps – Central Park, he assumed – he deserted the Harley in a quiet alcove and ambled out across the browning lawns. He'd done his best to conceal it, but the whole area seemed to be crawling alive with knots of raggedy-looking people, and no amount of security was ever *going to stop a truly determined thief. He searched his feelings for a moment or two – still not quite sure if he was seeking divine solutions, subconscious rationality or plain old trippy make-believe – and decided he wouldn't be needing the trike any more anyway.*

(The defining moment in this decision was a fat bear, made entirely out of smoke, waddling past with a claw flicking dismissively towards the vehicle. "Hope you're right," Hiawatha said. If he'd been in a more rational state of mind, he might have felt slightly dumb addressing such an obvious figment of his imagination. As it was, it not only seemed utterly natural, but far more real than the mundane shit going on around it.)

He shouldered the sack of guns he'd taken from the general store, and followed the flow of the crowd.

Somewhere ahead, in a copse of spindly trees, a great cheer went up. It seemed to hang in the air. Hundreds of hands clapping, voices laughing and shouting, and a single booming tone raised above the others. The rodent-like people nearby seemed to be gravitating towards it, sticking to little groups of two or three for as long as possible, then awkwardly mingling as the numbers locked together. Hiawatha saw luminous tags hanging above each one's head, wrapping ethereal chains and brambles around each neck. He understood without knowing how that these visions were brands declaring each persons' ownership. Each to a different tribe; like the Beaver-Lodge tattoo on his own left shoulder, but far harsher – symbols not of familial ties but of property, like a name tag sewn into valuable clothes. The people's cautious movements marked them out as rivals, awkwardly picking their way into someone else's territory at the mercy of their curiosities, unaccustomed to mixing.

Hiawatha began to understand this was unprecedented. A crowd like this; a gathering like this. Hopeful glances traded between bitter enemies, slaves electing a new master...

In his mind, there was a blanket of gold hanging above the park.

It was all deeply peculiar.

Every now and again a better-dressed man or woman – most in red, with feathers pinned in their hair – would point and shout accusations, snarling "you fucking Globies get outta the park!" or "Gulls only! Gull scavs only! No fucking Mickies! No fucking Strips!" Their shouts meant little to Hiawatha, and went mostly ignored anyway. Eventually the crowd just surged around them, and they wandered off, forlorn, towards the edge of the park, casting hateful glances back towards the source of all the cheering.

He began to catch snatches of conversation as he picked his way through the trees, letting the cheers grow up around him; feeling the excitement of the hordes. But what little he overheard seemed nonsensical at best, and he scowled and forged on through the storm of random commentary.

"...figures he told 'em if they wasn't with him, they was out on they fuckin' ear, man..."

"...got fresh rat here, fresh rat, barter for clothing, barter for burns... fresh rat..."

"...says any 'n' all welcome. Never seen nothing like, man, and I bin here years..."

"...wassa-wassa-wassa fucking Liiimey? Never hearda no Liiimey..."

"...sent the rest to tear down the territory poles... got plans, he says..."

"...rabbit meat and rats, rats and rabbits, get 'em while they're hot..."

And so on.

On the shores of a truly revolting pond (which formed a great miserable face in Hiawatha's mind, moaning plaintively for aid) he found the stranger; stood on a ramshackle podium built of logs and sheets, set-up in front of a great ghastly building that sprawled across the lawns like a living ooze.

He also found the largest crowd he'd ever seen.

In the ravages of his memory – from a time before his mind was prised open by the expedient application of mystical mumbo-jumbo and hardcore perception-altering pot, from a time even before the great Cull – he remembered concerts he'd visited, student rallies, great gatherings where all personal differences were thoughtlessly disregarded in the shared reverence of a single band; a single demagogue, a single voice.

This was like that.

But more so.

The stranger spoke surprisingly softly. He had the look of a character unused to such attention; far better suited to the quiet application of force in secret, covert places. Hiawatha guessed that under other circumstances the man would have passed for utterly unremarkable. A forgettable face, cropped hair, a physique neither tall nor short, vastly over-inflated nor ultra-weedy. Just a guy with a crazy accent and a hopelessly British manner, whose words managed nonetheless to silence a crowd thousands strong.

If it hadn't been for the blood drying in thick streaks down his cheek, the matted tangle of gore-splattered rags on his back – once patched in every conceivable colour, now stained to a uniform brown-grey – and the glossy rifle hung nonchalantly over his shoulder, nobody would have looked at him twice.

"Where," the man said, into a silence as deep and dark as the sky above his head, where the quicksmog oozed out of the stratosphere, "are the Children?"

Hiawatha shivered.

No, no... scratch that.

The whole fucking crowd *shivered.*

As he stood there, playing the reaction like a pro, the stranger was patched-up and fussed-over by an elderly black man wearing the most ridiculous clothes Hiawatha had ever seen. It was all part of the spectacle, he supposed; holding an ever-growing host spellbound.

"I don't see them. Do you?" The stranger glanced about theatrically. "Look. Look at you. Not a single kid in the whole place."

Here and there people muttered, but whether in anger or fear Hiawatha couldn't tell. The bright stars above the crowd – figments of his imagination, he was pretty sure – had turned to an angry scarlet, pulsing along with Hiawatha's own heartbeat.

"I'll tell you where the kids are, shall I?"

He smiled, almost paternal, just a little *too sweet to be genuine.*

"They're sleeping. Just over there." He nodded off to the horizon, to the south east. The crowd muttered just a little louder. "Like little angels, they are. Come from all over the world, the dears. Sleeping off a hard day of... of dutifully learning their scriptures. Preparing for big things. Getting ready to... lead the world into a new age of glorious civilisation. Right? That's right. That's where they are."

He sounded sincere. It was hard to believe he was being sarcastic, hard to believe he was forming dangerous words, but the crowd were off-balance. What was this? Rebellion or respect-paying?

And then the stranger leaned down low to the front rows, dipped his head so he was staring from beneath grimy eyebrows, and shouted so loud that everyone jumped.

"Bollocks! Fucking bollocks*!"*

Hiawatha didn't know what bollocks were, but he got the gist. Everyone got the gist.

"If they're locked away," the stranger growled, "in that... that fucking prison, *why don't we see them? Why do they never come out? Didn't you people ever stop and* think*? Didn't you ever smell a bloody* rat*?"*

Somewhere near Hiawatha, a couple of rows to his left, a woman started crying. It was a mystifying reaction. In any other place, at any other time, he would have expected the crowd to rise-up against the sanctimonious prick giving them a dressing-down; to react with fury at the open accusations.

But no. No, this crowd was a chastised kid. A naughty child who knew it deserved *to be punished.*

The stranger rung his hands together. "Didn't you ever... Didn't you..." his voice tailed off, lost to the frustration. He stood silently for a moment, and Hiawatha wondered if he'd run out of energy, if the anger gobbling him up had overtaken him.

But:

"Fuck!" he shouted. "Fuck – come on! *Even if those shits-in-dresses are telling the truth, even if your sons and daughters* are *hidden away in there, don't you tell me you're* happy. *Don't you tell me you handed them over with a... smile and a fucking song in your heart. Don't you tell me that!*

"No, no. You gave them up because you were told to. I get it. *Because... because maybe if you said 'no,' they would've just been taken anyway. Because you're nobodies. Because the shits in the Klans with the... the guns and the drugs, they said that's what you scavs* do. *That's what you're for. Right? And maybe you told yourself over and over it was for the best, that the kids would be going somewhere better, somewhere more* hopeful... *but people, I don't believe that. And I don't believe you believe it either.*

"Here's the truth, ladies and gents. These people... these fucking scum*" – and here the stranger raised a crooked finger towards a line of men standing at the back of the podium, held in place by scrawny scavs with knives and guns – "They've. Stolen. Your.* Children.*"*

Silence.

Thick, heavy, accusatory silence. On the stage the hostages shuffled their feet and traded glances. Scarlet eye-rings hiding furtive fear and the first glimmerings of tears. One of them – the scrawniest, whose face was contorted not with fear but with hatred – wore ruby-red sunglasses, as if to protect his eyes from the moonlight's glare.

Their robes had been stripped away, their weapons taken.

Neo-Clergy, fallen from grace.

Hiawatha almost snarled with joy to see them so humiliated.

And then, as had happened in every crowd since creation began, the prerequisite asshole at the front opened his mouth.

"For the glory of the New Dawn!" came a shrill voice; a scrawny man in stained rags leaping up and down, stabbing a finger towards the podium. He had a scarlet tattoo around his left eye, and a pistol raised in his right hand. "Your selfishness betrays you!" he shrieked, drawing a bead on the stranger. "Your wickedness shall..."

He never got the chance to fire. A blade snicker-snackered in the crowd somewhere behind him, hands reached out to snake around his neck and his arms, and within an instant the mob had swallowed him up and closed over him. His cries grew muffled, then tailed away into silence. The crowd's head twisted, as one, back towards the stranger.

He sighed.

"Any other morons?" he said, letting his eyes rove, like a teacher peering across a rowdy classroom. "Any other stupid bastards? Anyone else thinks their kids are better off cuddling a bible instead of their own flesh and blood? Anyone else want to tell me they did the right thing? They like *it how it is? The Klans and the killings and the fucking Tags? Anyone else want to tell me they* believe *the Clergy?"*

He was almost shouting. Voice hoarse. Anger dribbling over his eyeballs and into his words.

"Because, people, they're building us all a better tomorrow. Remember? That's what they say. And wouldn't it just be the best thing in the world to believe them? Wouldn't it just be so easy to shout 'hallelujah!'? To pray every night and... go with the flow? To feel like you did the right *thing, letting them take your kids? Wouldn't that be the dog's-sodding-bollocks?*

"Too right it would."

He spat on the floor. He took a deep breath.

And he drew a long knife out of his pocket.

The crowd stopped breathing.

"But believing it – really and truly, *I mean – in your guts, people. That's a tough call. That's a tricky business. And I'm going to go out on a limb here, and say I really don't think there are many of us who do. Not really. Not deep down.*

"So let's find out. Let's cut the crap."

He smiled.

"Let's see how many of you really love the Clergy. Let's see who's willing to stop me."

And he turned to the line of men, those captive Choirboys stood behind him, and he smiled.

"I came here from across the ocean," he said to the hostages, but loud enough for everyone to hear. "It was hard fucking work, let me tell you. But I came. I didn't let them stop me, your pals in London, although they tried. I had to kill all sorts of people on the way. And all because I wanted to ask you a question, matey, face-to-face. Nice and simple."

He leaned down towards the first goon.

"What I wanted to ask you, is:

"Where are my children, you kidnapping, indoctrinating, psychotic pieces of cancerous shit?"

The goon stared at him. The goon spat in his face with a sort of doing-it-by-the-script doggedness.

So the stranger cut out his throat.

The crowd made a noise. Not quite a cheer. But definitely not a scream of horror.

The man went down, his legs shivered and thrashed, his blood oozed, and in Hiawatha's eyes something dry and unpleasant fluttered up from the corpse to lose itself in the spreading quicksmog.

The stranger turned back to the crowd. No one made a move. No one breathed.

Hiawatha could see the lie. He could see the red taint of dishonesty hanging above the stranger, glittering and mewing like a mutant cat. This man, this unstoppable Brit with his boring face and his quiet voice, he had no interest in the scavs gathered in Central Park. He didn't care one bit about punishing the wicked. He couldn't give a damn for doing the right thing.

All he had was an agenda – whatever the hell it was – and Hiawatha could see, burning bright in his third eye, that this man would do anything *to get what he wanted. He would lie about an abducted family, just to make a crowd of allies empathise with his rage. He would slaughter his way through as many hostages as it took, to show them they didn't need to fear the Choirboys.*

He wouldn't stop until he got his way, and whilst Hiawatha couldn't bring himself to admire such apathetic selfishness, such casual manipulation, it just so happened that the Limey bastard's goals and his own were – briefly – aligned.

So he smiled, and started to clap.

And the whole crowd picked up the applause.

Later, the second goon went the same way, although his resolve left him as the stranger's question went unanswered and the knife blurred upwards towards his throat. He cried out wordlessly, gurgled, then dropped.

The fifth man in the line – the wiry one with the thick glasses, whose aura seemed to crackle with an orange edge – shouted something to the two remaining thugs. Hiawatha caught the words 'reward' and 'Heaven,' and could imagine the rest.

The goons sprang forwards, rushing the scavs who held them at gunpoint, shouting and snarling as their naked flesh rippled in time to their meaty swipes. The black man with the bandages dived to the floor, hands over his head; the stranger shouted – more angry than surprised – and the scavs opened fire.

The crowd shuddered. Muzzlefire lent the whole drama a lightning-storm animation, and between freeze-flashes, specks of blood appeared across the faces of the crowd.

When it was over, when the gunsmoke cleared and the scavs were cooling off and the crowd was in uproar, four naked goons lay bleeding on the stage, and the rat-like bastard with the sunglasses was gone, pushing his way through the recoiling crowd, through trees and undergrowth, shouting and laughing all the way.

The stranger swore. Loudly.

The crowd swore with him.

By four in the morning it was no longer a crowd. It was an army.

It was a tired cliché, but that didn't make it inaccurate. As Hiawatha watched, buffeted by awe and abstraction, he could think of no better description:

It was like a tidal wave.

The captured AV went first, followed by the smattering of vehicles the stranger had liberated from the Red Gulls. As their new de facto *leader, he was more than entitled to requisition them for his own ends, but a gutsy minority of the Klansmen had reacted badly to the idea of throwing off the feudal yoke and rising up against the tyrants, and had holed up inside the Gulls' base to stop anyone getting in.*

In the end, the stranger had had to kill pretty much all of them.

Hiawatha had stayed out of the way. It wasn't time yet. He'd sat to one side, beneath the great boughs of old, dead trees, and listened to the spirit-voices whispering mournfully inside them. As the first fires started burning deep inside the Gulls' lair, he had taken the stick of blacking-paint from the bottom of his pack, and began to slowly mark his face, chanting quietly to himself, feeling the silver needle in his pocket chiming along with his words.

Afterwards, when the armouries were opened and their bounties distributed, the crowd didn't wait for the dawn. It was like a crusade; a great wedge of people, shifting together along empty streets, swelling as they went. A magnetic pull.

And on the edge of the city, in Hell's Kitchen, squished up against the black waters of the East River, they faced the United Nations building, and advanced.

He – the stranger, the man whose name no one had bothered to ask – went first. It was all deeply medieval. All deeply mythic. But as the crowd roared as one and the vehicles gunned their engines and the guards inside the compound shouted and shit themselves, it felt right.

The AV ploughed through the main gates of the UN headquarters like a harpoon through whale meat, bullets rattling off its sides; slivers of shredded steel and tangled barbed wire thrashing in its wake. Even as it sat steaming in the forecourt, dents opening up across it, the Clergymen in the guard-nest were realising their mistake. Betraying their positions in the darkness with tapered candles of muzzle-fire.

The second wave of vehicles thundered through, guns firing. Sandbag-packed nests ruptured, grenades tumbled from heavy launchers and choked out red-black plumes of soot and smoke and people dying. Somewhere up on the roof of the Secretariat a heavy auto opened fire – thundering its payload down into the crowd – but at such a range and in such darkness its accuracy was far from perfect, and the spooky trails of tracer-fire stitched themselves neatly through panicky Clergymen as evenly as rioting 'scavs. Eventually someone had the presence of mind to order the ceasefire, and the artillery fell silent.

In odd corners, fires took hold. Sparks billowed and roiled, and beckoned with tongues of white light at the crowds waiting in the shadows, eyes gleaming. It was like an invitation.

The horde swarmed from the streets, in every hand a weapon, in every mouth a scream, and everything went straight to hell. Gunfire, above grenade-blasts, above human roars, above dying screams, above engine purrs and the horrified gasps of unprepared Clergymen.

Cy had forewarned them, maybe. But still. But still.

Yeah, *Hiawatha thought.* Just like a tidal wave.

It surged and boiled, fuelled by years of bottled anger. It lapped against the walls of the compound and spun in eddies of violence. Whirlpools with isolated Choirboys at their centres, screaming out as the mob circled and slashed and shot. It frothed at its edges; the glowing foam of muzzleflash and the warm spume of impact-craters, spitting dust and mortar and blood.

The AV gave up the ghost in a spectacular fireball, fuel-tanks finally punctured, hefting itself in warped fragments off the crowd to spin lazily in the air; but by then the crew were well clear, and its messy end served only as a distraction from the true violence, close and personal and vicious. In dark corners, men and women pushed blunt blades into robed sides, struggled muzzle-to-muzzle to bring poorly-tended pistols to bear on the thugs who had terrorised their worlds, beat and battered with crowbars and tyre-irons at the tattooed faces of the pious pricks.

"Where are they?" they screamed. "Where are the fucking children?"

Not much of a battle cry, but it worked.

Hiawatha stayed at the rear. Oh, not through cowardice – the spiralling dreamhaze had done away with that *– and he lent his aid where he could; firing calmly and accurately into Clergy lines where the other scavs hooted and panicked, picking off stragglers in their grey robes with a savage sort of joy. He felt like all the Sachems stared through his eyes, and laughed and giggled and passed around the beers with each new kill. The Haudenosaunee, it would be fair to say, did not much like the Clergy.*

But no, no, that wasn't his major role, here. He worked his way carefully along the edges of the mêlée, eyes darting, dreamsenses spinning; seeking out the stranger.

"Almost time, now..." *the wind said, hot with the breath of fuel-fires and roasting skin.* "Almost time."

The purple cloud ran like a thread through the crowd, and Hiawatha realised with a start that the stranger had snuck away. He'd got what he wanted, access to this barbed-wire compound, and had left behind the agents of his aid the instant they'd ceased to be of any use. It was cold and brutal and logical, but it had worked.

The trail led into the Secretariat.

Hiawatha skidded on blood, marvelling deep down at the raw apathy of a man who could bring about such wanton violence in the sole pursuit of... of what?

He stepped into the gloomy building, and went to meet his destiny.

CHAPTER FOURTEEN

I COULDN'T HELP smiling. The heat coming up from the fires, the smell of unpleasant things cooking, the acid stink of gun smoke.

Yeah. Let it out. Let the grin break through. *You're so close. Enjoy. You deserve it.*

Then with the guilt. Screams and blood and desperate people cutting chunks out of each other, just because I told them to. Just because I needed to get past those big fucking gates. I lied to them. Worked them up like a sculptor hammering clay.

Monster. Manipulator. Don't you care about anything? Don't you –

Then with the irritation *at* the guilt.

You trained for this. This is what you DO. *This is who you* ARE.

Round and round and round.

Fuck it. Fuck them all.

Don't feel guilty.

Look at what you did. Enjoy *it.*

From the third floor, looking down through the Secretariat's shattered mirror glass, it was quite a sight. Barely visible in the darkness, the undulations of the throng could easily have been mistaken for a gloomy sort of fog; wafted about by contrary breezes, lit internally by wyrd-lights and wil-o'-the-wisps; all of it sped up by a factor of ten and replayed to a BBC *Sounds of War* effects tape. Now and then, something solid differentiated itself from the mêlée – a moonflash along the edge of a blade, a torn strip of pale robe, an effervescent burst of cranial fluids. Little details, like individual brushstrokes discernible within a completed painting.

They didn't last. Big, crazy spectacles have a way of homogenising like that. Little by little everything was sucked inside; reabsorbed by the heaving, living, collective amoebic monstrosity that was the crowd.

"Jesus," I muttered, not really thinking.

Being stuck in a fight on ground-level, that's a messy, brutal, untidy sort of shit. No time to think. No time to gauge the way it's going. Just act, react, dodge, stab, duck, shoot. Gunfire ripping from left to right, contrary angles of devastation, panicky shouts and thoughtless responses, friendly fire.

But from above...

Oh yes. From above you get a pretty good idea of why generals get to be such arrogant arseholes. Why politicians don't talk about individuals, just 'the people.' Why the guys who make decisions – the top dogs, the head honchos – get to be sadistic fucks with no concept of human expenditure whatsoever. From above, it's all... *neat*. Tidy. Like playing war games with over-expensive models, rolling dice to determine movements, accuracies, wounds.

Nobody ever rolled a dice to determine how many sobbing loved ones each dead model leaves behind. How much the poor bastard suffered before he was removed from the playing table.

It takes a funny sort of brain to see a crowd of people, and mentally note them down as a 'diversion.' 'Cannon fodder.' 'Acceptable losses.'

Guilty as charged.

Again with the guilt.

Something exploded down below, and lit them all up. Just for a fraction of a second, they were *people*. Different faces, contorted in anger and pain and fear. Individuals, locked together. All unique.

For just a fraction of a second, fat with guilt and empathy and all that other bollocks, I wasn't the cold-hearted manipulative scheming *fuck* I thought I was.

Then the light faded and the mob coalesced in the shadows, and I was back to enjoying the spectacle, congratulating myself on getting inside the Secretariat without a scratch, being *me*.

"You... *ah*... you don't want to go help 'em?" Nate rumbled from somewhere behind me. He'd followed me up here like a puppy dog. He looked even worse now, twitching and sweating and jerking. I couldn't be bothered to ask what was wrong. Not when I was this close. Not when nothing else mattered.

I ignored him.

The fight was all but over anyway. Still a few pockets of resistance. Clergymen scrabbling behind improvised cover to mow down scavs in their dozens, stuttering cones of perfect light drizzling lead into onrushing walls of black rags and snarling flesh. The bodies piled up like human ramps, twitching and groaning, but there was more to come, more plugging the gaps, more stolen vehicles blasting away with heavy weapons.

Little by little the Choirboys were becoming isolated; cut off from buildings, rounded up in coils of the mob and gradually ringed in, hemmed, set upon.

None of them went quietly. And after the first few who tried to surrender were torn apart – limbs wrenched clean away, eyes put out, scalps sliced off and ribs broken – none of the others bothered to throw themselves on the scavs' mercy. They'd seen the look in their eyes. The excitement, the primal joy of being caught up in... in *something.*

The pack instinct. That old-brain thing, rustling inside my head, howling to go and join its brothers. But no mercy. None of that.

One or two of the Choirboys sang hymns as their ammunition ran out and the crowds seethed forwards. Mostly they didn't get past the first line.

There were fewer robes out there than I'd expected.

Where are the others?

I turned away. Pretty soon the big, spectacular part would be over and the scavs would be slinking inside the buildings. Kicking down doors under the auspices of finding their lost children; secretly yearning for nests of resistance, dorms piled with sleeping Choirboys, easy targets.

Let them.

Oddly enough, the Secretariat itself was almost deserted. On floor after floor, the plush offices of another time – structured with all the ergonomic ingenuity of too much money, in broad stripes of grey and beige and airy spaces and comfy sofas and padded swivel-chairs and blah-blah-*blah* – sat silent; deserted. It reminded me, in a homesick sort of way, of Vauxhall Cross, my base for the past five years, where once the SIS had controlled its agents all across the world, keeping fingers on the pulses of foreign threats, adjusting and prodding regimes they didn't like, sneaking about with a distinct absence of Martinis, pithy one-liners, Q-Department gadgets and obscenely horny chicks.

Well. Mostly.

The difference was that the offices back in London had a dangerous sort of mystique lacking here in the Secretariat. Sharper edges, maybe. Deeper shadows. Tight corners and internal windows. *Em-Eye-fucking-Six*, the place said. *Don't you cock around with us.*

The Secretariat just looked like an expensive software corporation.

Still, at least it felt *lived in.* Most of its airy floors had been comprehensively violated. Desks and waiting sofas used as sleeping palettes, walls covered in neat lines of devotional graffiti (*Book of Revelations*, mostly, which I guess is sort of *de rigeur* amongst insane apocalyptic cults). I figured the Clergy used them for sleeping dorms, store-rooms, pantries, whatever.

Which sort of begged the question: Where *were* they all?

The battle outside was still raging, still going strong, but there was no way in hell the scavs had overrun every last Choirboy in this place. It was *enormous.*

So where *were* they?

Nate and I had bumped into a few of the little shits on the stairwell on the way inside. Mostly they were sprinting down from above, guns and heavy packs stowed on their backs and crooked beneath overladen arms, and I'd been obliged to shoot them as they came clattering down the last flight without waiting for them to arm up. I'd be discreetly ashamed, if I could be bothered. No; more worrying was the reason for the sudden evacuation. These grunts weren't dashing off to join the defence of the outer gate, or form a second layer of repulsion. They were getting *out.* All possessions carried, scampering off through the vast lobby (now strewn with military netting and a blotchy mural of John-Paul) and out, towards the wide shape of the General Assembly Building.

Something was going down.

I couldn't give a flying fuck.

On the third floor we came across a shattered desk covered in telephone switchboard pins, and I rummaged through piles of discarded paperwork whilst Nate stood watch with that same nervous foot-to-foot hop. Amidst crumbling cards and files I found, finally, a yellowing printout of floor designations. Thirty-nine levels; thirty-nine busy little worlds dedicated to 'World Peace.'

A spray of stray bullets knocked out the windows beside me. Kind of ironic.

'32-35,' the printout said. 'Sci/Tech Research Administration,' with a list of departmental names as long as my arm and the telephone extensions of each. Someone had ringed one of the entries in green ink, with the bored assiduousness of someone who was tired of being asked for the same department over and over.

Towards the end, I guessed, as the Cull turned the city outside into a ghost town, the phones would never have stopped ringing.

Fl 34. Ext 34033. Epidemiology.

"Right," I said.

"You found what you been looking for?" Nate grunted, trying not to look too interested. He'd been pretty good so far, I supposed, at not asking out loud what the hell I'd dragged him into. He'd got his payment. He'd got his protection, and a little sliver of fame as the guy who's with the stranger. He was doing *okay*, and the Clergy hadn't tried to kill him yet.

But you could see it in his eyes. The curiosity was killing him.

I wondered if I should take him with me.

But.

Something not quite right...

Still that sensation of disquiet. His eyes twinkled over his soggy dogend, his teeth sparkled with every smile. He cooked a fine rat. He told a fine story. He looked a clown and acted a clown, and his shaky-handed approach to medicine had saved my life at least twice. Nothing to dislike about the guy, right?

Right.

But no. No. *Something not right.*

Something besides this new twitchy, sweaty routine he was going through, something besides the weird behaviour since yesterday.

A little tentacle of memory uncurled. A voice cut-through with exhaustion and inebriation, curdled with heavy breathing and fresh sweat.

Bella.

I only knew her a couple of weeks. Planning for the airport, mostly. Getting provisions, working out where to hit, how to get through, who to target. Mostly.

Except the one night we got smashed on whatever brain-killing homebrew the local survivors had been cooking up in their bathtub stills. Lost track of our conversation.

Ended up fucking on the bar in the abandoned pub we'd been using as home.

Even off my face, even after five years of hardcore celibacy, even in a world as careless and repercussion-free as this one, the guilt!

Didn't matter, in the end. We fell asleep all cuddled up on the trapdoor behind the bar, and as I dozed off I got confused and kept kissing her forehead, like she was someone else. And she started telling me things. Stuff I hadn't asked about, hadn't expressed any interest in. Stuff I barely bothered to listen to.

When she was finished there was a long silence, then she said:

"Doesn't matter. Not your problem. But that's why I'm going."

Back on the fifth floor of the United Nations Secretariat building, with people shouting and dying outside, I turned to Nate and said:

"Go help the others. Find the kids. Look everywhere."

He stared at me like I was mad. Half relieved, half terrified.

"But..." He waved a hand, searching for the right words. "*Why*, man? Ain't like you *care*. Ain't like you expect 'em to *find* anything. Why the sudden ch..."

Doesn't matter, she'd said, sweat making the grime on her face streak and run. *Not your problem.*

I snapped. Just a little.

"Fuck*sakes*, Nate! Just fucking... Just..."

His eyes bugged. I looked away.

Took a breath.

"Just... just go help them, will you? Please? I'm going upstairs. Might be dangerous. Just give them a *hand*."

Outside, a fireball licked at the edges of the building and blew-in the rest of the windows, letting in the screams from outside. Nate grunted.

I started to climb the stairs.

From the thirty-fourth floor I couldn't even see the fight outside. This high up, the green-glass windows were all intact, and I couldn't hope to see down to the base of the tower.

I was sweating heavily, by the time I arrived. Not a good sign. Since the Cull robbed us all of a functioning power grid, elevators had been a survivor's wet dream. Judging from the lack of empty food cans and discarded sleeping-mats, very few Clergy goons had taken the trouble to come this high. Even the walls were mostly free of nonsensical graffiti, and any plundering of office supplies appeared to have been more a matter of overturning desks and causing a mess than looking for useful stuff. If I'm honest, as I climbed the stairs I was quietly entertaining the suspicion that sooner or later I'd come across floor-after-floor of children, packed together in tiny bunks, poring over mass-produced bibles and reciting the day's lessons like good little acolytes.

Bella's words, getting to me.

"Not your problem."

It's a funny thing, convincing a horde that something was a lie whilst dimly suspecting it might just be true. I guess, deep down inside – *maybe* – there was a little bit of me expecting that the scavs *would* find their kids. Behind the carefully maintained disinterest, behind the rock-solid focus on my own goals (*Don't you fucking give up, soldier!*), it was lurking there, an irritating little piece of humanity.

The looks in the eyes of the women, standing outside the gates last night.

The way Malice rocked her child to sleep in the midst of the Wheels Mart, knowing she had four more years before the little mite was whisked away.

The edge in Bella's voice.

Was it so unlikely that they'd find them, after all?

Why did the Clergy *want* the kids, if not for their grand future-shaping scheme? Why fly the little buggers in from overseas, from all over the bloody world, if not to train them in the ways of the Lord, to fill their heads with destiny-based-bollocks? It's not like the Clergy were running a secret sportswear sweatshop, or mass-producing child meat pies...

No. They *had* to be here somewhere, somewhere inside the compound, hidden away.

But not here. Not a soul. Just the dim moonlight through thick plate glass, a morass of overturned desks and stalwart filing cabinets, and endless silence.

I started searching.

Once or twice I heard voices from the stairwell, torches wobbling in the gloom, puddles of hard light wafting past walls and windows. I froze every time, hands reaching for the M16, convinced they'd followed me. They knew what I was after.

Then they went clattering past – upwards – and were lost to the endless silence. I half-wondered what was on the roof that was so bloody important, then rammed my head into another heap of cluttered files and forgot all about it.

I found it forty minutes later.

Tucked away in a chrome cabinet (locked, but fortunately not bullet-proof), inserted between vile-green separators like the most unimportant thing on earth, rammed between bulging files marked PAL-, PAN-, PAO-, PAP-, it was a slender, unremarkable thing. A faded project-report, listing funding allocations, resources, classification levels, diplomatic passes, locations, and personnel.

I had to sit down.

Take a breath.

Look away. Out across the dark landscape and that brightening patch of sky to the east, promising – eventually – a new sun.

Then I looked back and re-read the title:

PROJECT PANDORA

It made me shiver, which is quite a thing to admit when you've spent most of your adult life killing people in secret.

I rifled through the loose sheets inside like a man possessed, fingers trembling, spilling useless documents and paperclipped photographs. It all seemed like it was happening to someone else.

I found the name I was looking for near the back.

Vital statistics. Origins. Code numbers. Re-assignment location.

There was a photo pinned to its rear.

I stared at it for twenty minutes.

The sun edged higher.

And then abruptly I was ready to leave, and stuffing the papers into my pockets, and staggering upright, fighting the shivers, and casting my eyes across the photos I'd dropped, stopping to retrieve my rifle, and –

Oh shit.

And there he was. Staring at me. Pictured in black and white, a decade or two younger, smart in dress-uniform and sergeant's stripes, smiling with officious intensity at the camera.

JOHN P. MILLER.

Lacking only for a vast white mitre, a snowy robe, and an exaltation to the Lord on his lips.

John-Paul Rohare Baptiste.

Why the *fuck* was *he* in the file? What the hell was *he* doing *th* –

Snkt.

This is a sound I have heard many times. This is a sound I am acquainted with intimately, and have been responsible for creating in the vast majority of cases.

This is the sound of a semi-automatic pistol being armed, in close proximity to someone's head.

The head was mine. The pistol was Cardinal Cy's.

"Fuck," I said.

"Yeah," he said.

Nobody moved.

"How did you find me?"

"On the way up. Heard a shot. Took it nice and slow."

Opening the filing cabinet. Bugger.

Still the same, strange voice. Little stammered bursts of thought, tones just a *touch* too high for comfort.

"Given us a chase. Haven't you? Troublemaker. Caused all sorts."

"What's on the roof?" I said. Stalling. It didn't matter. He had no reason to keep me alive now. Just showboating. Just being curious. Just playing with me.

"No concern," he said. "What you looking for? Up here, huh? What's got you into this?"

"None of your business," I deadpanned.

He punched me in the kidneys, giggling horribly and as I went down I made it look *good*, cried out, and staggered, and threw up my hand to ward him off, letting the photo of John-Paul flap about, and –

– and in the confusion sneaked my other hand onto the Uzi in my pocket, and –

– and the gun was back on my scalp, only this time I was kneeling.

"Fuck."

"Hands. Lemee see. On head."

He giggled again. Not right in the head.

I did what he said. The Uzi clattered to the ground beside the photo of John-Paul, and somewhere behind those impenetrable red specs I guess he snatched a glance.

"That who I think?"

"Yeah."

"Looks young."

"Yeah."

"What you doing here?"

"Looking for something."

"What?"

"Information."

"What information?"

"You really want to know?"

"*What information? Fuck! What information?*" The muzzle jabbed against my temple.

I sighed.

Tensed.

"I'm after the location of a secret UN research team sent to find a..."

And I struck. Always mid-sentence. Always unexpected.

Turned. Arms swiping across the pistol muzzle. Knocking it to one side.

He got off a shot – angry and loud and shocking in the silence – and the muzzleflash vanished in the wrong direction, and I was standing and snarling, and then wrestling with the gun between us, and *oh fuck oh fuck oh fuck...*

He was laughing.

He was stronger than me.

The gun came up slowly like the sunrise outside, like a perfect black 'O' opening to swallow me, and I pushed and fought and put everything into it, and –

Don't you fucking give up soldier!

Sir, no sir! etc, etc.

– and it still wasn't enough.

Hooked a leg behind his knee. Tipped us up. Rolling on the floor. Grunting, dribbling, spitting, sweating. The cords in his neck stood out like ropes, and still he wasn't going to stop laughing, the bastard, still he was giggling like his sides had bust.

He took a hand off the pistol, and for a second I thought I'd won. Redoubled my efforts. Forced everything I had into snapping his wrist.

But it made no difference, and he was still laughing, and he was still stronger than me.

With all the time in the world, he picked up my own rifle in his spare hand – fat fist wrapped round the muzzle – and hit me so hard on the head that my teeth rattled, my lips went cold, my eyes burned with a sudden whiteness and faded back to an awful half-gloom, and the sound that reached my ears shivered around inside my empty skull like an endless echo.

Still laughing. Standing over me, gun in hand.

Still laughing in between telling me he's going to shoot off my kneecaps and let the Abbot have his fun. Spitting on my forehead. Warm rain.

Still laughing when he aimed the pistol and took a breath.

Still laughing when the blurred shape that had been creeping up behind him for the past thirty seconds – tall and dark, dappled with stripes and patches in blue and red – swatted his wrist to one side, ignored the spastic misfire of the pistol, and jabbed a hunting knife so hard into his skull that it slid inside with a *crack* and stayed there.

And *then* he stopped laughing, the shit.

Which is about when I lost consciousness, and went skidding off into my own head.

From somewhere, the sounds of engines. *Big* engines. A *lot* of engines.

People were shouting ("They're going! They're getting out! Stop them!"), guns were chattering like woodpeckers in a distant forest, and two voices were arguing.

"Fuck were you *doing*?"

"You mind your *business*, man! The hell are *you*, anyways?"

"What's in the pack? Hey! Hey, I'm *talking* to you!"

"You back *off*, Tonto!"

"What did you call m..."

And so on.

Oh, and an ugly throb of motorised *something*, slinking off into silence.

...thrpthrpthrpthrp...

I didn't even bother opening my eyes. It was all too much trouble.

"I had a kid," she said. "That's all."

She was beautiful, I suppose, in a stretched-out way. Gangly almost, but not clumsy. Not my type, but I could appreciate her. With little beads of sweat catching the fire on her compact little breasts, and her legs sort of wrapped over-then-under mine, any man could.

The sex had been... okay. Nice.

A little awkward, maybe. Heart-not-quite-in-it, but...yeah. Nice.

"They took her last year. Just turned five. I hid out for months, moving about. Eventually some small-town fuckwit sold me out for a bottle of meths and a new shirt. I kicked his bloody teeth in, when I could walk again."

I pressed my nose against her hair. It smelt of dirt and damp and woman.

Oh-ho, the guilt...

"You're lucky they didn't kill you," I said. "The Clergy. Not big fans of tithe-dodgers."

"Nah." Her shoulders shrugged against my chest. "Why bother? Another woman left alive, another baby-machine to spit out more brain-dead bible-thumpers."

Then quiet. She was a deep breather and didn't fidget quite as much as –

As some people do.

"Who was the father?" I said, trying to sound interested. In truth the guilt was eating me up, chewing on my stupid prick-controlled-brain and cursing the nettle brandy (or whatever the hell it was) I'd been drinking all night.

Not that I wasn't interested in what she had to say, exactly. Just that I'd heard it – or something like it – a hundred times before. Just that I had my own worries.

Shit, five years since the Cull it was still a selfish motherfucking world.

"No one," she said, and her voice said otherwise. "Just some... guy."

"Before the Cull, right?"

"Yeah. Year or so. Prick." She sighed and nuzzled her way backwards until her bum was squidged up against my groin, and pulled the blanket we'd found tighter round herself. "Seemed like he knew everything, at the start. Smart guy, capable. Knew everyone.

"You get to feel like you're safe *with someone like that. You know? I mean, Jesus... I was only... what? Twenty-one? Living on the street. Spoilt rotten as a kid, I was. Ponies, swimming pools, four-by-fours, you name it. Thus the flying lessons. Got bored of that too. Same as anything."*

I was already tuning out. I know, I know. I'm scum. "I only got halfway through uni," she said, building up momentum for an entire bloody life-story. "Had a bit of a... hiccup. Took a look at myself. All the money, the materials. Probably got a bit too far into the whole student thing, if I'm honest. Just kind of... backflipped. Dropped off the radar. Wound up on the streets, getting by. That's where I met Claystone."

"That's the father?"

"Yeah. And then the baby came. Aaand... and give him his credit, you know... he hung around. Brought in some money, once in a while. Knew who to ask, get favours. Fingers in all sorts of pies. We got ourselves a little place, no questions asked – proper little family. Even tried to clean ourselves up. Stop using, y'know?"

I tangled a finger through the ringlets of hair next to her ear, then realised what I was doing and stopped. All these little betrayals, all these guilty little things.

If she noticed, she didn't show it.

"Then the Cull."

"He died?" I said.

She laughed, bitter.

"No. No, he didn't die. Stuck about for a while. Just long enough to see little Shayla hit one. Went out every day for food and togs, came back... now and then.

"Then one day he just didn't come back at all. Left a note. 'Couldn't handle the responsibility.' Prick."

More quiet.

"Sodding cliché, ain't it?" she said. I jerked back awake, realising I'd been slipping off.

"What?"

"Single mother, whingeing on."

"Yeah. Maybe. Though it's kind of different when you can't just nip to the local supermarket for nappies."

"Exactly. Anyway." She shrugged again. "We survived. Me and Shayla."

"And Claystone?"

"Pfft. Saw him about, once or twice. Heard about him all the time. Everyone *knew Claystone. He worked for everyone, sooner or later. Had a way of... of finding the best groove. Like... things got tough, he knew a comfier slot. Gold fucking medallist at living an easy life."*

Her voice dripped bitterness.

"But he never came looking for me. Vanished, eventually. Wound up in the river for all I know. All I care.

"Prick. Prick! *Well shot of him."*

Somewhere outside the pub's shattered windows, a fox loped by with its weird baby-scream call. Bella shivered.

"You know what it's like, when your whole world is focused on one thing?"

I scowled, uncomfortable with the thought. "Yeah," I decided. "Yeah, suppose I do."

"And then six men in robes come one day and take it away from you, and kick the crap out of you into the bargain, and put things in your mouth, and tell you to behave and do what you're told, then scuttle off into the night. And then you hear that thing – that... that centre of your universe *– get loaded aboard a plane and fucked-off to Yankland.*

"What then, mate? What do you do then?"

I didn't answer.

We lay like that for a long time, and I could tell from her breathing she wasn't asleep.

Eventually she mumbled:

"Doesn't matter. Not your problem. But that's why I'm going."

I was already asleep, and heard it only on the fringes of a dream.

I WOKE UP, and almost shat.

There was a face about a foot from my eyes; curved nose sharp like the edge of a scimitar, mouth tugged down at each corner, lost across a jutting chin to a network of weather-lines. Its hair – long, perfectly dark – was trussed-up in loops of red and yellow PVC-tape, so it stood upright like a tower then spilled down on either side to box me in.

From the hairline to the bottom of the eye sockets, the man was black. Not just Afro-Caribbean black, but *black* like ink, pressed-up tight against dark eyes that shimmered inside their puddle of shadow. But below the eyes – face bisected in a straight horizontal line across the bridge of the nose and down each angular cheekbone – the man's skin was tanned a ruddy red. He looked savage. He looked terrifying.

He looked like an ancient God of war (or rather, how I assumed an ancient God of war might look, never having met one), and in the fuzzy moments of half waking, with my whole head throbbing from the sharp pain in my scalp, I remembered the wax figures in their diorama displays in the museum, and wondered if one of them had come back to teach me a lesson for using him as a decoy.

The only detail that somewhat spoilt the prehistoric spectacle was the head-to-foot biking leathers in blue, black, red and white.

"He's awake," the effigy proclaimed, rising up and away from me. At a distance, he stopped being the most terrifying thing I've ever seen, and became a young man wearing face paint. I relaxed my sphincter.

"What? You *what*?" A familiar voice. I felt myself smiling, happy at the note of familiarity in the midst of all this oddity. Nate appeared on the edge of my vision like a man possessed, pushing the boy aside and stooping down to poke and prod at me. He was no longer sweating or shivering; a total transformation that left him grinning massively and mumbling to himself.

"Ow," I said, as he pressed his crinkled fingers against my temple. He did it again.

"Miracle," he said, grinning, cigarette hanging off his bottom lip. "That's what it is. Damned miracle. Asshole all but opened you *up*."

He tittered to himself.

I picked myself up slowly, fighting the urge to vomit every inch of the way. My head felt like a meteor had hit it – or possibly a speeding elephant – and judging by the dry tightness of my cheek it was appropriately blood-splattered. Added to the bandaged remains of what had once been an ear, the slashes and scars across cheeks and forehead, the aching wounds – messily fixed up – in my left arm, right shoulder and nape of my neck, I imagined I was starting to look just as patchworked as my coat. One of these days, I decided, I was going to have to find a functioning shower.

I tottered to my feet, lost the battle with my gyrating inner-ear, and barfed like a trooper. I was hungry enough to consider asking someone for a spoon.

Nate watched me cautiously, like he expected me to fall down any second. His pupils looked even bigger than usual, pushing against the bright whites of his eyes, and he was clinging to a red plastic box – like a power drill case – like it was a lifeline. Where he'd got it and what the hell it *was* were queries I never got around to asking. My surroundings swam into focus, and my senses came online.

The prevailing sound was: engines.

I was back at the Wheels Mart. The same raggedy little tent, by the looks of it, that Malice met me in before. Through the tattered openings I could hear the braying crowds and see the spastic danglings of the MC, shouting out his endless stream of nonsensical bid-acceptances. The smell of cooking meat underwritten by the heady chug of noxious fumes, the whooping and arguing of punters. It made my head hurt, if possible, even more than it already did.

"Brought you here in a *car*!" Nate whooped, doing a little dance. He was clearly on something. "Borrowed it, yes we did. Fucking Clergy, heh!"

"What... what happened?" I murmured, wincing at my own voice. "What happened to the priests?"

"Fucked off!" Nate sat down suddenly, cross-legged, and nodded like a flapping wing. "Trucks, hidden away. Took off all at once. You scared 'em off! City's free!"

Then he slumped against the wall of the tent with no warning and just... *switched off*, smirking. He dribbled a little.

High as a kite.

Hmm.

The young man in the leathers stood nearby, leaning against a tall wooden pole, arms folded, watching it all without movement. I found myself looking for the bow and quiver of arrows over his shoulder – hating myself – and dipped my eyes back up to his own to cover the up-and-down staring.

He didn't move a muscle.

"You saved me, huh?" I said, remembering the red and blue blur behind Cy, the knife cracking through his skull.

He shrugged. "You needed saving."

Nate *tsked* quietly behind me, then giggled again.

I held out a shaky hand to the boy, which he took with a suspicious sort of glance and shook firmly.

"Hiawatha," he said.

I nodded. "Pleasure. Want to tell me what you were doing on the thirty-fourth floor of a hotly-contested building swarming with insane priests, Hiawatha?"

He smiled. Sort of. I don't think there was much humour there.

"Saving you," he said.

Uh-huh.

Which is around about when Malice came in. Different.

She looked bigger, for a start. It took me a while to figure she wore body armour beneath the black threads. Pointy football-pads over each shoulder, skateboarding shields on elbows and knees, and a bloody enormous anti-stab vest that made her look like a samurai. Guns and knives poking from belts and straps on every conceivable surface – and that *included* the baby's wicker support-cage, still humping from her back like a dorsal fin.

She looked like an ice hockey player who was too hardcore to bother with a helmet.

Oh, and someone had beaten the shit out of her.

"Still alive, then," she said, not even bothering to make eye contact. She sounded disappointed, dumping an angular bag on the floor with a metallic crash.

"Uh. Yeah. Yeah, I guess." I tried to stop staring at her bruised face. "What happened?"

She rummaged industriously in a couple of crates nearby, then paused to glower at me. "Clergy happened, retard. You're a popular guy."

I suppose I should've guessed. Back before The Tag and the siege and all that, when Cy dragged the big Mickey-chief back to the UN with tales of the Limey psycho driving about on a clapped-out quad. Wouldn't have taken the Choirboys long to work their way back to the Wheels Mart.

I wondered whether she'd told them anything worth a damn.

"Sorry," I said.

"Skip it. We're ready to roll when you are."

"Excuse me?"

"We're loaded up and ready. Awaiting your pleasure, your majesty. And payment, of course."

"Sorry, I'm... I'm not with you..."

"I *said*," Nate grumbled. "Didn't I *say*? Let him wake up, I said! Just goddamn wait! Let him decide himself!"

Malice ignored him, hooking a thumb towards Hiawatha. "Last of the Mohicans here said you'd want a ride. Long distance. Heavy protection. No expense spared."

Hiawatha stared at me.

"But..."

"North-west," Malice said. "That's what he told me. You saying he's been wasting my fucking time?"

She didn't look in the mood for games.

I groped in my pocket and felt the crumpled sheet of paper I'd taken from the Secretariat with its Reassignment Location and the smooth photograph. Undisturbed, right where I'd left them.

I stared at Hiawatha.

"How did you know that?" I said, off-balance. "What's... how... how did you know?"

"Lucky guess," he said, then turned back to Malice, pointing a finger at the bag she'd brought with her. "That's mine."

"And?"

"They confiscated it at the door."

"And now I'm bringing it back, Tonto. Keep your fucking scalp on..."

"No, I mean... I mean you might as well keep it. It's for you anyway."

He strolled over and kicked open the drawstrings, letting dozens upon dozens of glossy guns – rifles, pistols, autos, semis, weird spiky things I didn't recognise and antique bloody revolvers – spill into the dirt.

"Figure that'll cover the rental costs," he said, into the silence.

Malice gaped.

The *Inferno* was waiting for us outside.

CHAPTER FIFTEEN

THE KID CAME too.

Right before we left, I had a half-hearted sort of attempt at talking Malice out of it. Over the roar of the fire-truck's engines (extensively tinkered with, a sweaty little man called 'Spuggsy' told me, to "purr like a lion on stee-roids an' go like a cheetah got a rocket up its ass"), I appealed to her sense of responsibility, reminded her we were taking the *Inferno* instead of some suped-up speeder because we might easily blunder into trouble, and finally had a stab at convincing her the little brat would keep us awake at nights.

It was pretty lame.

Malice just glared, scratched absent-mindedly at the split lip the Clergy's goons had left her with – as if to remind me whose fault it was, and who therefore had no fucking right to be suggesting *anything* – then went back to loading ammo-belts into the truck's hold. I'd half expected her to be vaguely grateful – it was arguably thanks to me that the Clergy had been kicked out of the city – but evidently she either refused to believe the news coming out of Manhattan or was a grudge-bearer of championship standards. She pretty much ignored me after that.

The kid, for the record, never even made a sound.

Ten minutes out of the Wheels Mart, as the solid wall of noise thrown up by the engine started to normalise inside my head, the diminutive gunner who called herself 'Tora' – fast-talking, flirtatious as hell, mad as a box of badgers – leaned close to my ear and whispered:

"She left her kid behind once before. That's all. Rental mission just like this. Some moron trying to get to Miami, I forget why. Figured we'd run into some crazies *en route* – 'specially with the dee-see *hole*, shit – so she laid out the responsible mother bullshit, left him behind. No *way* the Clergy gonna try collecting tithes inside the Mart."

"And?"

"And that's why she's only got *one* kid, 'steada two. And ain't a fan of the Choir."

Ah.

Still. Tensions aside, cramped and sweaty lack of comfort aside, snarling engine-volume aside, this was travelling in *style*. The *Inferno* slipped through New York like an icebreaker; stately and magnificent, oozing a *don't-mess-with-us* air and *explode-your-ass-muthafucka* intent. Weaponry on prominent display, promising instant overkill.

I kept catching myself wishing I could get out and have a look; standing in the street like all the wide-mouthed scavs and Klansmen, who bristled and hid as it slunk past like a nuclear armadillo. We wended our way in silence, across the meandering Triborough bridge – its girdered pillars flaking paint, flocked with hundreds of gulls that picked and squabbled over a dead sheep, hung upside down for no appreciable reason – and skirting the edge of the Bronx on Highway 87, peering solemnly into a deserted wilderness that seemed to have been frozen in time. Cars packed together in cryogenic traffic-jams, skeletal shadows sealed within.

Now and then we passed territory poles – or the remains of them – and gaudy wall murals where the local gang wars were meticulously chronicled: long lists of names, each one crossed through where some other mob had taken over. At some point the internecine squabbles had ended, and some thoughtful soul had added a broad scarlet circle to the foot of each list; unquestionably proclaiming the *true* rulers, regardless of which banana-republic Klans they allowed to govern in their stead. Every time we passed such ownership tags a fresh round of spitting, swearing and tutting would circulate round the truck's interior.

That was about as close as we got to conversation, in those first hours.

There were eight of us altogether, not counting the baby. Malice drove, mostly; the wicker basket transferred to a special harness on the cab wall beside her. Even in the city, where she was obliged to take it easy to avoid vehicle wrecks and pits in the macadam, I could tell she wasn't about to make it comfortable on her passengers. She throttled where any sane person would have braked, skewed the machine at hairpin corners round ancient riot-control vans with their panels stripped off and their remains burnt to slag, and every time I stared in horror at her recklessness there was a savage smile on her face.

Great.

She never hit anything and the rest of her crew were entirely at ease. Eventually I stopped staring ahead and decided to take in the scenery, just as the Yankee Stadium went sailing by on my right. Gone, mostly – just a few shards of tangled black spaghetti at the heart of a splintered parking-lot continent – but the determined observer could just about make out the sagging remnants of an aircraft's tail hanging over the edge of the burnt-out shell. I wondered what had happened, then decided I'd rather not know.

Someone had painted 'Thicker than water' in black tar across a fifty-foot expanse of the parking lot. I wondered if it would be visible from space.

Next to Malice, in the cab, was where Spuggsy sat. Well, reclined anyway. Lazed.

Slobbed.

Spuggsy, from what little I'd seen, wasn't much of an engineer. Granted, he had a gift for smoothing out the most angular of mechanical kinks, although I couldn't help noticing his technique tended to involve hitting things hard with a spanner until they started making the right noises. He was short and plump, and as bald as a cueball, and sat there flicking lazily through porno mags with an expression of unconquerable boredom. His one concession to arousal was the copious sweat oozing off his chubby face, but given that it remained even when he *wasn't* browsing *Anal Carnage*, *Wet Domination* or whatever the hell it was, that didn't mean much. When he spoke it was with an enthusiastically sleazy good nature – like a mischievous schoolboy who discovered German hardcore before he discovered snot-eating contests – and I found myself liking him and wanting to disinfect him in equal measure.

The Cross Bronx Expressway petered out in a fug of chipped road segments – mottled like they'd been in a firefight – and then the Hudson was below us, wide and shimmering and almost passable for clean. The George Washington Bridge stood just as solid and untroubled as always, as if this 'end of humanity' business was a passing fad by which it was neither impressed nor concerned. A couple of scavs had hanged themselves from the rails on one side (I like to think it was a tragic death-pact between lovers despairing of this cold new world... but it could just as easily have been a drunken dare) and a crowd of others was tugging them down as we passed by. Tugging a little *too* violently, actually, with knives and roasting-sticks in hand and a fat man building a campfire, waving away the gulls like the unwanted competition they were.

Tora kept them covered from the pintle-cannons all the way past.

"Fucking *cannies*," she spat.

Tora was sort of weird. She came from Japanese stock, she said – a heart-shaped face and dark hair (dyed deep blue at its tips), with a delicate sweep to the edges of her eyes and a nose like a button – and was one of the most mixed-up women I've ever known. Not beautiful exactly, but she knew how to move, had an attitude you wouldn't believe and could easily have flirted for her country. But it was *skewed* – the whole thing – like you knew somehow she was damaged; fucked up deep inside, and everything she did was just a façade to create the impression of humanity. She used sexual friendliness like a battering ram. Like an act of aggression. Her arms were covered – wrist to shoulder – in thin little scars where she'd cut herself, and she sat in the dangling canopy above our heads – half poking out to man the guns – singing a pretty song and carving new tally-marks into her skin. I asked her about it, later on. She shrugged and said:

"Why do you scratch when you've got an itch?"

"To make it feel better."

"Uh-huh."

I never found out what had happened to her – shit, maybe she was just born that way – but you could see it every time she looked at you, or spoke to you, or smiled. Like... just behind the veil, behind the spunky playful bollocks and cleavage-jutting body language, she was eyeing that scalpel and wondering just how deep she'd have to cut to make *all* the itches go away.

We bounced into New Jersey in a blur; Malice finally able to throttle up all the way. Fort Lee, Leonia; names on crooked signs that drifted by without any sensation of reality. Just echoes of something that might once have had some significance, but now... nothing. Skeletons on the edge of the road – picked clean – and blasted wrecks that jutted and trailed, forcing us to slow. Highway 80, place names fogging-by.

Hackensack.

Saddlebrook.

Elmwood Park.

At one point, Malice muttered something darkly to Spuggsy – spotting something ahead – who huffed and dropped his magazines and scrambled back towards us, poking Nike and Moto awake from their nest of sleeping bags and telling Tora to stand by. The *Inferno* jinked hard to one side; overtaking.

It was strange to see another vehicle on the open road; but even stranger to see one so... *normal.* I'd expected dune-buggy gangs, flame-jobs, hotrods and... oh, I don't know. Nuclear-fucking-powered bulldozers, maybe. Skull-hurling catapults. Something a little more... *survivalist.*

Passing an HGV hauling a trailer marked *Cheesy Snax* was pretty surreal. A couple of heads poked warily from the roof – guns arrayed cautiously towards us, just in case – and I spotted square slits in the corrugated sides of the container, bulging with naked flesh and squinting eyes.

"Workers," Tora told me, swinging in her harness. "'Burb Klans. Scavs work the fields, different shifts going back and forth all the time."

"Dangerous?"

"To us? *Pfft.*"

But still, but still... It was tense, as we passed them by, and Moto stared back at them – through the square porthole above the rear gun mount – for long minutes afterwards.

Moto and Nike kept themselves to themselves, mostly. The former was a well-built young man with startling white hair and an almost perfect face. I figured before the Cull he was maybe a model in cologne commercials, or a male escort, and he looked simply *wrong* – out of place, somehow – in the midst of all us raggedy bastards in the back of the *Inferno*. Actually, scratch that: he looked *almost* out of place. His one concession to chaos and ugliness was worn proud on his cheek. A mess, shredded and rippled in all kinds of gravely keloid contours, so that his lip and eye were all but joined by the matted tangle of scarring. He'd been whipped with barbed-wire, Spuggsy told me later with an indecent grin. Held down by a bunch of thugs and whipped carefully – lovingly, almost – by Nike. He didn't say why.

Towns went by. The quicksmog came down, hid the distant rooftops and tree-lined avenues, then went back up again.

Denville.

Roxybury.

Netlong.

Hills and gorge-blasted roads, the weak sun, the *Inferno* rumbling ever on.

That scar on Moto's cheek, I figured it was like a brand. Like some jealous tribal elder, maybe, defacing his young spouse to dissuade all thoughts of adultery. Maybe it was punishment. Some quiet misdeed, some jealous retribution. Fucksakes, who knows? The types of people out there these days, for all I knew Nike might have done it to *improve* the poor kid's face according to his own twisted tastes.

Either way, it was a mark – a signature – left by Nike, that said loud and clear:

Mine.

Moto said pretty much nothing to anyone except Nike for the whole journey, and when he *did* it was quiet and deferential, and he turned his face to one side so that all anyone ever saw of him was the scar. He seemed quite happy. *They* seemed quite happy.

Love, huh?

Nike, by comparison, was tall and skinny, quite old, I'd guess, and a perfect gentleman in every way. He nodded and smiled, and passed the time of day, and traded dirty songs with Nate. Towards the end of the first day, when Malice swapped with Spuggsy for a kip, Nike chatted to me about what sort of state London was in. He told me how he used to be a teacher – American history – and collected model aircraft for a hobby.

Everything about him oozed calm, rational, intelligent, polite decency.

And then you happened to glance at Moto, staring like a devoted dog at the older man, face all fucked up like that, and you *wondered*.

We stopped for a bite to eat on the freeway, just outside a place called Knowlton. Nate cooked, giggling and dancing annoyingly. The *Inferno* carried a heap of supplies as part of the cost of rental, and amongst the tins and rats there were three actual chickens and a genuine, freshly baked loaf of bread. If it's possible for your tongue to have an orgasm, mine did.

Mostly we sat by the fire – silent – although Tora stayed on the roof of the *Inferno*, keeping one eye on the road, and the man who called himself Hiawatha took it upon himself to perch, cross-legged, some distance away. He looked like he should have been meditating – communing with some indefinable infinite – but instead was smoking an enormous spliff and starring at the sky, nodding or shaking his head at random intervals. I still wasn't too sure what to make of him.

Earlier on, when all my questions were exhausted and his enigmatic bullshit responses were getting right on my wick, I'd got bored and asked him where he got the weed from.

He smiled mysteriously and said it wasn't just weed.

Moron.

"Surely," I said, with just a tiny guilty hint of pomposity, "there are more important things to be growing?"

"Yes," he said. "We grow them too."

I left him to it, after that.

It was around then that Malice decided she'd had enough sulking and sat down next to me, only slightly frosty. She offered me a flask of water.

"Ta."

"Your friend," she said, too quiet for anyone else to hear. She nodded towards Nate. He was picking gristle out of his teeth, fiddling with the red case he'd had with him ever since the Wheels Mart.

"What about him?"

"He okay?"

I scowled, glancing at him again for any obvious signs of damage. It occurred to me that in all the excitement and strangeness of beginning this weird journey, I'd barely spoken to him. Certainly I hadn't asked him if he was sure he wanted to come along. He just... *had*.

"He looks okay," I said.

"I *mean*... is he trustworthy?"

I stopped chewing and stared at her. Skin prickling.

I don't know why I didn't blurt out, "*of course he is,*" straight away. I don't know why I didn't tell her he'd saved my life a bunch of times since I'd met him, had expected nothing in return but a few condoms and a pot of dog food, and was even more in danger from the fucking Clergy than *I* was. I don't know.

"Why do you ask?" I said, intrigued despite myself. Was she getting it too? That feeling. That *sense* of...

Not quite right...

"'Cause the motherfucker's been outta his tree all day on whatever shit he's got in that pack, and he ain't slowing down."

I scratched my chin, brain flopping over. "There a problem with that?"

(Actually, there *was* a problem with that. Two problems. The first was, I hadn't noticed. Hadn't being paying attention. Too busy watching the road, watching the others in the group. Letting myself down. The second was, where the hell did the sneaky old bastard *get* it from?)

"No," she said, wobbling the harness on her shoulders. "No, I guess not. Only he keeps staring at my baby. All the time. *All* the time."

I told her not to worry.

Highway 80.

We hit Pennsylvania pretty soon afterwards. It looked a lot like NJ.

Towns. No longer paying attention. Letting the names roll together, like some great American gestalt; an obese vehicle with a thousand names that used cheeseburgers for fuel and liposucked fat for tyres.

I get surreal when I'm bored, and *boy* was I *bored*!

Stroud.

Kidder.

Black Cross.

Out across the fields, unlikely contraptions wobbled and smoked and steamed; hybrids of a hundred combine harvesters tended by hordes of miserable locals. At one point a bunch of guys on motorbikes overtook us, not even slowing to stare or glare. They wore strange silver puffer-jackets and jauntily-positioned bowler hats, gunning Harleys with hair flapping behind them. Each vehicle had skulls bouncing in its wake, like cans tied to the back of a bridal limo, and a smattering of guns hoisted on its pillion.

Tora tracked them the whole way over the horizon.

Hiawatha, who hadn't moved from his corner since we came aboard, except to roll and smoke occasional joints, turned his head to watch them go by. I wondered what he was seeing. I wondered how he'd even known they'd been there in the first place, when he wasn't sitting anywhere near a window.

Actually, there was a *lot* I wondered about that boy.

He said he came from a place that was once called Fort Wayne. He said, actually, it was just outside the city; the rolling plains of Ohio where the Haudenosaunee convened once a year, with all its scattered lodges coming together to plan and barter and talk.

He used long words that I'd never heard before and didn't understand. All the time.

He spoke with a natural sort of rhythm that was as off-putting as it was hypnotic. Like a mother reading a nursery rhyme or a poet picking his way through pentameter.

Like an evangelist, too. Like a mantra.

The weirdest thing was, every now and again there was a *crack* in what he said. Just a little fissure, a hint of something beneath. You notice that shit when you're me.

The voice changed, the eyes blinked. For a second or two he was just some kid; confused and wrapped up in something too big to understand, who didn't believe his own mumbo-jumbo any more than I did and had all the attitude of a scared young thing caught in the company of double-hard bastards. Too much testosterone for his own good, too much insecurity for his own safety.

I preferred him, in those tiny moments.

He said someone called the 'Tadodaho' had decided that my course and his were... well, he used the word "aligned." It seemed too weird, to me. I'd never heard of this guy and he already knew where I was headed, what area I'd be passing through, who I'd be up against.

Hiawatha said:

"It's all been seen. It's all been dreamed."

Enigmatic Bullshit.

Listen: I believe in moving fast, taking opportunities, focusing on what's ahead and getting the job done. I believe that anyone who gets in my way is dead. I believe in my own ability to deal resourcefully with any situation, and kill the fuck out of any stupid wanker who tries to stop me.

I believe in:

Don't you fucking give up, soldier!

I believe in:

Know everything.

Cover the angles.

What I *don't* believe in is Thunderbirds and dream-quests and voices on the wind and patterns in the sky, which is the sort of stuff Hiawatha talk/recited about right after he'd smoked one of his spliffs. Outside a town called Mifflin, as the afternoon wore on, Malice lost her temper and shouted at him to quit murdering her baby with his second-hand cancer gas. He smiled, shrugged, and blinked once or twice at the baby, like he was about to deliver some quasi-wise rebuttal.

Instead he just looked somehow... sad.

"Yeah," said the real-life-insecure-boy lost behind all that mystical arsebilge. "Yeah."

He climbed up to smoke on the roof, after that, and every time he went Nate watched him go, muttering and rolling his eyes, groaning in pleasure.

I caught him shooting-up, once or twice – sat in the dark corner at the back of what had once been the *Inferno's* pump-housing. *Hey,* I told myself, *as long as he's happy.*

But still. But still.

Lamar.

Boggs.

Lawrence.

Pine Creek.

Place names harder and harder to read with every mile. Eventually the sun slid like an old turd behind the hazy west and even the road signs – decorated variously in graffiti, dangling bodies and hungry looking crows – vanished into the ocean of dark beyond the *Inferno*'s lights. At some unspecified moment, ducking and weaving between the mangled remains of some long-gone pileup, Spuggsy declared out loud the road was "covered in more shit than a nuthouse wall," and declined to go any further until it was light.

We pulled up and ate again, in silence.

Up in the hills, and across the landscape to either side, tiny embers of light shivered away, like fireflies. Families, maybe. Cannibals, psychotic mountain-men, diseased brain-dead mutants or whatever. But most probably just families – normal people, or as good as – trying to stay warm and stay together.

Poor fuckers.

I chewed rat and didn't think about it.

Somewhere nearby, Nate was singing a song to himself and laughing after every verse. Totally wasted, totally out of his tree. It would have been funny – would have been endearing – if he didn't glance up every now and again, all casual, and stare at Malice's kid. I was noticing it now. The little hint of... what? Intensity, that visited his face in those moments.

I shivered again.

The crew slept in shifts. Two on watch at all times. Malice volunteered to take the last shift alone and I offered to accompany her. She shrugged, like:

Do what you want, asshole. It's your lack of sleep.

I dreamed of seagulls wearing robes, man-sized spliffs running up and down along the George Washington Bridge on little stubby feet, and of a great wound in the heart of New York, bleeding a fine mist of quicksmog up into the air, where it separated into colossal blood cells that floated and wobbled like lava-lamp clouds.

I dreamed of Bella saying:

"*Doesn't matter. Not your problem. But that's why I'm going.*"

Then she flopped over in my arms, gave me a look of bored disinterest, and poked me in the rigs.

"*Hey,*" she said. "*Hey, Patchwork...*"

Malice, waking me up for the watch. I tried to conceal my hard-on.

"So."

"So."

"What's this all about?"

I scratched my manky ear through its equally-as-manky dressing. "Which 'this,' specifically?"

She nodded out into the dark.

"Going west. Highway 80. Lake Erie. What's there, patchwork man?"

I smiled.

"Probably nothing."

She thought about that for a moment. "That's a long way to go. Lot of trouble, for probably nothing."

We sat in silence for a minute or two, listening to the deafening silence of the world. It wasn't a cold night, exactly, but there was something... *shivery*, yeah, about such profound darkness. Like living in oil.

Yeah, we had a rifle each. And *yeah*, we could scramble inside and be manning Tora's collection of hardcore artillery within a second or two. But still, we were *tiny*. We were nothing. There were stars and sky and road and hills, and nothing else, and we were just parasites. Fucking *fleas* on the back of an elephant.

I told you already, I get abstract when I'm bored.

"Okay," I said to Malice, suddenly feeling talkative, catching her eye. "Long way to go. You're right. You mind if I ask you something?"

She shrugged.

"It might piss you off."

"Would that stop you?"

"Probably not."

"Then shoot."

I fiddled with the rifle, keeping my eyes fixed – uselessly – on the night. Somewhere far, far away I thought I could hear engines, a muted throb that died away almost instantly, and left me doubting my own senses.

"Let's say there's something you want," I said. "Let's say you... you had it once. Lost it. Want it back."

Her eyes narrowed, just a fraction. I wondered if she knew Tora told me about her other kid, and if she'd blow my head off for raking up the past. She didn't look the type to enjoy in-depth discussion about personal tragedies long bygone.

I know the feeling.

"Let's say," she said, coldly.

"Right. Now let's say you find out there's a chance. This thing, getting it back, it's... it's the world. It'll make everything better. It's *important* – and, shit... not just to *you*. To *everyone*."

She didn't move. I blundered on, forcing myself not to jump when a bird launched from some perch out in the dark, cawing noisily.

"Far as you know, it's gone. For good. And okay, that's a shitter, and you'd pay money for it to be otherwise, but what's done is done. You're a realist. You bottle it up, you put it away, you *get on*. You get by."

I could see it in her eyes, and in that quiet little instant we were so *the same* I could have reached out and touched her and felt my own fingers against my own arm.

The silence got a little thicker.

I stared at her. "And now suddenly there's a chance. One in a million. Defies all logic, as far as you know. No reason to *believe* it, no reason to give it headroom. But still...

"*Just in case.*"

She swallowed, lips tight.

"How far," I finished, "would you go?"

Her jaw rocked back and forth once or twice.

"Long way," she whispered.

I nodded.

We sat.

We waited.

I smiled.

"You should go inside," I said.

She glared. "Pardon me?"

"You should go inside." I drew the knife from my belt and passed her the rifle.

"And why the fuck would I do that?"

"Because there are two men approaching the truck from two different directions, and we're sitting ducks up here."

Even in the gloom, I could see her eyes go big. Disbelief, maybe. Surprise.

"They pulled up a mile out on motorbikes. Probably from that crew that passed by earlier on. Listen."

"But I don't he –"

"There. A twig. And another bird. Fucking *amateurs*."

She just stared.

"Don't worry," I said, and I smiled again because I couldn't help it, and I couldn't be bothered to stop. "I won't be long."

And I slipped off the edge of the truck and onto the concrete, panther quiet, and went out into the shadows with a savage joy.

Don't you fucking give up, soldier!

It snarled. It *burned.*

Sir, no sir! etc, etc.

WHEN I GOT back Hiawatha was sitting on the roof, waiting, fiddling with something small and silver.

"You get 'em?" he asked.

I wiped blood off the knife and stared.

Letting the humanity come back into me. Slowly.

Reluctantly.

First rule of stealth combat. Advanced training, third year:

Don't fear the predator in the dark.

Be *it.*

"I can see you," Hiawatha said, conversationally. "Properly, I mean. All that... *conditioning.* All those changes. You're a wolf, mister Englishman. You know that? Inside your head. They made you a wolf."

The adrenaline was still up. Heart still going. Beast still *just* below the surface.

I spat on the ground. Couldn't be fucked with any more mystical bollocks.

Hiawatha smiled and said nothing.

"Who were they?" I said, not bothering to sound impressed or spooked out or anything but bored. My hands were shaking with the desire to hunt and hurt, and this snotty little idiot was getting on my tits.

"Collectors," he said, after a pause.

"And they are?"

"They're... I mean..." He stopped and scowled, and I could see again the person coming through, the scared kid chipping away at the know-it-all straitjacket. Then it was gone.

"They're scouts," he said, voice rising and falling in that same lilting chant. "Men of money and misery. Mercenary filth. Cells of aggression, unfaithful, unloyal, sent ahead of the crucified god and his robed horde to..."

"Cut the crap, yeah? Just tell me who they are."

He blinked.

And slowly, boyishly, smiled.

"Fuckheads," he said.

"Fuckheads. Right. And what do these fuckheads want with us?"

He shrugged.

"Clergy sends them, mostly. Or at least, that's where they get their shit. Trading with the Clergy. They... roam around. Outside of cities. Finding things the Church'll pay for."

"Things like what?"

"Like guns. Food. And... mostly... mostly kids." He looked away. Jaw tightening.

"Kids."

"Yep. No Klans out here, see? No loyal fucking scavs to hand over their own kin. Only the Clergy and the scum they pay, helping themselves. That's... that's what this is all *about*. You being here."

"I don't follow."

"I know. But you will."

I huffed and shook my head, too tired to push it. "Whatever. Doesn't explain what they want with *us*."

"No... but they came from behind, on the road. From the city, probably."

"And?"

And then the boy was gone, and fucking Hiawatha was back, smiling and staring and rolling his eyes.

"And perhaps this holy man, this John-Paul, this withered thing... perhaps he knows where you're headed. Perhaps he sent word to slow you down."

"How the fuck would *he* know?"

I remembered the personnel file. The name. The photo.

Cy, staring over my shoulder.

Hiawatha ignored the question and stared off into the night.

"Tomorrow," he said. "We'll find the rest tomorrow. They sent out these two to take us in the dark. Explosives, yes?"

I grunted, patting the pockets of my coat. There'd been four sticks of C4 on each corpse, with some surprisingly sophisticated remote detonators. Out in the dark, when the fat fucks had stopped shivering and bleeding and trying to shout with their windpipes torn-through, I'd helped myself.

"So if we're lucky, the rest won't know we survived."

Hiawatha smiled and nodded.

We weren't lucky.

CHAPTER SIXTEEN

We hit Ohio first thing, and they were waiting for us.

Outside a town called Hubbard, rammed up against the edge of the I-80 like a gaudy reminder of a long lost time, was Truck World. Truck World did exactly what it said on the tin.

There must have been twenty or so vehicles. Vast things, these fuckers; like whales built for the road, basking outside a long derelict burgers-n-barf joint and a once-snazzy truck wash. And not the poky little beasts we used to get in the UK either, but *monsters*. Bloody great behemoths with bulging engines and recurved exhausts, chrome snouts and brightly painted bodies. And yeah, they'd been graffitied and smashed up – what hadn't? – but they were still *awesome* to see, lined up like that. Like hibernating ogres, waiting for a wake-up call.

I was still staring at them through the window when Malice hit the brakes.

Still staring when Hiawatha – who had his eyes closed – shouted: "Fuck! Fuck, they're *waiti...*"

Still staring when Tora – bless her cotton socks – opened fire with the Mk19 and everything went nuts.

The Collectors weren't stupid. Their two boys didn't come home to them with the dawn. They'd taken precautions – obvious, really – and big dumb Precaution Number One was to block the road.

Truck World, when all was said and done, had represented one big sodding barricade on wheels. They'd strung them out across the interstate, those road-whales, two deep and three across, with no room to edge the *Inferno* past and no hopes of ramming through.

And the Collectors – leather junkies with artfully matted hair and once-expensive sunglasses, silver jackets patched and frayed, bowler hats arrayed like a long line of tits, lounging back on purring choppers like middle-class morons who'd watched *Easy Rider* once or twice too often – they *swarmed.*

The day before, when the little gang went zipping by, there'd been maybe six or seven. Lightly armed. All mouth and no trousers.

Now there were twenty, easy, and as the *Inferno* squealed to a halt and Malice wrestled to reverse, swearing inventively as she went, the windshield blew in like a metaphysical fart, glass frothed through the air, bullets rattled like drumbeats on the firetruck's skin, and everything *shook.*

Bikes. Engines growling in every direction. Smoke-bombs and sound overkill. Voices whooping and shouting, closing in. Someone with a fucking boom-box, playing *Metallica* at double speed.

Thump-thump. The Mk19.

Thump-thump, then – distantly – the hard-edged crack of a detonation, tarmac spewing and smoke gushing. One of the bikes fell apart, lifting up and out on the rim of a fireball, and Tora shrieked like a joyful psycho, chugging-out lead with the autos and re-sighting with the grenades.

Nike and Moto opened fire, which meant the arseholes had surrounded us. Heavy *things* thumped against the walls of our dark little cell, and I found myself torn between the frustration of sightlessness to the rear, and confronting the ugly situation through the windows at the fore. The *Inferno* twisted and flexed on the road, three-point-turning under a withering storm, and every whirligig impression through the flying glass and shifting landscape was a scene of spinning rubber, gun flare and snarling faces with too many piercings. Nate started screaming – fucking junkie probably didn't even realise what was happening – and outside, Tora found another target. Another shuddering clash of sparks and steel, and a scream lost to the rolling thunder.

But it wasn't enough, wasn't enough, wasn't enough...

One of the tyres exploded.

The *Inferno* pitched to one side, wobbled. Malice shouted. A deeper growl came out of the tumult and Spuggsy was yelling like a kid – "No! Oh, no, no! *No!*" – staring through his window, eyes wide.

Then he was just...

Paste.

It was another juggernaut – though I didn't figure it out until the world stopped rushing backwards and the *Inferno* went back to standing still. They'd taken the opportunity as we crept sluggishly away from the blockade, firing up the nearest HGV and ploughing directly into the cockpit; an acute angle that left the ramming truck speared on the *Inferno*'s jagged nosecone – driver chuckling insanely through shattered glass and bloody teeth, his ride mashed all to fuck and venting radiator steam into our cab – but it'd done its job. Spuggsy was crushed, with barely time to scream, and as the impact shunted us away he was a thing of fractured angles and limp bones, head lolling, skull slack, porn mags fluttering uselessly amidst broken glass.

And then footsteps. Heavy thumps on the roof. Collectors scrambling off the cab of their own truck onto the *Inferno*'s back. One hopped down onto the hood, sleek black auto ready to fill the interior with lead, but Malice calmly shot him in the forehead and watched him sag out of view.

Not enough. Not enough.

The baby started to cry.

Moto and Nike were firing continuously now, screams and shouts intermingled with stamps and bootfalls on the ceiling, and Tora's dangling rig swivelled around and around like a drunken ballerina, spitting grenades and bullets at whatever target she fancied. She was shouting too, high voice clearly discernible above the racket – "Too many! Too many!" – and a world away, Malice was fighting to restart the truck, its engine coughing uselessly.

"We're screwed," she said, quietly, calming the baby in a maternal little bubble of her own.

"Fuck that!" Tora wailed. "Fuck thaaaat!"

Thump-thump, thump-thump.

Bikes detonating. Men screaming.

Didn't matter.

Faces leering at windows, batons crashing against reinforced glass. I leaned out the window and emptied the last clip of the mini-Uzi into the fuel tanks of a dirty red Harley, smirking as the rider was shredded, his whooping comrades doused in burning gas, his bike reduced to a rubberised shrapnel-bomb.

But it wasn't enough.

Then Tora was just *gone*. Vanished upwards through her circular lookout, feet thrashing, screaming and spitting and calling for help. The voice was carried off, away from the truck, dwindling to an echo of a scream on the smoky air.

And then they came in.

Three of them. Bullet-vests under leather, hockey-masks over heads. A knife and a pistol each. Shock troops.

Repelling assault-squads. Kill the last one first.

Advanced training, year two.

He's the best. He'll send cannon-fodder ahead. Useless rookies.

He'll come last, wait 'til you're tied up.

So you kill him first.

Nice thought. But the *Inferno* wasn't a big space, and by the time Bastard Number Three slid down the chute, I was up to my elbows in the first two goons.

Savage again. Reacting without thinking.

"They made you a wolf..."

Well woof-the-fuck-woof.

I killed Number One pretty quick. Only fired once – back on the M16 again – but the startled motherfucker grew a hole in his forehead and another in his cheek, knocking out his lower jaw and spraying us all, so I figured Malice was playing along too over my shoulder.

The second guy was luckier. Used his mate for cover, even held him up like a human shield – hand on the hem of his jeans – and pumped three panicky rounds into Nike's legs, hanging from the gun mount above, before I pushed up close and shot him through his buddy's throat. Even then he took his sweet time, bashing about, trying to get a bead on my head as he squirted from his neck and screamed like a bullhorn. I had to bash his fucking brains out against the heavy iron edges of the gun-mount above, and he stared at me – eyes burning, accusing; lips spitting and frothing – all the way.

Somewhere a great noise went up. Like... like an army of hyenas, all laughing at once. I had no time to think about it, no time to try and place it, no time even to notice – in any sense except one of pure instinct – that outside the *Inferno* the gunfire had stopped...

The third man to tear into our little space, the man I should have killed first, he was *hollering.*

Ignoring everyone.

Throwing down his gun in contempt.

And leaping onto Hiawatha with an inhuman scream.

"K-k-kiiilled *Sliiip!*" he growled, knife held above the boy's eyeball, wrestling and grunting and rolling. "Fffucking kill *you!*" Beneath the Cullis of his helmet his face was a mass of festering wounds, skin scraped clear, bloody welts from chin to brow, nose a smeared mess.

Hiawatha was babbling, eyes wide, tears on his cheek, both hands wrapped around the hilt of the blade, shrieking "sorries" and "pleases" and "ohGoddon'tkillmes." Human again. A boy, scared and lonely and pissing himself and –

And I placed the muzzle of the M16 against the man's head, feeling abruptly calm, and said:

"Hey."

He looked at me. I shot him through the eye. So it goes.

And then everything was quiet. At least, quieter. As quiet as it *could* be with Hiawatha sobbing for his mother, Nike yelling and moaning, Malice's kid screaming like a dying cat, and my own heart pounding in my ears.

But no more gunfire. No more biker engines. No more grenades detonating or trucks rumbling towards us.

I stared out the window – through the crazy spider web shatter-patterns on what little glass remained – and saw why.

"Fffuck," said Malice.

The Collectors had been scared off. I knew how they felt.

There was an army. Hundreds upon hundreds of men and women.

Guns.

Bikes. Cars. Horses.

They looked kind of pissed.

His Holiness John-Paul Rohare Baptise closed his eyes and kneaded his temples.

Inside his head a sealed gate was opening wide. Every time he stopped to think, every time there was no distraction – nothing to stare at, nobody to talk to, nothing to think about – it was like... like stepping into a great bazaar, full of painful exhibits he'd never seen before.

Or... worse, like a labyrinth. Yes. That was it. The memories didn't come pouring out, exactly. He had to go in and explore, hunt them down, look for them. Afraid, tentatively digging into dark corners.

Never too sure what he'd find.

He'd always known there had been buried treasures. Always felt, instinctively, that for whatever reason, his mind had shut him away, closed itself down to him. He'd called it, privately, a gift from 'Above.' A purification designed solely to plant him firmly in the Now and the tomorrow. Never concentrating on 'then.' Never looking back. It was as if everything that had existed about him, from before five years ago, had been stripped away in a rush of balefire. God had severed his past, he felt, because he was no longer a creature of history. His was a role of divine prescience. Shaping the world for the new dawn.

Why should he need a personal past for that?

And now this.

"Hmm."

It was all terribly confusing.

John-Paul Rohare Baptiste was remembering what it was to be something he hadn't been for a very, very long time, and it was giving him a headache above and beyond the state of near-intolerable pain he spent the majority of his life experiencing. The 'something' he was slowly remembering was:

Normality.

The car shuddered – just another pothole, probably, or at worst a car wreck being bumped aside by the snaking convoy – and he straightened out the crumpled sheets of paper in his lap. He supposed it could *have been a coincidence... the English scum, the destroyer who'd come so close to finishing the Apostolic Church of the Rediscovered Dawn, rummaging about in old records... coincidental that he'd just* happened *to find... this...*

This.

This sheet. This crumpled personnel dossier with its clipped photograph and personal details, its family affiliations, service history, recommendations and citations.

One of the Cardinals had brought it to him. Found in some nameless file in some empty part of the Secretariat.

There was a story attached, he recalled – something about a struggle, a death? He couldn't remember. It hardly seemed important, now. Compared to this file, nothing *seemed important.*

John-Paul fingered the sheets and licked dry lips.

He'd always known his real name, at least. That had never been a shock. Back at... at the start, when he wandered into the city out of the west, alone and confused, filled only with the certainty of his own divinity and the exact requirements of his body in order to preserve it, even then he'd known. He'd had his birth certificate with him, hadn't he? Or... or maybe he faked it? Maybe he...

Anyway.

Anyway, it didn't matter. He'd known he was John P. Miller, somewhere at the back of his skull. He just hadn't cared, until now. Didn't want *to remember where the name had come from, who he'd been, what he'd done, what he'd been like as a person before he became more than a person; before he became John-Paul Rohare Baptise, Abbot of the greatest institution existing in the world today, architect of Tomorrow's Civilisation.*

In a roundabout sort of way.

Another group of robed outriders swept past the limousine on his left. The driver was being boringly silent – probably star-struck, the poor devil – and John-Paul found himself craving conversation, or distraction. Something of interest to stare at, perhaps, rather than the bland hills and blander roads of suburban nowhere. Something, anything, to take his mind off the sheet.

But no.

Sergeant John P. Miller. NATO liaison officer.
Assigned 4332/GGfT/332-099#1
Project Pandora.

It was a lot like watching a film. Like the trigger on a projector, immersing the viewer immediately in a cannonade of scenes, shots, impressions, memories. The only difference was, it was all inside his eyelids.

It all came right back to him, and for the fiftieth time he struggled with the desire to vomit. Soon he'd have to tell the driver to stop, to get the Acolytes up here, to prepare the Host.

It was a lot to take in.

And this, at his age. At his time of life. In his current state of health. Oh, was there no end to the tests he must pass?

He mumbled a prayer and tried to ride out the nausea.

He'd seen his empire shaken to its roots. He'd seen his fortress invaded by heretics and filth, his perfectly structured city ripped away from his grasp and – worst of all – his link with the world denied to him. The great satellite dish on the banks of the East River, the great studios and broadcast suites his loyal children had pieced together inside the General Assembly buildings. The means of speaking to the world.

The means of reaching out.

Spreading the Good Word.

All of it taken away. Destroyed, ripped apart, trampled underfoot by the ignorance and hatred of those who could never hope to understand his Divine Plan; who were led by the Man. The Stranger. The...

The fucking Devil.

John-Paul muttered a second prayer, shocked at the crudity of his own thoughts. Perhaps, though, it didn't matter. Perhaps... Mm. Perhaps being reawakened to his past was no simple coincidence, but an act of the Lord in itself?

Yes. Yes, that was it.

His tribe was beaten, but not destroyed. His home was taken from him.

What better time to recall another place? A better place. A hidden place, where once he'd served a far lowlier authority than the Lord. A place with communications facilities of its own. With defences and secrecy.

A place to start again, and grow strong.

He found himself clenching his jaw.

And if, in the course of this Holy Exodus to new lands and new futures, he should come across that same troublesome bastard, that Limey cumrag, if *that should occur – and the Collectors had been sent out to make fucking sure it* did –

Then fine.

Fine. Whatever the Lord willed, of course, but... Yes. Mm.

If. If they met him...

There would be a reckoning.

* * *

HIAWATHA WAS REAL again. Curled on the floor, shallow breathing, fighting tears and trauma, the dead Collector hunched over beside him with his brains leaking out.

This was how the poor kid must have been, before. Before he came all the way to find me, in a city he'd never visited, with a head full of mumbo-jumbo and a mission I still wasn't any closer to understanding.

It was like the whole thing with the psycho and the knife – the guy with his face scraped off – had been the last straw, and whatever weird-arsed personality he'd been hiding behind these last few days, inhaling it up through each of his sweet-smelling spliffs, it was comprehensively gone.

Thank *fuck*.

In the sudden silence after the fight, as we traded glances and worked ourselves over to find wounds and scars, as we eyed the horde gathered outside the truck with growing anxiety, Hiawatha wiped his eyes and started to laugh.

We all stared at him. Even Nike, crippled on the floor, fussed over by Moto (who clearly had never expected to be the one to do the fussing), looked up from his pain and misery in shock. Even Nate, curled in smacked-up otherworldly confusion, stared and muttered.

Hiawatha took one look out the window, grinning at the hordes of silent figures standing there. Just standing, staring. He smiled like he'd overcome constipation and shat a gold brick, then rummaged in his bag for the dope he'd been smoking and threw it with undisguised satisfaction through the mangled hole where Tora had been taken.

Like he didn't need it any more.

"We're home," he said. "We're fucking *home*."

"But. Uh. Hiawa –"

"Rick," he said, shaking my hand warmly. "My name's Rick. Everything's going to be fine now. Come on."

He wriggled up and out through the gun-perch. I glanced significantly at Malice and checked the load in the M16. Then I went after him.

"Careful!" Nate giggled, eyes rolling. "Injun's a... injun's a fucking liability."

Junkie.

Hiawatha was down on the ground, walking away. I went to follow him, then stopped.

There was a man on the roof of the *Inferno*.

I don't know how long he'd been there. I hadn't heard footsteps since the Collectors fucked off, and he didn't look the sort to go *anywhere* quietly. The wind moved in his hair, and the beads under his ears, and the feathers on his shoulders.

Which was sort of weird.

Because –

(*What the fuck is going on?*)

Because there wasn't any wind.

The sky smiled.

"Welcome," he said. And his face moved as he talked in ways I didn't understand, and the skin beside his eyes was a red desert that shifted with continental patience, and his eyes sucked in the universe, and the great decorated robe he wore, furled like the wings of a bat, danced in my eyes.

Messages in patterns.

The smile on the corners of his lips.

The –

The walkie-talkie poking out of his cloak.

What?

It hissed.

The man looked away for a second.

"*kkk*... llo..?" the radio said.

This vision before me, this ancient God of plains and prairies, this magnificent man with skin like leather and whorls of black and white across the bridge of his nose, with a great feather-totem spread across his shoulders and a long war-club held in his hand, he shifted from foot to foot, and said:

"Uh."

"*kkk*...cking *talk* to me, asshole motherf...*kkk*... *said*, is he *there* yet?... llo?... *kkk*... oddamn food's nearly ready an..."

The man rolled his eyes and sighed.

"C'mon," he said, turning away with a despondent beckon, reduced abruptly from awesome Earth Deity to an old bloke with a crazy costume. "Let's get a beer before the old bitches get pissy."

The *Haudeno... Haudanosaw... Haw...* oh, fuck, the Iroquois weren't what I expected at all.

Listen: I'm English. Only exposure I ever got to indigenous life was a school trip to a Stone Age village when I was a kid, and a whole shitload of John Wayne movies. You ask me, a Native American lives in a wigwam, says "How" a lot, and has a name like Two-Ferrets-Fucking. I know, I know. It's despicable, stereotypical and downright unforgivable. But I yam what I yam.

Still, I was *ready* to be educated, you know? As the quiet tribesmen loaded us all into cars and trailers, patching up Moto as best they could, and swarmed around the *Inferno* in our wake, I was prepared to have my eyes opened. Rick – Hiawatha, whoever he was – babbled the whole way about the 'new' Iroquois. About how, in a cruel post-Cull world, the Old Ways worked best. He said the people who'd come out here, they forgot all that bullshit we used to call 'society' and went back to the land. Back to basics.

Funny thing is, he sounded sort of bitter as he said it.

Rick told me it was a popular movement. Sure enough, at least half the tribesmen around us – variously wearing scavenged trousers, leather jackets or woolly jumpers, all with beads and mouse-skulls and intricate tattoos decorating heads and faces – were whiter than white. It was funny to see them like that. Embarrassing, in a way; like being seen in public with a raging tourist who doesn't mind stopping to take a photo every five seconds, and wears a hilarious t-shirt saying something like:

I CAME TO LONDON AND ALL I GOT WAS THIS LOUSY STD!

But they looked so earnest, smoking their cigarettes and hefting their guns, and they acted so friendly as we drove, that I kept myself from pointing and laughing. It was a struggle.

The point is, I guess I was ready to be... impressed. Stunned by the allure of this atavistic lifestyle. I was awaiting nomadic groups, great tribal fires, comfy lodges made of wood and mud.

Oh, piss... I admit it: I was expecting a *spectacle.*

Instead I got thirty caravans, assorted Winnebago clones, two dozen pickups and one of those prefab mobile homes, like a cheap Swiss chalet, on the back of a lorry. I almost choked. They stood formed together in a rough circle around the prefab, on the banks of a clean-looking reservoir, in the shade of a huge bridge carrying the I-80 to the opposite bank.

The old man who'd greeted me, who'd introduced himself as we clambered into the waiting car as a 'Sachem' named Robert Slowbear, caught my look of vague disappointment. He seemed to bristle.

"Just a mobile base," he said, defensively. "Not regular at all. We're a long way from home too, stranger."

"Yeah?"

He settled back and smiled. "You should see the lodges, Englishman. Fields giving crops. Herds of swine all through the forests. More people coming every day..."

Hiawatha muttered under his breath. "Caravans as far as the eye can see..."

Slowbear threw him a *shuddup, kid* look.

"You all live in the same area?" I said, intrigued by the vision of some sprawling trailer park in the middle of Indiana.

The Sachem shook his head. "No, no... The *Haudenosaunee* is a... a confederacy, not a state. Settlements with the right to roam. Mostly they stay still... farm, raise livestock, fish... Others move with seasons. We come together, now and then. Trade news. Share stories and lessons."

"Party..." Rick murmured, slightly more enthusiastic.

Slowbear ignored him. "The means of living vary, stranger. That is my point. Does it matter if a man sleeps beneath a pelt or a... a *duvet*? In a wooden lodge or a... hah... a TrekMaster 3000? The circumstances by which he acquired items do not lessen their value. It is the *ways* that matter. The councils. The families. The beliefs."

I felt my fists tighten, just a tad. Bugbear.

"What beliefs?"

He met my gaze, and we held eye-contact for a long time, without any sense of threat or status. It was an extraordinary sensation.

"Consider," he said, pausing to slurp on a flask of something that smelt like lager. "What is unchanged?"

He passed it to me. It tasted okay.

"What do you mean?" I said, wiping froth off my lip.

"This... this Blight. The 'Cull.' Call it what you like. What *didn't* it affect?"

I wasn't in the mood for a guessing game. "Tell me."

"Ha. The world."

I scowled.

"Do the animals care?" he said. "Did the deer fall down and die? Or the crows in the trees? Did the soil turn barren, or the rains stop? Did the earth *care*?"

"I guess not. Unless you count the minor case of nukage..."

"I don't."

"Figures."

"The point is, why look to some... heavenly God? Some crucified idiot born of mortal man." He stretched his arms out wide and gestured across the fields and hills, the glittering water of the reservoir and the clear sun in the sky. "Isn't this *enough*?"

I gave it some thought. It was a cute speech. Tempting, even. But still...

"Sounds a lot like just another faith-specific boys' club to me." I said. "You don't believe, you don't get to play along."

He didn't look offended.

"You must understand," he smiled. "It's not the tasks a man performs that defines who he is. That's just staying alive. That's just *being.* It's what sings in his heart as he does so."

Out of the corner of my eye, I caught Rick rolling his eyes.

"And what sings in these peoples' hearts?" I said, only a *little* wry, gesturing around me at the beered-up white-man-injuns with their polished guns and rattling pickups.

Slowbear smiled faintly, and took a long time to answer.

"Freedom," he said.

I stared at him. Worked my jaw. Thought about it. Said:

"Just another way of saying 'nothing left to lose'..."

We finished the journey in silence.

They took Moto away to be looked after and sat the others down to eat and drink. Pork, bread, freshly harvested vegetables, thick soups and wooden bowls of porridgey-paste and whiskey. I eyed it all longingly as Slowbear led me away. Nate tried to follow, shivering as he came-down off whatever he was on, but a couple of big guys wearing freaky blue masks politely told him to get some food in his belly, and steered him back towards the campfire.

I made a mental note to have a word with the guy. He looked like death warmed-up, and things had been far too crazy for far too long for me to find out what he was taking.

Where he'd got it from.

What the hell he was *doing*...

The big mobile home was a lot more impressive on the inside than the out. Someone had stripped out most of the dividing walls and blanketed the floor in a cosy mish-mash of cheap Persian rugs, animal skins, fur-coats and a thick pile of carpet off-cuts. It was like wading through the shaggiest patchwork in the world, and contrived to give the structure an earthy, russet-brown air; helped along no end by the chipboard walls. Each panel was so industriously graffitied with a swirling combination of text, iconic drawings and childlike scribbles that each component ceased to have any meaning on its own, and became just a part. A raw *splat* of language, of *culture*.

I caught myself getting abstract again, and noted the thick pall of smoke in the air, the sweet-sour smell of something that wasn't just tobacco.

Ah-ha.

It was weird. It was like I'd stepped through the door of this whitewashed suburban kitschism and entered some magical beaver-lodge. Some ancient cave, or skin covered bivouac. It just happened to have a few more right angles than you'd expect.

Slowbear lurked at the door and waved me inside.

"Who'm I looking for?" I asked, irritated by the mystery.

"The boss." He grinned, and closed the door.

At the end of the hallway I came to a large chamber, where the windows were boarded up and the high ceiling lost behind a canopy of drooping skins and weird shapes. Knotted ropes and dyed fabrics, a mournful cow-skull and a stuffed eagle turning on a string tied to the roof-joists. There was a very old man sitting beneath it, hunched over an electric fire, wearing a bland little chequered shirt with a brown waistcoat. His hair was almost white, and pulled back in a silvery ponytail that left his face uncovered; magnificently uplit by the glowing heat. Each line on his face was a fissure in a great glacial surface; ruddy-red but still somehow icy, like it radiated age and a slow, unstoppable determination.

There was absolutely no doubt at all that this man was in charge, in every sense, and despite the lack of gaudy costumes and outrageous symbols, I had to wrestle with my own desire not to dip my head.

He was smoking a pipe in the shape of a bear-totem. It looked cheap.

"Please," he said, and waved to a low chair placed opposite him. I made a move towards it, not thinking, and hesitated. Call me shallow, but the memory of the food cooking outside and the hole in my stomach was more powerful than I'd expected.

"No offence," I said. "But is this likely to take a while? I'm fit to fall down, here."

And then I smelt it.

Rich. Gamey. Good enough to kill for.

Vegetable aromas mixed with the smoky emanations of the old man's pipe, underscored at all times by the unmistakable scent of cooking meat. I realised with a stomach-gurgling jolt that the chamber led – via an archway in the corner – into a kitchen, and from inside caught the shadow of movement and a fresh burst of steam and smoke.

I almost dribbled.

"It is on its way." The old man smiled. He had a kind voice, and spoke with the thoughtful enunciation of a man to whom English is a second language.

I sat.

"Who are you?"

"*Tadodaho*," he said. "You would say... chief. Over all the *Haudenosaunee*. Over the sachem council."

"And why have you brought me here, chief?"

He puffed on the pipe, letting white coils billow upwards with that curious slowness of silt sinking through water, but reversed; rising to the surface, lifting up to –

Abstract bollocks.

Hold it together.

"You are here for a talk with the highest authority within our great Confederacy." He smiled, rotating the pipe in nimble old fingers. "The *Haudenosaunee* have been waiting for you."

"You knew I was coming?"

"Yes."

"You sent that kid to fetch me."

"Yes."

"How did he know where to look?"

He held out the pipe.

"A better question is: how did he know *how* to look?"

I pursed my lips. Stared at the pipe for a long time, then slowly shook my head.

"No thanks."

Clear head.

Know everything.

Cover the angles.

If my refusal constituted some big bloody cultural insult, or whatever, the old man gave no sign, shrugging good-naturedly and continuing to smoke himself.

Eventually, as the silence was killing me and the desire to blunder through to that kitchen and go crazy was starting to hotwire my muscles, he sighed through eddying clouds and said:

"My blood is not like yours."

"Excuse me?"

"Blood, Englishman. Blood *types.* I assume you are normal? Type 'O.' Rhesus negative. Yes?"

It was fucking weird, I don't mind telling you; sitting there in that warm lodge with a genuinely creepy tribal mystic, listening to him go off on one about bloody pathology. Like a brontosaurus with an MP3 player.

"Well..." I said, a touch too sarcastic. "You'll notice I'm technically *alive*..?"

"Mm."

"Then *obviously* I'm O-neg... What the fuck *is* tha – ?"

"I, on the other hand, am not."

He stared at me. His face was still. And in his eyes, oh fuck, I could see, I could just *tell*:

He wasn't lying.

"You're...? I don't underst..."

"Nor do we. Not fully. I tell you this because it will help you to understand why we have brought you here. We know you have desires of your own. Agendas. It is our hope that ours might briefly... compliment your own."

I swallowed. My mouth suddenly felt dry.

"Tell me more. About the... about how come you're still alive."

"I cannot. I do not understand such things. What I know is that of all my people alive before the Cull – my *true* people, stranger, by blood and birth – less than one half perished. Regardless of blood type.

"This, we hope, is welcome news to you.

"This, we hope, will give you some hope of your own."

He knows.

The old bastard, he knows what I'm looking for...

But if he's right. If he's telling the truth, then couldn't it mean that –

– don't even THINK *it! Don't even dare to hope –*

– that there's a chance?

That I didn't come here for nothing?

I must have looked thunderstruck. Sitting there, mind back-flipping. The Tadodaho was tactful enough to say nothing, watching my face, and when five old ladies magically appeared in the doorway to the kitchen, each bearing a wooden bowl, each bowl smelling like it'd come direct from an all-angels edition of *Masterchef*, even then my excitement at the feast couldn't quite sever my thoughts.

Some people. Some people lived through it, who shouldn't have.

Look at these folks.

Look at John-fucking-Paul.

Wasn't it possible?

I started eating like a man possessed, nodding thankfully to each woman as they delivered venison, sweet-potatoes, beans, sour-bread... In the confused fug of my thoughts – made sluggish by surprise and smoke – I noticed the last of the entourage wore flowing robes of a particularly vibrant red and had a cute little radio-mic clipped to what passed for her lapel. I squinted, trying to remember why this was significant, but couldn't. I thought the group might shuffle out of the room as they'd come in, but they gathered instead in a huddle of smiling faces and crinkled skin behind the Tadodaho, and stood there staring at me.

"The men of the Church," the old man said, watching me eat, "have their own interest in our survival."

I scowled, wiping sauce off my chin. "Why?"

"We don't know. All we understand is that their Collectors come to our lodges every day. In greater numbers. With guns and bikes and metal cords. Every day they come, every day they steal away our people."

"They take your kids?"

"There are no children left to *take*, Stranger. They have... widened their attentions. Any Iroquois, by birth. Any redskin. Any who survived the Cull, who should not have.

"They are killing us, little by little, Englishman. And we would like your help."

I stopped eating. I hadn't expected him to wrap up so soon, and it felt like every eye in the room was boring into me.

Worse, the eyes *shifted*. Swirled. I shook my head to clear the sensation.

"And... and that's why you brought me here?" I mumbled, trying to stay focused. "To help you beat the bastards off?"

The room suddenly seemed far less angular. Tapestries became rocky walls. The steam from the kitchen was an underground river, spilling through sweaty caves.

"Sorry," I said, shaken. "My fight's not with the fucking Clergy. They got in my way, I took what I wanted. End... end of story."

Somewhere, a million miles away, I felt the bowl fall from my hands and spill across my legs. I felt the room move sideways. I felt the skins drooping from the roof writhe and flex.

"We understand," the Tadodaho said. "We know. And do not think us so crude that we would attempt to convince you otherwise. You are a stubborn man, Stranger. We have always known it."

"Then... thuh... then why... brng... me here...?"

Slurring.

Not good.

Something in the food.

Drugged.

Panic.

"I told you," the old man's voice said, from far, far away. "You are here to talk with the highest Authority within our Great Confederacy."

"Buh... But..." Every word was a struggle. Every syllable a living beast that fluttered from my mouth and scuttled across the air, leaving trails of purple and green fire. "But we bin... bin *talking* alrrdy..."

Somewhere out in the soup of my senses, the Tadodaho's face coalesced.

"Not me." He smiled. "Not me."

And then five shapes – five woman-faces that rippled like ploughed earth and swarmed with a host of stars and fireflies – bulged together around me, hooked soft fingers beneath the skin of my mind and dragged me down to the past.

CHAPTER SEVENTEEN

THEY'RE WATCHING ME, but maybe there's not much I can do about that just now.

They're in every detail. Flaws, mainly. Like when you remember something with such crystal-clarity that you know every line, every shape, every resonance...

...and then you look up expecting to see London's grey skies, and there's a face looking down instead.

...and then you shake the blood off a knife, or finish retching with the force of your anger, and the droplets splattered across the floor form eyes, and stare right at you.

These memories, they're full of rage and violence and weirdness. And the thing with weirdness is, there's always room for more.

Things keep changing. Time keeps jumping. There's a roar in my ears like I'm underwater, but I'm not scared. They're watching me – those withered injun women – but so what? They're talking to me, too, and their voices are pretty, and maybe I'm talking back or maybe I'm not, but either way: they're in here with me. Spying on my past.

Back to the start.

Back to London.

After I got the signal, in the comms room of the old MI6 building at Vauxhall Cross – where I'd whored myself to the SIS for years – I sliced up some people good. Clergy. I don't recall how many. I was too focused.

We'd all seen the planes. Every rat-human crawling in the filth of London knew they were there. Blue-painted, marked with the red 'O' of the Church, going up, coming down. Why? Who knew? Who cared?

I went to Heathrow. My mind was a needle. Too angry to speak. Too focused to negotiate.

Pandora, Pandora, Pandora... like a mantra, see?

Nothing would turn me. I'd impale anything that dared get in my way.

And I waited. Cut and slashed in the night. Hacked open necks. Cut off fingertips. Made grey robes run red.

Not because I hated the Clergy.

Not because they had anything to do with anything.

Not for any reason except they were convenient, and they had something I wanted.

Took me three days of torturing to work my way up to a Clergy-bastard of sufficient hierarchical power to be worth taking hostage. I think – I know *– I stopped being me for a bit there. Let the animal thing take over too much. Let the rampage-instincts out of their box.*

It was a weird time.

I made sure everything felt significant, everything felt like a step in the right direction, and by God's own piss it felt good. *I let everyone I came across seem responsible, took it all out on them, mixed up the anger with the focus, just like they taught me in training:*

Made it personal.

So what I did, back at the start, I strolled into the airport as bold as brass, with this pigshit priest under my knife, telling every gun-wielding arsehole who came near to back off or get splashed.

And this guy, this hostage, this high-up canon or whoever he was, he leaned down so the knife was pressed up against his neck... and he shook his head.

Slit-slat-slit.

Faith. That's what. Obvious, really. Never take any wanker prisoner who's prepared to die for his beliefs.

So bang went my clever-clever attempt to hijack a plane alone, which is all I ever wanted out of those child-stealing sadistic delusional fucks. Bang went my momentum, bang went my anger, bang went the feeling of progress, of inertialess drive. The juggernaut rolled to a halt.

Cue running away, hiding, rethinking.

Cue a realisation or two: doing it alone wasn't going to work. Focus wasn't enough.

Enter Bella.

I found her waiting outside the airport, just standing and staring. Like she was shellshocked, maybe, except it looked like she'd been that way for years. Watching every plane, mumbling to herself. Waiting for something to happen.

I *happened.*

Cut forwards in time.

Bella telling me she knew how to fly.

Recon of the airport.

Preparing. Arming up.

Getting drunk one night and fucking, and not caring except to feel the guilt, and letting down the shields for five seconds and discovering – holy shit – I'm still human after all.

Telling myself I didn't care what her story was. Listening anyway.

They took her kid.

They took a thousand kids. Every week, another load. Off across the ocean. Off to be with the skeletal bastard Abbot off the TV. Off to a better life, or a worse one, or who knew what, except that it was OFF.

Scared. Crying. Can't you just imagine them?

(The faces in the clouds are watching and nodding, and saying yes we can, *and wiping tears and telling me to get on with it.)*

And then there was Bella, saying:

"Doesn't matter. Not your problem. But that's why I'm going."

And then the time comes and we make our move, and con our way inside, and kill our way further, and gather guns and steal drugs, and then it's sprinting across tarmac, and guns opening fire, and pain in my shoulder, and Bella dragging me up the steps, and then –

And then away. Stateside-bound.

And then the story started.

And Bella died in fire and pain and chaos.

And Nate and the city and blah-blah-blah.

"Doesn't matter," Bella told me, as we clung to each other in the dark. "Not your problem."

After everything she did for me. After she flew me and died for me. After she gave me back my humanity, and stuck a booster up my hope.

"Not your problem."

And all the others. The people of London who bartered and fed me, and said hello every day, and didn't care that I didn't say hello back. The scavs of New York, who died and cried and followed me, despite my lies, into the jaws of hell. The Iroquois, who sent their scared little envoy to watch over me, then saved me themselves on the road.

All of them. Children stolen away. Tears long since run-out. Dead inside, but still fit to help. Still fit to see hope for a better tomorrow. Still fit to smile and think the best, and do something good.

And here's me. Here's me pursuing my own goal and forgetting the rest. Damn the world. Damn every motherfucker alive. Ignore it. Let it happen. Be selfish, why not?

Nothing to do with me.

"Not your problem," she said.

Well, shit.

About time I made *it my problem.*

THEY WERE COMING. So said the Tadodaho.

(Or, rather, so said the matriarchs, who whispered and sighed in dark corners then told the chief what to say and do. It amounted to the same thing.)

I didn't bother asking how they knew. Scouts, surveillance, divine-bloody-intuition, I didn't know. Or care. I'd just taken a lazy stroll through the psychedelic bullshit of my own mind, and if the weirdest thing to greet me on my return was the rock-solid assertion that the Clergy were *coming, here, en masse*, then frankly it was a taste of reassuring normality.

They were following me, I guessed. We'd got past their psychotic Collectors, but it didn't matter. Their base in NY was overrun and they'd came pelting out here in my wake. Why?

Revenge?

Maybe. But it sounded like a lot of hard work to go to, just to kick the arse of the guy who'd rattled them up. So why else? Unless...

Unless they were going to the same place as me.

"What's the plan?" Nate said, hours later, when my head stopped spinning from its heavy barrage of hallucinations and synaesthetic memories. We were still sat at the fire between the caravans, watching the evening roll-in, just the two of us. Nike was laid up in one of the 'vans, dosed out of his skull, and Moto refused to leave his side. Tora... Tora's body had been found near where the Collectors caught up with us. I didn't like to ask what state it was in. Malice went and oversaw a quiet cremation outside the camp, and I'd figured it would be rude to invite myself along. She hadn't said anything, but there was an unspoken accusation in her eyes as she wandered off:

You brought us out here.

This is your fault.

I told myself I'd imagined it. I told myself they were all mercenaries who'd known the dangers, and it was a little late in the day to start complaining about the risk when two were already dead and one mangled to shit.

It didn't help.

So. Me and Nate. Warm and full of food (still chowing, in fact, on a second portion of everything to make up for the stuff I puked first time round). And again the old bastard's jaw was lolling, cheeks pinned-back in a rictus-smile, pupils dilated big enough to turn his eyes inside-out.

"What's the plan, what's the plan, what's the plaaan?" he said, giggling, wobbling around like he was dancing to some silent beat. "Got any more burns? Need a burn? Needaburn-needaburn?"

I stopped chewing. Looked at him and shook my head.

I guessed... oh, sod it. I guessed now was as good a time as any.

I put down my bowl.

"Look at you," I said. "Nate. Seriously. Look at yourself."

"Eh?"

"You're bombed. You're off your face, mate."

It took him a while to react, and his smiling face crumpled like a hollow mountain.

"Am not!" he shouted, far too loud, standing and pointing. "Am fucking not!"

I just stared, getting bored. Eventually he sat down.

"We had a deal," I said quietly, slurping on more of the homebrewed beer. He reacted jerkily, like he couldn't control his own defence.

"Yeah? *Yeah*, so?"

"So I paid you good scav and I kept you alive. Right? You were in pigshit up to your neck after the airport."

"I know that! Did I say I didn't know it? Fuck *you*, m..."

"And all you had to do in return was play at being a doctor."

I picked up my bowl again and spooned some potatoes into my mouth. Tasted good. Ignored the old man's rolling eyes and hurt silence.

"And... and I have!" he yelped, like a kicked puppy dog. "Didn't I? Didn't I? I've done *good!* Patched you up over and over. You know it, you know it, you know it!"

I glared.

"Yeah. And Nike's in a Winnebago over there with his legs shot to shit, and you haven't lifted a hand to help."

Nate's lips moved. Searching for words.

"But... h-hold it, he's... but..."

"But he's not part of the deal? Is that it?"

"No! No, I just... I thought your, your injuns here would take care and..."

"Some doctor, Nate."

We sat in silence for a long time then; darkness spreading above us, fire drooling embers upwards.

"The Secretariat," I said, eventually.

"Wh... what?"

I sighed, shaking my head. "Oh, nothing. Just thinking. Our little deal. Never seemed quite right to me."

"But... I don't understand. What's – ?"

"You didn't seem to get much out of it, I mean. I was wondering why you were sticking with me, to be honest. Now I know."

He looked suddenly angry, thick sarcasm souring his voice. "Oh, you know. You *know*, do you? The fuck do *you* know? You gonna make shit up and say you *know*, then you can kiss my –"

"The Secretariat. I sent you downstairs. Told you to go help the others find the kids."

His eyes went narrow. Chin jutting. "S-so?"

"So that's the only time you could've found that shit." I pointed at the pack next to his knees, unsurprised to see his fingers coiled securely through its handle. "Stole it from the Choirboys, didn't you?"

He almost exploded, hugging the bag to himself as he stood and shrieked, irrational and embarrassing. "The fuck's wrong with *that*?" he snarled. "You saying, you saying I shouldn't *steal* from *them* assholes?"

"Course not. I'm saying don't steal shit that'll turn you into a prick. Sit down."

"Fuck *yo* –"

"Or, don't steal shit that'll bring an army of motherfuckers chasing after you. Sit *down*, Nate."

"That's not why they're *comi* –"

"Or even better, don't steal shit when you're an ex-junkie."

Quiet.

He sat.

"Tell you what *I* think," I said, feeling sharp things moving in my words but not caring. Bella's face was swimming behind my eyelids, and for some reason it made me *angry*. "I think you never quit."

"What?"

"Back in London. You used to live there, you said. You said you quit, remember?"

He didn't say a word.

"I think maybe you were telling half a truth there, mate. I think what actually happened is, the supply ran out. Tough call, getting smack right after the Cull." His white eyes dipped, firelight reflecting. "But then along comes the Clergy and tells you they can fix you up, sort you out. All you got to do is clear off stateside and look after some kiddies on the way through..."

"That's... wasn't *like* that..."

"And for a couple of years it's all gravy. Probably wasn't even smack they gave you, right? Some weird new military shit. Am I right? Even better. Double the high.

"Then some dumb English fuck arrives and screws the whole gig, and before you know it you're out on your ear. Right? Am I right?"

He was just staring at the fire, face closed-down. Nothing to say. Nothing to deny.

I noticed a stain on his trousers and wondered if he'd even noticed he'd pissed himself.

He swallowed and looked up at me. "I... I just..."

"Why should you stay with me? Oh, fuck, there was all that shit about me protecting your life, blah-blah. Didn't buy it for a second, mate. But then we get to the Secretariat and *bang*, you've got right what you wanted. That big case right there. And I'm thinking... That's a *big* place. How did he find it? Unless maybe he knew where to look..."

"J-Jesus..."

"And *that* makes me wonder how you knew we'd be going to the Secretariat at *all*."

His eyes gave it away. In the end.

Flicked away from my face. A split second, no more, to the green sack hanging on my shoulder.

The penny dropped.

"The map..." I said, kicking myself. "Fuck. Of course. Of *course*."

I always knew he looked through my bag, back at the start, as I lay dying on the tarmac. I assumed he'd lusted after the booze, the Bliss...

But no. He went straight to the map. The New York City map, marked with a bloody-red ring around the UN Headquarters.

"So you saw where I was heading... Right? And you thought... Well now... Maybe I'll just... *tag along*?"

I glanced up.

He stared.

"You didn't even have the guts to tell me the truth, Nate."

I wouldn't have cared, if he'd been honest.

I *don't* care, even now. Don't give a shit what he does to himself.

I just don't like being wrong.

He opened and closed his mouth like a fish.

"Parasite," I said.

I stood up and walked away.

I WENT FOR a walk.

Took a look around. Found Malice and sat down to talk and draw maps in the sand. Scheming. If she was pissed about the *Inferno* and the others, she didn't show it.

Around midnight I went and fetched Robert Slowbear, and he took me to the Tadodaho. I politely declined anything to eat or drink.

Around four o'clock the camp moved, all at once, across the great concrete bridge spanning the sinuous lake, and by six I was up to my armpits in cold water.

By seven we were ready.

They didn't keep us waiting.

THE MEANDER RESERVOIR was a twisting strip of spilled water, dividing Youngstown from the green ocean of fields surrounding it. On the Tadodaho's map – an ancient and laminated thing, long-faded and well-worn – the lake was an obvious part of a chain, connected by creeks and ditches, that ran south all the way from Lake Erie. It wasn't a huge watercourse, I suppose. Maybe five or six miles, tip-to-tip. It wouldn't have taken too long to go around either, if someone'd had to, but what was perfect about it was this:

The I-80, straight from New York, spanned the lake dead across its centre on a single, exposed, vulnerable and oh-so-deliciously-narrow bridge.

If ever there was a better place for an ambush, I would've liked to have seen it.

For the record, somewhere – deep down at the rotten core of my mind – I shouted and cussed at myself, waggling a subconscious finger at this daft display of time-wasting.

Not my problem, it kept shouting. *Focus on the mission!*

And my response, my considered reply to this seemingly watertight argument, went something like this:

Fuck off.

The Clergymen came out of the quicksmog on the horizon at dawn, and the sound of engines reached us long before we saw them. The air went electric.

There were three other bridges too – two smaller roads, a mile on either side, that forded the water at its narrowest points, and a larger bridge far to the south where the Ohio turnpike turned northwards, with no easy access or turn-ons. We could ignore *that*, at least.

At about the same time we heard the engines, the *Haudenosaunee* vanished. All of them, dipping out of sight without so much as a word. It was incredible to watch.

Vehicles bundled off rapidly to the west, parked behind knots of trees and dips in the road. Bikes laid down on their sides and covered with grass and leaves. Men and women lugging improbably huge weapons squatted on the banks to either side of the central bridge, and simply –

– *disappeared.*

One moment there was an army, hundreds strong, arranged silently along the banks of the lake, staring off into the fog. The next: nothing.

Well. *Almost* nothing.

The *Inferno* had been dragged to the centre of the road on our side of the bridge. It was a sad sight, mangled and unsteady, lolling to one side with its cockpit torn open and its sides dented to hell. But the guns still worked, oh yes, and wedged up on either side of it there stood a pair of Iroquois caravans, untidily blocking the road, holding it upright.

It looked like the world's crappiest blockade.

Rick – Hiawatha, whoever he was – had volunteered to man the *Inferno*. He'd done so with the chin-jutting defiance of someone too young to know better, trying to prove something; to himself, I guess. If it'd been down to me I would have told him to stop being a macho prick and leave it to someone more capable.

"Good," the Tadodaho had said. "Good."

The youngster opened-fire right on time.

Down in the shade cast by the bridge, covered in a loose mesh of twigs and brambles, I had a perfect view. Malice grinned openly to my left, and even Nike – sprawled in a mess of splints and crutches behind her, with Moto mothering him wordlessly – chuckled to himself. Could've just been the painkillers, I suppose.

The bikes came first.

And went down like dominoes.

Outriders; scouting ahead of a far larger convoy that could barely be seen amidst the far fringes of the quicksmog; Clergy corsairs with white helmets and dark robes, some on military bikes with sidecars containing Uzi-waving idiots, others sprinting ahead on powerbikes re-sprayed grey and white.

Rick exploded them one by one.

The shape of the road funnelled them naturally, drawing them together, bunching them like skittles. As they ripped onto the far span it was to be greeted by a wave – a *wall* – of lead and fire and shrapnel. They should have been more cautious. They should have looked ahead at the obstruction and taken their time, but no. Straight in. Still accelerating when the ordnance closed on them and the world shook.

Thunder and smoke and muzzle-flare, and the first two bikes skidding in hot rubber and screaming chrome, and torn leather and blood on the road, and the next idiots flipping head-over-saddle as they smashed into their fallen comrades, and *then* – only then – did the brakes slam on and the situation slow.

By which time it was far too late.

The kid aimed with only the vaguest accuracy. He simply poked a cautious head through the *Inferno*'s turret, steered the great mass of oiled death mounted there towards the far edge of the bridge, and held down as many triggers as he could.

It was like...

Bonfire Night. Or the Fourth of July, depending.

Or maybe just a war zone. Maybe just a field-spotter's guide to hasty death.

The Mk19 lobbing its tumbling shells, spit-crack-flare-smoke; a brace of machineguns vomiting spent cases and angry tracers; dust and tarmac rising up; splinters of air and rock tumbling; bikes shivering in haloes of sparks and then dissolving – just *going away* – behind great balls of incandescence. The whole bridge shook with each grenade-flare, and underneath it all came the sharp ring of Rick's voice, shouting and laughing.

On the edge of the bridge, through curtains of hot smoke and fire clinging to shattered bodies and disassembled bikes, the blunt shadows of blockier shapes nudged at the edge of the quicksmog. Beside me, Malice's face dropped. The rest of the convoy, perhaps.

If Rick had noticed, he didn't care. The Mk19 spat its last grenade and whirred on, empty chambers cycling uselessly, but the rest of the arsenal kept going. Throwing curtains of dust and sparks at the far shore, as if daring the knot of bikes that had turned aside and backed away to *come get some...*

Nobody seemed keen to oblige.

The blocky shape began to solidify; angular panels and reinforced glass, painted sky-blue in defiance of camouflage. I recognised the boxy nose of an armoured vehicle – some ex-military ground car or other, heavy with ablative plates and sensor-gear – and let my eye wander quickly to the gun in its rear. Autocannon. 25mm, maybe 30. Against a crippled fire truck with armour made of corrugated iron, frankly, it wouldn't make much difference.

The bikes zipped off in either direction, clearing a corridor. Rick's petulant salvo rattled uselessly off the AFV's hull, and after a second or two he allowed the guns to fall silent, uncertain, letting smoke waft across the bridge.

Everyone held their breath.

The autocannon opened fire.

A *lot* of fire.

Somewhere deep in the tedious equip-details drummed over the years into my mind, I recognised the sound. The angry rattle, the hollow retorts of heavy calibre shells thumping – *stamping* – against the *Inferno*.

M242 Bushmaster. 25mm chain cannon, 200 rounds a minute. Probably ripped from some heavy-arsed Bradley tank and installed messily, incongruously, in the rear of that stupid little AFV. The whole thing shuddered and shifted backwards with the recoil, brakes clawing at the earth, but it didn't matter. Didn't make a fucking spot of difference.

The *Inferno* simply *tattered.* The shells didn't dent the sides, they ripped them. Metal shredded like cheap fabric, panels peeling back in lacerated strips, exit-wounds worthy of cranial trauma that blasted an organic gore of shrapnel and slag through the blockade's rear quarters.

Only a matter of time before the fuel tanks went up.

And then Rick was running, hopping between geysers of fire and dust, leather trousers ripped and bloody where shards of concrete had jumped up to slash his ankles, and the gunner swept the cannon to find him – thunderous blasts picking apart macadam, drawing close to his heels –

– and he was gone, diving with a shriek over the edge of the bridge, lost to the waters below. The gunner turned back to his first target with a dogged sort of *well-I'll-be-blowed-if-I-don't-get-to-have-some-fun* determination, and finally – throbbing at the air like a stuttering bass – found the fuel tanks.

The *Inferno* tried to fly. A heavy jet of black flame glommed from its belly, blew out its arse, lifted it up in a halo of flapping damage and slammed it down, keening on its side, to creak and vent fire.

"That's coming out of your deposit," Malice whispered. I smirked.

From across the lake came an uproarious cheer, broken and muffled by the fog, but *loud.* Wide. Spread out. Hidden there in the fog, waiting to emerge, were a *lot* of people.

And onwards they came. The AFV jinking to one side, making way for a lumbering colossus that might once have been a truck-cab but now – via the careful application of welds, armour plates and a fucking enormous dozer-scoop – looked a little more like a medieval dragon, lower jaw hanging open.

The Iroquois remained hidden.

Behind the hulking machine came others like it. HGV cabs bristling with guns, AFVs plugging gaps, converted civilian vehicles painted in the Clergy's colours and distorted by weaponry, spikes, ramming-noses. It poured from the quicksmog like a tide of filth, like an armada emerging from sea fog; robed figures standing at arms on every surface. Behind it came the carriers. Vast lorries, armoured but unarmed. Buses and coaches riding low on their suspension, figures crammed behind mesh windows. Plated limousines and SUVs, blue-and-scarlet flags fluttering like a presidential cavalcade.

I realised, then, why the resistance had been so lacklustre at the Secretariat building. Why so few Clergymen were left to guard the gates, and why so many ran, as we swarmed inside, towards the other parts of the compound.

They'd known we were coming. Cy's timely warning, spies on every street. They'd known we could wash across them despite their sternest defences, and so they'd loaded themselves aboard a long-prepared convoy, and taken the only course open to them:

Exodus.

And now here they were. All of them.

I understood, abruptly, why the Tadodaho had brought me here. Why this moment was so important to him, and Rick, and the rest of the tribe. And more than that: to the scavs in the cities, to the people back home in London, to Bella – if she'd been here to see it...

To me.

A chance to cut the heads off the bloody Hydra, if you like. Not my business, nothing to do with me, not my problem, but still. Something I had to do.

The Iroquois remained hidden.

The dozer-scoop behemoth inched towards the flaming wreck of the *Inferno*, preparing to shunt it, and the caravans beside it, to one side. I wondered how big a threat the Clergy had estimated this curious little blockade to be, and sincerely hoped the answer was:

Not big enough.

The radio in my pocket hissed.

"*...kkk...* orth bridge..."

"Go ahead," I whispered, watching the convoy crawl cautiously forwards.

"...ot outriders up here... crossing now. Ten bikes, two AVs..."

A second voice cut in – the thoughtful tones of Slowbear:

"...ame here. South bridge. They've sent a lorry over as well..."

"Stand by," I said, feeling the adrenaline coming up, imagining the two groups away through the haze, one on each of the smaller bridges, sneaking round to flank us. I saw them smirking and tittering, feeling oh-so-bloody-clever, mumbling bullshit about classic pincer movements, surprise attacks, blah-blah-blah.

I fished in my other pocket and handed a small black box to Malice, pointing to the top button. "The honours," I said. It seemed only fair.

She smiled, dipped her head with *faux* graciousness, and stabbed at the button.

The dozer scoop in front and above us hit the *Inferno*'s side and squealed in protest.

And then ceased to be the main event.

The light came first. Obviously. From both directions at once; a sudden flicker of white and yellow, pulsing across the entirety of the quicksmog like a firework lost in the clouds, then building more focus as the first flash of the explosion gave way to a pair of dancing fireballs; one on each side, great pyrotechnic monsters that clambered into the air and dissipated into the mist.

Then the sound. Almost perfectly synchronised; two rolling thunderbolts that echoed and coalesced in the eerie fog, becoming a single sub-aqueous *roar.*

And then screams. Even at this distance, even separated by water and haze, the shrieks of the maimed and the groans of the dying. Ghostly. Haunting.

The Collectors had left behind their C4 and their snazzy little detonators when they tried to kill us in the night. It would have been rude to waste them.

"*kkk...* orth bridge... Got 'em... *got* the fuckers... bridge is down, bridge is down!"

"...owbear here, same for the south. Hoo-ee! Can't see for smoke yet, but they're not coming any further..."

The dozer-scoop shunted the *Inferno* like a casual distraction, bashing as it went into the side of the nearest caravan. The driver wasn't watching. I guessed he was staring in shock at the baleful firelight hovering on either side in the distance, or shouting into a radio, or just wondering *what the fuck is going on.*

Distracted, one way or another. Otherwise he might have noticed the cables. Iron cords, tied off to the railings at either side of the bridge, each one carefully tensioned, leading in through the shattered windows of the caravans.

Each one holding aloft, in the stripped-out spaces inside, a dangling gallery of jam jars.

Each of which contained a single fragmentation baseball grenade, pin removed, trigger prevented from releasing by the glass of the jars.

Fort Wayne barracks, Slowbear had told me during the night. One of the few armouries that hadn't emptied its supplies into the Clergy's hands. Forget bows and bloody arrows. These injuns were *packing.*

The first caravan shifted. Jerked against the other, like marbles colliding.

On both sides of the bridge, the cables went slack. A tinny sound of shattering glass filled the air, and maybe I was imagining it or maybe I suddenly went fucking *psychic*, but I swear to God I could hear the driver in that colossal sodding rig mutter:

"Aw, piss."

A second or two, with the echoes of the C4-detonations still ringing, and then:

Think Baghdad. Think Hiroshima. Think surface of the fucking *sun.*

It was big, and flashy, and I could feel the heat from my cover. Frag-shrapnel turning the air to razorwire, men somersaulting out of gunner-mounts on the cusp of the blast, flesh sliding off bone, fingers clutching at air then clutching at nothing. The lorry-rig bounced onto its rear, its nose in the air, then crashed down in dust and death on the vehicles behind, bouncing in a way that something that big *shouldn't.* Driver and gunners alike screamed and died, sliced to ribbons; soot and black smoke washed over the top of the bridge and the tarmac *gaped* where the explosives had tripped. The caravans were gone. The *Inferno*'s shredded corpse was gone. What remained was modern art.

And finally the Iroquois rose-up from their cover, screamed like an operatic banshee, and let loose.

It would have been a massacre. We had them boxed-in. Exposed on the bridge, unable to back out at speed. We had machineguns and grenades and autocannons. We had a couple of rusty old mortars that found their range after two watery explosions (by which time Rick had already clambered, panting, ashore, so no damage there) and a crateful of anti-tank rockets which all the Haudenosaunee had been clamouring to play with.

Above all we had surprise and stealth, and well-camouflaged men and women using smoke and shadows and patience. We had so much lead and fire raining down on those pricks that they never realised how much knifework went on, how much scurrying and slicing was taking place in the noxious gaps between packed-in vehicles.

I know. I was there. I was *doing* it.

It *would* have been a massacre. It started out just dandy. The Iroquois vehicles came tearing back up, the bikes slipped onto the bridge to sow madness and death, AVs and lorry rigs popped like fiery bubbles with each shrieking mortar-round, and *oh, God yeah* it felt good. Malice and me with pistols and knives, scrambling over bonnets and under tankers, slipping grenades through open windows whilst drivers shouted and raged at the back-up, then scuttled off to listen for the *boom*...

Great times.

And fine, the convoy just kept getting bigger and bigger. More and more lorries oozing from the haze, trying to back up, trying to manoeuvre in the madness. Fine, there were a lot more of the bastards than we expected, a lot more guns and psychos slowly getting their act together and returning fire. Fine, it would have been *messy.* But we *had* them. We could've *taken* them.

And then my radio hissed, and everything changed.

Malice and I were holed up behind the vast tyres of an earthmover, waiting for the wanker in the cab to stop blasting our end of the bridge with whatever fat-shell cannon he was manning for long enough to sneak up there and blow his brains out, when Slowbear's voice broke through the maelstrom, tinny and tense.

"...ou there? Oh shit... oh shit... This is Slowbear! Are you there?"

"Yeah, here. What is it?"

Something bit at the rubber tyre next to me and made the whole vehicle shudder. Malice winced.

"The lorry! The... shit... shit... *kkkhh*... the lorry on the south bridge!"

"We got it, right?"

"Yes! F-fuck, yes, it's not that, it's..."

"Slowbear?"

"...t's full of children! You hear me?"

Malice's eyes bulged.

"...orries are all full of fucking *children!*"

It *would* have been a massacre.

We turned and ran back to our lines without another word, and as we strafed through optimistic fire streams I caught a glimpse of Malice's eyes, and the liquid glistening inside them. She'd left her baby with the matriarchs in safety, but still... it didn't take a genius to figure out what she was thinking.

It'd been her that pressed the button, after all.

A weird noise filled my head. Like an engine, but airier; filtered through the fog and the gunfire, distorted by the screams and shouts all around. I wondered if I'd damaged my ear more badly than I'd thought, then shook my head and stopped worrying. What, exactly, could I do about it anyway? I spotted the incline facing the bridge where we'd left Nike and Moto, and together with Malice I scrambled up the bank, forgetting all about the noise, concentrating on staying alive.

...thrp-thrp-thrp-thrp-thrp...

Nike and Moto were hunkered-down with five Iroquois holding shoulder-launchers. Nate was there too, watching, staying apart and looking shifty. I ignored him and he ignored me, making a show of staring directly upwards into the turbulent quicksmog. It seemed to be getting worse. Odd bursts of fire snapped at the tops of the ridge, off-target but getting closer, and before I could take the time to work out *how* someone was keeping track with us, at this distance, at this elevation, we threw ourselves down into safety. Rick was standing below the grenadiers, sopping water and trying to catch his breath, dishing out the tank busters.

"Aim for the lorries..." he was saying, unable to keep the twinkle of testosterone-choked-male out of his eye. He'd done his part. He'd lured the fuckers into the trap. No wonder he sounded older.

Nike was already lifting himself gingerly into a sitting position, head above the edge of the ridge, tube to his shoulder, when Malice gathered her breath and shouted:

"No! Stop! Don't fire!"

The older man swivelled his head to look at her, brows furrowing.

"But wh..."

The hesitation almost killed him. A round caromed dustily off the ground beside his face, within inches of splitting his head. He swore out loud and let gravity pull him back down into cover, the rest of us tugging him along in a knot of shouts and grunts. When we'd got him back down to the bottom of the ridge Moto flopped down next to him and clutched at his arm, horrified.

"Fuck..." Nike said, eyes wide. "Did you... fuck. Did you *see* that?"

And then his head really *did* split open.

Suddenly I was wearing him. Bits of blood and brain in my eyes, shards of bone stinging the exposed skin on my face. His body slumped and smoked, and next to it Moto's mouth went up and down like nothing made sense, like everything had gone dark.

How? My brain was screaming. *How did someone...?*

We're in fucking cover!

Out in the haze, the noise again. An angry dragonfly-throb, cut through with a motorised grind.

...thrp-thrp-thrp-thrp...

Moto's face had gone perfectly slack.

He picked up the rocket launcher. Malice scrabbled against his arm, trying to pull him off, and he hit her – hard – on the cheek. His expression didn't change. She fell; he turned. Rose to the top of the bank. Aimed.

And then everything went white and black, and I realised with a giddy sort of uncertainty that either the rocket had misfired, or someone had shot the launcher, and now – look – I was flying, and my hair was on fire, and everything hurt.

I landed and lay and didn't move. Staring straight up, as fire and smoke and chaos thundered all around me. I wondered if anyone else was still alive.

...thrp-thrp-thrp-thrp-thrp...

The quicksmog billowed. Surged. *Boiled.*

And finally I recognised the sound. Finally I figured out how the fuckers had shot Nike, I figured out how come they'd been taking potshots at me and Malice ever since we scrambled up here. How they'd blasted Moto's launcher before he could even squeeze the trigger, and blew us all to shit.

Why Nate was staring straight up.

There were lights above me. Rockets zipping down in all directions. Iroquois screaming, vehicles exploding. A sniper rifle *krak-krak-krak*ing from on-high.

And as the pain in my ribs exploded behind my eyes, and I sucked hard to get anything resembling a breath, my last thought was:

Nobody told me *the fuckers had helicopters...*

CHAPTER EIGHTEEN

Rick could move his arms. Broadly speaking.

He'd never been in a 'copter before. Big novelty. The vibrations had woken him, he supposed. He'd always fancied going up in a chopper when he was a kid, but he'd never imagined it'd be like this. Lying in pain on a grille floor, feeling something sticky that was probably puke on his cheek, knowing full well there was a trio of Clergy-fucks standing nearby with big-ass Russian guns aimed at his head.

He had opened his eyes a moment ago. He was still regretting it.

They'd left the bay doors open. They'd laid him out right next to the damned thing, so his first sight was green fields and jagged hills, gushing past below.

A long, long, long way below.

Yeah. Big fucking novelty.

To be honest, he couldn't even decide if he really was awake or not. Even with his eyes closed again, lights kept dancing weirdly in front of him, odd sensations were shooting up and down his left arm, and every time he tried to concentrate on anything the world went grey and prickly. Eventually he came to the conclusion he must be concussed. Maybe brain-damaged. Maybe dying.

Whatever.

He cast his mind back to the battle on the bridge, and tried to sort out what had happened. He remembered diving into the lake. Swimming to safety. Finding the little knot of Haudenosaunee fighters – all from different lodges, none of them recognisable – and staggering over to get some help for his bleeding legs. He remembered the way they'd looked at him – looked up *at him – and instead of rushing round to check he was okay and pat him on the head, they'd pointed at the tank buster grenades and asked him:*

What shall we do?

A couple of weeks ago he would've avoided the war-painted pricks with their stupid clothes and daft ceremonies, and living-off-the-fucking-land, and 'Great Spirits' and 'Earth Initiates' and 'Ghost Dances' and yadda-yadda-yadda, and here he was: a leader.

Well then, he'd thought.

Might as well lead.

He remembered telling them what to do. Remembered the itch at the rear of his head, just like he'd felt back in NY, back when he was Hiawatha, except this time it was him *in charge and that older, wiser, weirder voice consigned to an echo that he could attend or ignore as he chose. Best of both worlds.*

He remembered the dull flicker of green and purple fire on the edge of his subconscious, and turning round on cue to find the Stranger sprinting up with that sexy black chick in tow, and that old guy Nike going splat, and the kid with the scarred face flipping out, and reaching out to stop him, and –

And then something about light and fire, and pain.

And then confused blur-memories of a lot of people screaming and a lot of people dying, and men in grey and white laughing and shouting, and chanting in choral voices whilst guns chattered. And a radio hissing something about they're all fucking dead, they're all fucking dead, *and a general retreat, and then the howl of rotors.*

And that was about all.

Rick figured he'd been blown up. It certainly goddamn felt *like he'd been blown up. He wondered how come he was still alive at all, and why these robe-wearing assholes were dragging him off to who-knew-where, rather than just... squashing him. He felt like he should be more scared than he was, but inside the sweat-lodge of his skull Hiawatha sat and played strange songs on stranger instruments, and everything was okay. Nothing hurt, except in the physical sense.*

Which somehow just... didn't count any more.

Rick risked opening his eyes again, this time turning his head with a nauseous lurch to the other side, ignoring a muttered command from somewhere far away that might have been "stay still, fucko."

Yeah, yeah. Whatever.

He wasn't alone. Three other shapes, bundled side-by-side, head-to-toe, lay beside him. He kept his face down, focusing close through clouds of greyout blur.

All he could see of the recumbent figure directly next to him was a pair of boots. Muddy and bloody, fastened over tattered combats and the hem of a raggedy coat. Blazing, from the corner of his eyes, with a warm fiery glow.

The Stranger.

Beyond him was Malice. Her face was gone. Her skin was charred and burnt, her hair singed away in great bloody patches all over her scalp. If she was still alive, she didn't look it. Her eye was open. Unblinking. Staring straight at him.

Next to her were Nate's feet. Crazy red sneakers with army regs tucked into them, tied-together with a single loop of wire. He couldn't see past Malice's charred body to check if the old junkie was still alive or not.

All three lay, like him, on their bellies; arms twisted into the smalls of their backs, where pairs of black cuffs held them in place. Rick tried to move his own arms, unsurprised to feel a fresh tsunami of agony (all a million miles away, not worth worrying about) swarming along his left wrist. They felt impeded, sure, but there was something loose *about the whole arrangement, a sort of dried, gluey stickiness rather than metal solidity.*

Weird.

He tilted his head as best as he could, to peer down towards his own feet; hogtied, just like everyone else. Next to them, the Stranger was looking at him. Eyes open and alive, jaw clenched. Blood and flesh covered his face, and it was difficult to tell how much of it was his. They stared silently at each other for a moment or two, then the Stranger's eyes flipped downwards towards Rick's back.

Then back up again.

"Your hand's gone," he whispered.

"Shut the fuck *up!" one of the Clergymen screamed, stamping hard on the Stranger's head and mashing one lacerated cheek against the grille. Rick barely noticed, exploring his own body with a morbid sense of certainty.*

The stranger was right. His left hand. His left hand was gone.

Well, shit.

It felt like they'd bound it up, maybe. Rags or bandages, tied at pressure, holding the arteries closed. Then they'd slapped the same old cuffs over the top of it and left him to it, maybe expecting him to die from blood loss, maybe just not caring.

He could move his wrist. He could unglue it from the sticky mess of dried blood and pull it free from the cuff. And if he could do that, it meant his other hand – no, his only *hand – would be free to move.*

Hiawatha sang a new song. The wind against the back of his head, from that great drop beyond, tousled his long hair and whispered strange things in his ear. Something about... about a gift?

He shifted his weight, trying to determine if any other interesting parts of his anatomy were missing. The pockets of his leathers had been chock-full of ammunition and handguns before the blast knocked him out, but now all he could feel about his person was a shitload of bruises and something tiny – sharp, but swaddled-up – in the zip-pocket on his ass.

The wind giggled.

The gift, *it told him.* Remember?

And then he knew what to do.

Poor kid.

Shell-shocked, I thought. *He's been blown up. He's woken up dangling over an abyss surrounded by fanatic goons, and he's got a bloody hand missing.*

Shit, *I'd* be shell-shocked.

Outside, the green blur of land streaking past began to turn sooty and black. A sharp smell – like burning oil – filled the chopper, and above my head the three Choirboys muttered to one another, shuffling discreetly towards the open bay to see below.

The Haudenosaunee camp, I guessed, set-up far back from the war zone at the bridge. I couldn't see past the edge to whatever they were marvelling at, but I could imagine it. Blackened vans and charred wagons. The Tadodaho's weird mobile-home collapsing in embers and smoke. What else could it be?

We'd been roundly beaten; us plucky idiots with our ambush and our rebellion. Slaughtered and routed for our hubris. Taken prisoner. Taken away.

The smoke got thicker. I decided not to look.

Nor, evidently, did Rick. With the guards distracted his arms were moving slowly, gingerly releasing the swaddled stump of his left wrist from the cuffs and, thus freed, his right hand easing – *inching* – towards the pocket of his trousers.

What did he have in there, I wondered? What had the idiot-goons missed when they went through our stuff, rifling for weapons? What cunning escape plan was he cooking up?

"Lord Almighty," one of the Choirboys grunted, half reverential, half cursing, staring out into space, now almost completely choked with black smoke. The dancing light of flames lit his face from below, giving him and his comrades an eerie, devilish look. I imagined the tribal matriarchs screaming as they burned. The Tadodaho coughing on the thick pall. Malice's baby, left in their care, breaking its silence and starting – briefly – to wail.

Rick drew a folded rag from his pocket. Manipulated it with careful fingers, unwrapping it millimetre by millimetre. The cloth fell away with a dreamlike slowness, and I discovered myself holding my breath; desperate to see what he'd squirreled away.

My heart dropped.

It was a silver needle. Long and sharp, barely thicker than a hypodermic, slightly distorted by its time in his pocket. Not quite the weapon of mass destruction I'd envisaged.

There was a time, once – somewhere in the Middle East, I recall, on business – when I got into some bad shit and found myself up against a knifeman with nothing to defend myself but a table fork. Don't laugh. This shit happens.

For the record, he perforated my right lung before I got close enough to stab him through his eyeball – and that was without having a bruised and battered body up-front. Without gun-wielding maniacs watching. Without sodding handcuffs. With a fucking *hand* missing.

Good luck, kid.

Rick was staring at me again, needle held concealed in his hand.

"Sorry," he whispered. Then: "Trust me."

And then he was moving. Sudden and unexpected, face contorted, hefting himself off the floor and onto my back, flexing his legs to get towards me.

"Fucking limey asshole!" he snarled. "Fucking prick! You said you'd stop them! You said you'd save us!"

"What?" I hissed. "But..."

"*Kill* you, sonuvabitch! Look what they did! You said you'd stop them! Just fucking *die*!"

And then he was pressed over me, and his mouth was next to my neck, and *oh my God* he was *biting* me. Trying to rip out my bloody throat. I shouted and hollered – more confused than anything – and tried to shake my body to get him off. The guards were reacting slowly, turning back from their sightseeing in a chorus of curses and exclamations, throwing horrified glances up and over my shoulder to the bulkhead that led into the chopper's cockpit.

From where – cold and forced, like steel scraping cobwebs – there came a voice.

"What," it said. "The *fuck*. Is going on?"

Rick's teeth dug in further, but in an abstract section of my brain – not actively shrieking and demanding answers of this ludicrous situation – it occurred to me that by now he *could* have killed me if he'd wanted to. He wasn't even biting that hard.

The guards grabbed him and tried to wrestle him off.

And between us, in the secret concealed shadows of the ruckus, something sharp and tiny punched into the fleshy meat of my right buttock, buried itself there, and went still.

What the – ?

And then Rick was gone, hauled away, severed hand squirting blood through its disarrayed bandages. The guards clung to rails and handles, bracing him, facing the owner of that cold, grating voice.

"Sir?" one said.

"Hold him," it hissed. I recognised it, sort of. It was sharper than before, more strained, like it'd been pushed through a filter of trauma and hate.

It can't be –

But it was. He stepped over me, dainty steps untroubled by the chopper's shuddering, and crouched down to stare directly into Rick's face.

The boy smiled. "I should've pushed harder, huh?" he said.

Cardinal Cy snarled.

The knife was still embedded in his head. From behind, I could see its ghastly angle, hilt decorated with antiseptic patches and freakish lumps of bandaging. It had gone deep. Deep enough to fuck with his brain.

It didn't seem to have slowed him down.

He put a hand – almost tender – on Rick's cheek. "Old man says... old man says. Bring troublemakers to him. Ones who caused all this. Fuss. Likes to tidy things up personal. Y'see?"

Rick spat on the surface of his red glasses.

"Mm." Cy smiled, wagging a finger. "Mm. Except, except, except. Never even *saw* you, did he? Doesn't even know. So. Maybe you're too much trouble, eh? Don't you think? Maybe I should tidy up. Personally."

He twisted Rick's face to the side, hand digging deep into his cheeks and brow, forcing him down and round, making him stare out into the empty sky below the chopper.

I stayed silent. Wondered at the weird pain in my arse – the silver needle, I supposed – and watched. Waited for Rick's face to contort in horror as he saw the remnants of his tribe's war party burning away.

I couldn't have been more wrong.

"Lake Erie," Cy said. "Know what I heard? Used to be... so much shit came downriver, man could almost walk across. Some years, surface caught *fire*. Believe that?"

He pushed Rick's head further down, forcing him out, smoke billowing round him, held up only by the arms of the guards.

"Course... nowadays, all sorts. Weird shit pouring in. Oil from them... big refineries up north. All deserted. Gas, debris, timber. You name it. And pal... no fucker left to put out them fires.

"Now, the old man. When he kills a guy, just got one way. But me? I'm understanding. Got *mercy*. So what it is... Giving you a choice. How to die.

"Three options. Number one. You drown. Number two. You burn. And number three. You fall from on high."

The Cardinal put a hand on Rick's chest.

"Decide on the way down. Huh?" he said.

Rick said something in a language I didn't understand. His face changed. *Smoothed out.*

And then he smiled at me, and I cried out something wordless, and Cy pushed, and he was gone.

Below, wow!

Below, thunderbirds soared on fiery thermals. They keened and screamed as he fell, and squabbled to catch him.

And the trees sang and the wind murmured, and far away buffaloes grunted moronic greetings, and he settled as light as a feather on the back of the greatest fire-crow of all. It laughed and laughed, and so did he, and in its eye was lightning, and as it rose across the burning lakes Rick-Hiawatha felt something dull and insubstantial continue to fall away from him: something heavy and clumsy and solid, which he didn't need anymore.

The thunderbird kept pace with a garishly-painted helicopter for a moment, then veered off into the smoke, heading for the sounds of the plains.

IT'D END HERE. I'd figured that much out already.

Don't call it a hunch, or a spooky sensation. Call it reality. Call it there's-no-fucking-way-I'm-getting-out-of-here-except-dead-or-victorious.

Call it: I know when to stop chasing.

It would end on this green-and-brown splat of land, choked up by the curtains of smoke that hid the horizon and denied the mainland ever existed. It would end, for better or worse – probably worse – in the middle of a sludge-like lake, whole patches of which were flaming away happily, with a trail of dead people behind me, a psychotic cardinal with a knife in his brain bearing a grudge, and a throbbing pain in my right buttock.

Way to go.

They'd chained me to a sign. Mottled and half-cracked where a small golf-buggy had toppled into it (and indeed sat there still, crumpled and rusting in the tall grass) it was the only thing to keep me amused whilst the world turned blithely on around me, and I'd read it several times already.

It announced that in 1813 a bloke by the name of Oliver Hazard Perry kicked the shit out of a fleet of British ships on Lake Erie. I'm paraphrasing. It was a minor engagement, all things considered, but had a knock-on effect that ensured that a year down the line the peace talks were in full swing. Eventually some bright spark decided a memorial to the guy in charge was exactly what was needed, and it only took a hundred years to raise the cash. This was considered a triumph of human persistence rather than a lamentable token of inefficiency.

The sign was obviously intended to enlighten any visitor unfortunate enough to find themselves stranded on South Bass Island, and was crammed with interesting facts regarding the construction of said monument. At any other time I'd have expected to see fat tourists clustered around it making "ooh" sounds and taking pictures.

Alas, today, there was nobody but me to enjoy the info-feast. Instead there were dozens of armed Choirboys – men and women alike – spreading out across the tiny arsecrumb of land to convert any locals from their savage un-Christian ways to –

– well, death, probably. As it happened they hadn't found anyone yet, though they continued to kick in each mouldering door and holiday-home porch with optimistic enthusiasm. In the meantime I'd been left chained here with Nate – still not talking – to watch the two Clergy choppers ferry people from the shore. It was boring. It was boring and it was underscored by the imminent probability of my own death, which made it even worse. It was like these pricks had dug a hole in my stomach, told me to make peace with my maker, placed the gun against my head, then told me to amuse myself for a while.

As they dragged me out of the chopper I'd asked Cy what happened to the rest of the *Haudenosaunee*. He'd sneered and ignored the question. I couldn't work out if that was good or not. I couldn't work out if I cared.

The monument itself, for the record, stood nearby. I glanced up at it for the fiftieth time, on the off-chance it might be doing something interesting. Like so many military monuments it was basically a giant penis, cunningly disguised as a three-hundred-and-fifty foot Doric column with a bronze 'urn' (eleven tons, you'll be fascinated to learn) in the place of a throbbing glans, which was constructed, apparently, to *inculcate the lessons of international peace by arbitration and disarmament.*

Which was odd, because to me it looked a lot like it had been built to inculcate the lessons of international one-upmanship, specifically by stating: *my cock's bigger than yours.*

A foghorn blasted nearby, and I watched with a minor flicker of interest as the clapped-out old ferry they'd found deserted at Port Clinton made its third journey towards us, this time bearing two blue lorries and a school bus, undoubtedly crammed with scared kids in white robes. Next to me Nate stiffened, reminded of the innocuous job he'd held down for two years before all this mad shit started with a plane crash and a –

No. No, hang on.

'Innocuous' my arse. He was driving kids to a prison, or worse. And he knew it.

I hadn't entirely made my mind up yet how I felt about Nate.

I leaned back against the pillar of the signpost and sighed.

The long and the short of it was: the Clergy had invaded a nowheresville island in the middle of the burning Erie, *en masse*, and were in the process of transferring their *entire* stock of idiots, arseholes, arsenals and initiates. Don't ask me why. Don't ask me what they expected to find here, or how they thought it would advance their march towards a new future. I didn't know.

All I knew was that this place, this island, this dull little shithole, was where *I* had been diligently trying to reach too.

That sheet of paper from the file in the Secretariat, remember? The photo.

Reassignment Location, it said.

UN Installation Saffron. South Bass Island, Ohio.

The tourist map they'd chained me to didn't mention any UN installations. That would've made it too easy, I guess.

I sighed again.

There seemed to be a lot of activity around the base of the column. I couldn't see clearly from where I stood, but it looked like a lot of figures were waving a lot of hands, pointing and nodding profusely.

There was someone in a wheelchair with them, and it struck me that every now and again the crowds' gesturing hands would freeze, their heads would twist to stare down, and then a fresh wave of nodding and scraping and bowing, in response to whatever the chair-bound figure had said.

John-Paul, then.

The group disappeared behind the great stone column in an excited bundle, and I waited for them to emerge from the other side, pleased to be watching something mildly diverting. They never reappeared. They'd vanished.

"Huh," I said to myself. Nate glanced at me, briefly, as if maybe he thought I was about to talk to him.

I looked away.

My arse hurt. More specifically, my buttock hurt where a tiny silver pin had been rammed into it, and every now again I felt a fresh dribble of blood down the back of my leg. Every time I moved it stung, like it was worming deeper into the muscle, and every time that happened it made me think of Rick.

Tumbling off into smoke and death with a smile.

And that made me think of Malice.

Dumped, thoughtlessly, over the edge of the pier where the chopper landed, when one of the Choirboy crew bothered to tell Cy she looked like she'd croaked during the flight.

And that made me think of Bella.

And that made me think of... of something else.

And that made me think of all *sorts* of shit, which made the hole in my stomach burn and writhe, and my teeth clench, and my eyes sting, and –

You get the idea.

So I stopped thinking about the pain in my arse and ignored the voice growling – no, *shrieking* – in my skull:

Don't you fucking give up, soldier!

Dull, dull, dull.

The ferry docked, and the trucks rolled off. Someone shouted at someone else.

Gulls wheeled overhead on smoky updrafts. A hundred miles south and east, a bunch of dead Iroquois were going hard in the sun.

The chopper headed back across the lake. Somewhere in the distance came a short burst of gunfire, and I figured the goons must have found a local or two after all. The chopper wheeled off on a new course, vanishing into the smoke.

Time stretched on.

My arse continued to hurt.

In my head, Rick continued to tumble backwards, smiling.

Malice continued to sink and burn beneath the waters.

Spuggsy squished, Tora dragged off to be squabbled-over by human animals, Moto shot.

Bella screaming and thumping like a boneless doll against the insides of the pla –

"You think they'll kill us?"

Nate was looking at me. There was something like... *pleading*, in his eyes. Something that cut through all the shit, all the anger at how he'd used me, tagged along to get his fix, lied. Something that whispered frostily in my ear:

But didn't you use him too?

"Yeah," I said, not unkindly. "Probably."

I looked back at the monument. It was something to stare at, I guess. Didn't move, didn't change: just stood there, defying the wind, a granite prick raping the sk –

"Whoa," said Nate.

The monument moved.

At the top, the tip of the great upturned basilica creaked, squealed in protest, then opened.

"Well there's a thing," I mumbled.

It was like a flower blossoming. Petals rattling into place, unoiled pistons groaning deep inside the rock. Without being entirely sure when it changed from one to the other, I suddenly wasn't looking at an enormous phallus any more.

I was looking at a bloody gigantic broadcasting dish.

And then Cy was standing in front of me, sneering.

"Time to go," he rasped.

CHAPTER NINETEEN

With each new room, a new calamity of memory. A new disastrous, deadly (wonderful) explosion of sights and smells and sounds, bubbling up from the past, like liquid pouring into a mould; taking its time to slip into the deepest recesses.

Or, like dust blowing free from a hidden treasure.

Like cataracts dissolving.

His Holiness the Abbot John-Paul Rohare Baptiste allowed his minions to wheel him through the great, secret facility beneath South Bass Island, saying nothing, and felt his memories slither back one by one. They gathered pace the deeper he went, with each new level, each new string of concrete walls, each new dim light fixture that flickered and illuminated as it sensed movement.

Until eventually he remembered it all, like it had just been yesterday.

He'd arrived here, on the Island, five years ago: angry and bitter. It was beneath *him, he'd thought. A man of his experience – of his record – sent to keep an eye on a bunch of backroom nerds.*

Sergeant John P. Miller, the reassignment form had said. NATO Liaison Officer.

It should have said: fucking nursemaid.

But still the facility had been a pleasant surprise. Hidden away beneath the monument, below vaults supposedly for the Lake Erie dead – in fact crammed with generators and feeds from the solar panels above – down creaking elevator shafts and plunging stairwells. Always the drip-drip-drip of condensed water.

Oh-so-very exciting. Oh-so-very impressive. It almost made up for the ignominy.

Here and now in the present, his assistants wheeled him past doors marked LAB #1, LAB #2, LAB #3...

He didn't like using the chair – it created the wrong impression – but it'd been an exhausting journey from the city and he wasn't as spry as he was. He was forty nine years old. He looked approximately seventy.

This was living with anaphylaxis. Constant pain.

This was living with AIDS, and more drugs than he could count, administered by Clergy-doctors who'd have their testicles ripped off and fed to them if they breathed a word to anyone.

This was three anti-coagulation shots every day, and antihistamine solutions three times a week.

This was the AB-virus, eating his blood cells every second, staved off only by communing with the divine.

This was living by numbers.

This place, it'd been a nuclear bunker once. So his superiors told him. Secondary or tertiary governmental; an alternative to the presidential chambers beneath Washington and NY. Somewhere safe to rule an irradiated country. Somewhere cosy for a ragged government to sip clean water and make comforting addresses.

The whole thing had been converted at short-notice to the requirements of the UN team. Dormitories and armouries stripped-out, curious equipment shipped-in for days on end. 'Project Pandora,' they'd called it. An international attempt to stop the virus in its steps.

Out loud, as his wheelchair squeaked its way down the ramp to the sub-third floor, he mumbled:

"When all the evil spills out, there's still a... glimmer of hope..."

Pandora's box.

His chief minder must have heard him. An effete man named Marcus, good for very little but wheeling a chair and kissing arse, he gave John-Paul a concerned glance and crouched down to address him, unintentionally condescending. John-Paul approved of ignorance and ineffectuality. The soldiery were all very well; the cardinals and their units served a purpose, but one couldn't trust them. They were too full of their own ideas. Too focused.

"Your holiness?" The man said softly. "Did you say something?"

"Mm? No, no..." he closed his eyes and let the memories absorb him again, enjoying the concern on the man's face. "Everything's fine, Marcus."

He remembered wondering, at the time, why they'd sent the team here. *Why not to some scholarly lab in New York? Why not out in the open?*

And then the riots had started. They'd listened to the news every day before work, gathered together in the social room. Riots and police actions and union strikes, and embassies closing down at a rate of knots.

Then the diplomatic wrangling.

Then the rumours of DefCon escalation.

Then the standoffs and false alarms and real-actual-genuine-fear-of-Armageddon type talks, and suddenly everyone was living in a bad disaster film, and Sergeant John P. Miller became very very grateful indeed that his superiors had sent him deep underground.

Even then, *he'd been bored out of his brain. The team's progress was just so* slow.

No – correction: the team's progress was non-existent. *It just took them forever to figure that out.*

Outside, the world went to hell in a handcart, and inside... inside, test-tubes clinked and microscopes whirred and men and women in white lab-coats made fussy notes with fussy biros. A lot of them had families. A lot of them looked unwell.

More rooms glided past the wheelchair, now circuiting the fifth level. Comms, Resources, the door names went, Records, Studio, Engineering...

The place was enormous. He remembered thinking that, *too, all those years ago. Far too big for the research team. They'd set themselves up in their little corners and got on with it, and with nothing to do but file reports that said* 'No progress,' *he'd taken to wandering, exploring, poking in the dark.*

A mothballed war room, with its displays darkened and tactical consoles disconnected.

A water purification plant.

A dozen storerooms marked Non-Perishable. All empty.

And the communications room. And the broadcast suite.

And the Presidential Address studio. Plush red and blue walls. Elegantly draped flags. TV cameras jacketed in plastic wraps and rubber covers.

That *was it.* That *was what brought him back here, now. In the flash of a triggered memory – those records unearthed from the Secretariat, presented to him by Cardinal Cy even as the doctors fussed over his bleeding skull – he'd remembered the place, the resources, the cameras and broadcasting equipment and security.*

And as the exodus convoy had slipped away from the overrun UN headquarters – lost, futureless, despairing – that crumpled file from all those years ago had been like a bolt from the heavens. A sign. In that perfect instant he'd known, clearly and immediately, where to take his Clergy to find safety and security.

It was perfect. An island with its own tiny airstrip. Easily defendable. Perfectly secure quarters for the luminaries of the sect. Plentiful housing for the soldiery and devotees. Vast holding-rooms below ground where anything could be conducted in secret and silence. Airports a mere spit away in Cleveland, Toledo, Detroit...

And the studio. It couldn't be *any better.*

Halfway down the main hallway of the fifth sub-level a priest stood waiting, dressed strangely. He wore not robes but overalls – oil-stained and heavy with tool pockets – but in deference to his spiritual allegiance they were pale grey, with a scarlet circle on the breast, and the same pattern tattooed over his left eye.

Marcus waved towards him with an introductory nod. "Chief Engineer Maclusky, your holiness."

"Mm. Yes? Yes?"

The man dipped in a bow that combined deference, religious awe and sphincter-tearing-terror. John-Paul resisted a smirk.

"Studio's up and running, your holiness. Cameras work fine. Shocking, frankly, but then again they built this shit to last and I guess we can't be surpr..." The man stopped. His eyes snapped wide as his brain caught up with his rambling and noticed what it'd just said. "Uh... E-excuse my French, your holiness, i-it's n..."

"Please go on, child."

"W-well, uh."

"The cameras."

"Yeah, yeah, well... they ain't maybe as advanced as we're used to, but..."

"That doesn't matter. We can find new ones, eventually. As long as we can broadcast."

"Yeah, yeah." Another mad little bow. "The dish needs some tuning – but no problem. Up and running whenever you want it."

"Good. Very good. One hour."

The man's eyes bugged out again. 'Whenever you want it' clearly hadn't included 'right now.'

"One hou...! B-but..."

"That's a problem?"

"B-but... uh, no. No, your holiness, no. It's just... I assumed you'd want to wait for Sunday. H-how will people know we're going to be broadcasting?"

John-Paul treated the sweating man to a look that contrived to inform him his assumptions weren't worth a scrotumful of diseased spunk, then broke into a friendly little smile.

He liked to keep people off-balance.

"Aha." He said. "The people *aren't my first concern, my child. The Cells need to know we've moved. London, Paris, Moscow, Beijing...*

All those little mini-churches, happily ferrying the Divine Initiates to LaGuardia. What will they do, I wonder, when they get there?"

The terrified man shook his head. He dripped.

"No, no. What we need is a message of reassurance. Just to... let them know where we are. Where to re-route. A permanent broadcast. A loop. You can manage that, I trust?"

"W-well, yes, I should think that would be..."

"Good. One hour, then. I believe I will be feeling rather stronger, by then."

The wheelchair squeaked on, and left the engineer behind. John-Paul hummed to himself.

At the end of another corridor, round a pair of sharp right angles, was one final doorway. It was marked:

DETENTION.

His smile dipped.

Here.

Here was where it all began.

It made sense, he supposed. A nuclear bunker, containing dozens of important personalities and their families, all crushed together for an extended period. It was inevitable, perhaps, that tempers would fray. Behaviour would slip. A wise precaution, then, including somewhere to let troublemakers cool down. To keep them out of harm's way.

Another aide opened the door, infuriatingly casual, and John-Paul felt cold prickles shivering across his entire body. Didn't they know? Didn't they understand?

Here.

It began here.

Five years ago, this was where it happened.

The research. The virus getting inside. The first symptoms. The discovery of the trend – the O-negatives unaffected, the antigens revealing their secrets – and the broadcast to the UN to let them know. Then the luckiest ones shutting themselves away, fearing the anger of the dying. The place was supposed to be airtight. How did the disease get in? Who was to blame?

For just a little while, the place became... hell.

There were gaps in what he remembered. Something a little like insanity had gripped the bunker, for a time. But here in this room he'd let God touch his blood, and let his memories swallow themselves up, and let purity cleanse his bitter soul; and then there was nothing... nothing at all... until he staggered out of the haze and into New York, to claim his destiny.

It was a curious sensation, returning.

They wheeled him into the dull little chamber, stepped formally aside and let him see.

The prisoners.

He smiled. He smiled with a vicious little glimmer of glee at seeing these fuckheads, these arch-devils, stripped of their clothes and humiliated, beaten and captured. He stared with an imperious smirk at their exposed genitals and the bruises criss-crossing their bodies. He sneered and smiled and tittered quietly. He was smug and arrogant and self-righteous, and the best thing was: he didn't care.

"Leave us," he told the aides. "Wait outside. Someone find Cardinal Cy. He'll want to watch, I think."

They were smart enough not to argue, leaving in a silent gaggle of grey and white. John-Paul called out to Marcus as he reached the threshold.

"Y-yes your holiness?"

"Prepare the equipment, Marcus. Hurry back."

"The... the cameras?"

"No, Marcus. The other *equipment."*

"Oh... oh, y-yes. Of course." The young man swallowed, blinking. "Where would you like to... uh..."

"Here, Marcus. Right here. I shall... commune... *with the Lord before we broadcast. I will perform the miracle, I think. People must see that all is as it should be."*

"I understand, your holiness."

"See to it."

"Y-yes, uh..." he lingered, shifting his weight awkwardly.

"What is it?"

"The... the communion. *Would you like me to fetch an... an initiate?"*

John-Paul stared at him for a moment or two, then broke into a wide smile.

"No," he said. "No, Marcus. My friends here are all I require."

And he smiled up at the prisoners, and Marcus scraped and kowtowed his way through the door. It swung shut with a heavy clang behind him.

And then there were three.

His Holiness the Abbot John-Paul Rohare Baptiste turned to face the pair of bruised fucks who'd caused him so much annoyance, and said:

"Blessed are the children."

"You what?" I grunted.

He smiled.

My arse, for the record, continued to hurt.

The detention room was a boring cube with a grille-fronted cell set into each of the three walls unoccupied by the door. Rather than sling me and Nate into the cells themselves – oh no, that would've allowed us all sorts of unfair luxuries like being able to bloody *sit down* – Cy and his goons had cuffed us with our hands behind our backs to the front of the grilles themselves, then taken great pleasure in stripping off our clothes and covering us from head to toe in foul-smelling antiseptic powder. The upshot was that we were standing there buck-naked, stinking like necrotic kippers, unable to either turn, sit or slouch without dislocating our shoulders, and now faced with an unlikely audience with a chairbound old git with a gargantuan hat.

My top ten surreal moments had a brand new highest entry.

"The children," he repeated, watery little eyes glimmering. "Blessed, blessed, blessed. Mm. Yes."

He twitched and giggled.

I exchanged a silent look with Nate. Whatever unspoken enmities might exist between us, this overrode them all. I looked back at the mummified vision and chose my words with care.

"You," I said, "are mentally diseased."

Nate moaned quietly. For the fifth time he tried to reach out with his foot towards the red case on the floor, the same pack he'd been lugging about ever since the raid on the Secretariat. Cy had positioned it carefully next to our discarded clothes with a gleeful sneer, ensuring it was *just* out of Nate's reach.

Glancing now at my companion, in this light – with none of his daft costume-clothes to cover him – I could see the needle marks, the collapsed veins, the train-track bruises of a lifetime's using. He was sweating. Coming down again.

John-Paul Rohare Baptiste barely even looked at him, sitting directly before me and jerking strangely to some silent beat. He had eyes, as they say, only for me.

"They called the prophets insane," he said quietly, like he was talking to himself. "They called the apostles madmen."

I shook my head and looked away, more *disappointed* than anything. All this grief, all this bloodshed, all this *struggle*: caused by an incontinent chimpanzee in a squeaky chair.

"They had a point," I said.

The first shock was: his frailty. On the telly, during those annoying bloody broadcasts, he looked old, true enough. He looked old and calm and maybe a tad doddery, like a friendly old boy who'd had his share of an eventful life and more besides. He looked like the sort of human raisin who'd fall asleep halfway through his favourite soap opera but could shout and rant with the best if someone mentioned the War.

He looked, in other words, like an old man with a lot of life left in him.

In the flesh, in that cold detention room, under strip lights that strobed *just* too fast to notice, he was a cheap zombie special effect from an art-student B-movie. Skin so paper-thin you could make out the veins beneath the surface, hands so withered they looked like finger bones dipped in molten plastic. His eyes were set so far back in his head the sockets looked like volcano calderas, ready to bubble-up with pus and rheum.

Nice image.

This close up, under these lights, without the benefit of makeup, he *wasn't old*. He was *sick*.

I remembered the photo I'd seen inside the Secretariat. The NATO Staff-Sergeant, sat with an expression of quiet seriousness, staring into the camera. Forty, forty-five years old, well-groomed, no-nonsense.

The man before me hadn't got older. What had changed about him had nothing to do with age. It was simpler than that.

He'd just... *withered.*

He saw me staring.

"The Lord has sustained me," he said, like he could read my thoughts. With one hand he reached down to pluck a long coil of rubber tubing from a pocket on the side of the chair. "The Lord has shown me the Way."

"The Lord has taken a shit in your brain," I told him.

The second shock was: his smile.

It wasn't friendly. It wasn't pure. It wasn't the beatific expression of extreme serenity that basked in the studio lights every Sunday in the weekly broadcast. What it was, was:

Fucking vicious.

"The Lord has given me life in the midst of death. He has scoured the world with plague and fire, and wiped away those who bore his mark, and only I – whose blood runs with impurity – have been spared by his hand. The Lord favours me, Englishman, and in the hour of my greatest need – when the arch-Satan stormed at my door – he has delivered me from evil."

"The arch-Satan?"

"The arch-Satan."

"That'd be me?"

He smiled again. He smiled and underneath the God-talk, underneath the brimstone bullshit, I think maybe I saw...

– yes, I'm *sure* of it –

...a rational man staring out. A rational man who knew the truth.

A rational man who wasn't such a nutter after all.

Just a great liar.

"What happens to the children?" I said, suddenly exhausted. My body ached. My head hurt. Felt like it always had. I couldn't be *bothered* any more – not with any of it. With my own journey, with the goals I'd picked up *en route* like a travelling orphanage, with the whole twisted plate of crap this stupid bloody journey had become.

Don't you fucking give up, soldier!

Training. Secret Intelligence Service. MI6. Drill Sergeants screaming and yelling, shattering conventional wisdom, plumbing the depths of each grunt's soul for reserves of anger, for animal resilience, for the snarling shadow-lurking wolf loping about in the pits of the mind.

"The children?" John-Paul said. "Oh. Oh, yes. Oh, I see..."

Don't you fucking give up, soldier!

Blah-blah-blah-the-fuck-blah.

Not your problem, said Bella, and I believed her.

"That's it, isn't it?" the little man sniggered, chair squeaking. He carefully fitted a bung to one end of the rubber tube and drew back the fabric of his sleeve. A plastic cannula, stoppered up, sat in the crook of his elbow, lodged deep in the vein underneath. "That's what it's for. That's why you came to get me." He looked pleased with himself.

I scowled. "Come again?"

"A little boy, was it? A little girl? Hmm? Did I... Did I *steal* one away from you? Some little blonde slut, eh? Some filthy little brat with his finger up his nose?

"Came all this way, did you, Englishman? All this way to get back your kiddiewinks?"

Slowly, lip twisting, he pushed the tube onto the end of the cannula.

"Think you're the first, do you? The first disgruntled daddy to come get his brat?"

I could see the way his brain was working. It was logical, I supposed. It made sense. It was the same lie I'd told the scavs in Central Park; the same idea of aching loss, borrowed from Bella and Malice and all those others, who'd surrendered or deserted or *handed over* their own children.

It was the best rational reason for someone – someone like me – to do all that I'd done.

To clamber over piles of bodies. To cross oceans. To lock horns with the great Church.

It was so wrong it was funny.

"No," I said. "I don't have children. Never have."

The old man's eyebrows furrowed together. He stopped fiddling with the rubber tubing, let it hang loose in his hands.

"Then... but. Then *why*? Why did you come after me?"

I laughed, and I admit it must have sounded manic. Even in my head, the stupidity was too much to bear. The arrogance. This dried-up old lizard, this piece of desiccated skin.

He thought I'd come all this way for him. He thought this thing, between him and me, was *personal.*

"I didn't," I said in between chuckles, which grew thicker and damper with each breath, until my eyes fuzzed with water and I could barely see. "You silly old twat. I didn't."

I said:

Listen.

Her name was Jasmine Tomas.

She was... she was more beautiful than a new moon reflecting off a perfectly still sea. She was so beautiful I spouted corny old movie bullshit like that all the time, and I could get away with it and not get even a little bit embarrassed. She had skin and hair the colour of coffee – one with cream, the other without – and curves in all the right places. When she laughed it was too loud and made people look, but they always looked then smiled, because when she laughed it was like... an infection. Like everyone caught it straight away.

We disagreed about almost everything, but we disagreed in a weird way. Like it meant we thought just the same as each other, but would go hammer and tong to disagree over details. Ha. The colour of wrapping paper. New music. Pretentiousness of art. We couldn't start a conversation without arguing. It was great.

We loved each other so much it scared the living fuck out of me.

An aide came shuffling into the room, then, as silent as death. He didn't speak. He wheeled a medical stand before him, carrying a small steel machine with a glass front and a system of tubes dangling below it. I ignored him. I carried on talking.

A week before Jasmine Tomas moved into my flat, she told me to get rid of all the photos I'd taken of her. This was six years' worth. She said... she said when we lived together all our photos should be of both of us, or neither of us.

She said that sort of thing a lot.

The thing about Jasmine Tomas was, it would be easy to mistake her for a romantic. It would be easy to be fooled by the things she said, the gestures she made. And then just when you figured you'd got her pegged she'd switch on the footy, or tell a sick joke, or come home from work with stories of scalpels and infections. One time, I cooked Jasmine a stew. I mean, fuck... my job was to go overseas and kill stuff. I don't cook. Still, it turned out okay, you know? Cheese, leeks, you name it.

So I took the lid off the stew when she arrived – wearing the purple-and-blue dress with the earrings I got for her birthday – and oh, God, I wanted her, *and everything was just* perfect, *and the first thing she said was:*

Looks just like the inside of a gangrenous leg.

And then she laughed too loud, like a drain, and I laughed too. I couldn't help it.

The aide took the end of the rubber tube John-Paul had fitted to his arm. He slotted it neatly onto a spigot on the side of the steel machine, and turned towards me. He avoided my gaze.

My arse hurt. I kept talking.

He pulled a needle out of a plastic wrapper, and came forwards.

The first time I met Jasmine Tomas, for the record, she was teaching a group of wankers with too much testosterone about biohazards. All part of the training. She'd been seconded to the MOD from some governmental research-team or other – had more letters after her name than an episode of Sesame Street *– and there she was, stuck in front of a room of leering arseholes who spent far longer staring at her tits than at the projector presentations she brought along. So... a few of those same arseholes dared another arsehole to ask her an embarrassing question about the dangers of sexual infection during fieldwork, and she didn't skip a beat. Told him she'd examine his infected areas after the lecture as long as he promised not to leak pus on her, then kept on talking over the top of the laughter.*

I was the arsehole. I went and apologised after she'd finished. She took it well.

A week later we got dinner, then coffee, then the best fuck I ever had.

Three years later I was still killing people for Her Divine Majesty's Government, only now I was looking forward to the weekend just like every other guy, bored of his job.

Jasmine Tomas was *my weekend.*

The cannula was in my arm, somewhere. Fitted to the tube that was fitted to the machine. I couldn't see behind my back.

My arse continued to hurt.

The aide flicked a switch with a devotional smile towards his master, then stood with his back to me, fussing over the machine.

And the tube – oh, fucking hell, I understood – the tube that led from me to the machine to John-Paul, it filled with blood like a long thermometer; red mercury bulging upwards.

My arm felt warm and cold at the same time. A prickling sensation. Pins and needles, killing my cells, spreading across me. And oh, Jesus fuck shit, I got it; I got it, you withered old bastard, and I felt sick and weak and faint, but I kept talking because it's all I could do.

I said:

Listen.

I was never really designed, you know, for the romantic thing. Wasn't sure how to do it, I guess. But then nor was she, so we got on fine.

Squabbled and sniped and smarmed our way through it all, awkward as you like. Never happy for long, but never sad for long either. Fuck fairytales. Fuck 'perfect.' We loved each other like nobody else, and that's enough.

So she decides to move in. I asked her, she said yes. The thing is, she works all day, every day and I'm... out of the country. Business trips. Frequent flyer, blah-blah. So we figure we'll see more of each other if it's all cosy. All domestic. No need to schedule it every time.

Then the disease started. You remember? Right at the very beginning, it was just... some new thing. Nothing to worry about. They sent me to the East, to... well. It doesn't matter where or why. I got back and Jasmine Tomas was supposed to move in that week, and all I got was a bloody text message telling me we'd have to postpone.

She'd been reassigned. Couldn't say where. Couldn't say why.

So I waited.

And the world died around me.

John-Paul just stared.

With my blood pouring out of me, filling him up like a greedy mosquito, bringing colour and warmth to his shrivelled face, he just stared and listened. He groaned once in a while, like a man in the throes of passion, and it made me feel sick to imagine him balls-deep in someone, grunting like a pig.

I felt sick in a lot of ways.

The world wobbled around me. Nothing was the right shade. Greyness was creeping out of every corner, and stinging the insides of my arms. My eyes rolled. My arse hurt.

I twitched my fingers behind my back, certain now that the aide was too busy watching the machine to turn around. I worked with all the speed and focus I could muster as everything slid away into bloodless limbo.

I kept talking. I kept fucking talking.

It was all I could do to cling on. To stay awake. To stay alive.

I said:

I did some digging. Pulled some strings at the SIS; found out what she'd been sent to do. Where she'd gone, even.

UN mandate. That's all I got. Reassigned to a secret location as part of an international research team. Supposed to find a cure for the AB-virus.

'Project Pandora,' it was called.

John-Paul looked up.

And moaned, softly.

My fingers moved behind my back.

My arse stopped hurting.

Blood moved on my hands.

I said:

Listen.

Everybody died.

Jasmine Tomas, who I loved in that old-movie way... I never heard from her again. Not for five years.

People died and lay on the streets, ambulances rushed back and forth, the world shat out its own guts and sat there like Elvis, poised on a toilet, dying by degrees.

I went back to Vauxhall Cross. I checked her records. Blood-type AB+.

As good as dead.

John Paul wasn't listening any more. Not so you'd know it, anyway.

His eyelids fluttered and his lips twisted in a smile, and I could see the strength filling him up, my own blood giving him life, turning him back into that man in the photo, the man on the TV, the calm and peaceful saint.

He communed with God through the medium of my fucking blood.

Blood-type O, rhesus negative. Safe to transfuse into anyone, more-or-less. Not quite good for him, not quite recommended. Risk of anaphylactic shock if conducted too fast, but still, but still...

My fingers twisted.

My body slumped. My brain started to slip away.

Something clicked quietly behind me.

I said:

For five years, I didn't exist.

I was just... alive.

And then one day the machines in the SIS comms-room chattered to life, and the correct passwords slotted into place, and the power fluttered through the consoles, and in a string of exchanged information a single word rushed-by.

'Pandora.'

And a voice said:

"Are... Are you there?"

And it's a long shot. And maybe it's coincidence. Maybe it's fluke.

She should be dead. I know that.

But...

But you listen to me, you fucking leech. *You listen to me, because you're still alive and you should be dead, and so nothing in the whole world – you hear me?* – nothing, *no one, no fucking old reptile or his gang of delusional pricks, would stop me from finding out.*

So here I am.

And John-Paul Rohare Baptise smiled, like he'd been catching-up on what I was saying, and his eyes weren't sunken any more, and his lips were red, and he said:

"Mm, yes. Yes. Here you are. And... hah... And maybe you aren't the arch-Satan after all. Maybe you didn't come to get me, eh? Maybe I just got in your way? That's it, I think. But it doesn't matter, you see? No. No, it doesn't. Because here you are, and here you die."

And I smiled despite the weakness. Despite the nausea. Despite the rushing in my ears.

"It won't be as perfect," he said to himself, eyes closed, rapturous, "as a child. A child is perfection. The communion is... perfection. Yes. Mm."

His eyes opened.

He looked right at me.

"But you'll do. For today. It's only fitting. After all the trouble you've caused, mister. It's only fitting that you make a donation."

I smiled and I dropped the handcuffs to the floor by my feet, and the sliver of metal that had been buried in my arse tinkled from the lock – the lock it had helped me pick – to the floor.

And John-Paul Rohare Baptise was opening his mouth to protest, to shout for help, to cry out in baby-like shock, but it wouldn't do the old fucker any good, because my fist was already in his face and his teeth were already shattered, and I was already moving onwards and head butting the aide and cracking his nose, and he went down quick and quiet, and I was turning back to the groping old bastard with my knuckles bare and bloody, and this time I didn't stop until he was silent on the floor, and lying in his own juice.

Scratch that:

My juice.

And then I pulled out the tubes from my arm, and threw up like a trooper.

CHAPTER TWENTY

WHEN CY CAME blundering in fifteen minutes later, things were a little different.

I wasn't naked any more, for a start.

"You wanted me, your holin – ?" he started.

And stopped.

I tried to imagine how he must have seen things, in that cold moment when we all froze and stared at each other. But I didn't know him, and could only guess what his brain *did* in moments like this.

Would he have fixated on the blood? There was certainly enough of it about: great thick pools, already congealing, from where Nate's shaking hands had tried to puncture the comatose aide's artery with the crude transfusion tube. Third time lucky, in the end.

Or maybe Cy's eyes, hidden away behind those stupid shades, went straight to his Lord and Master? The great Abbot John-Paul, slumped on the floor with his teeth smashed out, whimpering as consciousness came slinking back?

After I'd cut Nate free, as the old junkie staggered and whinged and gagged, he told me I needed more blood – quickly. I'd wanted it from the Abbot – take back what he'd stolen. It seemed only fair.

But no, no, no. Nate had shook his head, eyes unfocused, shivering in need of a fix, telling me *no*. The old man had a different blood type.

"'Member... 'member the TV show?" he grumbled. "'Member the clumpin' cells? Clots inside. Wrong type. One way only."

So he'd swapped the tubes and let me leech off the spindly little aide instead. I would've felt bad, if I had the energy. If I gave a flying fuck.

So John-Paul was still lying where I'd left him, moving slowly, scrabbling in the blood. Was that what Cy saw first, when he stepped in?

Or was it me? Maybe that was it. Instant fascination. The English *bastard* who'd blown-up his airport, who'd wiped out his unit of grunts, who'd run rings round him in New York, who'd almost executed him following the Tag, who'd led the army that ejected his gang from their base, who'd held his attention as an honest-to-God red injun snuck up and stabbed him through the skull, and who'd beaten up the withered old man he worshipped.

I guess you couldn't blame him for being a tad grumpy.

Was that what he focused on, as he came marching in? Me standing there, looking and feeling like I'd died, wanting nothing more than to curl up and sleep for a year, letting my body adjust?

No.

Fair enough, the freaky shithead pulled a gun on me the second he appeared – quicker than I could see – but his heart wasn't in it. He wasn't going to shoot.

No. What Cy looked at as he stepped inside was this:

Nate's bag.

"Ah," he said. "Hm."

"K-kill... kill them..." the Abbot groaned from the floor, bent double. "Look what... they did..."

"Yes, holiness," Cy said, voice flat, not even looking down. "Get out now, sir. I'll deal with it."

And so the Abbot John-Paul Rohare Baptiste, spiritual head of the Apostolic Church of the Rediscovered Dawn, turned his back on the arch-Satan and wobbled away on his hands and knees, trailing blood. The door swung closed behind him.

And then it was just me, and Nate, and Cy. And a gun.

And Bella saying:

Not your problem.

"Well, now," said the Cardinal.

Nate was a wreck. Sweat poured off him. The effort of dangling there off the cell bars, then thinking straight long enough to hook me up to the whitewashed aide, must have finished him. He could barely stand, snot and tears and vomit decorating his face. I wondered how long it had been since his last fix. Certainly since before the battle by the bridge. I wondered what sort of weird-arsed home-made shit he'd been chasing anyway.

"Nigger looks like death," said Cy, grinning.

Nate swayed where he stood. "J's... Jus' need my... my..." He blinked, trying to focus. "Medicine."

A lot happened at once.

Nate lurched towards the red pack with his arms outstretched, gurgling from his guts upwards. Cy moved even faster, gun shifting to freeze the man on his spot. He had the sense to stay.

And I took my chance.

Pounced.

Fists raised. No *way* he could turn back to cover me in t –

– fuck, he's fast –

The pistol muzzle sat on my forehead. Cy smiled.

"Now," he said. "Just you back up. Back up, there."

I didn't move.

"Limey. Limey, you hear?"

I worked my jaw. "I hear you."

"You back up. Or the nigger gets shot."

"Not me?"

"Hah. Not you. No guns for you. Not 'less you make me."

I didn't move. Didn't care.

Let him go for Nate.

(But –)

No buts.

(But he saved my li –)

No excuses. You know the rules.

Don't you let yourself owe anyone anything.

Don't you fucking give up, soldier!

(Sir, no sir, *etc, etc.*)

Let him do it.

Let him try.

The second the gun moves, he's mine.

Cy said: "Don't say. Didn't warn you."

And then Nate was on the floor, and a gunshot hung in the air, and the stink of guns and the shock of movement, and the pistol was back against my forehead – hot, singeing my skin – before I'd even tilted forwards.

Too fast to see.

He, I decided, *isn't natural.*

Nate screamed. His foot was a wreck. Bones poked at fractured angles from a fragmented red sneaker, fountaining blood and singed fabric.

"Back up," Cy said again, and still the grin. "Back up. Or next. His face."

I backed up. Nate's screams turned to moans, then whimpered away. Cy kept the gun aimed squarely at me, sidestepping around the growing slick on the floor, squatting to his haunches beside the heavy case. The muzzle never wavered. The dagger-pommel poked from his head like a rubber cock, and I bit down on the cheap joke.

"Didn't have time," he said, smiling like a Cheshire cat, "to grab my own. Back at the Secretariat. Shit, limey... you shoulda seen the stashes. Junk coming in from all over. Collectors collecting. Scavs bartering. Even had us a team of geeks. Geeks *making* it. New kinds. Mixing it like fuckin' *artists*."

"Drugs?" I said. The word sounded... *naïve*.

"Best currency." He licked his lips and rummaged in the bag, not even looking. "'Cept for God. Heh. 'Cept for kids."

He withdrew a sealed hypoderm. Bit the rubber flange off the needle and spat it away.

The gun didn't waver.

"Put it to good use. Trickled it out. Some to Klans, some overseas. Let them know who's boss. See? Rewards for good boys. Sweeties for ignorant masses. Heh. Manna from heaven. Always kept the best shit for ourselves."

His stupid syntax was pissing me off. "Until the ignorant masses rose up and kicked your arse, you mean?"

"Uh-uh." He shook his head. "'Til this nigger stole it." He kicked Nate's ruined foot, drawing up another round of tortured screams.

Then he lifted the hypoderm to his neck, still staring right at me, punched through the skin and squeezed the plunger. His whole body went tense, cords straining.

"What is it?" I said, morbidly fascinated, watching the liquid vanish inside him.

His lips peeled back.

He hissed, like a boiler reaching critical mass.

Then grunted.

Then he yanked out the needle with a girlish giggle and chucked it away, letting it smash on the floor.

"The fuck knows?" he said, voice abruptly smooth, body moving with a weird liquidity. He stood up straight and peeled off his glasses, ignoring the tiny dribble of blood hanging on his neck. "Gave up reading labels years back."

His eyes were almost red. So bloodshot that they bulged, capillaries swollen and angry, pupils dilated to swallow dark irises that brooded at the heart of hot, insane scarlet.

It took me a moment or two to find my voice.

"Good to see there were no adverse effects, mate."

He giggled and winked. It looked painful.

"Now then," he said, moving slow. "You recall the Secretariat? You recall before the injun arrived?"

"What about it?"

He grinned. And then carefully, letting me see what he was doing every step, he tucked the pistol away in a holster inside his robe and cracked his knuckles.

"Let's... pick up. Hm. Pick up where we left off?"

The first lunge was almost too fast to follow. Maybe I was still groggy.

Maybe I was just too slow.

It didn't matter, really. I knew it'd be a feint before he'd even started, and was ready when he blurred left-right-left – confusing and showy – then sent a foot arching down towards my shins.

Looking flash, playing dirty. Trying to break my ankle, the arrogant fuck; that or push me backwards, keep me on the defensive, box me against a wall.

Best form of defence is –

I stepped forwards, through and under his guard. Took the force out of the kick with a sideways swipe of my right hand and rolled with the weight, down on one knee – letting fists strike uselessly at the air above my head. My left hand snapped palm-open, thrust forwards with a tiny snarl on my lips.

There's no word for what happens when you hit someone as hard as you can in the balls. It's like... it's like somewhere between a crunch and a squelch. It's like hard-and-soft altogether, and you can barely do it without wincing in sympathy.

What I did was: gripped.

Fact: it's possible to kill a man this way.

We must've stood like that for a second or two. That shocked sense of calm after a flurry of blows and kicks too quick to be handled intelligently. You just *react*. You just *let it flow*.

I waited for him to crumple.

And waited.

And looked up.

He winked again, then laughed.

And then his fist was slow-mo-ing and my cheek was all white light, and I was on my back, and the world came back bit-by-bit.

He stepped back and shook his arms, like an athlete warming up. Like there wasn't a great bloody stain oozing through his robes around his crotch.

"Round two." He giggled, every muscle shivering. "When you're ready, limey."

Fuck.

I stood up carefully, overplaying the grogginess. Hamming it right up. I swayed on my feet, waving him forwards with the punch-drunk bravado of an amateur. Trying to be *clever* about this... He was quicker and stronger and meaner, but if he was as dumb as he *looked* maybe I could –

Now.

And he was on me again. Expecting it to be easy; an elbow thrown out at my cheek as he spun past, a low leg orbiting at the edge of the curve. I took the elbow in both hands and wrenched, letting his weight overbalance him, chasing him down so the roundhouse arced uselessly. I fucking *pummelled* him, knuckles mashing on cheeks and lips, knowing it did no good but enjoying it anyway, leaning my arms on his chest as his back hit the ground, forcing the air out of him and feeling his ribs crackle, then planting both fists in his guts.

Hard.

Trying to get the shithead bleeding inside. Emptying him of oxygen. Playing it carefully, thoughtfully. Not a brawl but an amputation, not a fight but a fucking *dissection.* He coughed blood and tried to lever himself up, sucking back air, and I broke his nose with a smile and kept hitting, sat astride him; pounding away until my fingers felt broken and my arms ached from wrist to shoulder.

Intelligent application of force.

Yes.

Yes, you *fuck.*

Controlled violence.

Thwap

Thwap

For Rick. For Malice and the others. For Bella, you *shit.*

Yes.

For Jasmine.

I took him apart, little by little, and no brain-surgeon was *ever* as precise as me in that glorious flurry of aggre –

Snuk

My fists stopped moving.

Cy smiled through teeth smeared with bloody spittle, gripping my hands in mid-swing as if he'd caught a pair of tennis balls, then sat up in a single continuous movement and nutted me on the bridge of my nose. Something snapped.

Fact: It's possible to kill people like *this* too.

I went over backwards. A fist in my eye helped me down. Warmth spattered off my lips and chin.

And I lay there panting as he dragged himself out from beneath me, and stood with no obvious aches or pains, spitting the blood away and clearing each nostril with a viscous rasp of snot and gore. He rolled his head as if he'd fallen asleep in the wrong position; jumped up and down in his spot once or twice, then gave me a great, bright smile.

"Let's go," he said.

Fuck.

It took a long time to pick myself up. Every inch a mountain. Every movement a defeated consolation.

I couldn't win. This... this *thing* wasn't even human any more. With his veins clogged-up with freaky narcotic shite, nothing would work. Clever fighting. Precision and stealth. Fuck it. Fuck it all.

I've seen guys on PCP. I've seen guys go psycho on Yaba crazy medicine. Twenty bullets, major organs shredded. Doesn't matter. Takes the body longer to realise it's dead than it takes to kill whoever's killing you.

Cy was worse.

Cy soaked it up then smiled sweetly. He didn't rush. Didn't race to squish me before the wounds caught up on him. He just...

Enjoyed it.

So what happened was, my brain went away.

The conditioning shivered somewhere deep, unflexed like a great squid-thing, untangling from the murk. I'd held it down too long. Let it grow in the dark.

It took a hold of me and blurred away all those insignificances, all those useless extremities of thought and intelligence. Sharpened me as it blunted me down.

The trainers at the SIS would have been proud.

Good little soldier. Good little killer. Good little machine.

The wolf came out from its shadows, and its eyes glowed in the gloom, and I stopped thinking. Let the instincts take over.

Don't you fucking give up, soldier!

Sir, no sir, etc, etc.

And this time when he rushed me I was already hitting him, and when he scooped at the air to knock me back I was ducking into his belly with a knee, and when he snarled and spun and kicked out I *let* him, and enjoyed the pain in my hips because it meant I was *close*, and *hungry*, and I lamped him so hard in the ear that the skin on my fist popped.

Chased him down to the ground.

Snapped his shin with my boot.

Took out his eye with a finger.

Caught a hold of his jaw as it flapped open and yanked down so hard something shattered and tore.

Grabbed a handful of his neck and balled my fist 'til the skin broke and the cords underneath moved in my hand.

Punches raining on my face.

Like I care.

And I locked my fingers round his throat, bloody and slick and crackling down deep, and *squeezed.*

His eye bulged and bled. He gurgled.

And then the gun was in my face.

The wolf loped away.

Cy's lips twitched into something like a smile.

I sighed. "You said no guns. Not for me."

"N't...*nk*... n't less... yuh... *made* me..."

His finger tightened on the trigger.

And from the corner of my eye a black hand reached out from nowhere, gripped the rubber handle still poking from Cy's head, and *pulled*.

It made a noise something like a champagne cork.

He rustled as he died, and a soupy sort of stuff oozed out of his skull, and Nate – shivering on the floor with the knife in his hand, foot still pulsing blood – grinned his pearly grin and said:

"'Nother... 'nother one you owe me."

IT WAS STRANGE.

To have come this far for a *maybe*...

To have fought and killed and cut my way across... shit, across half the fucking world, on the strength of a feeble radio transmission and the half-a-chance idea of someone who *should* be dead *not* being dead.

To have shut myself off, to have *sliced* across any prat who stood in my way, because:

If John-Paul can do it, maybe Jasmine can too...

I'd come a long way. Following the voice in my head every step. Listening to its orders. It told me not to give up, and I didn't. It told me to know everything, and I had. It told me to cover the angles, and I covered them. Though it left me bloody and broken and knackered, I fucking did as I was told.

Right?

My head hurt, and the world spun around me. I giggled.

The voice, the voice. That was it. At the end, when the time came to find some things out, to finish it, the voice told me not to get distracted, to do the job, to stay focused. It told me:

Not your problem.

I wondered if I'd done the right thing, taking the syringe from Nate's bag. It made the world... different.

I giggled again.

I stood outside a room on the fifth sub-level of the South Bass Island UN Bunker complex, and shivered, trying to concentrate. Things were happening, somewhere. People running, voices raised, footsteps clattering and guns being armed. Right now, nobody was paying me much attention, which made a refreshing change. Earlier on, as I staggered out of the detention room with my eyes watering and my head spinning, a couple of guards had got lucky and noticed the red patches soaking through my stolen robes. I'd lifted them from the Clergy aide on the floor, whose blood was currently filling my veins. It had seemed elegant, somehow. Like... regardless of whether the damp patches came from him or me, it was all the same thing. Ha-ha.

Should that be funny?

(The two guards who'd spotted the blood hadn't thought so. I tried to explain it as patiently as I could – not even slurring much – but they kept on telling me I was stoned, and asking me who the fuck I was, and poking me with their fingers. It got boring quickly. I like to think I left them alive – just – though to be honest I can't say I was subtle about it.)

The point was, I was free to roam. And right now I stood outside a door, on the deepest level of the complex, and stared in confusion at the sign.

COMMS

This was where it came from. The transmission. The word PANDORA. The voice. This is where she sent it. I could almost *taste* it. Could almost reach out and pluck her from the air, and remind myself of all the guilty sensations that time had stolen. The smell of her hair. The slant of her nose. The exact shade of her eye.

I could remember them all. Ish. But memories are like regrets, they linger and haunt you, but they *evolve* with time. They lose their edge. Become idealised.

I wondered, in some quiet giggling abstraction, if I'd even recognise her when I saw her again. Then my brain reminded me she was dead – *must* be. Had been for five years.

Idiot. It said.

All this way, for nothing.

Without even realising it, I'd placed a hand on the door handle and begun to push. And that, really, was all there was to it. Inside this room I'd find out. Had she been here? Was it really her that sent me the message?

I felt like a pilgrim who never expected to *get* to his shrine.

I relaxed the pressure on the door and stepped back. The air was full of light. Hallucinations turned my brain upside-down; twisted synaesthetic confusions swapping sounds for tastes, musical tones for physical feelings, emotions for colours.

Scents for light.

In the detention room, the syringe I took from Nate's pack had been marked: SNIFF.

I recalled a time that seemed long ago, and a chase through city streets, and a big man in red injecting another man with... Well. With something that made him a little less than human. That sharpened up his senses. I recalled being pretty fucking impressed, at the time.

And now here I was. A wolf in the true sense.

And I turned away from the Comms Room with my nose in the air, and followed a pulsing trail of light-stink that moved and shifted like electrified neon, because maybe it *wasn't* my problem, and maybe it *wasn't* part of my mission, and maybe no one would care but *me* –

– but some things need to be finished, whether it's your job to finish it or not.

Jasmine could wait.

She'd waited five years.

I FOUND JOHN-PAUL Rohare Baptiste in a room decked in red and blue velvet, with flags hung up behind him. The country they signified was dead.

It had been easy, closing in on him, down bunker tunnels and twisting corridors, with lights shimmering before and behind me, sniffing the air.

He smelt of me.

He was sloshing with *me*.

He was talking as I stepped quietly inside, through a door marked:

STUDIO

"...and... and so I'm putting this message on... onna loop..."

He was swaying unsteadily. Face all busted up – cleaned of raw blood but clearly bruised – eyes crossed. He was holding himself upright on the barn doors of an old TV camera, staring deep into the lens. The red light was on.

"...We've... had some troubles. You c'n... c'n see from my face, I think. But... h-hallelujah! We have prevailed, my sons and daughters. God's righteousness has... has shone through. We have been sorely *tested*, and faced down the... the evil of ignorance. We have endured our great Exodus, and in the... in the process have found our 'Promised Land.' My children... we have been found *deserving* of glory."

There was nobody behind the camera. Nobody behind the glass window in the control booth set to one side. Not any more. Not since I stopped off to say hello.

It had been impressively soundproofed. John-Paul hadn't even noticed.

There was nobody listening to him. Nobody except me, and the world. What was left of it.

"I send out this message to say to you all: do not be alarmed. We have moved, as God's will has dictated. But our mission remains steadfast. We must build a brighter tomorrow. We must open the eyes of the children! *Amen.* Mm. *A-men.*"

His eyes rolled and closed up; communing with the divine. His withered face creased in a perfect smile.

"And... and so I say to you all, continue to send me the architects of the future. Continue to bring me your sons and daughters. Bring them to Cleveland, and Toledo, and we will reveal to them the paradise we are building here.

"We will take them and raise them up, and... a-and...*ah*..."

His voice tailed off. His eyes fluttered open.

I pushed the silver pin a little harder against the frail skin of his neck. He hadn't even heard me approach him. Hadn't been aware I was behind him, looming like some great fucking bat, until the sliver of metal was pricking his throat.

The sliver Rick gave me. Buried in my own flesh.

John-Paul gurgled.

The red light continued to burn.

"Wh... who... who's there?" he asked, not daring to move.

"I'm the Holy Ghost," I said. "I move in mysterious ways."

"Y-you! You would... you would commit this sin before the world? Y-you would expose your evil?"

I leaned down until I was close to his ear, senses alive with the drug, tasting his fear. *Enjoying* it.

"I will if *you* will," I said.

"Wh... what d... do you m...?"

"The children, Abbot. You were about to tell us about the children. About how you 'raise them up.' That was as far as you got. Why not... *tell* us about that?"

"B-but... But I..."

"Now, now. The world watches, your Holiness." I pressed harder with the pin. "Let's not scrimp on details."

And so he told them.

He told them how he'd survived. He gibbered and snotted and cried as he went, and he dressed it up in holiness. Didn't matter. Still came across like a desperate man polishing a turd.

It wasn't murder, he said, it was the Touch of God. It wasn't blood, it was divinity itself.

Listen: people might be a little short-sighted when confronted with miracles. And okay, maybe humanity has a hole in its common sense where the idea of deity sits nice and firm. Maybe there's something to be said for the infuriating fucking gullibility of mankind, but here's the thing:

You can only push it so far.

I think the message got through.

I think what they heard, out there, clustered round TVs for weeks to come, as the message looped and re-looped over and over, was *not* a divine prophet delivering words of hope and purity...

...I think what they heard was a wretched little freak, explaining with patience and politeness how he'd stolen the blood of a thousand kiddies, how he'd convinced the world of his perfection, how his acolytes had flocked to serve him, just to fend off the virus that was killing him.

He told them that there were no 'marks.' No angels pouring out their vials onto the earth. Nothing. Just people with a particular type of blood. Whole ethnic groups, with genetic traces that he neither understood nor cared about, but had nothing to do with the wrath of God.

He told them that the virus was just that: a virus. Biological. Predictable. It killed certain people and left great swathes of others alive. The O-negs. The Native Americans. Eastern Asians. Australian Aborigines. He told them he knew this because he'd been with the group who found it all out. They'd seen what the virus killed and what it spared, and they'd failed utterly to find out how to stop it. They'd hidden away down here in the bunker until the virus caught up with *them* too, and there was a time of madness and... and things he couldn't remember, and then...

Then he was reborn as John-Paul, the Holy.

Stealing blood to stave off the virus. Whole transfusions of O-neg, to replace the juices the Blight guzzled every day. Injections of plasma from Iroquois captives, to plant whatever genetic armour they possessed deep inside him.

He told them *everything.* Then his voice went quiet and his face went slack, and he told them that children were better than adults.

Purer, he said.

More perfect. Like drinking the blood of an angel.

More beautiful.

And...

And when they were weak from blood loss, he said, when the Light of God was in them...

They never said "no" to *anything...*

He went on and on and on, and when he was done I patted him on the head like he'd done well, pushed the silver needle into his jugular so the blood went out of him like a balloon losing air, and when he was on the ground I stamped on his head with a noise like a cockroach crackling.

And there were choirs of angels singing, and shafts of light, and the warm gaze of divinity to assure me I'd done well. But then again I was hallucinating like a motherfucker, so I ignored the whole stupid show and told myself – one way or another – I'd made the world a slightly better place.

"Architects of tomorrow," John-Paul had said.

Heh.

Sometimes architects have to tear down before they can build up.

CHAPTER TWENTY-ONE

Predictably, the place was in uproar. Things were moving too quickly now, cascading towards a shit-littered abyss before anyone could even prepare for the fall. I wondered why. I wondered what was going on. I wondered why I couldn't give a damn.

Tangled cords of scent-trails braided and split apart in the air of the bunker; a three-dimensional map in the hallucinogenic chambers of my mind that documented fear and panic and confusion. Men in Clergy robes sprinted along corridors, rushing up tangled stairwells and queuing five deep at the cavernous elevators. Somewhere high above, on the first or second sub-level, shouts filtered downwards. Everyone seemed to be ignoring me.

The drug made me giggle. Or maybe I just felt like it. I don't know.

With my senses on overdrive – whole body *thrumming* to some internal beat, like an iron butterfly flapping great wings inside my chest – it was all too much to bear. The noises and smells and sights. Eventually I stopped paying attention, turned away and just... *walked.*

I found myself, eventually, back outside the Comms room, and slumped to the floor on the opposite side of the corridor. Just staring. Wondering.

Was she here, once?

Did she... did she die here?

Where are the bodies?

I killed some time picking lumps of brain and bone out of my boots.

The drug was doing something to me. Not just hotwiring my senses and overloading my brain, but picking away at parts of my mind, doing something insidious and unwelcome. Something that involved the wolf, somehow. Something that tugged at the upper layers – those useless skeins of civility and rationality – and went nestling *below*, into the 'Old Brain,' into the scratching suspicions of the subconscious and paranoia.

Something *gnawed* at me. Something that had been gnawing for a long, long time... Something I'd noticed and disregarded, or ignored without concern. Something that had been clanging and shouting to grab my attention, formless and silent; beginning to piece things together moment-by-moment, to build me a message.

To show me something.

It had to do with Bella, I think. With something she'd said.

Doesn't matter. Not your proble –

No, not that. *That* was solved, now. I'd *made* it my problem. For her and Rick, and the crew of the *Inferno*, and the scavs and citizens and misguided Klansmen and *everyone*, I'd made it my problem. A regular little hero. But that wasn't it.

My brain itched.

What else?

What else did she say after we'd fucked, in the pub outside Heathrow, as we lay on the barrel chute and I curled my fingers through her hair, thinking of someone else? My Jasmine. Thinking of my Jasmine and feeling guilty and dirty and wrong, and not evening listening to what the poor girl, poor little Bella, was saying.

Further along the corridor, a hurrying Choirboy limped towards me, hood-up, a red pack slung over his shoulder, with a medical stand used as a support. I knew it was Nate without even looking around. The drug made him smell of sweat and fear and chemicals.

And guilt.

What?

"Th-that you?" he said. "What you doin'? We gotta get out of here."

I stared at the door of the Comms Room. Was I ready for it yet?

Instinctively, I felt it should be the *last* thing that I did. It should be the last mystery to be solved. I should get everything else out the way first.

Don't you get distracted, boy.

Don't you let things slip.

Know everything. Cover the angles.

"Just thinking," I said.

"Yeah? Well... well you do it and *walk*, man. Crazy *shit* goin' on." He leaned down and waved frantically at the other goons, face buried in the folds of his robe. I didn't ask where he'd got it. "They saying... they saying the Abbot's *dead*. You know 'bout that?"

I shrugged.

"They saying there's boats out on the lake. Circling round and round. They saying one of the choppers been knocked out. They saying it's the... Hau... Howdenoh..."

"The Iroquois?" I said, barely interested.

"Yeah! How the fuck 'd they do *that*?"

I shrugged again. *Good for them.* Wouldn't have been difficult, I guessed. Impossible to invade the island, but easy to prowl the lake. Sneaking about, exploding a lorry or two, taking down the choppers from afar. No big undertaking, for enough people.

I wondered how many survived the fight by the reservoir. How many of them got away because Cy and his shitheads were so busy collecting me and Nate.

I wondered if the Tadodaho had planned it all along.

Who knew?

Who cared?

I imagined Malice's baby, gurgling on the distant shore, listening to the fireworks.

I cared.

How annoying.

Nate tried to pull me upright. I shook him off.

"C'mon!" he burbled, eyes bulging. "N-now's the *time*! We can... we can slip away, maybe. Huh? In the confusion, you know? It's your *show*! 'S what you *do*, man! We gotta... we gotta look out for each other!"

I translated in my head. It was almost pitiful.

You've got to look after me! I saved your life! Protect me! Protect me!

He tugged at me again, staring off down the hallway.

"Ain't no fucking *way* Nathaniel C. Waterstone's gonna die here today..."

And there it was.

I stared at him. He was struggling out of his robe, yanking the eye patch out of his pocket to cover the tattoo, muttering under his breath.

"Nate?" I said.

"Huh?"

"What's... What does the 'C' stand for?"

He stopped with the robe looped round his neck and stared at me, like I was insane.

"What?"

"The 'C.'"

"The fuck you wanna..." He rolled his eyes and shook his head, like he'd decided to humour the mentalist to hurry him along. "Stands for Cassius. Why you wanna know?"

"Like... Cassius Clay?"

"My pop's hero. S'where they got the name."

The pieces slotted together.

I should have seen it before.

No more mysteries. No more excuses.

And finally Bella's little voice in my head, saying over and over *not your problem, not your problem*, that voice had an answer from the wolf, its eyes glowing in the dark.

Problem solved, it said.

"Nate."

"Huh?"

"We need to talk, Nate."

"Shit, man – it can *wait*! We gotta go –"

"You remember I called you a parasite?"

He went quiet, then nodded and waved it away.

"Yeah. Yeah, I remember. Forget it, man. It was a... tense time. No need to apologi –"

"I wasn't going to, Nate."

"Wh... what? Oh."

"I was right. You *are*. You *are* a parasite." My voice was cold. I couldn't change it for the world. I was on autopilot.

Not your problem, Bella said. I shushed her gently and looked up at Nate.

His mouth formed words, trying to find something to say. Clergymen shouted nearby.

"L-look. Fucksakes! I... listen, you got something to say, okay. O-*kay*. But you do it when we're out of here, huh? Or we both die right no..."

I pulled Cy's gun on him. His eyes bulged. He looked angry.

"What the... what the *fuck*, man? Are you out of your fucking *mind*? I saved your *life*, limey! I saved your goddamn life, like, *ten times*! I got shot in the goddam foot, man. Don't you point that thing at my –"

"Nate."

"Don't you poi –"

"*Nate*. Listen."

He listened.

"You're good at favours, Nate. Good at finding people to take care of you."

"Now hold o –"

"No. Be quiet." I armed the gun. It sounded like bones scraping. "You told me you went over to England in the eighties, right? Got taken out there by your exec-bitch? Lived the life of Larry, blah-blah. Cushy sort of arrangement. Right."

"Look, this ain't the ti –"

"Then you fucked her pal and screwed it up."

He sighed. Looked down.

"Bummed your way around. Attached yourself to people. Yeah? Did the bare fucking minimum to make yourself *useful*. Got taken *care* of."

He wouldn't look me in the eye.

"Same as later on. You told me so yourself. The Clergy showed up, offered you a job. Nice and cosy, safe as houses. And who cared if the job was ferrying kiddies to get themselves sucked dry? Huh? Who cared? You just pretend like you don't *know*."

The look in his eye told me: *he knew*.

"Oh, and there was the smack, too. You forgot to mention that. You told me you got clean back in London. Maybe you did, for a while. Must've been too good an opportunity, right? When these robe-wearing pricks showed up with all the skag you can shoot?

"Bare minimum effort, maximum reward. Easy life."

"L-look. It's... it's not like..."

"It was the same when *I* showed up. Shit, Nate, don't look at me like that. I know. You see this psycho Brit, all fired up – who cares about what? – and he can make sure you don't get *dead*, and he can lead you back to the supply, and all you've gotta do in return is patch him up when he needs or wait for him to die."

"Don't you gimme that," he hissed, real anger in his voice. "Don't you act like I used you. You done the same! You lied to all them scavs. You had yourself a goal, same as me, and you used any motherfucker you had to to get it."

"That's true, Nate. Thank you for that." I smiled, cold fury doing something sharp to my belly. "I'm not a very nice piece of work either."

He nodded. Like he'd scored a *point*. "Well then."

"Except, the thing is, Nate... Responsibilities."

"What?"

"We've all got them. Don't always benefit us, but they're there. You think I gave a shit if John-Paul lived or died? Had nothing to do with me. Just got mixed up in this. But I tell you what, Nate: I *finished* it. Too many people died on the way not to. Too much at stake."

"Make your point, limey."

"The point." I worked my jaw. Sighed deep. Saw Bella's face. "The point's name, Nate, was Shayla."

He stopped breathing.

Looked up.

"H-how... how did you..."

"She would've been, what? One, when you ran. Shit, you even left a note... 'Couldn't handle the responsibility,' Bella said. Rare moment of honesty there, Nate."

"You... you know B-bella..?"

"You latched onto *her* too, didn't you? Nice young thing, bright as a button, rich family. I mean... there's you, out on the streets, no place to live, and here's this stupid kid. What an opportunity..."

"Y-you... you shut the fuck up, now..."

"Made her love you, right? Used her money. Got her hooked on shit and right up the duff. Then just when the cons outweigh the pros, just when there's a kid in the picture, off you toddle. Off to the Choirboys, waiting with their job. Off to the U-S of A. Something like that?"

He was glaring, now. Wondering whether to run or punch me.

"Malice kept wondering," I said, "why you wouldn't stop staring at her kid.

"Guilt, right?"

The gun was heavy in my hand. I sighed.

"Bella helped me get here." I said, voice tighter than I'd expected. There was something like a choke rising in my throat. "She's dead now."

"How long have you known who I was?" Nate said, quietly.

"I think..." I scowled, looking inwards. "I think from the beginning. Heh. Maybe I *am* like you, Nate. Maybe I ignored it because you were useful. Was only just now, sitting here, that it all clicked.

"'Claystone,' Bella called you. Nathaniel Cassius 'Clay' Waterstone. Small world."

"Small world," he muttered. Almost a whisper. Then: "How's... How's the girl?"

My jaw clenched.

"That's just it, Nate. That's what I meant about responsibilities. Y'see, that girl, that little Shayla... she turned five last year."

Nate's eyes bulged. He saw it coming.

"They raped her mummy and dragged her away, screaming, to an airport just outside London."

"Oh... oh, God..."

"They loaded her onto a plane with a dozen more, all crying, and shipped them to a shitty little airport outside the Big Apple."

He moaned, knees giving way.

"And you'll never guess who was waiting for them, with a kind word and a silly costume, to ferry them off to see a nice old man."

"...No, no, no, no, no..."

"Bella told me... Bella told me it wasn't my problem. I wonder if she knew you'd be waiting there, at the other end?"

Tears oozed out of his eyes, falling in thick blobs to the floor of the corridor.

"I wonder if she knew I'd *make* it my problem?"

His lips parted.

"Wait. please! Just, wai –"

And I shot him in the head, through the centre of the tattoo over his eye, and watched as smoke coiled up from the hole.

Then I stepped into the Comms room with a clear head.

HER DIARY WAS there.

The goons had moved it all to one side. Bits of old detritus, files and notes and sheets. Enough paperwork to keep anyone busy for months. They'd swept it all aside and got-on with preparing the place for John-Paul. On the TV above the control board the withered old man died, mid-confession, over and over again. Stuck on a loop.

Her diary was there.

I almost didn't see it. Almost mistook it for just another book of notes, more tedious laboratory results to be communicated back to New York.

I bought her that diary. It was just... just this stupid thing. An idea for Christmas, one year. We gave each other notebooks, wrote down all our thoughts, everything we'd done, all the stuff we'd seen and said... then swapped them back at the end of the year.

Seems daft, now. It's not like I would've been allowed to write down half the stuff I got up to.

But hers... hers were always full. Fat with notes.

My heart almost exploded. *Her* handwriting. Neat little letters, unjoined, in neat little columns. Page after page. Different pens, different colours. Dated at the top, and always the same beginning:

My darling.

My eyes went fuzzy.

She'd been here. She'd been here once, but how long ago?

My fingers were clumsy, suddenly. Pages stuck together, paper tore. I scrabbled through the tears and shakes to the last pages, blinking at each date in turn.

Towards the end, she'd started using a page per week. Then per month.

Space was running out, as the back cover nudged closer. I didn't read a word, just let my eyes dance from date to date, not understanding, flicking further and further back.

The last two entries were separated by six months.

The last one –

Oh...

– the last one was made three months ago.

I was on the floor, then. Not understanding. Lights in front of my eyes.

Panels clicked and lights flickered on the consoles. My head swam.

This room. This was where she contacted me. This was where the signal started.

This was where my journey began.

And the greatest revelation of all, the one that all the others presupposed, but that somehow took far longer to settle; that blew them out of the water one by one and left me curled in a ball, head in my hands, teeth grating together, choking on dry sobs.

She's alive.

Oh, God.

She's alive.

Above ground, the Clergy ignored me. In my robe I was just another figure, and they had more than enough to be worrying about.

Wailing and screaming at the death of their master.

Hunting for Iroquois warriors, as their rusting ferry was sabotaged – listing in the water – and distant rumbles shook the island.

Some were taking over-optimistic potshots at the canoes and rowing boats just visible though the smoke, dodging between flaming patches of scummy liquid. The rest were just sitting, watching, waiting. They'd all seen the broadcast. They all knew.

It was over.

Soon, I'd swim out to the Iroquois in the boats. Nudging aside fiery drifts and scalding slicks. Maybe the *Tadodaho* was expecting me. Maybe I'd get medical treatment and food and thanks for my help.

Maybe not. Who cared?

I took the diary and the papers, bound up neatly. I stepped past arguing clerics and screaming soldiers, and let the world turn on around me.

She's alive.

The sun was setting. Through the settling quicksmog it was a distant spotlight, misted and artificial, and by its waning glow I read through the final pages of my lover's life.

Find me. The last page said. *Come and find me, my love.*

The fires of Lake Erie burnt around me, and the sky choked up with smoke and haze, and I flicked through pages and found –

Yes. There.

– found where to go. Found where to find her.

And smiled.

Don't you fucking give up, soldier!

Sir, no sir, etc, etc.

THE END

Simon Spurrier is an award-winning writer of novels and graphic novel fiction. He's worked extensively for the UK's talent-factory title *2000 AD*, has published novels with Abaddon, the Black Library and Black Flame, and has won a series of accolades and prizes for screenwriting. He's worked as a cook, a bookseller, a BBC Art Director and a film student. He lives in London because the night sky is a far better shade of green there than anywhere else.

KILL OR CURE

REBECCA LEVENE

For Carrie O'Grady,
without whom I'd never have been able to
figure out the plot of this damn thing.

And also because she's a top bird.

PROLOGUE

You know what they say – about being able to see yourself reflected in the pupils of someone's eyes? Bullshit. When you're standing that close to a man, all you can see in the centre of his eyes is darkness. But when I looked at him, I did see myself. In an epileptic flash of memory, I saw myself back when I'd first met him. Jesus, how was it possible to ever be that young? And then in an epileptic flash of the future, I looked at him and saw what I would become.

He smiled, a vivid flash of white against his dark brown face. And, despite everything, I smiled back. "Jasmine," he said. "How did this happen? How did you and I come to this?"

I raised the gun and pressed the muzzle hard into his cheek, the soft flesh yielding around it. I gave him the gun, because it was easier than the answer.

The answer started months before, back when my world was a hundred foot square and clean and white, and there'd been no one to share it with for five years. I didn't mind, though. I didn't care very much about anything then, as my mind – and everything that made me me – snoozed contentedly under a warm blanket of opiates.

I don't know if you've ever got high. It's like a golden glow that spreads out through your veins and rushes into everything; into every dark corner of you. It makes you feel that everything is absolutely fine, like main-lining optimism. Forget the physical high, the orgasmic rush – it's that unshakeable sense of being *fine* that makes it all worthwhile.

Or at least, that's what it's like to begin with. After the first few times, it's more like scratching an itch. And the longer you feed it, the deeper and crueller the itch gets. Normal people find it almost impossible to stop. Junkies get clean in prison and swear they're never going to let that shit screw up their lives again.

But when they're out and their life just isn't fine, but they know something that will make it feel that way... people who've tried it don't call it junk. They know better than that.

For junkies it's hard, but for me it was impossible. Because the morphine in my veins was the only thing that blotted out the Voice in my head. I could always hear it, whispering and giggling at the edge of my consciousness, but with enough drugs inside me I couldn't quite make out the words.

That morning started the same way every morning had for the last five years: first the Voice and then the drugs. It was always the Voice that woke me, growing louder as the protective blanket of morphine slipped away. Maybe outside, there might be something to distract me from it. In here, there was nothing. Just a small white warren, five corridors, two labs – one half-wrecked – and an office holding a long-fritzed computer and the corpses of two of my colleagues (desiccated now, embracing in the cleaning cupboard where I locked them until the smell of decaying flesh became bearable). There were only two books, one by Geoffrey Deaver and the other a microbiology textbook, both of which I'd read so often that I could recite them pretty much by heart. The morphine helped with the boredom, too. And the terrible loneliness.

There was a cannula in my arm. I'd treated enough smack addicts in my time to know that you didn't want to keep digging fresh holes in your veins, because pretty soon the ones in your arms would be on the point of collapse, pocked with gaping, pustulant sores, and then you'd find yourself moving on to the ones in your thighs, your eyeball. I'd seen junkies without penises, rotted away where they'd kept on injecting, even as the flesh festered and died, the pain less important than the hit.

So I fixed a cannula in my arm, like a terminal patient in a cancer ward. All I needed to get my fix was to empty the ampoule into a syringe and push the needle through the rubber tube permanently hanging from the crook of my elbow, like the open, hungry mouth of a baby bird. I could feel the excitement build up as I put the tip of the syringe in place, my heart rate speeding as I anticipated the rush. Junkie thinking, I knew. But what else did I have to live for?

Yeah, there was one answer to that, but he was on the other side of the world and probably dead and, anyway, I couldn't give him me without giving him the Voice, and I thought that was one thing I should keep to myself.

That day, though, I wasn't even thinking about him. I didn't think about anything much by then; the thoughts in my head had begun to wear thin, like an old video played over and over. All I thought about was getting the drug into my system.

I'd started pressing down on the plunger of the syringe, the first molecules of opiate trickling into my blood, when I heard it. A voice.

A voice, not the Voice. It was coming from the one break in the whiteness, the mound of rubble from the explosion which had trapped me in here, back when the world still had some hope in it.

It was coming from outside.

Christ.

My brain was still fuzzy from yesterday's drugs and the white noise of the psychosis they helped to mask. It couldn't quite process this. I had to think this through one step at a time. Voices meant people. Voices meant people inside the base – deep inside. The explosion had only sealed off the innermost areas. They couldn't have just wandered into a hidden military base on an island in the middle of a lake. They'd come here deliberately. They were looking for something.

Were they looking for me?

Who was looking for me?

For a moment I felt a flare of sharp, bright hope – a spike of emotion stronger than anything I'd ever got from the drugs. It was *him*, it had to be. Who else would come to this place, after all this time, to hunt me down?

But a moment later, reason swum up sluggishly through the murky waters of my thoughts. If it was him, why hadn't he tried to contact me? The comms unit had been sealed in along with me, powered – like the rest of the base – by generators built to survive a nuclear war. If he thought I was alive, he'd know where I was. But there was no way he'd think I was alive. I shouldn't be alive. I could have let him know different, but for five long years I'd chosen not to, because the price I'd paid for survival was too high, and I preferred him to remember me as I was rather than as what I'd become.

And then I heard the voices more clearly, calling out instructions to each other about clearing the rubble, and I knew for sure that it wasn't him. Because his voice was deep and just a little gravelly and these voices were light, with an accent I couldn't quite place.

"Getting thermal signs of a living body behind here," one of the voices said with sudden clarity. Shit! They knew I was here. These strangers, whoever they were, were coming for me – to take me away, to kill me, to do whatever they wanted with me. And suddenly, all the reasons that had kept me from getting in touch with him didn't feel like enough, and I wanted to hear his voice one last time before I died.

The comms unit was two rooms away, tucked into the back of the base. A part of me wanted to stay and face whatever was coming head-on. But I could hear the *clang* of heavy machinery and I knew that they'd be through the rubble soon; I'd only have this one chance.

The opiates were beginning to flush themselves out of my system, leaving behind a dull ache in my limbs, a cold sweat and an emptiness in my head – just the kind of vacuum that nature abhors. The Voice grew louder as I walked, filling the void, its cadence following the rhythm of my footsteps, echoing through my mind in time with the shakes now beginning to wrack my body. I could make out words now – 'blood' and 'cure' and other, more brutal words that I didn't know lived anywhere inside me – but I ignored them.

I hadn't entered this room since the first few weeks after I'd been trapped. Too tempting, if I was there, to call him. I was shocked by the layer of dust lying over everything, like a thick brown snowfall.

I eyed the communications equipment, sharp edges softened by the dust, and wondered if it was even functional. It had been built to last, but it had also been intended to be maintained. I had done nothing useful the whole time I was trapped down here. The drugs took away motivation along with everything else.

Behind me, I heard the muffled crump of a controlled explosion. They were through, or soon would be.

Two sweeps of my hand cleared the worst of the dust from the controls. My fingers were clumsy on the keys, but in thirty seconds or so I'd punched in the code for the headquarters in London. I'd no guarantee he'd be there – no guarantee he was even alive – but that was a thought I didn't let myself think. I knew him; if he was alive, he'd have found the safest, most defensible place in London to hole up. And that was the MI6 building, somewhere only a select few even had access to.

For a painfully long moment, the comms unit was silent. The gritty sound of debris being cleared echoed through the corridors behind me. Then, sharply, there was a crackle of static, and the hungry silence of an open communications link.

"Are... are you there?" I said, paralysed suddenly. What do you say to a lover you haven't spoken to in five years? Or to whoever else it might be who was listening, far away across an ocean and half a continent? Or to the emptiness of a deserted building, everyone who might have found their way into it already long dead?

And then it came to me, the flood of words I wanted to say to him, everything that had been dammed up inside me by drugs and loneliness and fear. And I started speaking, but a moment later I realised that the expectant silence I was filling had become the silence of dead air. Every light on the unit had gone out.

But those first few words had gone through. I was sure of it. And if he'd received them, he'd know where they'd come from.

My bedroom was two doors down, but I could already hear other footsteps. The invaders were through. It took a desperate scramble to find my diary, buried under a mound of unwashed clothes and discarded food packaging; personal hygiene hadn't been high on my agenda for a while. When I finally pulled it out, a grease stain from a discarded half-eaten ration pack on its front cover, I was shocked to realise how long it was since I'd last written. The clock on the wall gave me today's date. The last entry was six months before. Writing in here was the one thing I'd tried to do. When I got the balance of the drugs just right, I'd sit down and I'd think about him and I'd write him words which I knew he'd never read.

And now I had just a few minutes to write the last entry; there was a chance, perhaps, that he would see them. Behind me, I could hear voices, footsteps. They were outside the room. Going slowly. Treating the base as hostile ground. I had a minute, tops.

Find me, I wrote, the pen stiff and awkward in fingers that had forgotten the simple motion of writing. *Come and find me, my love.*

He never will, the Voice said in my head. *You're all alone in the world.*

But I wasn't. The intruders had arrived.

THEY TOOK ME to a flying boat, bobbing outside the base on the quiet waters of the lake. They were keeping a careful distance, their guns and their eyes on me. I knew why. I was shivering almost uncontrollably now and a cold, sick sweat was slicking my skin. My eyes must have looked quite mad.

Diseased, they were thinking.

Just crazy, I wanted to say, and maybe I did. Just a crazy junkie.

My mind didn't seem able to settle on any one thing, like a bee in a flower field, constantly caught by details. The gun that was pointed straight at me, barrel thin and long. *He* would have known what it was: make, calibre, stopping power. On our second date he had taken me to the Imperial War Museum. The next day I took him to this little collection of antique surgical instruments they used to keep up in Camden somewhere.

The gun flicked and I realised that the person holding it was waving me on – a distant blur at the periphery of my attention. I looked down and something else caught my eye, hooking into my mind and dragging it there. A little flower, yellow and drab, struggling up through a crack in the concrete of the helipad.

I hate flowers. I was sick once, very sick, when I was seven. Leukaemia. Everybody brought flowers. The hospital room was full of them, the smell so strong it muscled out the stink of antiseptic and old vomit. But I preferred the stink. It was what that place was all about. The flowers were a lie.

They had to carry me on board the flying boat. My muscles were cramping by then and the shakes were so hard they were close to convulsions. When I was halfway in, I vomited. I don't know what I hit. One of my captors, if the shouts of disgust were anything to go by. A part of me knew that I could die from withdrawal this severe.

Tell them you need the drugs, the Voice said. *It's obvious they want you alive.*

This made perfect sense, but I suspected the Voice had its own agenda. I tried to ask for anti-psychotics instead, the one thing I hadn't been able to obtain inside the base. But my ears were deaf to my own voice and I'm not sure how much of it there was left. I was sobbing helplessly with the pain by then.

Pain. That brought back another memory. The strongest of all. The first time the madness came and brought the Voice with it. Twice in my life, I've had a disease that wanted to kill me. And each time the pain it brought had a different quality. A terminal quality. This was a pain that was trying to drag you down with it, drag you away somewhere you weren't coming back from.

When the Cull struck, it was a quick death, but it wasn't a clean one. When you're bleeding out of every pore in your body, but you're still conscious. When your brain's frying inside your skull. When you're thirty years old and you know that you've only got two more days on this earth, and each of them will be filled with this same, unending agony...

And if the Cull was bad, the thing we did to ourselves to avoid it was unendurably worse.

The first time the Voice spoke, I thought it was one of my colleagues, the O-neg staff members who were the only ones left on the base to treat the many of us who were dying. The pain will end, *it said, suddenly and clearly.* If you surrender, it will leave you. *It seemed like a dumb thing for a doctor to be saying. Nothing but death would end this pain, not even the painkillers they'd been pumping into me. Or was that what they meant – that I'd be better off just letting go and dying? But that didn't sound like something one of my colleagues would say either.*

And then I realised, as I was thinking this, the pain had lessened. That terrible tearing in my muscles, the feeling of my body ripping itself apart. Gone. And my breathing was easier, too.

My head felt clearest of all. Clearer than it had ever been. Yes, *the Voice said,* you can hear me now. *A distant part of me realised that this was a symptom of psychosis – maybe even the result of a high fever, or maybe just approaching death – but the Voice was louder and stronger, and the new rush of energy surging through me didn't feel like death. It felt like rebirth.*

I opened my eyes for the first time in days, weeks. Before, every attempt to do this had been met by a blinding sear of white-hot light. Now I could see everything, more than I'd ever seen before. Colours were richer, more vibrant. I stared at the wall beside my bed for a moment, fascinated by the way the light reflected from the tight grain of the white-painted concrete. I could see, just by looking, that there were precisely five thousand three hundred and seventy-one grains of sand on the surface of one square inch of wall. Each one seemed to be sparkling at me individually.

The euphoria of returning health, I told myself.

No, *the Voice told me,* it's more than that. You're different now.

I knew that it was right.

You need to get out of here, *the Voice said, and I knew that was right too. There was no question of arguing with it, not because its command was so powerful, but because it seemed to make so much sense. It felt like the voice of reason.*

You know how they say that madness feels like sanity? That delusions feel like a new and wonderful clarity?

No shit.

I turned away from my study of the wall to look carefully around the rest of the room. There were five other beds, all empty, some surrounded by the detritus of emergency medical procedures. My memory was hazy still, but I knew that I hadn't been the only one Culled on the base. Or the only one Cured. There was no sign of them now.

Don't worry about them, *the Voice told me.* You can find them when you're free.

My arm was hooked up to an IV tube, my chest to a heart monitor. I detached both, unhooking the monitor from the power so that it wouldn't make a betraying noise. When I pulled the tube from my arm an ooze of blood followed it, darker and thicker than was healthy. I watched, mesmerised, as the viscous drops fell in perfect globules to shatter on the floor. I expected to feel weak when I rose. But I didn't feel dizzy, more like I was floating. As if I could do anything. I looked down at my legs under the short hospital gown, expecting to see them somehow magically transformed, muscles bulging. But they were still thin, pale and wasted, from illness and long confinement underground.

When I looked up again, it was to find someone standing in the doorway, watching me. He was wearing a white coat, but he was also carrying a gun. "Dr Tomas?" he asked cautiously. A prominent Adam's Apple bobbed in his thin throat. I recognised him as one of the soldiers who guarded the base, but I couldn't remember his name. Military and medical didn't mix.

Kill him, *the Voice told me,* Kill him before he realises what you've become. *It made perfect sense.*

I smiled at the boy, little older than eighteen, whose name I suddenly remembered was Andy. "Yes," I told him. "I'm feeling much better." I took a hesitant step towards him, as if I still had almost no strength, and tried to calculate how close I'd need to be before I could wrench the gun out of his hand, put my hands around his neck and snap it.

I watched his eyes as they tracked the blood still dripping from my arm to the floor, the unplugged IV, the dead heart monitor. "No," he told me. "Dr Tomas, you're not well at all."

A sudden flash of the present intruded, and I opened my eyes for a moment to see a sickening, vertiginous view of trees and water far below. The base was receding, just a grey dot on the horizon. My mind floated above it for a moment, trying to cling on to the past, but then it tore away and for a while there was no coherence to my fever dreams, just fragments of images as jagged as pain.

The plane landed at some point, a sickening lurch and then a nauseating sway on water. I was shaken roughly and kicked, but no force on earth could get me to my feet, and eventually I was carried out of the plane and onto the large pontoons that held it over the shifting surface of the waves. A wash of warm saltiness revived me and I saw that they were carrying me towards a boat, a big one. A sailing yacht.

Faces watched me from the deck as I was hauled up the side like a sack of potatoes. I watched them for a moment, round circles of brown and black and pink. There were black gashes in their centre, open mouths: in smiles or grimaces, it was hard to tell. My eyes drifted away and, instead, I watched the sweat pouring off me, as it dripped and fell into the ocean below. Salt into salt.

After a few minutes I sprawled on the deck. The sun blazed down on me but I felt cold, drawing my knees and elbows in. The faces blinked above me, watching.

"This is what you bring me?" one of them said. I thought I recognised the accent as Eastern European.

I saw one of my rescuers shrug. Felt it, too, as if my skin was now so hypersensitive that the slightest shift in the air moved agonisingly against it. The Voice was screaming at me to get away, but the pain was screaming louder and I put all my energy into ignoring them both.

"She's a scientist, a doctor. Last survivor of the research centre. That's got to be worth something," my rescuer said.

"She's a junkie."

I couldn't argue with that. The junk was flushing itself out in my sweat as they spoke, leaving a hungry void behind.

I felt them stop and look at me. "So," my rescuer said, "she'll live or she'll die, and then we'll know if she's any use. All we need to do is wait."

So, she'll live or she'll die... The words echoed hollowly in my head, banging against other memories, knocking them loose.

"So," I SAID, right back when this all first began, "either we'll live or we'll die, but at least we'll know. We know we won't be safe here forever. No matter how careful we are, or how airtight we think this place is, the virus is going to get in eventually. I'll take a punt on a zero-point-one per cent chance of survival over no chance at all."

The others nodded. They knew I was right. And sitting there, safe with their O-neg blood, they were in no position to be giving lectures on safety to someone sitting right in the crosshairs of the virus. The room was crowded, the top brass of the base all gathered together. This, after all, was what it had all been about. Why we'd all been brought here in the first place, safe from the horrific fate of the rest of the world. There was a thick smell in the room, too many people who got to wash too infrequently. Put us all in one place and it became unbearable.

I saw Corporal Wetlock, brown face washed out by too long spent underground, staring at a speck of dirt on the wall as if it might hold some sort of answer. I'd noticed that a lot over the last few weeks. The saved unable to look the damned in the eye. Not often, I guess, that you get to work up close and personal with real-life walking corpses.

But maybe not. Not anymore – not if Ash and I had got it right.

"Zero-point-one per cent?" General Hamilton asked. "That's all you can offer me – after all this time?" Her chest was a mosaic of medals. I wondered when she'd had the time to earn them all.

We all knew that time was running out. Deaths were in the millions worldwide, maybe hundreds of millions already beyond saving. No point getting angry at her impatience.

"I don't see any other project offering you any odds at all," Ash said, pissed off nevertheless. He glared around the table, over the proud arch of his nose, and more people looked down. There were seven separate research programmes going on here, coming at the problem from every sensible angle and a couple of straight-out crazy ones. The nearest anyone else had got to a vaccine was something that gave lab rats intestinal cancer within two days of injection. Nothing else had even progressed to in-vivo testing.

"Okay," Hamilton said. "But testing on yourselves? You're the last people we can afford to lose in the ninety-nine point nine per cent likelihood that all it does is give you pancreatic cancer or cause your brain to bleed out your goddamn ears."

The bleeding out the ears had been one of our earlier attempts. Poor rats.

"General," I said, "If it doesn't work, if this avenue's a dead end, we're useless to you anyway. By the time we've started a new line of research..." I shrugged. "We'll be bleeding out of pretty much every part of our body."

"Fine," she said. "Try it."

And that, right there, was the single worst decision anyone could have made.

CHAPTER ONE

Going cold turkey is no one's idea of fun. It's a private kind of hell. What can I say about it that hasn't been said already? Just sobbing and puking and sometimes fitting and nearly dying. I didn't know where I was – but I was somewhere. We'd arrived. The visions of my past eased up after that first rush, leaving nothing to relieve the monotony. That's the biggest secret about illness and pain. How monumentally fucking boring it is.

People drifted in and out, shot things into my arm and sometimes forced them down my throat. Some of those things must have been anti-psychotics, because after a while the Voice faded into silence. My mind felt clearer than it had in five years. When I stopped screaming in agony, I guessed I'd be grateful for that.

On the fourth day, I realised that the rocking sensation I was feeling had nothing to do with drug withdrawal. I was still on a boat. Something about the motion told me it was a big one, an order of magnitude above the yacht which had brought me here. I spent ten minutes lying there, wondering if it was worth the effort to get up and walk towards the port hole I could see to my left. The shutters were closed over it, a relic of the stage when any light stabbed into my eyes like a knife, but the diamond-splinter pain behind my temples had faded to a dull ache, and I thought I could risk a look.

If I could make it the five paces across the floor to the porthole... my knees buckled the instant I stepped out of bed. My joints felt like they were held together with weak glue. I caught a glimpse of myself in a mirror against one of the dark-stained wooden walls. Dark shadows circled my eyes like bruises and my hair hung lank and unwashed around my face, grease turning the dark brown almost black. My skin was so pale it looked yellow, faint black veins showing on my arms. I realised that this was the first time I'd seen myself in years. I'd deliberately smashed the one mirror in the base after the first few months of staring at my blank, desperate eyes. I'd hidden the fragments of glass in the closet along with my colleague's corpses.

The catch on the porthole was tight. I had to stop to gather my breath four times before I finally managed to twist it open. I flinched from the light that poured in when I finally did, but my eyes adjusted without problem. I suddenly realised that I felt alive, really alive. It was a weird sensation.

The sky was only a little paler than the sea, a brilliant, tropical blue. The water was far below, fifty feet or more, the waves smacking against the hull in sharp little peaks and troughs. The ship was even bigger than I'd realised. There was a coastline ahead of us, a crescent of pure white sand leading back to dark trees and rising into jagged volcanic peaks. Almost certainly the Caribbean.

A long way from Lake Erie. I wondered what the people who'd found me had been searching for, all that way from home. And I wondered why they'd bothered to bring me all the way back here, when they hadn't thought I was worth the trouble of saving. Had I said something in my delirium that had made me sound valuable? But what use was an expert in a virus that had killed everyone already?

I heard the sound of a key turning in the lock of my door and realised for the first time that I had been a prisoner. The man who stepped through was big, blond and handsome in the kind of way that just wasn't very interesting to look at.

"Dr Tomas?" he said. He had a faint Scandinavian accent and a lighter voice than I'd expected from such a large man.

I nodded, and a wave of dizziness washed through me. I leaned an unsteady hand against the porthole for support, feeling like I'd been on my feet for ten hours, not ten minutes.

The man seemed to realise what was up, because he strode over in two long paces and carefully supported my arm under the elbow. Or maybe he just wanted to make sure I wasn't going to make a run for it.

"I have a lot of questions," I told him.

"Yes, I guess so." It was immediately apparently that he wasn't going to be the man to answer them. "Are you well enough to...?" he nodded at the door.

I wasn't, but I couldn't stand the thought of spending a moment longer in that room. A waft of cool, fresh air was drifting in through the door and I realised for the first time that it stank in here. I reeked of old sweat and the toxins that had washed out of my body along with it. "Yeah, I think so," I told him. "Maybe I could take a shower first."

"After," he said.

I wasn't going to argue with him. I'd just noticed the handle of the semi-automatic poking out of the waistband of his jeans.

THERE WAS ANOTHER person waiting outside the room – a tall woman with olive skin and a face as elegantly sculpted and impassive as a mask. She didn't say anything, just fell into step behind me as the man led me forward. The ship was a warren, corridors snaking fore and aft, lined with cabins. The carpet underfoot had once been expensive but was now frayed and a little threadbare. The chandeliers hanging from the ceiling were covered in grime. I was almost certain now that I was on board a commercial cruise liner. It seemed so improbable, a relic of a time before the world had sickened and died.

We passed other people, some of whom nodded greetings to my two guides. No one ethnic group seemed to predominate; a mixture of brown, black and white faces. They were all dressed colourfully, many of them in leather and silk, and there was something old-fashioned... a little studied about their clothes. They almost looked like costumes, or a bizarre sort of uniform. I felt their curious eyes following me as I passed. So, a big ship, but not that big a crew; small enough, anyway, to notice a stranger among them.

At the end of one interminable corridor we came to a lift. The walls were entirely covered in mirrors, dusty but clear enough to give me an unwelcome view of myself. I'd seen homeless junkies on the streets of London who looked more promising. No wonder no one wanted to talk to me.

The lift rose for a very long time. I felt the sea-breeze the moment I stepped out, tasted the salty tang of it. Five paces and we were out in the open. The sun deck of a ship, even larger than I'd guessed – a floating city.

And here, at last, was a crowd. They were as colourful as the people on the lower decks, and far noisier. The babble of talk hit me the moment I stepped out, and I found myself physically recoiling from it. People are a habit it's easy to lose. I felt like a wild animal encountering humanity for the first time.

In the centre of the deck was a big rectangular pit which I realised after a moment was a dried-up swimming pool. An over-sized wooden chair had been placed at one end of it, and though not everyone was facing it, it was obviously the centre of the gathering.

I realised that I'd stopped short when I felt something pressing into my back, nudging me forward. It might have been my escort's finger, or maybe her gun, but either way I wasn't arguing.

The woman on the chair watched me all the way. Her eyes were brown and cynical, a shade darker than her coffee-coloured skin. Mixed race, I guessed, and definitely part Afro-Caribbean. Her hair clung to her head in tight cornrows, then hung down her back in a long cascade, stiff with beads. I could feel the power emanating from her. This was a woman who ruled – and these people were her subjects.

She smiled, finally, when I was only a few paces away from her. The expression was startling, suddenly making her seem entirely normal, like someone you'd be introduced to at a friend's party who turned out to work for the local council. She was quite young, maybe in her late thirties. But the lines around her mouth told me that she didn't smile very often. She was dangerous, however friendly she seemed.

"Thank you Soren, Kelis," she said to the two who'd accompanied me. I was surprised to find that she had a British accent, quite a refined one. I don't know what I'd expected, but it wasn't that.

Soren nodded and fell back to the side of the woman's chair. Behind me I felt Kelis shift, but I knew that she hadn't gone far. And everywhere around me there were guns. Knives too. And the brightness on some of the clothes was blood.

I looked back at the leader of this informal army. "Thank you for rescuing me."

She shrugged. "It wasn't intentional. We were just scavenging and there you were."

"Still," I said, "I'm grateful."

"Are you?" she studied me closely. "You'd been taking industrial quantities of opiates and benzoids." So, educated too.

"Yeah. The time in that bunker just flew by."

She smiled slightly at that. "How much time, exactly?"

"Five years. Give or take."

"Since it started."

I nodded. "We were a government research project, but... the shit hit the usual apparatus. There was an explosion and half the place collapsed, with me on the wrong side of the rubble." It was close enough to the truth.

She seemed to accept it. "And what were you researching?"

"The cure."

I felt a buzz pass through the crowd like an electric current. The woman's face remained unreadable, though. "Did you find it?"

I cocked an eyebrow and looked around me.

"I guess not," she continued. "But you – you told us you needed anti-psychotics. Those aren't usually needed for opiate detox."

"I have mild schizophrenia," I told her. "Totally controllable, with the right medication."

She seemed to take a little longer to accept this half-truth. Or maybe she was just wondering what the hell kind of use a head-case like me was going to be to her. Some, she must have decided, because then she asked, "You're a doctor, right?"

I nodded.

"Academic?"

"And practical. I was a haematologist before." I didn't need to say before *what*. Time was now divided into 'Before' and 'After.'

"Can you set a broken limb? Sew up a cut or take down a fever?"

"Yeah," I told her. "Give me the right equipment and I can do all that." I glanced over the deck to the distant shoreline, palm trees leaning over the pure white beach. "I know my stuff when it comes to tropical diseases, too."

She smiled fully and stood up. She was exactly my height, our shoulders level as she reached out to embrace me in an impersonal hug. "Then welcome to my kingdom," she said. "I used to have another name, but now people just call me Queen M." She smiled, as if it was a big joke. But I knew damn well that she was a queen, and I'd better be sure to treat her like one.

QUEEN M TOOK me on the tour herself. The flagship was just what I'd thought: a luxury cruise liner which had been stranded off the coast of St Martin when the Cull struck and its crew were too sick to think about anything but dying.

"We threw off the corpses, scrubbed down the decks and took her over," Queen M told me. She was standing at the prow of the small catamaran they'd launched from the belly of the cruise ship, the wind rattling through the beads in her hair.

"Where do you get the fuel to move her?" I asked.

Queen M looked at me, judging the question. Why did I want to know? Was I figuring out their weaknesses? "We don't very often," she told me eventually. "But it's useful to know that we can if we need to."

The catamaran circled the prow of the boat and I got my first view of the rest of the fleet. Hundreds of vessels, almost all of them sailboats, some big enough to carry a crew of fifty, others barely big enough for one. There were fishing boats as well as luxury yachts, and somewhere in the middle I saw the flying boat which had taken me from the compound. After a second I noticed that all the vessels were all flying the same flag: a stylised drawing of a red blood cell – the outline of the platelet picked out on red against a white background. A survivor's celebration. And also a subtle sort of warning.

"All following you?" I asked, watching one ship hove away from the fleet, the wind billowing its sails.

"I brought them together," she said, a non-answer.

"And the rest of the world?" In the back of my mind, always, were thoughts of him. Of what had happened back in London, and whether there was any chance he might have survived it.

She looked at me almost with pity. "You don't know?"

I looked away, not liking what I saw in her eyes. "I can guess, but..."

"Yes," she said. "Everything you've guessed, and worse. There's no government left in Europe or America. The Cull took most people, but other illnesses, and fighting, and just outright stupidity, took a lot of what was left. Infrastructure broke down. The rule of law. There are crops rotting on the plains of the American Midwest while the people of New York starve. You wouldn't believe, would you, that civilization could fall apart so quickly?"

I shook my head. But I saw in her face that she'd believed it – and had prepared for it.

After that, the catamaran headed for one of the more distant islands, a small hump on the horizon. We passed more ships as we travelled, some with long thin lines stretching into the water from their bows, trawling the deep waters for fish.

"Yours too?" I asked.

She nodded at me and then at the dark-skinned fishermen on the boat as they shouted a greeting. Nearer in to the island I saw something stretching across the waves, barring our way. "Fishing net?" I guessed.

"Wave farm." The turbines stretched entirely around the shore, ringing the small island in steel. They must have generated enough power to supply everyone on board the flagship and then some. Civilisation might have collapsed elsewhere, but it seemed to be alive and kicking here.

"Food?" I asked. She didn't answer, just waved an instruction to our skipper. The catamaran veered sharply to starboard, throwing up a wall of water as it turned, and we headed for yet another island.

At first I thought a massive fire had scorched the island's soil, but as we drew nearer I realised that it was just black, volcanic sand. The interior was flat, stretching off to a distant horizon, but it was vibrantly green. Closer still and I could see the pattern to it, a patchwork of fields with flourishing crops. There were people there, slowly working their way up the lines of crops, planting or weeding, whatever the hell you did when you were a farmer.

"Food," I said.

"The Caribbean's a fertile place," she replied.

"And that's why you came here?"

"One of the reasons. My mother was Trinidadian, you know. We used to come here on family holidays when I was a child." Her face had a faraway look for a moment, drifting in memory.

"It must have taken a while to set this up, though. Time to gather resources..."

She smiled. "The scarce resource these days is people. And all you really need to do to gather them is offer a tiny bit of hope."

I looked over at the island again, the crops thriving in the region's benign climate as field workers sweated under the tropical sun. Maybe she was right.

After the tour they took me back to the flagship, to a different room from the one I'd detoxed in, bigger and cleaner. I had the impression that I'd passed some kind of test. But the instant I stepped onboard, my two shadows joined me: Soren and Kelis, falling into step behind me as naturally as if they'd been doing it for weeks. I kinked an eyebrow at Kelis – figuring she'd be the more communicative of the two – and she seemed to understand the question.

"Bodyguards," she said. "For protection." She had a Latin American accent. A pleasant, light voice with an air of lethal competence about her. Kelis looked like she could kill without even raising a sweat.

"And what exactly am I going to need protecting from?"

Kelis smiled slightly. "I didn't say we were going to be protecting *you*."

I shut the door of my cabin on her smile and Soren's frown and heard the key turn in the lock. As soon as I was alone I realised how exhausted I was. There was so much I should be doing, so many things I needed to find out about my rescuers, but there wasn't an ounce of energy left in me to do it. I lay on the bed, closed my eyes and that was all I knew.

When I woke it was dark. I had no idea what time it was but it felt late. I realised that I needed a watch and ridiculously, it was that, more than anything, that made me realise I was back among people. I wondered if I should try sleeping again, but I knew it wouldn't come. It would take some time to get my body clock back in sync with the normal, sunlit world.

There was a small bathroom attached to the cabin, with hot and cold running water. Someone had even left me towels, soap and shampoo. And when I emerged, naked and still a little damp, revelling in the sensation of finally, finally feeling clean, I found that the wardrobes had been filled with clothes, the same colourful silk and leather as I'd seen everyone else wearing. I didn't quite get it. It was like they were dressing up as pirates. What wasn't I being told?

Something else had been left for me too. A vial of a strong anti-psychotic with a new, sterile syringe. Just one vial. There was something about that I didn't like, the implication that the drug was to be rationed, the threat of its withdrawal used as a way to control me.

Still, I pushed the dose into my arm, and slipped on a loose pair of maroon trousers and a tight-fighting white blouse. When I looked in the mirror I saw that I was still far too thin and far too pale, but washed and dressed I could at least pass for heroin-chic rather than straight-out junkie. My eyes were still ringed with black circles. I wondered if those would ever fade, the knowledge that had drawn them there was not something I could unlearn.

I tried the door and Kelis and Soren were there waiting, looking as if they might never have moved from where I'd left them hours ago. I nodded a wary greeting to Kelis, then to Soren. Only she bothered to return it. His eyes looked almost as shadowed as mine.

"It's three o'clock," Kelis told me when she saw me surreptitiously glancing towards her wrist. "We saw you were awake." That meant a hidden camera. Shit.

"Sorry," I said, although really why should I apologise?

"Let's go for a walk," Soren said. "You can explore the rest of the ship." So maybe I wasn't a prisoner anymore. It seemed that Queen M trusted me now. We set off along another of those endless, intestinal corridors which seemed to fill the entire vessel. The cabin doors were all shut, but it was impossible to tell if they were occupied.

"Are these all used?" I asked Kelis, but it was Soren who answered.

"They will be, eventually."

"By new recruits?" I asked, but that seemed to be it for him, conversationally.

At the end of the corridor was a larger room with marble stairs leading up and down from it and glass-fronted shops lining the walls, long-emptied of their goods. No cash economy here, I guessed. At the foot of the stairs was what I'd been looking for, one of those cross-sectional maps of the ship that long-ago voyagers had used to orient themselves.

Jesus, it was huge. The ship must have carried thousands of passengers when it was a cruise liner. I had a sudden, unwelcome vision of the way it must have been for them when the Cull struck. No time to make it to shore. A ship of the dying. Suddenly desperate for homes and families that they'd never realised they'd said good-bye to for the last time. Queen M's crew must have had a strong stomach to clean all that out. The decks would have been literally running with blood.

But maybe Queen M's crew didn't mind the sight of blood too much.

We drifted along the corridors and decks of the ship like ghosts, my two shadows wafting along behind me. The whole place was eerily quiet. If I'd been a superstitious type, I might have thought it felt haunted.

I found the casino next, still fully stocked, piles of chips on green baize tables.

"Queen M opens this every Friday night," Kelis told me. "People come from all the ships."

I picked up a blue hundred-unit chip and spun it in my fingers. "And what do they gamble for?"

"Duties," Soren said. "Jobs no one wants."

"Like body-guarding cleaned-up junkies?" I asked, but only Kelis smiled.

I wandered for a while among the tables, threw some dice on the craps board, spun the roulette wheel. It seemed appropriate, somehow, that it landed on double zero. Everything you'd gambled lost.

But perhaps not everything of mine was. Somewhere, maybe, I had a man. Did I want to tell them that? He was – well, he was a useful man in anyone's army. If I told them about him, there was a chance I could talk them into looking for him, bringing him back here.

I opened my mouth to tell Kelis – then slowly closed it again. No. I still knew too little about what was going on here.

After the casino I found the ship's kitchens, deserted at this time of night but still obviously in use. Kelis and Soren watched impassively as I pulled open store cupboards and refrigerators, poked my nose into spice racks and big bowls of dried herbs. They didn't go hungry here, that was for sure. A walk-in cool room was hung with animal corpses: tiny rabbits, birds, and something so big that I thought it could only be a horse.

I found four separate dining rooms, six bars, a theatre and a cinema. There was an indoor pool and a gym that looked like it still got use.

After a while, Kelis and Soren seemed to get into the spirit of it. When we hit a corridor we knew was unoccupied we went into the cabins, saw what was in the wardrobes, the dressing tables. They'd cleaned the corpses out when they'd taken the ship, but left the possessions behind. All these relics of unfinished lives. In one room there was a digital camera, the battery still miraculously charged. Morbidly, unable to stop myself, I flicked through the pictures in its memory. Almost all shots of an older woman, standing on a series of interchangeable beaches, sometimes with a chubby, grey-haired man beside her. In the last photo the two of them looked scared, but I didn't think they knew yet exactly what lay in store for them. I put the camera down and we didn't go into any more rooms after that.

Instead I headed down, below the water line, into the bowels of the ship. For the first time I sensed reluctance from my two guards, but neither of them said anything until I'd bottomed out into a drab metal corridor that looked like it belonged on a submarine, not a cruise liner.

"Time we went back," Kelis said.

I ignored her and walked further down this corridor that seemed to lead nowhere.

Her hand clamped on my arm like a vice. "Far enough."

I turned to look at her, but there was no humour in her face now. "Why?"

Soren shifted, just a little, and for the first time since we'd set out that night I got a glimpse of the gun he kept tucked in the waistband of his trousers. "No reason," he said. "I want to go back to sleep."

"So go," I said. "I can find my way back."

Kelis slowly released my arm, but she didn't look away from me. "Believe me, Dr Tomas, there's nothing down there you want to know about."

After a second I shook my head and smiled as if it was no big deal. But I tried to memorise the route to that forbidden corridor as we wound our way back to my cabin.

Not that I was given much chance to use it. It seemed like the entire crew of the ship had something wrong with them and had just been waiting for a doctor to show up and fix it. Another day passed, and then another, and then a week and I still hadn't been allowed a single second in the ship without my two bodyguards doggedly following at my heels.

Then, on the eighth day, everything changed. I woke to the sound of pounding on my cabin door. They didn't wait for me to answer and a second later I opened my eyes, disoriented, to find Soren's blue ones looking down at me. He didn't speak.

"So, I guess you want me to get up," I said eventually.

He nodded. I wondered suddenly what he did when he wasn't traipsing around after me. He was one of those people you couldn't really imagine relaxing, knocking back a few drinks with his friends or sunbathing with a good book. He didn't look like a man who ever really enjoyed himself.

"Why?" I asked him. "Has something happened?"

"No," Kelis said. I realised for the first time that she'd been hovering by the door, brown skin almost the same colour as the mahogany panelling on the wall behind her. "It's time for you to really earn your keep."

A catamaran took us to the island and from there a car drove us to the airport, just two strips of tarmac cut through the trees. There were twenty others with us, and this time there were none of the bright colours, the play-acting at pirates. This time it was clear that I was travelling with a regiment from someone's private army.

Soren was dressed all in black. There were ammunition belts slung over both his shoulders and he was carrying more guns than he had limbs. It was almost absurd, but I could see the way one of his thumbs was tapping a jittery rhythm against the barrel of the largest rifle and the small drop of blood forming on his lip where he couldn't seem to stop chewing it. Anything that made Soren nervous made me very nervous.

Kelis's face was as calm as ever, her body entirely motionless. Only two spots of colour, high in her cheeks, told me anything about what was going on inside her. I'd been given combats to wear, an ugly olive green. I felt ridiculous, a little girl playing at being a soldier.

They'd given me a medical kit but they hadn't given me a gun.

The small jet took off from the runway, wheels bumping alarmingly along the pock-marked surface, without anyone having said a word to me about where we were going. After an hour, though, as the sea crawled on endlessly beneath us, I was sure that we were travelling east, crossing the Atlantic.

"May as well sleep," Kelis told me. "We'll be nine hours yet."

Going all the way to Europe then. Bringing me closer to *him*, a small, hopeful voice said in my head.

BUT NOT, IN the end, close enough. I woke up seven hours later to a rising sun and the approaching coastline of a country that I knew wasn't England.

"France," Kelis said.

"Okay," I answered. "Why?"

"Recruitment drive," one of the others told me, a middle-aged white man with leathery skin and a thin, mean face. He'd introduced himself as Curtis, though whether this was his first or his last name I never found out.

I remembered what Queen M had told me, that people were the scarce resource now. I thought about pirates and the British Navy of old, and the weapons that everyone but me was carrying – and I began to guess what we were. A press gang.

PARIS APPROACHED. MORE golden than I'd remembered it; like a vast human honeycomb. There were blots of darkness in the gold, relics of a recent burning. As the plane sank lower I saw that whole streets and neighbourhoods had been reduced to rubble. Strange, how people can face a disease that wants to kill them all and still have the energy to kill each other.

The plane sank lower still, low enough that I could make out the insect forms of people on the city's streets. Never alone, always in crowds of ten, or twenty, or greater. Safety in numbers.

Soon, the plane was low enough that I could see individual faces. I could also see the Eiffel Tower, prodding the sky above the heart of the city. I began to wonder where, exactly, they were planning on landing.

A few minutes later and we were a hundred meters or so above the roofs of the buildings and a few hundred meters away from the start of the Champs-Élysées. "You have got to be fucking kidding me!" I said.

Kelis grinned, making her look like a little kid for about a tenth of a second. "What's the matter?"

I settled for, "What about the cars?" I'd seen news broadcasts in the bunker, the streets of every major city choked with vehicles, abandoned when their owners sickened and died.

"Cleared them the last time we were here," Soren said.

And when was that? I wanted to shout. *How do you know people haven't been piling the road high with broken-down cars and trucks since you left?*

No time left for that. The plane had started its final, fatal plummet to the ground. Now I could feel the breakfast I'd eaten four hours ago rising up to choke me and I think I might have screamed for real, because roads are narrow and aeroplanes are wide and no one in their right mind tries to set one down on top of the other in the middle of one of Europe's biggest cities.

The golden blur of buildings rushed by on either side. I looked across at Soren but he was just frowning faintly, like a man wondering whether he'd forgotten to buy milk that morning. Kelis was still smiling, the expression more feral than happy.

And then we were only twenty feet above the road. There were cars there, three of them right ahead of us, but there was absolutely no way we'd be pulling up now. The wind screamed past the wings and I screamed too, but it didn't matter because the back wheels had finally hit the ground with a noise louder than I could have believed possible. The plane jerked underneath us like a wild horse which had just been saddled for the first time. Suddenly I wasn't the only one screaming.

I was buckled in, but the strap nearly broke around me as we swerved violently to the right. There was a hideous crunch beneath us, as if we'd just run over the world's largest cockroach, and we passed the first of the cars. But there were still two more to go. For just a moment I wished that I hadn't taken the drugs which had killed the Voice inside me. That I could have heard it still, telling me that everything was going to be okay, that I was invincible. But maybe even the Voice would have had a few doubts right then.

Another swerve, to the left this time. Another horrible crunch. A firework display spat past the windows; after a second of confusion I realised that it was the spark of the undercarriage dragging over metal.

There were screams outside the plane too now. We must have come out of the blue sky without warning. I wondered if anyone had been caught beneath it, if some of the crunches we'd heard had been bone, not metal. But I didn't wonder too hard. Other people's deaths don't count for much when you're facing your own.

Then, incredibly, we were slowing down. The awful rasping sound of metal on tarmac was still deafening, and the plane was still shuddering. I guessed that we were pulling one of the crushed cars along with us, the drag of the undercarriage fighting against our vast momentum. We were going no faster than a car on a motorway now, the buildings rushing past on either side finally individually distinguishable. And then we stopped altogether.

There was a second of one of the most profound silences I'd ever heard. Then one of the men beside me whooped and the rest of the crew joined in, and I did too because Jesus, it felt good to be alive.

When we got out, we saw that we'd stopped just ten feet shy of the Arc de Triomphe. I wasn't the only one who let out a jagged, slightly hysterical burst of laughter at the sight of the plane's nose, sniffing at the base of the world-famous landmark. The plane itself had seen better days: one of the wheels had torn off, and an engine was hanging loosely from the wing.

Soren scratched at his short cropped hair. "Guess we're going to have to do some work on that." I couldn't see it being a quick job. But then I had no idea how long we were supposed to be here.

"Philips, Mitchell," Curtis said. Two of the crew turned to the plane, others standing close by to guard. "The rest of you – it's time to rock and roll."

Every single person in the party, save me, was suddenly holding some very serious ordinance in a very serious way, and the few ragged people I'd seen melting out of the side streets around us were melting right back into them. There was a *don't-fuck-with-us* vibe going on, that made me feel safe and uneasy at the same time.

Paris was eerily quiet. This was the first time I'd been in a major city since the Cull. I'd known, intellectually of course, what it would be like. Less than two per cent of the population left alive by now – the place was bound to be a ghost town. But nothing prepares you for the sight of somewhere you've seen full of people, noise and motion suddenly so still. Worse, because the buildings – the bones of the place – were mostly intact, with no visible reason for what had gone so wrong.

Still, but not deserted. There were subliminal flickers of motion out the corner of my eye as we walked the narrow side streets in strict military formation: point man, scouts, rear guard. They'd placed me in the centre of their small arrow of personnel. For protection or to stop me escaping? I couldn't tell, and it didn't make much difference. There was no way I'd be heading off into these mausoleum streets alone.

We were being watched – everyone knew it – and not by friendly eyes.

Still, the attack was unexpected when it came. Queen M's people were watching forward, sideways, behind. They were watching above, scanning the roofs of the buildings for snipers or spies.

They weren't looking below.

Being right in the middle is no protection at all when the attackers are coming at you out of the sewers. There was a quick, loud grate of metal as a cover was shoved aside. And then the whine of bullets and the crack of their impact as someone stuck his arm out and fired round a full 360 degrees. I felt a stinging graze on my right thigh.

Not everyone got off so lightly. Kelis let out a grunt, blood spraying from one side of her ribcage. Another of the men went down and didn't get up. More bullets thudded into his corpse, the blood now oozing slowly out without a functional heart to pump it.

A second later, Soren had stepped in front of Kelis, pushing her to the ground behind the tree-trunk solidity of his body. His semi-automatic was firing and firing, and even over the noise of them, I heard the splash of our assailant's body falling into the filthy water below.

But he wasn't alone. Drain covers were popping up all over the street, figures pulling themselves acrobatically out of the sewer. Our formation was shot to hell. Everyone had scattered after that first, shocking burst of gunfire. I felt horribly exposed, unarmed and unprepared. My first instinct was to fall to the ground, but that's where the threat was coming from. Instead I found myself kneeling beside the bloody body of our lost man. Up close I could see that he was young, maybe still a teenager. His eyes were open, blankly reflecting back the last daylight he'd ever seen.

I didn't know exactly what I was doing there. My body seemed to be moving without my mind having to give it any instructions, as if it had realised that this was more than the conscious me could deal with. I wondered for a second if I'd meant to try to help him, but then my hands were reaching for the gun he'd never had a chance to fire, sliding the barrel back and forward to load a bullet into the chamber. Before I'd quite registered what I was doing I'd fired a round point-blank into the head just emerging from the dark hole of the sewer in front of me.

The force of the shot twisted the man round, giving me a perfect view of the exit wound ripped out of the back of his skull, the bloodied shards of bone and the white meat inside.

I heard the ragged breath of someone behind me and twisted, firing at the same time. The shot was wild but good enough to take the man in the chest. He fell, gasping, with hands clutched against his body, trying to keep in everything that belonged inside. It was a battle he couldn't win, and after a few seconds his hands slackened and fell. I'd taken two lives.

After that I made it to the side of the road, crouching in the lee of a small brick wall. I could taste the adrenaline in my mouth, a bitter tang. It had flooded my system the moment the fight had begun, but already it was washing back out again, leaving fear and weakness in its wake. I saw my hand holding the gun begin to droop and shake. I brought my other hand up to steady it, but that one was shaking so hard now too that I was afraid I might pull the trigger by mistake.

After a moment, I let it drop. Only three of our attackers were still alive and above ground. As I watched, Kelis kicked one of them in the knee, snapping the joint with a wet crack I could hear from fifteen feet away. When he was down she reached around and snapped his neck. The other two didn't last much longer, and as suddenly as it had begun, it was all over.

Only then did I notice the uniform our attackers had been wearing, sashes draped round their shoulders in the old revolutionary Tricolore. Old tribalism revived, I thought. And old instincts coming back, even in the most civilised of us. The cold ability to kill or be killed.

I thought I might be sick but in the end I wasn't. They hadn't even spoken to us before they'd opened fire, and I wasn't in any way sorry they were gone.

"Hey, you okay?" Kelis asked, crouching down beside me and staring at me in unexpected concern, as if her own body wasn't leaking blood onto the cobbled pavement.

"I'm fine," I said. "Bullet grazed me, that's all. But let me take a look at that."

She frowned for a moment; whether unsure if I really was alright, or just not keen to let me treat her, I couldn't tell. But then, with the heat of battle wearing off, her pain must have begun to register, and she slid down the wall beside me and nodded.

The wound wasn't as bad as I'd thought, although she hissed in pain as I probed it with my fingers. "I think one rib's cracked," I told her, "but the bullet's gone clean through and hasn't nicked any major vessels."

She looked down for a moment longer, as if mesmerised by the sight of my fingers moving against her skin. I realised that I was closer to her than I'd ever been, and for the first time really registered her as another person, with thoughts and feelings inside her head that I couldn't know.

Then she swatted my hand away impatiently and nodded over to the other side of the street. "Go see to Michaels. He took one in the leg and he doesn't look so good. I can bandage this up myself."

It took me half an hour to patch us all together. Michaels needed something more major than the field surgery I could offer him, but he was safer with us than alone so I improvised a splint for his leg and shot him so full of opiates that he wouldn't care if it dropped off on the journey. I had to fight the urge to turn the needle around and plunge it into my own arm, feed the hunger which would never quite die. I succeeded, this time.

The constant, never-ending war of the addict. Not this time. Not the next. The one after that? Yeah, that one you're never quite sure about.

One of our attackers was still alive. She was groaning quietly, body slumped half in, half out of the sewer. She looked to be middle aged and bald, from some skin condition that left her looking like a medieval leper. The woman had taken a bullet to the gut but I probably could have saved her. Curtis spared me the effort though, not even wasting a bullet on her; he just smashed the butt of his rifle hard against her head, driving it down into the pavement until the skull shattered.

"Stupid fuckers," he said. "Try to get us every fucking time. Never fucking learn."

We walked off east, one man light and even more cautious. But I guess news of the fight travelled, because no one else challenged us and the pressure of unseen eyes against my back eased.

The streets soon broadened again, into the grand, tree-lined boulevards of central Paris. I started to recognise the buildings we were passing from a romantic holiday he had taken me on. Palais de l'Elysée. La Madeleine. Our route led straight through La Place de la Concorde and I wondered again just where we were going. Who we were looking for.

No one had taken the gun from me after the fight, and it hung limp and useless from my hand as we walked. I guessed it was a sign of trust, but I didn't feel particularly flattered.

Kelis saw me looking down at it and gently pried it from my fingers. "Might want to reload that," she said, doing it for me. When she handed it back I tried to hold it in a firmer grip, but it still felt alien in my hand.

He'd taught me to shoot, back when we first met, said it was something everyone should know how to do – almost as if he'd seen all this coming. But I'd never learned to love guns the way he did. I didn't like the potential for death I could always feel curled up in their barrels.

When we stopped at the huge glass pyramid, I thought for an insane moment that we'd come sightseeing, that this was what it had all been about. But the set of Kelis's shoulders, and the sudden wariness around Soren's eyes, told me different. This, for whatever reason, was our target.

"So we're what?" I said to Kelis. "Stealing artwork? Desperate to get our hands on the Mona Lisa? Unable to go another minute without looking at the Venus de Milo?"

She flicked a quick, hard smile at me. "Long gone. We're here for something much more valuable."

"Is it going to require the use of my gun?"

"That's not the plan, but..." Kelis shrugged.

Right, because when did anything ever go according to plan? My hand tightened on the trigger, so hard that I almost let loose a volley when the lone figure emerged from the glass pyramid. But he was unarmed. Hands held high.

Curtis wasn't taking any chances. He waited until the figure walked right up to him and then grabbed him round the neck, pulling him into the shelter of an old magazine stand.

The man didn't resist when Curtis frisked him, and he proved not to be armed. He was thin-faced, deep laugh-lines etched at the sides of a wide mouth, hair so brown it was almost black. Curtis finally released him and the lines deepened as he grinned at us, as if he wasn't staring down the barrels of enough heavy ordinance to take on a small army.

"My name is Jules," the man said, his French accent only faint. "Welcome to Paris."

"Yeah, it's been real welcoming so far," Curtis said. "I'll be giving it a five star write-up in my travel guide."

The man frowned. "Ah. I think perhaps you have met with the Revolutionary Guard. They see it as their duty to protect this great city against incursions from elsewhere."

"No kidding," Kelis said. "And what about you? You planning to live up to the Parisian reputation for warm hospitality?"

He turned to face her, hands lifted in a conciliatory gesture. "We are always keen to welcome newcomers." And then, for just a moment, the smile slipped from his face. "We also have twice as many armed men as your numbers, and not all of them are inside the pyramid. But this does not matter, I think, because you are not here to make war."

Curtis's mouth pulled into a thin line. "No. That's not what we're here for at all."

It surprised me how readily Curtis allowed his men to surrender their weapons, leaving half his force behind to guard them while the disarmed contingent – myself included – was led into the pyramid by Jules.

Kelis hadn't been kidding. Everything of value was long gone, hoarded by some unknown collector for some unknown purpose. The bare walls of the gallery looked like an accusation, or a metaphor. Stripping away from this new life everything that wasn't purely functional.

Still, there was no denying it made a great base. There were fifty-six of them here, camped out in the shell of the museum, sitting on a stockpile of weapons and ammo they'd scavenged from who knew where. They weren't soldiers – there were families, children as young as two and a silver-haired old woman well past eighty – but they knew how to fight. Or they'd learnt, in these last five brutal years.

They had food too, fresh food. After we'd toured the empty, dismal galleries of the museum and seen the homes they'd carved out for themselves in the shell, they took us to their farm. I smiled when I saw it. The Twilleries, the formal gardens long dug up, rows of lettuce, beets, potatoes, planted in place of the roses and neatly mowed lawns.

"How can you defend all this?" Kelis asked.

Jules shrugged. "We have guards."

But she shook her head. "Not enough. Not for this."

He looked at her narrowly, assessing. Then he nodded. "No, not for this. But without us it would not grow so well, nor the hydroponics underground. We have scientists among our number, agronomists and biochemists. We make medicines too. They, the Revolutionary Guard, and others like them, let us make the things they need. They take what we give and we make sure that the price for taking it all would be too high."

Curtis looked impressed. Or maybe he was just pissed off – he had the kind of face which made it hard to tell. "We want to trade," he told Jules. "Groups like yours and ours need to connect, share technology. Rebuild society from the bottom up."

Jules nodded, but said, "Trade requires the possession of something that another desires. And we have everything we need."

"When was the last time you ate a pineapple?" Curtis asked.

Jules smiled. "That wasn't tinned?"

"Coconut, too. Peaches, lemons, oranges. Fresh fish, fresh meat. And that's just the basics." It was the most animated I'd seen Curtis. His face was filled with an almost evangelical fervour and for the first time I considered that Queen M's kingdom might be something her people actually believed in. "We have higher technologies too. Some manufacturing. We have access to oil fields."

Jules looked suddenly wary. "You have all this, and yet you would cross an ocean to trade with us. What is it we have that you want?"

Curtis's expression shifted, just a little, and I knew that whatever answer he was about to give, it wouldn't be the truth. But for the moment the conversation moved on, and soon they were bartering, figuring out exchange rates in a world without currency. They talked about technologies, the possibility of getting generators running again without enough people to staff them. There was drinking and eating, too, and after a while some chatting and bonding. It felt strangely ordinary. Just one group of people visiting another and chewing the fat. A little boy came to sit in my lap, his curly brown hair brushing against my chest as his head turned backwards and forwards, following a conversation he couldn't understand.

Some time after midnight, it all began to wind down. Jules hesitated, then told us that we could sleep in the safety of the Louvre with them.

I was the only one watching Curtis's face as he said it, and I knew instantly that he'd made a terrible mistake.

THE ATTACK CAME at precisely four in the morning. At the first sound my eyes snapped open, then snapped to the clock on the far wall – an instinct I'd picked up years ago when he and I had been living together, and there was no telling when he might get called away or where to. Four o'clock is the deepest part of the night – the time when most people who die in their sleep pass away.

But there weren't many deaths that night. Not as many as there would have been if our crew had struck during the day. I guess that was the point. By the time my eyes were open and I was fully awake there were already three bodies on the ground by the door. I could hear the sounds of fighting further out and Curtis was holding a big black Beretta against Jules's head. Understanding spread like a ripple through our hosts and, one by one, the weapons they'd picked up were dropped to their sides.

Somewhere at the back of the room a baby was crying. I could hear the desperate whispers of its mother as she tried to quiet it down. She was probably afraid that our people would kill it, if she couldn't get it to stop. I wasn't sure they wouldn't.

For a moment, Jules's eyes glared into mine through the gloom and I read a bitter accusation there. I wanted to tell him that I hadn't known this was going to happen – except that would be a lie.

Soren had a gun in his hand and he looked happy, or at least satisfied. He herded our hosts out of the gallery, pushing them towards the grand marble stairs that led to the ante-chamber below the glass pyramid, then up into the big, empty square. The sky was dark and starless above us.

Kelis carried one of the women who had been wounded in the brief crossfire, blood oozing from her side onto Kelis's t-shirt. She avoided my eye as she walked past, and I wanted to believe that it was because she was ashamed, because I'd thought I might be starting to like her.

There was more sobbing now, not just from the baby. They thought we were going to kill them all, a death squad come to end their little social experiment. But that wasn't it at all.

They divided them up: men, women, old, young. The four oldest were pushed into a far corner, away from everyone else – discarded. Historical memories washed up, of other times when one group of humans had sorted another in this way, but I let them ebb. We weren't a death squad. I was sure of that, at least.

"Check them over," Curtis said to me.

I folded my arms, not wanting him to see them shaking. "Check them over for what?"

He frowned. "Disease. Injuries – you know, doctor stuff."

"Treat them like animals, you mean."

I saw his hand tighten on the trigger of his gun, the barrel twitching reflexively towards me.

"I'll treat the wounded," I said, and there was no disguising the shake in my voice. "That's the only 'doctor stuff' I'm prepared to do."

"Listed, lady. We've been doing this for a long time before you joined the show. And we can carry on just fine without you."

"So why do you need me at all?" I asked.

His lips curled in a sneer, but Soren stepped forward before he could speak. "Check them all out," he said, "and you can treat that lady. She'll die if you don't look at her. You can see that."

I could. The bleeding from her side hadn't slowed, and her face was the ivory pale of someone a few pints short of a full load. "Promise me no one will die," I said.

"No one will die," Curtis said, so quickly that I knew there had to be some kind of catch. "You've got my word on that. If everyone plays nicely, no one gets hurt," he added. I didn't think he was lying.

The woman's injuries took half an hour to patch up: a pressure bandage, some stitches and antibiotics. I wanted to give her some painkillers too, but Curtis's hand clamped around my arm as I reached back into my medicine bag. "She'll live without that, won't she?"

I nodded reluctantly.

"Then it's time to do your job."

I approached Jules first. His face was numb with shock. I stood awkwardly in front of him for a moment, wondering what exactly I was supposed to be doing. Taking his temperature? His pulse? Holding his balls and telling him to cough? In the end I settled for the first two and rolled back his eyelids to check for anaemia. Curtis was still looking at me impassively, so I took his blood pressure too – sky high, but that was hardly surprising – and then I examined his tongue. After that I turned to Curtis and shrugged. What the hell else was I supposed to do?

"Strip," Curtis said, and for one moment I thought he meant me. Then he turned to include all our captives in the instruction. "Strip – all of you."

Now it really did look like something from the darkest pages of history. I saw the women look at each other, look at the men, look at their children. But when there are fifty-odd guns pointing in your direction, there isn't much time for modesty. And they'd heard Curtis's promise that no one would get hurt. I was clinging on to that hope too. Quietly, trying not to look anyone in the eye, I gave each of them a more thorough exam, peering at bellies sagging from childbirth or the bitter scars of acne on a teenage face. After each one I gave Curtis a report, a run down of past ailments, possible present conditions. A young woman's eyes stared at me, wide and uncomprehending, when I told her she was in the late phases of breast cancer, almost certainly fatal.

After me it was Kelis, questioning each of them about their background, their qualifications, their skills. They were kept shivering and naked as they answered in the chill Paris air, dank with a mist which smelled as if it had come straight from the sewers.

And then, finally, Curtis began pointing. There were seventeen empty seats on the plane and fifty-six people to choose from. I could do the math. The true scarce resource these days are people, Queen M had told me. And I guess however many plantations and wind farms you build, you can still only pump out new people at the same old slow rate.

Unless you go and steal them from somewhere else, of course.

A lot of jet fuel for seventeen new subjects, but you're looking at a lifetime of work. Especially if you pick the young and the healthy, and you leave behind the old and the barren. The seven-year-old child – bright-eyed and full of energy – had been sorted into the wheat; worth the investment of a few more years training. But the baby, the child's sister, got left behind – a chesty cough that might just be a cold, might be something more serious.

I saw the awful realisation of what was about to happen in the mother's eyes a second before she started screaming. Curtis didn't say anything, just backhanded her across the mouth. She fell to the ground, the scream boiling down to a desperate whimper.

"Whatever you're doing," Jules said, "don't do it. Please. We're happy here. We're... we'll trade with you. We'll give you what you need. We'll... anything."

Curtis shrugged, looking bored. I wondered how many times he'd witnessed this little scene before. Just variations on a theme to him by now, I guessed, the same words coming out of different mouths. "Yeah, we'll take some technology back with us," he said. "But the only thing we really want is you."

"Then take us all! You're separating husbands and wives. Families. You might as well kill the people you are leaving behind – you know they have no chance on their own." Jules voice was soft and persuasive, but I could tell he already knew that Curtis was deaf to any plea or persuasion. His face hardened.

"Fine. Take us. Point a gun to our heads and take us – but do not expect us to work with you. Do not imagine that every second of every day we won't be searching for a way to pay you back for what you have done."

And that was the one thing I still didn't understand. Queen M could take them, but how could she control them? How do you keep a whole slave kingdom docile? I'd seen the scientists working on her flagship, the people in the fields – unguarded.

It was Soren who put the final little piece into the puzzle, the picture springing out clear and clever, and ugly as hell. He drew something from his belt that I'd taken for yet another gun. But I saw now that the barrel was too thin to spit out conventional bullets. It was meant for something else.

He approached Jules first, and the man flinched away. But when Soren dropped to his knees in front of him, he looked briefly taken aback, not quite sure where this could be heading. Before he'd even begun to guess, Soren grabbed his leg, pressed the barrel of the strange silver gun against his thigh, and pressed.

Jules let out a scream of profound agony, dropping helplessly to his knees as Soren moved on to the next woman, shooting whatever it was into her too. He turned back to me before the third victim, waiting for this one, struggling and screaming, to be restrained by our soldiers. "They'll need dressings for that," he said.

There was no point refusing. The wound on Jules's leg where the gun had fired was small but wept thick crimson blood, where the wound had penetrated the bone marrow. It would get infected if I didn't cover it soon. I tried to figure out what had happened as I worked on him and the rest. The only thing I knew for sure was that the hole wasn't empty – something was lodged inside.

The process didn't stop with those who'd been chosen. The discards, too, were shot. Only with the baby did Soren hesitate, before a short, angry jerk of Curtis's head urged him on and – face turned away – he pressed the gun against his tiny leg too. The child's agonised wail went on and on, overlaying everything that followed.

"You've all been fitted with tracking devices," Curtis said flatly. "Long range, ten years of battery life. And that," he said to Jules now, seeming to take a sort of pleasure in it, "is why you'll be doing every fucking thing that we tell you. Because not only will we know where you are at any time, we'll know where they are." He pointed at the small, frightened group of those to be left behind. "And if you do something we don't like, they'll be the ones to suffer."

I realised suddenly that Kelis was hovering at my shoulder, watching my face rather than the bloody little drama playing out in front of us. She touched my shoulder lightly. "We're taking them to a better life, you know. We're rebuilding society – the only people who are."

"And that makes this alright, does it?" I asked bitterly. "That's how you live with yourself?"

She shrugged one elegant shoulder. "I live with myself because I haven't got any more choice than they do." She rolled up the rough green cotton of her combats, and I saw a small white scar on her outer thigh, right where her own implant had gone in.

It only took me a second to understand it all. My fingers shook as I rolled up my own trouser leg. And even though I was expecting it, the sight of the puckered little scar on my right thigh still sent a wave of nausea through me, the bile rising in my throat.

"I don't have a choice," Kelis said. "And neither do you."

THE PLANE WAS fixed by the time we returned, but there wasn't much of an air of celebration as we climbed onboard. The newcomers were silent, shell-shocked. I caught the eyes of the little seven-year-old girl as we taxied and took off, and read a dawning knowledge in them that someone that young wasn't meant to have.

I'd been sleeping, fitfully, when I felt the plane begin to descend. A glance at my watch told me we'd only been airborne a few hours, and I looked out of the window and saw the green-grey land beneath us. No way was that St Lucia, or anywhere else in the tropics.

Ireland, I realised as the plane landed, more cleanly this time, a strip of concrete that might have been a road once. Curtis didn't take everyone this time, just Jules and me and four of the others – no explanation, just a brusque order to follow him.

The people he was looking for were nearly a mile's walk away, over the hills and the long wet grass. There was a fresh smell to the air, cleansing after the decay of Paris, but I didn't find it refreshing.

When they saw us they raised their hands to their heads, three little matchstick figures in the distance. They must have known we were trouble but they didn't try to run. Perhaps they'd realised there wasn't any point.

Curtis was watching them through military-grade binoculars, still and silent for two minutes. Whatever he saw must have satisfied him because he made a sharp gesture and we all walked forward. They stayed stock still, waiting.

"There were six of them when we came," Curtis said. "We took two. The rest were too old or two weak. They had the trackers put in, same as you. But I guess they just didn't believe us."

Close up, and they'd gone from stick-men to stick-thin real people. I guess subsistence farming isn't so easy when you have a climate like Ireland's and no wind generators. I thought they were probably younger than they looked, but fear and hunger had hollowed out their faces. They could have been in their sixties, three women and a man, stooped over the hoes with which they'd been tilling the fields.

A fine drizzle had started as we walked, plastering everyone's hair to their heads, dripping from the tips of their noses. The same nose on each of them, with a little up-tilt at the end that must have looked cute back when they were children. All the same family, I guessed. The separation must have hit them hard.

"They ran away," Curtis suddenly said, to us and to the forlorn figures in front of us. "Your sisters or wives or, who the fuck knows, maybe both. Just so as you know who to blame for what's about to happen."

Then he pulled out his gun and shot all four of them – two in the back as they'd finally realised that they needed to run away. Even the blood looked grey in the watery sunlight. I wanted to look away, but I didn't. Everyone ought to have someone watch, and care, while they die.

And then we went back to the plane. Lesson over. Of course, there was no way of knowing if what he'd told us was true, if they really were the relatives of runaway slaves. For all I knew, they could have been some random strangers he'd seen from the air.

But in a way, that was the point. Because now we knew exactly how ruthless he was. We knew he didn't make empty threats.

I saw in the hopeless droop of Jules's shoulders that the knowledge had broken him. He'd do whatever Queen M wanted him to. And, in time, maybe he'd even come to enjoy his new life. Now that he knew he had no choice, he could forgive himself for his desertion – I knew how people's psychologies worked. Self-justification. Cognitive dissonance. We need to believe that what we're doing is the right thing, always. If our beliefs say it isn't, we're more likely to change our beliefs than our actions. I guess human beings are lazy that way.

In his own brutal way, Curtis had given Queen M's newest recruits a sort of freedom – to embrace their new life without guilt.

But not me. I'd learnt a different lesson. If I wanted to escape I'd have to be very clever, and very, very careful.

CHAPTER TWO

IT FELT ALMOST unreal to be back under the clean sunlight of the Caribbean. As soon as we landed I was given a list of patients and put right back into the routine I'd had before the flight to Paris, as if nothing at all had changed. The slowly healing bullet wound in my leg was the only concrete reminder of what had happened. Everywhere I went, Soren and Kelis came too. For the first two days I refused to speak to either of them. Soren took the snub with his usual stoic restraint, or possibly indifference. Kelis didn't say anything, but there were tight little lines around her eyes, deepening every hour I ignored her. For some reason, my opinion seemed to matter to her.

Good. I could use that.

On the third day, we were eating breakfast in our customary silence when Kelis suddenly said, "You can keep this up forever, I can tell. You're stubborn as hell. But really, what's the point? You've made the same decision we have – to accept what's been done to us and to live rather than die."

My mouth tightened. "Yeah. But my decision involves curing people and yours involves killing them. Excuse me if I don't see the equivalence."

Soren grinned, his blond hair blowing in the sea breeze. "You cure them so that we can kill them later," he said. "Excuse me if I don't think that makes you any better."

"Soren," Kelis said, frowning at him. "You know that isn't –"

But I interrupted her. "No. He's right. Where do I get off thinking I'm any better than you?"

And yeah, it was a calculated move. First the punishment, then the forgiveness. But at the same time, it was true. I wasn't any better. And if they'd found *him*, then left him behind somewhere with a tracker in his thigh and a death threat hanging over him, would I even be thinking about escaping?

Of course, he'd have found a way to remove the tracker – probably amputating his own leg – and have tracked me down by now, taking out Queen M's entire army in the process, but that was another story. I've always remembered an interview I once saw with a survivor of one of the Nazi death camps, someone whose job it had been to drag the corpses from the gas chambers to the ovens.

"Until you find yourself there," he'd said. "You don't know the things you'll do for just one more minute of life."

I guess something of that acceptance must have registered in my face, because the third week after we returned I finally woke to find that Kelis and Soren weren't outside my door. "Recruiting mission," someone told me at breakfast on the big communal tables out on the deck, but they didn't explain. No one else had anything very much to say to me either, and I wondered what Queen M had told her people about me. I realised I was lonely without my two constant shadows.

I spent the morning running a small surgery on the ship, giving the once-over to people suffering everything from colds to colitis but mostly VD. I didn't have to hear the noise from some of the cabins at night to know how most of Queen M's crew killed the idle hours. Nothing like living through the apocalypse to reawaken your lust for life. If they kept going at this rate, we'd be developing antibiotic-resistant strains of syphilis which were just going to be a whole bundle of laughs.

After lunch a call came through that there'd been an injury on one of the plantations on St Kitts. A machete wound; deep, by the sound of it. I was required to treat it and get the man back in working shape. And if I couldn't... I could already imagine the cold little cost-benefit analysis going on in Queen M's head. I'd seen her only once since my return from Paris, and we hadn't spoken. She'd just looked into my furious eyes and smiled, patronisingly – as if I were small child throwing a temper tantrum that would be indulged at first and then, if necessary, punished. I don't think, up to that point in my life, I'd ever hated anyone so much.

But when I got the order to go to St Kitts, I went, just like she knew I would. What was I going to do, leave the man to die of his injuries?

The small schooner which took us bounced on the waves like an over-eager puppy. I was eager to get to the island too – my first unescorted trip away from the ship. The shoreline was rocky, rising quickly to a forested, hilly interior with terraces that had been cut into the hills. Fruit trees and sugar-cane plantations were slowly eating up most of the fertile land.

We made landfall at a small jetty on the sort of beach that would once have been heaving with fish-belly-white British tourists. Just two people were waiting for us there that day, a tiny Chinese woman who looked as delicate as a doll, and a big North African man whose face was deeply marked with tribal scars.

I hopped off the boat onto the sand. My sandals sank in, grains seeping in over the side to cascade grittily over my toes.

"The doctor?" the Chinese woman asked.

I nodded, and to my surprise, turned to see that the schooner was leaving, none of its crew of four staying to baby-sit me. "We'll be back at sunset," the captain told me. "When you're finished with the patient you can relax, take a tour of the island if you want. Queen M said you'd earned a holiday." He grinned at me like he expected me to be grateful, and I managed a thin smile back.

They brought the injured man down to the beach, transporting him on the back of a rickety donkey trap. They'd given him a leather cord to chew on, but muffled whimpers were escaping. The edges of the wound were already blackened, starting to rot in the humid tropical air. His eyes stared into mine, pleading. I guess he knew what the price of my failure might be. It all depended on the state of his ligaments, but I didn't tell him that. I just shot him up with enough morphine that he wouldn't be worrying about anything very much for a while.

After that I injected local anaesthetic around the wound and got to work. It was jagged and deep enough to have nicked the bone. At the edge of the nick I saw a small piece of metal and after a second I realised that I was seeing a tracking device. Finally – a piece of luck. Except not really, because now I knew that it was embedded right in the bone. No way to remove it without breaking the bone around it.

Nothing about this was going to be simple.

I sighed and carried on with the job I'd been brought to do. There was dirt in the cut too, and I could see the beginning of sepsis. As I irrigated the wound and cut out the tissue that was already past saving I found myself drifting back into that trance-like state I'd first learned when I was a junior house officer putting in sixty-hour weeks at the Royal London. You couldn't see the person you were working on as a person. It had to be a job, a little bit of technical expertise you were displaying. Saving a life was only secondary. You focussed on the skin and subcutaneous fat and bone until it was just another material you were sculpting.

I was so caught up in it that it wasn't until I'd nearly finished, delicately sewing the edges of the wound together with the smallest stitches possible – as if he was going to care about the ugliness of his scar – that I noticed someone watching me as I worked. Not just watching. Drawing. I caught the brief blur of a pale face and dark hair, the *scritch-scritch* of pencil on paper.

When the bandage was in place, I took a moment to look closer. A Japanese guy, younger than me probably, with a slightly rakish air. His hair was gelled into sharp little spikes and his clothes looked like he'd spent too long thinking about them.

Without asking for permission, I took the sketch pad from him. I blinked, twice, and then I let out a small, helpless laugh. I'd expected something lifelike, a medical journal illustration or a *vérité* style of war-reporting maybe. But he'd turned us into a comic: soft, round curves and big doe-eyes which made me look like a ten-year-old mutant. The guy I'd been working on was drawn screaming in pain. There were Japanese characters coming out of his mouth in a speech balloon which I guessed loosely translated as 'holy shit that hurts.'

I looked up from the drawing to the artist. "Okay, who the hell are you?"

He smiled. He had shockingly white teeth, so straight you could use them as a spirit level – but there was a wide gap between the two front ones. It turned his rakish look to something slightly goofy and I instantly found myself liking him more. "I'm Haru. And you, I think, are Jasmine. I'm very pleased to meet you." His voice was strident, accent a little Japanese, a little American.

"Yeah. You've clearly heard of me but strangely no one's said anything to me about you."

He looked a little offended. "Really? Well, I'm the court artist." I laughed, which pissed him off still further. "No, I'm serious. Queen M knows that a society isn't just about the physical things, the food and the power. Without art and culture we may as well return to the stone age."

"Funny," I said flatly, "she didn't seem too bothered about the artistic qualifications of the people we left behind when I went recruiting."

He winced. "Yes, well – I guess culture's a luxury still. You can only afford so much of it." His eyes skittered around, trying to avoid mine, and after a moment I looked back down at his work, flicking through the drawings.

They were good. They were all in the same style as the first, some of them divided into actual panels, super-heroic figures leaping across the page in tight-fitting, brightly coloured costumes. I was pretty sure the beefy guy in the blue spandex rescuing a little child from a fire was supposed to be Soren. I wondered if that was something which had actually happened. "So I'm guessing you were a Manga artist in a previous life," I said, looking back at him.

He shrugged. "Wanted to be. Never seemed to find the time to go professional."

"Then Queen M came along. Lucky old you. She just leaves you free to wander, does she? Draw when the inspiration strikes?"

He flushed slightly. "I travel the islands. I guess you could say I'm the court reporter. A sort of... photo-journalist."

"So you've been pretty much everywhere?" And this, suddenly, was interesting. A short cut to finding out what I needed to know if I was ever going to get out of here.

"I've been here seven months now so... yes, I'd say I've seen most of it."

"Good." I smiled, almost sincerely. "Then you can give me the tour."

He took me round the plantations first. It was cotton-picking season and the fields were crowded with people of pretty much every nationality, backs bent achingly over the scrubby plants. It was like a scene from three hundred years ago, given a United Colours of Benetton makeover. I wondered how many people here were natives of the island, survivors of the Cull. Had Queen M used the already available resources or had she wanted a clean sweep, no complications from people who saw this place as their home and her as an interloper? For once, without Soren and Kelis watching and judging every move I made, I felt free to ask.

"I'm going to speak to some of them," I told Haru. "Find out if there are any parasites, diseases, something that might get passed on to the rest of the crew."

He shrugged, not very interested. When I looked back at him a few moments later he was already sitting cross-legged on the ground, sketchbook on his lap.

I could see the workers snatching quick glances at me as they toiled. There were two women, armed, lounging at the edge of a field. But they seemed more concerned with the game of dominoes they were playing than with watching the workers. I ignored them and they ignored me as I headed over to the cotton pickers.

"Hi," I said to the first person I came to, a petite white woman who couldn't have been much older than twenty. Her hair was flame red, darkened by sweat.

She smiled shyly but kept on picking.

"I'm Jasmine. The new doctor."

"You come to treat George, then?" Her accent was hard to place. Czech maybe.

"Is George the guy who got too friendly with a machete?"

She nodded.

"Yeah. He's going to be fine."

"It wasn't an accident, you know."

I raised an eyebrow, and she finally looked right at me. "Yochai meant to hit him. George was making moves on his woman."

"And what's George going to do about it now he's staying in the land of the living?"

She became very interested in her work; small, clever fingers pulling out the cloud-puffs of cotton, and I knew that I wouldn't get any more out of her. Still, this was interesting. Queen M's rule wasn't absolute, if nasty little squabbles like this broke out. There was some freedom of movement in the chains.

I spoke to more people: a dockworker from Portsmouth who'd been chosen for his knowledge of ship repairs; a Jivaro from the Amazon, picked, I guessed, for his sheer brawn. It was hard to tell from his few words of English. There were several Americans, mainly from the South, and there were people who'd been born and raised on St Kitts, then watched, five years ago, as everyone else around them died. They'd been trapped here with food rotting in the fields, the corpses of their friends and family for company, before Queen M had come. They didn't see Queen M as an interloper; they saw her as a saviour.

Some of the others though – they were a different story. Hidden in their eyes was the same burning anger I felt in myself, tamped down now but ready to burst into flames at the right provocation.

I believed that they would rise up, if they were given the chance. But I didn't get the slightest sense that they'd begun to plan it yet. There was no underground railroad spiriting slaves away, here, as there had once been in the Deep South. Most of them barely spoke each other's languages. They'd never met before being brought here, terrified and powerless. I began to appreciate Queen M's strategy, the reason she was willing to burn jet fuel, travelling to every corner of the world. These people's diversity, their disunity, was her strength.

And she didn't make their lives too unbearable. There was one day's rest a week; food and drink for everyone in the evenings, along with parties, good times. They had something to live for and therefore something to lose.

Still, there was a power in their buried fury, here under the relentless Caribbean sun, the brilliant blue skies. I had to hold onto that hope.

After an hour, I went back to Haru. He looked up when my shadow fell across the page and flipped round the last sketch he'd been working on without my asking: the workers in the field, bent over the crop. It was a surprisingly melancholy picture. He'd captured the blankness in some of the eyes, the sense that the labour was given unwillingly. A sort of hopelessness.

"It's good," I told him.

"Yeah." He looked back down at his picture. After a moment he carefully tore it from the pad, rolled it up and shoved it into his backpack. "Maybe I won't show that one to Queen M."

I could still see it in my mind, though, all the faces, the people I'd talked to today. And I knew that escaping wasn't enough. I had to free them too. Don't get me wrong – my motives weren't that altruistic. A big part of it was because it would piss Queen M off, and I really wanted her to realise that she'd underestimated me. But it was also because if he were there, I thought it was what he would do.

I ASKED HARU to take me to some other plantations. I spoke to more people, who told the same stories, only in different languages. But that wasn't really why I was there. By the third plantation I'd figured out that there were two guards for every hundred people, and neither of them stayed the whole night. There was only one permanent garrison on the island, according to a rickety old Barbadian, but the soldiers there tended to stick to themselves. Queen M was pretty bloody confident in her power over these people.

Pretty bloody confident of her power over the guards too, I realised. The people she armed and let out of her sight.

"How are people chosen for guard duty?" I asked Haru.

He looked at me suspiciously, a raised eyebrow asking why I wanted to know.

I shrugged. "Seems like a pretty plumb job to me – sitting on your arse all day when everyone else is working in two hundred degree heat. I just wondered how people landed it."

"Thinking of signing up?"

"Guns have never been my thing," I told him. "I don't like the feel of them, you know? The knowledge that you've got something in your hand that could kill everyone around you and you wouldn't even raise a sweat."

"Really?" He frowned. "I think I like them for exactly the same reason. That incredible potential to change the world, in such a small thing. But the soldiers – she chooses them because they're big and strong and maybe a little stupid. Same as everywhere, I guess."

"People with previous training?"

He shook his head. "Not usually. She prefers to train them herself."

Prefers people who know only what she wants them to know. But I didn't say it.

Still, Haru wasn't stupid. His black eyes narrowed, considering me. "You're wondering how she makes sure they're loyal, right?"

I tried to look casual. "Well, it must be a concern."

"I guess. What I heard is she chooses people who have no family, or people whose whole family is here."

Of course, that made sense. People who could be loyal to her unambiguously.

The sun was beginning to sink towards the horizon as we walked back along the rough tarmac road towards the beach. I watched it for a while, the astounding reds and pinks as the light refracted through thicker layers of polluted air. Dirt making beauty. I was sure Haru would have something to say about that.

When I looked across at him, he was still studying me, and I thought maybe he had been this whole time. "Yes, there aren't many guards," he said quietly. "But it's not that simple. To escape, you need a way off the islands, or all you are is a sitting target and Queen M can come and deal with you when she wants. More importantly, you need to take care of the tracking device. No one will leave her while they've still got it in them. You might think you can persuade them, but you're wrong. You'll tell them that if everyone goes, she won't be able to hunt them all down. And they'll know that's true – but she'll hunt some people down, and what if that person's you?"

I shook my head as if I didn't know what he was talking about.

He grabbed my arm, fifty metres from the beach. The schooner was waiting for me in the water, the figures of the crew black silhouettes against the sunset. "I can help you. If you'll trust me. I know this place better than you, the people too." He was talking in an urgent whisper, as if afraid that the distant figures of the crew might overhear us.

How can you help me, I wanted to ask him, *when you don't even have the courage to say what you're saying out loud?* But all I said was, "I'm not interested in escaping. I don't have any family out there, either. And I've got a cushy job too."

He released my arm, but he didn't stop staring at me. "Are you going to report me to Queen M?"

I shook my head, turning away from him.

I caught his crooked smile out of the corner of my eye. "Then you're not the happy little citizen you pretend to be, are you? I'll be waiting – when you're ready to talk."

THE CAPTAIN INFORMED us that the flagship had moved, so the journey back would take us a couple of hours. The stars were crisp and bright, and I guessed that our crew, grizzled islanders who looked like they'd been born on the waves, were using them to navigate. I tried to talk to them about it, but the replies they gave were monosyllabic. After a while I gave up and went to stand in the bow, as far from Haru as I could put myself on the small boat. I watched our white wake, disappearing into the distance until it was impossible to distinguish it from the waves.

There's something very peaceful about sailing at night, the solitude of it. The noise of the sails as the wind caught them suddenly seemed very loud. And there it was again: a sharp flap that was almost like a whip-crack.

Except that it wasn't our sails.

There was absolutely no reason to panic. We were in friendly waters; the sea was filled with Queen M's ships. But when I saw the expression on the sailor's faces, the sudden flush of fear in Haru's pale cheeks, ghostly in the starlight, I knew that what I'd heard was the start of something very bad.

"They're windward and gaining," one of the sailors shouted, voice hoarse with panic. I was shoved aside roughly as the others hurried to the sails and swung the boom right around. The wind caught the sails again and the deck tilted sharply as the ship veered. I'd been completely unprepared. The motion flung me like a rag doll against the starboard railing – except that the railing wasn't there, it was ten feet lower than it should have been and instead of the bone-thumping crash I was expecting I just kept on falling.

The ocean looked dark and deep beneath me, and somewhere out there was whatever had caused this sudden, frantic flight. Without any conscious thought, I flung my arm out, grabbed hold of the railing as my body arched over it.

My fingers caught and held, the weight of my body yanking at them as I fell. The pain in my shoulder was indescribable. I was sure it was dislocated. My fingers felt like every single one of them had been broken at once. But I held on, until I felt the brutal thump of my body against the side of the ship, my chest bruised to the bone by the impact. I let out a shout of mingled relief and pain.

My body bounced once, twice, against the hull. I thought I heard the sound of a rib snap, or it could have been something on the boat breaking. I was too dazed to tell. My eyes flicked shut, wanted to stay shut. My brain wanted to switch off. I wished all that noise would just go away so that I could go to sleep like I wanted to. All the shouting, the screaming. That infuriating whimpering.

My fingers had almost slipped from the railing when something inside me shouted and I jerked back into consciousness. For a second, it had sounded like a voice. Like the Voice – willing me not to let go just yet. But it couldn't be, could it? The anti-psychotics were supposed to have killed the Voice for good.

And then I didn't really care about it anymore, because my head swung round as I tried desperately to claw my other arm up to the railing, to drag myself back onto the deck – and I finally saw the boat which had been pursuing us.

At first I thought I might be delirious, that the side of the boat had cracked my head as well as my ribs. Because the people on that boat... they shouldn't have been alive. Not in any sane universe.

They were still fifty feet away and closing fast, and I could see their eyes glaring at us, even at that distance, as bright and flat as coins. They were dressed so normally, in chinos, t-shirts, loose flowing skirts... as if there was nothing wrong with them at all. But their bodies... their faces...

Twenty feet away now and I could see all five of them, leaning over the side of their boat, grappling hooks in hand, almost panting in their eagerness to get to us. Animalistic. I could see a string of drool trickling down the chin of one, a fifty-something woman. After a moment, her tongue flicked out to lick it up and I saw with a nauseous shock that the tongue was split down the middle, wriggling hideously.

The other damage was more obvious. One of her hands was gone entirely but no one had done anything to set or heal the wound. I could see a stump of bone, poking through the centre of her arm, white in the newly risen moonlight. There were deep, infected cuts on her face. Ten feet and I could smell the corruption pouring off her, off all of them.

They shouldn't have been able to walk. Not the teenager with the gaping hole in his body where his spleen must once have been. Or the older man with the festering pit where he once had an eyeball and the fingers of one hand all hanging off, swinging in the sea breeze on strips of skin. They should all have been screaming in agony.

But I was the one who was screaming. Ten feet now and the first grappling hook sank into the hull inches from my head. Desperation gave me strength and, an inferno of pain in my shoulder, I managed to drag my other arm to the railing. Another grappling hook pierced the hull on the other side of me and I could feel the shift and sway as our schooner was slowly dragged off its course. I didn't have time to look, I knew the other boat was drawing closer, side on. If I didn't move soon I'd be flattened between the two vessels, slowly enough to feel every second of it. I didn't know if that would be preferable to the alternative.

My arm felt like it was tearing itself out of its socket, but inch by inch I managed to draw myself upwards, towards safety. And then another grappling hook hit the side of the boat, failed to find purchase and splashed down into the water fifteen feet below me. A gout of seawater splashed up, spraying across my eyes, and for just a second I lost concentration as the salt burned. My arms straightened and I was right back where I'd started, facing one sort of death or another.

"Fuck!" I screamed. "Fuck!" It just couldn't end like this. How could it, when I didn't even know if he was alive? When I'd spent the last five years doing nothing but shooting junk into my veins, and now those were going to be the last five years of my life.

With one last adrenaline-fuelled burst of energy, I flexed my arms and lifted myself up. I couldn't see anything now because the other boat was so close, the stars above me were nearly gone. I was rising. And then it wasn't just my own force bringing me up because someone else had hold of my arms, and *Jesus* it hurt, but it didn't matter because I was over the railing and lying on the deck, gasping in fear and shock. Haru's face, three inches from mine, looked like it had aged twenty years since I'd last seen it.

"What..?" I said, but he didn't let me finish, just yanked on my arm – my injured arm, and this time I managed not to scream, biting down on my tongue until it bled – and dragged me as far away from the other boat as he could.

"Don't touch them!" he screamed. "For fuck's sake, don't let them touch you!"

But how the hell didn't you touch four people who were climbing onto a thirty-foot wide boat with you? And why not? Were they contagious? Christ, could we turn into what they were? I suddenly wished, fiercely and hopelessly, that Soren and Kelis were with us. Or if not them, at least one of their guns.

I was unarmed and Haru didn't have anything more deadly than a 2H pencil, and the crew of our boat were sailors, not soldiers. I saw one of them now, wrenching open a lockbox under the tiller with desperate fingers. The youngest of the... things which had boarded our boat trotted over the deck towards him. I'd been half expecting them to shamble, like B-movie zombies, but somehow, these people were still alive.

The other three were watching the sailor, heads tilted as if in idle curiosity. But they were leaving the boy to take him on alone.

"What do you want?" I said, not expecting any sort of answer.

The one-eyed man turned to face me. "Nothing you'll give us willingly," he said with a light Spanish accent, a voice you could have heard on the street and not thought about twice.

Even on the other side of the boat I could hear the sailor's teeth chattering with fear. The boy was almost within touching distance now, but then the key snicked into place and the gun was out of the lockbox and in his hand. He might not have been a soldier, but the kid was standing right next to him. Even with his hands shaking so hard that he could barely hold the weapon, he managed to put three bullets straight into the boy's chest.

The boy staggered back a few paces – then kept on coming. *Not enough stopping power*, my man's voice said inside my head. The little girl in me who was still afraid of the dark was gibbering in fear of the unnatural things that couldn't be killed. But I was a scientist; nothing was irrational, only yet to be understood. I'd seen soldiers walking around with injuries that should have laid them out cold, because the body's own anaesthetic had kicked in and they just didn't know how bad things were yet.

But there were some injuries no one walked away from.

"The head!" I shouted. "Aim for the head!" After I'd said it I let out a choked, hytserical laugh, because maybe we were in a zombie movie after all.

The sailor turned to look at me, as if he was about to ask me if I was certain, and for a moment I wanted to kill him myself. When he turned back, the boy's hands were only inches from his throat, but the gun roared one final time. The bullet tore through the boy's left eye and exited messily out the back of his head. He let out one quick, surprised cough, then dropped on top of the sailor like a marionette with its strings cut.

The sailor screamed an almost unearthly wail of complete panic. I thought he must have been hurt in some way. Maybe the boy had been carrying a knife, although I hadn't seen it. But then he pushed the boy off him and shoved himself to his feet, his mouth still open and screaming. His whole face and his white t-shirt were drenched in the boy's blood, black and shiny in the moonlight. *Infected*, I realised. He thinks he's been infected.

And by the time I'd realised that, it was already too late, because the sailor turned wide, desperate eyes to us for just one second and then turned and leapt over the side of the boat. Another second later, and the remaining three infected turned their heads to us, moving in an eerie kind of unison.

The sailor had taken the gun with him, out of reach into the depths.

Still, I knew they could be killed now. Haru was huddled behind me, whimpering. His stock of courage seemed to have been entirely used up dragging me over the side. Now he was hugging the boom as if it might offer him some sort of comfort.

The boom.

I pushed Haru out of the way, not really caring when I heard his head crack against the deck. He swore viciously in Japanese. The boom was tied off – of course it was.

Fuck!

How could a rope that thick be knotted that tightly? My fingers picked at it feverishly, and then Haru was with me, helping. *Shit!* They were spreading out, the three of them fanning across the deck. There was no way I was going to get all of them. Abruptly, the boom was free. Haru and I heaved on it together, and for once things were going my way because it swung easily, quickly, well-oiled and beautifully counterbalanced. They can't have been surprised by the move, but they weren't expecting it to come so fast. It took one, then two of them, and swept them clean off the deck and into the water.

"They'll come back!" Haru said. "They'll climb back onboard!"

"Then stop them!" I screamed because, for fuck's sake, did I have to think of everything myself? "Get rid of the grappling hooks – or use one to hit them with if they try to climb the sides!"

He nodded, jerkily, but he still just stood there. His eyes were so wide that I could see the whites all the way around them. I yanked his shoulder round to turn him in the right direction and then shoved him on his way. He stumbled, then kept on walking, and I caught a flicker out of the corner of my left eye. She was coming straight for me.

I felt like a creature of pure adrenaline. My senses were hyped, the smell of the invaders almost making me gag, only made bearable by the salt smell of sea water that seeped through everything. Like a vague buzzing in the back of my mind, a half-recalled memory, I felt the pain of the bruises on my side, and my dislocated shoulder, but they weren't enough to distract me.

Later, I'd wonder if that was what *he* felt when he went on those missions he could never tell me anything about. He'd always said danger was a high and I'd thought *yeah, that's the cliché, but really isn't danger just frightening?* In that instant I understood that it was absolutely both. And this, this moment when my actions would decide whether I lived or died, was the purest of my life.

The thing was smiling at me as she walked forward, not a sneer or a grimace of rage but a real grin. Up close I suddenly saw that her cheekbones had the same angles, her eyes the same tilt as the dead boy's. *Her son,* I thought, but she didn't seem to care that he was dead. She just seemed... happy.

Her split tongue flickered out, lizard-like, through her smile.

I didn't have any weapons, not even a knife. The boom was over the other side of the boat now. Even if it swung back, it would hit me and not her. And if I let her touch me, it was all over. She walked forward and I walked back, a pace at a time. One step for her. One step for me. Two. Then three. I was nearly at the railing and after that there was nowhere else to go but into the water.

"What do you want?" I said to her again. "I'm a doctor. I can help you with... whatever the hell it is that's wrong with you."

That made her stop, just for a second. She held up the jagged stump of her right hand, eying the protruding bone as if she hadn't really noticed it before. Then she looked back at me. "But why would I want to change?" she asked in a warm, friendly Jamaican accent. "Everything's perfect just the way it is."

And then she took one last step forward, and instead of stepping back I stepped forward too. I put my hands on the lapels of her denim jacket and I dropped back, bringing my foot up and into her stomach. It had been years since I'd learnt this. Since he'd made me go to self-defence classes, then made me practice with him at home, again and again, because London's a dangerous place and he couldn't bear it if anything happened to me. But I guess he was right, that once you've learnt it you never forget. It took no effort at all to pull her over my head and then kick off with my heel and flip her over the railing. Less than a second later, I heard the splash as she hit the water.

I lay there for a second, shaking. She hadn't touched me. No part of her had touched me, I was sure of it. But the adrenaline had burnt itself out, purpose served, and all I could feel now was the desperate, paralysing fear I should have been feeling earlier.

It took us another forty-five minutes to reach the flagship. There was a radio on the boat but a bullet had taken it out and there was no way for us to let anyone else know what had happened.

Haru and I spent the time keeping watch, peering uselessly into the dense night for any more pursuers. The sailors had wanted to tip the infected boy's body overboard but I'd persuaded them not to. I'd need to study it, figure out just what the hell was wrong. Grumbling, they complied, taking the wide detours around his body and the pool of blood spilling from it.

When we got back to the flagship I asked to be taken straight to Queen M, but it was near midnight and the only person I could find was Kelis, back from whatever mission she'd been out on. She told me that it could wait until morning. I needed to sleep or I'd be making no sense to anyone anyway.

I let her lead me back to my room because I was exhausted – my whole body was one big ache – and also because she just hadn't seemed that surprised when I told her about the people who attacked us and what seemed to be wrong with them. I needed some time to think about what that meant.

The morning dawned bright but cooler. I shivered when I went out on deck in my shorts and tank-top, squinting against the piercing light of the rising sun. The blue sky, the blue seas, the distant palm trees suddenly looked a whole lot less reassuring than they had when I'd first arrived. Trouble in paradise, and then some.

Queen M was already enthroned in the empty pool, lounging back with one leg slung over an arm of the chair, looking like she hadn't a care in the world. She stood and smiled when I approached, and I guessed she'd been waiting for me. Only a few people were out at that time of the morning and they drifted away when they saw me.

"They come from Cuba," she said when I was ten paces from her. "My people call them the Infected."

That stopped me in my tracks. "Cuba?" I don't know why it surprised me; there was just something too known, too package-holiday about Cuba for it to be the source of that terrible affliction.

But she nodded. "They don't make any effort to disguise it, their boats are easy enough to track."

"And has anyone gone there to find out what's going on?"

Her bright eyes narrowed. "Would you go?"

I felt the throb of the deep bruises covering my legs and chest and I shook my head.

"I sent some people, back when they first showed up," Queen M said. "Twenty-four went, five returned. Back then it wasn't the whole of the island. Now as far as we can tell it's everyone. And it's started to spread. They say there have been cases on Haiti, some of the other Greater Antilles. As for what causes it..." She shrugged.

"But you're sure it's infectious?"

"How else could it be spreading?" Her eyes were still staring into mine, weighing everything up. She knows I want out, I thought. And this is her way of getting me to stay.

I sighed because, yeah, she might be manipulating me, but whatever it was that was coming out of Cuba was more important than my anger at her, or my desire to escape. The world just couldn't take another Cull. It would be the end of us. "I'm not just a doctor," I reminded her. "I'm a researcher. I was part of the team investigating the Cull, so I've picked up a thing or two. We brought one of the Infected back. I can do an autopsy on him if you like, get some blood work done, whatever you've got the equipment for. See what I can find out."

She smiled like a cat that had just been given detailed directions to the creamery. It occurred to me then that I'd never been told why the flagship had moved while I'd been on St Kitt's, or why she'd so unexpectedly decided to give me the day off.

What I knew now was that she was the kind of person who was more than happy to kill a sailor or two if it got her what she wanted.

* * *

The lab was in the bows of the ship, tucked away behind the casino in one of those areas that Kelis and Soren had steered me carefully away from. I thought it might once have been a crew kitchen; the gleaming metal surfaces and sinks were obviously original, but the pipettes, Bunsen burners and centrifuges were more recent additions. As was the autopsy table right in the centre of the room.

I had a sudden flash of it being used by Queen M for other purposes, living subjects, the runnels to carry away the blood at the sides a convenience when you were trying to extract information from someone you didn't want to die quite yet.

The current occupant of the table was very definitely dead though. Now I could see him under the halogen lights I realised he was even younger than I'd first thought, barely into his teens. There were three others in the room when Kelis and I arrived, white-coated and bending intently over their workstations, test-tubes and Petri dishes spread out in front of them like a particularly unappetising meal. I gestured at the corpse of the Infected. "Mind if I take a look?"

The nearest scientists, a harried looking woman in her forties, shrugged. "He's all yours. I'm an agronomist. Corpses aren't my thing."

"We're both electrical engineers," the man beside her said, nodding over at a third man who was peering through a microscope at some kind of circuit board. "You're the crew's first pathologist."

"Yeah," I said. "Except I'm not. I'm a doctor and a biochemist, but I haven't performed an autopsy since medical school."

"At least you've done one," the first woman said. "I wouldn't have a clue where to start."

Kelis hovered at my elbow, peering over at the body with open curiosity. "First one you've seen close up?" I guessed.

"Yup," she said. "Queen M always told us to steer clear, leave them be. Only recently they started getting aggressive, coming after us."

I looked down at the boy's body, the gaping bullet wound where his left eye had been, and lower, were something had cut into his chest. Now that he was naked I could see other wounds too: a chunk out of his left thigh, two toes hanging off and another two broken and twisted. It was easy enough to tell which injuries were the result of the confrontation on the boat and which had been around a while. The new ones weren't running with puss, oozing yellow and green into the surrounding flesh.

I decided to take a look at the wounds to his legs and stomach first. The edges of the cuts had been blurred by swelling and infection, but on the leg there was one little area that had remained relatively unscathed and it told me everything I needed to know. "Teeth marks," I said to Kelis, pulling back on the flesh and standing aside so that she could get a clear view.

She turned her head aside and made a face. Funny, you wouldn't think a woman doing her job could be squeamish. "*Joder!* You're saying they eat each other?"

I shook my head. "Not human. Shark, I think, though I've never treated a shark attack victim, so I can't be one-hundred per cent sure."

She held a hand over her nose in a futile attempt to ward off the stink and leaned a little closer. "Doesn't look like they did anything to it after the attack. There's no stitches, nothing. Why would anyone let an injury like that go untreated?"

"Yeah." I looked at his stomach, sure now that the flesh had been torn in the same incident. The level of infection was consistent too, both injuries dating back a couple of weeks. "It's like the shark bit him, he fought it off, climbed out of the water and then carried on like nothing had happened."

"But that's not possible, is it?"

I shrugged. "Short term, sure, it's amazing what a flood of adrenaline can do for you. Long term – no, it shouldn't be. He should have been in agony."

"Any sign of brain damage maybe?" She peered at the boy's head, what was left of it. "Something that might explain why he can't feel any pain?"

She was quick. I needed to remember that, in my plans. I sawed the boy's skull open but the damage from the bullet was too extensive to make out any subtler trauma around it. "Brain damage might explain what happened to him, but not the rest of them. It's too much of a coincidence for them all to have suffered the same condition."

After the brain I went for the other organs, cracking open the ribs to get at them, wincing as blood splashed back at me from the corpse. The gown and mask caught it all and the examination didn't tell me anything I could use. The state of his liver would suggest too much drinking, but alcoholism just wasn't going to explain the things I'd seen on that boat. I used a scalpel to slice off a sliver of it anyway, along with the heart and the lungs, but I wasn't really expecting to find anything. I thought Kelis was probably at least partly right: whatever was wrong with these people was wrong with their brains.

After I was done with the body, hauling a sheet over it because I didn't want to look at the ruin of that young man a second longer, I took the samples over to one of the microscopes. And yes, I'd been right – they told me nothing. Normal. Which left only... but I'd been putting that off since I came into the room, almost as if I'd known from the beginning what I was going to find.

"What about his blood?" Kelis said, watching it soak through the thin white sheet covering his body like a guilty secret that wanted to be known. "Aren't most infectious diseases blood-borne?"

"They can be air-borne too, transmitted by touch..." But I was just talking, the words didn't mean anything, because she was right. I had to look at the blood. My fingers trembled as I prepared the slide, and I wondered if Kelis had noticed. And then I wasn't thinking about anything at all because what I could see in front of me was what I'd somehow feared without even knowing it, and the memories washed back over me, too strong to resist.

Most of all I remembered the excitement, a taste in the back of my throat that was very much like fear. My heart pounding, loud in my ears and heavy in my chest. And maybe it was fear, a little, because what if we were wrong? If we doled out hope and then took it back again, would anyone there forgive us? With the way nerves were on edge, tempers frayed – it would only take one spark, and that might be it. But...

"I really think this is it," Ash said, and there was an edge of excitement in his normally cool voice.

I looked at the slide again, at the lab work, the electron microscope images and grainy NMR scans, but they were all telling us the same thing. "This is... you know how fucking dangerous this is, right?"

But Ash was grinning now, that smile I remembered from college but hadn't seen in a while, when he knew he'd done something clever and was planning on being insufferable about it. "Yeah, because dying in agony while your brains slide out of your ears isn't dangerous at all." The lab felt too small to contain him when he was in a mood like this.

I ignored him and took one final look at the slide, the papers. As if the facts might have changed while I wasn't looking. But of course they hadn't. "It really is O-neg."

"Yeah," Ashok said, "and before that, it really was AB. This is it, Jasmine. Stop second guessing and start celebrating!"

"Shit," I exclaimed. "Shit. We are geniuses!"

He swept me up into a hug. "Yeah, babe, we really are."

"Twisted geniuses."

He gave me a last squeeze, and then let me go. "The best kind."

"Because what we did here is mental. You know that, don't you? I mean, we're generally in the business of curing retro-viruses, not creating them."

"Not to mention the military tech in there that would make al-Qaeda's eyes light up. If they weren't, you know, dying in agony along with everyone else."

"And the stem cells – don't want to forget them."

"How could I? But the FDA's out there melting right alongside the terrorists we also don't have to worry about."

Our jubilation had tipped over into near hysteria, and we must have been shouting pretty damn loud, because Abuke poked his head round the door and frowned. Then he saw our faces and his frown slipped into another expression, harder to define.

"You did it?" he said. "You've found it?"

I smiled. "Yeah, I really think we have."

But a vaccine that turns a rat's blood from one type to another isn't necessarily the same as a Cure that does the same thing for humans. In any normal medical research there'd be years of testing to go before we moved on to live subjects. Fat chance. It was live testing or nothing, and there weren't a whole lot of subjects to choose from.

The five of us lay in identical beds wearing hospital gowns, tubes in our arms, expressions of unease on our faces. I guess it was flattering in a way, that the other three were prepared to put so much trust in mine and Ash's work. Or more likely it was just desperation.

Yesterday, the base had seen its first Cull. The rest of us would follow; weeks or days later, who knew, but it would be soon.

On the bed beside me Ash smiled, but it was strained. The muscles in his cheeks tensing and releasing as he ground his teeth, a nervous habit I'm not sure he knew he had. "Ready?" I asked him.

"Jasmine..." he said softly, and I realised that he was going to say something serious, probably about us – but I had a man at home.

"We'll be fine," I said hurriedly. "I've got faith in us."

"Yeah." His eyes closed slowly, then opened again, and he knew I didn't want to hear what he wanted to say. "I'm glad I'm here with you," he said finally, "whatever happens."

And then we both took the needles nestling in the cannula in our arms, and pushed. A second's hesitation, then the other three did the same. The Cure, mainlined, spreading through our system like the virus it was. Taking our DNA and changing it. DNA transcribing to RNA, coalescing and knotting to form the templates for alien proteins inside us, closing off the source of the AB blood cells that marked us for death. Telling our bodies that we'd been O-negs all the time, we just hadn't realised it yet.

Doing all of that – and something else too. A second after the small pain of the injection came a pain that was a thousand times worse. It felt as if something essential was being ripped loose right in the heart of us, and then again, and again, and again, until I couldn't imagine that it would ever end. Ash was the first to start screaming and once he'd started, he didn't stop. None of us did.

* * *

AND NOW, HERE, as I looked at the slide, I knew exactly what I was seeing. Except, of course, that it shouldn't be possible. I turned to Kelis, hoping she couldn't see my shaking hands, that she wouldn't notice the way all the blood had drained from my face. Blood – ironic how everything comes back to that.

"Hey," I said, and tried not to wince at the fake casualness of it, my inability to seem normal when everything inside me was screaming as loud as it had when I first took the Cure. "Any chance you can scare up some food? I didn't have any breakfast earlier."

She looked at the boy's corpse, and then at me, eyebrows raised. "You're hungry – seriously?"

"Yeah, what can I say – I'm a doctor. Gore gives me an appetite."

She shrugged and headed out the door, maybe glad to get away from the gore herself. Strange to think of a killer being queasy at the sight of blood. But then *killer* didn't quite capture her. It implied a love of it, or a clinical efficiency. Soren was a killer. Kelis had gone about killing with a kind of weary resignation, like it had been her third-choice career while there was a kid at home with an out-of-work husband and she needed to bring in the dough.

I'd brought my medical bag with me. The sterile needle and syringe were right where they always were. I had to stop myself shooting edgy, guilty looks at the other scientists as I drew out my own blood from the crook of my elbow and carefully smeared it onto a slide. They wouldn't think there was anything odd about it. Why should they? I was just a fellow scientist, going about my scientific business.

The slide clicked into place beside the one I'd taken from the Infected boy. I already knew what I'd see, but like a lump of vomit stuck halfway up my throat, I was still reluctant to bring it all the way into the light of day. I took one deep shaking breath, a second, then put my eye against the microscope and focussed.

The slide of my blood was on the left. The boy's blood was on the right. I remembered that – but there was no other way to tell. The two slides were identical, the same sickly, deformed red blood cells, twisted into a shape that nature had never seen before Ash and I had had our bright idea, five years ago. When we'd believed we might be able to save the human race.

The cobbled-together, wing-and-a-prayer hybrid we'd engineered in a lab from cutting-edge medical tech and code-black military wetware had driven me insane. Somehow, it had done something very different, but equally terrible, to the people of Cuba.

Ash and I had meant to cure one plague. Had we managed to start another? I guess I should have been feeling guilty, for letting loose this thing that could wipe out the last, ragged remnant of humanity. But that wasn't what I was thinking about right then. What I was thinking was that Queen M had been right: this thing was infectious, and I was a carrier. Hell, I was Patient Zero. And if she ever picked up even a hint of it, I'd be shark meat.

Suddenly escape was looking a whole lot more urgent. Fuck everyone else. I had to get out of there right now.

CHAPTER THREE

I'D FINALLY MANAGED to discover the location of the camera in my room, hidden in the handle of my wardrobe where it had a perfect view of the bed. I hoped whoever watched the footage enjoyed the view. I hadn't changed anything about my routine when I discovered it, not even giving in to the temptation to start undressing in the bathroom. Couldn't let them know I knew. Besides, there was probably a camera in the bathroom too, but that one didn't matter.

I couldn't set my alarm, not sure if there was sound recording in the room as well. It wasn't essential to my plan. Since my medical student days I'd always been able to wake when I wanted.

At exactly ten past four in the morning my eyes blinked uselessly open in the absolute darkness.

I'd spent five days learning my way around the cabin by touch. Subtly brushing a hand along the dresser, counting the paces from door to bed, feeling the rough patch in the carpet with my toes. I let my eyes slide shut as I felt in the wardrobe for my clothes, twisted the clasp on my blouse shut, slid my sandals over my feet.

There's something about the dead of night that seems to amplify sound, every rustle of cotton, every scrape of a zipper echoing in the seemingly cavernous room.

That night my fingers fumbled at my shoes, fingernails scraping against a buckle, and I froze for a second, my heart pounding.

Nothing. No sound of my shadows waiting outside my door. When I was dressed, I slid my feet over the carpet to the door, counting footsteps. One, two, three, four, five. The handle was right there and I turned it. The lip salve I'd casually smeared last night from my lips to my finger to the latch seemed to have done the trick; the door eased open without a sound.

The night lights in the corridor seemed momentarily far too bright and I had to fight the urge to flinch back. I knew where the camera here was too, ten feet away from my door. Fixed, no rotation. Nobody would see me leaving, but whoever was watching would see me walk past.

Not a problem. Like any tribe, the soldiers here liked to find ways to distinguish themselves from the common herd. They always wore red, somewhere on them, when they weren't out on a mission, boots rather than sandals, dog tags scavenged from God knows where. Those had been the hardest to get, but it's amazing what you'll find lying around in places where ninety-three per cent of the population didn't get to leave any kind of last will and testament.

They'd know my face, of course, if they were really looking. But why would they be, if I walked with confidence and looked like I knew where I was going? Stupidly, like someone picking at a scab on their finger when their whole leg needs amputating, that was the part of the plan I was most worried about. *He'd* always joked that I had no sense of direction and I'd quoted him psychological research about how men found their way using maps and women did it with landmarks; but both were equally good. Then he'd challenge me to find my way from Leicester Square to Covent Garden – and he was right. I couldn't navigate for shit.

There'd only be so long I could stand, looking at one of those wall-mounted plans of the ship, without it looking suspicious. I thought I knew where I was going. I *thought* I did. So I worried about that rather than worrying about the camera, after camera, after camera I was passing with my face visible for God and everyone to see. Or the fact that I had only the vaguest idea how to pilot a boat, even if I could get to one. I particularly didn't think about what Queen M would do if she caught me. About that autopsy table in the lab, and the runnels down the sides to carry away the blood.

The ship felt haunted at night, by all the people who'd been so happy right before they died. I walked through the endless, bland, carpeted corridors; down the marble stairs and through the empty galleries with blank bare windows that used to hold things the dead people had wanted to buy. Soldiers passed me now and then, glanced once and looked away. They had the white, weary look of people who were missing their beds. They didn't want trouble, anything that would force them to act. I made myself easy to ignore.

And I went steadily down, towards the water line. On Deck Four I took a wrong turn, left rather than right. I realised it two strides too late. No turning back. That would be too noticeable, too much the act of someone who didn't belong. All I could do was carry on, to the next staircase, down to the next deck, hoping it was built on the same plan as the previous one as I turned right this time and, yes, it was. Because suddenly the stairs were metal, the walls a dull institutional brown.

I was out of the guest quarters and into the parts of the ship only the crew were meant to see. My feet echoed loudly on the metal treads, but I didn't care. I was nearly there.

So what was I going to do about that little fragment of metal in my leg? I was going to get clear of the ship, get to one of the islands Queen M had only recently begun to colonise – Isla Marguerita, or St Thomas, somewhere there weren't too many people around – and then I was going to operate on myself and remove it.

I'd only be using a local anaesthetic, obviously, and I'd be digging deep through muscle and into bone. I'd probably be breaking the bone. There was a chance I wouldn't survive the procedure and the likelihood I couldn't walk away from it. But I was desperate and willing to try.

One more flight of metal stairs and I was on the tender deck. Little detachable jetties led from here into the water only a few feet below. I could hear the slap of it against the hull of the ship, always more violent than you expected after you'd seen it from the sundeck far above, so tranquil and blue. Sometimes the tender boats stayed overnight. Sometimes they went back to the islands when they'd unloaded their cargoes. But so many came and went, there had to be one still here, right?

And there was. Right at the far end, an open hatch in the side of the ship. The waft of salt air and the audible bounce and crash of a small boat moored outside drifted through the hole as it hopped on the rough waves.

I was only ten feet away from it when I realised that the floor beneath my boots was covered in a thin rubber sheath, good grip for when the water washed in. The floor was rubber, but I could still hear the echo of footsteps on metal. Two sets of them.

I turned round to face Soren and Kelis. "So," I said. "I guess this doesn't look good."

Soren huffed out what might have been a laugh.

Kelis looked... almost upset. Like I'd let her down, somehow. "You were thinking you could operate on yourself, take it out, right?"

I shrugged. "Or maybe I just wanted to stretch my legs."

"It wouldn't have done you any good." She came closer, but her hand was empty. She wasn't pointing a gun at me, just yet. "The tracker system's more sophisticated than you realise. There's a roam-zone programmed for every individual. An alarm goes off when anyone breaches it."

"And I just breached mine," I guessed, but she shook her head.

"Twenty meters out in that boat and you would have. We thought we'd stop you before that happened." She glanced at Soren and he stared straight back at her. For the first time I registered the way he leant subtly towards her whenever she was near, like a plant responding to the sun. He doesn't care about me, I thought. He came because she asked him to. Another piece of information I could file away for later use – if there was a later.

Their hands were still nowhere near their guns. They weren't looking like they thought I was any kind of threat. *Tackle Kelis*, a voice inside me said, *surprise her, take her gun. Shoot Soren.* Possible, maybe. But I wasn't going to do it.

"So... how exactly did you find me?"

Kelis shrugged. "I knew what you were planning – you'd been twitchy all day. Acting too casual. I was a corrections officer, back before. You learn to read the signs." That startled me. Not so much the information, because it wasn't that hard to imagine, but the fact that I'd spent so many hours with her and I'd never asked about her previous life, hadn't even really wondered.

The Cull was like a big black wall cutting across the past. You couldn't climb it, so why would you want to know what was behind it?

"So you came down here and waited, right?" It was dispiriting to realise I'd been that transparent. "Why?"

She shifted and, for the first time since I'd met her, looked unsure of herself. It was Soren who answered. "Queen M would kill you if she knew what you were planning."

"And you didn't want that?"

He shrugged and looked at Kelis. "She didn't."

"You're here to stay," Kelis said. "Accept it."

"And what if I can't?"

She looked away, out into the dark void of the open hatch, and didn't bother to answer me.

NEXT DAY I was back in the lab, researching a problem whose answer I already knew. Still, the source of the infection might be obvious, but how it had metamorphosed remained a mystery. A couple of years as a research assistant had taught me to perfect the art of looking busy while remaining essentially idle, and I didn't think the other scientists in the room had any idea that the tissue cultures I was taking, and the slides I was carefully preparing, were entirely meaningless. The only thing I managed to establish for sure was that the virus was transmitted though blood and not an air-borne contagion. That at least was something I could tell Queen M.

Kelis and Soren were back, shadowing me from the moment I woke up. Their decision, I guessed. I wanted to believe that Kelis hadn't told Queen M what happened the night before. My eyes twitched briefly, involuntarily, to the autopsy table in the centre of the room. To the convenient little grooves to carry away the blood.

I felt the tension in the lab before I saw her. I felt it most of all from Kelis, and when I looked up to see Queen M standing in the doorway of the room, I didn't know if it was because she'd betrayed me or because she hadn't.

Queen M smiled and I still didn't know, her expression as unyielding as an investment banker. "Come and walk with me," she said, nodding at Kelis and Soren in a way that let them know that they weren't included in the invitation.

A little trickle of ice-water seeped down my spine.

"We haven't really spoken properly since you arrived," she said when we were out of the lab, heading up the stairs which would take us to the sun deck and the empty pool.

"I'm sure you've been very busy." I injected a note of irony into the words. She knew I didn't like her and she'd get suspicious if I started pretending that I did.

"I used to be an academic, did you know that? Reader in evolutionary psychology at the LSE."

My head snapped round to look at her: cornrows, beaded braids, wide, thoughtful eyes. It wasn't that difficult to believe. "You've come up in the world."

"Down is what you mean," she said, then held up her hand, stopping my protest almost as soon as it had formed on my lips. "No, it's okay. I know exactly what you think of me. You hold me responsible for those deaths you witnessed, you're imagining many more and you're completely right. I am responsible, and there were more. You think I'm a monster."

I looked away from her again because I didn't want her to see exactly how true that was.

"But you're in a unique position," she said softly. "You're the only person in the world who didn't see what happened after the Cull. You can still go on thinking all those cuddly things about human nature that four thousand years of civilisation allowed us to believe. Have you heard of Hobbes's Leviathan?"

I shook my head.

"But you've heard about life being nasty, brutish and short, right? That was Hobbes, telling it like it is – when there isn't a state around, an all-powerful Leviathan, to force people to listen only to their better angels."

"So – what? You knew how bad people could be and you decided to be worse? Becoming a monster was inevitable so you decided to embrace it rather than fight it?"

She smiled at me, the small patronising grin of a professor who's about to score points from a first-year undergraduate. "Hobbes saw, and the Cull showed, what human beings become in the absence of a state monopoly on violence. You think I'm bad, that this society is bad, but that's only because you haven't seen the rest of the world. I have to be a dictator, or someone has to, because the only other option is chaos."

"Those people in Paris seemed to be doing okay, 'til we came along." My words were marinated in two weeks of bitterness.

"No, they really weren't. Three quarters of them were already dead. Half the women had been raped – and not always by rival gangs. That baby, the one you left behind? Her mother didn't know who the father was – it could have been any one of the men who caught her out after dark one night and spent the next seventeen hours doing exactly what they wanted with her. You think this is bad, Jasmine, you think I'm a monster, but that's only because you haven't seen the alternatives."

It was the first real passion I'd heard in her voice. Her eyes were finally alight with something other than a cold amusement. "They don't just stay because of the tags in their legs," she said finally. "However much you might want to believe that."

"And why are you telling me this?" I asked eventually. We'd reached the top of the ship. The sun, the distant sand, even the sky was white and fierce. Hard.

She was looking out over the ocean rather than at me. When she turned back, her face was closed again. And though I knew the earlier openness had been real, I also knew it had been calculated. "You are only staying because of that tracker in your leg, and that isn't healthy. I want you to believe in what we're doing here. I'm not looking for slaves, I'm looking for followers – committed ones. And I never want you to try again what you did last night. Because the next time you do, I'll kill you. And it won't be anything like as quick and pretty as the deaths you saw in Ireland."

I smiled bitterly and didn't say anything. What was I going to say? I believed her threat absolutely. I nodded to her, not sure what I meant by it or what she'd think I meant. Then I walked quietly back inside, away from the punishing sun.

* * *

Haru was still where I'd seen him that morning, hunched over a vivid line drawing of a young girl being ripped apart by zombies. The Deck Ten children's pool beside him was filled with a thin slurry of pond scum.

"Okay," I said. "Why should I trust you?"

He looked surprised only for a moment. Then he smiled. "Because I want to get out too, and I think you can help me. You know we've got a much better chance together."

"Your life here isn't so bad. Why would you want to change it?"

He opened the leather portfolio that was always with him, and for a moment I thought he was going to show me another drawing. But the thing he pulled out was a photo, a little dog-eared around the edges: a young boy, maybe ten, sitting hunched in a wheelchair, frail legs twisted like pipe cleaners in front of him.

"My son," Haru said. "Back in Japan. Not at all the sort of person Queen M wanted in this brave new world."

"Then," I said, "let's talk about what we need to do."

The day after Queen M gave me her strange little pep talk, Haru introduced me to Ingo: blue-black skin, soft, deep African accent. A boyish face that was probably older than it looked.

"I run the network," he told me, taking my hand in a firm, enveloping shake. He had long artist's fingers, but I could see that most of the bones in them had been broken some time in the past, and reset crooked. I didn't need to ask why he wanted to escape.

"The computer network?"

He nodded.

"And I'm guessing your job involves more than telling people to switch it off and then switch it back on again?"

He didn't smile. His face was so unlined that I wondered if he ever did. "I take care of it all," he said. "Including the tracker system."

"You can disable it?"

"Of course." And he did smile then, but it was little more than an upward twitch of his lip.

"Permanently?"

He shook his head. "She had me set up the central core so it was password protected, and she has hard copies of all the information."

"But it was you who set up the password, so..."

"She is not stupid. There were four of us who worked on this. I was the project leader, but each of us oversaw the other's work. And she told us – if one of us saw something and did not report it, we would be punished just as if we had done it ourselves. There is no backdoor. The system is unbreakable."

"Okay then." I looked down, disappointed. "But you can take it down, at least for a little while."

"Yes," he said. "That I can do."

After I spoke to Ingo I waited until, a week later, I got what I needed: a fresh corpse from the plantations and an excuse to perform an autopsy on it. Twenty years old, fit as a fiddle, and dead for no reason. I caught myself almost smiling at the family when they told me what had happened; how he'd been talking about the weather one minute, dead the next. Their numb, tear-streaked faces looked back at me, hoping I'd have some explanation for their sudden wrenching loss, and the smile faded into nothing.

I radioed the ship, asking for the lab to be cleared so I could perform an autopsy on a potentially infectious vector. "I'm sure it's nothing, just a weak heart," I told Queen M. "If you prefer I can cut it open out here, take a quick look. Then the family can have him back and buried by the end of the day."

"No," she said. "better to be safe. The equipment you've got out there isn't sophisticated enough to pick up anything important. Bring the boy in – and keep yourself in quarantine until you can give me the all-clear. I don't want anyone but you coming into contact with that body."

"Fine," I told her, "but you'll need to keep the family in isolation too." The smile was back again and this time there was nothing I could do to suppress it. I ended the call before Queen M could hear it in my voice.

I didn't look at the man's face as I cut him open. I was sure I'd read an accusation there, that I was desecrating the only thing left of him in this world for no real reason. Chest first and yes, I could see it, the hole in his heart that had killed him. But there was no one in the lab to share the find with me, the spectre of an infectious agent that much more terrifying in a post-Cull world. I carried on cutting, as if I was still searching for something more elusive.

Getting the chip out should have been easy – cut into the thigh, through to the bone, and that's it. Except that Queen M would only have to take one look at the body and she'd know exactly what I'd done. And I was damn sure that she'd look at the body.

But the organs – those I had a good reason to poke around in. I took out the liver and the pancreas, the coiled crimson length of the gut, releasing the stench of half-fermented shit into the antiseptic atmosphere of the lab. The human body really is like an overstuffed suitcase. You look at everything that comes out of it and can't believe biology ever fitted it all in there.

I took tissue slides of each organ and looked at each of them under the microscope – his liver was like a sixty-year olds; he must have moved straight from breast milk to rum. Nothing of note in the kidneys or the testes, but then I hadn't expected there to be. Finally, I went back to the whole point of the exercise: burrowing down through the now conveniently empty chest cavity to drill a small plug out of the pelvic girdle. I took the bone, slick with blood and worse, and slid it into the pocket of my slacks, into the little zip lock bag I'd hidden there earlier.

Then I burrowed deeper still, through the flesh along the edge of the bone. I had unwelcome flashbacks to cooking for *him*, carving the raw meat as he looked away, pretending he was too squeamish to watch. Letting us keep up the fiction that his job wasn't the inverse of mine, making death out of life. *You're better off without him*, a voice said inside me, and I wasn't sure if it was the Voice, waking up from the drugged haze I'd put it in those last few weeks, or just the voice of reason I was never able to hear when he was near. Love isn't blind, that's the trouble. You see all the faults and all the insurmountable problems – you just don't care.

I still didn't. That, in the end, was why I needed to get out of there. I could tell myself all kinds of comfortable lies about freeing myself from despotism, but in the end it was all about him. While I was there, I would never see him again. Out in the world, maybe – and that was just about enough.

And there, at last, it was. The chip, inserted tight into the bone but not tight enough that I couldn't pry it out. It went into my other pocket and then all I had to do was stuff all those organs back into the body and sew it up, stitches as neat as I could make them because this was the body his family would be burying, the last sight they'd have of someone they'd once loved. Not much recompense but the best that I could offer.

Then I went to see Ingo.

"Magnetism," he told me. The chip looked tiny in the pink cradle of his palm. "If it is strong enough, you will degauss it."

"Great," I said. "Because a giant magnet is just the kind of thing we're going to find lying around on a ship."

"No," Ingo said, entirely seriously. "I think you are mistaken. It is highly unlikely that there will be a magnet of sufficient size anywhere in the fleet."

Behind his back Haru rolled his eyes and I had to suppress a smile, but it wasn't really very funny. If we couldn't solve this problem then the plan was dead. The chips had to be deactivated.

We'd met in a little room to the side of the main lab, home to the centrifuge and a collection of embryo-filled specimen jars which gave Haru an excuse to be there. He was sketching as we spoke, some kind of squid monster emerging from the machine in the centre of the room. One of its tentacles was about to grab, or possibly indecently assault, the most humourless of my lab mates. Ingo was inspecting my laptop, which I'd reported as broken. I reckoned we had another five minutes of talk before our little gathering started to look suspicious. Then we'd be back to using Haru as our go-between.

My eyes drifted back down to my own work, a fruitless tissue culture I was growing from the now half-decayed Infected. I was no closer to finding out how the hell the Cure had turned from a vaccine to a virus, and my lack of results was starting to seriously piss Queen M off. Yet another reason we had to figure out a way past the chips.

"What about electricity?" I said. "Could we fry the things?"

"Yes," Haru said, his hand busy sketching lightning bolts around the squid monster. "And fry us in the process."

"It's possible for the human body to survive a lightning strike. A current that would kill the chip might leave us alive. Right?" I said to Ingo.

He tilted his head, considering this with his usual infuriating slowness. Then he nodded. "Yes, that is possible."

"'Might'?" Haru said. "'Possible'? These aren't the words you want to hear when you're talking about putting twelve thousand volts down your spinal column. How about words like 'definitely' and 'entirely safe'?"

"What about that kind of electricity?" I asked Ingo. "Can we find that anywhere on the ship."

"The engine room. Maybe." He shrugged. "I cannot say for sure. My work uses currents considerably lower."

"You'll need to search then," I told Haru. "See what you can find."

"Sure, why not? Maybe it will give us superpowers, turn us into Team Electro – if, you know, it doesn't kill us all first."

Then Barbados, and Haru was showing me his sketchbook again. The pictures were getting wilder, more fantastical, as if the approaching escape was firing his imagination, or maybe just letting the darker recesses of his subconscious peek through. I wondered what Queen M would make of it all.

I wondered if he showed them to her at all, now that there was something else there – hidden in the logo of a t-shirt, the pattern of the carpet. For the last two weeks he'd been painstakingly compiling plans of the ship: each deck a different drawing. And here, in the seemingly random leaves of a tree, the outlines of the islands, each military base picked out in darker green. The waves on the ocean in another drawing were a complex circuit diagram, a wiring plan for the ship. And in each night-time picture the stars were the charts we'd need to navigate our way to freedom.

"This is everything?" I asked him.

"I've been everywhere on the ship. Even into Queen M's quarters. It's all here."

"And nobody suspected anything?"

"Do I look suspicious?" He grinned boyishly, flashing the gap between his front teeth and, no, he didn't. He looked like the likeable nerd who didn't get the girl at the end of a John Hughes movie. Which, given how much of this plan depended on him, didn't exactly fill me with confidence.

"So we're ready to go," he said.

"Yes," I said. "I guess we are."

When I woke up at four that morning it was to find that the Voice had returned, sliding through the thoughts at the back of my mind. *You need to be careful*, it told me. *You can't trust anyone.*

But I knew that already. I took my morning dose of anti-psychotics, a lower dose than I really needed, but it was the only way I'd been able to hoard enough to last me for the journey, until I could find an abandoned pharmacy somewhere on land. *If* I could find a pharmacy. The Voice, so blessedly absent from my mind since my rescue, had become a restless whisper at the edge of my consciousness. The panicky knowledge of its presence was a threat that one day would be made good.

Perhaps this whole escape plan, the desperate need to leave, was itself coming from the Voice. Madness feeling like sanity.

Fuck it – I'd worry about that once I was away.

There was no need to keep the lights off this time. Thanks to Ingo, the cameras in my room would be feeding back a constant loop of my sleeping form. So I've watched a few heist movies in my time – if an idea works, it works.

Haru met me outside the door. He gave me a tense, uncomfortable smile. Then he gave me a gun, a hefty Magnum with a silencer already clutching the end of its barrel. Haru flicked through his sketches, navigating our way through the ship. We had to follow the exact route we'd agreed with Ingo, otherwise his little trick with the looping tape wouldn't work. We'd timed it to the second, stopping at the end of each corridor and the bottom of each stairwell to check it off against the timetable Haru had hidden in a picture of Queen M's braids.

Ingo had memorised the timetable. Eidetic memory, he told us. Asperger's I would have said, but not to his face.

The ship was as quiet as the night of that first aborted escape attempt. So quiet that our footsteps, the gentle rustle of them in the threadbare carpet, felt like an offence. The ship wanted to rest, and here we were waking it up.

Empty too. We'd chosen to do this when two different grab teams were out on missions, and another batch of soldiers was on St Martaan for R&R. As we walked down a flight of stairs, across a deck, through the echoing emptiness of the casino, down more stairs, I thought that perhaps we wouldn't see anyone at all.

Not possible, of course.

I recognised the woman's face as we rounded the corner to see her leaning up against the closed lift door, sneaking a fag that she must have been hoarding for weeks until she could enjoy it away from the grasping hands of her colleagues.

She looked up at us, startled but not afraid, and I remembered suddenly that her name was Jeannine. I'd heard someone shouting it across the mess, maybe two weeks ago. For one paralysed moment I just stood there. But then her eyes began to narrow in suspicion, her hand inched towards her gun, and as soon as it became her or me the choice was that much simpler.

A harsh exhalation, muffled by the silencer, and the bullet took her through the throat. Not where I'd been aiming, but it did the job. The jet of arterial blood splashed the lift door, droplets of it landing on my cheek and in my hair. Her hands came up to cover her throat, uselessly. She had that look of shock young people sometimes get when they're dying. Disbelief that their lives really can be ending this way.

I felt Haru's hand pulling at my arm and I realised that I was standing frozen, wondering how I could possibly treat her. If I could cure her.

Once a doctor, always... but not really. I couldn't call myself a doctor now.

I let Haru drag me away, down another flight of stairs and through the dim, endless corridors, like players of a particularly lacklustre first-person shooter. We were running now. Once the first body was found it was game over.

The next person I shot, I didn't stay to watch die. The bullet struck him in the head this time, and there wasn't enough left of his face for me to recognise anyway.

With the third person the bullet went wide, and the sound it made as it hit the bulkhead was too damn loud. The next shot took him in the chest, his own gun still tucked into the waistband of his shorts, but the damage was done. Anyone in earshot would have known exactly what that sound was. I could already hear raised voices, the first inkling that an alarm might be raised.

We were just ten paces from the door when they got to us. They were expecting resistance this time and they knew that I was armed. There were no silencers on their guns and they roared as they spat their bullets at us. The one that missed my head by two inches deafened me, ringing in my ear long after we'd dived through the open bulkhead and slammed it shut behind us, spinning the wheel that would lock us in one of the few rooms on the ship that was designed to be sealed from the inside.

The server room looked like something out of a seventies sci-fi movie: big silver boxes and lots of flashing lights. There were six dull thuds against the door as someone unloaded their gun into it. Tough shit. That thing was designed to resist pretty much anything bar heavy duty explosives.

Haru was flicking frantically through his sketchbook. "Shit. Shit! Where is it?"

"It's in that picture of the giant robot – the New York skyline."

"I know what it is!" he shouted. I realised that he was terrified. His face was dripping with sweat, his breath was panting and ragged.

Seeing his fear made me notice my own for the first time. "It was the last sketch," I told Haru, my voice suddenly shaky and weak. But I was right. The skyscrapers on the skyline had a careful pattern of light and dark, an exactly blueprint of which cables we needed to pull and which needed to be left. My hands were shaking as well as my voice. Everything inside me was saying *for fuck's sake, hurry, they're right outside*, but I clenched down hard on the panic and continued to slowly, methodically work my way down the side of each server, each router.

We couldn't afford to disable the wrong equipment. We'd need it later.

Outside, the banging had stopped, but I could hear the muted sound of more voices. They would probably bring some explosives, pretty soon. But they'd think a while before they used them, because the servers in here were pretty much irreplaceable. Besides, they knew that we'd have to come out eventually.

Only we wouldn't. When you put a whole load of delicate computer equipment in the bowels of a ship you'd better be pretty damn sure that you can cool it – and the ducts that let the air in were just big enough to let people out. The hatch was in the far corner of the room, just above head level. It took a minute to unscrew and then we were out.

Jesus, the tube was narrow. I tried to force my body through a space that was only meant to take air, my face pressed up against Haru's thighs as he forced his way through ahead of me. I felt the walls pressing in around me, squeezing the air out of my lungs. I tried not to think about the fact that Haru was bigger than me. If he got jammed there'd be no way forward and no way back.

Behind me I heard the sudden sharp sound of an explosion and a second later felt a wash of painfully hot air rocket through the shaft. I'd managed to prop the cover shut behind us, but it wouldn't take them long to figure out where we'd gone.

I hoped they didn't have the schematics anywhere to hand. If they did, they'd know exactly where we'd be emerging and we'd be sure to meet a welcoming committee on our exit. I saw the autopsy table again.

But maybe we wouldn't be getting out at all. In front of me, Haru had stopped cold. I could hear the harsh sound of his breathing and I could smell the acrid tang of his sweat. He was panicking, on the point of losing it.

"Keep moving!" I shouted, the sound muffled by our bodies, almost lost in the short distance from my mouth to his ears. "They're right behind us."

"It goes up," he shouted back. "I can't... I don't think I can get up there."

"Well try!" I shouted back. Behind me, louder than our voices, I'd heard the screech of the cover being moved. The duct had run straight, up to that point. As soon as they pointed a torch in they'd be able to see us.

Haru just wasn't moving. Frantic, I reached my arms out in front of me, pressed my hands against the soles of Haru's shoes, and pushed.

Instead of moving him forward, the pressure moved me back. Laws of physics I'd known since I was ten. Behind me, only a few feet behind me, someone else was starting to climb into the duct.

"Fucking move!" I screamed at Haru. And finally, somehow, he did, bending his back at an impossible angle and pushing himself forward with his toes. I slithered after him, desperately. But when I reached the kink in the pipe, almost forty-five degrees up and then only a foot later back to flat again, I knew why he'd found it so hard. My shoulders jammed in tight against the roof of the passage, my knees pressing agonisingly against the metal floor. My head twisted at an angle one degree away from snapping my neck. And now *I* wasn't moving. Ahead of me, Haru was opening up a gap, moving faster now, body flattened to the metal. Behind me, someone was closing on us fast. A voice I recognised as Curtis's shouted, "Stop! Come back!" but there was no way in hell that was happening. I didn't really know how I did it, but suddenly I was up and over the bend, and the shot that rang out through the duct behind me took the last of the hearing from my good ear, but the bullet passed harmlessly beneath me. Curtis was a big guy, too, and there was no way he was getting around that bend after us.

When we spilled out onto the deck above, Ingo was waiting for us.

"So, everything went smoothly?" he said.

I looked at Haru and we both laughed, a tinge of hysteria in it. His trousers were ripped and my chest was marked with long, parallel cuts where my t-shirt had rucked up and allowed the floor of the duct to skin me like a cheese grater.

"Is the tracker down?" Haru asked him when we'd got our breath back, already heading down the corridor. We were all carrying guns now, no need for careful timing any longer, only speed. There were three of us against a crew of four-hundred and thirty-seven. We needed them to make the obvious assumption, that with the tracker down we'd be making for the tender boats.

But we weren't going down, we were going up.

"The whole computer network has crashed," Ingo told us. "It will take them at least twelve hours to repair. I think more likely a day."

We turned a corner, then another. Two soldiers, and Ingo took them out without blinking, without even seeming to notice. The next turn and a woman came at us from a side corridor, looking startled. She hadn't been hunting for us but I shot her anyway, the finger-twitch on the trigger a mindless reflex. The first bullet went clean through her shoulder, embedding shards of bone in the insipid watercolour on the wall behind her, white lumps in the white clouds over Botany Bay. I recognised her too late. A kitchen worker, just a cook, nothing to do with the soldiers chasing us. Collateral damage, I told myself bleakly, moving on. You couldn't stay and think about these things, because it only got you killed, and that was two dead bodies without one good reason.

He'd taught me that, too, on one of those rare times he talked to me about what he really did.

We killed seven more, moving on before their bodies even hit the deck. *They don't matter*, the Voice whispered to me, and I really wanted to believe it. Beside me Haru's eyes looked wild, Ingo's just blank. Then, at last, we were there. And no one was waiting for us, not one single guard, because the one ship they would never have expected us to take was the one we were already on.

I slammed the door shut behind us and twisted the wheel to lock it. This was another room designed to be secure. *This'll show you, you self-satisfied bitch*, I thought. *You're not quite as clever as you think you are.*

There were only two men at the controls, eyes heavy with tiredness, and they spun to face us just a second too late. Ingo's bullet took the one on the left and mine the one on the right, almost as if we'd rehearsed it. And then we had the bridge all to ourselves.

Stealing an ocean liner is much, much easier than you might expect. Ingo took one look at the controls and nodded, satisfied.

"You're sure?" I said.

He gave me that peculiar almost-smile of his. "Definitely."

Ingo's hands glided over the controls like a musician's, the crooked bones looking almost elegant as he worked. Far beneath us, a deep bass roar began, the sound of the ship waking from its sleep. My stomach turned over in time to the engine. As soon as she heard that, Queen M would know exactly what we were doing and then every last soldier on the ship would be heading straight for us.

"Set a course and lock it," I said to Ingo then, to Haru, "Show me how to work the PA."

Haru's hands shook as he worked the dials, as if they'd be more comfortable holding a pencil and drawing things which weren't real. But after a second he nodded and mouthed ready at me.

"I need it to be everywhere and I need it to be loud," I whispered back, my hand over the mic. He nodded again and I took my hand away and began to speak. "Wake up," I said. "Wake up!" I waited a second, and then, "Okay, I hope you have, because there are two very important things I need to tell you. Firstly, the entire tracking system's been disabled. So if any of you have been thinking of taking a short – or indeed permanent – vacation, now would be the time to do it."

I could see Ingo looking across at me from the controls. His expression was mild but his actions were more violent, smashing his fist into the console, snapping leavers and twisting knobs until they detached entirely.

"The other thing you need to know," I continued, "is that we're currently on course for Cuba. The controls are locked, and we're going to make landfall in the not too distant future. Have a nice day." As soon as I'd switched off the mic I smashed it. No need to leave Queen M the means to tell everyone that I'm lying.

Besides, I wasn't. In two hours the Infected would be swarming all over us.

The instant Ingo was finished we bolted for the door and swung it open. If there were soldiers outside, we were finished. I was betting that pretty much no one was going to be obeying orders right now.

I was almost right. Soldiers had been waiting outside, two dozen of them. For a second, I was staring down the barrels of twenty different guns. Military and precise, like a firing squad. Except that these guys were looking us in the eye. They looked just about as frightened as we were. One of them said, "Is it true?"

I swallowed past a bone-dry throat and said, "Take a look for yourselves," but they didn't bother because something in my expression told them that yeah, it was the truth, and the twenty seconds they wasted checking it out could be the difference between making it out alive or getting up close and personal with one of the Infected.

They ran, all military cohesion gone. Now they were just individuals, scared for their lives.

The ship was full of them. They weren't trying to stop us any more, now they were just in our way, clogging up the stairwells and corridors, feet heavy on the threadbare carpet. I smelt their rank, night-time breath as they pressed past me. Their faces looked pinched, almost yellow in the pale lighting, rodent-like. The ship wasn't sinking, exactly, but the rats weren't taking any chances.

They knew that there weren't enough tender boats for all the people on board. That was the biggest gamble of all, that we'd make it down there quick enough to get one. It had to be this way, everyone else knowing that same stark fact.

I saw Haru grabbed by a woman who was half his size but twice as desperate. She flung him aside and sprinted past him, then vaulted over the stair rail to drop two decks below. I heard the scream as her ankle buckled and broke but she didn't stop running. I thought I could see a jagged shard of bone poking through blue-black skin.

I hesitated for a moment, but I didn't stop. I knew Haru wouldn't have stopped for me. We weren't friends, just useful to each other. And if I got to the boat first maybe I could hold the others off long enough for Haru to reach it. Or maybe I'd head straight out.

I didn't get the chance to find out. Two more decks down and Haru had caught back up with me. He grabbed my hand as soon as he was in reach and I didn't snatch it away. There was a sort of comfort in it, this contact with a virtual stranger – even one I'd been quite willing to leave to die just a few seconds before.

Shots were ringing out above us and the second body that came falling down the staircase wasn't alive any more. I touched my own gun, pushed roughly into the waistband of my trousers, but I didn't pull it. In the crush of people as we plunged deeper and deeper into the ship it would have been useful as a cudgel and nothing else.

The noise level ratcheted up and for a moment I thought it was just the same old din of voices, and frantic breathing, and the occasional scream, but then I realised that it was also footsteps, hundreds of them, ringing out on metal stairs. We were almost there.

There was one final thing we had to do before we could get out. I'd told myself that it had to be left to the last minute, because afterwards, we weren't going to be in a state to do much running around. The truth was I'd left it 'til the end because it scared the shit out of me, and I wanted to put it off as long as possible.

Ingo had found the place for us, near the engine rooms and the tender boats, where the electric wires that channelled the current that fed the ship were thickest and most accessible. He'd said a lot of other things, but I hadn't really listened. Only the words ten thousand volts had really registered, along with the words I'd mentally added: commonly fatal. But Ingo had said that that was the current we needed to guarantee burning out the chips.

"It's here," Ingo shouted, voice barely audible above the screams of the crowd.

We began to shoulder our way towards a narrow corridor that snaked off to the left. I got an elbow in the ribs, another in the eye. Behind me I heard Haru shout as someone snagged his t-shirt and pulled him roughly out of the way. He stumbled and I grabbed his arm a second before he could fall. He gasped out a thank you, lost in the din. A fall would be fatal. This crowd wasn't stopping for anyone. Their feet echoed against the metal floor, filling the lower decks of the ship with a sound like an army on the march.

I could see the entrance we were aiming for, five feet away now but still impossibly out of reach. There were six people, ten, between us and the entrance and not one of them was going to move out of our way. Just for a second, I thought about the gun jammed into the waistband of my trousers. But no, not that.

In the end, I was a pace past the door by the time I'd managed to make it to the left-hand wall. Only Haru saved me, grabbing my arm this time and pulling me back and sideways, abruptly out of the crowd and into a dark, silent room.

"Well," I said brightly, "who wants to go first?"

"It would be better for me to go last," Ingo said, with his usual blank seriousness. "Since I will be the one administering the shock."

"Hey," Haru said, waving a hand at me in a gesture that would have looked more suave if he hadn't been visibly shaking. "Ladies first."

I wanted to say that maybe I should be last, since I was the doctor who would treat whatever injuries this insane process was going to leave us with. But the truth was we'd either live through it or we wouldn't, and no amount of medical training was going to change that.

"Fine," I said. "Do it." I rolled up my trouser leg and tried not to shake too visibly. It almost made me laugh, the way the wire was spitting sparks, like something out of a Frankenstein movie. But I thought if I opened my mouth the thing most likely to come out would be a sob of fear, so I pressed my lips together and turned my eyes away.

Strange, isn't it, how anticipated pain is so much worse than pain you aren't expecting? It felt as if every cell in my body was on fire, the fire sparking into my brain, nerve endings forgetting that they were designed to do anything other than tell me how much they hurt. My muscles contracted, agonisingly, then slackened uncontrollably. I was glad I'd known to empty myself in preparation. If there'd been anything in my bladder or my bowels, it wouldn't have stayed in.

A second later as I lay on the floor twitching, I heard a harsh, high scream and then Haru was beside me, spine arched, only the back of his head and his heels touching the floor.

It occurred to me that maybe I should have told him not to eat or drink because there was the sudden stench of urine and shit combined, and I could see the dark puddle of liquid spreading out beneath him a second before his convulsion ended and his buttocks felt right back down into it.

But, gasping and gagging, he was still alive and so was I. His hand scrabbled along the deck beside him and I wondered what he was searching for, until his fingers clasped his watch. Of course. He must have put it aside before the current went through him, because flesh can be healed but the delicate mechanism of the watch was irreplaceable. Machines were more valuable than people now.

Finally there was Ingo, his round, placid face showing no fear. He hesitated a moment, then jammed the wires into his own bare skin. The shock of it pushed him backwards like a giant hand, thumping into the far wall with a deep *clang.*

Feeling even weaker than when I'd been going cold turkey and wishing I could die, I dragged myself to my knees. My head hung low as I fought a sudden, intense nausea. I took a moment more to gather myself, to convince myself that motion really was still possible, and then I pushed myself to my feet.

Soon, you'll be stronger than ever, the Voice told me, louder than a whisper now, as if it had somehow drawn energy from the current as it coursed through me. I laughed at the idea that I'd ever be strong again. Then I saw Haru looking at me, puzzled, and I remembered that the Voice was something only I could hear.

But I just laughed louder. His hair looked exactly like a cartoon character who'd stuck his finger into an electric socket, a wilder caricature of his normal gelled spikes.

"I'm glad that you're enjoying yourself," he said, rasping.

I shrugged and offered a hand to pull him to his feet, though I had to lean my full weight backwards to give him any kind of leverage. I bent down to do the same for Ingo and realised for the first time that he hadn't moved since the shock. I couldn't see his chest moving.

"Shit!" I said. I knelt hurriedly beside him and fumbled for his pulse, with fingers still only half under my control. After a moment I felt it beating, inconsistently, faintly. The corridor was dark, but I thought I could see his eyeballs rolling beneath the closed lids. It was impossible to say what this meant: that he was about to wake up? That he'd never wake up? With that kind of shock, damage could easily be permanent.

"He's unconscious," I told Haru.

He shrugged, hair still a wild shock, but not looking so funny now. "He's done his part – we don't need him any more."

I reached down and shook Ingo's shoulders gently.

"Come on," Haru said. "We're running out of time. Two out of three making it is better than we could have hoped for."

He was right, but looking down at Ingo's soft, boyish face – at the crooked fingers of his hand, resting outstretched against the metal floor – I didn't feel ready to make that kind of decision just yet.

"One more minute," I said to Haru.

I thought he wouldn't wait for me, but after a second and a sour twist of his mouth he turned back, eyes fixed impatiently on Ingo's.

Another second and Ingo's eyes flicked open. I could almost see the knowledge seeping back into them, and with it an expression of pain so profound that I found myself leaning away from it. A moment more and it was gone, and Ingo's eyes were as dark and untroubled as ever.

I offered him my hand, surprised at how big and warm his palm felt in mine. His youth had somehow tricked me into thinking he was smaller than he was, more helpless. Jesus, I realised, I'm feeling maternal towards him – just the kind of sentimental shit I didn't need right now.

Ingo nodded at me, the most thanks I'd get, and then we were running into the corridor that led to the boats and back into the crowd. Except that the crowd was gone, the flood of people had thinned to a trickle. When we emerged into the larger space of the launch deck, our footsteps echoed hollowly in the emptiness.

Panicking now, I sprinted to the first launch bay. The boat was gone. Then the second and that boat had gone too. Same story with the third. I hoped, prayed, that one boat had been left. This had been the only part of our plan that relied on luck as much as planning and now I was cursing my decision to leave this final, crucial stage to chance. If it didn't work, it would all have been for nothing. Less than nothing. I thought about the autopsy table, the blood, Queen M's cold, calculating eyes. The beginnings of despair set in.

Don't give up, the Voice told me, *your plan hasn't failed yet.*

It was right. There in the fifth bay was a small motorboat. As we approached, five others pushed past us, walking away. "It isn't working," one of them said. "No key."

I nodded and shrugged and carried on walking with Ingo and Haru beside me. When we got into the boat, Haru pulled the key out of his pocket and put it into the ignition. We were pulling away from the side of the ship before anyone on board had realised what was happening.

As soon as they did I heard a roar of fury and then every person left on that deck was heading our way. There was five foot of water between us and the ship when a huge white man with brown hair and a vivid red scar running the length of his face reached the side of the ship and launched himself straight off. His dive brought his fingers into contact with the side of our boat.

Haru swung the boat hard to starboard but it didn't dislodge the man. I saw the fingers tense and whiten and then he was pulling himself up by sheer force of will. A few more seconds and he'd be on board. I had a sudden clear memory of my own panicked attempt to drag myself on board the schooner when the Infected attacked. Not letting myself think about it I pulled my gun and aimed. But I couldn't shoot him, not when I'd been the one who told him to escape in the first place. Not when all he wanted was exactly the same thing I did – to get away.

I'd set out to free everyone, and now all I seemed to care about was freeing myself. The Voice told me to do it, that he didn't matter, but it was still quiet enough that I could ignore it. I'd left five, maybe ten, corpses behind me already and I suddenly found that I couldn't add another. I grasped the barrel of the gun instead and used it to slam the butt hard against his fingers. Index finger first, then the ring finger – two slams to dislodge that – and finally the last two. He let out a roar of rage and pain, and disappeared into the waves.

I fell back into the boat, feeling the ache in my joints to sweep through me as the rush of adrenaline swept out. I felt as if every bone in my body had been broken and reset, sparks of electric pain still firing off randomly in the neurons of my brain.

Around us, the sea was choppy and restless, waves in ragged white-tipped ranks. The sky was just pinking with the first light of dawn at the distant horizon. The other ships were dark blots in the water around us, some already lost to distance. Ahead of us, a larger, darker blot.

Cuba.

I'd always assumed that Queen M would be able to get her ship back under control before it ran aground on the Cuban coast. Now I wondered. The island couldn't have been more than a mile ahead of us, maybe less. The humps and mounds of its mountains looked enticing in the growing morning sunshine, glints of gold catching off patches of sand on its beaches. Like pretty much everything seen from a distance, it seemed harmless. But it wasn't.

The rest of Queen M's fleet was heading out to open water, fleeing the island with all the speed the wind offered. Most of them were sailing boats and they could go where the wind went. None of us knew how to sail and we'd been forced to steal ourselves a motorboat. There was enough fuel in it to take us to Cuba – or to leave us stranded in open waters. No other land was in reach.

Another problem we'd anticipated, but hadn't been able to avoid.

I was so focussed on looking at the shoreline that it took me a moment to register that there were four figures standing behind me where there should have been two. The first thing I saw as I turned was Haru, his face frozen with fear. To the other side of him was Ingo, looking startled and a little annoyed, that anything could have interfered with his neat little plan.

Between them were Kelis and Soren. They were each holding a large gun, and both of them were aimed at me. Soren smiled, an expression that was more like a snarl. Behind him, the tarp they'd been hiding under was flung carelessly aside, so obvious now it was too late.

"So," Kelis said. "I guess you weren't expecting us."

CHAPTER FOUR

KELIS LOOKED HURT, as if everything we'd just done had been a personal slight. "Yeah," I said. "This is certainly a surprise." I tried edging a little closer to her, a millimetre shuffle forward of each foot, but a quick twitch of her gun stopped me in my tracks.

"We told you not to do this," Soren said in a dull, heavy voice. For the first time, in the bright morning sunlight, I noticed the strands of grey in his ash blond hair and the fine wrinkles raying out from his mouth. There was something a little off-centre in his pale eyes. We'd broken something he never thought could break and now he wasn't sure about anything.

I shrugged. "You told me I wouldn't be able to. Not the same thing."

Kelis stepped forward until the barrel of her gun was pressed into the thin material of my t-shirt.

I carefully didn't look at it, only into her eyes. "As a matter of academic interest, how exactly did you find us?"

"A boat with no keys and a full fuel tank. You're not that subtle."

"No, I guess not. But you're free too now, you know. That's a good thing, isn't it?"

Soren frowned. "Maybe we didn't want to be free."

"The sea around here is full of people who did," I said. "So are the islands. I wanted to be free, and I'll die before I let you make me a slave again." With a confidence I didn't feel, I pushed my fingers against the barrel of the gun pressing into my chest. There was a moment of resistance, then Kelis let me brush it aside. Soren shot her a look and didn't let his own barrel drop. I ignored him and turned back to the wheel of the boat.

"And how many people did you kill to get free?" Kelis asked. "How many of my friends?"

That hurt more than I thought it would. I was sure she could see the sudden tension in my shoulders, but I kept my voice light. "I don't know, I didn't keep count. Did you?"

I felt Haru's sharp intake of breath, but I thought I knew Kelis now. She didn't need things sugar-coated. She didn't like them that way.

"You could come with us, of course," I said, when there'd been a moment without either a reply or a gunshot. "We've got the brains covered, but now we're out we could do with some muscle."

"That's one of the least flattering offers I've ever received." I risked a look at Kelis and saw that she was almost smiling. "What makes you think that we won't just take this boat ourselves and push the rest of you overboard?"

"I don't know. Maybe the fact that you haven't already?"

"No, they cannot come," Ingo said suddenly. He seemed completely unconcerned that two very large guns were now being pointed right at him by two pretty pissed-off people. He just frowned, as if mildly annoyed that they couldn't see it for themselves. "Their tracking devices are still functional. Once the computers are back on line, Queen M will be able to find them."

"Yeah?" I said, before Kelis could actually shoot him. "And how is Queen M going to get the network back up, now her entire crew has fled?"

"Fled from the ship," Ingo said. "The islands are still hers. And there is nothing to say that the loyal will not return to her once the danger of Cuba is passed. It is that, not freedom, which drove many away."

In the time we'd been talking, the prow of the boat set on a straight course, the island had grown larger, the details of the coastline clearer. I could see individual palm trees now – and there were people, streaming towards the golden beach. To starboard, and slowly drawing ahead of us, was another vast bulk between us and the sun: the flagship, still on a collision course.

"If the danger of Cuba does pass," I said.

"But taking them remains an unnecessary risk," Ingo said stubbornly, and I wanted to punch him.

To my surprise, Soren just laughed. "Yeah, well, it's a risk you're going to have to take."

Ingo opened his mouth to protest some more and this time I did stop him, grabbing his arm hard. "They're with us. Accept when you've lost and move on. Besides, they'll be useful. I hear it's a dangerous world out there."

Kelis holstered her gun. A warm salt breeze blew up and the boats all around us bobbed on the waves, and it almost felt like we were pleasure cruising, somewhere where nothing could harm us. But plenty of things could and some of them were heading right towards us.

"Those aren't our boats," Kelis said, eyes straining against the brilliance of the Caribbean sun.

Haru squinted short-sightedly. "How can you tell?"

Kelis gave him a look of contempt. "How about because they're coming from Cuba?"

They were. The sea ahead of us was suddenly dark with vessels, small and fast, darting across the waters towards the refugee fleet. The other boats were beginning to realise the danger. The fleet began to split, no longer a unified shoal, now just a series of individuals, happy to leave everyone else behind if it saved them from the predators. Soren put his beefy hands on the wheel, ready to swing us around and join the panicked flight.

The swarm of Infected was gaining fast, five hundred meters and closing. The wind was in their sails; if we turned we had little chance of outrunning them.

I held Soren's hand firm against the wheel. "No. Keep course – straight for the shore."

He looked at me like I was going crazy and he wasn't the only one. Maybe I was, but I didn't need the Voice to tell me that this was the right thing to do. "They're all in the water," I said. "If we can get past them, they'll have to turn into the wind to follow us – and why would they, when all the other ships are straight ahead?"

"She's right!" Kelis said. "Straight on, full throttle."

Soren obeyed her without question. We powered forward and now we were three hundred meters from the Infected.

"Head for Cuba – are you crazy?" Haru screamed. "So what if their boats are all at sea? Who's to say there aren't twenty more of them on the island? There could be thousands of them, just waiting on the beach for us to arrive."

"No, this is a good plan," Ingo said firmly.

Haru sagged, realising that he was outnumbered.

"We don't need to land, we can skirt the island," I said. "All we need to do is get past the Infected."

They were barely a hundred meters away now – too close to change our minds. We were the nearest of all Queen M's fleet to them, the most obvious target. I could see the crew of their leading ship, leaning forward in the prow as if they couldn't wait to get at us.

Behind the yacht were five jet skis, with two Infected clinging on to each. Fuck. The yacht would never turn in time, but the jet skis... I turned to Soren, thinking maybe it wasn't too late to turn back.

He read my expression and shook his head. No time.

"Then give me a fucking gun. A big one. Take one yourself and give Haru the tiller."

"Hey!" Haru said, at the implication that he'd be useless in an actual fight. Then he glanced up and saw the Infected. Closer now, close enough that we could see their faces – the festering cuts and sores. He took the wheel without protest.

Soren hauled aside the tarpaulin that he and Kelis had hidden themselves under, revealing a cache of arms and ammo. He tossed me a semi-automatic rifle that made my small pistol look like a toy and handed out the rest, taking two for himself. Kelis gave a very small smile as he did.

To starboard, the great hulk of Queen M's flagship was finally beginning to turn, as unwieldy as a cow on a race track. I gave it even odds whether it would run aground or skim the shore and make it back out to sea. Whatever happened, it couldn't outpace the Infected. Their ships were swarming around it, little insect-figures of people already beginning to scale the hull.

Not my problem if the people I'd once thought to rescue had instead been brought here to their deaths.

Ahead, the Infected yacht was heading straight for us, prow sharp as a knife, ready to cut through our little tub. It was a game of chicken which we could only lose, playing against a ship full of people with no fear of pain or death.

"Hang on!" Haru shouted, his voice high with terror. Almost before he'd finished speaking he pulled the tiller hard around, flinging us desperately out of the path of the approaching ship.

I grabbed a thick metal ring set in the floor as my body was flung against the starboard railing. I heard a crack that might have been the boat or might have been a rib but I held on grimly, splashed by an arc of seawater as we tipped at nearly ninety degrees.

A second later there was another crack that was neither the boat nor a rib. A neat little chip appeared in the deck five inches from my face, and I realised we were being fired on.

Somehow I'd managed to keep my grip on the rifle. But I'd need two hands to fire it, and one of them was still desperately clinging on to the metal ring that was keeping me out of the water. The boat tipped a little further, so far that I could feel a salt sting in my eyes. A lurch, and suddenly we were tipping the other way, faster. I felt a fierce blow against my back as we hit the water and my jaw slammed shut on my tongue. There was a trickle of coppery blood down my throat. And all around me now, the insect whine of bullets.

My back clenched, protested, but I fought against the agony and dragged myself to my knees. One quick glance to the side and I saw that Haru had done it. The Infected yacht was beside us for one moment and then past, drawn helplessly onwards by the wind. I swivelled to fire off a brief burst. I thought that maybe one figure in the stern dropped the rifle it was holding. But then we were past and the hail of bullets eased, and for just a second our path looked clear to Cuba's golden shore.

Then the jet skis were all around us. The odds were still against us.

The worst thing was the way the riders were smiling, a polite little social smile, as if none of this mattered very much. Their hands on their guns were relaxed, fingers engorged with blood, not white with tension like mine were around the trigger of the rifle. Nothing about them said they cared – about anything.

The stream of bullets from my rifle took one of them right through that social smile. Teeth shattered, fragments of enamel sticking to her ruined cheeks.

Haru was screaming, a constant noise that might have contained words. Kelis let out a whoop at her own shot, straight through the heart of the grey-haired man on the leading jet ski. She was enjoying herself, high on the adrenaline. I understood it, but I couldn't feel the same. The air was full of death, meaningless and sudden. I didn't want to die. I wasn't ready.

The people I'd killed weren't ready either. But that didn't stop me from firing again, missing my first target but winging the second. Another jet ski veered and faltered, and now there were just three. Suddenly the odds were favouring us.

The Infected seemed to realise that a frontal assault wasn't working. Now they were hanging back, using the fronts of their skis as shields, heads bobbing around each time they let off a shot.

I fired back, a short, controlled burst. The bullets hit the water, sending up little geysers of crystal. I jerked the rifle up, over-correcting, and the bullets flew wildly high, arcing over the heads of the Infected. My finger was pressed hard against metal but nothing was happening, and I realised that I'd run out of ammo. Reflexively, my hand reached down to my belt for a spare clip, but of course I hadn't thought to bring any.

The ammo I needed was five meters away, still hidden under the tarpaulin. It might as well have been five hundred meters. The Infected was coming straight for me, closing fast. The gun in his hand had plenty of ammo and all of it was headed in my direction.

I felt a sudden, fierce pain in my right calf as a bullet tore straight through my leg. Blood trickled hot into my sandals, mixing with the sweat between my toes. The Infected was nearer still and now his smile looked predatory; there was no longer any way he could miss.

My hand was still grappling uselessly at my belt. Except that now it had found metal and, of course, it wasn't useless. My conscious mind, numb with fear, had forgotten. But my subconscious knew that there was another gun in my belt.

I smiled too. I didn't remember bringing the gun up, but now there was no one guiding the jet ski. The Infected teetered for a moment on one leg, like a cut-rate circus performer. His eyes told me he was already dead, but his body didn't want to recognise it and, for just a second, it looked like he might leap off the ski and drag me down with him.

He fell, and I saw his body sink through the clear waters. He didn't go far. We were over coral reefs now and there he was, like a cancerous growth on the rock, something for the multi-coloured fish to eat. I laughed, crazily, because every second from now on was a second when I hadn't thought I'd be alive.

Except, fuck, why was the water so clear, the sand so golden beneath it? And suddenly everything Haru was screaming became clear, like a radio that had finally tuned in: "– we're going to hit land!" And the Infected's plan became clear too, the way the jet skis had surrounded us, herding us like cattle. They hadn't needed to kill us, just to get us somewhere someone else could do it for them.

The bottom of the boat scraped against coral. The vibrations shot through the soles of my feet, a gentle, almost tickling sensation. Then rougher, more violent. I saw Haru try to wrench the tiller around. The boat bucked and swerved but kept on moving forward, momentum carrying it now because the engine was out of the water. And, finally, like a crippled animal, it dragged itself onto land to die.

The Infected were everywhere. Haru had been right after all – the beach was crawling with them. They'd been climbing into boats, joining the swarm attacking the flagship. But unlike us it had somehow managed to stay at sea, picking up speed as it headed back out into open waters.

I almost felt it physically, the moment when two hundred pairs of eyes turned from the flagship to us. The beach was blank, a few desiccated palm trees above the tide line. This was a tourist beach, a cheap one. Behind the sand I could see the plain concrete blocks of hotels, little parasols with cracked tables and chairs that weren't even comfortable when they were new. The harsh midday sun shone down on it all, unmoved.

Soren and Kelis flanked me and raised their guns. Ingo too, looking just a little startled, as if he'd discovered one too many zeroes in a complex calculation. Haru cowered in the cockpit, like a child who thought that if he couldn't see them, they couldn't see him. There was no way that we could survive this, there were just too many of them.

"Fuck!" Soren shouted. "What the fuck do we do now?"

Kelis dropped one hand from her gun and I thought that she was going to reach across to offer him some sort of comfort – but it was my arm she grabbed instead.

The moment seemed frozen in time: the sand, the sun, her arm, the barest whisper of a breeze. The oily smell of our burst fuel tank. The Infected, their guns. A story with only one ending.

"Jasmine," Kelis started. Her eyes were wide and wild. I didn't know what she wanted to say to me, but it seemed somehow right that the last words I ever heard would be hers.

"Stop," a voice said, resonant, male and unexpected – and all around us, the Infected did just that. They cocked their heads to the side, each of them the exact same angle, and they waited.

Haru lifted his head a little above the dip of the cockpit, searching for the source of the voice. After a second he found it – a loudspeaker high on a pole at the far end of the beach.

I lifted my gun. Beside me, Kelis and Soren did the same. The muzzles wavered as we each picked out one target among the many. We didn't fire, though, because a bullet might have woken them from this sudden strange stillness.

"The invasion is over," the voice crackled again from the loudspeaker. "Leave the coast and go back to your homes. Enjoy yourselves."

There was an abrupt hubbub and I jumped, nerves still on a knife edge. But it was just chatter, two hundred people suddenly behaving like people again and not like zombies. All around us the Infected were sauntering and running and breaking up into social little knots and groups as they left the beach. The only odd thing about them now was the way they completely ignored us.

I stood and watched in startled silence and then, almost helplessly, I started to walk after them. I'm not entirely sure why. Maybe to convince myself that they were really going and this wasn't just some cruel joke. After a moment's hesitation, the others started walking too.

When the Infected reached the road that ran in front of the beachfront hotels, they separated, veering off to left and right. Heading home, I guessed – just like they'd been told to do. We walked a little further, between two of the hotels and into the beginnings of the city behind.

The first thing that caught my eye was a poster, fresh and bright where the plaster on the building was peeling and faded. For one second I thought it must be Castro, a holdover from the times before the Cull.

It wasn't Castro, but it was a face I recognised. Just like I'd unconsciously recognised the voice that the Infected had obeyed so unquestioningly.

The voice belonged with the face – both of which belonged to a person I'd never expected to see again. Or maybe I had, and hadn't wanted to admit it to myself. But now the memories wouldn't be held back.

I looked down at the body of Andy, an eighteen year-old soldier whose neck had snapped in my hands like a piece of balsa wood. For just a second I felt a twinge of guilt. Hadn't he once helped me to carry some equipment into the lab? I'd thought then that he might have a little crush on me. But no, there was no need to think like that. The person he'd flirted with was gone, and the person I was now had more important things to worry about. That was what the Voice told me.

A last vestigial flicker of something – my humanity maybe – made me reach over and press the lids down over Andy's blank blue eyes. Then I took the gun out of his slack fingers, chambered another round, and headed for the door.

Get out of the base, *the Voice told me.* It isn't safe for you here anymore.

In the distance I could hear gunshots and the cries of people in pain. The base was tearing itself apart, a microcosm of the world. People turning savagely on each other, as if the Cull had infected everyone in some way, loosing something primal and cold within them which had been waiting all these years to get out.

You're different, *the Voice told me.* You're Cured.

The door opened before I could reach it, easing cautiously back as if the person on the other side wasn't quite sure what he'd find inside.

And he, *the Voice told me,* is Cured too.

I didn't need the Voice to tell me that, I could see it in his eyes. They'd always been distinctive, so brown they were almost black and sparkling with an inner life that was the most attractive thing about him. Now they were burning, and nothing about the smile he showed me was human.

"Hi, Jasmine," he said and I heard the Voice echoing through his words. I saw it in his face, the same ruthless certainty that was in mine. There was a knife in his hands, sharp and clinical. Its blade was smeared with blood, more blood smeared across his hand, up the length of his arm. He reached out to brush a lock of brown hair out of his eyes and left a streak of red there too, like a tribal mark across his cheek.

"Hi, Ash," I said as I studied his face.

The same face I saw now. The face staring back at me from a poster on the streets of Havana.

CHAPTER FIVE

WE'D BEEN IN the town-centre apartment for three days now. There'd been one excursion to scavenge food. Pointless. The stores in the crumbling heart of the city had been picked clean long ago. I guessed the Infected must have been getting food from somewhere, but wherever it was we hadn't been able to find it. We found a chemist's, though, virtually untouched, and among the bottles of prescription medicines, a week's supply of anti-psychotic pills. I took one gladly, then forced myself to put the rest back in my pack. It wasn't enough to kill the Voice entirely, but it would have to do. God knew when I'd be able to find any more. There were clothes shops too, windows smashed and wares dragged out over the pavement, but enough left for us to find a few changes of clothing.

Ingo was looking very dashing now in a pair of black trousers and a garish purple shirt. He seemed fond of it. I'd see him stroking the material sometimes, a far off look on his face. Haru had managed to put together a leather outfit that made him look like an extra in Mad Max. It must have been hot as hell in the stifling Cuban heat, but he sweated it out, a triumph of style over good sense.

I didn't ask where Kelis and Soren found their khaki combats. Stripped off one of the decayed corpses that littered the street, I suspected.

Clothes and drugs that first day, then back to the apartment with its peeling plaster and non-functioning taps, and there we stayed.

The Infected were everywhere. Queen M must have been right that whatever ailed them was contagious, because the population of Cuba alone couldn't have accounted for the numbers of them. They must have been recruiting.

They walked around in little family groups, in pairs, on their own, as if nothing about the world had changed in the last five years. To see them here, on their home ground, you couldn't imagine what they'd been, the berserker rage when they'd attacked us. But then...

...then you saw them up close: the suppurating sores on their faces; the fingers hanging from hands by ragged threads of skin. The missing eyes, ears, noses; white bones poking through gangrenous flesh. That first day, as we carried our findings back towards the centre of the city, I saw a toddler trip and fall over a jagged chunk of masonry. Her mother didn't seem to care; she didn't even notice. And the child just got up and carried on. No tears, no screams no nothing. Her little brown ringlets bounced as she followed her mother down the street.

But I saw her leg, the place where a broken-off nail in the concrete had caught her as she fell: the four-inch cut, the muscle exposed beneath greasy yellow fat. Blood streamed down her leg, pooling in her little trainers as she ran, but it wasn't enough to wash away the brown clots of dirt and rust which the nail had gouged into her flesh. It would be gangrenous within a day, beyond saving in three.

"Shit," Kelis said, watching them trot away along the narrow alley ahead of us. "What the fuck is wrong with these people?" It was just a whisper, but she might as well have been shouting. The Infected acted like we were invisible. I guess they hadn't been told to see us.

There were loudspeakers everywhere on the island. Loudspeakers and cameras – Ash's eyes and ears. And his face on posters everywhere, watching us. Four times a day or more, his voice would ring out, issuing instructions. Sometimes they were just for one person, some name we didn't know being ordered to go somewhere we'd never heard of. Sometimes he'd order boats out to sea, maybe to recruit more Infected. His presence was everywhere, in total control of the island.

That was why, after that first day, we stayed in the apartment. Between us we had enough food to last a week, and we'd managed to get a few bottles of clean water from a river on our way up. We were safe inside for the moment, out of sight of the cameras. But we knew that one day Ash's voice might be issuing instructions about us, and suddenly we wouldn't be invisible and there'd be nowhere to run to.

The others wanted to leave the island. "Our boat's toast," I told them on the second day in the apartment. "There's no way we can salvage it. We'd need to steal another: one of the Infected's. How much do you want to bet that as soon as we get close to one of them they'll start paying us some attention?"

"I'd bet a few dollars," Haru muttered sourly. He'd been twitchy and ill at ease ever since we'd arrived.

"Do you want to bet your life?" Kelis asked dryly and he scowled at her and shook his head.

"Can I just say that if Haru wants to risk his life, I have absolutely no objection," Soren said. "Why don't you go steal a boat on your own, and if it works we'll all join you?" For some reason, the big Swede had taken an intense dislike to the artist.

"We need to figure out what's going on here," I said. "Work out who's controlling them and how we can stop them."

A lie, of course. I knew damn well who was controlling them. What I wanted to find out was why. That was why I'd chosen this apartment, right here in the centre of Havana on one of the city's small hills. It had a clear line of sight to the biggest building in the district: Castro's old headquarters. I was sure that was where Ash would be holed up. He'd replaced the old dictator's cult of personality with his own, torn down Castro's posters and put his own face all over the island. Why wouldn't he take the old man's home too?

So I made sure that we stayed in the apartment, out of sight of the cameras, and watched. I had to find out what Ash up to, how he was spreading a Cure that was no longer needed and why it had turned the Infected into whatever they were. Most of all, I needed to know what his long-term plan was. Because he'd have one. I'd silenced the Voice in my head, but Ash had embraced it, and the Voice always had a plan. I'd just never listened to it long enough to figure out what it was.

So we waited, and we ate as little as possible, and we sweltered in the humid air. But day after day, no vehicle came or went from Castro's palace. I didn't see a single person walk through its gates. Nothing happened, nothing changed. The Infected carried on walking the streets, slowly rotting away, and I learnt absolutely nothing.

And after six days, we were short of water and even shorter of patience.

"This cannot carry on," Ingo said on the sixth night. Our stock of candles was running low. One was flickering on the table now, casting everyone's faces in a dim, devilish light. Ingo's eyes were entirely shadowed, his face unreadable.

"The boy's right," Soren said. "If we wait here any longer we'll have to start eating each other." His eyes strayed to Haru.

"We can't stay, we can't leave – what can we do?" Haru said.

"We need to understand," I insisted. "We can't risk going out there 'til we know what we're up against. I need to study one of the Infected, up close."

Kelis frowned. "But you've already done that. And you told me you found nothing."

I felt a quick twinge of guilt, swiftly suppressed. What was the point of telling the truth about the Cure? It wouldn't get them off Cuba any quicker. "I'm talking about a live specimen," I told her.

Haru laughed. He stopped quickly enough when he saw I wasn't joking. "Are you crazy? I thought the whole reason we'd been hiding out here was not do draw any unwanted attention."

I stared him down. "They wander off on their own plenty of the time. And the cameras aren't everywhere. There aren't any in the street behind this apartment – that was why we chose it. All we have to do is wait until one of them goes down there alone."

"And then?" Soren said. He was sitting in the furthest corner of the small room, a congealed lump of darkness. But I could hear the *click-clack-click* as he compulsively disassembled and reassembled his rifle, a nervous habit that had become almost constant in the last few days. "What do we do then?"

I shrugged. "Capture them."

I wasn't winning the crowd over, I could tell. Even Kelis looked sceptical. "How do you catch something alive when it doesn't feel any pain? That's the thing about them, isn't it – no fear and no pain?"

I nodded. "There's something wrong with their nervous system – I could figure out that much from the corpse. But they've still got one, and anything with a nervous system can be anaesthetised." I held out the ampoules of Suxamethonium I'd liberated from the chemist along with the anti-psychotics. "This paralyses all voluntary muscles. Put enough of that into anyone, even one of the Infected, and they'll drop like a stone."

"Yeah?" Soren said. "And did you get a tranq gun along with the drug?"

"No," I told him, smiling slightly. "I thought this way it would be more of a challenge for you.

"Remember," I added more seriously, "the infection's blood-borne only – touch can't transmit it."

He stared at me blankly for a long second, leaning forward into the candlelit so that it caught highlights in his blond hair. Then he leaned back and laughed. "Why the hell not? It's not like I've got anything better to do. But I've never given an injection – you'll need to get up close and personal yourself if you want to put that stuff into them." I noticed he didn't mention that the person giving the jab would also be the one most likely to get sprayed with any blood.

"Yes," I said. "Won't that be fun?"

* * *

Nothing on earth would persuade Haru to join in our little adventure. Besides, I'd seen him in a crisis already – I'd feel safer if he was nowhere near us. Ingo came, though, as impassive as ever. He was almost like one of the Infected himself, all his emotions dialled down near zero.

Ingo took up position in a first floor apartment in the same block as ours. The window gave him a clear sight line up and down the alley and we left him with the nearest thing we had to a sniper rifle. Insurance policy. If something went wrong, he could take out the Infected before it did us any damage.

Yeah, right. Still, I felt better for knowing he was up there.

Kelis was crouching in the shadows at the far end of the alley, where it opened up into one of those big, nondescript squares that might once have been pretty before Communism had turned it into something proletarian and bland. Once the Infected was through she had to make sure it couldn't turn back. Her gun was holstered. Instead she had opted for a pool cue, something that could incapacitate without killing. She was holding it like she'd used one before, and not for potting the black.

Soren and I were halfway down the alley, standing in doorways to either side. If more than one Infected came through we'd let them pass and hope that they treated us with their usual indifference.

But if one came down alone, we were ready. Soren had his usual two guns in the waistband of his jeans. In his hands he was holding a fishing net. We'd had to chance a trip out to the harbour to get it, just me and Kelis, clinging to the shadows and shrinking back from the Infected whenever they passed us. A big risk, but probably worth it. It was our best chance of subduing one of them without doing permanent damage.

Then it was just me and the Suxamethonium. I looked at the needle in my hand, a fragile little spike, and thought that as plans went it lacked a certain finesse. I carried on looking at it, and sometimes at Soren, who was as patient as a rock, or at Kelis, fading into the distant shadows, as hour after hour passed with no sign of the Infected.

Could they know what we had planned? Was there any way they could have overheard us? I had the sudden, nasty thought that the apartment might be bugged and Ash could know everything that we said and did. My mind worried at the thought, teasing it apart, finding it more and more convincing as the morning brightened into noon. The sun arcing to blaze down directly over the alley.

When it finally happened, it happened fast. She was an old woman, hair entirely grey, body bent and frail, but she moved like greased lightning. She was past Kelis before we even noticed she was there. From the startled expression on Kelis's face I thought she might have fallen asleep leaning against the wall at the end of the alley, but she snapped out of it and took up her position.

No need. The old woman showed no intention of turning back. God knows what she was running to, or from. She was thirty feet from us now and I could already smell her, the heavy, putrid stink of gangrene. I wondered what part of her she was about to lose.

Fifteen feet and I knew the answer. There was a cavity where her ovaries should have been – just two deep holes, black in the centre and yellow-green around the edges. I gagged, holding the nausea in with a fierce effort of will. That wasn't a random, neglected injury. That had been done to her deliberately.

No time to worry about it now. Five feet and Soren was on her. The net caught in her grey hair, dragging it against her face as he pulled it down over her shoulders, down to her waist. Instantly she was struggling and screaming, a high sound like the distant cries of the seabirds. I could see that she was strong though, stronger than a woman her age should have been. Soren had clamped his fists around her arms, but her leg lashed out and caught him squarely between his. He bent over in pain, bringing his head closer to hers. Instantly, her mouth snapped at him through the netting, missing his cheek by millimetres.

"Now would be good!" he shouted at me, glaring, angry and afraid.

I squirted a needle of liquid from the syringe in my hand. No point putting an air bubble in her veins and killing her before we could talk to her. Soren had both arms clamped around hers now. Her mouth continued snapping, uselessly, at the empty air in front of her. The animal rage radiated from her like a physical force. She kicked him again between the legs, and again. Soren's face, covered with sweat, grimaced in pain. Another kick and I saw his arms loosen a little, his body jerking involuntarily away.

He gritted his teeth and tightened his arms again, spinning round so that the old woman was facing me. Her eyes blazed into mine, bright with madness. One of her shoulders was twisted at an unnatural angle and I realised that she must have dislocated it as she struggled. She writhed and I heard a crack that might have been a bone breaking.

The needle slipped easily into the loose flesh of her bicep. But she twisted at the last minute and I felt a jar as the point bottomed out against bone. She pushed further forward and I realised what she was trying to do, to snap the point before the syringe could deliver its load. It was too dangerously easy to think of the Infected as mindless animals. But it was their feelings that were numbed, not their intellects.

I pulled back, just enough to move the needle away from bone, and depressed the plunger, shooting the anaesthetic straight into muscle.

Now I just had to hope that her circulatory system was still functioning in something like a normal way – that her brain and body would respond to drugs the way a normal person's would. I was so intent on watching her eyes, waiting for them to glaze over into sleep, that I didn't see the movement coming until it was too late. Her head jerked violently towards me and her teeth clamped over my nose with a vicious strength.

Soren made a sound that was halfway between a grunt and a laugh. Yeah, I might have found time to think it was funny too, if I hadn't been in sudden agony. He made an attempt to pull her back and I grabbed desperately at his arms as her teeth tugged at my nose. I knew that she wouldn't let go, no matter how hard he pulled. The only thing that could give was my nose.

Somewhere on the periphery of my attention I was aware that Kelis was running towards us. I saw Soren looking over my head helplessly, hoping his partner would know what to do.

"Pull her jaw apart!" I gritted out through a throat that only really wanted to scream.

"I can't!" he said. "If I let her go..."

Then Kelis was there, and she had her hands round the woman's mouth, circling me from behind. I could see blood slicking down over her wrists and I knew that it was coming from me. The word *Infected* was ringing in my head like a mantra. Infected. Infectious. Her saliva in my blood. My mouth was filling with a coppery taste as the blood from my nose dripped into it and I thought that I was probably swallowing her saliva too. I'd already had the Cure, but did that mean I was immune to this twisted new strain of it?

Kelis's fingers were white with strain on the other woman's face, digging in to her skin so hard each nail had torn the flesh, leaving a perfect semi-circle of red in the wrinkled old skin. Other than that, she was achieving nothing.

I could feel the teeth sinking further into me. I felt the rasp of enamel against cartilage and the pain intensified. Her legs kicked and kicked, forward backwards into Soren and forwards into my shins. The discomfort was lost in the larger pain, a whisper drowned out by a shout.

The syringe was still in my hand, braced between my body and the old woman's. *Use it!* my mind was screaming at me. *Straight in her heart. That will stop the pain.* Or maybe it was the Voice, released by the rush of adrenaline through my body. But using the syringe that way would kill her, and then this would have been for nothing. So we stayed there: her teeth in my nose; Kelis's hands on her face; Soren's arms around her. Stalemate.

The pain was almost unbearable. I realised that my hand was creeping up despite myself, the needle a glitter of silver pointed straight at the old woman's heart. The instinct to survive was stronger than anything, even my own conscious will. I watched, mesmerised, as inch by inch my hand moved towards her. I wanted to stop it but I wanted to live, damn it. I wanted the agony to end. A few seconds now and the needle would be in her chest and this would all be over.

My nose was still a blaze of agony, but the pressure had let up. Her jaws had relaxed. In front of me, her eyelids were flickering, the muscles in her face slackening. Blood rushed back red into Kelis's fingers as they relaxed too. Soren's arms loosened, supporting the old woman rather than restraining her.

A second more and she was entirely off me. Her jaw flapped open, strings of bloody red saliva hanging from her teeth and dribbling down her chin. I staggered back, the syringe dropping from my hand as I clasped it over my nose. "Jesus fucking Christ!"

Kelis rested a hand against my shoulder. My eyes caught hers and I saw that she was uncertain how to help me. I managed a shrug. Nothing she could do. We both looked up as we heard the rumbling sound of Soren laughing. "Well," he said, "you sure have a strange idea of fun."

WE SECURED HER to the heavy wooden table in the kitchen before I let her come out of the anaesthesia. We'd put strong wire bindings at her wrists, elbows, ankles and thighs, wound over strips of cloth to stop her tearing her own flesh if she struggled. Not that we were worried about hurting her. I *wanted* to hurt her, after I'd caught sight of my nose in the apartment's one cracked mirror. Her teeth had scored deep marks on either side, marks that would leave permanent scars. The nose itself was swollen and bulbous. I wanted to hurt her, but I didn't want her to get loose and I was afraid that, given the chance, she'd happily saw off her own limbs to escape. She was struggling even before her eyes had opened, complaining softly when she found that she couldn't move.

"Give her the anti-psychotics now, before she wakes up," Haru said nervously. Even with the woman securely bound he refused to come within five feet of her. I'd noticed that he was leaving five foot of clear space around me too, and he wasn't the only one. Soren hadn't come within spitting distance of me since the old woman bit me.

I'd swabbed the wound on my nose with antiseptic when I got back, injected myself with antibiotics and anti-virals and told the others that that would take care of anything. They didn't look convinced, and why should they? The truth was if there was something to catch I'd got it, and the only defence I could count on was that my bloodstream was overloaded with the same infection already.

"I don't want to give her anything 'til she's conscious," I told Haru now. "Seeing what effect it has on her will tell me something about what's wrong. Besides, there's no saying how long it will have an effect. Supply's limited and I can't afford to waste any on a sleeping subject."

A moot point anyway. Her eyes were wide open now and flicking around, sizing us up.

"*Habla Inglés?*" I asked her when her gaze caught mine. Something in the set of her face told me she'd understood, but she didn't reply.

"We need you to answer some questions," Kelis said, continuing in Spanish. "We won't hurt you if you cooperate." But she looked at me as she said it and I shrugged. We both knew it was an empty threat, and sure enough, the old woman didn't bother to respond. Up close, I had a grandstand view of the gaping wounds in her abdomen where her reproductive organs had once been. What could we possibly threaten her with that was worse than that?

"Okay," I said, Kelis translating into Spanish for me. "I'm going to give you an injection that might clear your head a little. It's just a standard anti-psychotic – there won't be any long-term effects." I didn't know why I was bothering to explain it to her, but it seemed very important to me to keep up the pretence of being a doctor now that I had so much blood on my hands.

I thought the old lady might have shrugged, but her movement was too restricted by her bonds to be sure. It was as much permission as I was likely to get, and I yanked down the edge of her rough black skirt and pushed the needle into the sagging flesh of her buttocks. I nodded at the others that they could leave us in peace. Intra-muscular drugs took some time to diffuse through the system, particularly ones that have to cross the blood-brain barrier. Ingo seemed happy enough to go, and Haru couldn't get out of the door fast enough, but Kelis and Soren both stayed.

"Could be at least an hour before we'll know if it's worked," I told them.

"But you're staying," Kelis said.

I shrugged. "Someone needs to."

"Then we'll keep you company," Soren said, looking at Kelis and not me.

"You really think this will work?" Kelis asked.

I shrugged again. "I think it might. And if it doesn't, that will tell us something as well."

"Yeah, but what? What exactly is it we're waiting here to find out?"

I looked at her, casually picking her teeth with a fingernail, leg slung over one arm of the chair. The posture looked deceptively relaxed, but it also kept the holster of her gun right next to her hand.

"I want to find out what's made these people sick," I said. "I think we need to find out, before it's too late. Because otherwise there might be nowhere in the world that's far enough to run to."

She stopped picking at her teeth and sat a little more upright in her chair. "You think we're looking at another Cull?"

Soren was watching me too, out of the corner of his eye.

"Yeah, I think that's exactly what we might be looking at," I told them, and it was pretty much the truth.

After that, she lapsed back into silence, and I was free to study our captured Infected as the anti-psychotic spread slowly through her system. I looked at her eyes most of all. She was studying the room, looking for escape routes. Everything a normal person would be doing in her situation. That wasn't what interested me, though. I was looking for something else, something I'd seen in my own eyes for the last five years.

There's a little game they make medical students play when they teach you about mental illnesses: Hearing Voices. One student interviews another – but the whole time a third student is talking in the interviewee's ear, just a stream of nonsense. It's supposed to give you an idea of what it's like to experience auditory hallucinations, and I guess it kind of does. But the most interesting thing is the expression on the person's face. Once you've seen it, you never forget it: the momentary distraction, the subtle blankness, the focus pushing to the horizon as the attention turns inward.

I studied the old woman, but I just didn't see it. If the Infected was hearing voices, hearing *the* Voice, there was nothing on her face to show it. Still, because I was studying her so closely, I was able to see the moment when the anti-psychotic began to take effect. It wasn't difficult, because the moment the madness went, the pain came.

I'd been prepared for that. "Does it hurt?" I asked her in my own broken Spanish.

"*Si, senora*," she said, her voice little more than a whimper. "*Me duele mucho.*"

I didn't need Kelis to translate that for me. The painkiller was lying ready and I injected that too. The relief washed over her face like a wave and I felt an intense stab of envy. I knew what that felt like, that wash of contentment, and not a day went by when a part of me didn't want it back.

"Better?" I asked, and this time Kelis translated for me.

The old woman nodded. She pulled feebly against the bonds, seeming puzzled by their presence. They looked cruel, now that she was just an old helpless woman with a wound in her body that would shortly kill her. But the anti-psychotics wouldn't last long and my nose was still throbbing. She stayed roped up.

"Do you remember how you came to be here?" I asked her.

I could see her thinking, her eyes clearing as memory returned. "You captured me," she said, Kelis translating.

"Yes."

"Why?"

"We wanted to find out what was wrong with you," I told her, "and then see if we could cure you."

"But I'm already cured."

I shook my head. "I've given you anti-psychotics but I'm afraid their effect is only temporary."

Her face cleared, looking suddenly relieved. "So... my mind will be better soon? This... feeling will be gone?"

Kelis and I exchanged a look over her head. "You're saying you felt better before we captured you?"

"Of course." Her eyes drifted out of focus for a moment. "I was cured."

"If you were cured, why were you acting the way you were? Why wouldn't you speak to us?" I gestured at my swollen nose. "Why did you do this to me?"

She laughed. "You were trying to stop me from doing what I had to do. I didn't ask you to attack me."

"And now?"

"I don't..." She looked momentarily lost. "I don't know what it is I'm supposed to do. And I... feel."

"But you didn't feel before, did you?" I said. "You felt no pain."

"No pain," she said. "No guilt, no fear, no loneliness. That was the cure we were promised. The cure you can have too, if you want it."

Ingo and Haru had re-entered the room as she spoke. I looked at their faces. There was a flash of something on Ingo's, I wasn't sure what, but I thought that maybe it was temptation. The death of feeling held some appeal for him. Haru just looked appalled.

"Who cured you?" I asked her. "Who is it that can cure us?"

"The Leader. He plans to cure everyone." The anti-psychotics wouldn't have worn off, but the mad light was burning in her eyes again; the bright light of absolute conviction.

"Where can we find the Leader?" I pressed. "If we want the cure for ourselves."

"The palace, of course," she said. "The Leader has always been in his palace. And he finds you – there is no need to seek him out. He speaks to anyone who wants to listen. Please, *senora*, I have told you everything I can. Please release me." She was sweating, trickles of it running off her forehead and into her straggly grey hair. I thought for a moment that the painkillers were wearing off, but it wasn't that.

"Oh God," she said. "I remember. I don't want to remember. Jorge!" And then she was screaming, louder and longer than when we'd captured her outside.

"Jesus," Haru said. "What have you done to her?"

"Allowed her to feel again." I said flatly. "Who's Jorge?" I asked the woman, but I wasn't sure that I wanted to know what it was that had happened, that was pulling the terrible sound out of her. There was no reply anyway, just more piercing screams. Haru scurried out of the room as fast as he'd entered it, but Ingo stayed, staring at her. I wondered if there was anything hidden away inside him, some secret that made him want to scream the same way. There sure as hell was inside me.

I turned to Kelis, meaning to tell her to put the old woman out of her misery. But I closed my mouth as soon as I'd opened it. What, so I could keep my hands clean and keep kidding myself that I was someone who saved lives and didn't take them? No. I pulled out my own gun, turned my face away and put a bullet through the old woman's skull. There was only a very little blood.

We set out for the palace three hours later. The Leader wanted to cure everyone? That wasn't something even Haru thought we could ignore.

The walk through the streets of Havana was nerve-wracking. One of us might have hoped to slip through the shadows and side-streets unnoticed. Five of us? No chance. So we walked, calmly and quietly, as if we had every right to be there and knew exactly where we were going.

The first time we passed a cluster of the Infected I expected it all to fall apart. Surely they'd found out what we'd done to the old woman? But they just passed us by, not even sparing us a glance. Kelis let out a little huff or relief. Haru shuddered and wrapped his arms protectively around himself.

Next were the cameras, silent silver eyes on every street corner. All it would take was some simple face-recognition software. Soren ducked self-consciously as we walked past, but I yanked on his arm and forced him to face forward. Conspicuously hiding from the cameras – there was software that could pick that up too. Either they'd recognise us or they wouldn't. My hand drifted down to the gun hidden beneath my baggy t-shirt.

All we could be was ready.

But all around us, the world carried on as if we weren't in it. The streets were dusty with ragged fragments of cloth and paper blowing down them in the hot wind. The Infected seemed to be in no hurry, walking slowly down the narrow streets to nowhere in particular. Bloody remnants of wounds stood out stark red on their faces, hands and legs; but no one seemed to care. Once, as we walked past, a man with a seeping sore over his left eye fell down on the pavement and didn't get back up. No one reacted, they just adjusted their paths round his body and carried on walking.

For the first time, I realised that some of the piles of cloth on the pavement had once been people, worn away by time. Dead and left to rot where they fell. Why bother to bury your dead when you just don't care that they're gone?

After thirty minutes walking, the scruffy residential streets gave way to broader, bleaker roads with the concrete hulks of government buildings squatting on either side. Barbed wire lined the tops of tall fences, but there was nothing to keep out any longer. The streets were deserted, none of the Infected in sight. The buildings too had the unmistakeable look of desertion about them. Only the ever-present cameras peered out from their walls. Within there was an echoing emptiness, evident even fifty feet away.

We walked on. The sky was hazy above us, caught between sunshine and rain. No shadows anywhere, just a pervasive muted light. Another fifteen minutes and we were there.

The street outside was entirely empty. There was a tall fence, security gates, cameras, guard towers. And again, that air of desertion.

"You're sure he's here?" Kelis asked.

I shrugged. "That's what the old woman said."

"Yeah," Soren said dryly. "And why would she ever want to lie to us?"

I saw Haru swallow hard, then square his shoulders. "Well, we're here now. And look..." He pointed over the gate, deep inside the palace complex. "There's light in there. There must be power. Why would they waste electricity on a place that was empty?"

The cameras to either side watched us blankly. There was no question that whoever was inside knew we were there.

"So..." Kelis said. "Do we go in?"

I looked at the cameras again. "Nothing to lose now. I guess we climb."

Kelis boosted each of us over the high fence, using that deceptive strength of hers. Soren went last, pulling her up and over as if she weighed nothing at all. His hand lingered on hers before he let it go. I saw her notice it, the slight unease as she finally pulled her fingers free. That was never going to end well.

Inside, we all paused a moment – waiting for the other shoe to drop, I guess. But no guards came pouring out, no sirens started blaring and after a moment we got moving deeper into the silent concrete complex.

When I was a kid, no older than nine or ten, I read *The Day of the Triffids*. I remember having to sneak it past my parents, because they would have thought it was too scary for me. But it didn't scare me at all. The image that stuck in my mind, the one I absolutely loved, was of the hero wandering through a deserted London, where everybody else was dead.

I remember finding that an incredibly seductive idea. To be able to wander into everybody's houses, see what went on behind doors that were usually closed. To have it all to yourself. Maybe it was a legacy of the time I'd spent in hospital when I was very young, and had had no privacy at all: even the inside of my body became public property then. Maybe that was why I could imagine being so alone without finding it lonely.

Wandering through those echoing, empty rooms made me think of that, with a sudden sharp stab of nostalgia for a childhood that could never be relived, not even through children of my own. There wasn't a soul in the place. No bodies, even. Nothing. We passed through living quarters, utilitarian barracks, plush sleeping chambers, impersonal guest rooms, through offices and finally through labs. Three of them, fully equipped but not purpose-built. These had been offices once, I guessed, before Ash put them to better use. There was no sign that they'd been left in a hurry, or during any kind of emergency. No signs of flight, or disaster. The people who'd once occupied them were just... gone.

"Okay," Kelis said as we looked around at the benches, Bunsen burners, pipettes and all the usual apparatus of a working lab, "I guess this is just a front. He must have his real base somewhere else."

"It could be anywhere," Haru said. "How will we ever find it?"

"But you were right to begin with," I told him, "the power's still on. Something's still happening here." Halogen light shone done from the ceiling, flattening our features.

"A relay station," Ingo said. His voice was soft but startling, because it was always so easy to forget that he was there. "Remote control. There were satellite dishes on the roof, transmitters. The feed from the cameras goes out, the signal for the loudspeakers comes in."

"Goes out where?" Soren said. "Comes in from where?"

"Off the island," I said with sudden certainty.

Kelis raised an eyebrow. "You think?"

I gestured around me, at the carefully abandoned lab. "This was his headquarters. He was doing whatever he was doing here. Why would he bother to pack it all up just to shift somewhere else on Cuba? The only reason to leave would be to go somewhere else entirely."

"Okay, I buy that," Kelis said. "So what was he doing in this place? This lab – it's not original, is it? He built it, just like Queen M built hers."

"Yeah," I said. Only he built it better, because Ash was a real scientist. I walked away from the others, along the length of the benches, scavenging for any clues. They weren't hard to find. I don't think when he'd left here he'd meant to erase his traces. He'd just taken what he still needed and left the rest behind.

It was all very familiar-looking, and no wonder. The same set up we'd had back at the base. I recognised the Petri dishes with carefully cultivated cultures, left to die or breed alone. In the furthest corner of the room there was a laptop, plugged in and switched off.

"Paydirt," I told the others as I booted it up.

"Why did they leave it behind if it's still working?" Haru said dubiously.

I shrugged. "Because they didn't need it anymore and they didn't expect anyone to find it."

I was right, though a part of me knew that Haru was right as well. This was all just too convenient. Did Ash want me to find it? Why? But even if he'd meant me to have this information, for whatever twisted game he was playing, it didn't mean it wasn't worth having.

"Anything?" Kelis asked.

I nodded as I skimmed through the directory before I delved deeper, because you'd be amazed how much people give away just in the way they name things. "Definitely something."

Thirty minutes later I could tell her exactly what. It wasn't a surprise, not after everything else I'd seen, but the certainty still sat like a sour lump in my gut. Guilt too, because a part of me had suspected all along, even back when there was still something I could have done to prevent it. Memory again, sharper than pain.

Ash out of the lab, taking one of the few sleeps we allowed ourselves back in those frantic days when it still seemed possible that we could stop it all, if only we could do it in time.

I was feeling wired that night, I remembered that. I wasn't sure why, maybe it was the message I'd had from him, a quick email which had taken three days to reach me. It must be getting bad out there, I knew, if information itself was beginning to sicken and slow. He hadn't been able to say much, with the security checks at his end and ours. But I could hear his voice saying every line and it had left me itchy to see him, to hear his voice for real. I knew that I probably never would again and it was almost unbearable. When you love someone like that it seems impossible that the love itself can't overcome every obstacle between you. If love can't do that, then what's the point of it?

So I was restless and unhappy and, as I usually did, I sublimated it in work. My computer was slow to boot, some bug the techies hadn't been able to fix, so I switched on Ash's instead, unthinkingly using the password he'd told me long ago when we were students together and the only thing he had to hide was the fact that he'd been cheating on his girlfriend for the last three months.

I was planning on logging onto the shared drive, not even looking at his private files. I didn't expect there to be any private files. When would he have time to do anything but work?

Except there were private files – and *they were to do with work. Not our work; the job I thought he'd left behind him when he came here. I knew, of course, that for the last few years he'd been employed by the Department of Defence. There hadn't seemed anything sinister about it, there were plenty of good reasons why the DoD might want to employ a virologist.*

I'd known, too, that some of the ingredients we'd been mixing into this 'Cure' we were creating came from classified sources. The cutting edge gene therapies, the more esoteric retroviruses, borderline unethical stem-cell research. These weren't things available to the general public. But here they were in Ash's files, files with dates going back months, years; long before he knew we were going to use them. This was the stuff Ash had been working on before the Cull struck. Wasn't it just the mother of all coincidences that it turned out to be exactly what we needed to make the Cure?

No, I told myself, as my heart raced. It was just selection bias. Ash had been recruited into the project precisely because his experience was so exactly what we needed.

Except. Except... here was a file on gene-therapy for sickle cell anaemia. There was another on the use of stem cells in adult neural rewriting. It was obvious that the RNA we were carefully sculpting to change A and B to O-neg was a mash-up of both of these. But why the second? As far as we knew, the Cull wasn't neuro-active.

"What are you doing?" Ash asked from right over my shoulder.

"Snooping through your files," I told him, because he and I had never been able to lie to each other. Or at least I hadn't. For the first time, I was beginning to wonder about him.

"Find anything interesting?" he asked, so nonchalantly that I instantly relaxed.

"Yeah, highly classified defence department files. It said something about killing anyone who read them – but they were just kidding, right?"

He smiled and we got back to work and I never did ask him what exactly that research had been about, and why exactly it had fitted our needs so precisely. I never asked – but sometimes, late at night, I wondered.

"Find anything interesting?" Kelis asked me now, and I knew that I was pale when I turned from the laptop's screen to face her.

"Yeah, I guess 'interesting' is one word for it."

"And what would be another word?" Ingo asked, as literal as ever.

"Terrifying."

"It's the Infected, isn't it?" Haru ran a hand nervously through the dark spikes of his hair. "This was done deliberately. The Infection – it was designed, not accidental."

I nodded and Haru grimaced and turned away.

Kelis was still studying me carefully, her intense brown eyes narrowed. "That's not everything, is it?"

"No, it isn't. The thing is, he did create the Infection deliberately." A perversion of the Cure I was carrying in my own blood, but I wasn't ready to tell her that yet. "He deliberately made it contagious. Blood-borne at the moment."

"At the moment?" Haru's eyebrows were so high they were lost in his hairline.

"That was the best he could do to begin with. But he was researching other forms of transmission."

"Airborne?" Ingo asked, and even he sounded hushed. Everyone knew that the Cull had been airborne too. It couldn't have done what it did otherwise.

"Maybe. But the trail here had reached a dead end, and he abandoned it about six months ago. That's the date of the last update to any of the files." And that really was as much as I could tell from the fragments of half-finished research on the abandoned laptop.

"We need to find him, wherever he is now," Kelis said, and I felt a warm rush of relief, because I didn't want to be the one suggested it.

"How?" Haru asked.

Ingo held up his hand, like a child in class asking for permission to speak. "Somewhere in here there must be a central computer co-ordinating the information going in and out. If we can find that, I can tell you where the transmission is being sent from."

"Good," I said. "When you find it, there's one other thing I need you to do."

Have you ever watched a whole city burn? There's a wild kind of pleasure in it, giving free reign to a force of nature that we're more often trying to contain. The truck we'd commandeered raced over the cracked tarmac of the road, but the heat travelled faster, clasping at our throats as we tried to outrun what we'd done.

All around us, the loudspeakers were still blaring the same message: "Everyone must come to Havana immediately. Come to the centre of Havana and await further instructions." They'd been saying the same thing for the last two days. We hadn't been able to wait any longer, but it hadn't been quite long enough. All around us, Infected were still flooding into the city, calmly walking into the flames which had already consumed thousands, tens of thousands, of lives. The fire wouldn't get all of them – there'd still be pockets of them in the furthest reaches of the island – but it would get enough.

So I was a mass murderer now. And in the end it had been so easy. All it needed was for Ingo to splice together audio tracks from a few of Ash's previous messages. The words didn't sound quite right, the emphasis in the wrong places, elision between syllables which didn't belong together. But the Infected didn't seem to care. It was their master's voice, and they had no choice but to obey it. The cameras were put on a loop, so Ash wouldn't be able to see what we'd done, while his own audio feed had been cut. We'd left him no way to save this terrible experiment of his; we were putting the Petri-dishes in the furnace and burning the cultures away for good.

After that, it was just a few cans of petrol over some central buildings, a hot day and a strong wind. Fire is endlessly hungry – it doesn't need much of an invitation to consume everything. I leaned against the cab of the truck and looked back, like Lot's wife, knowing there was a price to pay but helpless to avoid seeing for myself what we were leaving behind.

There's a Pink Floyd album cover: a burning man shaking hands with another, oblivious to the fire which is eating him alive. It's almost funny, the way he just doesn't seem to care. There were hordes of them, all walking into the furnace, on and on as their flesh blistered and burned, red fissures opening in skin like the cracks in the surface of a volcano that tell you another eruption is due. The smell was overwhelming. The meaty, greasy smell of human beings burning.

I saw a girl no older than eight walk calmly down the narrow alley between two buildings. The doorways of the buildings belched yellow fire at her, little sparks of it drifting ahead of the body of the flame. Her hair caught first, burning a bright orange against her skull, but she kept on walking. She kept walking until her legs gave way, the bones snapping in the heat.

Finally, when the girl's body was lost to sight and the crowds on the streets had begun to thin and the flames receded into the distance, I looked away.

Kelis caught my eye. "We had no choice," she told me in a voice that said even she didn't believe it.

"It's done now," I said. "They won't be going out recruiting for a while. And they won't be trying to stop us from leaving."

"So now we find the dear Leader and stop him doing anything worse," Kelis said, offering a sort of comfort.

I looked ahead in my mind to the ocean fast approaching, and beyond to our destination, across the waters and most of the way across a continent. All the way to Las Vegas where, one day soon, I'd look Ash in the eye and make him pay. Not so much for what he'd done, but for what he'd turned me into.

CHAPTER SIX

It was ninety miles to Miami by boat. We'd found a light aircraft on the island, but since none of us could fly it, it looked like we'd be going to Vegas the long way. I didn't look at Cuba as it receded into the distance behind us; just took the wheel of the small pleasure craft we'd commandeered – the fastest we could find – and looked forward over the calm seas. As we'd sat on the shore and waited for the world to turn and the sun to rise, I'd decided that I was done with regrets.

The journey was peaceful, no one in pursuit, nothing but us and the seagulls hovering over the waves. After an hour or so I handed the wheel to Ingo and went to the sundeck. The others were all lying there, lazing in the sunlight, stripped down to shorts and t-shirts.

We looked, I realised, like a bunch of American university students on Spring break. For the first time since I'd left the base, for the first time in five years in fact, I felt myself begin to relax. Haru was pissing over the side of the boat, watching the spray blow away in the wind, and for some reason that made me smile. There was something so young and male about it. Ingo always used the privy, carefully locking the door, and that made me smile too. Modesty seemed so redundant in the new world.

"You look a million miles away," Kelis said, and I realised she'd been studying me for a while.

I shrugged. "Just thinking."

She smiled. "Yeah, that can be tough sometimes."

"It's strange for me, you know, being back among people. I don't think I'm quite used to it." I didn't know why I told her that. She was hardly the poster child for opening up and sharing. Except that it was strange, being around other human beings again after so long, and I suddenly wanted to know them, really *know* them. To connect, to bond – all those terrible, psychobabble words. But humans are social animals, and I knew I'd lost something essential in the years I'd spent alone. The person who'd gone into the base would never have done the things that the person who came out of it did.

I wanted to blame the Voice, but I wasn't sure I could.

"It was strange for me too," Soren said unexpectedly. "When I was recruited. That was the hardest thing, being back in such a crowd."

"Harder than the things she made you do?" I asked. "The killing?" I think there was more curiosity than accusation in my voice, and Soren didn't seem offended.

"For me, yes. I was home in Sweden, the fishing village I'd lived my whole adult life. A tiny, cold place on the north coast where the sea was always icy, even in midsummer." The focus of his eyes pushed out as his attention pulled in, looking at memories I suspected he'd kept hidden away for years. Then he smiled self-consciously. "Sorry, I forget what I was trying to say."

"No," I said, "Don't stop. I'd like to know what it was like for you, before Queen M. I want to remember the world before the Cull."

"Before the Cull?" He looked from me to Kelis. Something in her expression must have persuaded him to carry on, because he suddenly shifted position, pulling his legs beneath him to get comfortable. I suppose somewhere inside we all want to be known. How else would therapists stay in business?

"Sweden was an orderly country, you know? We weren't a nation that liked to get too excited about anything; we left that to the Danes. Orderly and neat and prosperous. I'd grown up in Malmö, down in the south, but as soon as I'd finished my degree I moved away. There were too many people in Malmö, too many tourists. It was too noisy, always full of traffic and the fog horns of the boats in the harbour. What's the point of living in a large country with a small population if you can't enjoy the peace?

"So I went north, away from everyone, where the winter nights were so long you barely saw the sun rise. I went as far north as I could until I was on the edge of the arctic circle, where I could watch the Northern Lights at midnight and listen to the never-ending sound of the sea. I bought myself a log house out in the forest, a fishing boat and an axe. And then I got myself a broadband connection and every day I worked with people I never had to see. Once a week I went into the shop, and that was the only time I saw another person, except maybe a few other fishing boats, far out at sea. People are much easier to enjoy, I think, if you don't have to actually talk to them. Out there I started liking my fellow country folk for the first time.

"Then the Cull struck and everyone was – well, you know how it was. But I thought, less people in this overcrowded world, why is that a bad thing? I suppose people died in the village but I hadn't known them before the Cull and I couldn't pretend that I cared. The shop emptied after a while but it was no big problem. I knew how to hunt and fish, and planting simple crops wasn't difficult. I had an axe and finding trees to use it on wasn't a problem either. There was only myself to feed. After three weeks, maybe four, the radio that I kept went silent and that was the end of it, I thought. Civilisation had collapsed, somewhere off-screen. But for me nothing really changed.

"It was so beautiful there. The trees are evergreen, all year round they look the same. Very dark, impenetrable as soon as you're away from the coast. The cliffs are grey rock, almost the same colour as the sea. I read a guidebook once. It called our coast 'forbidding,' but I never understood that. What was forbidden there? It seems to me that it's only in a place like that you're allowed to be yourself, without other people telling you what you should be.

"And then Queen M came." He shrugged, his face losing its faraway look. "I guess you know the rest. Back to join the rest of humanity."

"Or what was left of it," Haru said, and I was sure the double meaning was deliberate. The remnants of humanity, and the remnants of their humanity.

Kelis looked at him through narrowed eyes. "It's easy for you to be smug. Japan dodged the bullet while everyone else was bleeding out. It wasn't just the O-negs who were spared there, was it?"

"No," Haru said, "something in our genes saved most of us, in the good old Land of the Rising Sun." He looked at Kelis, questioning, and she shrugged – meaning, why not? We've got ten hours to kill and what else is there to fill the time?

"Okay," he said. "You want to hear my story? The thing you have to know about Japan is, we're a little like Soren, here. We don't really need anyone else. For years we were this closed island kingdom. Then along came the Western empires and we thought we might like to get an empire of our own. Everyone knows how that ended for us. So we went back to doing what we do best – minding our own business. I suppose you'd say we're the ultimate voyeurs. We like looking at other people and sometimes we like imitating them, but we don't want any actual contact.

"So when the Cull came and spared us, but took everyone else, it seemed like a sign. Shut yourselves in. Shut yourselves off. There wasn't much protest when the government locked the borders down. The economy was in a mess, of course – we relied on high-tech exports to buy low-tech imports. But China was just sitting there, no longer in any kind of position to fight us off, so we went in uninvited and got everything we needed. Then we just... carried on. You know the thing I noticed most? That there were no new Hollywood films. Nothing new from Spielberg, no big dumb action movies, no more X-Men. I stopped going to the cinema and that was the biggest way my life changed.

"Oh, there were deaths, of course. A lot of them. But we buried them and we moved on. Only for me, I kept imagining the rest of the world. All my life I've been drawing the apocalypse. Giant robots, mutants... and now here was a real apocalypse – the genuine article – and I was still a wage slave in a grey suit.

"So when there was a movement for colonisation, I joined – to go back out in the world. I took my son away from the security of Tokyo to New Zealand, where the government in its wisdom had voted to set up New Kyoto. I had to fight to take him; he was... well, he wasn't well. But they had trouble recruiting enough colonists and in the end they let us go. I remember how I felt on the flight, how excited I was. I watched the sea scrolling away beneath us and I thought that this was a real new beginning. I didn't imagine for a moment that I could be making a mistake."

He smiled thinly and trailed off and I remembered what he'd told me about the son he left behind. "And then Queen M took you and not him," I said.

"Yeah." He ran a hand back through his hair, messing up the spikes, already stiff with salt spray. "I took him away from safety for no goddamn reason and then I just left him there, on his own."

"He would have been looked after," I said, "by the other colonists."

Haru just shrugged and looked away. I guess we all had our own burdens of guilt to carry, and no one to share them with.

When I looked at Ingo he stared back, blank and maybe a little challenging. "You hope to know about my home?" he asked, and I realised I didn't even know where that was. He smiled mockingly and I could see that he knew that too.

"The Congo," he told me. "The Democratic Republic of Congo. For twenty years the West wanted to know nothing about my land. Four million people died in a war that no one noticed, and now you ask me for our history?"

"Listen, friend," Soren said. "We're not the West. We're us. But please yourself – I'll survive the disappointment if you don't feel like sharing."

"There is no story," Ingo said. "There is nothing as neat as a story to tell about my country. First the Belgians robbed us and sometimes they murdered us, and when they finally left we put our own men in charge – and they robbed and killed us too. Our neighbours abused us and the refugees of Rwanda came and made everything worse, bringing the terrible ghosts of their past with them. There was war, and where there was not war there was disease, and everywhere there was hatred and greed. The women were raped and then they were driven from their villages because they had been raped, because of the shame. Mothers killed their own sons and daughters for witchcraft. But why did we need witches when we already had men? The warlords fought over blood and diamonds. The West held concerts for the starving of Ethiopia but they turned away from us, and do you know why?"

"I know why," Haru said quietly. We looked at him and he twisted his mouth into an expression of wry amusement and shame. "Video games."

For the first time since I'd known him, Ingo really smiled. It wasn't a good sight. "Yes," he said. "Coltan from our mines made the games machines of the West. Our children died in slavery so yours could have just one more toy. I have seen you, Jasmine, looking at my fingers and I think you assume this happened when Queen M found me. No. They were broken long ago, when I was seven and a man stood on my hand when I reached for a knife to stop his friends from violating my sister. You ask how it was when the Cull came? I will tell you – it was exactly the same as it had always been. My land was drenched in blood, and nobody cared."

There was a silence after that, deep and uncomfortable. Finally, it was Ingo who turned to Kelis. "You still have a story to tell."

"Anyone want to hear it now?" Kelis asked self-mockingly, but I nodded and so did Haru.

"We showed you ours..." he said.

She paused a moment, then nodded and leaned back so that she was looking up at the pale blue sky rather than at us. "New York. Who'd have thought that one day a rain really would come and wash the streets clean? Only it wasn't the dirt that was washed away – sometimes it seems like the filth was the only thing left. But *mierda* never stays smooth. It clumps and congeals and that's what it did in the city. First just little groups, the old street gangs, and then new ones came. It was quite funny really, to see Manhattan lawyers walking the mean streets with guns. Funny until they started shooting at you.

"After a while it got more formal. The gangs turned into Klans and you were either in one or you were left to beg for scraps – no middle ground. That's what the Cull took away – the safe centre. And all my life I'd been begging for scraps, working as a secretary in some crappy little law firm that made your average ambulance chaser look classy, getting spat at and worse, guarding prisoners who thought they were something because they ran crack on their little corner. So I decided – enough, you know? Why shouldn't I start over? Why shouldn't I be better than I was?

"I joined the Midtown Men and I found that I was good at it. My daddy, he'd taught me to shoot before he... yeah, back before the Cull. So I could handle a gun and I found that I could handle myself too. I made myself useful and I was completely loyal; pretty soon I was one of the elite. People were eating *my* scraps – and it felt good.

"But it doesn't matter how high you climb, there's always someone above you. And if you're looking out for number one you can be damn fucking sure that everyone else around you is doing the same. We had a lot of things in New York, but we didn't have high tech. And the gangs, they had an arms race going on – doesn't take much to get one of those started. You get handguns, I get semi-automatics, you get rocket launchers, and I get myself an Apache helicopter. Leave it long enough and they'll go nuclear, I'm not kidding.

"So when Queen M came and offered the kind of tech we were never going to find for ourselves... we were racing to say 'yes' before anyone else could. The only thing she wanted in return was a few soldiers. New York, soldiers are easy to find – ten waiting to fill the place of each fallen man. We said yes. *I* said yes, when we voted on it. Didn't think for a minute they were gonna pick me."

She looked over at me and smiled. "I guess right about now you're thinking that I got pretty much what I deserved. But I was only trying to survive. I remember learning about Darwin back in school, when it was still okay to teach evolution. He said we're all the children of survivors. Every ancestor we've got won some kind of fight. I don't think it's any surprise we're killers – the surprise is how we sometimes manage not to be."

She was still looking at me, her expression more uncertain than her words, and I realised that she was looking for some kind of forgiveness, or at least for acceptance. I smiled back, awkwardly. "I'm not going to judge you. Hell, I'm long past judging anyone."

"Yeah?" Her expression lightened. "Shame my girlfriend didn't feel the same. When I told her I was gonna have to leave her behind... well, let's just say I don't think she's keeping my bed warm back in Washington Square."

Her girlfriend? Oh. *Oh.* I saw the way she was looking at me, as if she wanted me to understand something without having to explain it. And I saw the way that Soren was looking at her, and how his face darkened as he followed her eyes to mine. There was no way this was going to end well.

"What is your deal?" Haru said, turning to me. "You were a scientist, you said, trying to find a cure for the Cull. What happened?"

"Well," Soren said dryly, an edge of hostility in his voice that hadn't been there before. "I'm only taking a guess, but I'd say she failed."

"Not entirely," I said and only as I said the words did I realise that I was finally going to have to tell them the truth. Because they'd opened up to me? Not really. More because lying is tiring and I was using all my energy trying to keep the Voice inside me down to a murmur. I didn't have energy left over for anything else. And maybe because I'd done so many wrong things over the last few weeks, I wanted to finally do something right.

"Not entirely," I said again. "We did find a cure, but we found it too late."

"I never heard that," Kelis said with wonder. "That's... I don't know, that makes everything so much worse, somehow. To know that someone got so close to stopping it all."

I shook my head. "No, not really, you see..." I laughed harshly, because this was harder to do than I'd imagined. "You see, I haven't been entirely honest with you."

At that I felt four different people stiffen around me and I remembered suddenly that all of them had guns. Maybe this wasn't such a good idea, but I could see their faces, closed and untrusting, and I knew that it was too late to back down now.

"The Infected, on Cuba – I knew exactly what was wrong with them. I knew it because I recognised it. Jesus, I helped to design it."

"They'd been given the cure?" Kelis said slowly.

I nodded. "Yeah. A version of it. The Cure stopped the Cull, you see, but it didn't leave the people we gave it to unchanged. It caused auditory hallucinations, delusions, the whole schizophrenic works."

"*You* were cured," Haru said in amazement, and one by one I saw the others understanding.

I smiled with unexpected relief. It felt great not to have to hide myself any longer. "Yes. We tested it on ourselves, me and Ash, and on a few of the others."

"That's why you need those drugs," Kelis said. "The ones we went hunting for in Havana."

"Yes," I said again.

"And what exactly happens," Haru asked, "if you stop taking them?"

Like Kelis, earlier, I leaned back, looking up at the sky rather than across at my companions. "Bad things. Worse things than even I imagined. You see Ash – he was another scientist, a bio-weapons expert – he took the Cure too. We were both sick for a long time, days of pain when we didn't think we'd survive. When we finally woke up, there was... the Voice." I could hear it now, on the edge of my consciousness, hissing at me to keep quiet, to go on keeping its secret. But I found that with these not-quite-friends around me it was possible to ignore it.

"It spoke to me, inside my head. It still does. It's not my voice – it's not the voice of anyone I know. And it's not – I don't know how to describe this, to someone who hasn't felt it. The Voice doesn't make me obey it. There's no compulsion about it. It's just that when it speaks, everything it says seems to make such perfect sense that there's really no question of not listening to it."

"Yeah?" Haru said uneasily. "And what kind of thing does this Voice say? Are we talking along the lines of 'kill them, kill them all'? Because speaking as an objective observer, that sort of thing really doesn't make sense."

"Sometimes it says that kind of thing," I admitted, feeling the atmosphere thicken around me. "But it's not..." I laughed. "It feels absurd to talk about the Voice as a person, but in a way it seems to be, or that's how I experience it: as something independent that has its own agenda. And that's what it's about, when it tells me to do terrible things. It doesn't want them because it enjoys seeing people suffer. It's not psychotic – except in the clinical sense. It just wants what it wants and it doesn't care who gets hurt in the process."

"So," Kelis said, "not so much psychotic as sociopathic."

"Yeah. Yeah. It doesn't care about anything, except maybe me, and even then I think it just sees me as a means to an end."

"You realise this is crazy, right?" Haru said. "This voice isn't real. It doesn't want anything. It's just, I don't know, repressed urges inside you getting out, right? The things you don't want to admit to wanting."

His pale cheeks were flushed and I thought that he really was only a few seconds away from shooting me where I sat. "I thought that too," I told him. "I mean, it's the only thing that makes sense, isn't it? Except how could I have gone my whole life without even beginning to guess that I wanted to do those things? And if the Voice really is just my subconscious, why does it seem to be working to a plan that I'm not privy to?"

"You keep talking about a plan," Kelis said softly. Her face was a closed book again. Before, she'd been trying to tell me something about the way she felt about me, but I knew looking at her that whatever that was it wouldn't save me if she decided I was a threat. It was like she'd said – everyone there had survived for a reason, and one of those reasons must have been that they didn't let sentiment get in the way of necessity.

She held my gaze for only a moment, then looked away. Best not to look in the eyes of a woman you might be about to kill. "What is the plan? What is it that you think this Voice inside you wants?"

"I don't know. I didn't want to know, that was why I started taking the drugs to silence it – first the opiates, then the anti-psychotics. I never let myself hear the Voice clearly enough to find out what it wanted."

"I still do not see the connection to the Infected of Cuba," Ingo said. "You are not telling us, are you, that it was you who infected them?"

"No," I said. "It wasn't me. It was Ash."

"The face on all the posters, the Leader," and Kelis was there again, too quickly for comfort. "That was the other scientist you worked with?"

I nodded. "The thing about Ash was, he *liked* the Voice. When I first woke up, after the Cure had run its course, I... killed a young soldier. The Voice told me to do it. And I think that's probably how I was able to resist the Voice long enough to suppress it. Because however much the Voice told me to, I couldn't forget the look in the soldier's eyes just before I snapped his neck. But Ash... he found me just after I'd done it, and I could tell that he didn't feel any guilt at all, even though I found out later that he had a lot more blood on his hands than that.

"He'd woken up before me, you see. I don't know why – maybe just a faster metabolism. So he'd had time to speak to some of the others on the base. I didn't see it at the time but I read the accounts of it later in the logs. There was videotape too, from the security cameras. Ash was like a messiah. He had this incredible self-belief when he spoke, and it made other people believe him too – even when he told them to do terrible things."

"What sort of terrible things?" Kelis asked.

"Turning people against each other, soldiers against scientists, soldiers against soldiers. People who'd once been friends. Ash sowed doubt in everyone's minds and in the end the only person they trusted was him. I guess it didn't work on me because the Voice in my own head gave me a kind of immunity. When Ash wasn't watching me I sneaked away and found some opiates and I injected enough into my veins to make sure I didn't give a damn what the Voice wanted me to do.

"The trouble was, the opiates stopped me caring about anything – including trying to stop Ash." I swallowed as I realised that maybe this was the real reason I hadn't wanted to tell them the story. Not because I was afraid of their anger, but of their disdain. Old guilt is like wine. It doesn't lose its strength, it just turns to vinegar – sour and corrosive. "He was trying to get everyone else to take the Cure, you see. Even back then. I'd almost forgotten it – I guess I'd just dismissed it as a part of his madness. But now... now that I've seen what he did in Cuba, I know that it wasn't incidental to what he wanted. It was central to it."

"And was that where the first Infected came from?" Kelis asked. "Those soldiers and scientists on the base?"

I shook my head. "They would have been, I suppose, but Ash wasn't the only crazy person there. There was a soldier – Sergeant Miller, I think? – I remember that he started some kind of fight, a stand-off between Ash's men and his. I just tried to get away from it all, hiding deeper in the base. Then there was an explosion and I was left on one side of it with them on the other. And that's where the story ends."

"Not Ash's story though," Soren said. "Seems like his story has quite a long epilogue."

"Yeah." I took the wheel again and looked out over the waves ahead of us, where the American coast was finally approaching. "I can only guess what happened next. He must have made it away from the base with his followers. I suppose he tried to give them the Cure like he'd been intending, but my guess is that it didn't work. It was designed specifically for non-O-negs. I don't know what it would have done in its original form to anyone who was O-neg, but I suspect it might have been fatal. So he would have had to do more research, refine it. If he took what he needed from the base when he left, that would have been possible." Now I thought about it, some of the equipment in that laboratory in Havana had looked familiar. I shrugged. "Then at some point he came to Cuba and tested it out."

"But why?" Soren asked. "What exactly was he hoping to achieve?"

"I don't know, but I know it's nothing good. When I heard the Voice, something inside me knew that it was the voice of madness, and I rejected it. But Ash embraced it, and I think maybe he wants everyone else to embrace it too. Cuba was just the start. It was a failed experiment – that's why he abandoned it. But there's no question in my mind that he's going to try again."

"And you intend to find him," Kelis said. It wasn't a question.

"I have to," I said. "I'm the only one who can possibly understand what it is he's trying to do. Which means I'm the only one who's got a chance of stopping him."

"Okay," Haru said. "And why exactly should we help you do that?"

"Because Cuba was only the beginning. You can leave me if you like. That's why I told you the truth – so you can make a real choice. All I ask is that you don't make mine for me. Leave me free to follow Ash. Because you all might regret it if I don't."

I got up to take the wheel after that, leaving them free to make their decisions without me around. But the truth was, without them I was sunk. There was no way I'd be able to make it all the way to Las Vegas on my own. Even with them to back me up it was a long-shot.

"Why didn't you tell us this before?" Kelis asked. If there was anyone who might follow me, I knew it was her. For all the wrong reasons, though, and wasn't it wrong of me to exploit that? I shot her a quick look, but she was watching the waves, not me.

"I was afraid of what you'd do if you knew I was Infected too."

"Are you infectious?" she asked me.

I shook my head. "I don't think so. That's what Ash's research was all about, you see – making the Cure transmittable, because that wasn't how we originally designed it."

"Its weapons tech, isn't it? The Cure." Kelis said.

"Ash's contribution was, yeah. We put stuff in there that we didn't fully understand – or at least I didn't. We were desperate enough to try anything."

"Do you think someone somewhere planned this all?" she asked me. "The Cull and the Cure?"

"That's another reason to find Ash, isn't it?" I said. "To answer that question."

She nodded and I thought that maybe she was going to tell me that she'd made her decision and she would come with me. But instead her hand reached out to clasp mine over the wheel. Her eyes strained towards the distant coastline of Florida.

"What is it?" I said. There were black dots on the shore that might have been people, but that wasn't unexpected. Miami was a big place and there was no reason to think it would be entirely deserted after the Cull.

She didn't answer me, just called out for Soren. He leapt up to join her, Haru and Ingo hanging behind. Ingo's dark face was sweating lightly, drops of crystal on mahogany, no clue there about what decision he'd made. Haru would go where the group went, I knew that, seeking safety in numbers. And Soren, I supposed, would follow Kelis. But that was something else I shouldn't be taking advantage of.

"Shit!" Soren said. "You're right."

"Right about what, exactly?" Haru asked. Kelis's hand was still over mine on the wheel but she wasn't moving it and I kept on steering a straight course towards whatever was waiting for us on the shore. We were close enough now that I could make out little figures, flashes of red and brighter colours on their clothing. I felt the first stirrings of unease.

"Are those..?" I said.

"Yeah," Kelis said. "I recognise the formation. Standard when facing a sea attack. All the island garrisons practised it."

"Those are Queen M's men?" Haru said, finally cottoning on.

"I think so," I said.

"I know so," Kelis said impatiently.

"This is no surprise," Ingo said calmly. "The tracking devices were never removed from Soren and Kelis."

Of course he was right. Haru turned an unloving look on the two of them and I remembered that he'd been all for leaving them behind. "Okay," I said, "it's not a problem. I'll just turn and we'll make landfall somewhere else." I tried to shift my grip on the wheel to do just that, but Kelis held my hand firm.

"No point," she said. "While the trackers are in us, she can just follow us along the shore. We'll run out of fuel before she runs out of patience. Besides – she'll have boats of her own. Faster than this, probably."

"There are only two options," Soren said. "Fight or surrender."

"There's a third option," Haru said sourly. I knew he meant to throw Soren and Kelis overboard, and they knew it too. Soren half turned to him and Haru backed away.

"Then I guess we fight," I said.

CHAPTER SEVEN

I TOOK OUT my gun again. The weight of it had begun to feel very comfortable in my hand. I wondered if this was how it had been for my man: first a burden, then a useful tool and finally an end in itself. The adrenaline was already surging through my body and that was addictive too, the rush of it, even the bitter taste it brought to the back of my throat.

Haru had taken the wheel from me. I could see the white of his knuckles as he gripped it and I knew that he was forcing himself not to turn aside. I guess he knew that Queen M's men might kill him, but Kelis would shoot him for sure if he didn't do as she'd ordered.

The coastline ahead of us looked like a cleaned-up version of Havana: white sand and smart resort hotels. Like in one of those old make-over shows; Havana was the before and Miami the after. The people had been made-over too, not shambling wrecks but whole and tooled-up, and lethal.

The front of the boat didn't offer much protection, not if there was any heavy artillery facing us. We were gambling that Queen M wanted to ask questions first and shoot later. There must be a reason she'd followed Kelis and Soren specifically – to find me, I was guessing – and she wasn't the type to waste resources on petty revenge. She wanted something from us other than our corpses.

On the other hand, if our corpses were all she could get, I was sure she'd settle for that. Fifty feet from the coast now and I could recognise some of the faces. The hardcore loyalists who hadn't fled the flagship when everyone had their chance. It was no surprise to see Curtis among them, Queen M's top recruitment agent.

"Hold your fire," Soren said.

Kelis shot him a look and I think for a moment she suspected he was changing his mind. But he was right. The longer we delayed opening fire, the better our chances. If they wanted us alive, they wouldn't shoot first.

Twenty feet from the shore and we weren't slowing down. Kelis had clasped her hands over Haru's, forcing him to stay his course. His face was sweating and desperate. The boat began to judder and shake, jarring over the rocks in the sand, rising higher and higher above the water line. I clung on hard, knowing that if I fell that would be the end. The boat was the only protection we had.

There was a heart-stopping moment as the boat's keel scraped against a sand shelf beneath us and I thought we'd be grounded, still too far from dry land. But then the boat jerked over the ridge and suddenly I could see that we weren't going to stop at all.

The people on the shore could see it too. Their tight little formation began to fragment and then it was a free for all. Half a dozen ran to the left, another five to the right. Two morons tried to outrun the boat straight back, sprinting towards the regimented line of hotels. The boat shot onto the sand, bumping twice as it went over their bodies. I didn't hear their screams because by then the first shot had been fired.

I staggered to my knees as the boat finally ground to a halt. Haru was flung forward against the hard wood of the cabin. I saw a spray of blood and a shard of something white that might have been his tooth. His howl of pain was lost in the din of gunfire.

The boat splintered beneath the hail of bullets. The splintering wood was as dangerous as shrapnel, a threat to flesh and eyes. All I could think about was escape. I'd run twenty paces before I'd even thought about firing my gun.

The fighting was too close, too intense, for any kind of game plan. The only thing that saved us was numbers. The boat had scattered Queen M's troops in a wide circle and they couldn't fire at us without firing at their own. Instead they pulled out knives. The fighting would be brutal, bloody and personal, but it was better that way. I wanted to see the faces of the people I was killing – punish myself with reality.

Another five paces away from the sea and the first of Queen M's men was on me. It was Curtis, as stony-faced as ever, even as he swung a machete straight for my throat. I didn't feel a moment's remorse as I put a bullet through his chest. His eyes glared all the way into the dark. The last thing he saw was me smiling. I thought about the ghosts of Ireland and was glad.

I could hear a fierce whooping somewhere to my left: Kelis, filled with the berserker rage of battle. There was a whimpering too, and that had to be Haru. I think maybe I was laughing, but I didn't know why, except that there's a certain exhilaration in facing death. Another face and another bullet, but this one got his own blow in. I saw a thin line of red bloom and widen on my forearm, the flesh parting with surgical precision.

The agony followed a second later. I gritted my teeth against it and kept on fighting. I knew where I was heading now, towards the hotels that lined the beach and the grid of roads behind that offered the only possibility of escape. Not fucking much of one, but any hope will do.

Two more bullets, then a pause to reload. It left time for one of Queen M's men to duck right in and shove something bright and sharp into my chest. But the blade glanced off a rib, tearing through skin and flying away to the left. There was no time for a bullet before the next killing blow. I jammed the handle of the Magnum hard into his nose. A crack and a fountain of blood. I grinned ferally.

All I initially saw of the grizzled, grey woman now attacking me was a flash of silver as her knife swung for my back. But Kelis was there, sliding a blade between the woman's vertebrae. Kelis took down another one after that, as did I. But there were always more, and how could we possibly kill them all?

I looked at Kelis and her brown eyes stared back at me and we both knew that there was no chance.

Except we weren't the only people coming in from the sea. I didn't realise what they were at first, the ragged, blackened figures falling on Queen M's men from their rear flank. For a crazy second I thought it must be some kind of mutiny, an uprising that we'd somehow sparked.

But the newcomers had never served Queen M. They only served one leader and he must have ordered them to come here, to follow us in from the sea. Their skin was red and crazed, untreated third degree burns. It was astonishing they were even standing. They were barely fighting. It didn't matter, though. The presence of the Infected, like an old-fashioned zombie horde, routed the others. Half the people who should have been following us turned to face the new threat. The rest kept fighting, but there was a hesitation to their actions now. They knew what was coming up behind them, and something was screaming at them to turn and face it.

I only took a second to watch the new reality unfold. Then I kept on running, using the time the Infected had bought us. The others must have had the same idea, because suddenly we were at the road and astoundingly it was all five of us. Haru's mouth was a bloody mess, and there were droplets all over Ingo's face that might have been blood or might have been sweat. Nothing in his expression told me which.

We were almost clear, but much more vulnerable. Up here we were a tight little target and Queen M's people were all behind us. There was nothing to stop them using their guns. Concrete sprayed out from the sea-wall of the hotel as I dived for shelter behind it, but it was only five feet high and there was no way I could stay there. I lifted my head above the wall and emptied my clip at my pursuers. They dived for cover too, but for them there was nothing but sand. Soren's semi-automatic blazed beside my Magnum. A few moments of that and the sand was more red than gold.

I knew I had to get up and run. We'd bought ourselves only a few seconds. But my back itched at the thought of turning it on all those weapons. Soren got up and turned to go.

I don't know how he knew that I wasn't moving. Maybe all those years away from people had made him hyper-sensitive to them. He spun round, grabbed my arm and pulled me to my feet, then flung me in front of him. Kelis was already running, Haru and Ingo trailing her by only a few paces. Ingo was somehow managing to run backwards as fast as the others ran forward. There were two guns in his hands and he wasn't even breathing hard.

I sprinted. I couldn't believe that I still had the energy when my legs felt like they were made of over-cooked pasta. My stomach was churning and loose, wanting to spill out everything inside it. There was a grunt from behind me, hard and bitten off, but I didn't turn to look. The bullets were streaming all around us. Every moment could be my last, and call me selfish, but all I wanted to think about was me.

I almost laughed when we came through the narrow road between the low-rise hotels and into the main road behind. Queen M was smart, but boy was she cocky. I guess it never occurred to her that we might break through the line of men she'd left on the beach. Her people had left their rides right where we could get them, the keys still in the ignition. We took the nearest vehicle, a big red jeep with silver spoilers and paint that hadn't seen water or polish since the Cull. The back was stacked high with barrels of petrol. More guns and more ammo too. There was no food, but that we'd be able to find on the journey.

Kelis took the wheel and I took shotgun, while Haru and Ingo piled into the rear, both facing back and firing. She'd turned the key and started the engine before I even realised that Soren hadn't climbed in with us.

The second bullet took him in the shoulder as we watched, but that wasn't the one that was going to kill him. That one had gone in through his stomach, exiting raggedly through his back. There was no return from a wound like that.

"*Mierda!*" Kelis said. "Soren – get in here!"

He gritted his teeth at her, more a grimace than a smile, but we all knew what he meant. "Go!" he shouted. "I'll hold them off and disable the other vehicles." He'd already dived behind one; collapsed, really, onto his knees. But he didn't let go of his gun and I knew that he wouldn't until we were clear.

"No way," Kelis said. "No fucking way are we leaving you behind!" Her hand released the key and reached for the door.

I grabbed her wrist, hard, wrenching her round to face me. "He's dead already, Kelis," I told her. "His body just doesn't know it yet."

She wanted to argue with me, but she knew I was telling the truth. She looked back at Soren, face twisted in grief. Maybe she hadn't felt about him the way he'd wanted but she'd sure as hell felt something. Her eyes locked with his for a moment. His mouth opened but the only thing that came out was a gush of blood. He wasn't even going to get any parting words.

Kelis twisted the key and slammed her foot down hard. A bullet hit the back or the jeep, then another, but they were too far away to get a bead on us. Then we were gone.

None of us got to see Soren die. But we saw the explosion, the bloom of fire that must've taken out most of Queen M's men, along with any vehicles that the rest of them could have followed us in. A grenade, I guessed. He must have been holding it back, waiting for just the right moment. I wished I could find a tear for him, but I'd only known him a few weeks and the truth was, he wasn't a very likeable guy. I saved my pity for Kelis. The numb expression on her face and the emptiness in her eyes were all I could see as we headed out of Miami and away.

It should have taken us two days to reach Las Vegas, but nothing ever goes according to plan. All those weeks I'd been wondering what the world looked like after the Cull and now I could see it for myself I was suddenly grateful for all those years I'd spent hidden away from it.

Florida was a breeze, a straight drive along what was essentially a reclaimed sand-pit. We saw people, ragged bunches of them guarding their orange groves and their fields. They didn't bother us and we saw no reason to bother them. We just held our guns out, high and obvious over the side of the jeep, and kept on driving.

Orlando was dreamlike in its weirdness, the city a ruin, but Disneyworld itself was entirely untouched. And there were people there, more than you would have thought. The only word I could seem to find for them was 'pilgrims.' Some of them had trekked by foot all the way down the Eastern Seaboard to get there, because vehicles were hard to come by and petrol harder still. There were whole families of them, starvation-thin parents with their skeletal kids, like the ghosts of the bloated coach potatoes who used to visit before the Cull.

I don't know why they came. When we asked they just looked blank, as if they hadn't thought about it themselves. I guess the place was a symbol of something important. Of normality itself, I suppose. They sat on the silent rides, frozen in place among half-wrecked animatronic pirates, or waiting in vain for *It's a Small World* to start playing and the little puppet children to dance.

We hadn't wanted to stop there, but we needed electricity, a strong current, and this seemed like the best place to find it. We walked past the shambling tourists and into the workings of the rides, the machinery that made it all run. As I walked past the animatronic cowboys, bears and twirling teapots I felt obscurely guilty, like a kid who'd sneaked downstairs on Christmas Eve to confirm that yeah, Santa was just mum and dad. It all looked so shabby and second-rate.

It took Ingo five hours, before he finally got one of the generators working, jump-starting it with cables running from the car. Kelis didn't even flinch as he put the spitting cable against her leg. The force knocked her into the frayed, fungal wreck of what had once been a Mickey Mouse costume. She sneezed out spores when she finally came round, but didn't let out a murmur of pain or complaint. There'd be no more tracking by Queen M. All we had to worry about was every other damn thing on this continent.

The Gulf coast never had much in the way of a population, and it had even less now. We drove past deserted wind-swept beaches and wooden houses half-blown away by hurricanes that no one could any longer predict. There was oil still out there, under the choppy waves, but no one had the means to find it. Queen M maybe, before she'd met me.

Biloxi had a population. We had a real good scrap there. It was entirely one-sided, small sidearms against semi-automatics and Kelis's cool, trained aim. It could only have been desperation that sent them out against us, but I didn't have time for pity. Kelis's face was blank and cold as she shot them all dead and I wondered if she was thinking about Soren as she did it. Probably not. She'd been a killer long before he died.

Then we drove onwards, and even a road trip through Hell can take on a kind of monotony. The lowlands of Mississippi scrolled past us like the scenery for a video game that had run out of budget. We seemed to have talked ourselves out on the boat, because we couldn't find anything to say in all those hours. I drove for a while, then Ingo. The rest leaned over the side, guns drawn, trying to stay tense and ready for action when really we were just bored. You can only live in fear of your life for so long before you lose the energy to keep caring.

* * *

We'd talked about skirting around New Orleans, avoiding the trouble that was bound to be found there, but we needed fuel and food, and we were reckless with tiredness by then.

The outskirts of the city were like a third-world slum. It was hard to say if that was the work of the Cull or the aftermath of Katrina, still unhealed after all these years. Vacant-eyed people came out of their hovels to stare at us. We ignored them and drove on past.

After a few miles we were into the older parts of town. We saw more people and, floating above them, the harsh scrape of live bluegrass. Then somehow, without even noticing it, we'd driven into the heart of a carnival. I didn't know what date it was, not exactly, but I knew for sure that this wasn't Mardi Gras.

"Join the party!" a tall black man in a bright red bird mask shouted out as we drove past. Others walked along beside the jeep, like they were following some kind of carnival float. A few tried to climb on board, but we pushed them back and they didn't seem to mind. There was a hallucinogenic quality to the whole thing that might have been a product of sleep deprivation, but I didn't think so.

I don't think that the party ever stopped here. I guess in a city surrounded by sugar cane fields rum is pretty easy to distil, and after the Cull they probably couldn't see much reason for doing anything than drinking it. Everyone we saw there was at that stage of drunkenness where you're a heart-beat away from doing something extreme, but you can't be entirely sure what. Would they fuck, fight, vomit, kill? We didn't stick around to find out, just kept on driving. It was frantic but joyless. No one there was having fun, not even close, but they kept on doggedly going, like partying had become some kind of onerous duty.

Finally we found ourselves in the heart of it all, the old French quarter. Everywhere there was cast iron, brick facades and unlit neon signs for clubs and bars that hadn't been open in years. There were food stalls here, people barbecuing meat that was probably rat, but we took it anyway. We gave them bullets in exchange, one for each chunk of meat. It was red raw on the inside, but I didn't care as I tore it away from the bone and swallowed without chewing. For the first time I appreciated what Queen M had done, saving her people from this. A man came up and kissed me as I ate, grabbing my cheeks and driving his tongue deep into my mouth. I pulled away and Kelis slapped him savagely back, but when he was gone he'd taken half the meat with him.

"Guess he didn't love you for yourself," Haru said. I realised it was the first joke any of us had made since Soren died, and managed a tired smile.

Then we drove on. Ahead of us a pile of naked bodies writhed, fucking openly in the street. The men around them had their cocks in their hands, stroking them in time to the heaving pile of flesh. It looked vicious and unsafe, about something more primal than lust. Further down there was another crude ceremony, but this one had a victim.

The boy could only have been about five. When they slit his throat the blood jetted into the crowd and they lifted their faces, swallowing it down. I looked away as Ingo pressed down on the accelerator, face as impassive as ever. I wondered if he'd even seen it, or if he'd retreated far into his mind; contemplating numbers, equations and algorithms, because they were so much cleaner than people.

Another hour passed before we'd driven our way clear of New Orleans and its human ugliness. After that we cut through a corner of Louisiana and then we were into Texas. Flat, hot and endless. We avoided the big towns by unspoken consent, which meant, most of the time, all we had for company were cattle.

We'd taken it in turns trying to sleep but there was no rest in it. We were all pale and drawn. Our fingers tapped restlessly on our guns and I knew that if we didn't get some sleep soon we'd regret it.

After Texas we were into the corn fields of Oklahoma and finally we knew we had to stop. It was absurd really, caring about state boundaries in a world where they'd become meaningless. Except that when we crossed over that border something did seem to change. We drove through small towns and the people in them didn't run away from us. Some of them even stopped and smiled. The fields were tended and the people looked well-fed. There was a tightness around their eyes that spoke of a fear that never really went away, but that was hardly surprising.

"It's like we've driven into Stepford," Haru said the second time a crowd of children waved and laughed as we drove past.

"We should stop," I said.

"Why?" Haru said. "So they can take us away and replace us with identical robots?"

But Kelis was already slowing the jeep down on the outskirts of a bland, cookie-cutter town. Lower-middle class; no white picket fences but lots of square, clapboard houses with square, grassy yards around them. It wasn't a big place – I doubted the population was a thousand, even before the Cull. Now there was an air of neglect about the whole town. The grass was knee-high and choked with weeds. Children's swing sets rusted in the middle of unkempt lawns and unused cars rusted in the roads.

"We need to get some sleep," I said. "There's bound to be empty houses here and if we post a guard we can see trouble coming long before it reaches us." You could see anything coming here, across the endless expanse of the corn fields. In the distance I could make out the grey twist of a dust devil, sweeping across the great, empty landscape.

"Yeah, and what if the trouble's already here?" Haru asked. He nodded to the left, where a group of ten or more adults was sauntering towards us. There were no weapons on display, nothing to indicate that they were a threat, but my hand drifted towards my gun all the same. I'd been out in the Culled world long enough now to know that trusting the goodwill of strangers got you nothing but an early grave.

I saw the same distrust mirrored in their eyes, but there was fear there too and that made me feel a little safer. If they were afraid of us, maybe we didn't need to be afraid of them.

"We tithe already," one of them said as soon as he was within earshot. He was a big, red-faced bear of a man, but his shoulders were hunched and his gaze slipped away from mine. He reminded me of the Alsatian our neighbour had kept when I was a child, the one we'd heard yelping in the night when he'd beaten it. He had the same whipped expression. All these people had it.

"We're not after a tithe," I told him. I pointedly moved my hand away from my side, palm out and open, then frowned at Kelis until she did the same. "We just want a bed for the night. And if you've got any food to spare we'll trade you some ammo for it."

"We don't need ammo," a small blonde woman said quickly. "We're not looking to fight."

"Well, that's good then," Haru said, "because neither are we."

There was a small, awkward silence after that.

"So..." I said eventually. "How about that house over there? Anyone object if we camp out in it for the night?"

Finally they seemed to decide that we really meant what we said. The slump left their shoulders and the smile came back to their faces. "How long you looking to stay for?" the bear man asked.

"Just one night," I told him. "And we really would appreciate any food you've got going spare. We'll happily do some work in return." Haru frowned at that but I stamped on his foot and he quickly schooled his expression. We could take whatever we wanted from these people – which was exactly why we weren't going to do it.

"A TITHE?" INGO said later, when they'd left us alone in the big, run-down house with enough bread and cheese to feed a small army, along with a bottle of old, and probably precious, wine. They'd refused payment for it and in the end I'd given up trying to make them take it. Maybe the knowledge that we weren't planning to stay was payment enough.

I swigged back the wine. "Back to feudalism, I guess," I said. "The peasants till the land and the lords take a portion in return for not taking it all." My mind felt scraped raw, tiredness and a delayed reaction to the tension of the last few days. Even speaking was an effort.

"Why not just take it all?" Haru asked. "You're talking gangs right, armed gangs, maybe out of the city? It's not like the people here would put up much of a fight against them."

"But then who would grow the crops?" Ingo said quietly. "It is my experience that soldiers prefer fighting to farming. But it will not just be crops that they take when they come. They will have their pleasure in any way they wish, with anyone they want. I have seen it before."

Kelis shrugs. "Yeah, well, it's the farmers' choice, isn't it? There's almost certainly more of them – all they need to do is get organised and get armed."

"You think we should do a Magnificent Seven, train them up?" Haru asked.

She shrugged and looked quickly at me and then away. I didn't think she was really angry with the people here, just with everyone who made the kind of choice that Soren had and ended up dying for it.

"Maybe on the way back," I said, but it was just a salve to my conscience. I knew we'd never be back here. Even before the Cull, the world had been full of injustice, and at least these people got to live and eat in relative peace. There were worse fates. I'd already seen them.

I lingered over the last drops of the wine, suddenly unwilling to go to bed. The house we were in was big enough for us to have taken a bedroom each. Mine must have been the youngest son's, decorated with pictures of rappers and American football stars. The living room was still fully furnished, covered in thick layers of dust but otherwise untouched since whatever had happened to its occupants had happened. The mantelpiece was lined with ornaments – a picture of the Virgin Mary made out of seashells, a terracotta replica of the Basilica, an ashtray so thick and crooked it could only have been one of the children's pottery projects.

How must it be, I wondered, for the townspeople to spend every day living beside the houses of the dead? At least I couldn't put a face to the ghosts here. These people had lost neighbours, family, friends. No wonder they took whatever dirty little compromise was offered to avoid the same fate.

My imagination began to get darker as the wine hit a system which hadn't experienced alcohol for a long time. It jarred with the anti-psychotics and my thoughts started to twist. "I'm going upstairs," I said, getting abruptly to my feet. "We should get an early start tomorrow. Haru, why don't you take first watch, wake me after two hours."

Haru nodded without looking up, still stuffing his face with the last of the bread and cheese. Kelis didn't respond at all, but her eyes followed me all the way up the stairs.

The room and the bed were both small. I almost didn't have the energy to get undressed, tempted just to collapse straight onto the dusty blue bedspread with its little pictures of stars and planets hidden beneath the grime. But no, I needed a good night's sleep. With grim determination I made my fingers undo each button on my blouse, then the zipper on my khaki trousers. There was a full length mirror on the door of the wardrobe and I looked at myself in it once I was entirely naked.

If anything, I was even thinner than when I'd first been taken from the base by Queen M, all the food I'd eaten burned off by nervous energy. There were fading bruises on my ribs, a cut on my arm, a bullet wound in my leg, darker bruises around my eyes and a neat row of teeth marks against the bridge of my nose. Still, looking in that mirror, I almost recognised the woman I'd once been, the one who'd loved him. But then I looked into my eyes and thought, no, that woman is gone.

I was still looking at myself when Kelis came through the door. Her eyes caught mine in the mirror, dark and haunted. I wondered if she thought about the girlfriend she'd left behind – if she ever judged herself so harshly by someone else's standards.

I didn't turn round as she walked towards me, not even when her arms circled my waist and pulled me back against her. Her t-shirt felt rough against my naked back as she bent to kiss my neck.

"He loved me," she said. "He knew I'd never love him. Even if I'd... I never would have."

"Love is like that," I whispered, the sound trailing off into a moan as her lips found the nape of my neck.

"Blind, you mean?" She finally let go, allowing me to turn around and face her as she tugged her t-shirt over her head in one quick motion. Her breasts were bare beneath it, small, high and firm.

"Hopeless," I said, leaning forward to take one of her tight brown nipples into my mouth. It felt less intimate than kissing her. Her skin was lighter than mine, and soft beneath my lips.

"Is it hopeless?" she asked, and I knew she wasn't talking about Soren.

"Yes," I said, moving my fingers to the fly of her shorts, pushing them hurriedly down. "I've only ever loved one man and I keep telling myself he's half a world away, but the truth is he's probably dead."

She stopped for a moment, then her hands reached out to cup my breasts, kneading the flesh and pinching the nipples hard enough to hurt. "You can always pretend he's watching us," she said and she almost carried off the light ironic tone. Almost.

I didn't, though. I only thought about her and me as we fell onto the narrow bed. I wanted this, I needed it, and the least I owed her was to admit that for this one night it was all about her. I wanted human warmth, the warmth of her thighs around mine, her hand on me – in me. I wanted to feel connected to something in this world, where death could come at any time.

Afterwards I thought she'd get up and leave. I thought I'd want her to, but I didn't. I didn't want this to be that impersonal. I was glad when she pulled me against her, spooning her longer body around mine. It had been so very long since I'd been with another person this way that I found that I was crying. She didn't say anything, and I felt the wet heat of her own tears trickling down my neck. I closed my eyes as we drifted into sleep, and I let myself pretend that our tears were for Soren, because someone's should have been.

Haru's warning cry didn't wake me, because the gun shots already had. The window exploded inward in a lethal shower of glass. Only the thick comforter saved us from being cut to shreds. Bullets continued to thunder through the darkness, but by then Kelis had snapped awake and rolled off the bed, dragging me with her.

Our guns were in the discarded heap of our clothing, tangled at the foot of the bed. Kelis pulled out her semi-automatic and ammo clips while I fumbled for my Magnum. We didn't bother with the clothes – there wasn't time, and it wasn't like a t-shirt was going to stop bullets. The bed was between the window and thr door, shading us from the gunfire for the time being. We belly-crawled across the floor, the carpet rough against our naked stomachs. Ironic, really, that this was what would leave us with rug burn.

The stairs were sheltered, the inner sanctum of the house. The part of me that wasn't a fighter, and had never wanted to be, told me to stay there, safe, and let the others fight this out. But I could still feel Kelis's hands on my back, my hips, and I couldn't let her be just another corpse I'd left behind.

Haru was cowering at the bottom of the stairs, flinching as splinters of wood flew past. His gun was in his hand but I knew that it was cold and unused. He didn't have any problem letting other people do his dying for him. He looked at my face first, and after a second his eyes drifted lower – then widened in shock.

"Where the hell did they come from?" I screamed at him. He stopped looking at my breasts and looked back around the stairwell.

"I don't know!" he shouted back. "But they knew we were here – they must have done. They would have come straight in if we hadn't locked the door."

I could guess what was going on: the people of the town reporting the newcomers to their lords, like the well behaved peasants they were. No doubt whoever was out there thought we were planning on moving in on their property – taking the tithe that was their due. If they knew we were just passing through, they'd probably leave us alone, but I didn't see myself going outside and trying to explain that to them.

"They've got us surrounded," Kelis said. To me the gunfire was just white noise, sourceless and ceaseless, but she sounded certain and I supposed she must be right. No point ambushing someone and leaving them an escape route.

"Then we break out," I said. "We fight back. With any luck, they've forgotten what that feels like." Ingo had slipped through the shadows to join us. His eyes registered no surprise at my nakedness. It was possible he hadn't even noticed. "You too," I said to Haru. "We've got a better chance the more guns we can point at them – two out front, two out back."

The air was heavy with the smell of brick dust and hot lead. The living room was at the front of the house and what I could see of it, around the edge of the stairwell, looked like a war zone. The seashell Mary and the terracotta Basilica were gone from the mantel. Just dust now, like their owners.

I didn't trust Haru to do as I told him, but Kelis took him by the scruff of his t-shirt and virtually threw him towards the front door. I could his wide, terrified eyes but I didn't wait to see any more because Ingo had my arm and we were both barrelling around the corner of the stairs, towards the kitchen.

Bullets lanced through the air around us. There were fewer of them now, but it only took one. Maybe they thought we were already dead, or maybe they were just running short of ammo. We'd soon find out.

I didn't give myself time to think before I ran out of the door, confident that Ingo would be right behind me. They must have thought we were dead because they had started to walk out of the cover of the derelict cars towards the house. They looked almost comically surprised to see me – a naked woman running towards them, gun spitting death.

They were far, far younger than I'd expected. The first one I killed was barely into his teens and not one was out of them. They dived to the ground as soon as the first of them fell, and I realised that they didn't know what they were doing, not even slightly.

I shot another in the gut and Ingo blew the heads off two more, fatty grey matter splattering the long grass. The four left were now holding their hands up and screaming at us to stop. Suddenly loud, the Voice said, *What are you going to do, take them to a prisoner of war camp? Leave them behind to come back and try again?* I shot one in the heart, then looked away as Ingo took the rest.

I tried to remind myself what Ingo had said, about the things people like this did to the people they ruled. I tried to imagine one of the young girls who'd laughed and waved as we entered the town, screaming as these boys gang-raped her. But it was no use, all I could think was how young they were and that young people were the only hope left after the Cull.

There was nothing I wanted to say to Ingo when we were done. I walked silently through the back door and up the stairs. The house was a ruin. I put on a fresh set of clothes, then begun to shove my few possessions back into my bag. Kelis came in as I was doing it, her face lightly dusted with blood. I couldn't look her in the eye and she didn't seem to mind. I didn't need to ask if she'd left any alive. It wouldn't even have crossed her mind.

"Amateurs," she said dismissively.

"Yeah, neighbourhood kids gone bad." I could see their brutal little history as if I'd witnessed it. Children freed of all constraints, suddenly the strongest and the most powerful where once they'd been the weakest. Every town has a Trenchcoat Mafia waiting to happen.

"Want to have a word with the good people of the town?" she asked, after a few seconds of silent scrutiny during which I resolutely kept my gaze fixed on the bag I was packing. "It must have been them who tipped the kids off."

"No," I said. "I think we've done enough already."

Ten minutes later we drove away, through a few hundred more miles of cornfields and past a few dozen more small towns. We didn't stop. The Interstate, bland and featureless, took us out of Oklahoma almost as fast as I wanted. For mile after mile we saw nothing but vast billboards advertising products no one could buy. Then we were back in Texas, a little northern jut of it, heading towards the desert of New Mexico, scrubby and dry and mercifully free of people. Las Vegas was in reach of one long drive and I didn't need to ask to discover that none of us had the stomach for more human interaction. We didn't want to stop again.

But fifty miles from Santa Fe we came to the first road block. On the straight desert road we could see it far ahead, slabs of concrete laid across the length of the road, with the crouched figures of men behind them. "Should we go off-road, drive round?" I asked Kelis.

She shrugged and I could see her preparing to twist the wheel, but Haru reached forward from his place on the back seat and put a hand on her arm. "We can't risk damaging the car," he said. "Not out here."

He was right. Wreck our ride and we might not find another one before we dropped dead of dehydration and heat exhaustion. Kelis nodded and pulled the car to a halt twenty metres from the pile of concrete.

There was a moment's stand-off as we crouched, guns at the ready, and the men behind the block did the same.

"Well, this is productive," I said eventually. My voice carried clearly in the still desert air.

"We've got food and water back here," a husky female voice shouted back. "We can wait all day. How about you?"

"We only want to pass through," Haru tried. "We're not looking for trouble."

"But we're quite capable of being trouble if we need to be," I added.

High overhead, vultures were circling. I guess they'd been having some good years.

"Pass through on the way to where?" the woman asked after a beat.

We glanced at each other but there didn't seem to be any reason to lie. "Las Vegas," I told her.

My finger tightened on the trigger at a sudden movement, but it was just the woman poking her head above the parapet. Even from fifty feet away I could see the black, surprised 'O' of her mouth. "Are you crazy?" she said.

We drove to Santa Fe in convoy, our vehicle bracketed by two of theirs, strange solar-powered contraptions which looked like they'd been designed by a lunatic trying to recreate the moon unit from memory. They didn't top twenty miles an hour so the journey took a while, but we didn't try to break away. We might have been able to outrun them before they shot us, but I gave it even money. And besides, they had something we wanted: information.

"We work for The Collector," the woman had said when we'd finally dismounted from the car and approached the barricade. She was African-American and about as wide as she was tall. I couldn't be sure that all of it wasn't muscle. She told us her name was Jeannine, but that her friends called her Jen.

"Yeah?" I said cautiously. "And what does he collect?"

"Oh," she said, "stuff." Then she squinted at us, heavy brows lowering over small eyes. She took in the red and black of Kelis's clothing, the military way she held herself. Her eyes skittered over me, then Haru and Ingo. "You're Queen M's, aren't you?"

I twitched in surprise and then it was too late to lie. I shrugged. "We were... guests of hers for a while."

"Yeah," Jeannine said, smiling. "We heard she misplaced quite a few of her guests last week. Don't worry – people are the last thing our boss is interested in. There are enough mouths to feed as it is."

"Yeah, okay," Haru said. "Then what's with the road blocks?"

She shrugged. "Human intel. The most valuable currency there is."

It took us three hours to reach the outskirts of the city, its pale adobe houses like an extension of the desert on which they sat. We were only a few metres past the sign welcoming us to the place when I saw it. I did a double-take, but at the second glance I knew I hadn't imagined it: Rodin's *Kiss*, sitting by the side of the road, a grubby patina of dirt over the white marble. Kelis had seen it too. Her hand reached out to grab mine in surprise, then just as quickly pulled back.

Jeannine, sitting beside me in the back of our jeep, laughed at my expression. "We got a couple of copies of that, so he left that one as a kind of greeting. You know – make love not war."

I looked at the AK-47 she had strapped to her back and didn't mention that she seemed prepared for either contingency.

We drove more slowly now, through the drab suburbs and into the picturesque heart of the city. The town was full of people, more than the survivors of the Cull could account for. The Collector must have been recruiting, whatever Jeannine said. They didn't stop to greet us but I knew that we were being assessed and that if we hadn't been with Jeannine and her crew we wouldn't have got very far. The place had the feel of a fortress: slabs of concrete sitting by the sides of roads where they could be dragged out to block them, and nests that probably held machine guns, maybe even AA guns. This wasn't a place anyone would want to take by force.

The drive through town took an hour and Jeannine seemed happy to act as tour guide, pointing out local landmarks as we passed. I guess she, at least, was a local. I tuned her out and concentrated on getting a read on the place, a sense of what went on here. The Voice had become a constant dull murmur in the last few days, clear enough to hear, and it was telling me to be careful. Warning me that the people here weren't my friends. I did my best to ignore it. Maybe there were no friends here, but I didn't get the sense that there were any enemies either. More like people from a parallel world, benignly indifferent to ours. We finally stopped, at a building that looked like a honeycomb, with a half-collapsed sign that told me it had once been a hotel.

"Heart of the collection," Jeannine told me. "You'll usually find him here."

The heat was searing, dry as my mouth, and I wondered why anyone would ever have chosen to live in a place like this. Then, when we stepped through the big lobby doors of the honeycomb building, the cold hit us like a bucket of ice-water in the face. I guessed the air-con was solar powered, but it seemed like a needless extravagance.

"*Madre de Dios!*" Kelis said. "Why not just move somewhere cooler?"

I smiled, but the expression slipped from my face when I saw what was in front of me.

"Holy hell," Haru said. "You've got the Elgin marbles in your hallway!"

They had all of them, by the look of it. The delicate friezes of gods, heroes and monsters that I had last seen six years ago in the British Museum.

I looked across at Jeannine and she grinned back, looking amazingly impish for such a vast woman. "Like I said, he collects stuff. And the cold is good – helps preserve them, the paintings especially."

"Don't tell me," I said. "You were an art historian in a previous life."

"Curator," she told me. "He's very particular about who he recruits. Want the tour?"

They'd pretty much gutted the British Museum. The dining room was filled, floor to ceiling, with totem poles, leering animal faces staring out at walls covered in African tribal masks, which glared blankly back at them. The bar was filled with mummies, standing around in conversational huddles. A giant stone scarab sat in the middle of it all, impassive.

"No Rosetta Stone?" I asked.

Jeannine shook her head. "He's interested in art, not history."

The paintings were in the guest rooms, carefully preserved behind glass. Hanging on walls above beds and dressers, where once there would have been cheap hotel art. I saw Caravaggio's *Supper at Emmaus*, Andy Warhol's *Marilyn Monroe* and Grant Wood's *American Gothic*. Haru brought out his sketchbook, the first time I'd seen it since Cuba, and drew neat little pencil sketches of the works we passed. I glanced at one and saw the subtle way he'd changed it: the Madonna's eyes just a little rounder, her mouth a little smaller, the baby in her arms with a wild look in its eyes, as if what made him more than human wasn't entirely safe.

The grounds of the hotel were filled with sculptures. I stopped for a long time in front of Epstein's vast, chunky statue of Jacob wrestling the angel. The dusty pink of the marble blended with the red-gold desert sand. It made me think, suddenly, of the voice in my head, my own struggle with it. But was the Voice Jacob or the angel? I used to be quite certain of the answer, but the louder the Voice got, the less sure I became.

"That's always been a favourite of mine, too." said a man so slender he was little more than bone. His skin and hair were as pale as each other, as if one had been entirely bleached by the sun while the other was always hidden from it.

"Well, I guess no one from Tate Britain will likely miss it too much."

He smiled, open and friendly. "No one's voiced any complaints so far."

THEY COOKED A meal for us out on one of the hotel's patios, a barbecue. The warmth of the flame was welcome in the abrupt chill of a desert night. He ate delicately, picking at the chicken wings and beef steaks with his fingers as if testing their consistency. We ate ravenously, tearing at the meat with our teeth like animals. He watched us with wry amusement.

"This is what you've been doing, ever since the Cull?" I asked him.

He nodded. "From the moment the Cull started, once we could see where it was all heading."

"But why all the way out here?" Kelis asked. "Why not just take over the Smithsonian, somewhere you've got a head start and don't have to transport a million tonnes of rock over ten-million fucking acres of desert?"

"Because it's all the way out here," he said. "We don't get many visitors, and that's just the way I like it. And because this is my home, and why the hell shouldn't Santa Fe be the new cultural capital of the world?"

"There's more though, isn't there?" Haru squinted at him under lowered brows. "Being far away isn't a guarantee of safety on its own."

I remembered the Irish farmers, out in their lonely hills, and knew that he was right. The Collector looked at him a long time, and beside me I felt Jeannine tense. But then he smiled again, a cadaverous grin in his wasted face. "You're a clever boy. Yes, you're right, there's more to being safe than enough sand between you and your enemies. Like the good ol' boys in our neighbouring state used to say, an armed society is a polite one."

"Machine gun nests, AA emplacements. I'd say manners around here must be pretty damn good," I said.

He laughed. "Oh, those things are just gravy. What keeps the scavengers away is the stuff that used to lie buried beneath the earth, not many miles from here."

"You are talking of nuclear weapons," Ingo said calmly.

I wanted to laugh, because that would have made it a joke, but it clearly wasn't. "You've got nukes?"

"Just the two," the Collector said demurely.

"Nukes are a weapon of deterrence, not a weapon of use," Ingo said. "Will anyone believe that you would detonate them, simply to protect this?"

"Oh yeah," he said, his tight smile bringing out the subtle networks of wrinkles around his eyes and mouth. I realised he was much older than I had originally thought. "They know I will."

"Really?" Kelis said. "You'd really nuke anyone who tried to take your collection?"

"It's not mine. It's ours – humanity's. The things I have here, these are the best of us. They're the only part of us left that's worth killing for."

I remembered all the people I'd killed and the reasons for it, and I thought that maybe he was right.

LATER, WHEN HE'D opened a bottle of cognac and we were lounging on cushions in a room whose walls were guarded by the Terracotta Army, he said, "I hear you want to go to Vegas?"

"Yeah," Kelis said. "That's the plan. Know anything about what's going on there?"

He shrugged. "More than you, probably. Less than I'd like."

"Did..." I hesitated, but really, if this man was in league with Ash, it was already too late. "Did anything change there, recently, maybe around six months ago?"

His eyes narrowed. "You know something about this new guy who's taken over there?"

"Yeah, we do," I said. "And I can tell you one thing, this is not someone you want as a neighbour. Have there been any... have you noticed anything odd about his followers? He does have followers, right? An army of them."

The Collector shrugged. "He's got people working for him, that's for sure. Beyond that, no one knows anything. Soon as he arrived he sealed Vegas up so tight it's a wonder air can get in there. He closed it and he fortified it, and if you think we've got a few guns lying around this place, you should see Sin City. Rumours are he's got as much ordinance in that place as a small country."

"Rumours?" Kelis said. "So no one knows for sure?"

"No," Jeannine said, "on account of the fact that no one we sent in there ever came out again."

CHAPTER EIGHT

THE NEXT DAY Jeannine took us to see the other collection, a warehouse full of army-issue small and not-so-small arms. Kelis smiled for the first time since Soren had died. "Yeah," she said, wandering through the aisles of weaponry, "this is more like it."

"He's still going to cream your asses," Jeannine said. "No amount of guns are going to change that."

"So why are you giving us any?" I asked.

She shrugged. "Because you might do some damage while he takes you down, and that's worth a small investment."

"Gee, thanks," I said dryly, but in truth I was grateful to the Collector. Without his help we would have stood no chance at all. He was giving us food, water for the long drive across the desert and a new vehicle to make it in. The truck was big and green and ugly as hell but it looked like it could get into an argument with a rhino and win. I'd seen tanks which were less heavily armoured. We loaded it with the guns, grenades and rockets Kelis had chosen, then gathered round to plan our attack.

The Collector had given us maps of Vegas, too. Haru spread one of them out on the hood of the truck, peering at the network of roads and houses fading into the emptiness of the desert. "It's a big place," Haru said. "Do you really think he fortified it all?"

I looked at the tangle of roads and tried to figure out where I'd have put the bulk of my forces. *Everywhere*, the Voice told me. *You will never defeat him; you can only join him.* I didn't want to believe it but I knew it was right, at least about one thing. "He won't have taken any chances," I said. "He'll have surveillance, like he did in Cuba, and he'll have his forces deployed so they can respond to any point of attack as quickly as possible."

"No weak spots?" Kelis said doubtfully.

"So then, stealth would be better." Ingo suggested.

"Maybe," I said. "But this is a city in the middle of a desert. Sneaking in unnoticed isn't really an option."

"Okay," Kelis said. "So what's the plan?"

I shrugged. "Try not to get killed too quickly."

Santa Fe receded into the distance behind us, lost in the dust. Far ahead and to our right, the plain gave way to hills and then mountains, the scattered remnants of the Rockies. Out here, it was easy to forget the Cull had ever happened. People had always shunned this barren land, ghost towns already lost in the sand long before the deaths started, places where the young no longer saw any reason to stay. It was impossible to say how old the corpses of the cars and lorries that littered the roadside were. Some looked like they came from the nineteen-fifties. They had probably been rusting down to zero for decades.

It's hard to grasp the endless vastness of America, its landscapes which just go on and on. We drove for two hours and the mountains didn't seem to get any nearer. Maybe I'd died during the gun battle in Oklahoma, or on the beach at Miami, even back at the base, and this was the afterlife I'd been condemned to, this endless journey. Punishment for taking that young soldier's life.

The scenery was hypnotic in its monotony. I'd chosen to drive, glad of anything that used up cognitive space and stopped me thinking about anything else, like how the hell I thought I was going to face up to Ash. Or whether, when it came to it, I'd even want to. I was down to two doses of anti-psychotics now. In two days time, if I didn't find more, I'd *be* Ash.

At first the dust cloud was just a distraction at the edge of my vision. A micro-storm, I thought, a dust devil weaving a solitary path across the desert. Except, no natural storm ever kept going in a line that straight. A line that ran entirely parallel to ours, and had done for at least fifteen miles now.

Kelis saw what I was looking at and nodded. "Convoy," she said. "Off-road vehicles out in the desert."

She was right. I could see the glint of metal and something brighter in the heart of the dust cloud now. Another minute and I could make out the individual vehicles, bigger than cars or even trucks. Winnebagos maybe, sturdy enough to travel over sand and rock.

"They're heading towards us," Haru said.

Ingo nodded. "Our paths will converge in approximately ten minutes." Despite the cold jolt of alarm in my stomach I smiled. There was something reassuring about his inability to react in a normal human way to anything.

"Stop and fortify or try to outrun them?" Kelis asked.

My hands tightened on the wheel. "How do we know they're hostile?"

"How do we know they're not?"

We opted to stop, in the end. There was no telling what the maximum speed was on their vehicles. And even if we could outrun them, did we really want to be heading into Vegas with another batch of enemies on our tail?

The desert was eerily silent when we switched off our engine. The air shivered with heat, foxing my eyes as I strained into the distance, trying to see if our shadows were turning to face us or continuing on their original course.

"Why did I ever leave Japan?" Haru said suddenly. "I'm so tired of this. I thought danger would be exciting. Isn't that what the stories tell you? But all it does is wear you down."

"You're welcome to leave," Kelis said. She hooked a thumb back over her shoulder. "Santa Fe's three hundred miles in that direction."

Haru grimaced and looked away, but I knew just what he meant. I was tired too, of the constant fights, particularly the one going on inside me. Surrender seemed to be an increasingly attractive option. Just... giving up.

The convoy was definitely heading towards us. The dust cloud's shape had shifted, seeming to shorten as the vehicles turned and sped straight towards us. I could hear them now, the rattle of wheels over rocks, the grind of motors – and something else. After a few moments I realised that it was music. The deep bass beat of it seemed to resonate through the rocks beneath us and up into our bodies.

The closer they came, the odder the convoy looked. I could see now what the bright flash I'd seen earlier had been – solar panels on the roof of each of the dozen or so vehicles, iridescent and delicate as butterfly wings. The vehicles themselves seemed to be buses. But they were definitely home-made, because no factory could possibly turn out machines that crazy-looking; sides meeting at every angle except ninety degrees, paint covering every inch of them, and each inch a different colour.

The first of them swerved to a halt a hundred yards ahead of us, and I saw that there was a big yellow smiley face painted on its side, grinning out at us from beneath a painting of a dove. I felt the barrel of my gun slowly drooping from horizontal to vertical.

Kelis frowned at me. “Could be trying to lull us into a false sense of security.”

“It’s working,” I told her. Up close, I’d finally recognised the music: it was *Hello* by the Beloved. Either there was some very complex psychological warfare going on, or these people were no sort of threat.

Five of them came out of the first bus as the others begun to pull up behind it. They were all young, twenties to thirties, and the kind of dishevelled that took some effort to achieve. I stared at them, disbelieving, because I thought that kind of studied cool had disappeared from the world along with ninety-three per cent of its population. None of them was armed, which meant either that there were more people hidden behind the mirrored windows of the bus pointing something lethal at us, or they were suicidally stupid. Looking at their dazed, slightly vacant faces, I was going to opt for the latter.

“Hey,” the leader said, a tanned, sandy-haired boy who wouldn’t have looked out of place on a surfboard.

“Hello,” I said cautiously. My hand was still on my gun and so was Kelis’s, but he didn’t seem to mind.

“We’re not looking for a fight,” another of them said. She was tall and stringy with features that were okay individually but didn’t quite match up on her face.

“Us neither,” I said. “On the other hand, we weren’t following you, so I think we’ve got less explaining to do.”

Surfer boy laughed and so did the others, and for the first time I realised why they were so relaxed: they were stoned. I holstered my gun.

“Who are you people?” Haru said.

“We’re the party at the end of the world,” surfer boy said. “Want to have some fun?”

“You know what,” I said, “I think I’ve already had about as much fun as I can handle.”

He shrugged. “Also, we’re going to Vegas, and the Collector thought you might be looking for an escort.”

“So, IS LAS Vegas a big party town these days?” I asked later, when we’d driven in convoy with the party people until a few hours past sunset. We all stuck to the road this time, finally leaving it to park up on a camping spot they told us they’d used before.

There were stockpiles of wood here, twisted and bleached like bones, and they'd lit fires, several smaller cooking fires and one huge central bonfire whose heat radiated out into the night, chasing away the creeping cold. The flames were bright, although above us the stars seemed brighter, a perfect spread of them across the sky, pin-sharp. There wasn't a flicker of light pollution from horizon to horizon, probably not even back before the Cull.

Mike, the surfer-boy leader of the group, shrugged. "Everyone needs to relax now and again."

"You've been to Vegas?" I pressed. "Recently?"

A young black-haired Goth, who'd twined herself around his arm the moment he sat down, laughed. "Yeah, but wherever we go there's a party – that's, like, the point."

I looked across the cooking fire to Haru, clutching a metal bowl of soup between his hands. He rolled his eyes. These guys were worse than useless as a source of information, but if they could slip us into Vegas under the radar they'd be worth their weight in gold.

There were a lot of them, more than I'd realised; at least a hundred. They were sitting around their own small cooking fires in huddles of three or four. The flames of the central bonfire shot thirty, forty feet into the air, advertising our presence to anyone with their eyes open – but they didn't seem to care. They seemed supremely confident that nothing in the world would hurt them. Could be the drugs – could be something else. And if we were hooking up with these people I wanted to know for sure.

When the meal was done I turned to Mike and asked as casually as possible if it would be okay to take a look at the buses. "We're running low on fuel ourselves – solar power's got to be the way forward."

"Sure," he said, waving a lazy arm towards the distant, misshapen silhouettes of the vehicles. "Just be back in time for the burning – it's kind of a bonding ritual." His other hand was in the young Goth's hair, gently running the strands through his fingers, and I noticed for the first time that she was pregnant. Only a few months gone, the little creature inside her was adding just a slight roundness to her belly. For a second I couldn't take my eyes off them: the tenderness of his gesture, the blind hopefulness of bringing another life into this world. With an effort, I blinked and looked away.

Kelis was out on the periphery of the group, a darker blot against the night sky. I didn't like sitting with the vast emptiness of the desert behind me, but I knew she'd rather have that at her back than these strangers. When she saw me heading for the buses, she drifted to her feet and joined me. A moment later and Ingo was with us too, silent and thoughtful. Haru looked up and then back at his sketch, a delicate line drawing of the Goth girl that hinted at the body beneath her baggy black clothes. He kept the page carefully tipped up towards him, so Mike wouldn't see it. I shrugged and turned back to the others as we mounted the steps to the first of the buses.

"Are these guys for real?" Kelis asked.

I looked back at them, lounging contentedly around their small camp fires. "They didn't seem too bothered about us poking around. They haven't searched us, or asked for our weapons."

"Or asked us who we are or why we're going to Vegas," Kelis said. "Don't you think that's odd?"

I shrugged. "With anyone else, yeah. With these guys..."

And then we were inside the bus and I felt a sick lurch in my stomach. It was a lab, low-tech but unmistakeable. Fuck! Why the hell did I still trust anyone? I backed away, gun out of its holster, ready to make a run if it wasn't already too late. I looked to Kelis, expecting her usual hair-trigger reaction to threat, but she was still looking at the lab. Looking and laughing.

I relaxed, just a little, although my heartbeat was still pulsing in my ears. "There's something I'm not getting here, right?"

Kelis took in my expression, my hand clawed around the handle of the Magnum. "It's okay, its fine," she said, hand gently resting against mine, prying my fingers loose. Her tone was almost crooning, the voice you used with a hysteric. I must have seemed close to the edge, teetering on it. I guess I was. The Voice was constant now, chipping away at my calm and sanity.

"This is not the same as Ashok's laboratory in Cuba," Ingo said. He had a beaker in his hand, squinting at its thick brown-yellow contents.

"It's a meth lab," Kelis said. "Primitive, but it doesn't take much. Look." She gestured at a side table, which I saw now was piled high with opened boxes of prescription cold medicine. The ephedrine, I suddenly remembered – extract it and you were halfway to having yourself a batch of crystal meth.

Finally, I laughed too. "Tweakers. Okay."

Not just tweakers, it turned out. The next bus had a lab set-up that looked a lot more complex, but by then I wasn't too worried. Beside, they'd left a convenient pile of their end-product on one table, little off-white pills with the rough imprint of a dove on them. Old school. "Ecstasy," I said.

Kelis was inspecting a heap of white powder. She took a small dab on her finger and licked it before I could stop her. "Speed too, I think. Or it could be ketamine." She grinned, suddenly. "Give me five minutes – if I start fighting, it's speed, if I just lie there staring at my fingers, it's K."

"You have not taken enough for either effect," Ingo said. Kelis's eyes met mine, amused. A second later we looked away, the momentary closeness between us a reminder of things we didn't want to think about.

The third bus was a living quarter, crowded bunk beds and a filthy bathroom. The walls were draped with tie-died fabric and bad art. It looked like a squat I'd lived in for a week back when I was a medical student.

"How do these people survive?" Kelis asked as we walked into the fourth bus. "They're sitting targets." Here was something I'd seen in the squat, too: growing tanks, heat lamps, and a profusion of green. The unmistakeable harsh greasy smell of dope.

"Like the farmers," I said. "They've got the expertise to make this stuff, why would anyone want to interfere with that? And my guess is they give it away for free."

"We do," Mike said, a dark shape in the doorway of the bus. "We don't have the tech to make anything high-grade, but it's good enough to get rolling."

"It's a fair trade, drugs for food and safe passage."

He smiled, lopsided. "But the drugs are just a means to an end. It's the party we're about – the good time."

"Yes," Ingo said, "because a party is precisely what people need in this world."

Mike shook his head, taking Ingo's flat tone for sarcasm. But I knew that Ingo didn't do irony, and I thought that he was probably right. Mike and his people offered an escape, and that was more valuable than any pill, powder or plant.

LATER, THEY HAD a party for us. I hadn't intended to join in, but when they dragged out the effigy, a huge figure of wood and paper that must have been hidden away somewhere behind the buses, I decided that I'd stay to watch that, at least. I was flooded with childhood memories of Guy Fawkes Night, innocent memories too painful to look at and too precious to ignore.

It took twenty of them to carry the figure to the fire. They used a pulley to lever it upright and for a moment it teetered, a stain on the starscape, before it tipped over and burnt. As the flames licked up the wooden struts of its legs, turning them to ash, I felt other more unwelcome memories. The people of Cuba, burnt to death for a deal they'd made years before, whose terms they probably hadn't understood.

I turned away, sickened, to find Mike behind me, holding out a tray of pills. The doves mocked me, symbols of a peace none of us would know again. But I wanted to. Suddenly, I really wanted to. So I took one and put it in my mouth, quickly swallowing away the bitter chemical taste of it. I could feel Kelis's eyes burning into me, but I wouldn't meet them.

Half an hour later, the drug began to kick in, first a rush that was almost a panic, then the panic transforming into an energy that was also the most profound relaxation I'd ever felt. There was music playing somewhere, a haunting melody and a heavy beat. I let my body move to it, effortlessly.

Off to one side, I could see Haru with a joint hanging from his mouth, his eyes narrow and bloodshot but content. I smiled at him and he smiled back. I knew what I really thought of him, his cowardice and his moral vacuum, but for just that moment I didn't care. The love I felt was big enough to include him, to include everyone. To my new eyes everyone looked like an echo of the Goth girl, a young life curling and growing inside them, pregnant with hope.

I joined a circle of people dancing around the bonfire. My hand was taken by a thin brown one on one side, a blunt white one on the other. The family of Man, I thought, and laughed.

The hours stretched and warped and the night lasted both forever and no time at all. I took another pill, and then some of the powder which made me feel higher, or clearer, or happier; by then I could barely tell. The high couldn't last though – it was fighting against too much. The melancholy was lurking just underneath it. A moment's inattention and it crept back in and grabbed me.

I walked away, out from the others into the wide desert around us. Someone called out to me, but I ignored them and they didn't follow. The joy the drugs brought felt like a joining, but there was a profound selfishness at the heart of it, an attention only to one's own pleasure. I walked until the fire was a distant blur of orange and the stars were the brightest thing in the night. I could just walk forever, I thought. Ash needed to be stopped, but it didn't have to be me. For one moment I let myself entertain the fantasy. Going back, across the continent and then the ocean. Finding *him* and pretending that I was still the person he loved. He'd never know all the things I'd done, and I'd never have to tell him.

He's long dead, the Voice told me, *and you can't go back to being who you were. It's too late*. I sighed and took one last look around me at the stark solitude of the desert, then walked back to the light and the people.

WHEN I WOKE up the next morning I felt the lingering remnants of the drugs, a quiet echo of the absolute contentment I'd felt last night. Kelis wordlessly brought me a mug of coffee. I didn't know where she'd spent the night. She hadn't been in the truck when I'd returned to sleep there, curling myself in the back seat.

"Vegas in five hours," she told me. There was an edge of accusation in her tone – *do you really think that was the best time to get wrecked?* – but she didn't voice it.

The desert looked bleaker in the early morning light, or maybe that was the beginning of the come-down I was due any time now. I sighed and started the engine.

THREE HOURS OF driving later we hit the Colorado river, wide and powerful down here in the plains. We drove along its high banks for ten miles and then, suddenly, there was the concrete sweep of the Hoover dam, so vast you almost couldn't believe that it was man-made. I wondered how long it would be before we were ready to make anything that astonishing again.

The tarmac in the road over the bridge was crazed and broken, causing the convoy to slow almost to a stop. I felt a crawling sense of unease as we crossed, the sense that we were being watched.

"Cameras," Kelis said, pointing. She was right. There were two of them, high on the struts at each end of the dam, swivelling sleekly to follow us as we passed. I had the sudden, suffocating certainty that we were back in Ash's kingdom. I was sure the broken road surface was his doing, a way of slowing everyone down to let him examine them and decide whether to let them in. There were blocky buildings at each end of the bridge which I thought had once housed museums and tourist shops. Now they would be filled with his people, ready to push undesirables off the narrow road and far, far down to the waters below.

I turned my face away, keeping it as much in shadow as I could. My fingers itched to be holding a weapon, although I was sure that was just the sort of thing the invisible observers would be watching for.

The minutes seem to pass agonisingly slowly as the convoy inched its way over the bridge. My head began to throb with the tension. Even Ingo seemed uneasy, the dark skin on his round face looking stretched and old.

"Come on, come one," Haru muttered. He was rocking backwards and forwards in his seat, little jerky motions that I don't think he knew he was making. Ingo reached out a hand and pressed him back firmly into his seat. Trying to calm him.

But no one stopped us, and fifteen minutes later we were driving past the last buildings and away from the bridge. Haru let out a gasp of relief that was almost a sob and we drove on, an ugly green minnow in a school of gaudy angel fish.

There were five more checkpoints in the next sixty miles and they waved us through each one. As we passed I saw people lean out of the windows of the buses, throwing little parcels to the guardsmen, the price of passage. I looked at them out of the corner of my eye, trying not to let them know that I was watching. There was nothing about them that resembled the Infected in Cuba: just bored-looking men in khakis, smoking cigarettes and now the joints that the party people had thrown them.

"They look okay," Kelis said. "Like regular people."

"Yeah," I said. "And so do I. The Infected only look the way they do because Ash got it wrong. Maybe he's perfected it."

Haru scowled. "A city of lunatics."

"Or worse," I said, and we carried on driving in silence.

Finally we could see Vegas ahead of us, a dark stain on the sand that slowly resolved itself into a network of roads and then into trees, cars, individual houses. There was a burst of gold at the centre of it, bright in the midday sun, and I realised that the lights of Glitter Gulch were still blazing. That was just like Ash, I thought. As much a showman as he was a scientist.

The city blended out into the desert and we were driving into the suburbs before I'd even realised. There was no obvious check-point, but I guessed that the unseen watchers were here too. Cameras were everywhere, and people too. Some of them stopped and stared as we passed, none of the zombie-like inattention of the Cubans here. The women were wearing floral dresses, the men jeans and t-shirts. Different faces, different bodies, yet alike in some way I couldn't quite identify. If I didn't know better they could have been clones, the same few individuals repeated over and over.

"Is it just me," Haru said, "or are all the women here pregnant?"

As soon as he said it, I realised that I'd noticed it from the start, but my conscious mind hadn't quite processed it.

"Yeah, they are," Kelis said. "That's... creepy."

"It's the only way to repopulate," Ingo said. I hoped that it was as simple as that, but I absolutely knew that it wasn't.

Deeper into the city, but not quite at its heart, the buses finally stopped and we dismounted. Kelis looked a question at me and I nodded. The party people had bought us safe passage so far and we had nothing to gain by ditching them yet. I looked around. There didn't seem to be anything special about the place we'd stopped: tract housing on one side, the concrete cubes of a hospital on the other.

My nerves had been humming with tension, rising in pitch the nearer we came to Ash. I could sense his presence everywhere, and in my head the Voice was telling me that I should go to him. "Any reason we've stopped here?" I asked Mike as casually as I could.

He smiled and pointed at the hospital. "Medical check-up. No one's allowed in without one." Justified paranoia in a post-Cull world, to check that newcomers weren't bringing new diseases with them – except I knew Ash, and I didn't believe this was the real reason. The rest of Mike's people had dismounted the buses as we spoke. As I tried to back away I realised that we were surrounded, ten of Mike's people around each of us, subtly isolating us. I reached for my gun but they were so close there was no room to draw it, and even if I could take some of them before they overpowered me, I couldn't take them all.

I tried to catch Kelis's eye, or Ingo's, but we'd been separated quite efficiently and now the party people were moving towards the hospital entrance, pressing us along with them. "What's this about?" I asked Mike, trying to swim uselessly against the tide of people carrying me forward.

"It's just routine," he said. He was still smiling but the smile looked frozen now. Fake.

Helplessly, I was pushed through the hospital doors. I drew my gun finally, however useless it might be, because I knew this was where the storm I'd been waiting for was going to break.

A hand grabbed my arm and the gun was taken from me before I could even think of using it. I looked around but the woman had already backed away from me. She was big, armed and unsmiling. She was also pregnant. I heard a cry of pain to my left and saw Kelis drop to her knees. She'd been disarmed too. There were twenty or more women waiting in the room, all armed and all of them pregnant. As soon as they had our weapons they stepped in front of the doors behind us, blocking our escape.

I looked at Mike, leaning relaxed against one wall. "You didn't get any message from the Collector," I said. "It was Ash who sent you to pick us up."

He smiled and shrugged, as if none of it really mattered. "It's okay. They won't hurt you if you co-operate."

There were doctors in the room, men in white coats with friendly reassuring faces, and it almost could have been just a routine physical. Except I remembered Paris and there was something about the set-up here, about the way they herded the women to the right and men to the left, that sent a spike of unease through my nerves.

"It's okay," said one of the girls, the young Goth with the black hair. "They'll do the men first. And you're not... you know... are you?"

"I'm not what?" I asked, my voice a dry rasp. And then, before she could answer, a horrible suspicion began to form. "I'm not pregnant?"

"Right," she said and I tried to back away but there was nowhere to go and about twenty guns pointed right at me. I didn't think they'd hesitate to shoot through the girl to get at me.

"You'll need to strip," the doctor said to the men. Exactly like Paris, I thought, as the men from the buses stripped while Ingo and Haru watched, motionless. It was almost comedic, the sight of all that tanned, naked flesh and the two clothed figures in the middle of it, upright and tense. I was so focussed on Ingo and Haru that it took me a moment to work out what was wrong. It was only when Mike turned his dazed, not-all-there smile on me that I saw it.

Mike's stomach was flat, abs perfectly sculpted, a thin line of hair leading down from the middle of his belly to... nothing. There was nothing there, not even a stump, nothing left of his genitals but a white scar. I felt a rush of bile to the back of my throat and pressed a hand against my mouth to hold it in.

I looked past Mike at the other men. All of them were the same. Some of the scars were angry and red, recent. Some were clumsier than others, the mark of a more amateur surgeon. But every one of them was a eunuch. Worse than eunuchs – geldings. No longer men in the way that really mattered.

I saw Haru's face, frozen with horror, as he took it in. Beside him Ingo was utterly impassive. Mike turned his smile on them both. "It's really all right," he told them. "They'll give you an anaesthetic, you won't feel anything. And you can take hormones, if you want them, to replace what's lost."

"To replace...?" Haru said, voice high and incredulous. And then his paralysis suddenly broke and he was running towards the entrance. The men reached out for him but their hands slid away as Haru's desperate flight carried him past. He was only ten feet from the door when they finally brought him to the ground, five of them piling themselves on top of him. I could hear Haru's ragged, half-sobbing breaths from beneath the pile of naked men. When they slowly let him up, arms locked behind him, he was crying.

Throughout it all, Ingo had remained entirely still. He might have used the distraction to make his own escape, but he didn't. When Haru was finally subdued, Ingo calmly shucked first his own loose green t-shirt, and then the khaki trousers he was wearing underneath. When he was entirely naked, he turned to face me.

I don't know why I was so shocked to see the same angry red scar on Ingo's groin, the same absence beneath. I should have worked it out long before.

"You were working for him all along," I said.

"Yes," said Ash. "He was."

CHAPTER NINE

They didn't blindfold me during the trip. Why would they? The whole town belonged to Ash. They drove me deeper into the city on one of the buses, wedged between two of Ash's female guards, semi-automatics held away from their pregnant bellies and pressed into my sides. Ash himself wasn't with us. He'd barely stayed a minute after he'd checked that it was really me, Ingo was still his and Haru wasn't going to be a threat.

The bus stopped at one end of the Strip. The road was pockmarked and badly maintained, but the neon signs still glowed bright against the blue-grey twilight sky. At one end, the model of a cowboy waved, twinkling at us. The volcano outside The Mirage exploded on cue and, far above us, I could see the roller coaster thundering around the Stratosphere Tower. Only the human beings were missing; the whole place was a model town, working but unpopulated.

They took me to the Luxor, a monstrous pyramid squatting in the heart of the Strip. Inside, plastic mummies stared impassively at Egyptian-themed fruit machines that no one was using – row after row of them, unlit and silent. We walked past roulette wheels, backgammon tables, long abandoned games of craps. My escorts and I were the only people inside and the silence was more sinister for its contrast with the bright tackiness of it all.

Dim, emergency lighting led us through the vast gambling floor. There were no windows and no clocks; this hadn't been a place where they wanted you to tell time – and I guess Ash didn't much care about it either. The lift took us right to the top, where the high rollers had once lived. He was waiting for me in the penthouse suite, leaning on the railing of a balcony that gave him a view over all of Vegas. This, I thought, was why he'd left the lights of the Strip burning, a crazy extravagance just to make him feel even more like a king.

"Come up in the world, I see," I said when he turned to face me.

He shrugged and smiled, looking so much like the friend I'd once known that it was painful. But I could see the light of madness shining in his dark eyes, and I knew that that was all the explanation I needed for what he'd done.

"You know," he said, "when Ingo told me you were alive, I couldn't believe it. I was sure you'd died in the explosion. If I'd known, I would have returned for you – I hope you realise that."

I looked away. A part of me remembered the five years of terrible solitude and wished that he had. "Don't beat yourself up about it."

He laughed at little, but there was something studied about it, as if normal human responses were something he now had to fake. "Still, you're here now, and that's what matters."

"Thanks to Ingo. Tell me, if you thought I was dead, how did he manage to find me?"

"He wasn't looking. Ingo's job was to watch Queen M, when we were no longer neighbours. I wanted to know what she made of my Cuban... subjects. You were just a very unexpected bonus. A coincidence, I suppose, though in time one of my agents was bound to have found you."

He leaned over the balcony, staring across his kingdom. After a second I joined him. Las Vegas was a spider's web of light in the darkness of the desert. "You sent the Infected against her deliberately," I said, seeing it all suddenly. "You wanted her scientists to investigate them, and then for Ingo to report back what they found."

He was still looking out over the city. It felt almost comfortable, a distant echo of the companionship we'd once enjoyed. I remembered with sudden clarity the one time he'd come on to me, after we'd been in the bunker three weeks and it was all starting to seem hopeless. He'd pushed me up against a bench in the lab at three in the morning and kissed me with a sort of desperation.

I'd pushed him away and tried to laugh it off.

He hadn't let me, though. "I know you've got a boyfriend somewhere," he'd said. "But you're never going to see him again. Can't I be the last man you ever fuck?"

I'd just shaken my head and gone back to work and he hadn't tried it again. I wondered if he remembered that too, or if the Voice took away all memories of failure, if you let it.

"Why would I want to do that?" he asked now.

I shrugged, not very interested in playing his games. "Because you needed all the help you could get. I'd thought – I don't know why, I guess I just assumed – that you'd taken the Cure with you when you left. But of course, you didn't plan the explosion, and what wasn't buried beneath it was trapped with me." I looked at him, a slight frown on his handsome dark-skinned face, and I knew that I was right. "You recreated it, I suppose, from its remnants in your own blood. But you got it wrong. The Infected of Cuba weren't at all what you intended, and you were hoping Queen M would be able to tell you why."

There was a long silence and I thought that he was angry. He must be unused to challenges to his authority, after all this time surrounded by his worshippers. "Yes," he said finally. "That's true. But here, at least, I've got it right."

"I don't believe you. If you had, why would you need me?"

"Who says I do?"

"Ingo, and the trouble you went to get me here. Tell me just one thing, Ash. Was this planned all along – the Cull and the Cure?"

For the first time, I saw just a flicker of uncertainty in his face. "I don't remember. I've let go of that part of my life. But Jasmine, I want you to be a part of the new life I'm making here."

"If you think I'm going to help you spread the Cure, you've forgotten who I am."

"I could never forget you. And I don't need your help – not in the way you think."

"I'm not giving you any help."

He shrugged, dismissing my objections. "The thing is, I spent all that time, wasted it, trying to recreate the Cure – when I should have realised all along that it was unnecessary. The Cure's already inside me, perfect. The answer isn't to spread it, I know that now."

"A little too late for the people of Cuba," I said bitterly.

"They wanted what I gave them – I didn't force it on them. And I wasn't the one who burnt them to death."

A helpless shudder passed through me at the memory. "You left me no choice, Ash. Better a quick death than rotting away, piece by piece."

"Did you ask them that?" He waved a hand to silence me before I could object. "It doesn't matter. I realised that if I wanted to spread the Cure, I didn't need to infect people with it. There's a simpler and older method than that." He turned to face me fully, arms crossed over his chest. The moon was only a sliver of light above us and his face was in darkness.

But I didn't need to read his expression to know what he meant. I looked over at the two silent guards standing just inside the doors to the balcony. I looked at the round swells of their stomachs, pulling the material of their t-shirts tight. "Children. No wonder you wanted all the men castrated. Will every single child born in this city be yours?"

He nodded. "The Cure was an extreme form of gene therapy, you know that. It changed us. It rewrote our DNA and turned it into something more... eloquent."

"And that change will be passed along to your children," I said flatly, forcing the words out past the sudden nausea.

"Like all genes, the Cure only cares about reproducing itself. Given the biological raw materials, it can build the meat machines to carry itself, to propagate itself further."

"And they say romance is dead."

He didn't even smile. "Procreation has nothing to do with love. It's more basic than that, the replication of something older and greater than us. Genes are immortal, you know that. They're the only part of us we can truly send into the future."

"Well, I can certainly see the appeal of this little arrangement for you. What I'm finding harder to grasp is why anyone else would agree to it."

He spread his arms, a theatrical gesture playing to an audience of one. "They believe in me, Jasmine. When Jim Jones told his followers to drink poison and feed it to their children, they did it gladly. Suicide bombers turned their own bodies into shrapnel, back in that wonderful world we all remember before the Cull. People will do anything if they only believe, and I'm asking them for so much less than that."

"No," I said, "not so many, not that." And then, clear and unpleasant, I saw the whole picture. "But if you gave them a watered down version of the poison you gave the people of Cuba – then they might agree. Tell me, Ash, just what is in those pills your travelling circus is handing out like sweets?"

He smiled, almost pleased that I'd understood. "Only a little something to make them more... open to suggestion. I learnt from my mistakes in Cuba. The latest version doesn't leave any lasting damage."

"I don't think Haru would agree with you." For a moment I let myself imagine him and the terrible thing that might already have been done to him, all because he'd been foolish enough to listen to me.

"Your companion?" He shrugged. "In time he'll come to understand. That's the other thing I've found. Take someone's freedom, mutilate and brutalise them, and if you offer them a way to keep their pride, to tell themselves that it was all for a purpose, they'll take it. Humans have always lived a delusional life. I'm just giving them a different dream." He paused a moment, and when he carried on his tone was more fervent, almost fevered. I could hear the Voice, resonating through every syllable. "An incomplete dream, until now. But with you..."

"I won't join you. I don't believe, and I never will."

He shook his head. "You misunderstand. I don't need your co-operation, not in the way you mean. Your value lies elsewhere – in the Cure you're also carrying. All these children I've fathered with my wives here are only half-breeds. But our children, Jasmine – they could be the first of a new race."

I shook my head, horrified. The friend I'd once known had taken my rejection and accepted it. This Ash, the servant of the crazy Voice that I knew all too well, would never take 'no' for an answer. I backed away, hands held out in front of me to push him away.

He lashed out, fast as a striking snake, and grasped my wrist. I tried to twist away, to break his grip but he was too strong for me. Stronger than any human should be. I didn't stop struggling, though; this was something I would never surrender to. The balcony was a hundred feet above the city. I could throw myself over it, maybe even take him with me. Anything, anything, to stop this happening.

Another step, and now I felt other arms pinning me.

"No," Ashok said. "No, Jasmine, I would never do that to you."

I looked him in the eye, but there was no human compassion there. For the first time I accepted that every last trace of my friend was gone. "Yes, you would."

"Then let me rephrase. I don't need to do that. I have something else entirely in mind." He nodded at the women behind me and they began to drag me towards the door of the suite. I dug my heels into the thick carpet, resisting with everything that was left in me, but it was futile. They had some of Ash's crazy strength about them. I wondered if it came from the warped new life growing deep inside them.

After five minutes, I gave up the struggle. All I was doing was wearing myself out. I needed to keep my strength for whatever came next – wherever they were taking me. I knew, of course I did, that resistance would be as futile then as it was now, but I needed to cling on to a fragment of hope.

THEY TOOK ME from the top of the casino down to the basement, a vast room that must have run the full length of the building. The light there was neon-bright and flat. I thought it might once have been the kitchen but the only remnants of its old use were the long silver tables which lined it from wall to wall. The meat which lay on them was still living, but unconscious. There must have been a hundred of them, maybe two hundred. All women, all attached to drips and heart monitors. All naked. None of them was older than thirty. The youngest might have been sixteen.

"They're brain dead," Ash said. "It was easier that way."

"Are these the people who wouldn't believe?" I asked, sickened. Was this what lay in store for me? My mind gone, just a body to lie here, for Ash to use as he wanted. A part of me thought that might not be such a terrible end, if it meant that I could finally rest.

There were more men here, doctors. One of them approached us now, a syringe in his hand. With my arms still pinned behind my back I was entirely powerless.

"I wouldn't force myself on you," Ash said. "That way we could only make one baby every nine months. Inside you, you have the seeds of far, far more than that. All I need to do is harvest them and plant them somewhere else."

I looked at him, then at the rows and rows of comatose women. They were nothing but bodies now – just fertile ground. "No, Ash," I said. "Don't do this." But I there was nothing I could say to stop him. He nodded to the doctor and the man reached out, hand almost gentle as he lifted my t-shirt up.

The needle hurt like hell as it went in.

"Just some hormones," Ash told me. "We need you to hyper-ovulate before we harvest. Ten or twenty times and we should have enough."

"You'll kill me if you do that."

"Maybe, but by then you'll have given me everything I need." Then he turned away, as if I was no longer of very much interest to him.

INGO WAS WAITING in the room they took me to, one of the suites on the upper floors, smaller than Ash's penthouse but still plush and a little gaudy. I tensed when I saw him there, wondering what task he was here to perform. He looked almost tentative, and there didn't seem to be anything worse he could do to me. The hormones were already racing through my system, flushing my face and speeding my heart. The Voice was louder too, more and more difficult to ignore. They'd taken my anti-psychotics along with my gun. Maybe I should be glad that by the time they tore the ova out of my body I'd probably be a willing victim.

The guard pushed me into the room and then it was just me and Ingo now. I thought briefly about trying to overpower him, but what was the point? I ignored him instead, moving to sit on the long sofa at one end of the room. I stared at the large blank screen of the television but it had nothing to tell me. Ingo didn't move, didn't say anything. Eventually I gave up and turned to look at him.

"Why?" I asked him. "Why would you let him do that to you?"

"Take away my manhood? Is that what you mean?" His eyes were wide, face as open and guileless as ever.

"Yes," I said, though I meant more than that. I'd liked Ingo. I wanted to believe that he'd once been a person who wouldn't let the things happen which happened here. Why had he let Ash change him into someone who would?

"The priests of Isis, in ancient Rome, would cut off their own genitals with a scythe in honour of their goddess," he told me.

"Ash isn't a god, Ingo. He isn't even really a man anymore."

"I do not worship him. Is that what you think? It is his ideas that have drawn me, right from the start."

"To make everyone in the world as crazy as he is? As master plans go, I'd say it's one of the more deranged."

"Yes, I know that you believe this. But this is because you grew up in the one small corner of the world where reason ruled. I have seen the look in Westerners' faces in this world after the Cull. They cannot believe that it has come to this – that mankind can behave in this way.

"Look in the face of an African and you will see that they cannot believe that humanity could ever behave in any other way. I told you about my country and I think you felt some pity, but there is a part of you which will never really understand. I was five when I saw my first murder. Seven when they raped my sister in front of me. My father they killed, a bayonet to the belly so that it would be slow. I worked in the mines for four years, my lungs full of rock dust. It is there, still, murdering me too. I will not live another ten years. I saw children kill each other for scraps of food.

"Someone once asked, 'Where was God at Auschwitz?' and the rabbi replied, 'Where was man?'

"Where was man in the Congo? The Cull was cleaner than what my people did to each other."

"I know I can't understand," I told him. "You've experienced terrible things – but why do you want to take a hand in more of them? Ash wants to replace humanity with the Cured. It's genocide. Worse than that – the destruction of an entire species. *Your* species. Why would you help him with that?"

His eyes burned into mine, the first emotion I'd ever seen in them, a fierce certainty. "Because I lived twenty years, and I saw nothing in humanity that was worth saving." He left before I could say anything else, locking the door behind him, and I didn't know what it was I would have said anyway. That humanity was worth saving? I wasn't sure I really believed that any more.

Except, damn it, I'd met individual humans who were. Kelis was worth saving, and she was somewhere in this town, or this hotel, having God knows what done to her.

I paced the room, twenty paces along one wall, thirty along another, weaving between the gaudy furniture. There was no balcony here. The windows were closed and locked, and when I swung my fist against the glass it bounced back harmlessly. I guess too many people came up here after a bad night at the tables and thought about ending it all – but dead people didn't pay bills. The only way out was through the door, and Ash's guards were outside.

On a sudden impulse I switched on the television, knowing that the signal had died long ago. The dead static flickered into the dark room and I felt another flickering, deep inside my head; the edge of madness coming to claim me. This time I knew there was no defence against it. My medicines had been taken when I was brought here. I couldn't even dull it with a good strong dose of opiates. The craving for them was the strongest of all, the urge to just stop caring.

Listen to me, the Voice said. *Listen to me!* I wanted to refuse it, but I had no choice.

I can help you, it said. *I'm the only thing that can.*

And I didn't know if it was because I was already halfway down the slope that led to the place where Ash was, but I believed it. Listening to the Voice had brought Ash here, to this position of power. Letting the Voice speak through him had brought him his army of believers. If I wanted to fight him, I had to become him.

Yes, the Voice said. *Yes. Let me lead you.*

Okay, I told it, with every ounce of strength left in my mind. But only on my terms. As cautiously as a bomb expert defusing a nuclear device, I took down the defences it had taken me five long years to build. I could feel the monumental weight of the madness, dark and unknowable, massing behind the barriers, but I wouldn't let it all through. Just enough. Only enough to do what needed to be done.

No! the Voice screamed at me, a deafening roar now that I had given it a clear path through to my mind. It pushed its weight against my mind and I could feel my sanity bending, bending... With an effort of will more intense than anything I had ever experienced, I pushed back. There was a moment when everything was in perfect balance, until, step by painful step, I beat the Voice back. I could feel the sweat dripping from my body, every muscle in me corded with strain. But I wouldn't lose, I couldn't lose. I took what I needed, the knowledge and conviction that the Voice gave me – and then I slammed the door in my mind shut behind it.

Finally, I opened myself to what I'd let through – knowing that there was a risk that I'd already surrendered too much.

The feeling was amazing, my mind clearer, more focussed, than it had ever been. I felt strength flowing through me, a tide of wellbeing stronger than any opiate rush. I felt absolutely certain that I knew what to do. A part of me questioned this new certainty, the dangerous lure of it, but I pushed that down too. I had to do this.

I banged on the door five times before the guard answered it. She was small and dark-skinned, with wide-set eyes. Her fingers were a little tentative on her gun as she turned it on me. "It's okay," I said, holding my hands carefully in front of me, "I'm not going to try anything." Although a part of me felt that if I did, I could take her on – I could take them all on.

"What do you want?" she asked after a moment. I looked in her eyes and read everything I needed there. These people weren't like the zombies of Cuba. They could listen to reason.

"I want to talk to you," I told her. "I've got something to say that you're going to want to hear." My voice resonated with my conviction. She would want to hear what I had to say.

"I'm not supposed to talk to you."

"Did Ash tell you that?"

She hesitated a moment before answering, and I knew that she hadn't received any orders directly from him. "No," she said eventually. "But you're to be kept locked up. You're a prisoner."

"And did Ash tell you why I'm a prisoner?"

She looked away.

"Seems like he doesn't tell you very much, does he?"

"He tells me enough." She set her mouth into a thin, determined line. I was only a few words away from being pushed back into the room and having the door locked on me.

"Did he tell you I'm Cured, too?"

She tried to hide it, but I saw the slight flutter of the pulse at her throat, the nearly imperceptible tightening of the muscle in her jaw.

"It's true," I told her. "I knew Ash years ago, back before the Cull. We studied together, worked together – and developed the Cure together. Then we tested it on ourselves."

"That... that can't be true," she said. "He told us he was the only one."

I nodded. "Yeah, that's what he thought. He thought I was dead and so he came here and set about breeding this race of half-Cured children. Like the one you're carrying inside you. How many months gone?"

"Five," she said, reluctantly. "Five months."

"Four more 'til he's born. That's pretty amazing – carrying one of the first of a new race." Her smile was cautious. "Although not really an entirely new race, I suppose. He'll be more of a half-breed, won't he?"

And the smile was entirely gone.

I ploughed on relentlessly. My voice was soft, persuasive. "All the children here, they're only half of what Ash wanted. You can guess why he wants me here, can't you? Maybe you've seen the women downstairs, the ones he's keeping in a coma. He doesn't need their minds – all he's interested in are their wombs. I think you know what he's planning to plant in them."

Her face told me that she did.

"Our children – mine and Ash's – now they'll be the real thing," I continued, relentlessly. "The first of a new race. The culmination of all Ash's work, ready to start creating his brave new world. I wonder what place your child will have in that world."

"Ash would never..." Her voice was too loud and I saw her make an effort to quiet it. "This is his son too, he'd never do anything to hurt him, or us. He loves us."

"Yes," I said. "Yes, he does. It's just that he loves me, and what I can give him, more."

"I could..." She swallowed. Her hand was shaking. The barrel of the gun she'd raised to point straight at my heart was shaking too. I could feel it brushing against my t-shirt. "I could make sure there are no full-breeds."

I should have felt afraid. The tightrope I was walking had no net beneath it. I'd locked my fear away along with the Voice, and that alone made the bargain worthwhile. Everything you used to be isn't that high a price to pay not to have to live in fear anymore. Queen M's press gangs, the zombies of Cuba, the new serfs of Oklahoma, the party people – they could all tell you that.

"He'd never forgive you," I told her. "And he'll know it was you. Who else could it be? But if you let me go he'll never find me – then you and your sisters can have him and his children all to yourselves."

"Why would you do that?"

"Because if I stayed they'd be his children, not mine. I'm nothing but a brood-mare to him. But I won't be subordinate to anyone, not even Ash."

She finally lowered the gun and stepped back. "He'll know this was me too. He'll punish me anyway."

I shook my head – then, before she could react, I swung my fist straight into her face, twisting my hips to put the full weight of my body into the blow. She crumpled with only a small whimper of pain.

I'd broken her jaw and my knuckles were bloody and torn from where they'd broken her teeth. Nothing in me cared. I pulled the gun from her slack fingers and walked away, down the long, quiet casino corridor. My footsteps were muffled by the red carpet, which was the exact same colour as her blood.

One objective achieved, my mind was straight onto the next: find and release Kelis and Haru. There wasn't any kind of warmth about the thought, just cold calculation. I knew I needed allies.

I looked around, but there were no cameras up here at the apex of the casino. Ash wanted to watch, not be watched, and in his arrogance it would never have occurred to him that anyone could challenge him at the pinnacle of his power.

I walked through the corridors, confident and certain, and nobody challenged me. I didn't know where I was going, but that didn't matter as long as it looked as if I did. I let my eyes drift casually over the women I passed, as if I had nothing to fear from them. Twice, I saw women who had been there when Mike's people had betrayed us to Ash. Before I had listened to the Voice I would have tensed and given myself away. Now I walked past them without a twitch and, even though one of them looked right at my face, they didn't see me. This confident woman, one of their own, was nothing like the frightened prisoner they'd dragged here only an hour ago.

People see exactly what they want to see. Six years ago I'd looked at a world where children were sold into slavery before they could talk, where girls were genitally mutilated so that they'd never have a reason to betray their future husbands, where millions died in famines that never had to happen, and I'd seen somewhere that was just fine.

It seemed likely that Ash would be using the casino's old control centre as his command base. The place where they'd once watched the gamblers and tried to see who was cheating and who was card-counting. The lift was silver and gold and mirrored, vulgar and loud. My eyes stared back at me as I travelled down. There were no questions in them now, just certainty. I barely recognised myself.

The ground floor was more crowded, but it was easy to slip unnoticed through the ranks of fruit machines, between the green baize of the game tables. I came to a service door marked 'staff only' and walked right through. I turned left, then right, then headed down a long, dingy stretch of corridor. And then I arrived.

The banks of screens stared back at me as I walked in, images of neon and night from all over the city. There were three men manning the monitors, scrawny types who might once have been accountants. They looked up at me with wide startled eyes, but I wasn't even looking at them, as if they didn't matter in the slightest. After a second I sensed them looking back down at their screens. Ash, then the women, then the men. That was the order of things here.

And there on a screen at the far right of the room was Kelis, pacing the confines of a small room in a tight, angry circle. "Where is that?" I asked one of the men.

He startled, then bent forward intently, as if to prove how seriously he was taking my question. "Room 597," he said. "She's waiting to be processed." I didn't have to ask what 'processed' meant. I'd seen its end product laid out on silver slabs, waiting for little pieces of me to be planted inside them.

* * *

Her room was in one of the poorer parts of the casino, where the tourists from Wisconsin, Ohio and Leeds would have stayed. There was only one guard outside her door but there was a camera eyeing me from the far end of the corridor. Once this started we'd have no time. They'd know and we'd be running. I paused a moment to calculate whether rescuing her was really worth it. Benefits, costs. A second more and I decided that the former outweighed the latter.

The woman struggled when I put my arm around her neck, arms and legs thrashing back at me. But her windpipe was crushed, her carotid artery blocked, and a second later she dropped to the floor unconscious. I didn't waste a bullet finishing her off.

Kelis must have heard something through the door. She was waiting for me, when I entered, launching a roundhouse kick at my head. At the last minute she saw who I was and tried to pull back, and I tried to duck, and her foot ended up grazing the edge of my ear and she ended up on her backside staring up at me.

"We have to go," I told her. "They know you're free." I threw her the semi-automatic I'd taken from the guard outside.

She caught it easily, then pushed herself to her feet with her usual catlike grace. Her eyes, brown and deep, stared into mine for a long second. Then she pulled me into a rough embrace, hard enough to squueze the breath out of me. "I thought you were dead," she said. Her voice sounded choked, as if there were tears in it, but when she released me a moment later her face was as mask-like as when I'd first met her.

But just for a second, when she'd held me in her arms, the Voice had separated itself from me, and I'd known that here was something I did care about. Then the first guard came for us and I thought that maybe I had to let that part of me go, because it would only get me killed. But without it I was dead anyway and I chose to keep on caring. The Voice shouted at me but it was safely locked away again, behind the barriers in my mind, where I could ignore it.

The guards weren't able to come at us *en masse*. They'd had no contingency plan for this escape and so they came one at a time and that's how we took them down. The first people to find us were men, running towards us down the long red corridor that led to the lifts, and them I shot easily. They'd let Ash cut away the most vital part of them. I didn't feel anything about their death.

At the end of the corridor we made it into the lifts, and headed down, with a few seconds to breathe before it started again.

"Where's Haru?" I asked Kelis.

She shrugged. "I don't now. They just took me."

"Back to that hospital, then," I said. The Voice told me to leave him, that it was too late anyway. It was almost certainly right, but I refused to listen.

Then we were out on the ground floor and here I knew that we'd be facing the women. I knew now that every single one had a new life inside her and that I'd be taking two lives each time I killed. A screaming, blonde-haired woman came at us from a side corridor and my shot went wild, taking her in the stomach when I meant to aim for the head. Kelis was already running on and I knew that I should too, but I looked at the blonde hair splashed with blood and the face beneath, mouth set in a rictus of agony. I knew that somewhere inside that body a little life was feeling the same pain.

It only took a few seconds to throw up everything that had been in my stomach, and then I was running after Kelis. Her own face was pale and I knew that even she couldn't be indifferent to the lives we were taking.

Still, we took plenty more as we fought our way to the back doors, then spilled out onto the neon-brightness of the Strip. There were announcements over the loudspeakers now, Ash's voice a horrible echo of Cuba. The blood was pounding too hard in my ears to hear what he was saying, but I was sure it was about us. More and more people were heading towards us, gunfire spitting sparks from the pavement, the neon cowboy waving down at it all.

There was a jeep right outside the casino, keys still in the ignition, maybe the one that had brought Kelis here. Too convenient? No, probably just arrogance again, the certainty that no one would oppose him here, right in the heart of things.

I took the wheel and gunned the engine hard enough that the wheels screeched and skidded, leaving a layer of rubber on the road before they got traction and took us away. Kelis straddled the seat to fire behind her. Her semi-automatic was close enough to my left ear that the sound was deafening. If I looked in the mirror I would have seen the people she was shooting at, but I didn't want to.

I concentrated on driving down the straight deserted roads. Every second I expected more cars, a fleet of them, the full force of Ash's army to range itself against us. It never came, which left me wondering whether it was all an elaborate trap, yet another layer to his scheme that I'd have to peel away.

Listen to me and I'll tell you, the Voice said. The temptation was stronger than the junkie draw of heroin, but I'd learnt to fight that in the last month, and I fought the Voice too.

I don't know how I found my way back to the hospital. I hadn't thought I was paying attention when I'd made the trip the other way, but fifteen minutes later we were there, the building looming big and blocky against the night sky ahead.

No cars had followed us. "What in hell's going on?" Kelis said. "Don't they care that they've just lost their prize prisoner?"

For some reason they didn't. One guard met us at the entrance to the hospital, a sixty-year-old man with the wide-eyed innocence of a baby. I shot him through the left eye and we ran inside.

The doctors in the hospital were unarmed. They watched us run past and didn't try to stop us. "Where is he?" I screamed at one of them, but they weren't going to help us either.

We banged open doors to operating theatres – empty – to private rooms and to wards where a few patients lay in beds with broken legs and who-knew-what other injuries. A maternity ward, eerie and empty in the darkness, waited for the flood of occupants who would soon come.

We didn't find him until we came to the recovery room, and by then I already knew that it was too late. The room was small, only fifteen feet square, with two beds and a window high up on one wall showing nothing but darkness. One bed was empty. Haru looked very small lying in the centre of the other, as if he'd shrunk since we last saw him. "Sweet baby Jesus," Kelis said. Her brown skin looked a little green.

There was a thin sheet resting over his legs and midriff, but when I pulled it back I could see the bandages swathing him from the middle of his thighs to just below his belly. They looked clean and fresh, just one small spot of blood in the centre of them.

Haru's eyes flickered open as I leant over him. The moment full consciousness returned, he started screaming. He was still screaming when Kelis threw me her gun and scooped him up in her arms, flinging him over her shoulder. The scream increased in pitch, a sound of pure agony now, but she ignored him. We were running for the stairs, bounding down them, passing the same expressionless doctors we'd seen on the way in.

My finger itched to pull the trigger on them for what they'd done to Haru. But they'd done it to themselves, too, and they weren't to blame.

No one tried to stop us leaving the building. They stood and watched us in silence, our panting breaths the only sound in the deserted wards and sterile white corridors. Then we were through the front doors and out. Kelis put Haru down on his feet to walk the few paces to the car.

He'd only taken one step, face crumpled with agony, when they came. There were a few faces I recognised, many I didn't, but I'd only spent a few weeks on the boat and Queen M must have called in every reserve she had for this. She was right in the forefront of them, hair still in the same braids, wearing the same pastiche of a pirate's outfit.

Haru's face twisted into an expression it took me a minute to recognise as pure hate. "You cunt!" he screamed. "You're too late – look what they've done to me!"

Because of course Haru was *her* man. Of course he'd been hers all along. I remembered with sudden clarity, the way he'd removed his watch before letting Ingo pass the current through him that killed the tracker. A spare chip hidden in the workings of the timepiece, where none of us would ever have thought to look for it. It was the final betrayal which made everything else make sense.

I think I would have killed him then, except letting him live now seemed that much crueller. And anyway, someone I hated far more was standing just a few feet in front of him, smiling that infuriatingly patronising smile of hers.

CHAPTER TEN

There was a moment when I was facing Queen M across the tarmac, only ten feet between us, and it would have taken less than a second to kill her. Then the moment passed and her gun, and the guns of all her men, were pointed right at me. As soon as I drew mine I'd be dead, but I was going to do it anyway. I was furious, a red mist behind every thought, but I wasn't sure if I was angrier with her or myself. "I've been a fool," I said.

She smiled. "A useful one."

Kelis stood beside me, the muscles in her arms knotted with tension, a fierce, unforgiving hatred on her face. I thought she was remembering Soren's death and here, finally, was someone she could blame. "Why?" she asked, her voice tight with fury.

"She knew about my connection to Ash," I told her, but my eyes stayed on the other woman, watching for the slightest signal that the dying was about to begin. "That's why she came to the bunker. And that's why she let me go. She was hoping I'd lead her to him, the only person who was challenging her power in her little corner of the world. Someone whose slaves were even more obedient than hers."

"And here you are," Queen M said. "Doing exactly as I intended. Who'd have thought that someone so crazy could be so... predictable?"

"And here he is," Kelis said. "Did you predict that?"

But she must have, because the moment Ash's people came, the shooting began. Ash had sent everything he had: ground troops, jeeps and three helicopters, hovering over the battle like angry hornets. The noise was deafening. I took one second to think that, of course, this explained why Ash's people hadn't followed me and Kelis. They'd had bigger things to worry about.

Then it was all about surviving. I dived to the left. A moment later I felt Kelis's body land on mine, winding me. A rib might have cracked, the sharp pain like a knife in my side. I felt a stab of anger along with the physical pain. Then some other strong feeling I couldn't identify as I realised that she was shielding me with her body. Shards of concrete spat at us and fragments of metal that took lumps of skin with them. I knew we'd die if we stayed there.

It should have been a massacre. This was Ash's town and he held all the cards. Except every soldier he'd sent here was a man – his weakest force. He didn't want to risk the women, I realised, not now he thought these might be the only children he had.

Machine guns blazed from the sides of the helicopters, cutting through the ranks of Queen M's soldiers. I saw a spray of bullets catch one woman in the centre of her chest, just below her breasts. Her legs folded, her mouth still screaming in fear and pain even as her eyes glazed over. Then another of Queen M's people lifted a rocket launcher to his shoulder and that was the end of the helicopter; a molten mess of metal, shrapnel and, somewhere in there, scraps of flesh and shards of bone. I'd lost track of Queen M long ago, but I knew where she'd be, somewhere at the back of it all. Like Ash, she was happy to let other people do the dying for her.

Kelis's body was still a dead weight on top of me. I felt her shudder as something hit her. "Are you okay?" I asked.

She levered herself off me and I knew she couldn't be too badly hurt. "We've got to get out of here!" I shouted. She nodded, kneeling above me. I drew myself up to my knees too and tried to see any way clear of it all.

"Back through the hospital," Kelis said. She was right. Some of Queen M's men had taken shelter there, but the odds were still better than for any other route out. She leapt to her feet and I followed, shooting behind as she shot ahead, a move so fluent it was almost rehearsed.

I don't know if I hit anyone. People were dropping all around, the bullets were coming from everywhere. These were deaths I didn't have to own. Ten paces and we were at the hospital door. Kelis shot the two men before I could even train my gun, neat holes in the centre of their chests.

Then we were past them and into the lobby, and there was Haru, on his hands and knees, dragging himself away from the battle an inch at a time. A dark trail of blood flowed behind him and I could see that the bandage had come loose from around his waist. Thick black thread held shut the void at his centre – a horrible, ironic echo of the pubic hair which had once been there. His head swung around to watch as we approached him, looking like it was too heavy on his neck.

"That boy whose photo you showed me," I said. "Was he even really your son?"

"Yeah." His voice was a rough rasp. His hair hung over his eyes, limp and damp, face whiter than I'd ever seen it. "I didn't lie to you about that."

"And he's really crippled?"

"Please," he said. "You have to help me. She'll kill me if she finds me. I'm no use to her now."

"Yeah, it's a real great lady you've chosen to give your loyalty to," Kelis said.

He laughed but it turned into a cough and then a pained scream. "You gave her your loyalty too, once. You're the traitor – I never changed."

"And your son?" I asked. "The one she made you leave behind."

"Fifteen years I took care of him," he said. His voice was fading, but he kept on inching forward. "When she took me away I woke up that first morning and I suddenly realised that I had no one to take care of. I didn't have to feed him, or listen to him, or wipe his arse. Why would I want to go back to him, when for the first time in my life I was free?" He coughed again and this time I could see the blood oozing out of him, a dark spurt that was more black than red, something he couldn't afford to lose.

I didn't look at his face as I pressed the gun against his temple and I closed my eyes when I pulled the trigger. Kindness? Anger? I don't know, but there was no question in my mind then that I had to kill him. Kelis watched me and not him as he died. Inside my head, I felt something click into place, but I wasn't quite sure what. I took a moment to look down at Haru's empty eyes, then we both stepped over his body, and walked out through the rear of the hospital, bloody footprints glistening darkly in the moonlight behind us.

"We have to find Ashok," I told Kelis, the sound of the fighting now a muted roar behind us. She nodded, although there was no real reason she should follow me. Or there was only one reason, and it wasn't one I wanted to acknowledge because it wouldn't be right to use her that way.

But that didn't mean I wasn't going to.

We walked two streets before we found a working vehicle. It was a big ugly SUV with two child seats in the back, absurdly suburban. Kelis drove this time, retracing our route, back to the centre of it all. Occasionally a vehicle would roar past, travelling in the opposite direction, reinforcements for the fight. At first I saw men sitting in them, rifles and revolvers clutched nervously in their laps. Then as we got nearer to the Luxor, the cars were filled with women, and I realised that Queen M must be winning, somewhere back behind us, because Ash was starting to risk his most precious resources.

Did I want Queen M to win? Maybe. There was no question she was the lesser of two evils. But I didn't think that Ash would stay to face the music if her forces got the upper hand. There was no doubt an escape route already planned, another city he could flee to and start this all over again. I had to find him first.

The further we drove, the more dream-like it became. I felt detached from it, from the bodies I saw lying in the street, outliers for a conflict whose main body of data lay behind us, out of sight. I wondered for a second why I was thinking in this clean, clinical way, but the thought and the worry drifted away into nothing, as insubstantial as the world around me. The lights of the Strip blazed into the night sky ahead of us, near now, and I knew I should have been feeling... something.

I don't need feelings now, they'll just get in the way, I told myself, but the voice I was speaking in didn't seem to be my own. For a brief, horrible moment, a spike of emotion broke through the calm. I knew, in that second, that I was losing something of myself, as crucial as the part of Haru he'd left behind on the operating table. As vital as the gore he'd coughed up onto the hospital floor in the moments before he'd died. I thought some people might have called it my soul, but I didn't believe in that kind of thing.

"Kelis," I said, and I could hear that my voice was raw with fear and desperation.

Her head snapped round to look at me, fearful and then puzzled as she saw that there was no immediate danger in sight. "What?" she asked.

"Kill me," I said, forcing the words out through a throat that tightened against them. "Kill me now before I turn into him."

Her eyes were wide and shocked. "What the hell are you talking about?"

"I'm..." I said. "I'm..." But the words wouldn't come out. Something stronger than my will was holding them inside me.

Inside my head, one part of me clawed at another, desperate for purchase, but the new certainty within me was smooth, hard and impregnable, and everything else just slipped quietly away. The panic went with it and I didn't remember any longer why I'd been fighting this so hard.

Never mind. It was over now.

I glanced sideways and saw that Kelis was staring at me, the worry plain on her normally calm face. I wondered what my expression had revealed, in those brief moments of struggle. "Are you okay?" she asked.

"Yeah," I told her. "I'm good. I'm better than I've ever been."

* * *

Ash's people were there, massed in front of the Luxor when we drew up in the SUV. The last line of defence. I smiled when I saw them, because they meant that Ash was still inside. Kelis raised her semi-automatic, hunting rifle by her side, but she was looking at me and I shook my head. The odds were hopeless and there was a better way.

"Tell Ash I'm back," I shouted at them. "He'll want you to let me in."

"What are you doing?" Kelis hissed at me. "Do you want him to know you're here?"

"He already knows," I told her. "And he'll let me in. He has to. I've got something he wants more than anything else in this city – anything else in the world."

I could see the doubt in her eyes. There was a moment of poised stillness. Kelis and her guns. The ranks of women in front of us, the new lives they carried. The new me, the Cured me, didn't care about that. Those half-breeds were meaningless and the bodies housing them expendable. But a fire fight could kill me too and that certainly wouldn't do. It was very important that I get in to see Ash, although I wasn't quite sure why. The Voice only let me know as much as I needed to, and that was fine. It was just fine. It was so much easier to let something else do the thinking. I didn't know why I'd resisted this for so long.

A ripple started in the crowd, and suddenly a path cleared through the centre of Ash's army. "Go in," one of them said. "He's waiting for you."

Kelis hesitated, but I didn't give her time to pull back. The women stared at me as I walked between them and I could read the distrust and fear in their faces. They knew what I meant for the children inside them, they'd figured it out, but no one wanted to be the one to make the first move. One spark was all it would take to set this situation on fire.

I walked with complete confidence. The only way to survive this was to show them no weakness. Hundreds of eyes glared at me as I passed. I felt the weight of their regard, but I didn't bend under it. And then I was through, Kelis just one step behind me, and we walked past the cheap plastic statues of the long-dead rulers of another land, and into the heart of the casino.

The lift doors opened directly into the penthouse, the metal grate clinking aside to admit us. He was waiting for us, ten paces away, silhouette framed by the moonlight outside the big picture windows. There were only two women with him; big, black and heavily armed. I laid my hand over Kelis's before she could reach for her gun. Brute force wasn't going to get us anywhere here.

"You came back," he said. "Changed your mind?"

I nodded. "My mind has changed, yes."

His eyes widened, then narrowed, as he understood the full meaning of what I'd said. "You surrendered at last?"

"Yes," the Voice said through my mouth, "she's mine now."

And I felt Kelis stiffen as she understood my meaning too.

"Why should I believe you?" he asked. He took a step back, the two women flanking him. I thought maybe that he did believe me, and that it was this which was alarming him. I was supposed to be his tool, not his rival. His mouth opened to give the order to kill us both.

Kelis spoke before he could. "Jasmine." Her voice was shaky, her eyes a little wild. I looked back at her, and whatever she saw must have triggered something in her; she snatched her arm away from me and stumbled back.

My attention seemed broader now, able to absorb every last detail of the situation in one glance. Ash twitched, his gaze switching restlessly between me and Kelis. The two women's guns faltered, shifting their aim from me to her, sensing a more immediate threat in Kelis's sudden panic.

"Jasmine doesn't live here any more," I told her. Then, in the second before she could react, I pulled my own gun from its holster and shot her in the gut. She let out a choked gasp, in betrayal more than shock.

The instant I'd shot her I turned my gun on the other threats. One bullet through the throat, another through the heart, and both women were falling to the floor. A splash of arterial blood hit Ashok's cheeks, a dark stain in the dim light of the room. He gagged, bent over, and I knew that some of it must have spurted into his throat.

When he straightened, it was to see the barrel of my Magnum pointed at his heart. For weeks the grip had been uncomfortable in my hand, the shape somehow wrong, but now it felt as if it belonged there. "Just you and me now," I told him.

He nodded but said nothing. Behind me I could hear Kelis groaning. Without looking, I kicked back, knocking her fallen weapon away. Her hand reached out to grasp weakly at my ankle, her skin pressed against mine. Warm and still alive. In that moment of contact I felt... something. A spark of some feeling I couldn't identify hissed up the nerves of my leg and into my skull. It illuminated something there I hadn't been able to see – a part of me I'd forgotten existed.

I shook my head, trying to dislodge that uncomfortable spark and the unwelcome illumination it brought. I walked to the two fallen body guards and picked up their guns in my left hand, then shoved them into the waistband of my trousers. They were slick with gore and I wiped my hand against my t-shirt after I was done, leaving a perfect red palm print on the white cotton.

"I'm just as fast and just as strong as you now," I told Ash. "Don't even think about it."

"Why would I want to? We're the same now, you and me. We want the same things."

Did we? A half of me seemed to think so, but something else had shaken loose, blasted free by the shot I'd fired into Kelis. I felt a split inside me, a rift between two parts that had seemed like a whole. "I'm not your brood-mare," I told him, one thing at least that both halves agreed on. "I'm Cured too."

"I provide the seed, you provide the eggs – it's an equal contribution. And the end result will belong to both of us. They'll surpass us both."

My eyes drifted as my mind struggled with itself. I felt compelled to make these children, this new race. The feeling was so strong it seemed to fill every part of me. But then I saw the bodies of the two guards, the women I'd killed, and I saw the rounded swell of their stomachs, the embryonic lives inside which I'd murdered at the same time. "You need to save the half-breeds too," I told Ash. My voice was thick as I said it. A part of me was resisting these words.

"It's too late," he told me. "The death of my wives will buy time for you and me to escape. We can find another city, gather new receptacles. They're finished – but we can start again."

"No. You can still save them."

"How?" He was intrigued. He took a step towards me until he saw my eyes narrow and stopped. He was almost close enough to touch now.

"Tell them to surrender. Give the signal. Queen M will spare them if they lay down their arms."

"Or she might just kill them all," he said.

I shook my head. "They're fit, and they're fighters, and they're pregnant. Believe me – she'll want them."

He stared at me for a long moment. My eyes didn't waver, although inside I felt as if my head was tearing itself apart.

Finally he nodded. Holding his hands carefully away from his body, he walked to the control bank at one end of the room, incongruously high-tech in the middle of all the faux old-world opulence.

"This is your leader speaking," he said. Distantly, I heard the words echo back, and I knew that he really was doing as I'd told him. "Lay down your arms, the fight's over. You've served me well, but now I'm asking you to switch your allegiance. Join the forces you're fighting, take your commands from your new queen. This is the last order I'll ever give you. You're hers now."

I couldn't be sure that the order would be obeyed. Or that if it was, Queen M would believe it. But I'd tried to save them – and one half of me at least was glad of that.

I waited until he'd pressed the switch that ended the transmission before I stepped closer. My breath felt tight in my chest, my vision narrowed down to just his face, his eyes. My mind felt like an inferno, burning up.

"I guess that's all that I really need you to do," I told him.

I could see in his face that he knew what I intended. He didn't look afraid, exactly. The Cure didn't allow fear. But he didn't want this to happen and he refused to believe that it would.

You know that thing they say – about being able to see yourself reflected in the pupils of someone's eyes? Bullshit. When you're standing that close to a man, all you can see in the centre of his eyes is darkness. But when I looked at him, I did see myself. An epileptic flash of memory on my retina. I saw myself back when I'd first met him. Jesus, how was it possible to ever be that young? And then in a flash of the future, I looked at him and saw what I would become.

He smiled, a vivid flash of white in his brown face. And, despite everything, I smiled back. "Jasmine," he said. "How did this happen? How did you and I come to this?"

I raised the gun and pressed the muzzled hard into his cheek, the soft flesh yielding around it. I gave him the gun, because it was easier than the answer. "We did this to ourselves," I told him. "It's only right that we're the ones who pay the price."

"But our children," he said. "The new race. You need me."

He's right, the Voice said, somehow separate from me again, but louder than ever and almost impossible to ignore. There was another sound in the room, quieter but more profound, the sound of Kelis breathing. I fixed all my attention on that; each painful, rasping breath, every wet exhalation. In one, out two. In three, out four. On the fifth breath I pulled the trigger.

The bullet passed through his cheek, leaving a ragged hole. I could see the ruined remnants of his tongue through it, flapping in a wordless scream against the roof of his mouth. It only lasted a second. He looked smaller when he lay on the floor, as if his body had already begun to decay and fall in on itself. A pool of blood spread around his head like a dark halo.

"Mary mother of God," Kelis gasped. "I know it needed to look convincing, but did you have to shoot me in the fucking gut?"

I turned to face her. My gun was still in my hands and I saw them raise it until it was pointing straight at her. I'd fired four bullets since we'd entered the building – more than enough left. She wasn't looking at me as I said, "I meant to put it through your heart. I guess my aim was off."

She chuckled weakly, the sound turning into a gurgle of pain. But when she lifted her head to look at me the laughter died. "Jasmine?"

"I told you, Jasmine's gone." Somewhere inside me, something was protesting that, but the Voice was quite sure. It had lost Ash – there was no way it was letting me go too.

Face twisted in agony, Kelis pushed herself upwards, first to her elbows then slowly, painfully, to her knees. "No," she said, her voice just a thread. "You're still you."

I took a step towards her, stumbling over my own feet. "That's not true. I've killed hundreds of people. I've shot pregnant women. Jasmine would never do that. It must be the madness."

A thin trickle of blood leaked from her lips. She gasped as she struggled to form the words. "We'd all like an excuse for what we've done – but that's just cowardice, and you're not a coward. You killed all those people, Jasmine. Accept it and move on."

I took another step closer. My finger was tight around the trigger of the Magnum. Another millimetre, another milligram of pressure, and Kelis would stop saying those terrible words. "I don't know myself any more," I gasped.

Amazingly, she managed a smile. Her lips were crimson with her own blood. "That's okay, I know you. And you're not so bad." Her eyes wouldn't let mine go, no matter how much I wanted them to.

I could kill her. I wanted to kill her. I could surrender to the Voice and let it take all the decisions. Let it shoulder the responsibility. Or I could live with all the things I'd done. I could go on making all the awful, impossible choices that this world forced you to make. The only sane response was to go crazy. Let go. Just let go.

And yet.

Kelis's eyes. The lips that I'd kissed, only a few days ago. I had to take the responsibility for that. I couldn't kill her and let that death be nobody's fault.

I didn't know I'd thrown the gun away until I heard it clatter against the far wall.

EPILOGUE

I BANDAGED KELIS'S injuries as best I could. The bullet had done less damage than it might – a through-and-through which had missed the organs she'd need the most. The exit wound was the worst, muscle beyond repair, ragged scraps of skin. In front it was just a small hole, black and burned round the edges. The bandage stopped the blood loss, but I didn't give her five hours if we didn't get her some more serious care. And even then...

She was unconscious by the time I finished with her. My body felt drained, my mind almost a blank. And the Voice was still there, pushed down but not defeated. Another sort of addiction, a temptation that would always be there.

It was easy enough to figure out Ash's broadcast system. The message I sent was short, but I thought it would do the job. Then I sat down beside Kelis on the floor, rested her head in my lap, and waited.

It only took half an hour for Queen M to find us. She looked at us both, long and cold, then at Ash, the blood pooled around his head. "Well," she said. "It seems my confidence in you wasn't misplaced."

"Glad to be of service," I said, and in a way I was. The pirate queen's ambitions seemed almost charmingly small-scale compared to Ash's. And who knows, maybe the world needed her in it. When I'd chosen not to kill Kelis I'd had to accept that Queen M was right. The best of us are capable of terrible things.

"So," she said, but I held up my hand.

"I know what you're thinking," I told her. "You're thinking your little plan worked just fine, and I helped you neutralise the threat from Cuba along with a far worse threat you hadn't even known about. Kelis wasn't part of the plan, but it all turned out for the best. So I guess you'll just shoot me, because I'm not the safest person to have around now Ash is gone."

She was smiling as I spoke. I couldn't tell what it meant. Probably nothing good – her smiles never did. "You left out the part where I bring Kelis back to my flagship and then shoot her too, just so everyone can see what happens to people who betray me."

Kelis's head was still in my lap. I ran my fingers gently through her hair and I felt her stir a little. She didn't wake, though, and I thought that was probably for the best.

"But you don't want to do that," I told Queen M, "because I'm going to need her, and you're going to need me."

"Really? Seems to me you've passed your sell-by date."

"If Ash was the only person left who'd taken the Cure, you'd be right."

Her whole face stiffened. I knew that Haru must have told her everything I'd told him about the Cure and what it did. "Okay. Where are they?"

"I don't know. But wherever they are, they're a danger to you. Fuck, they're a danger to the whole world."

"And you'll hunt them down for me," she said, an edge of mockery in her voice.

I smiled, because this wasn't a job I wanted, but I knew I had to take it. "I'm the only one who can. I'm the one who understands them."

She looked at me for a very long time. Then she nodded once, sharply. She was smart, that had always been the problem.

It took two weeks for Kelis to recuperate. Queen M and her people were long gone by then, taking their new recruits with them. Ash's eunuchs had deserted the city when their leader fell. They'd never found Ingo and I hoped that, somewhere, he was still alive.

It was just me and Kelis in the sterile white hospital with its echoing, empty maternity wards. There were stocks of anti-psychotics there, more than enough to last me. I took them and forced the Voice back down into the depths of my mind, and tried to forget the things I'd learned about myself when I'd listened to it.

On the eleventh day we took the jeep that had been left for us, food and ammo and spare fuel piled in the back. Kelis was still weak, stumbling as she walked until I let her sling her arm over my shoulder. I took the wheel as we headed into the desert. The wind was hot and dry in our hair and I saw Kelis smile for the first time since the night Ash died.

The smiled slipped and her eyes closed, and I thought that maybe she'd drifted off into sleep. But after a moment, she said. "You didn't tell Queen M about the children."

"No."

"You didn't think maybe you ought to warn her?"

"No."

She turned towards me, opening her eyes again. "That's all you're going to say? Because if we are going to be spending the next God-knows-how-long together, I'd appreciate a bit more in the way of conversation."

I shrugged. "She would have killed them. And Ash could be wrong. He was crazy, after all – there's no reason to think the Cure will be transmitted into the second generation the same way it manifests in us. Who knows what those children will grow up to be?"

"I guess we'll find out in about ten years."

The silence stretched out between us, easy and comfortable, as the jeep ate up the miles on the long road. "You've got someone," she said finally, fifty miles down the road.

It hurt, but not as much as it used to. "Yeah. Or maybe. I'm going to go on believing that he's alive."

"And you don't want to go and look for him? Back home in England? That could be the first place we go."

"No," I said softly, then more firmly, "No. I'm damaged goods. I don't want him to see me like this. Let him remember me the way I was before."

She didn't look at me as she said: "Maybe he wouldn't care. Maybe he'd just be glad to have you back."

I watched the tarmac unspooling in front of us, the sun blazing down on it all. "Maybe one day," I told her eventually. "There's something else we need to do first."

"Yeah," she said. "Okay. And where do we start?"

"It's a big world," I told her. "We could start anywhere."

THE END

Rebecca Levene has been a writer and editor for fifteen years. In that time she has storylined *Emmerdale*, written a children's book about Captain Cook, several science fiction and horror novels, a novelisation and making-of book for Rebellion's *Rogue Trooper* video game, and a *Beginner's Guide to Poker*. She has also edited a range of media tie-in books. She was associate producer on the ITV1 drama *Wild at Heart*, story consultant on the Chinese soap opera *Joy Luck Street*, script writer on *Family Affairs* and *Is Harry on the Boat?* and is part of the writing team for Channel 5's *Swinging*. She has had two sit-coms optioned, one by the BBC and one by Talkback, and currently has a detective drama in development with Granada Television.

DEATH GOT NO MERCY

AL EWING

For Jon, Matt and, most of all, Tom.

CHAPTER ONE

THE DUCHESS

Skrr-rr-retch.

The knife was a combat knife, and it was sharper than a knife had any right to be. Put to use the right way, it'd cut bone; even in the hands of an amateur, it could gut a man from stem to stern and spill his steaming guts out on the dusty ground.

The trick was, when you sharpened it, to drag the blade over the whetstone, gentle-like. Cade was a man who could be gentle when he had to be.

Wasn't what you'd call his main skill, however.

Right now, the knife was only cutting wood, but Cade gripped it like he was cutting through a man's skull. And a man who was alive, at that.

Skrr-rr-retch.

Cade sat on the steps of his trailer, bringing the knife slowly up against the wood, letting it bite in and then flicking his wrist up so as to carve off one small shaving at a time. The work was slow and Cade's body was still – an intense kind of stillness, like that second of quiet before the artillery tears into brick and slate and flesh and leaves nothing but mist behind. When Cade was still and silent like that, there was a danger about him. That ain't to say clichés like 'coiled spring' could quite apply to the man – even the suggestion of potential motion was missing from him. But put your ear to his chest, the old-timers in Muldoon's used to say before the bad times came, and you wouldn't hear a heartbeat. You'd hear ticking.

Across the way, the Duchess was laying out solitaire. She'd found a poker set in Bill Aughtrey's trailer after Cade had taken his body out to the back lot for burning and burying – once upon a time she might have felt a little out of kilter about playing with a dead man's cards, but too much time had passed. They were just nice things going to waste, and the Duchess made it a point of pride to never let anything go to waste, especially not now Duke was in the ground more than two years.

Even in her middle sixties, even playing solitaire, looking at the Duchess was like looking into a burning fire. Every move she made, she shifted against her t-shirt – low cut and ugly pink, off the shoulder, what she called her 'show-off' top. She leaned – playing the ace of spades down into the space she'd marked for it – and the bounty of her breasts leaned along with her, heavy and gorgeous against the tight ugly pink cotton, moving just on the edge of Cade's vision.

She knew what she was doing. They did the same damn thing every day.

Skrr-rr-retch.

The knife cut deep.

Pretty soon, Cade figured, he was going to have to stand up and turn that damn card table over. The Duchess would say something appropriate and Cade would say something appropriate back. Then he'd carry her into her trailer and put her down on the old mattress and they'd get to it. The Duchess knew it. Cade knew it. Hell, the rusty bedsprings in her trailer knew it. It was coming, it was inevitable, and Cade knew it because it happened every damn day.

Not that Cade was complaining, exactly. There wasn't a hell of a lot else for either of them to do.

It was a routine they'd fallen into, on account of how routine was about all that was left for anybody after the bad times, unless you wanted to go stone crazy. But it was a pretty damn good routine for all that.

Cade just hoped she wasn't playing a winning game when he sent the cards flying. Be a shame to wreck that.

The knife handle twitched. The blade cut.

Skrr-rr-retch.

Woody Dupree was due any time. Another ritual. Woody would come and bring the insulin, and they'd maybe play cards a little. Or maybe they wouldn't. Maybe Cade would knock over that card table first, and they'd be in the trailer getting to it when Woody arrived, and he'd just have to sit awhile. Cade wasn't a rude man by nature, but sometimes it happened that way anyway.

But eventually they'd all be sat around the card table with a beer each and they'd talk about the weather, or about something Woody'd read in a book, or maybe about how the vegetable patch was doing.

The last three living people for miles. They'd sit. And they'd talk.

Mostly Cade and the Duchess and Woody Dupree didn't talk about the bad times – mostly they skirted around it, like old rats around poison. But occasionally someone would say something. A subject that big, that black, someone had to say something. Woody might mention his mother, or the Duchess would make an off-hand comment about Duke, and all of a sudden all of those old ghosts would be back in the room and things would get colder. The night would end in silence and pain and a few tears, with Cade left to watch the other two feeling things he couldn't.

Best to leave the past in the past, Cade figured.

Skrr-rr-retch.

More wood shavings fell on the ground, the fresh ones joining with old and rotting ones from the day before and the day before that.

The Duchess laid down another card, her body shifting on the edge of Cade's eyesight.

Cade cut.

Skrr-rr-retch.

He didn't even really know what the hell he was carving.

He just cut.

Skrr-rr-retch.

Cade was considering standing up and turning the damned card table over when he heard a rumbling noise from down the track, and turned his head to see Woody's pickup rolling up next to one of the empty trailers, saving him from his thoughts. The Duchess looked over and waved as Woody opened the driver's door and stepped out, then walked around to the back of the truck. Cade figured something was wrong right then.

Generally, Woody brought the insulin a box at a time, on the passenger seat. But now there was a big crate of the stuff in the back of the truck.

The Duchess's smile left her face, and she looked puzzled instead – puzzled and a little fearful.

Woody was breaking the routine.

Woody still lived in the same house over in Muir Beach, a couple miles away from the trailer park, and he spent most of his time there. He was a solitary man, even before, and since his mother died along with the rest of the folks in Muir Beach he didn't seem to need or want any company, beyond the time he spent with Cade and the Duchess. Sometimes he wouldn't come to the park for days, and when they'd head into Muir Beach to find him and drag him out for a beer in what was left of Muldoon's – another ritual they tried to keep to every week at least – he wouldn't answer his door. Him bringing the insulin to the trailer park every week was a way for the Duchess to keep an eye on him.

Woody was a fella who needed taking care of, she figured.

His hands shook as he tried to get a hold of the big crate. They shook most of the time, these days.

"Gimme a hand with this, Cade? I don't want to drop it."

Cade stuck his knife in the ground, got up and walked over. The crate wasn't that heavy, but Woody wasn't much of a physical specimen and besides, he had the shakes pretty bad. Cade figured it was best he took hold of it.

By now the Duchess was looking worried. She was scratching lightly at the needle marks on her arm, saying nothing as Cade laid the crate down inside her trailer. Cade figured he'd best ask the question.

"Woody?"

Cade was a man of few words.

Woody sighed, looking down at the ground.

"That's the last crate, Cade."

Cade narrowed his eyes. The Duchess spoke up, a tremor in her voice.

"Now, that can't be right, Woody. I – I thought there was plenty left in Brenner's..."

Woody shook his head, not looking her in the eye. "I thought so too, I did. But, uh, the crates in the back room of the store, the ones that have insulin written on the side, they're... well, they're all full of eye drops. I guess they ran out of eye drop crates at the factory, or there was some sort of mix-up or something... anyway, that's the last. There's sixteen boxes in there."

The Duchess shook her head, getting to her feet. She was blinking slowly as it dawned on her.

The Duchess had known the insulin would run out eventually, but she figured they had enough for a year, maybe two. Long enough to work something out.

"Woody, that'll only last about four months. What happens after four months?" There was an edge of panic in her voice.

Cade shrugged. No sense he could see in panicking. "We get more."

The words hung in the air for a moment. Woody swallowed. "Um, yeah, that's why I brought the whole crate up in one go. See, uh... I figure there's going to be more in the city, so I'm taking the truck down that way, and loading some boxes up..."

He tailed off.

The Duchess looked at him, blinking. "Jesus Christ, Woody, you wanna go down to Sausalito?"

Woody shook his head. "Sausalito's gone. I was thinking Frisco."

Cade looked at Woody. Woody who was out of shape, who still lived with his mother's ghost. Woody and his shaking hands and his twitch that wouldn't go away, talking about how he was going to take the pickup truck down all the way into San Francisco.

Ed Hannigan had taken a car down that way to see how things were there, about a couple of weeks after the last broadcasts finished and even the emergency band on the radio wasn't giving anything but static. He never came back.

After a couple more weeks, Woody had driven after him a ways. He'd stopped when he came to a skeleton hanging from a sign by the side of the road. He told Cade later there was an orange glow lighting up the horizon.

Sausalito on fire.

Since then, the three of them had pretty much given the cities up for lost, and now Woody Dupree wanted to go down and load up a few crates of insulin, because he felt guilty. He was terrified. You could tell just by looking at him.

Cade shrugged his great shoulders once, reaching to scratch the hairs at the back of his neck. It was pretty damned obvious Woody was about to get his fool self killed.

Hell with it.

"I'll go."

Woody looked at him like a drowning man looking at a rope. He shook his head, licking dry lips. "No, it's okay. I should have checked the crates earlier. It's my fault, I'll..."

"I'll go, I said."

Cade wasn't a man you felt comfortable arguing with, at least not when his voice carried that tone to it. Woody looked down at the ground. "Are you sure?"

The Duchess spoke, her voice dry as Martini. The scare had gone out of her, and Cade was glad of that. "If it's my life on the line, I want Cade to go. No offence, Woody."

Woody nodded. "I'll..." – he swallowed hard, unable to keep the relief off his face – "I'll leave the truck here. If... if you drive down to the town tomorrow morning, I'll help you load up with stuff." He licked his lips again. Nervous. "You know. From the gun store."

"Sure." Cade said. He didn't smile, but he probably would have made an attempt if he'd thought of it, for Woody's peace of mind as much as anything else.

Cade was never what you'd call the smiling type.

Woody looked at his shoes for a bit, and then waved, feeling foolish. His face was red as wine, and his eyes were wet, and Cade couldn't help but feel a little sorry for the man. The bad times had left their mark on him and he wasn't ever going to be the same, but he was a decent fella who wanted to do the right thing, and Cade knew that he hated himself right then for passing the buck along. Cade almost wished there was a way he could take that off the man's shoulders.

There wasn't, though. Not a way Cade could figure, at least.

Woody finished waving and turned. "I'd... I'd best get moving, if I want to get home before the sun..." The sentence trailed off, and then Woody turned and trudged back down the hill, leaving the truck where it stood, looking foolish.

They watched him leave, and when he was out of sight the Duchess eased the fullness of her body back into the picnic chair she'd been playing solitaire in and made a show of picking up her cards. Her hands trembled, just a little.

Cade went to pick up his knife.

"Hey."

Cade turned. The Duchess was smiling, or trying to. She was still scared, he could tell. It wasn't just the possibility of losing her insulin supply – or her life. It wasn't even losing him – he knew a lot better than that. She didn't much like Cade, except in bed.

What scared her was that tomorrow would be the end of the routine.

The Duchess shot a glance at the card table, and then a glance at him. Then she half-lowered her lashes, leaning back and raising her hands up into her dyed-blonde hair. "You want to come turn this over?"

Cade nodded, and went.

CHAPTER TWO

THE BAD TIMES

Cade met up with Woody the next morning, outside his mother's house.

Cade didn't know much about her, but then he hadn't known much about Woody before the bad times – carrot-topped, slightly overweight, working under Jim Robinson at the Post Office. Soft voice, hunched back, liked men better than he liked girls, and if Cade ever needed to kill him the best way was probably to sever the pulmonary artery. That's all Cade had known about Woody back then. He remembered Woody's mother as a kindly-faced woman in her middle seventies with the same soft, round, chubby look to her as her son. Mothered him a lot. Made brownies for the boys at the bar come Superbowl time. Nice woman, if you thought about such things, which Cade didn't.

She'd been one of the first, as he recalled.

Cade's constant silence made him a repository of confidences for the town of Muir Beach, and he was happy enough to listen to people's troubles, just so long as he wasn't imposed upon to care.

That night in Muldoon's he'd been drinking alone, watching Duke lose at pool to some hitchhiker come down from Seattle and breezing through town on the way to a stag weekend in Mexico, when Doc Hackett had sat down at his table, a double whisky in each fist, and it had all come pouring out of him.

Woody's mother had come in to see the Doc about a cough she'd had the whole afternoon that had turned bloody. Right there in his office, in the middle of telling him about it, her lungs had rotted down to liquid in her chest – she just keeled over like a sack of potatoes and let what was in her chest flood out over his white tile floor. He'd seen seven other people do the same thing - that or flow out through their ass – and there were more coming in, and the nurses were coughing their guts up too, and half the people in the street, and... and he needed a drink, goddammit.

Cade passed his own whisky across. The Doc downed it to keep the previous two company and went into a coughing fit, finally spitting a mix of blood and meat back into Cade's glass. Then he went into the toilet and never came back.

Cade had sat and drank, listening to the people in the bar starting to cough. He could've said something, but he figured there wasn't much anybody could do, and there was no mileage in starting up a panic. If this was his last whisky, he wanted to drink it in peace.

Jerry Muldoon closed the bar early – he was coming down with the flu or some such, he said, and besides most of the patrons had staggered out long before – and he died twenty minutes later, while Duke and the hitchhiker were singing in the streets, drunk as lords, not seeing the bodies in the doorways or hunched in parked cars. They were singing Meat Loaf, as far as Cade could remember, *I Would Do Anything For Love*, with Duke singing the female part in a high, shrill voice. He punctuated every line with a hacking cough until he had to stop, and when the hitchhiker, whose name Cade never learned, leant over and puked his guts in the street, there'd been blood in the vomit. The boy stared at it a second and then slumped face first onto the pavement, the seat of his jeans turning red as he bled out.

Duke made it home, at least, although he didn't know who the hell the Duchess was when she let him in. He called her by the name of a whore he'd known in Abilene while his guts turned to liquid and pooled on the kitchen floor.

Cade buried him the next day. Duke had touched a lot of people in his life, but only the Duchess was there to mourn him.

Everyone else in Muir Beach was dead.

They'd got a hard dose of what was going round – Cade had heard tell of folks hanging on for maybe a week or so with it, but Cade was kind of glad that wasn't the kind anybody in Muir Beach got.

Bad times should be over with quick.

Cade shook his head. He figured there wasn't any point in dwelling on it. He pulled up the truck next to Woody and leaned to open the door.

Woody nodded slightly and walked around to get in. His eyes shifted uncomfortably to meet Cade's for a moment, and Cade could see the skin beneath them was baggy and black. It was a sign of what kind of nights the man had had recently. Last night he probably hadn't slept at all. Apparently people didn't sleep too well when they were guilty, or at least Cade had been told that once. He had no way of knowing.

Cade hadn't felt guilty about much of anything in a while.

Woody muttered a 'hello' as he clambered into the passenger seat. Cade didn't say a word in reply.

It wasn't a calculated gesture, or one made out of dislike of Woody. Cade found Woody pretty much as bearable as he found anybody else. But Cade wasn't a man who said hellos and goodbyes – it was one of those social conventions he never did see much point in, like giving up your seat or opening a door for someone. Cade didn't see the point in that. Or shaking hands. Shaking hands was the worst.

If you reached out your hand to someone, you exposed the wrist. It was the easiest damn thing in the world to grab that hand and carve down the wrist with the blade of your knife. Then the other guy's busy trying to stop eight pints of blood hitting the dirt and he's no damn good in a fight, which means you can drive your knife right in the man's eye and kill him stone dead in less than a second. Shaking hands just seemed like a risk that wasn't worth taking.

That's the way Cade saw it, anyway.

Woody sat – nervous, fumbling with his hands. Then he reached across to grab hold of the seatbelt and draw it across what remained of his pot belly. He spoke softly, without looking at Cade, fingers fumbling with the seatbelt catch as it rattled in the slot. "I couldn't sleep last night, Cade. I felt terrible. It's my fault, all this."

Cade shrugged and shook his head.

"It is, though. I mean it, Cade." He sighed. "She was relying on me. She was relying on me and I let her down. I should have looked in the boxes, or at least... I don't know. It's – it's our most valuable resource. More than canned food. We've got more of that than we know what to do with. I... I should have..." He paused and swallowed, his eyes wet, still fixed on the road ahead, unable to go on. He seemed not to be able to look at Cade.

Cade didn't say anything.

"She could die." It was almost choked.

Cade didn't say anything. Not much to say. Woody wasn't to blame. Some damn fool had marked or packed the crates wrong and there'd been no way of telling. If Woody couldn't see that, there wasn't much point in discussing the subject. He'd have to work through it on his own time.

They drove through Muir Beach in silence.

Muir Beach was a small town – small and secluded, with about a hundred and fifty houses in all, and the trailer park just up the mountain. Everybody knew each other for the most part, even if only by sight, and while there was plenty to gossip about, the folks had respected Cade enough not to pry into his business too close, which was the way he liked it. Muir Beach had become his home after the business with Fuel-Air and the Captain and Sergeant A, which was a business Cade didn't like to dwell on too much. He didn't exactly regret anything he'd done, or even anybody he'd killed, but it'd been a hard day to live through and it was better kept in the past.

Muir Beach had seen better days.

Woody and Cade had managed to clean the bodies out of the places they went regularly and a couple other places besides, but for all that, the town had a rotting, decomposing stench to it, that got on the clothes and the skin. It was one reason the Duchess had moved out to the trailer park after Duke died. The air up the mountain was a hell of a lot cleaner, at least once they'd burned the few bodies that'd been in the trailers.

Woody'd stuck around. Cade didn't dwell much on why that might be. Punishing himself, probably. Cade looked over at him as he sat up suddenly, looking confused and pointing out of the passenger side window.

"The, uh, the gun store's down that way."

"We don't need them."

Cade used the 'we' out of courtesy.

"Um. Are you sure?" Woody finally looked at him, wet eyes wide and uncomprehending. "I mean, you don't know what kind of trouble you're going to run into there. You – you need something to defend yourself."

Cade shrugged. He never did like guns. They just weren't that much use unless you were on a battlefield, at least in his opinion, and Woody's idea that a gun'd help defend a man was full of holes. If someone saw you had a gun, they'd be *more* likely to shoot you, not less, and a gun wouldn't stop you getting shot either – not unless you were faster than they were, and that was a gamble, not a guarantee. But Cade's real problem with guns was that guns jammed. Guns broke. Guns misfired. They needed cleaning all the damn time. They could get taken away from you and used on you if you didn't know what the hell you were doing, and most people didn't. Guns were just plain unreliable.

When it came to killing, Cade liked things to be reliable.

That's why he carried a bowie knife.

"Hardware store's got everything we need," he said.

Woody paused, looking at Cade out of the corner of his eye, but didn't say anything more.

Instead, he looked out at the empty streets, as if he was wondering what it was going to be like to have to walk them all alone.

Cade didn't spend too long at the hardware store. He was mostly there for chain.

He settled on two lengths of it. The first length was of the kind strung between posts to make fences with; every third link was decorated with a diamond-shaped decorating weight. This was chain designed primarily to look pretty and line driveways and lawns, and there wasn't all that much in the way of call for it here, but the hardware store kept it in anyway, for reasons that died with Bart Oakley, who was in charge of ordering and died with his face in his cat's litter tray. The chain was useful, in that it was heavy and strong and the decorative weights on it would crack skulls and gouge out eyes should the need present itself. Cade looped it around his waist like a belt and fixed it in place with a combination padlock, which he closed and locked with one number off 0-0-0-0, in case he needed it quickly.

The other chain was lighter gauge, a little thicker than you'd find in a door chain. The sign next to the roll said it was the strongest on the market, and Cade took about five feet of it. It was a good length for strangling, and if looped on itself it'd hurt without killing. A good swipe of this would blind a man, which could come in useful. He looped it around his right bicep, putting it in place with another padlock. Then he though, hell with it, and took another length of the same chain for his left. Might as well.

A man couldn't ever have too much chain, in Cade's opinion.

Woody looked dubious, and that was good. Cade knew most people would look at it the way Woody did – as a decoration or an affectation. That was very good. That meant that when they took away his knives, they wouldn't take the chains. And they probably would take away his knives, Cade figured, even if he didn't know who 'they' were quite yet.

He had two knives. The combat knife, the bowie, his favourite and the one he knew best, was strapped to a holster on his belt. He also had a switchblade decorated with a skull, picked out in white ivory, that fit neatly in his pocket, waiting to come out. Both of these were good blades, although the switchblade was kept more for sentimental value, or as close as Cade got to sentimental, anyway. He made sure to keep them both in good working order. Cade figured between them and the chains, he'd have enough to work with.

The knuckledusters were insurance.

Woody watched in silence as he loaded up, then moved to get in the passenger seat again. Cade shook his head.

"I'm going to head out to Frisco from here, Woody."

Woody swallowed and looked at his feet. Cade figured he could walk from here without any problems, and he waited patiently while Woody searched for the right words.

"Thanks, Cade. For... for taking this on, I mean. Uh, when do you think you'll be back?"

Cade shrugged. "No idea. Depends."

Woody's head lifted. "On what?"

"Don't know. Might need to kill some people. Depends on how many and if they kill me." He scratched the back of his neck, frowning. He wasn't used to talking as much as this, and it sat wrong.

Woody nodded and looked at the ground again. Cade didn't feel like prolonging this any longer, and he figured he should cut it off where it lay.

"See you, Woody. Visit the Duchess regular. She worries."

With that, Cade figured he'd done about enough big speeches. He stomped on the accelerator and the roar of the engine drowned out Woody's reply.

DRIVING OUT PAST the far edge of town, towards the woods that lay between home and the big city, Cade felt something. Saying he felt his load lighten wouldn't be true – Cade was a man who didn't really lighten or otherwise – but there was something that lifted, all the same. The routine of two years of sunrises and sunsets.

Cade had a job to do in San Francisco. He was going to have to do what he did, and it'd been a long time since he'd done it. It might even be fair to say that he missed it, as much as he let himself miss anything or otherwise.

Cade was going to have to kill people again.

He might have smiled at that.

But he wasn't the smiling type.

CHAPTER THREE

THE VOICE IN GERMAN

DUKE HAD A story he used to tell. Kind of a story about a story.

There was a fella once up Russian River way, and Duke always said how dumb they were up Russian River way. But anyway, this fella made his money driving a big rig, an eighteen-wheeler, from a supply depot in Jenner down through the woods to Sausalito. Electrical goods for the most part, there and sometimes back – repairs, Duke figured – and occasionally he'd run a little coke down there from his cousin, or bring a load of reds back to Jenner with him if the Sausalito boys gave him a good deal. Usually his route took him through the Muir Woods area which, by a coincidence, were the same woods Cade was headed through now.

One time, this fella, the dude from Russian River, saw a body laying in the road in a pool of blood. Just laying right in the road and looking deader than hell. So this fella stopped, got out of his cab and went to check, whereupon the dude laying in the road got himself right up and pulled a Mac-10 out from under his belly, stuck it in the dumb fella's face, jacked his truck and drove off into the sunset with a hundred thousand dollars worth of Japanese cameras and half a kilo of coke under the front seat. They found the truck abandoned in Tiburon with the coke still sitting there, and the fella ended up doing about fifteen in San Quentin. War on drugs and all.

Turned out the blood on the road was ketchup.

Now this wasn't the end of Duke's story; it was just the point at which he got in another round of whiskies and maybe took a trip to the head if he had a mind to. The rest of the story went like so: one time Duke was taking the Mustang on a road trip down to Daly and the best way to get there was on the road through the Muir Woods, 'less you wanted to carry on down the highway and get backed up for your trouble. It's worth mentioning at this point that it'd been ten or eleven years since dumb-fella-whose-name-Duke-forgot got jacked up and busted, and in all that time Duke hadn't ever heard of anyone else having any kind of a similar experience – not in the Muir Woods, anyhow.

Lo and behold, as Duke would say, he'd driven roughly about a mile into the woods when he saw a body laying in the road. Not looking deader than hell so much this time, but laying on his front with one hand under his belly, like he'd hidden something there. Duke stopped the Mustang and got his shotgun out from under the blanket on the back seat. Then he walked towards the fella in the road, real slow, checking the situation out. There wasn't even any blood on the road this time, and Duke figured he'd best shoot first before the guy got his Mac-10 or Uzi out or whatever else he had and sprayed Duke with a few hundred rounds.

That was when the man vomited up his breakfast all over the road, which was evidently two bottles of bathtub liquor. Damn fool had just passed out in the road.

"I damn near shot up a drunk 'cause of that dumb Russian River bastard," Duke would say, ordering another round of whiskies. "What the hell was that fella's name anyway?"

The lesson according to Duke was that if it's a choice between taking the Muir Woods shortcut and going around the highway, you should go around the highway.

Cade didn't feel like going around the highway.

So he ran the truck on the road through the woodland, letting the giant redwoods rising up either side pass him by. Cade figured they hadn't much noticed the human folks dying, but they'd take advantage just the same. Gradually, those redwoods were going to spread out, first of all obliterating this little road, then the big highway, then any of the empty towns in their way, until they'd reached a size big enough for them to feel comfortable in. Muir Woods had been hemmed in by the people for too long.

Cade wasn't what you'd call an environmentalist, on account of how he didn't get too involved in politics on a general principle. He didn't figure he needed any more excuses to kill folks. Life provided enough as it was. Still, he figured it was only right that the great redwoods would take their land back over the generations, for practical reasons if nothing else. People wouldn't be gone forever. Those trees needed to get their numbers back up a little, if only so that men could come and chop them down again when the time came.

That was about all the thought Cade gave the subject.

He drove the woodland road in silence.

There wasn't much point in having the truck's radio on, since there were no stations to pick up anymore. On the few occasions he and Woody had clustered around Bobby Terrill's radio set – Bobby Terrill had boasted back before the bad times that he could get any station in the world with his setup, and Woody believed it – they'd heard nothing but crackle and static, apart from one voice in German, talking about who knew what.

Woody had been excited at that, and Cade had let him be. It'd lasted about half an hour, and then Woody realised that neither of them knew German and while it was nice to know that some German guy had gotten hold of a radio, they didn't have any way of talking back. Still, Woody took Bobby Terrill's radio set into his home and listened to the German voice sometimes on dark nights, long after Cade had lost interest in who else might be wandering around out there, and after the Duchess had decided it was better not to hope too hard.

Once, Woody'd turned up at Muldoon's during one of Cade and the Duchess's drinking sessions, all excited. "He was speakin' English today! Kinda, anyhow. See, I couldn't figure what he was talking about at first, but it was all thees and thous and it had a kind of rhythm to it and I figured it out pretty quick – it was Shakespeare! The man was reading Shakespeare, can you believe it? Out loud, I mean."

Cade had shrugged, and the Duchess had smiled maternally. "That's real nice, Woody."

"Ain't it? I figure he's been reading stuff over the radio to maybe keep himself sane. It's a good idea, y'know? I mean, maybe I could do that. Read books to whoever's listening. If we could broadcast, I mean."

"That sounds like a real good idea, Woody," slurred the Duchess, lifting up her eighth whisky. "So, you worked out how to do that? I'd like to hear it. You got a good voice. Ain't he got a good voice, Cade?"

Cade shrugged. Woody shook his head, not losing his smile.

"Nope. I figure, uh, we need a transmitter or an antenna or something. I dunno, I'd need to look it up, and I don't think we've got the books here. Still, it would be nice, wouldn't it? Sending all that literature out into the world. I got some Ed McBains I could read – you know, like those old detective plays that used to come on the radio. Wouldn't that be nice?"

The Duchess had laughed, and poured him a tall whisky, and they'd talked into the small hours about the books they liked to read. Turned out the Duchess had a thing for Harlequin Romances and J.P. Donleavy, of all people. Woody liked crime novels, most especially Donald Westlake in his Richard Stark days, the Parker novels.

Cade didn't read, at least not fiction. Nobody was surprised.

A few shots of whisky after that, with the Duchess passed out on a couch in back, Cade had asked Woody if he'd ever tried tuning in and finding something from the States. Maybe there was someone reading books in American. Maybe, said Cade, coming to the real point of the matter, the Government had managed to get themselves together again. Maybe they were organising, or broadcasting. Maybe there were some good times coming.

Woody had been laughing and playing with the dead shot-glasses, making cracks about old brat pack stars he'd have liked to take to bed, but with that question he suddenly sat up straight, all the good humour draining out of him like someone had pulled a plug at the bottom of his soul. Woody'd looked at Cade, pale and drawn, and downed his next whisky in one gulp. "Good times ain't coming, Cade."

Cade blinked. Woody swallowed, trying to clarify. "I mean they ain't organising, Cade. Folks are broadcasting, but... they – they ain't organising." His eyes were suddenly wet. "And they ain't reading no great literature out either, or any Harlequin Romance books or Parker novels or anything else. Trust me on that, Cade. They ain't."

Cade had shrugged and let it go. He had a pretty good idea of what Woody had heard when he'd tuned away from that calm voice of Germany, and he figured it wasn't anything he needed to trouble himself too much about, and especially not something he needed to burden Woody any further with.

Anyway, he'd know for sure now, or soon enough at any rate.

Cade left the radio off, and the only sound was the dull growl of the truck's engine and the occasional rustle from the trees as a bird took off and flew. Cade kept alert – in these woods, it wasn't uncommon for a deer to head onto the road, and if he wrecked the truck it was going to be a long walk. Not to mention the possibility of dying from being crushed to death by a dead deer.

Cade wasn't a man afraid of dying, but that'd be a pretty damn foolish way for a man to go.

In the event, he didn't see any deer. What he did see in the road was a man. Or a boy. *Young adult* probably fit him best, Cade figured.

The young adult in question was all of eighteen years old, certainly not much older than that. He was dressed in old, grubby jeans, boots, a t-shirt with a confederate flag on it and a lumberjack shirt. He had sandy hair, close-cropped, and a pronounced overbite. And he was laying in the road, looking like he was injured. But there wasn't any blood.

Cade thought about Duke's story – that time Duke nearly shot the drunk because of what had happened to the fella from Russian River.

Guess things did come in threes at that. Funny how it works out.

The young fella had his hands on his belly and his face suggested real pain. His posture as he lay suggested maybe a couple of cracked ribs, like he'd been beaten and left there to die, although there weren't any marks on his face beyond dirt.

He was laying right in the path of the truck. He didn't look to the layman's eye like he could move himself. If Cade didn't want to roll right over that boy and splatter him on the trail, he was going to have to slam on the brakes. Then he was probably going to have to get out of the car, keeping one of his knives ready at hand, and check to see if the boy was all right or if he was faking. And he wasn't exactly trained as a doctor.

Hell with it, thought Cade.

Then he slammed his foot down on the accelerator.

The boy's eyes went wide in shock and he had just about enough time to let out a squealing cry, like a pig in an abattoir, before the front left tyre hit his head and burst it open like a melon, spraying blood, brain and skull fragments across the dirt roadway. The truck skidded slightly, the front wheel churning in the boy's face as Cade gripped the wheel, fighting the swerve – then the neck cracked as the head went under the wheel. There was a jolt as the limp body thudded under the back wheels and was left behind.

Cade had figured the truck's shocks could take the collision, and he was happy to see he hadn't been wrong. He probably couldn't have hit a deer head-on that way, but then again, a deer was a sizeable animal. A kid wasn't going to do as much damage, especially when he'd been laying down.

It wouldn't have troubled Cade much if the young fella had been what he appeared to be. Things like guilt or remorse weren't especially in Cade's nature, although there were nights he had bad dreams, especially on the subject of Fuel-Air and Sergeant A.

But all the same, there was a certain satisfaction when it came to being proven right about something.

So when the two men charged out from behind the tree with the shotgun, Cade felt a little better. He could keep his foot on the accelerator, keep going, but there was a good chance they were going to blast away with that shotgun, maybe take out one of the back tyres. Then he'd have to abandon the truck. That'd be a real shame. Not to mention the fact that if he drove off now, they'd be waiting for him on the return leg.

And he'd gotten a little rusty. It'd do him some good to get back in practice on these folks.

Hell with it. If he was going to go to the trouble of justifying it to himself, he might as well just do it. At least driving over the kid had thinned them out some.

Cade put his foot on the brake and the truck came to a screeching halt. And then he stepped out of the truck and raised his hands.

The man with the shotgun had sandy hair in the same shade as the young feller's, grown down into a mullet, along with the same pronounced overbite and the addition of a ratty moustache. The other man had the same. There were some physical differences – mullet a little longer in front on one, belly a little pronounced on the other – but the only real difference was in their t-shirts. The one without the gun had a stained *Burn this Flag* tee, the other was wearing one advertising the Scorpions on their last tour. Scorpions's face was red and there were tears running down his cheeks, so Cade figured he was related to the boy somehow, but it was pretty obvious both these men were kin of some kind. Brothers maybe.

The man with the shotgun opened his mouth and screamed.

"Y'all killed my boy! Y'all drove over him like he was nothing!"

It was like an animal howling. The barrel of the shotgun was pointed right at Cade's chest. This was the moment. If Cade ran, or flinched, or looked like he was going to do something, Scorpions was going to pull the trigger. Cade just stared.

He figured Scorpions had a bit more to say on the subject.

"We was just going to rob you, you know that? We was just gonna take your fancy truck and your stuff, and then you killed my boy! My youngest! I dunno how I'm gonna tell Maw her youngest boy's dead..."

Cade wondered if Maw was a term of endearment or if Scorpions had gotten his mother pregnant. It wasn't outside the realm of possibility. Scorpions had the barrel pointed at Cade's face now, and he was moving closer.

Not quite close enough, though. Cade waited.

He could be patient when he had a mind to be.

"...but I reckon the tellin's gonna be a mite easier if'n I blow your head off and take her your goddamn brains in my hand, you son of a bitch! Look at me! Look at me when I'm talking to you! *Look at me!*"

Cade wasn't looking at Scorpions. He was looking over at Burn This Flag, sizing him up. Burn This Flag was looking back, a little wary. His mouth was half-open, like he was trying to work out what was going on.

Cade figured Burn This Flag wasn't the smartest in the family.

"Look at me! I wanna see your eyes! Look at me!"

The barrel of the shotgun was nudging Cade's chin.

"*Look at me! Look at me, goddamn you...*"

Cade made his move.

His right arm moved suddenly, almost a blur, grabbing the end of the barrel and twisting it to the left, while his left hand grabbed it further down, twisting it right. The gun went off, discharging close to his left ear, leaving nothing in it but a ringing noise. Cade hoped that wasn't permanent. He hadn't figured on the gun going off.

Rusty.

The shotgun landed on the ground between them as Scorpions clutched at his hand. His trigger finger was bent upwards, at a right angle. He stumbled back, looking at Cade with wide eyes, his mouth open in shock.

His face stayed that way while Cade took the combat knife out of his belt and cut his throat with it.

Cade sidestepped most of the blood, but still felt a wet gush of it hit his side. He'd probably need a change of shirt later. Burn This Flag was still looking at him, blinking, his mouth opening and closing like a fish. His legs were shaking a little. He wanted to run, Cade could tell. But he just couldn't make his legs do it.

Cade had seen that happen to people he'd killed before.

As he walked up to Burn This Flag, the redneck let his bladder and bowels go, soaking the front of his jeans with a growing dark stain as the back sagged under the weight of his mess. His eyes were still staring ahead and his mouth was still opening and closing, trying to form even one word, when Cade drove the point of the combat knife through his forehead and into his brain.

Burn This Flag took one step backwards and crashed down, convulsing on the floor. Cade figured he'd let the man thrash a little and then get his knife back. Then he'd carry on the way he'd been going, past what was left of Sausalito and into San Francisco. Not much point hanging around.

He didn't hear the growl.

His left ear was still ringing, and they came on his left. It was the big shape in his peripheral vision that warned him, but he wasn't expecting what he saw.

An old woman of about eighty or ninety, with wispy grey hair and that same damn overbite, standing in a worn polka-dot dress. That wasn't so surprising to Cade. He figured there'd be more from the family around these woods. What was surprising was what she had with her.

On the end of a chain leash, there was a brown bear – a grizzly. Up on its hind legs, teeth bared, eyes red. A grizzly bear in a killing mood, and this old girl had domesticated the damn thing somehow.

Cade was rarely surprised by anything. But this was one of those times.

After all, bears weren't common to the Muir Woods.

Cade scratched the back of his neck. The combat knife was stuck in Burn This Flag's skull, and he'd need a second to pull it out. He figured he most likely didn't have a second.

He looked at the bear.

The bear looked back at Cade.

The old lady looked around at the three bodies. Then she let go of the leash. Her voice was high, reedy and a little raspy. Cade figured this was Maw.

"Sic 'im, Yogi."

And Yogi did just that.

CHAPTER FOUR

THE BEAR

Now, YOUR STANDARD grizzly bear stands about eight feet tall and weighs about eight hundred, maybe eight hundred and fifty pounds.

Which is a hell of a lot of bear.

Yogi was a little taller. Cade figured that one good swipe from Yogi's claws was probably going to take his face off – just unzip the flesh from off his head and tear it loose like peel off an orange.

Hell of a thought. One swipe, knocking your head to the side, maybe cracking your neck, so's the one eye you got left gets to see something wet and red flying off to the side like a pink deflated balloon. Something with a nose and a mouth, wrapping around a tree, while your grinning skull waits there for the jaws to crack down on it and burst it just like an egg in a grown man's fist. Thought like that'll keep a man up nights.

It didn't trouble Cade overmuch, mind, but Cade had a habit of not troubling himself with the details. The important thing at this particular moment was to pick a weapon and stick with it.

He had maybe less than a second. Not much time at all – not near enough to go for the switchblade, or pop one of the lengths of chain on his arms. He'd have to take the bear on with just his hands, which was going to be a problem. That said, Cade didn't worry too much.

He had the knuckledusters on, and Cade was a man used to making do.

He snapped his right arm forward, slamming his fist into the bear's stomach, then did the same with his left, then his right again. The three punches took less than a second to throw, and he felt one of the bear's ribs go with the last one – on account of the lead weight sitting on the end of each fist, turning every punch into something like being hit by a sledgehammer.

Cade wasn't under any illusions. The bear wasn't about to get any easier to fight. Fact was, now he'd wounded it, it was going to be pretty damn mad – killing mad – and eight hundred and fifty pounds of killing mad bear could probably tear a man right open without even letting the thought cross its mind.

He'd just have to kill it before it did that.

The knuckledusters were simple but effective – studded lead weights that fitted his fingers neatly. They were a good pair of tools, and Cade had gotten a fair amount of use out of them in his time. Cade wasn't generally known as a man who got into bar fights – not as a rule – but once upon a time, he'd been ambushed in an alley on the way back from a long session at Muldoon's. Sore loser who didn't like having his money taken away from him by a straight flush and figured he could take it right back. Cade wasn't of the same opinion.

Cade had never learned the man's name. They'd found him in the alley the next morning and identified him using dental records, from the bits of jawbone laying a few feet away from what was left of his face. Cade never heard anything more about it, so he assumed the detective in charge of the case hadn't had much luck. Too bad.

The knuckledusters were useful, all right. But that was then and this was now, and there was a hell of a difference between a drunk with a blackjack and eight feet of pissed-off woodland killer.

Cade had his work cut out for him, in other words.

One of the razor-sharp claws came for his face, ruffling his hair as he ducked under it. The damn bear was howling up a storm now – Cade could see that in just about a half second the animal was going to spring forward and slam all that weight down on him. And while Cade was pretty capable of lifting a thing when he had a mind to lift it, he wasn't about to lift eight hundred and fifty pounds of bear, most especially angry bear. Not if that bear decided to grab his head in its jaws and crush it like a damn eggshell and then pull what was left off his neck like a chicken drumstick.

Yogi roared at the top of his lungs, showering Cade in bear spit. Another swipe from those claws... Cade veered back, getting far enough out of the way not to lose any more than a button off of his shirt, then stepped back inside the bear's reach and swung his left. Cade had a pretty fearsome left hook, and with the knuckleduster on, it could kill a man without trouble. But a bear's not a man.

The lead weight slammed against the side of Yogi's head, caving in half of the beast's teeth and most likely fracturing the jaw into the bargain – at least if that hard, flat *crack*, like a rock breaking underneath a chain gang hammer, was anything to go by.

It was a hell of a punch, no doubt about that. But it was a lucky punch, and Cade wasn't going to stay that lucky for long.

Next thing he knew, he was flying across the dirt road with a warm gash opening up in his side. In the moment he'd taken to register his own hit, the damn bear had backhanded him. On account of not having any hearing on his left side, maybe. He slammed into the dirt, the impact knocking most of the wind out of him and sending a wave of fire through the fresh wound on his side.

Yogi was already lumbering towards him as he rolled back onto his feet. At least he could get on his feet and still keep his guts inside him. Cade figured that meant he hadn't been tagged that bad – maybe a deep cut, but nothing a few stitches wouldn't cure, if the bear didn't decide to stick that smashed muzzle in it and root around for whatever it could get.

He braced himself as the bear charged.

Cade lashed out again, aiming for the head – a solid right, connecting above the eye with an unholy crunch, leaving a dent. The bear's momentum kept it moving, those eight hundred and fifty pounds slamming into him like a freight train, knocking him off his feet and damn near crushing the breath out of him. Cade snapped another punch up, into the jaw, a left hook that landed with the power of a drop hammer. Then a right, into the throat, crushing the windpipe. He felt it go – felt his hand sink into the flesh, rupture the organs the animal needed to breathe – and then he was buried in fur with eight hundred and fifty pounds crushing down on him, breathing bear. This was it. If the damn thing wasn't dead by now, it was going to rear up and those jaws were going to rip him into bloody pieces before it even thought about breathing. The pain from the broken jaw would just make it bite harder while it could.

The bear didn't bite. The jaws lolled, drooling spit and blood. The body shook, convulsing, as Cade managed to work himself out from underneath the dead weight of it, careful of the still-twitching claws.

The damned thing was dead, all right. So much cooling meat. Cade had killed it when he'd cracked the skull, probably put a few pieces of bone right into the animal's brain.

Lucky punch.

Cade stood, the corner of his mouth twitching slightly as his fingers moved over the gash in his side. Not even deep, just plenty bloody. Ten or twelve stitches would see to it.

Just as soon as he'd done something about the old woman.

She was standing, looking at him, a cold stare that didn't blink once. There was a lot of hurt in those eyes. Hurt and hate and frustration, because the fight was over and she'd thrown her best at him and she didn't have much of anything else to throw.

And he was still standing.

"You killed Yogi."

Cade nodded. It was a fact.

"You killed Yogi and you killed my boys." She swallowed, shaking her head slowly. "They was just going to rob you some. You didn't have no reason to kill 'em for it."

Cade nodded again. He didn't feel the need to say anything. She was right. He hadn't needed to kill 'em. But Cade only fought one way, and people didn't get up again after it. That was just the way the man was.

Nobody said anything else for a good minute. Cade looked at the dead bear, and the old woman looked at Cade until he turned those grey eyes of his in her direction again.

She shook her head. "It ain't right, that's all I'm saying. Ain't meant to happen this way, not to the family. We had the good blood – we could all of us live through the sickness. Good blood, kept in the family, that's what pappy said. Allus had it. We all kept our bloodline pure."

Cade looked into her eyes, old and confused. Crazy as it was, there was a hell of a lot of logic to it. There was that one blood type that the plague didn't hit; Cade knew that from the news reports, and presumably these people did too, before the news reports quit on them. Inbreeding might keep that special strain of blood flowing.

Once upon a time, these people were probably the scum of some community down south or in a trailer park somewhere even people as damaged as Cade and the Duchess wouldn't end up. A bunch of inbred hicks, a sick town joke. And then the bad times had come and turned the whole damned world into the punch line. And suddenly the hillbilly scum family everybody laughed at turned out to be the last survivors. Any of them who could read or switch on a wireless would put two and two together and the first thing such a clan'd do sure wouldn't be to stop screwing each other. Keeping it in the family would go from general policy to an article of faith.

Keep it in the family and you kept the blood pure.

The old woman's eyes glittered, hard little stones in the grey flesh of her face. "Who's gonna keep it pure now? Got Maybelle and the baby waitin' back in the woods. Their brothers are dead now – so who's gonna get 'em with child? Who's gonna keep that blood pure? You tell me that!"

She was crying.

"We was gonna start again! Gonna... gonna..." – she groped for the word, clawing the air with her fingers – "gonna repop... repopulate the world! You killed the world today, yes you did, killed the whole damn world! Killed the future of the world..." She shook her head. "You best kill me too. You better had – better put me in the dirt right now! Because *I'm going to come after you!*"

Cade looked at her. She was thin as a rake – malnourished, probably full of cancer.

She grinned, and there was one tooth in it. "I'm going to come after you! And I'm gonna kill you and anyone you love, like you killed *mine*, boy –"

Hell with it, thought Cade.

He figured you should take your elders at their word.

He swung his right into her face, the lead weight smashing just above her eyes, crushing the skull inward and turning the frontal lobes to jelly. She tottered back for a step or two, her head dented in like a car bonnet after a death-crash, whatever was in her bladder and bowels hitting the ground with a wet slap, then tumbled over like a rag doll. Twitching on the ground, she looked like nothing quite so much as a puppet with the strings cut.

Cade figured she was probably just crazy, but there was a chance she had some clout – maybe she could have caused him trouble on the way back. He was better off dealing with her now. Anyone coming across the scene would probably put the picture together, but Cade'd be long gone by then.

He reached down and gripped the handle of the combat knife, tugging it free of Burn This Flag's skull. Cade wasn't a man who worried himself a great deal, but there was a troubling aspect to the encounter. These were probably the most screwed up people he'd ever encountered outside the confines of his shaving mirror, but they made some sense. Their blood was an antidote to the thing that'd murdered a planet, so inbreeding made sense. Screwing your own family, bearing children by them, that made sense. Pretty good sense, in fact.

That worried Cade.

He wondered if there were crazier people waiting for him in Frisco. More dangerous people. And if there were, he wondered if they were going to start making sense to him too.

When Cade got out of the woods, he put the truck in gear and pointed it south, down Highway 101. Behind him, to the north, was what was left of Sausalito and Marin City. Part of him had been hoping Woody was wrong about that, but one look at the column of smoke still rising up towards the horizon was enough to set him straight. Woody wasn't wrong. Sausalito had most likely been razed to the ground, and the chance he was going to find what he needed there was slim to none.

San Francisco lay ahead, across the Golden Gate Bridge. Cade gunned the engine, narrowing his eyes.

There was something strung across the bridge. Something white and flapping, half-burned, stained with blood in places. A banner. Cade strained his eyes, and read:

HIPPY donT let thE sun set on yu HERE!!!

Cade didn't figure that was a good sign.

CHAPTER FIVE

THE ALPHA MALE

CADE KEPT THE truck on Highway 101, past the cemetery and along Marina Boulevard. The parks and suburbs around the Presidio looked as gutted as Sausalito had been – wrecked houses, smoking timber where trees and fields had been, dead bodies nobody had bothered to clear up. A lot of them looked dead from the bad times – bled out on the street or on the porches of their houses. Some of the corpses looked like they'd died some other way, though – there was one in particular, a pair of legs dangling by almost-rotted trouser cuffs from a telephone pole, the top half laying propped against a fire hydrant, mostly lost to rats and scavengers.

Across the street, there was another sign, of sorts. A fat fella – had to weigh a good three hundred pounds, and all of it blubber – was sitting naked on the road ahead, placed so that Cade had to swerve around him. He slowed the truck, taking a good look. The man was naked, and had been posed and propped up with a stick, sharpened and pushed into the meat of his back. His head had been severed, and the neck was ragged, as though it'd been pulled off. What was left of the head was sitting in the man's lap, and flapping out of the open mouth was something Cade thought at first was a thumb, until he got a little closer and saw it had a foreskin on it.

Carved into the chest were some words. It took Cade a few seconds to read them:

HELTER SKELTER

Not good at all.

Something bad had happened out here. Probably the same bad thing that happened to Sausalito, to Marin City. The destruction seemed to get worse as he went further down the boulevard, the last of the suburbs a still-flaming vision of something out of hell – then suddenly he took the truck past the line of Baker Street and he was on the city grid. And things were different.

He slowed the truck down to a crawl. The streets were empty, and they were mostly clean. There weren't any bodies laying anywhere – he figured they'd been dumped into the Marina, or piled up elsewhere, out of sight. Maybe even buried. He glanced right, down the length of Broderick Street. The same story. Clean, deserted, no dead, no garbage.

Cade figured he'd just crossed a boundary line. Either whatever had torched the Presidio had been turned back here... or it'd started out here. The hairs on the back of Cade's neck were itching a little, the way they had out in the desert when the officers were talking about their damn-fool strategies. Those hairs on the back of Cade's neck were antennae, of sorts. They flared up when something got to smelling bad.

Cade had to admit, this smelled pretty bad.

He figured he had a couple of options, as things stood. He could find the first pharmacy, load up with as much insulin as he could handle and get the hell out. Thing was, that wasn't much of an option for two reasons.

One, if he loaded up the truck with one drugstore's worth, he'd buy the Duchess maybe another year at most and then he'd need to do it all again, and he'd be a year older and a year slower and have a year less gas for the truck. And then the year after that – well, it just wasn't sustainable, was Cade's thinking on the matter.

No, Cade needed to find a big supply of the stuff, which meant he'd probably need to ask some questions, which meant, judging by the state of the Presidio, that he'd need to kill a few people. That was fine by Cade.

The other reason was a matter of security, and it'd been half in his head since he'd seen Sousalito, and now he'd crossed the bridge, he was sure of it. Muir Beach was a ways away from San Francisco, but if they'd trashed the Presidio and the suburbs, then gone for Sausalito, then Marin, then who knew where else up to the north – well, it was a matter of time before they headed west and got to be a serious problem. Whoever did what he'd seen, there was a hell of a lot of them. Either they were out to the north and he'd need to run them down, or they were here and he'd need to burn them out.

Either way, he needed to ask some questions. He needed to ask a few just to get the lay of the land, because it was pretty damn clear to Cade that San Francisco was as foreign a country as he'd ever been in and he didn't have a damn clue what the customs were or who the local boss was. All he knew for sure was that there wasn't a single soul on the streets.

Not one soul, alive or dead.

Which was a little weird in itself.

There's a hell of a lot of weight on a dead body. Woody and Cade had done the best they could with the hundreds of bodies in Muir Beach, although in the event Cade had done most of the actual work, cutting the bodies down and lugging them a piece at a time. Woody wasn't made to haul bodies – although he did as many as he could before he started crying and throwing up – and Cade didn't want to trouble the Duchess with it. Cade didn't exactly care about people, but there were a small number of people he nearly cared about, and he came the nearest with her. He wasn't about to put her through a nightmare he could take on his own self.

It had taken months to even make a few places in Muir Beach liveable again. That was a small town of a hundred and fifty homes and no cable TV, and they couldn't clear it entirely – had to give about two thirds up for lost.

San Francisco was a whole damned city. There were more people on five or six blocks than in the whole of Muir Beach. And by the looks of things, it was clean as a hospital wing.

Frankly, that just wasn't right.

The breeze coming in through the truck window was clean, with no trace of that rot that blew through Muir Beach when the wind went the wrong way. But it still stunk to high heaven for all that. The hairs on the back of Cade's neck were buzzing like death row.

"Hell with it," he muttered, and jerked the wheel right, turning the truck down Cervantes Boulevard. He wasn't going to be getting anywhere pissing about the edge of town.

His eyes narrowed as he crawled down the street, checking the buildings one by one. Something about halfway down the Boulevard caught his eye, and it took him about a half second to work out what the hell it was.

Neon.

BLARNEY'S, flickering on and off in green with a little shamrock. An irish bar.

With a neon sign.

Those neck hairs were dancing tango.

They had electricity; probably something rigged up in back, a cheap gas-powered generator, maybe, but someone had to rig that up and run it. And nobody was going to the trouble of making a neon sign flicker without a good reason. Neon signs were what Cade would call a hell of a luxury.

What that was, was a beacon. Maybe an invitation.

"Hell with it," muttered Cade, and parked the truck.

As he got out and closed the door – Cade knew better than to slam it – he was listening. There was a sound on the wind – low voices, men's voices, singing softly. Cade stopped for a moment, breathing in the clean air. There was something about that song that halted even him, something that gave him a little pause. Not the soft tone of the melody, or the reverence, but that such a thing should be at all.

"Amazing Grace... how sweet the sound..."

Cade scratched the back of his neck, and his mouth twitched towards a frown for a second. Cade wasn't generally a man who allowed himself to be spooked by much of anything, but he had to admit to himself that this was a touch spooky no matter how you cut it.

Back in the desert, Cade had been in a humvee with a guy named Fuel-Air. That wasn't his name – his name was Billy Dominguez – but the Sergeant figured nicknames were good for morale, so if someone looked like he was bucking for one, Sergeant A made sure it stuck. Fuel-Air got more Ripped Fuel than air, according to Sergeant A, so he ended up on a permanent caffeine and ephedrine rush. That made him a hell of a driver on no sleep, but made him a hell of a talker besides, which wasn't the best company for a man like Cade, who gave the impression in a conversation that he lost a year of life for every word he said.

Fuel-Air pissed Cade off no end. He never shut up, and he had a way with a phrase, short little explosions of profanity and bitter sarcasm mixed in with all the shitty DVDs he used to rent before he joined up. Fuel-Air Bombs, according to Sergeant A, who was a lot funnier in his head than he was in real life. Still, he cared about his men, and he did his damnedest to keep them alive.

He wasn't like the Captain in that respect.

No sense dwelling on that, though.

Fuel-Air was dead now. Dead before the bad times hit, which was probably best. Cade didn't think Fuel-Air could've coped with losing his guts out of his anus. That would've been *some five-star fucked-up undignified Stephen King shit,* as far as Fuel-Air was concerned. He'd have complained about it every damn second he was dying. Probably would've been one of the ones who lasted a week, just so he could discuss it at length.

Cade blinked and pictured his voice, yelling over the dull engine roar of the humvee droning in the background. Always yelling, always talking.

"This is some five-star shit, dog, some five-star Silent Hill *strange-ass* Children Of The Corn *shit! They're gonna put fuckin' bees on your head or some shit like that, man, like Nic fuckin' Cage!"*

He was dead before that film came out, though. Cade shook his head. He didn't know what the hell he was thinking about that boy for. He'd hated the little bastard.

Time to get to work.

Cade walked to the door of the bar and pushed it open, and the singing stopped.

The first thing Cade noticed was that all the taps had been torn out of the bar, and instead of booze on the shelf behind, there was bottled water. All kinds of brands, sparkling and still, rows and rows of glass and plastic bottles and not a single drop of anything alcoholic between them.

Each of the bottles had a cross drawn on it in magic marker.

That spooky feeling was getting worse.

Cade didn't like where things seemed to be headed. He counted the men – ten sets of eyes staring in his direction. Ten men, a couple bigger than Cade, and none of them looked like a man who wasn't used to fighting.

And he'd done interrupted their choir session.

This would not end well.

The muscles in Cade's back tensed, but he spoke gently, calmly. Truth to tell, Cade didn't really have another way of speaking but calm, and soft, and low. A lot of folks found that menacing, but Cade just wasn't the shouting kind. He hoped he didn't sound like he was trying to be menacing now. He wanted some information.

He didn't want to kill anybody.

If it came to a fight, Cade pretty much only knew one way of fighting, and that was fighting to kill. So if things got a little untoward, there was a good chance none of these people would be left in a position to say a damn word about Sousalito or any other subject you could name. They'd be a little busy being dead. Cade didn't want that. At least not just yet.

"Sorry to disturb you," he said, as a courtesy. "I've got some questions."

One of the men was chewing a stick of gum. A blonde guy, maybe six-five, had an alpha-male look about him. He stopped chewing, and his voice was a slow, lazy drawl, heavy with scorn.

"You a hippie?"

Cade considered the question. No, he couldn't say he was. He shook his head, keeping his eyes on Alpha Male.

"You look like a hippie."

Cade lifted his hand to his face and tried to remember the last time he'd looked at himself in a mirror. Cade pretty much avoided looking at himself in a mirror unless he had to. It wasn't a guilt thing, exactly. Cade wasn't a man who felt guilty as a rule. But it was a pastime he couldn't say he got an awful lot out of.

His fingers brushed through his beard. It was pretty furry there, all right. A good three months of growth.

And now he came to think about it, the Duchess had been saying she needed to cut his hair again. It'd been about eight months since she'd done that. She was saying he was getting to looking like a damn mountain man.

Cade ran his fingers through his hair. It was pretty long at that.

This was something he should've considered when he saw that sign on the bridge.

"I said you look like a hippie, boy."

Alpha Male was pressing his point. Cade was a fair-minded man when he had a mind to be, and he surely had to admit that there was a certain logic to Alpha Male's position. Cade probably did look a bit like a hippie, at least going by his hair, and his beard. Mind you, there was the big splatter of slowly drying blood on the side of his tank-top, and all over his fists and up his arms, but maybe in this light they just looked a little grimy.

Hell with it.

"Guess so." Cade nodded. No harm in being agreeable. "All the same, I've got some questions." He paused, looking at the men. The ones with glass bottles were carrying them by the neck now, like clubs. Cade figured he could see where this was headed. "Hoping you could answer them."

One of the men smashed his bottle against a table, the water splashing onto the ground along with shards of glass, leaving him with a weapon. Cade looked in his direction for a moment.

"I'd be obliged," said Cade, softly. He figured there wasn't much else apart from that to be said.

Alpha Male spat.

"You got a nerve, hippie. You're a long way from the Hashbury now, you know that? Satan doesn't have the power to help you here. This here is God's city." He grinned, and the grin lit up his face. There was malevolence there, but also a kind of fervour, a sort of ecstasy that shone out of those blue eyes.

It hit Cade, suddenly, that this talk of God and Satan wasn't an excuse.

Cade had met a lot of folks in the past who used talk of Jesus to excuse themselves when they figured they'd give Woody a punch in the mouth for sleeping with who he did, or take a tyre iron to Lou Greer's caddy because Maisy Greer was white, or tell Frank Bellows's eldest she was Lucifer's own murderous whore because she'd gotten herself pregnant and decided not to keep it. Cade had come across a fair few of those folks, and usually it was people like Frank Bellows – who didn't appreciate some damn fool making his only daughter feel even worse about something that wasn't their damn business to begin with – who'd ask him to make their acquaintance.

For the most part he'd gently let them understand that Muir Beach wasn't the best town for them to make those excuses in. Generally that didn't take more than a couple of fingers.

Those folks were just of a certain mind, Cade figured. If they were in some country where folks weren't quite so fired up about God and his particular wants on a subject – Sweden, maybe – they'd find another reason to bully folk. But Alpha Male believed every word, and so did the other nine.

In another moment, they were going to do their damnedest to kill him for the length of his chin hair, because in their minds, that's what Jesus had told them to do.

Cade couldn't help but wonder if they'd come up with that one on their own.

He cracked his neck, and popped the chain from around his waist. There was the sound of another bottle breaking. Then a third.

Alpha Male grinned.

"Praise be."

And then they charged.

CHAPTER SIX

THE FIGHT

As it turned out, Alpha Male was the first to go.

Alpha Male had a real name, of course. It was Marvin Wilton, and he'd been a basketball hero in college before settling down with the prom queen, who also sang regularly in the local church – which had unfortunately been wrecked during the roughest days of the Cull, like a lot of churches had been. He'd had three children, all of whom were now dead, and before the Cull hit he'd been a pillar of his community, albeit a little judgemental when it came to some of the people he shared San Francisco with. His neighbours would have been shocked to see him acting this way, had they lived. They wouldn't have thought Marvin Wilton capable of this kind of wanton violence.

But the Cull changed people.

Not that Cade gave a damn about Marvin Wilton. Cade had turned not giving a damn into a science, and if someone had tried to tell him Marvin's life story, Cade would have found something else to do by the second trimester. Alpha Male was Alpha Male, and that was the name he was going to die under as far as Cade was concerned.

It was a legacy of his time in the humvee with Sergeant A – Cade wasn't much on people's actual names. As far as he figured, he was facing down Alpha Male, Combover, Man-Tits, Skinny, Budget Ben Affleck, Ears, Never Forget, Tall Fella, Other Tall Fella and Global Hypercolour.

To be honest, he didn't even give them that much thought. But if he'd wasted a second looking at them, that's what he'd have called them, and it makes what happened next a little easier to describe.

What happened next was Cade doing what Cade did.

The heavy gauge chain whipped out, the combination lock on the end whirling through the dusty air like a mace until it slammed hard into Alpha Male's mouth. Marvin's perfect teeth cracked and splintered on impact and he reeled back, spitting out enamel fragments and blood, the remains lacerating cheeks and gums as he screamed – and then Cade swung the lock down on the top of his skull with as much force as he could bring to it. There was another flat *crack* and Alpha Male dropped like a sack of coal, bleeding from one ear. He was one of the lucky ones. He'd lost most of his teeth and he'd never be able to count to a hundred again.

But he'd live. For a while, at least.

In a matter of days, he'd have his jugular vein torn from his neck by a cannibalistic ex-finance director who hadn't bathed in two years, but that was in the future.

Man-Tits lunged with a broken bottle that'd once been full of some Brand X Perrier substitute. Once upon a time, drinking something like that in Blarney's might have been taken as the sign of a man who wasn't in full possession of his manhood. It might even have earned a medium-level ass-kicking, like as not from Man-Tits himself, who was the type to take offence at that kind of thing. But things had changed some since the Cull hit. According to the Pastor, alcohol was the work of Satan, and refined sugar likewise. Water was good for the system and good for the spirit, although anything that still managed to struggle out of the taps in San Francisco wasn't likely to be either of those and it was best to stick to the bottled variety, as passed out by the Pastor himself, blessed by his hand. Man-Tits had come to believe very strongly in the Pastor and his word.

Man-Tits was a man who believed strongly in a lot of things, especially if they were told him in a loud voice and it was implied that he was some kind of communist queer-boy if he didn't buy into them. Man-Tits was just that sort of fella.

Cade shifted to the side, then used his free hand to catch Man-Tits by the wrist and break his arm at the elbow, making sure to twist it so the broken bone pushed up through the skin. Then he snapped his head forward hard enough to break Man-Tits's nose. He could've left it there, but Other Tall Fella had a bottle of his own and was bringing it around to slash at Cade's throat.

Cade grabbed Man-Tits by the hair and swung him across, and Other Tall Fella's bottle went right into his neck, carving it wide open. Cade took a step back, doubled the chain in his fist and swung it so it raked across Other Tall Fella's face. It didn't do his complexion a whole lot of good.

The diamond-shaped weights in the chain – that made it look so nice and pretty when it was strung on the edge of a man's lawn – burst both eyes and broke a mess of teeth, which pretty much put Other Tall Fella out of the fight. His fellow men of God pushed him out of the way when he started screaming. He stumbled back, tripped over his own shoelaces and then toppled back like a falling tree, until the back of his head met the corner of the bar with a crunch that finished him off for good.

Probably for the best, considering.

That left seven.

They were a little wary now, though their blood was still up. Cade took a step back, and they took a step forward, shuffling around the bodies. Cade was swinging the chain in his hand, round and round, a slow circle. It made a little *ch-chink* sound every time it went round. A little whisper of metal on metal.

Ch-chink, ch-chink, ch-chink.

Global Hypercolour stepped forward, sweat dripping down his forehead and off his nose, big hot-pink stains spreading out from his armpits and down his chest. The rest of the t-shirt was purple, aside from the Global Hypercolour logo in white. Cade had never understood the appeal of those things.

He whipped the chain out and around Hypercolour's neck, then jerked him in, like reeling in a fish, grabbing the big man in a headlock and twisting his neck quickly until he heard it snap. It was as quick a death as he could make it, but Tall Fella and Combover were already rushing his flanks, and now his good chain was tangled up around Hypercolour's throat. Combover had a broken bottle, Tall Fella just had his fists, and Budget Ben Affleck was coming up in front to make three.

Cade didn't need to think too hard about it. He took a step back and caught Tall Fella's ear in the fingers of his right hand and Combover's bottle in the left. Then he pulled. Tall Fella had his centre of gravity a little far forward as things stood – the tug on the ear, hard enough to rip the cartilage, send him stumbling forwards until his feet met Hypercolour's thrashing body, and then over he fell. Cade kept his grip on Combover's wrist and moved the broken bottle so Tall Fella tumbled face-first into it. It made a sound like a shuriken hitting a twenty-pound steak.

Budget Ben crashed into Tell Fella and the two of them went down to the ground while Cade popped Combover's arm out of its socket, and once Ben was down on the floor Cade brought his boot down on the back of the man's head, hard. Cade figured he probably wouldn't look too much like Ben Affleck after that, but that was his own lookout.

Tall Fella was screaming his lungs out through what was left of his own face, so Cade gave him a kick in the side of the head to shut him up and then swung a right hook around to break Combover's nose and put him out as well.

The whole thing had taken about fifteen seconds so far.

Cade was a pretty quick worker when he had a mind to be.

He cracked his neck again, looking each of the last three square in the eye. Skinny and Ears looked like they might listen to reason at this point – especially with a couple of the bodies still thrashing and voiding their bowels on the floor – but the fella with the crying eagle tattoo and the Never Forget underneath it, he was going to be a problem. It wasn't just the tattoo. It was in his eyes. Never Forget wasn't a man to start talking in a situation like this.

Fella had something to prove.

Cade figured he'd try talking anyway.

"I've got some questions. Hoping you could answer them."

Ears swallowed. Skinny looked down at the dead, his face pale. Never Forget just stared. His lip was curling into a sneer. Cade didn't know whether it was on purpose or if his face was just built that way. He nodded, then spoke one more time.

"I would be obliged."

Never Forget spat on the floor.

Cade shrugged. Hell with it. Least he'd tried to do things the easy way.

"You got a nerve, you –" said Never Forget, and that was as far as he got, on account of the next second Cade's combat knife was lodged in his throat and he couldn't get the next word out through the blood flooding out of his mouth.

Cade was a man who was willing to give a fella a chance when he had a mind to.

But he didn't always have a mind to.

Cade went into a roundhouse kick, aiming the steel toe of his boot into Skinny's chest, snapping a rib and sending the man down to the floor. In the movies, folks tell you a broken rib ain't much of anything. They're liars. A broken rib's a hard thing to work around, especially when it breaks off bad and ends up going into a lung. Cade had made damn sure it'd gone into a lung, and now Skinny wasn't going to get up again in a hurry. He had his hands full just taking a breath without screaming.

That left Ears. He was already raising his hands to surrender, but Cade didn't catch it in time. Cade wheeled around in another roundhouse – what Duke had called his Chuck Norris move – and brought his foot up a little higher this time. The steel toe cap slammed into one of those big elephant ears hard enough to burst the eardrum. Then Cade followed up by smashing an elbow into the man's face.

That's another thing the movies tell you is easy – driving a man's nosebone into his brain hard enough to kill him stone dead. It's a hell of a trick, especially with the elbow.

Maybe Cade just got lucky.

Still, after he'd stepped back and taken a breath, he didn't feel quite as lucky as all that. Skinny'd passed out pretty much right away, which meant there wasn't anybody likely to answer his questions. He had a few more of them than before. Cade was a man who could put two and two together if he had a mind to, and he'd figured on there being some kind of old-time religion operating in Frisco – when the bad times hit, a lot of people had made some snap decisions about religion – but damned if he knew how far it spread or what the hell else might be going on. He wasn't any closer to finding any insulin, and he damn sure wasn't any closer to finding out what'd done for Sausalito.

He'd killed a bunch of folks, sure, but there came a time even that wasn't much consolation.

"Hell with it," muttered Cade, and reached down to tug his knife free of Never Forget's windpipe.

That was when he heard the voice.

The voice had a thin, reedy quality, a kind of soft hissing rasp that made it seem like a snake talking. It had a way of taking its time over the vowels, drawing them out before biting the consonants into harsh little snaps. The kind of voice that would make a man feel uneasy in the depths of his stomach, make him draw in his breath a minute and take a step back.

The Pastor had a way of making folks hear his word.

"O Lord..." It came out *Oooh, Loo-rrd-ah.* "O Lord, O Lord, what hast thou sent to tempt your faithful servant now? Why, a demon of vengeance, Lord, sowing wrath and murder among the faithful. Lord, thy tests are strange and terrible, yes indeed, but your servant shall not flee, oh no, oh no..." He clicked his tongue. "Turn yourself, Demon. Turn yourself to face the Lord's best-trusted servant."

Cade turned himself.

The man was about six-five, thin as a rake, and dressed in black with a white band at his throat – a man of God. Cade figured this was probably the fella calling the shots around here. The right person to ask, anyhow.

He nodded. "I've got some questions. Hoping you could answer them." He nodded down at the dead and the dying at his feet, and the growing pool of blood on the floor. Then he locked eyes with the man in black. "I'd be obliged."

The Pastor smiled, a smile that seemed to crack his thin face into a thousand wrinkles, but never touched his eyes, which were grey as Cade's own but with a touch of ice in them. Cade always figured you could tell a lot about a man from his eyes. From the look of it, this was a stone cold son of a bitch, and violent with it. Cade wasn't too happy about that.

Town probably wasn't big enough for two.

The Pastor let his face drop back into its normal expression – a serene half-smirk, eyes heavy-lidded, that gave the impression of a rattlesnake shaking its tail. "Wellt then, my son. I shall oblige you. Please, follow along with me." He nodded, stepping back through the door. Cade could see at least six men behind him – big fellas, armed with aluminium baseball bats.

That told Cade something. Muir Beach now had a population of three, and that was counting the trailer park. Now, admittedly, it'd been hit hard, and it was a small community. But all the same, it said a lot about a fella that he could get so many men together, train them and arm them – and the big fellas did look like they'd had training for some kind. Plus, this Reverend or Padre or whatever had no way of knowing Cade wouldn't just go to work on these six like he had on the fools in the bar. Which meant they were expendable into the bargain.

Cade was surely considering going to work. Something about the fella's smile, and those grey eyes of his, made Cade figure he'd be a fool not to. Put the son of a bitch down and find his answers another place.

The Pastor smiled, all teeth. "The Lord must be obeyed, my son."

Cade gripped the handle of the knife. Then he relaxed, put it back in his belt, and nodded.

"Hell with it."

Cade figured he could handle whatever the thin fella had to show him. And if he couldn't – hell, he'd have time to regret it later.

And he did.

CHAPTER SEVEN

THE PASTOR

"THIS-A-WAY, MY SON. This-a-way, to walk in the very footsteps of the Lord..." And a chuckle like animal bones cracking underfoot. Then the Pastor turned back to his shuffling walk, one foot dragging after the other, the shoulders jerking back and forth in time with the steps. It was eerie, like watching a cobra trying to walk on its tail like a man.

The more Cade saw of the Pastor, the less he liked it. Those damn neck hairs were standing up to be counted.

The streets were still clean, and apart from the Pastor and his guards, there still wasn't a soul to be seen in them. Cade followed along - the way he saw it, if he wanted answers, he could either walk in the very footsteps of the Pastor's God or just kill the guards and beat the answers out of the Pastor.

There were a couple of problems with that second option, attractive as it was. For one, Cade had done things to people occasionally that folk would call torture, and there wasn't anything about it that was reliable for getting information out of anybody. The only thing torture was good for was torture, and unless you were ready to own the fact that there wasn't any kind of purpose or reason to it besides that, you were fooling yourself. So Cade had to shake his head a little when he heard some damn fool talk about using it for an interrogation on the Iraqis or whoever the hell it was this week. That was just fool's talk from a bunch of clowns who figured the only way they could get another bunch of clowns to vote for them was by showing how very badass they thought they were. 'Course all it did was show they were clowns, but a clown's gonna vote for a clown anyhow.

Cade was a mite cynical when it came to politics.

Anyhow, aside from the practicality of beating a confession out of the Pastor, it was pretty obvious the man was crazy as a broke-backed snake and he was likely to say any damn thing that came into his head. Best Cade could do was follow along as the man's guest and hope he picked something up.

Hell, if Cade acted godly enough, maybe the Pastor'd help him out with his insulin problem, or at least tell him what happened to Sausalito. Acting godly wasn't something Cade had much practice in, but he figured if he kept his mouth shut, that'd about do it.

Keeping his mouth shut was something Cade specialised in, after all.

The Pastor smiled, bobbing his head and moving with that gentle, sinister, shuffling gait as he led them down Cervantes Boulevard to where it intersected Fillmore Street. Ahead of them was the Moscone Recreation Centre – a big grey and white building. Cade shot the Pastor a look. It wasn't exactly a threat, but there was a hint in his eyes that he could just as soon go straight to the killing if he was forced to, and he'd take a certain amount of pleasure in doing just that.

The Pastor smiled his cracked-face smile, his eyes as cold as January morning. "They had basketball here once. Did you know that? One of the best places in the city, I was told." He chuckled softly, like a glass file rubbing against a shard of bone. "We have other entertainments here now. Oh, yes, we do..."

Cade was starting to wonder if beating the Pastor's head against the concrete until it cracked open wasn't the best plan after all. Cade wasn't a man to be unsettled easy, but there was something in the Pastor that just didn't strike him as right. Part of him was already clocking the positions of the guards with their baseball bats, working out who to kill first, who'd make a good shield, who he should take his blade to and who he could just disarm and put down with a simple neck-breaker or a dislocated leg. Cade had a pretty good strategy worked out by the time they'd pushed the doors open and walked down to the basketball court. That was when the smell hit him.

He'd spent a day at the San Diego Zoo, once upon a time. Hell of a place to spend time, and even a man like Cade could find a point of interest in it. He'd spent a while in the monkey house, on account of he liked watching them – Cade was of the opinion that monkeys were people with most of the bull taken out of them.

Now, the smell of shit there was overpowering, but you got used to it quick. Cade had spent a good couple hours there, watching the monkeys do what the monkeys did. After a while the smell stopped bothering him, and he didn't even notice it. And when he'd gone to get himself a Coke from a vending machine, the fresh air had smelled sweet as rosewater. A few minutes later, he went back to the monkey house and there it was again, strong as ever. Monkey shit. Didn't matter if you'd gotten used to it – one breath of fresh air and you were primed for it all over again.

The nature of shit was to stink. There was a lesson in there somewhere.

This was a similar situation. Cade had lived around Muir Beach, with its corpses and old bones, for a good couple of years. He'd smelt some sweet air in the Pastor's territory, but now it was like heading back into that damn monkey house. Only this time the smell that was hitting him wasn't monkey shit.

It was dead folks.

Rotting dead folks.

Cade had a feeling he should start the killing there and then. But when the doors swung open and he saw what the Pastor kept on those courts, he figured he'd hang on a little longer. He figured anything that fucked up had a story in it.

The Pastor smiled, breathing out his words in a soft hiss, like air escaping from a balloon. This time the smile touched his eyes, and they shone.

"Oh hear, sinner man, oh hear... oh *hear* the word of the Lord! Oh, *behold,* sinner; let thine eyes *feast* on His word and His work! Sinner man, can you not see it? Can you not see the *glory* of the Lord your God?" He laughed, and the laugh was a rustle of pages in an undertaker's book.

Cade could see a hell of a lot. He could smell a lot, too.

He maybe wouldn't call it glory, mind.

Set up in the basketball court were about a hundred wooden crosses, and nailed to each cross was a rotting skeleton. Once, there'd been people on those crosses – living people – with nails pounded through their wrists and ankles for who the hell knew what. And they'd been left there until they'd died, one by one. After that, the putrefaction had set in – the writhing maggots that still coiled and squirmed over the last scraps of a long-vanished face, the seeping, blackened mire that clung to thighbones and scraps of mouldering cloth. A couple of the ribcages were homes to rats, that skittered and gnawed on the bones, giving the cadavers a kind of twitching motion, a parody of life that stilled the heart and sickened the gut.

Cade knew for a certainty that the Pastor came in here every chance he could, to watch it happen, day by slow day. And he knew for a certainty that – while his men might have helped hold them still and keep them in place – it was the Pastor his own self who'd nailed every one of those souls up onto their crosses with his own withered hands.

He heard the sound of a breeze rushing through a graveyard. The Pastor was breathing it in. Savouring it. His brittle body shook like a leaf in a storm. Cade had seen folks taking their first hit from a needle who didn't look half so transported as the Pastor did in the presence of his works.

Cade wasn't a blushing virgin in the ways of death, and he figured he knew a thing or two about horror. He'd seen a hell of a lot and done a hell of a lot too. He'd figured he had a pretty good idea of how bad the world could be when it had a mind to be.

Now he knew he'd been a damn fool all the while.

He turned to the Pastor and nodded, once.

"It's something at that." His voice was steady, and level, and his eyes were boulders. Cade wasn't a man who got mad, exactly, but those few who knew him as well as anyone could would have said he was as close as he could get to it.

An eyebrow twitched. Questioning. The voice dropped, just a shade quieter than before and cold as stone. The question was almost under Cade's breath, but there wasn't a body in that room who didn't hear it.

"How come?"

The Pastor was still smiling that weird cracked-skin smile of his, eyes still sparking for joy. When it came, his voice was just as quiet and just as focussed. "Perversion. Men laying with men and women with women. Godlessness and atheism. The worship of drugs that steal the soul from the body, a terrible affront to the Lord... but that wasn't the question, was it? No, no, it wasn't the question at all..." Another chuckle, like a trickle of cut glass along a knife blade. "You're not concerned about their crimes. You want to know why I chose this path. Why the *Lord* chose it... well, sinner man, you will hear it. Hear now the word of the Lord..." He closed his eyes, reverentially.

Cade marked the positions of the Pastor's men again. Then he listened. He figured he'd more than bought his ticket. He ought to get the whole show.

The Pastor walked between the crosses, occasionally putting his hand on the bones, breathing in deep. "When I was a young man, I decided to serve as a chaplain in Vietnam, to bring the word of the good Lord to the men fighting there for freedom from the seeping coils of communism..." He turned, and gave Cade another of those cracked-face smiles. "I was young, you understand. Naïve. I did not heed the Lord, nor did I understand His word, nor His glory. I knew very little."

His smile was wide as a cat's. His eyes were like two rivets nailed in his face.

Cade had a feeling he knew where this was going.

"The firebase I was stationed at had been long abandoned by command, and the men there were now fully under the power of demons, oh yes... I saw it with my own eyes, O Lord, the debasement of the spirit in that dank and lonely place! You say Hell is not real, sinner? I saw it! The degradation, the fall" – his voice rose, calling out like he was giving a firebrand sermon from a pulpit – "I say to you, *the very fall of Man!* And there were times, oh yes, sinner, there were *times* when I could no longer *feel* the hand of the Lord upon me! When I could not *hear* His foot treading in the shadow of my own, when instead – instead I heard a hoof! *A cloven hoof!*"

His nostrils were flaring, and his shock of white hair was plastered up on his head. The eyes were bloodshot, where before they'd been clear. Cade wondered if the man was working himself up to a stroke.

Might save him the trouble.

"I felt the most alone I've ever felt in that place, with those men who were destroying themselves faster than the Viet Cong could do it, those men who had been abandoned and who had abandoned themselves and their souls in turn. Oh Lord! Didn't I *tell* them, Lord? Didn't I *warn* them what was coming? But I could not teach them! For I could not teach what I did not know, and sinner, I did not truly *know* my God! I did not *hear* his word! Not then!"

The Pastor hissed the words, eyes narrowing.

"Not until those devils came for *me!*"

He whirled, stabbing his fingers at the guards, who dropped to their knees, faces transported in joy.

"Charlie rose against us, rose *up,* I say, and murdered every man in that camp, whether he fought against them or lay in stupor! The ground ran red with *blood,* I tell you, *red* with the blood of sinners! And in that fire and fury I felt You *rise,* O Lord! I felt Your *hand* upon me! I felt you *working* in the fire and in the blood! In the screaming and in the dying! I felt you, Lord, and your name was *death!* And *Hell* came with you to that place! And I prayed, Lord, oh I *prayed!* I prayed for you to *enlighten* me! To show me the *way!* To bestow upon me the *reason*! I prayed for a *sign,* O Lord, and a sign *came,* oh yes, oh, my *Lord,* my *God... a sign did come!*"

Cade blinked. He got the impression the Pastor had kind of forgotten he was there, and to tell the truth he could see how that might be. Cade had lost himself for a second in the fire and fury of the man. He could figure how other folk might end up losing themselves for good.

"I was the only one to survive. They saw me praying, saw me kneeling, and the spirit of the Lord moved in them. And they *took* me, O Lord! They dragged me under the earth! To their *tunnels!* They beat me with sticks and with stones! They cut me with *knives!* They broke my legs again and again until I *begged* to be killed! I spent three years in a bamboo cage, three feet by three, O Lord! I faced *torments! Torments of Hell itself!*"

The Pastor gulped air, steadying himself on one of the crosses. Cade wondered how a man could breathe in gulps of that rotting air without passing out – the stench of the corpses was still in his nostrils with every breath he took, and his stomach did a slow, lazy roll every couple of minutes. The smell of a body that's been dead a long time was a hell of a thing to put up with, even for Cade.

Eventually, the thin man spoke again. He seemed to acknowledge that he was speaking to Cade now – the fever in him had passed. "The good Lord spoke to me. For three years... the Lord, the *good* Lord, was my helper through those terrible days and nights. He spoke of His plan for the world to me, you see. That one day, one day, there would come a terrible *scourge* upon the Earth... and those of purest heart would be saved for the final task, O Lord, the most *sacred* task... the culling of the last sinners from the Earth." He chuckled, sweat beading on his brow. "You've a great power in you, boy, a great power. The Lord hath placed a terrible *judgement* in your hands..."

Cade narrowed his eyes. This was starting to get a mite personal. He turned towards the door. "Got things need doing." Cade never had believed in wasting words.

The Pastor smiled.

"You've a great power in you, and I have great power in *me,* son. I have scores of pure souls in my flock, all waiting to do the word of the Lord and work for His glory, Now correct me if I'm wrong, but the kind of things a man like you might want to get done... well, they could need that great abundance. Many hands make light work, they say. And you have set yourself a great task..."

Cade stopped, and turned his head.

"Oh, I can tell just by looking. You have the look of a man on whom the Lord has placed his hand. A man with a mission." He chuckled. This time is was like the shattering of a test tube containing some deadly bacillus. "I will help you, if you will help me, my brother. Place your hand in mine and I will place the hand of the Lord in yours, and He will guide you in your works and bring you aid from every corner of this great city. Only aid *me* when the time comes. Help me in my time of need, my brother." The Pastor smiled his crack-faced smile, and ran a hand over a thighbone, caressing it. His eyes glittered. "Help the Lord in his righteous work."

Cade took a look around the room – at the skeletons hanging from the crosses. There were men there, and women too. A couple of kids. He could see one skeleton at the back, rotted down to bones, and it was no bigger than a chicken's might be, held to the cross with a single nail.

A baby.

Cade took a deep breath of the air in that room. The heavy, sick-sweet, rotted air.

Then he gave his answer.

"Deal."

CHAPTER EIGHT

THE FLOCK

It was a lie, of course, but it seemed to be good enough for the Pastor.

Cade was glad to get out of that room. The same air in the corridors that'd seemed tainted when he walked in now seemed sweet on his tongue, and he took a long breath of it. Then he turned to the Pastor, shuffling along next to him with his cobra walk.

"You did the sign?"

The Pastor narrowed his eyes, confused. Cade almost sighed. If there was one thing he hated, it was using a bunch of words when a couple would do.

"Sign on the bridge. Figured someone had a problem with hippies. Figured it was you." Cade didn't elaborate any further than that. Either the Pastor'd know what he was talking about or he wouldn't, and that'd be an answer in itself.

The Pastor chuckled his little dry-bone laugh. "Yes it was, my friend, indeed it was. Or rather, it was the work of my people, performing a public service for the glory of the Lord. The goodly in this city, the *saved,* feel it best to warn off them that'd spread their sin and wickedness, their *pestilence,* to our beautiful city –"

"Huh," Cade grunted, cutting the Pastor off before he got started. Cade wasn't in the mood for a big speech. He had things to find out. "You burn Sausalito?"

The Pastor chuckled softly. "No, my son, no. When the Lord visits the terrible necessity of taking life upon us, it is with purpose, yes it is, a *great* purpose, the cleansing of *sin* from the community... so that the chosen people of the Lord might go about their works without its taint amongst them. Now what you speak of there is a thing of *chaos,* my friend, of chaos and *dam*-nation; a *serpent,* I say, let loose upon the earth; a terrible beast of rage and flame, yes indeed..." He stopped, suddenly, his whole body shaking like a leaf in a breeze. Then he tilted his neck and turned those cold grey eyes on Cade, seeming for a moment to look deep into him. He hissed out the words, spitting them like venom. "The *Devil's* work!"

Cade stared for a moment, then nodded slowly.

"So who did?"

The Pastor frowned sternly, drawing himself up, the snake-walk quickening in pace. "You should learn to heed my words, sinner man. Heed them well, for they come from the *Lord,* yes indeed, from the very mouth of the Lord on high! Didn't I *say* it was the Devil? Didn't I *say* we were fighting those that spread their sin? Did you not *believe,* O sinner?"

Cade figured he'd caused some offence with the question. Hell with it. He knew who the Pastor was getting at. "The hippies."

The Pastor grinned, and the grin didn't touch his eyes. "The *hippies.* The *godless.* Satan's own. They burn and they destroy, yes they do, enact the Devil's commandments and bring the Devil's punishment down onto all that stand in their way. It's the truth I bring you, brother, the truth of the Lord. Do not doubt." He chuckled, a high, snickering sound, like a rat skittering in a glass ribcage. "I speak the word of the Lord!"

Cade nodded, but what the Pastor had to say didn't seem right. He'd been down the Haight-Ashbury a couple of times back before the bad times, and while it wasn't the Summer of Love anymore by any stretch, most of the folks he'd seen there were peaceable enough folk, and the man walking next to him definitely wasn't that.

Still, Cade knew how the bad times could change a body. Wasn't nothing quite like losing everyone you ever knew to make you crazy. He figured he'd reserve judgement until he knew the score a little better, but he was going to need to head east pretty soon and check on Haight-Ashbury for himself.

Right now he had other problems.

He heard the sound of the crowd through the front doors before he saw it. Somewhere between a hundred and a hundred and fifty people were choking the street outside – men at the front, the biggest first. At the back, Cade could see the womenfolk, huddled, not looking up. That made some sense, at least. Maybe Cade could be charitable and say that the Pastor didn't want the womenfolk hurt, but he was building a new society for himself that nailed people to crosses for reasons provided for him by a voice in his head claiming to be an Old Testament God of death and pain and damnation. Traditionally there wasn't a big role for womenfolk in a system like that.

A couple of the women were pregnant, and Cade figured probably more of them were than showed. Breeding the new generation of the saved.

Cade looked around the crowd, and frowned. There were a hell of a lot of them, and though he wouldn't put it past the Pastor to baptise him into the faith in front of an audience, it was a lot more likely that he'd brought these people around because he figured even Cade couldn't kill a hundred people.

And Cade couldn't. Not these hundred, anyhow.

It wasn't just the women. Cade had never killed a woman – though he'd been accused of it – but he wouldn't have a problem if the circumstances came up. It wasn't the numbers, either. Cade didn't have a problem with dying, and he'd take as many of these sons of bitches as he could with him before he went. The ten or so that finally did for him would know they'd been in a fight, that was for sure. Neither of those reasons would have been enough to stop Cade going to work right there.

It was the children.

Little faces with big eyes, peeking between the women's skirts. Ready to hide if things got bloody, but brought out to see something. A show. A lesson, maybe. Their mommas had brought them to see the sinner.

Cade drew the line at killing kids. As weak spots went, that was one he could about live with.

Cade looked at the Pastor. He didn't bother saying anything. He was a little curious how the Pastor'd got the word out – maybe one of his guards had passed a signal while Cade had been watching the Pastor froth at the mouth in there – but beyond that things were pretty clear.

The Pastor smiled back, and stepped into the crowd. Not a word was said as they swallowed him up. Just an eerie silence, like they were all waiting for Cade to speak. He didn't bother.

"The children of the Lord," came the Pastor's voice from inside the throng. "They who have heard the word, the good word of the Lord in their ears. *You* want to join my flock? A *sinner?* A *killer* of goodly men? Your sins are black, I tell you *black,* inside your soul!" The voice rose, an edge of hysteria creeping in. "You call yourself my brother, with your hands steeped in your black and evil sins! If you touch me, you *defile* me! Your sins are black as *pitch!* You must be *shrieved,* O sinner, you must be *purged,* your sin must be driven *from* you..."

Cade frowned, taking a step forward. The crowd took a step forward too. As one.

"Hell with it," he muttered.

The Pastor's voice laughed, his bone-rattle laugh. Cade cast his eyes through the crowd and couldn't see a sign of him. It was as though he'd simply melted into the mass of people. "Oh, sinner. *Oh,* sinner... your sins have found you *out!*"

The crowd surged.

Cade had a couple of choices at this point. He'd left his good chain back at the bar, but his best knife was in his belt and he could get his knuckledusters on quick, maybe pop a chain from his bicep, then wade in. Swing the chain in a wide arc, slash the knife with the other hand, cutting through a swathe of people – the ones he didn't blind with the chain would find their guts hanging on the floor. Then he could advance into the mob, slashing, cutting, keeping a wide circle around him, and then...

What?

Cade had fought big groups of folks before, but it'd take a lot of doing to fight a crowd this size. Most likely he'd tire, or leave an opening sometime – with that number it'd only take one. That was when they were going to drag him under. If most of them were dead on the ground, that'd just make the rest more likely to kill him. And even if he killed a good hundred men – and he figured that he probably could, given time and a hell of a good dose of luck – then what? Start on the women?

The children?

Cade could do that if he had to. But it'd most likely be a death sentence to start, and he wasn't sure there was too much of a need for it. If he was gonna die here, he'd die here.

But he was willing to gamble on the Pastor having something else in mind.

He stepped into the crowd, hands raised, and the crowd folded around him. Dozens of men, jostling and pushing at him, herding him through into the middle of the street, hands roaming and pushing at his back, grabbing at his shoulders and forcing down.

For a second, Cade resisted, and then someone behind him kicked into the back of his knee, sending that knee crashing into the concrete. Cade's expression didn't change, even when they forced him onto his back. He didn't make it easy for them – he fought as much as he could. But the trouble with Cade was that so far as he was concerned, fighting meant killing, and he'd decided he wasn't going to kill any of these people.

Not just yet, anyhow.

Cade wasn't a man who enjoyed being held down, and he flexed his arms as well as he could, but there were two or three big men for each arm or leg. He wasn't going anywhere.

"O sinner man... are you prepared to embrace the Lord, your *master?*" The voice was soft and almost soothing as the Pastor stepped out of the crowd, shuffling. He had a pair of railroad spikes in one hand – big, sharp steel things, giant nails. In the other, he had a hammer.

Cade was starting to wonder if he'd gambled wrong.

He flexed, but they had him pinned. He still wasn't going anywhere. Suddenly he was very conscious of how warm the tarmac was against his back.

He didn't bother saying anything. There wasn't much to say.

Gently, almost lovingly, the Pastor pressed the tip of one of the spikes into Cade's palm. Then he brought down the hammer.

Cade didn't flinch. The spike went through the palm, kicking up a gout of blood as it lodged fast in the tarmac. The Pastor raised the hammer again, and brought it down hard enough to drive the spike another inch in. The pain was like a red hot knife carving all the way down Cade's arm, and he wondered if he'd be able to use his hand again when he got that spike out.

If he got that spike out.

Another blow from the hammer and the spike was deeper into the road. Then a third. Each of those blows of the hammer was like someone sticking battery acid into Cade's palm and shooting eight hundred volts down his nerves. It was a hell of a thing to take and not flinch or cry out, but Cade didn't figure crying out was going to profit him all that much, and flinching was just going to tear his hand up worse.

Another blow. The sound of the hammer on the spike was like a ringing bell. Cade started wondering about infection. The spike was most of the way into the tarmac now. The Pastor stood, panting slightly. "Oh Lord," he breathed, his face flushed, his eyes shining. "Oh Lord."

The Pastor was stronger than he'd looked, to swing the hammer that way. Cade wondered how many times he'd done this before.

Probably a few.

That gamble was starting to look like the worst bet Cade had ever made.

Cade's thoughts were starting to run away from him a little. He tried to focus. He'd been a damn fool to let himself get took. He could've run. Running wasn't his nature, but all the same, he could've hid out, got his answers another way.

He could feel his forearm getting sticky as the blood pooled under it.

The pain was gigantic.

The Pastor moved to the other hand, pushing the point of the railroad spike into the flesh. Cade was ready for it now, when it came, anticipating that first brutal blow of the hammer. But the Pastor was ready too. The hammer didn't move.

Cade looked up and saw that cracked, crazy-paving smile, the eyes glittering above it.

All he could hear was the slow, steady tic, tic, tic of someone's watch.

Cade scowled.

The son of a bitch was making him wait for it.

Cade's lips twitched, nearly baring some teeth. He came pretty damn close to saying something about that. Then he realised that even a cross word was giving the son of a bitch a measure of satisfaction, and the hell with that. Cade took a deep breath, and relaxed, letting the pain in his pinned hand be its own thing, not touching him.

Above the crowd, the sky was a slowly deepening blue. The first stars were starting to come out. Cade looked up at them, letting everything else fade away.

Crang.

The hammer came down, hard, and another white wave of pain smashed down Cade's arm, then crackled and burned like hot coals as the hammer rose and fell, rose and fell, rose and fell. The Pastor wanted to get it done quick now, Cade figured. Good for him.

The men in the crowd let him go and stood back. They still hadn't said a single damn word, which might have shown an impressive command of internal discipline, under other circumstances. Right now, Cade wasn't concentrating too hard on that. He was pinned, arms spread wide, palms nailed to the tarmac, and that was where he was going to be staying. He figured he could probably pull himself free if he wanted to – except that'd drag those metal spikes through the flesh and bones of his hands, tear them both apart. He'd probably cripple himself for life.

Might have to come to that.

The Pastor knelt down, grinning like a snake in a gerbil's cage.

"Oh, sinner, your sins are black as *pitch*... but have faith. Trust in the good word of the Lord. Oh, sinner, *hear* his word!" The Pastor's bony hand crept to Cade's combat knife, pulling it out of Cade's belt. Then he laid the blade against Cade's chest and the black fabric of his tank-top. "You got the *Devil* in you, sinner! You got the hand of *Satan* on you!"

He laughed, and it chattered like skeleton's teeth rattling in a cracked glass jar. "Cast him out, Lord! Cast... him... *out!"*

Then he cut.

Down first, through fabric and flesh, then across, the blade bit, slicing as keenly through Cade's skin and muscle as it did through anything else. Carving a bloody cross.

Cade swallowed. That was just overkill – plus it wrecked a pretty decent vest. He just hoped nobody he'd cut up earlier had any kind of blood diseases. These days there wasn't any telling. A man should be careful.

The Pastor stood, passing the knife to a man in the crowd. That was it. The whole mass of people walked away, not saying a word, most of them heading back down Cervantes and filtering off into the streets and buildings. Within five minutes, Cade was alone.

The agony in his hands and chest had become a steady drumbeat of pain. He could feel the blood matting what was left of his top and the hair on his chest. He was very conscious of the hard blacktop under his head, and how uncomfortable the chains on his biceps were, all of a sudden. He wanted to flex a little, but with the soft tissues in his hands pierced by a pair of railroad spikes, that wasn't a good idea.

Cade breathed in, and breathed out. Far away, a dog howled.

It was going to be a long night.

CHAPTER NINE

THE GHOST

ANOTHER MAN MIGHT have screamed.

That's not to say a man couldn't deal with being nailed to tarmac in the middle of the street without screaming. That would certainly be possible, if a mite unlikely. But another man might have found himself gasping out, or grunting, or groaning, or making little noises every time he breathed to help himself deal with the pain. Another man might, after the first nine or ten hours rolled past and the pain in his hands turned into an itching that didn't stop, and the freezing night turned into a baking day, and all in total silence, with just the blowing of the breeze to listen to – well, another man might start to cry. Or start howling in the night like a damned wolf, shrieking at the top of his lungs until those lungs gave out and his vocal chords ruptured, just to break things up, just to hear a sound, any sound at all...

Not Cade.

Cade just lay there and took it.

It wasn't until the sun dipped below the horizon again, and he realised how dry his tongue and throat were, and how he'd been laying there with his mouth open for a couple hours because he'd forgotten to close it and his throat was like sandpaper – it wasn't until then that Cade made a single sound, and even then, it was a slow sigh.

As if to say, *Hell with it.*

He didn't say a word until the second day.

That was when Fuel-Air turned up.

He was sitting on the tarmac next to Cade, his boonie hat pushed back on his head, grinning. He looked wired.

Holy fucking shit, dude, he said, although Cade didn't *hear* him exactly, more *felt* him speak. *That's some Jesus Christ on the motherfuckin' cross shit. You messiah-acting motherfucker.*

Cade scowled.

Serious, dog, this crazy fuck's got some sort of king-size fucking hard-on for your ass. I mean, this is some awesome shit, man.

Cade swallowed. "Reckon?"

He could hardly hear his own voice – it was a rasping croak, like a toad baking alive in the middle of the desert. That wasn't any damn good. He could use some fluids pretty soon. Maybe Fuel-Air had some Red Bull or Jolt Cola or something.

Sorry, dog, all I got is coffee granules.

He was eating them raw. Cade shook his head. Goddamn Fuel-Air.

What, I'm supposed to be bringing some magic sponge for your ass? Man up, bitch, you can handle this shit. You did a year in the hole and you didn't blink, man... shit, you were one Steve McQueen-ass motherfucker, know what I'm saying? This should be a walk in the fuckin' park.

"Had a drink back then." Cade didn't know why he was talking to Fuel-Air. It just encouraged him when he was alive, no reason why it should start making the boy see reason now.

Something about that didn't seem right, but Cade couldn't put his finger on it.

Hate to bring this up, dog, but that was urine. You were drinking piss the whole time you were there.

Cade almost shrugged, then remembered his hands. They were almost numb now. He rolled his eyes instead. Piss was sterile, and he'd needed the liquids. Come to think of it, he wouldn't say no right now.

I ain't gonna piss in your mouth, man. I know how you fuckin' think, dog, and that's some very homo-erotic I Am Curious Yellow *shit and I ain't fuckin' doing it. Shit, man, is that even legal in this state? What I look like to you?*

Cade took a deep breath, counted to ten, then let it go. Goddamn Fuel-Air always managed to annoy the hell out of him. Maybe the Duchess could talk some sense into him when they got back. Had they met?

Why hadn't they ever met?

Cade closed his eyes for a second, fumbling for the words. "Fuel-Air... aren't you..."

He opened his eyes. There was nobody there.

Hell of a thing.

The sun crawled across the sky, beating down like an oven. Like a kiln. Baking the tarmac until it burned hot all around Cade, baking him just the same. The heat made his hands scream, and the carved-open wound on his chest throb and itch, pulsing raw and red. The sun blazed into his eyes, even when he closed them, and it seemed to pulse to that same hellish drumbeat.

Another man might have passed out.

Cade just took it.

By now it wasn't just his hands, or his chest. His whole body was itching, aching, wanting to move. His leg kept twitching. Shaking. He couldn't seem to stop it. Every time his leg jerked, it sent a little bolt of pain down his arms from his hands.

His mind kept coming back to the heat.

The noon sun up above him was a like a blowtorch searing him, burning him alive, just sitting up there without a care in the world. Roasting him to death and there wasn't a cloud in the sky to stop it. He tried not to think about it, but then he had to swallow with a mouth as dry as bone on sand, or blink away the sweat in his eyes, or shift his weight and feel the burned skin scream at him for it, and there wasn't much option but to let his mind revolve around it, coming back to it again and again, like a planet revolving around the sun, that damned burning sun...

So in the end, Cade just took it. He could take it. Cade had taken things like that his whole life. That was pretty much all he did, was take things. Take and take, soak up punishment like a man on the ropes in the final round. In the desert, they'd said Cade was made of stone. Cade was a rock.

If you hit it hard enough, a rock would crack.

Cade suddenly decided he was going to rip his hands free.

Hell with it. It'd hurt like the devil, but it'd be worth it. He'd like as not never use his hands again, but he'd be able to sit up at least, get out of the damn sun. Get some water. Ruined hands – he could take that. Cade could tough it out. Just a matter of gritting his teeth, flexing and...

Semper Gumby.

Cade blinked, and turned his head. Fuel-Air was sitting a ways away. He had some dip in a can and he was chewing on a wad of it.

Stay flexible, dog. Semper Gumby, you know? This ain't something you can tough out, man. Gotta adjust yourself. Go with the flow.

Cade blinked, and then breathed in, counted to ten, and breathed out, letting his head rest against the cold concrete. He was pissed off with Fuel-Air – he was always pissed off with Fuel-Air – but he was more pissed off with himself. He'd near as dammit persuaded himself to tear his hands to pieces, and for what? Nothing he wouldn't get later. There'd come a time when he'd need to make that choice, but that time wasn't yet. Not by a long shot. Fuel-Air was right.

Goddamn Fuel-Air.

"You said to man up?"

Shit, dog, you gonna hold me to everything I fuckin' say? I told you fuckin' ages ago, ass. Circumstances have fuckin' changed. You gotta adapt your strategy, you know? This is some ungrateful-ass shit right here, bitch. Fuckin' ingrate pussy. I'm spending my fuckin' Sunday keeping your sorry ass company and you're acting like a whiny bitch. I'm fuckin' ashamed of you, dog. He spat. *I ain't spittin' in your mouth either, dude. You know you were gonna ask.*

Cade rolled his eyes. "Didn't know it was Sunday already."

Every day's fuckin' Sunday here, dog, like in that emo-ass song. You're in God's country, ain't you been told? He laughed, a little snort, then spat another thick wad of tobacco-spit onto the road. Then he wiped his nose on his sleeve and carried on talking.

Fuel-Air never could shut the hell up.

So it's like I was saying, man, this Reverend dude, he loves your ass. All this shit right here is some kind of Man Called Horse *ritual shit, dog. He's testing your ass, 'cause you're so goddamn perfect. Shit, you saw those dumb assholes in the bar, and if you hadn't been such a bitch and let them nail you down, you could've taken those baseball bat wielding motherfuckers easy. You're one deadly-ass motherfucker, dog.*

Cade shot Fuel-Air a look, then rolled his eyes again. Kid wasn't worth the spit it'd take to hold up his end of the conversation.

Fine, be that way. Point I'm trying to raise is that you're a motherfuckin' stone-cold killer, dog. That's some fuckin' useful-ass shit right there. Fuckin' Pastor ain't got one motherfucker in his army who could fuck shit up good as you. Why'd you think he didn't kill you? Hell, he didn't even nail your damn legs – 'cause he needs you to walk for him later. Shit, I figure the only reason he ain't put you to work right away is that maybe he's worried you're not as stone-cold a motherfucker as he figures. Maybe you're gonna fold or betray him or some shit. So he puts you in the jackpot, dog, gives you the fuckin' Passion Of The Christ *shit, see if you make it. If you're dead, fuck it – you ain't no problem no more and he gets his bone on from nailin' you up. Probably let you rot out here, make a roadsign out of ya. This way to fuckin' Albuquerque. Helter Skelter. But if you make it, he knows he's got a fuckin' gold mine.*

"Might kill him." Cade was considering it.

What, after days with no food and water and big fuckin' holes in your hands? I ain't sayin' you couldn't, but he could probably get his hundred motherfuckers to kick your ass all over again, only this time they'd cut your head off and shit. Or maybe he'd just keep doin' this shit over and over. Up to you, dog.

Cade nodded. Fuel-Air made some sense. That worried him. That, and something else dancing in the back of his mind. He closed his eyes, breathing in through cracked lips, then breathing out.

There was no getting around it. He'd have to say something.

"You're dead, Fuel-Air."

Fuck you. What are you, Bruce Willis now? Fuck you, bitch. You don't get rid of me that easy.

He heard the kid snicker, and spit. Cade felt it landing on his cheek.

No, that wasn't spit.

It was raining.

Cade relaxed as the drops fell faster and faster, hitting his cracked, parched lips. He saw the flash of the lightning through his closed eyelids, then heard the thunder boom overhead. The storm had come out of nowhere.

When he opened his eyes, Fuel-Air was gone.

Time passed.

At first, Cade lay there, his mouth open, drinking in the rainwater, refreshing himself and quenching the terrible thirst that had built up over the past couple of days. But after a spell, the rain wasn't refreshing or soothing. It was just rain. And it kept on. And on.

The sun had sunk below the horizon again. Cade knew better than to miss that burning heat, but all the same, when he tried to bring it to his mind, he couldn't remember the way his skin had seared and his throat had seemed to scrape like a match lighting every time he swallowed. He just remembered he'd been warm and dry, and now he was wet and cold.

Scratch that. He was freezing. His bones were freezing inside him and he could feel every drop of rain chilling him colder yet, like meat in a locker. Cade was probably the toughest, meanest, most ornery son of a bitch you could ever hope to meet, but he was a man for all that, a human being, and he was getting pretty close to his breaking point. He let his mind spin, looking for distractions, looking for something to keep him from that rain, that chilling ice rain, the ice storm beating down upon him harder with every second that passed, pooling in the bloody scar on his chest and the holes in his hands, so the itching and the pain came in icy waves, something to keep him from coming back and back and back to that, over and over...

He couldn't think of a damned thing.

He should have figured he was in trouble when he'd seen Fuel-Air, that stupid, doomed little bastard, always talking even though he was dead. Goddamn Fuel-Air...

Cade narrowed his eyes, then he turned his head and asked the question.

"Why not Duke?"

What the fuck you on about now, dog?

Fuel-Air was standing in his utility dress, the rain dripping off his helmet. He still had that goddamn grin on his face, like a damned skeleton. Cade shook his head, trying to get the rainwater out of his eyes.

"Duke's dead. Why you?"

Fuckin' Duke? What the fuck is this, election day? You wanna pick the guy who you like having a fuckin' beer with or the guy who gets you out of the fuckin' shit when it hits? Duke was fuckin' army, dog, what the hell do those fuckers know when the shit goes down? I'm the dude who drives the fuckin' humvee and gets you through the shitstorm. You know how many times I saved your ass, bitch?

Cade frowned. If he was going to go crazy, he figured he had a right to pick. He wasn't going to start arguing with a dead man, though. Wasn't any profit in it. His head sank back on the tarmac and he relaxed.

Shit, dog, what the fuck do you want? Some fuckin' Patrick Swayze in Ghost, *I-ain't-gonna-quit-you best buddy motherfucker treatin' you to a fuckin' beer and a game of cards while you rot your ass off in the fuckin' street? Fuck, I kept your ass alive in the fuckin' desert, bitch, I'm keeping it alive here... you got tough when you needed to get tough, and now you're nice and fuckin' flexible and Semper Gumby and shit, letting all this bullshit slide off your ass while you wait it out. You been doing everything fuckin' right in this fuckin' ass-ugly situation you made for yourself. You know why, dog? You want to take a guess?*

Cade didn't speak.

'Cause you hate me. He laughed. *Shit, dog, ain't you worked that out yet?*

Cade nodded. The little prick had a point. Maybe he'd have given up in front of Duke. But damn if he was going to screw up in front of goddamn Fuel-Air.

Cade spat, and Fuel-Air's ghost grin widened a notch or two.

Attaboy. Figure you last the night, we're almost done. Just stay cool like Ferris Bueller and shit, don't let it get to you. Almost done, dog. I guaran-fuckin'-tee it. Just stay loose.

"Semper Gumby." Cade muttered the words, and closed his eyes, letting the torrents of water trickle off him and onto the road. Things could be a hell of a lot worse. There could be a dip in the tarmac right about where he was nailed to the road – that'd drown him. Hell, they could've cut his balls off. A man could still be a good killer without any balls. They could've stuck his dick in his mouth like they did with the fat guy on the road in.

If that was them. And not some other bunch of crazy bastards Cade hadn't met yet.

Things could always get a hell of a lot worse, Cade figured.

The rain kept on lashing him, pooling in the wounds in his palms, washing the dried blood off his hands and chest and off the road and carrying it into the gutters. Cade turned his face to the side, so it wouldn't drown him.

Then, finally, he slept.

In his dream, the Duchess was sitting in front of him, naked as the day she was born, her breasts falling their full distance without the support of her bra, the blue veins on her thighs visible as her legs spread. She grinned, in that way she had, laying down cards on an old card-table: tarot cards, and every one was Death.

"You got to be ready, Cade. Things are going to get worse and you're going to feel them getting worse right in your soul, but you can't go making mistakes. You just bought something, and you'd better use it, that's all. And watch out for Fuel-Air."

She held up five Death cards, and smiled, starting to sing softly, the way she did sometimes in the mornings.

"Gotta know when to hold 'em, know when to fold 'em..."

"You should've showed up earlier," Cade said. He was wearing his uniform, behind the wheel of a humvee he didn't know how to drive. He needed some coffee. Maybe the Duchess had some of those instant granules – he could eat those raw. "You got coffee?"

The Captain barked back at him, face red as a damn beetroot. "Wake the hell up! Danger close *is coward talk! Wake the fuck up, pissant! Just wake the fuck up!"*

Cade woke up.

The rain had stopped, and the sun had come out and dried him off while he slept. It was high noon. His palms throbbed, a regular, hot drumbeat of pain. It didn't feel so bad, Cade reckoned.

In fact, Cade felt pretty good.

He turned his head, and saw someone standing next to him, wearing black.

"Fuel-Air?"

It wasn't Fuel-Air.

It was the Pastor.

CHAPTER TEN

THE GENERAL

"EASY NOW, CHILDREN... easy now. The Lord's touch is *gentle*, yes it is..."

The Pastor crooned softly, keeping his eyes on the spike as it slowly worked free. The man holding the long-handled pliers gave careful little tugs, trying to do as little damage as possible, but the blood had started flowing again despite that. Cade's right hand was already free, and he held it up in front of his face, slowly opening and closing the fist. Every time he did it, his hand seemed to catch fire and burn, the pain igniting his nerves like electricity. He was a little amazed he could move his fingers at all, after what the Pastor had done. The man must have the mind of a surgeon.

Or maybe he'd practiced a hell of a lot.

Anyway, Cade figured he'd feel pain any time he held anything for a long time. Maybe for good.

Cade would probably come to resent that later. Right now, he didn't mind it so much. Not now the spikes were coming out.

The spike in his left hand pulled free with a little rush of blood, and Cade raised that one too, the blood trickling down his forearm as he tested it. This one was a little harder to close – he was going to have to watch himself if he used that hand to work with, and hitting with it was going to be murder. He was going to have to test that out soon.

No time like the present.

Cade stood, his feet unsteady for a second from the long hours on his back. The Pastor watched him, careful as a hawk. Then Cade wheeled and punched the man with the pliers in the forehead, hard enough to send him crashing onto the tarmac, out cold.

The Pastor didn't blink, but Cade did. His mouth twitched. His hand was in agony, glowing like a hot coal. He growled slightly when he spoke. "Wanted to check."

"Oh, I understand, my brother. A soldier in the service of the Lord must test himself." He chuckled, and it still made Cade uneasy, even after all that he'd done already. Shattered glass tumbling from a polished skull. "We should get your wounds seen to, lest the Devil enter and infect the flesh. The sin is driven from your heart, but your body may still succumb to the evils of Satan..." He smiled, and turned, shuffling up Fillmore Street towards North Point. Cade followed, leaving the man with the pliers where he lay.

Cade didn't bother asking the Pastor why he'd had the sudden change of heart. He figured a man who liked the sound of his own voice that much would let him know the reasons soon enough, and in the meantime he'd stick with Fuel-Air's theory – that the Pastor was testing him to see if he'd break, either nailed to the road or after. Testing him to see if he was going to try and kill the Pastor right now. Cade could tell when a gun was on him, and he figured there was a fella at a window somewhere who had orders to make damn sure that if Cade raised a hand to the Pastor it'd be the last thing he ever did.

Cade wasn't in the mood to raise a hand to anything except maybe a sandwich and fries. After close on three days laying on tarmac with just rainwater for drinking, he'd noticed how hungry he was. Unless he got some food in him pretty soon, he wasn't going to be much use to anybody, never mind the Pastor.

The Pastor turned his head and smiled that weird smile of his. He seemed to know what Cade was thinking.

"We have food and drink, and a place to rest in my sanctuary. My place of peace in the midst of war, where my flock gather to come together in the glory of the Lord. You have seen my purgatory, my brother, now shalt thou know my paradise, oh, yes you will. Now shall you understand the *joy* of service to the Lord..." He chuckled his bone-rattle laugh as they turned to move west up North Point Street, heading towards some kind of big supermarket. Cade figured that was where they were headed. It made sense. Lots of room, lots of food – hell, if they'd rigged up a generator to the PA system, he could even give sermons. Seemed like a pretty sweet setup.

He flexed his fingers a little, frowning slightly at the firestorm of agony that shot up his arms. There was still a steady throb of pain in both hands and Cade knew it wasn't going away. Maybe not ever. It wasn't going to stop him doing anything he needed to do, but it was an additional distraction he didn't need.

The Pastor glanced at him. "You have a choice ahead of you, brother. Many are tested, yes, but few are chosen to serve in the glory of the Lord. Now your sins have been wiped from your soul and you are again clean, born anew. Tell me, are you still willing to serve the Lord in all of his splendour?" His voice was soft, but there was a keen edge to the question.

Cade shrugged. "Might as well." He shot a glance at Fuel-Air, who was leaning in a doorway with a jar of Ripped Fuel, grinning that smart-ass son-of-a-bitch grin.

Told you so, dog.

Goddamn Fuel-Air. It was a little unsettling to see him again. He remembered the Duchess telling him to watch out.

Well, he hadn't done any harm so far. Might have kept him alive, in fact.

Fuel-Air grinned.

"Got my knife?" Cade looked over at the Pastor, not blinking. He was pretty fond of that knife, and he'd sharpened it and got the balance the way he liked it, and it'd be a hell of a shame to start from scratch. If he had to start from scratch, he'd have to seriously consider snapping the Pastor's neck and using his body as a shield against sniper fire.

He might need to do that anyhow. He hadn't decided yet.

"We have your knife, and we have your chain – the big one with the weights, I mean. We've got all the tools you'll need to be a warrior in the service of the Lord your God, and that's what you'll be, make no mistake." He smiled, turning his eyes up. "The Lord your God has a *mission* for you, my brother, a mission of great import, oh yes, a mission *vital* to the work of God on Earth..." The Pastor was starting to breathe faster, his hands waving and clutching the air as he warmed to his theme, still shuffling with his broken snake-walk. "Will you *follow* his path, O my brother? Will you bring your sharp sword to *bear* on the unbelievers, the tools of *Satan,* the followers of the Hor-ned *Goat?"* The words were spat, his eyes rolling in his head in a fever.

Cade shrugged.

"Sure."

The Pastor led Cade up Buchanan Street, around to the front of the place. "There are powers in this city, O faithful servant, yes there are...

powers ranged against the glory of the Lord, powers arrayed to *destroy* His works, to commit acts of *murder*, to foment crimes of *perverse lust!*" He walked faster as his hands shook and danced, weaving between the abandoned cars still sitting in the parking lot.

Cade figured that line about murder and perverse lust sounded a little like the pot calling the kettle black, but there wasn't much mileage in saying so – leastways, not until he'd got his knife back. "The hippies?"

"*Lust and murder! Satanism and destruction!* You saw their handiwork yourself – do you think *your* community will be safe if their filth is left *unchecked?*" He hissed it, looking at Cade with that odd ferocity of his as they passed through the doors. Cade frowned. The man had a point. If the hippies – whoever the hippies were, wherever they'd set up – were the ones doing the burning, Cade needed to deal with them.

If they were. Cade wasn't in the habit of trusting people who nailed him to the middle of the street.

The supermarket had been gutted and rebuilt – most of the shelves had been dismantled and taken out, their place taken by a sea of mattresses, most crusted with piss and filth, and the occasional tent-like structure. Dozens of people – men, women, some of the children Cade had seen earlier – were sitting on the mattresses, some singing softly, some reading from Bibles. A couple were eating from tins, taken from the still-standing shelves on the far side of the supermarket. These shelves were stocked entirely with cans and a small quantity of canned drinks, as well as a vast reserve of bottled water – Cade figured any food with an early sell-by date had been eaten long ago. The shelves were guarded by the big men with the aluminium bats from before.

It was a crude setup. Cade could've put something better together in two days, and working alone at that. Most of the men and all of the women looked thin and pale – the kids looked malnourished, with that greyish skin Cade had seen a lot of. The food was probably rationed, maybe one can per meal if they were lucky. Cade looked around, and saw a set of double doors, locked up tight with strong chain and a padlock. That would be where the supermarket storage area was. Cade figured there'd be more food back there.

Unless they were using it to keep something else.

A picture was starting to develop. The hippies, the Satanists, the defilers: if they had control of the Haight-Ashbury, they'd be near Buena Vista Park, Golden Gate Park, the golf course, Corona Heights, all kinds of decent farming land. Cade had slung the word 'hippies' around pretty casually along with everybody else, before the bad times and after, but he knew it could mean a hell of a lot of things; some teenager with long hair, some fella with liberal views, hell, pretty much anybody in San Francisco as was, if you were standing outside it. But now Cade was thinking about communes, collectives, organised groups of people living off the land, growing crops like the Diggers in the sixties. Hell, if they had a working generator or two, they had hydroponics on their side too. As far as food was concerned, they'd be sitting pretty.

Meanwhile, the Pastor's people – who'd maybe been used to having things done for them, used to putting their faith in a higher power and slobbing out in front of a TV set or a pulpit while other people got their snack packs ready for 'em – didn't have a clue where to start when it came to farming and weren't in a position to do much about it except pray and keep on praying, because their crazy Pastor had seen to it that they only had one book to read. And now food was running short – what they needed was someone to grow food for them, someone who already had the knowledge. Maybe a slave class, maybe just some warm bodies to turn cold so all their food stocks could be stolen and taken away.

Cade liked this theory. It fit pretty well, and it meant that the fella who'd killed a hundred-odd people for his Old Testament God and then nailed him to a road for three days on top of that was the bad guy in the equation. Cade'd know exactly where he stood, and that'd be pretty damn good to know. Trouble was, there was a big piece missing that Cade couldn't get to fit.

Somebody'd burnt down Sausalito, and Cade was pretty sure it wasn't the Pastor's people. He didn't trust the Pastor, and the Pastor might have been lying – hell, he probably was lying about a hundred things – but these people liked their territory a little too clean and tidy for them to be burning everything outside of it. Still, even that could be worked in. There was just one thing that couldn't be.

Helter Skelter.

That wasn't a Jesus thing. The Pastor hadn't done that.

That was someone else.

Wasn't any way around it, Cade figured. He was going to need to investigate anyhow. Might as well do it for the Pastor as anyone else.

Still, he figured he should set a couple of things straight first of all.

"You run this?" He gestured around him.

The Pastor looked at him, one eye narrowed. He drew himself up to his full height and launched into a speech: "It is my calling to lead the chosen people of the Lord to their salvation, and to bring *fire* and *fury* upon the –"

Cade cut him off. "Reckon you need a war chief. Like a General. You need them hippies dealt with – kept an eye on, at least. That's my job. You run things here." By Cade's standards, it was a hell of a speech. A regular sermon.

The Pastor scowled, which seemed to crack his face up as much as smiling did. "I *have* a mission for you, my friend. A chance, a very *special* chance, to be a warrior in the glory of the Lord. To do His will upon this earth. To be His *sword* in the *war* on the forces of Hell. Now the *fool*, in his vanity and pride, might want *more*, but to him I say –"

Cade sighed. "War needs planning. Scouting. Intelligence. Won't get it done otherwise." Cade was getting pretty damn tired of explaining every little thing. He shrugged. "Not like you've anyone else worth a damn."

The Pastor raised one eyebrow, then looked past Cade, over his left shoulder.

Cade turned.

The man standing behind him was blond, tan and about a head taller than he was – a muscle beach type. The fella's muscles had muscles on them. Cade figured this guy didn't have to worry himself overmuch about food rationing – he was obviously getting a hell of a lot more than his share. There was a smacking noise as the big man slapped a steel knuckleduster into his palm in a slow, golf-clap rhythm. Cade reached into his pockets for his own.

He didn't bother looking at the Pastor. "Another test?"

The Pastor smiled. "Meet Jurgen, brother. You could call him my General."

Jurgen grinned, speaking slowly, in a thick Austrian accent. "Der Leader already hass an advisor to help him viz makink decisions. I am in charge of planning der long var against der Godless – he hass no need of a girlie-man like you."

Cade nodded, looking up. The man had to be a good seven feet tall, and he was a walking advertisement for steroid abuse. Great thick veins like cables stood out on the man's biceps. Cade didn't say a word.

Jurgen smirked through gapped teeth. "I am talkink to you, girlie-man. I haff business viz der Pastor. If you vant to be useful, you can try cleanink der toilet. There iss a lot of sshit in it." He smirked a little wider, jabbing a finger into Cade's chest. "I think you vould be good at pickink up sshit, girlie –"

Cade moved.

There was a snapping sound as he yanked the finger backwards and broke it. Then he moved with his left, wincing slightly as the fist slammed hard between Jurgen's thighs, smashing against the steroid-shrivelled bits of flesh he kept there. The punch sent a wave of molten lava up the nerves in Cade's arm. Hurt like hell.

There was some consolation in knowing it hurt Jorgen a hell of a lot more. He doubled over, making a high-pitched whining sound as his eyes bulged, at which point Cade let go of the man's finger and pulled back his right.

Jurgen tried to straighten up, but he couldn't make it before Cade's fist slammed into his jaw. Cade didn't get angry as a rule, but he'd been nailed to the street for three days, putting up with Fuel-Air of all people, and that didn't do much to ease a man's temper. There was a fair amount of anger in that punch, and a hell of a lot of power, and the lead knuckleduster he'd slipped out of his pocket besides.

The impact tore the jawbone off Jurgen's face, sending a gout of blood spattering over Cade and onto the floor, the flesh of the face torn to strips as the jawbone dangled by a thread of muscle. Jurgen's eyes bulged, and he raised his hands to his face.

Cade's hands got there first, closing about the dangling jaw and tearing it free. Then he swung it around, smashing it into Jurgen's temple, sending him crashing down to the ground. The Pastor nodded approvingly.

"With the jawbone of an ass, he will slay his thousands. The Lord was right about you, brother, yes He was."

Cade nodded. "You need a new General."

The Pastor smiled. "Why? The old one's still alive."

Cade tossed the jawbone aside as Jurgen raised his head, scrabbling helplessly with his remaining fingers at what was left of his face, his tongue flapping uselessly as blood and drool mingled on the cold tile floor. Cade brought his fist down once, crashing the lead weight of the knuckleduster into the back of Jurgen's head, smashing the skull into fragments.

Jurgen slumped forward, deader than hell. He hadn't thrown a single punch. A couple of the children started to cry.

The Pastor turned, raising his hands to the crowd. "Be not afraid! For even the angel of *death* himself was but a noble *soldier* in the army of the Lord! Brother – name?"

"Cade," said Cade.

"Brother Cade is here to do the will of the Lord and pro-*mote* his glory! Brother Jurgen was *weak!* The *Devil* was in him! Brother Cade is a strong right arm for the Lord, a man who will do works of *greatness* in His name! Do you not *believe* in the Lord? Do you not *love* your Lord? If you love your God, do not fear! Only the *godless* need fear! The hippies! The *pre*-verts! *Satan's own!*"

The children had stopped crying. They were looking at Cade, mesmerised. If they'd seen a monster standing there before, they were seeing something else now. A biblical hero, ready to slay his weight in unbelievers.

Cade suddenly realised there wasn't a toy in the place.

The kids didn't have toys. He'd figured the adults weren't allowed books, but there wasn't even a magazine or an old newspaper. There wasn't anything that wasn't food or water or a place to sleep. Or a bible. He already knew nobody drank, but that was the tip of the iceberg – the

Pastor had taken everything from these people except the chance to kneel and pray to his Lord.

Cade was almost impressed. The man knew how to put a cult together.

One by one, the men and women stood, bowing their heads and saying their 'amens.' Cade leaned forward and muttered. "We should talk."

"In the morning, Brother Cade." The Pastor smiled, walking into the crowd, laying on hands. Cade followed a pace or two behind. He wasn't in the habit of feeling good about himself, and he felt a mite ambivalent now, but he had to admit he'd played this one pretty well. He had a home base now, while he was in San Francisco – somewhere he could lick his wounds, get food supplies and hopefully medical care, if the Pastor allowed things like band-aids and stitches in his handmade heaven.

He was going to need to kill the Pastor, of course. That went without saying. Probably he'd need to kill a good load of the rest of these fools into the bargain.

But he figured that could wait.

At least until the morning.

CHAPTER ELEVEN

THE WALK

Morning came soon enough.

Cade had managed to get some sleep and a little food – pork and beans out of a can – and now he was in the Duty Manager's Office, looking at a map of the city the Pastor kept there. The thin old man stuck one bony finger out, drawing a line across the map, marking the edge of his territory.

"Pass this line, and you're outside my reach, Brother Cade. All you have is the Lord at your back, and you must trust, you must *trust* and *believe*, in the mercy of the Lord and the power of the Lord to *shield* you from the evils of the Devil..."

That suited Cade just fine. He didn't trust the Pastor further than he could piss, and he had a feeling it was mutual. They were using each other – or at the very least, not killing each other – but no more than that. Cade needed a base, and the Pastor needed some eyes. Everything else was window dressing.

Of course, that meant the Pastor figured he needed a pair of eyes that could take being staked down on the tarmac for three days and then get up and kill near seven feet of solid muscle without thinking twice. That was a hell of a pair of eyes.

Made a man wonder what might be waiting out there.

"Ain't the first."

The Pastor drew back, surprised and slightly confused. Cade looked at him, that look he took on when people didn't catch his meaning right away, and the light dawned on the Pastor's face. "Ah... no, I have sent men out before. I have to *know,* you see; what he's doing. But nobody ever comes back."

Cade shrugged. "Converts, maybe."

Folks not coming back didn't necessarily mean they were dying. Could be that they took one look at the hippie setup – which probably included decent fresh vegetables, books and a toy or two – and decided they'd just as soon stay there forever as head back to the Pastor. If Cade had been the kind of man to have a sense of humour, he'd have said they'd been tempted into the ways of sin.

Instead, he leaned back in his chair, studying the Pastor carefully. "Who's 'he'?"

The Pastor hissed, crunching the paper of the map in a bony fist. "The *Devil!* Devil among devils, prince of demons! How many souls did he *condemn,* O Lord, how many souls did he send with his own hands into the eternal *fire?*"

Cade frowned. "Couldn't tell you. Who is he?"

"*Doctor* Leonard Clearly!" the Pastor spat the words, his eyes narrowing, the lines on his brow becoming deep, furrowed trenches. "A botanist and bio-chemist, *they* called him: the media, the liberal apologists. He wasn't anything but a pusher! A *dealer* who spoke with the forked and hissing tongue of *Satan!* The teacher of worldly pleasure! I knew the man, before the Lord brought His wrath upon this land. I... I *debated* him. In a lecture hall. A special event." He spat. "*Hah!* A setup by the *liberal elite!* They *ambushed* me with their questions, their *science!* As if their science knew better than the voice of *God!*" The Pastor turned his eyes to Cade's, and there was pain in them, all of a sudden, an old humiliation. "He called me a *lunatic!* Can you imagine, Brother Cade? He said I should be taken to the booby hatch and locked away with the nuts – his exact words! Because I dared stand up and tell him that happiness came from your *soul!* From the *glory* of the Lord! Not a *pill-bottle!*"

The Pastor sank into his chair, releasing the map from his grip. He raised his hands to his head. Cade leaned forward a little. This was the first time he'd seen the Pastor rattled, and he couldn't help but get curious.

The Pastor exhaled a long, shaken breath. "They laughed at me. A whole roomful of young people. Students. Just young. They weren't real hippies then, you see. They weren't tools of the Devil. Not *then.*"

He shook his head. "But they didn't *hear* me. Wouldn't listen to the holy word, no... and all the time, he was talking about – about *mind alteration.* And... *open sexuality.* We know what that means, don't we, Brother Cade? You can dress it up all you like, with your *words,* your fancy liberal *words,* but you can't hide from the *Lord* with words, no you can't, you cannot conceal your sins from His gaze..."

He raised his head, and there was pure hatred in those ice-grey eyes. "*Free love.*" He let out a harsh, barking laugh, bitter and poisoned. "We know where that leads! *Oh* yes! Freedom to love – *love,* they call it! There's only one love, yes indeed, and that's the love provided by the Lord! That's right, the Lord in His glory and His purity and His... His *chastity...*" The Pastor let out a sob, covering his eyes.

Cade didn't say anything. There wasn't much to say.

The Pastor swallowed. "Free love leads to sins that cannot be forgiven. Profane *lusts* – evil and heathen *perversions!* It's not me that says so, oh, no! No, *sir!* It's the *Bible!* Those crimes are outlined for all to see in the very written word of the *Lord!*" He pounded his fist into his palm. "They're crimes against nature and God, crimes that gotta be paid for, yes sir, paid for in *blood!* The blood of a *sinner!* You got to see that!" His tone changed suddenly, as he leant forward, his hands out in supplication. "You – you see that, don't you? You *gotta!* You do – you *do* see that? Don't you? Don't you see? Don't you see I was *right?*" He was almost begging.

Cade thought about the skeletons on the crosses. He just stared. He wasn't about to give the Pastor absolution – he didn't figure he could if he wanted to.

And he didn't much want to.

Some crimes can't be forgiven, all right.

Eventually, the Pastor stood, shaking his head. "Oh, he was a devil, that Doc Clearly. A *fiend!* He corrupted hundreds, *thousands,* yes he did... Too many to count! His words were a *poison* that blanketed this city and inflamed *sin* within all they fell on! He preached *Satan's* word! Condoned *psychedelics* to muddy the mind and doom the soul – why, he even *created* some! Things the law didn't cover! Drugs to chain the mind and heart so it might be brought quicker to the Devil's grip!" He slammed his hand down on the map, as if trying to crush the man he hated under his palm.

He stood like that a moment, shaking his head... then he sighed, and his body seemed to wilt a little, held up by his hand pressing on the map.

"Then the end came."

Cade just watched.

"The end came, and billions died, and *Doctor* Clearly... he wasn't one of them. No. The Lord... the Lord must *test* a man. Only the *worthy* can enter His kingdom. He sets us *challenges...*" He looked up suddenly and jabbed a bony finger at Cade. "*That's* why I put those iron spikes through your hands, you see? That wasn't *my* idea. *I* didn't think of that. It wasn't my test to give you. The *Lord* spoke in my ear, *whispered* it. He said to me that you could do *great service...*" He blinked, shaking his head, and then reached into the desk and pulled out the knife, still coated with dried blood, and the length of chain. "So, then. Do great service *now,* Brother Cade. Bring me word of Doctor Clearly, or if you can, bring to me his *head* that I might offer it in *sacrament* to the Lord..."

Cade reached for them both, slotting them into their proper places. "Obliged. Now I just need my truck."

The Pastor smiled. "Our need is greater, Brother Cade. We have a use for your vehicle – it will be the chariot that will carry our... *gift.*" He chuckled like a dusty mirror cracking in a haunted castle. "Judgement as a gift. I like that. Walk south and west, Brother Cade – towards Alamo Square. Take Lombard Street and Divisadero... *don't* walk down Van Ness Avenue."

"Sure," Cade muttered, locking the padlock on the chain. Lombard and Divisadero was the direct route. He wasn't planning on walking Van Ness anyhow – that'd take him far out of his way, and there was no reason for it that Cade could see.

Except there was a reason the Pastor could see. Might prove interesting to see what that was.

The Pastor shook his head, as if to clear it, then brought the topic back where he'd left it. "Clearly... he's a persuasive Devil. He has a silver tongue. I don't think you'll be fooled *easy* by his words... but so many have been. So, so many. I don't know if you'll return to us."

"I will," murmured Cade. He stood, checking his gear. He'd be back soon enough, all right.

The Pastor grinned. "He *is* the burner, Brother Cade. The force of chaos. He's the one you're looking for, the one who took the torch to Sousalito, yes he is... the Devil is a man of *fire.*" He chuckled, like a knife dragged down a sheet of glass, then raised a bony hand to wipe the sweat from his brow. "Kill him, or find his weakness, and then we'll talk. The Lord is a powerful *friend,* Brother Cade. The Lord provides for many needs..."

Cade nodded, once, and walked out.

His hands still itched, and they shot fire every time he moved them. For a moment, as he walked through the supermarket, between the mattresses, listening to the soft singing and praying of the people there, he wondered if he was going to walk out and find a big crowd with railroad spikes in their hands... but when the doors opened, all there was was a parking lot and a sunny day.

In fact, it was the most beautiful morning Cade had seen in a while.

That's some eerie shit, dog. Fuckin' surreal is what it is.

"Don't have a need for you now, Fuel-Air," Cade said, walking past the thin figure in the utility gear, chewing dip and grinning that fuck-you grin of his. "Get lost."

You'll need me later. Guaran-fuckin'-tee it. And you got me now anyway.

He laughed, a caffeinated little giggle.

I'm gonna keep an eye on you, Cade.

Cade didn't bother to reply. When he looked back around, Fuel-Air was gone.

Cade scratched the back of his neck, mouth twitching a little as the pain in his hand bothered him, and then turned right, heading towards Van Ness Avenue.

The Pastor didn't want him to know what was down there, and Cade figured that was reason enough. He set to walking.

VAN NESS WAS a walk, and then some – a couple of miles of straight road. But Cade didn't exactly mind. After what he'd been through the last couple of days, it felt good to just move – good to get one foot in front of the other. Good to just breathe. Even the garbage he was starting to see on the road was starting to look good.

Shit, man, what are you, some garbage con-o-sewer now? Fuck, that's some fucked-up American Beauty *shit...*

"Thought I told you to get the hell out." Cade wasn't in the mood for Fuel-Air right now. He had business to be getting on with, not to mention finding whatever the Pastor didn't want him to see on Van Ness Avenue. He was getting damn tired of being pestered by a ghost.

Fuck you, bitch. You're missing some elementary fuckin' shit here, you know? How come that garbage looks so damn good to your dumb ass?

It was a sign Cade was outside the Pastor's territory – away from all his religion, his rules and regulations, his damned crosses and the rest of his assorted bullshit. Every empty bag of corn chips blowing about the streets was like a dove with an olive branch in its mouth as far as Cade was concerned. A sign that things were getting halfway back towards normal. He didn't bother saying any of that out loud. Fuel-Air would pick it up anyhow, he figured.

Okay, so you're sentimental for the days people didn't bother picking up their shit, fine. Something's still missing, dog. Check it out.

Fuel-Air walked past him, humping his pack on his back, tin lid on his head. He pointed across the road. Cade looked – there was a converse trainer sitting on a step, another one a little further down the street.

"So?" Cade was trying to sound like he didn't see what Fuel-Air was trying to say, but he was getting a sinking feeling. He'd seen it the second Fuel-Air had pointed it out.

You got shoes over there, dog. Where the fuck are the feet?

Cade didn't say anything.

No corpses, you dumb motherfucker. You got nobody picking up the garbage and shit, but people are picking up the fuckin' bodies off the ground and burying them or some shit. Ain't a single one here. Means you got another faction operating, one the Rev didn't want to mention. You're in enemy fuckin' territory, dog. Better get your shit together.

Cade nodded. Much as he hated to admit it, Fuel-Air was right. He needed to get his shit together. He'd been making damn fool mistakes ever since he'd reached San Francisco. He'd lost the truck, damn near lost his hands and probably lost his damn mind if a stupid kid he'd seen get blown to pieces with his own eyes was dropping hints at him from six feet in the ground. He wasn't noticing things he needed to.

Hell, maybe this was the mythical Doctor Clearly at work. If the hippies were growing food, they'd need fertiliser...

That boat don't fuckin' float and you know *it, dog. Shit, man, where's your fuckin' head at?*

"Shut up, Fuel-Air," Cade snapped, raising his head. Then he froze.

Fuel-Air wasn't there.

Instead, Cade saw a boy of about eight or nine, with hair down to his shoulders, covered in dirt and dust. He was barefoot, wearing a ragged t-shirt and a cut-off pair of jeans that had both seen so much assorted crap that they'd lost any colour they might have once had. The boy was holding something in his hand – Cade couldn't work out what it was at first.

Then the boy grinned with a mouthful of rotting teeth, raised it up to his mouth and bit into it, tearing off a strip and chewing. Cade watched, eyes narrowed, looking at the thing the boy was biting on like it was a strip of beef jerky.

The thing was wearing an earring.

CHAPTER TWELVE

THE BOY

CADE LOOKED AT the boy.

The boy looked at Cade, and chewed his ear. His eyes were heavy-lidded, slow-looking, a cow's eyes. Cade knew you could go crazy pretty quickly from eating human meat – it caused lesions on the brain. Affected you a little like CJD.

There was a good chance he could get to the boy before the boy made a run for it. Whether he could answer a question would be another matter.

Cade counted to three. Then he moved.

The boy moved too – breaking right, making a bolt towards Grove Street, heading east. He was quick – fast as a whippet. Cade was a good couple of heads taller than him, but he was having some trouble closing the gap. Probably still weak from before.

Should've taken a day off, dog. Got a couple nights sleep and shit. I know you hated that motherfucker but that didn't mean you couldn't eat his food and sleep on his fuckin' piss-stained mattresses until you got your strength back. Shit, you didn't even change that fuckin' shirt.

Cade spat. Goddamn Fuel-Air.

Fuck you too, bitch.

Cade was gaining slowly, but the boy didn't seem to tire. At this point Cade was wishing he had the truck – remembering how he'd dealt with the last crazy kid he'd found.

Youth of today, man. What the fuck you gonna do, dog? Kill 'em? Oh yeah, that's you all over. Fuckin' baby killer. Come on, catch that motherfucker, bitch.

Cade cursed under his breath. It was hard enough keeping up without Fuel-Air criticising his damned moral choices.

Shit, fuck you then, baby killer...

The boy gained another couple of feet on him. By now they were heading past Larkin Street, and Cade could see Market Street coming up. The boy was angling to the left. Where the hell was he running to...?

Cade cursed again, and spat. He wasn't a film-going man, but he'd seen enough of them in his time to know a cliché when he saw it. The little bastard was heading up Market Street, towards the Civic Centre. Towards the BART.

Cade put on a spurt as they rounded the corner, trying to catch him, but it was like trying to catch the hare at a greyhound race. He was in shape, but he wasn't a runner, and this kid obviously did a lot of running.

The hare at a greyhound race. Something about that made Cade uneasy. He slowed as the boy darted around the building, letting the dirt-coated kid get some distance and skitter down the steps into the darkness of the BART station. Cade slowed to a walk, catching his breath, walking carefully forward...

The hare at a greyhound race. That was a hell of a comparison. Because this kid did a lot of running. Like that was his job.

Cade could hear Fuel-Air laughing at him.

Because... the job of a mechanical hare at a greyhound race wasn't just to move fast.

It was to get the dogs running after it.

It was bait.

The air filled with screaming.

"Hell," said Cade. There wasn't time to say much of anything else.

Out of the mouth of the Civic Centre BART Station came about two dozen men and women, all screaming their lungs out, covered in dirt and filth, teeth rotting, naked but for ragged jeans and cutoffs or torn business suit trousers and skirts, a couple of them not even having that. They had madness in their eyes, and they were fast as the boy – hell, they were faster.

And they were headed right for him.

Cade cursed out loud this time. Then he drew his knife out of his belt and swept it around in a wide arc, cutting into the first wave as they came for him. The lucky ones got their arms up in time, coming away with defence wounds as the blade glanced off the bones in their forearms. The unlucky ones reached up too late, grabbing hold of throats that were flapping open and gushing blood.

Cade only had time for the one swing before they were on him. These people made the Pastor's mob seem gentle – they slammed forward, not giving a damn if they trampled over their own, pushing their dead to one side, a couple of the pack splitting off to drag the convulsing bodies away and tear into them with their rotten teeth. The mass of bodies hit Cade, one of them impaling itself belly-first on his knife, rotten breath washing over him. Cade couldn't tell if it was a man or a woman.

Their broken fingernails clawed at him, tearing at his ruined top and the wounds on his chest, the stench of their bodies hitting his nostrils hard enough to make the bile rise in the back of his throat. He flashed back to the corpses nailed to the crosses on the basketball court. It was like they'd come to life now, rotting flesh and all, to swarm over him and drag him down into the dark.

He hit out at best he could, feeling his fists slamming into jaws, breaking bones, sending rotting teeth tumbling onto the precinct as they fell from suppurating gums, feeling ribs snap and legs break, and none of it doing a damn bit of good. He could beat on them until sundown and they'd still keep coming. It was in their eyes – crazed, rolling orbs, swinging about in their sockets. It was in the sounds they made, not quite human any longer.

He could still beat them. If he could get free of the crowd, he could make a run for it, maybe get into one of the buildings –

Something slammed into the back of his head, blurring his vision and making him see stars. He hit out with an elbow, smashing in someone's nose, then turned his head, trying to see what'd hit him. He caught a glimpse of someone holding a human thighbone.

It had teeth marks on it.

Another bone slammed into his ribs. They were armed. Cade tried to fight his way free, swinging his fists and snarling like an animal whenever they made contact and he felt the pain slam up his arms, but the best he could do was block the bone clubs as they swung at him. He wasn't going to be able to break free of them. The knife was out of his reach – they were already eating the one with the blade in his belly. Cade didn't rightly know why they weren't eating *him.*

They would soon enough.

He'd screwed this from beginning to end, since he first set foot in the city. He'd acted like he knew what the hell we was doing and he'd screwed up time and again, and now he'd screwed up for the last time. Now he was going to die for it. Cade wasn't someone who felt fear, exactly, but he felt something like it now. A cold certainty that sat like a frozen stone in the middle of his chest. He was going to die down there, in the dark. Maybe they figured they'd cook him first. Maybe they just wanted him out of the sun before they tore him to pieces and used his bones for tools.

He kept fighting even while they dragged him to that dark tunnel, the sheer weight of numbers forcing him down the steps, into the darkness, the pitch black, and there were even more of them there, a sea of monsters, human beings made less than human, running their ragged nails over him, scratching and clawing him, trying to tear his eyes out of his head.

Cade figured his eyes were probably a delicacy. That and the testicles.

The only light was coming from the street above, and that was mostly blocked by the crush of bodies, but Cade could make out piles of bones and skulls, sigils drawn in blood on the walls. They'd been eating the dead, those dead from the plague and anyone else they'd managed to catch since – eating their own when they had to. San Francisco was a big city. Cade wondered how many there were down there...

Fingers found their way into his mouth, nails scratching at his tongue, trying to yank it out. He bit down and his mouth filled with blood. They were going to tear him into pieces.

Cade felt a kind of calm wash over him. That was it. He figured they'd do him in quick. Too bad about the Duchess, but maybe Woody'd head north and get something from one of the small towns up that way. Hell, maybe they'd both move north and get out from under the jackpot that'd hit Sausalito.

Wasn't his problem anymore.

Cade relaxed, closed his eyes and waited for them to get it the hell over with.

"Let him go. I want to talk to this one."

The voice was deep and rich, in every sense of the word. It was a television voice, a radio voice, a money voice. A voice used to getting what it wanted.

The cannibals let Cade go. He nearly fell backwards before he steadied himself on his feet.

When he opened his eyes, he was damned near blinded – someone was shining a light right at him. The cannibals were creeping back, shielding their own eyes. Some of them slinked up to the surface, looking to join the ones who'd stayed up top to eat the fallen. Some crept towards the barriers, vaulting the turnstiles and disappearing deeper into the system. A handful stuck around to watch.

Cade spat out the severed fingers in his mouth, swallowing the blood. "You in charge?"

The voice chuckled. "Straight to the facts, light on tact. That's good. No place for small talk in a negotiation situation – shows weakness. In this frankly chronic economic crisis... you need to be strong. Trust me... I'm Strong." Cade narrowed his eyes. It sounded like the start of a TV show. He was pretty sure it was one.

The voice lowered his lamp, putting it on the ground. Cade blinked a couple of times and then took a look.

The man in front of him was about Cade's height, black, handsome, well-groomed – or as well-groomed as you could get living in a subway station. He had on a white suit that was pretty much untouched by the dirt, shiny black shoes and a gold watch. His gaze was steady – none of the eye-rolling the others had. His teeth were clean and white, apart from one gold one, slightly off from the centre. It had a diamond embedded in it that glinted when he smiled. He was smiling now.

Put him in the middle of a Hollywood premiere, he might have looked a little shabby. Put him in the Pastor's supermarket, he would've looked like a prince. Down here, surrounded by human wreckage twitching and grunting and smearing their own waste on the walls, he looked like a God.

But his breath had the same stink of raw meat on it.

"Washington Strong. Your money-saving, flesh-craving host with the most – of any currency you name, I can put you to shame. Of course, stocks and shares don't have the same exponential potential that they once did." He grinned, and his tooth flashed. "These days... you could say I'm an investor in people."

Cade was trying to place the name. He'd seen the man on the TV in Muldoon's, with the sound down – taking up three minutes on the evening news some nights, an hour-long show at the weekends, pointing to graphs of plummeting shares, playing with props, taking phone calls from worried old folks who'd lost everything they had. It was coming back a little now.

Washington Strong, CNN's money maestro. Blue or white collar, he'd protect your dollar. News flash, here's where to put your cash. You could trust the man with the million-dollar smile.

Only it turned out you couldn't. Cade had a hard time remembering the news from before the bad times - financial meltdowns had a way of paling into insignificance when everybody you knew was dropping dead in the street – but he remembered the old woman in Tennessee who killed herself after putting her last thousand dollars into Washington Strong's Investment Success Superscheme™. He remembered the endless pre-trial hearings as Strong put off going to prison on a dozen counts of investment fraud, embezzlement and tax evasion. It would've been a hell of a trial, but the trial never came. The bad times turned up first, and suddenly nobody gave a damn about the man with the million-dollar smile.

Cade nodded. He figured he should say something. He'd never met a celebrity before.

"Nice smile."

"An affectation that befits my station." Strong grinned. "Can't have a king with no bling, a ruler without a jeweller. You want loyalty – be royalty. Down here, a man's leadership skills can be a matter of life or dinner."

Cade shrugged. He'd take the man's word for it.

Strong stepped towards Cade, looking down at the severed cannibal fingers and stepping neatly over them. "You fought back pretty hard, pard. A display that made my day. Moves with something to prove. Got a name, my hard-fighting, finger-biting brother?" He still talked like he was on his TV show. Combined with the wash of rotten meat coming off his breath and that never-ending diamond smile, it made the whole situation seem unreal.

"Cade," said Cade.

Strong put a hand on Cade's shoulder.

"You've made the grade, Cade, my bone-breaking, life-taking, widow-making buddy. You've got the greed you need to succeed. You're what you might call... hungry for success." He grinned, gesturing upwards at an imagined sky, his shadow making hideous clawing gestures on the wall. "I saw a lot of guys like you up in the towers, looking down on the ordinary joes, the pathetic shmoes... now we're under the ground looking up, but it's the same game, different name. We're sharks. We survive by taking lives. Once upon a time that meant taking every dime, but that was small time. If you've got real *cojones*, you take the meat from their bones..."

Cade was about ready to punch that diamond out of his face, but he figured this wasn't the best time for poetry criticism. He looked around him, at the crowds of half-human things down in the BART station. A hell of a lot of them were wearing the rotted remains of suits. One of them had a tie.

And those jeans had designer labels on them. No wonder they'd lasted so well.

Cade took another look at the walls, the symbols drawn in blood. Dollar signs. FTSE, scrawled on the wall like a magic word. Dow. Jagged lines, smeared in human fat, rising up, up, up.

Cade figured he knew what these people had been before the bad times had hit.

He never knew San Francisco had such a thriving banking community.

He turned back to Strong. "So?"

"So, my ultra-violent, practically silent friend, there are two types of people in this brave new world. The eaters and the eaten. I think you've got the power to devour, Cade. I think you've got a bone-crunching, human-munching predator inside you, just waiting to get out. I think... you need to decide which side of the food chain you're really on. Right now. Because the offer I proffer comes with a deadline, my time-costing, patience-exhausting brother. And this Rolex I'm wearing is just a shade fast."

Cade got the message. Either join the program or join the menu.

"Sure," he said.

"Wise move. But I'd like a practical demonstration of your dentation, Cade. I'd like to know if you're serious about being deleterious." He paused, then smiled wider. "Eat someone for me."

Cade narrowed his eyes. "Told you I'd do it."

"I'm from Missouri. Show me."

"Who?"

Strong grinned, and looked over to the corner of the room. Cade followed his eyes, and saw the boy who he'd chased to get here. The one who'd got him into this. He looked at Strong.

"Him?"

Strong grinned. The diamond flashed.

"Him."

CHAPTER THIRTEEN

THE POLITICIAN

Cade looked back at the boy, sizing him up. The boy looked right back at him and snarled like a stray dog. He'd heard what Strong had said – didn't like it much. Cade figured this would probably be a test for the boy as much as for him. If Cade didn't kill the boy and get eating, the boy was going to try and kill him, and he'd probably have an even chance. He'd have killed already – if he was being used as bait to lure suckers or other cannibals in, he was most likely trained to kill fast if he had to. Cade had killed his first man at age eight. He knew how easy it was once you'd started, kid or no kid.

Even if Cade managed to put the kid down without killing him, he'd fail the test and the cannibals would come back for him, and Cade knew he wasn't going to be able to beat them all. This wasn't a crowd of normal folks – they were crazy as rabid dogs. They weren't going to hold back or try to avoid getting injured. They were just going to bury him and then tear him to pieces.

That's unless he killed the kid. Cade wasn't comfortable killing children.

But Cade wasn't exactly in his comfort zone.

He looked around the BART station at the men and women in their stained, dust-covered clothing, their rotten teeth. He was right out of options – he wasn't getting through that crowd unless he turned cannibal himself.

He shot Strong a look.

"Got a question."

Strong grinned, and the diamond flashed. "You got a meal to eat, Mister Cade. Call it an *hors d'ouvre* that must be obeyed."

Cade didn't move. "Got a question. How come you're in charge?"

Strong looked at Cade for a moment, then at the boy. The boy hunched like an animal, readying himself to pounce, his teeth bared. Strong shook his head.

The boy backed down, slowly.

"That ain't the question you were suggestin', Mister Cade. What you want to ask ain't why am I in charge. It's why should I be in charge of *you* – if I'm a product that's safe to invest in." He smiled again. "Let me ease your mind. I'm in charge because I have what it takes, Mister Cade. When the plague hit, a whole lot of the survivors – the movers and shakers and money takers in my particular circle – they looked around and they panicked. They thought they weren't going to make it in this new economic scenario. No more TV, no more internet, no more phones, everything falling to pieces. The only way forward was to maximise your survival potential, and that's where I stepped in. Washington Strong, the man with the million-dollar smile. The man who can tell you just what to do."

Cade kept his eye on that flashing diamond. He figured if he looked at the boy, the boy might see it as a challenge. Better to keep Strong talking.

Cade figured Strong was going to.

Strong chuckled. "If they ever bring TV back, you should try getting on it, Cade. You don't have to know much... you just talk like you do. You got authority, you set the priority. When you tell people to jump, they don't ask why, they ask how high. They were used to following me, even after all the scandal. They wanted to put their money where my mouth was." The chuckle became a laugh, the light dancing as the lamp in his hand shook.

"So... people were panicking. A few people were looting, but a lot were just breaking what they could find, burning things, running wild... they needed someone to tell them what to do, and I happened to be there. I told them the truth. It's a dog-eat-dog world, Mister Cade, and there are luxuries you need to set aside to abide. All those things you don't need to feed... like a conscience. Morality. Laws. All the things that stop you just taking what you want. And it's easy to take what you want when you're up against weaklings who won't, Cade. People who don't go that extra mile to live in style. My people already knew that – hell, they'd been feeding off folks for years. They didn't take much convincing." He smirked, and that gold tooth of his sparkled. "All I'm doing now, my hesitating, procrastinating brother, is feeding off people literally instead of metaphorically. And if you're on my team, you can live the dream. Eat like a king, live like a predator, do all the things you always wanted to do but didn't want to get caught doing. There's nobody to catch you any more, Cade, nobody but you."

His smile vanished.

"So go ahead. Hold back. Make out you're better than us. It'll last just long enough for you to die. And then we'll forget you were ever anything but the main course."

Cade nodded.

"So. You're in charge 'cause you're the biggest bastard here."

"That's right," said Strong, smiling. "Now, you gonna eat the boy? Or is the boy gonna eat you?"

Cade shrugged.

"Neither."

Then he moved.

Strong was still smiling right up until the lamp crashed to the floor, lighting everything up like a horror movie and throwing dark shadows onto the walls. He tried to bring his hands up, but they weren't quick enough. Cade's teeth were already in his neck, biting into the jugular.

Cade snapped his head back. There was a tearing sound that made the people skulking by the walls lean forward, anticipating.

Strong couldn't quite believe it. He kept not believing it when Cade starting ripping chunks of flesh out his throat and chest with his fingers, using the switchblade in his pocket to carve. He died not believing it.

The last thing he saw was Cade chewing on his meat.

Cade swallowed. It didn't taste too good, but he figured he needed to eat plenty if he wanted to make an impression, so he cut off a little more. Strong hadn't expected that. He'd spent a little too long with folks who either took orders or died quick. He'd starting thinking he was as invulnerable as his own image. The man was a sucker for his own hype.

Bad mistake for a man to make.

Cade tossed a chunk of meat to the boy. "Eat up." The boy looked at him for a second, then tore into the scrap. Cade figured there was more where that came from if he needed it, and it'd stop the boy doing anything stupid for the minute. Right now he had other fish to fry.

He stood up and turned to look at the cannibals. There were more coming now – trickling in to see what the fuss was. Some of Strong's blood had got on the lamp, drenching Cade in red light. He tore into another strip of flesh with his teeth, and the hot iron taste of Strong's blood made his head swim. Hell of a thing.

Half of them were shrinking back against the wall, trying to take in what had happened. These had been people, but they'd given Strong everything they had, right down to their humanity, just to survive. Cade figured they'd be easy work.

It was the others that he didn't like the looks of. The ones who were leaning forward, eyes narrowed, almost salivating. Animals had a habit of challenging the alpha male for pack dominance – or Cade had heard something like that on Discovery, anyhow. He figured if he wanted this lot on his side, he was going to need to apply a little carrot-and-stick.

He looked each of them in the eye, one by one. Then he growled, deep in his throat.

"I'm in charge now."

He kept looking, looking for the challenge, looking for the eye-fuck. There was a big one, long hair, biker tattoos, matted beard – he'd muscled his way to the front. His teeth weren't just rotten, they were black, most missing. This one hadn't come into it out of fear. He'd come into it because he liked the idea.

This was going to be the one. Cade locked eyes, eye-fucking him right back, then spat. If the biker backed down now, he was a coward. Cade was hoping he wouldn't.

He needed some stick to go with his carrot.

The biker charged, lanching himself forward, letting out an animal roar. Cade stepped to the side, catching the biker's head in his hands and twisting. There was a loud crack, like a branch breaking, and the biker's body stumbled forward to crash onto the tile floor.

Cade looked back at the crowd. Some of the eager ones were leaning back, mistrustful, weighing it up. They knew that what happened to the biker was probably going to happen to them, and that was the lesson Cade wanted them to take away.

Time for lesson two.

He leant down, using his skull-handled switchblade to cut a fat strip of meat off the biker's calf. Then he tossed it to the furthest man forward. Then he did that again, carving up the biker, tossing scraps of meat to the crowd. The growls turned to mutters of satisfaction – occasionally even gratitude. Once or twice, Cade heard human words.

A couple of the cannibals still didn't get the message. Any time one of them got within a couple of feet, Cade slit him across the throat with the switchblade and then opened up his belly. Then he used their meat to feed the rest. The message was pretty simple. *I'm in charge. Act up, you die. Toe the line, you live and get fed.*

Cade might have been cynical about politics, but he was pretty good at it.

Eventually, the ragged people in the BART station all had meat in their hands and in their mouths, and Cade was a mess, coated with clotting blood. Occasionally he still chewed on a piece of Strong, just to keep the illusion up.

He was the leader now.

Time to lead.

"Okay. Round here's deserted. Nobody left to eat. You been following bullshit." He wasn't used to making speeches, but he didn't have to say much. They were already looking at him with heads cocked, curious, like dogs following the stick before you threw it.

"Head north – up Van Ness, up Franklin, towards Marina Boulevard. Big Safeway – that's where the meat is. Meat in cans" – there was a rumble of discontent; he was losing them – "Raw meat. On the hoof. Human meat. Weak meat. Use kids as bait, you'll starve. You got to hunt."

He stopped, and looked at them. They blinked back at him, unsure.

Cade growled. He'd drawn them a goddamned map. What the hell more did they need?

"*Git!*"

They got.

As the throng of barely-human, half-naked things scuttled and scuffled up the steps towards the failing light, Cade noticed Fuel-Air standing in the light, shaking his head. On an impulse, Cade put his hand on one of the cannibals – one who looked a little more like he knew what was going on.

"No women, no kids. Someone eats a woman or a kid, I kill ten of you for every one that falls." The cannibal looked at him, opening his rotted mouth. "I will do it. *Git*."

The cannibal scurried into the shifting crowd, passing the word on in halting, broken English. Cade looked to Fuel-Air, but Fuel-Air was gone.

Cade wondered if he'd have thought of that on his own. He wondered if he'd have cared one way or another.

He looked at the marks on the wall and mused for a second on just how people – human beings, bankers and stockbrokers, CEOs, educated folk – could fall so far in just a couple of years. Then he shook his head, figuring himself for a damn fool.

Hard part wasn't falling. Falling was easy as hell.

Hard part was standing up in the first place.

Pretty soon they were all gone and it was just Cade – and the boy, gnawing on a piece of tattooed skin, looking at him with narrowed eyes. Questioning. Cade turned to look at him.

No point in sending him out to die with the rest of them. The Pastor's men were going to take a hell of a hit, but they had at least a couple of sniping rifles and a hell of a lot of other weapons. Cade figured the cannibals were going to knock his cosy paradise for a loop, maybe shake the faithful up a little bit. Make things harder.

Then when Cade came back, the Pastor's paradise might just be open for a coup. Worth trying, anyhow.

Cade would've made a hell of a politician.

He nodded at the boy. "You. Go get me my knife. I think I left it in a fella out there."

The boy looked at him warily for a second, then vanished. He was back a couple of minutes later with Cade's knife.

Cade took it from him, slotted it into his belt, and saluted. "I'm abdicating. Rule wisely now."

The boy looked uncomprehendingly at him as he climbed the steps. Cade figured he was better off alone than he had been with the rest of them. And he was a hell of a lot safer in a deserted BART station with a couple of dead folks than he would've been with Cade.

What the fuck was that shit? A salute? You growing a sense of humour in your old age, dog?

Fuel-Air was sitting under a tree with a porno mag and an open can of coffee granules. Cade nodded to him, then set off down Market Street, heading for the intersection with Oak. "Sure."

About fuckin' time, man. Shit, you look like all ten fuckin' Jason movies. You planning on washing some of that shit off before you meet the fuckin' hippies? They're gonna think you're Charles Manson or some shit, dog... fuckin' helter skelter n' shit, right?

Cade narrowed his eyes for a second, wondering what Fuel-Air knew. There was something about Fuel-Air that Cade was starting to find troubling, beyond the fact that he was a sure sign Cade was going nuts.

Hell with it. He needed to wash off the blood and find a change of clothes. Fuel-Air was right about that, at least. Cade nodded towards him.

"You coming?"

Fuel-Air flashed his usual shit-eating grin. Cade noticed he'd gotten a gold tooth from somewhere. With a diamond lodged in it.

Thought you'd never ask, my meat-chuckin', Pastor-fuckin' brother. Thought you'd never fuckin' ask.

Cade scowled, picking at the dried blood on his arm.

Goddamn Fuel-Air never could take anything seriously.

CHAPTER FOURTEEN

THE WAR

No dead on Oak Street.

Cade didn't know whether that was on account of the cannibals having eaten them, or whether he was in hippie territory and they'd picked them all up to use as fertiliser. Either way, he wasn't comfortable. He never thought he'd want to see a rotting corpse laying in the street, but now it came to it, he missed them. They were a sign people weren't around to screw things up.

Cade was missing the dead and resenting the living, and he figured that was more than a little fucked up. So when he saw the coffee shop after the intersection with Divisadero, he figured it was as good a place as any to wash up and rest for the night.

The taps weren't working, but there was an old cooler behind the counter with bottled water in it, and he managed to get a fair amount of the blood off his hands and face with it, although he had to get rid of his tank top. After that, he checked in the back room.

That was where he found Frank.

Cade didn't know it was Frank – all there was, as far as he was concerned, was a skeleton that stank to high heaven. He didn't know it was Frank's white t-shirt he found in the back of a closet, either. But he was pretty grateful to Frank anyway. Frank being there let him know the place hadn't been found yet. It meant he was as safe as he was going to be for a few hours. It meant he could get a little sleep, tend to his wounds, think about what he was going to do next.

Frank had a little whisky too, which Cade poured into the holes in his hands and over his chest, letting the alcohol burn into the cuts, saving a little for drinking purposes. It wasn't exactly standard medical practice, but he figured it was better than just letting the wounds fester, especially after his pierced hands had pulled a few bodies inside out. It was a miracle he hadn't come down with an infection already.

After he'd cleaned up and washed his wounds as best he could, there wasn't much else left to do but watch the street. The coffee shop had a second floor, and from there Cade had a good look at anybody who might be coming from Haight-Ashbury. Plus, sitting with a view to the west, he got a good look at the sun going down. Cade wasn't a man who had much appreciation for natural beauty, but he wasn't about to turn it away when it got handed to him on a plate.

And it was a hell of a sunset. Boiling pink clouds scudding across a sky filled with fire and brimstone, blood and copper. Cade hadn't seen a sight like it in forever.

Kind of reminds you of something, don't it, dog? Sky all on fire and shit.

Cade shook his head. He knew what Fuel-Air was getting at, and there wasn't any point thinking about it that he could see. That sunset wasn't anything like an artillery strike. And Cade wasn't going to think about the artillery strike anyway, so it didn't much matter if it was.

He looked up at Fuel-Air, who was sitting in a booth on the other side of the room, sipping a frappucino. Half his face was missing, and he only had one arm, plus his guts were hanging out on the table. So the frappucino was slurping out through his ruptured throat and what was left of his guts, pooling on the table and the floor.

He still had Strong's gold tooth shining out from what was left of his mouth, though. Goddamn fashion plate.

Shit, dog, sorry. I should get myself together. Bringin' back painful memories and shit, I bet.

Cade spat, and took another sip of whisky.

"Where'd you get the coffee?"

Ways and means, bitch. Fuel-Air grinned, flashing his new diamond. Cade hoped he got sick of that thing fast. It'd been irritating enough on Strong.

Say what you like about Strong, at least he knew enough to stay dead.

Cade could feel the memory pressing on the back of his mind. It wasn't going away any time soon, but he was damned if he was going to spend time reliving it. He was getting enough of Fuel-Air anyway without remembering the way his voice shook as he huddled next to the humvee.

Shit, dog, you reckon the Captain knows there ain't no motherfucker out there? Figure he's just getting his total up for the Commander – shit, is this dumb motherfucker actually in charge?

He didn't need to hear Sergeant A standing up for the chain of command the way he always did when there was a clusterfuck going on all around him.

There's a chain of command, Killer. It's there for a reason. If the Captain says artillery, we go with artillery. The Captain's the Captain and what he says is what... Jesus, Killer, what the fuck do you think you're doing? Sit down! Cade, I said sit down...

He sure as hell didn't need to remember the Captain barking into the radio set, laying down co-ordinates that were maybe a hundred and fifty metres from where they were sat, calling up an artillery strike on some bad intelligence, a damn phantom Chinese whisper that'd made its way up and down the comms. They were close enough to see with the naked eye that there wasn't any Republican Guard in that field, and even if there had been, Cade could have blown them away without breaking a sweat whether there'd been a squad of trained Marines to back him up or not. But Captain Chaos, in his infinite wisdom, was calling up an artillery strike. A hundred and fifty metres away from them.

Sir, I'm respectfully asking you to rethink this. It's danger close...

The Lieutenant. Nice guy, at least by Cade's reckoning. Named Hunter Cragg, if you can believe that. If Cade had seen that name in a movie, he'd have laughed. Hunter Cragg was a good man, though. Hunter Cragg had seen the elephant. Had a lot of combat experience. Ran his men right, gave them shit when they needed it, let it ride when they didn't, smart enough to know which was which. In another war – say, a war where the people running it had any kind of plan – Lt. Hunter Cragg would have been hailed and respected as the leader of men that he was. They'd have put a medal on him. They'd have made him Captain, maybe Colonel. Maybe General. Hell, maybe President.

Cade figured as long as he was wishing, he'd like a pony.

Hunter Cragg had been stuck in the war he was stuck in, and in that war folks like Dollings got to be Captain and folks like Cragg had to suck it up and be Lieutenant and do what they were told. And if they were told to jump in the shit, they were meant to ask how deep.

Cade took another shot of whisky.

He hated thinking about the Captain most of all.

Danger close? You little pissant, danger close *is coward talk! No such thing as danger close for a Marine!*

Cragg's voice came again. Desperate. A strong man begging.

Sir, please, call off the strike... at least delay it while we pull back...

And then that barking, angry, ugly voice of the Captain. Captain Paul Dollings, known in the lower ranks as Captain Chaos, born in the great state of Texas, enjoying his first taste of combat and divorced from any kind of shared reality. A first-class, grade-A dumb-fuck son of a bitch, to put it mildly.

Captain Dollings had never seen real combat in his life. He'd never seen the elephant. And every word he said made that loud and clear.

Coward talk! You had best wake the fuck up, Lieutenant, because the only place you're headed after this kind of gross insubordination is a military tribunal! I'm going to tear that bar off you myself, do you hear me, you damned coward? You're finishing out what's left of this war as a grunt like... who the goddamned hell is that? Jesus! Put that gun down! This is treason! This is...

It wasn't a happy memory, all in all. But that moment when the Captain had seen Cade raising his assault rifle, had seen the barrel swinging towards him, had looked into Cade's eyes and read the unmistakeable truth in them – that Cade was going to wipe the Captain out like a stain right there and then, and not because of any personal dislike of the man, or hatred of country or Corps or government or God or any other reason that'd allow the Captain to die a hero...

...but simply because Captain Paul Dollings was a dumb son of a bitch who was in the way and needed to be taken out of it...

...to have the Captain look in his eyes and understand his own worthlessness in the seconds before he died...

...*that* was a happy memory.

In his booth, Fuel-Air grinned, raising his frappucino.

You the man, dog. The look on that motherfucker's face. Fuckin' Kodak, man.

Cade raised his whisky, and nearly smiled. That'd probably been the second-best moment of his life, right after his first kill. Then Fuel-Air ruined it.

Too bad you shot the wrong guy, huh?

Sure, thought Cade. Too bad.

Too bad the Lieutenant had to go and be a goddamned hero by hurling himself in front of the bullets. Cade had liked the Lieutenant. Hunter Cragg was a good man, and he treated his men right. He'd seen the elephant.

Cade didn't know why he'd step in front of the barrel like that. Just couldn't figure it.

But he had.

The bullets had pretty much torn Cragg into pieces, which was a hell of a shame for his wife and his little boy. Cragg'd probably have survived it if he'd let himself hold back for a second. He'd probably have killed Cade, but Cade had figured on dying anyway. Probably wouldn't have been such a loss.

A couple of the bullets managed to find their way through the Lieutenant and smack into the Captain – one in the gut, one in the shoulder and a couple in the leg. None of them hit an artery, but the gutshot would have killed him eventually. Of course, he might have gotten medical aid, and Cade couldn't have that. There was no way this son of a bitch was going to stay alive one more second if Cade could help it.

It wasn't just the artillery. It was all the grabbing of souvenirs from the dead and the dying. It was shouting on open comms about how vulnerable they were whenever they were vulnerable, which was often. Mostly, it was that time he shot a five-year old – accidentally-on-purpose – and then wouldn't medevac him. Just watched him die with a grin on his face, talking about how mistakes were often made in war.

The artillery was something of a last straw.

Cade took another gulp of whiskey and tried to remember what it'd been like before that moment, back when he'd given a damn whether he lived or he died. For the life of him, he couldn't. Maybe he'd never given a damn. Maybe he'd only pretended.

Maybe he'd only pretended he didn't want to remember this.

Cade poured more whiskey and thought back, remembering, picturing that look of cold fear in the Captain's eyes, hearing the way the bark in his voice had turned to the whimpering of a kicked dog.

You can't do this! I'm a Captain! You can't do this! Please! PLEASE!

All of a sudden, Paul Dollings had seen the elephant. He was staring the damned elephant right in its eyes.

And the elephant was going to walk right over him without even stopping to blink.

Cade had brought the butt of his weapon down between Dollings's eyes hard enough to cave the skull in. He figured that was it for him too. Sergeant A had his sidearm drawn and was yelling something. He wasn't calling Cade 'Killer' anymore, and if Sergeant A stopped using a man's nickname it meant he was pretty mad.

Cade had raised his hands and turned. He saw Sergeant A yelling the words *chain of command,* over and over again, Fuel-Air behind him staring with his eyes almost popping out, the other men starting to run towards him, weapons drawn.

And then the strike had hit.

It was about a hundred and fifty metres off target. In their direction. Danger close.

Cade didn't remember much after that. He remembered reaching with a hand covered in blood and dirt, nothing in his ears but ringing, turning over a body and seeing Fuel-Air with half his face gone and his guts hanging out. No diamond tooth, though, which looking back was a mercy.

After that, all he remembered was waking up in the hospital. He wasn't the only one out of his unit to survive, but the other survivors hadn't got a good enough look at what had happened with the Captain and Lieutenant Cragg, and the bodies had been torn into pieces by the shelling. Cade had been lucky to escape with shrapnel and broken bones.

Lucky motherfucker, grinned Fuel-Air. *You had* guilty *written all over you, dog.*

Which accounted for the year in the hole, the dishonourable discharge and the promise – delivered to him through unofficial channels – that if Cade ever showed his face again anywhere, he was a dead man. Which suited Cade fine.

All he wanted was somewhere quiet to lay his head. A trailer park in the middle of nowhere, near the coast. Somewhere where they didn't investigate violent deaths too good, in case he had any problems. Somewhere he could forget himself until he died.

You really thought I was gonna let you forget? Shit, you should be so lucky, bitch.

"Yeah." Cade was tired. He'd had enough memories, and he'd had enough booze, and he hadn't seen a damn soul coming down that street. The sun had sank under the horizon, and all that was left now was the night and the dark. Time he got some sleep. He had a lot to do in the morning.

Big day tomorrow, dog. Those hippies sound like some Satan-worshipping motherfuckers, into all kinds of sacrifices and shit – 'least, according to the Pastor. You ready for some shit like that, dog? You think you want to put yourself in the jackpot with some crazy acid-head freaks like that?

Cade shrugged, finishing his whisky and stretching out on the leather of his booth seat.

"Sure."

Then he slept.

CHAPTER FIFTEEN

THE GANG

CADE DIDN'T DREAM.

It was after nine when he woke up. Cade was usually a dawn riser – he figured sleeping in like that was his body telling him it needed the rest. That and having something close to a real bed for the first time since he'd driven out from the trailer park.

Fuel-Air was gone. Cade figured he'd gotten what he wanted – Cade had had a chance to relax for an evening and he'd spent it reliving getting blown half to pieces because a damn fool figured his reputation was worth more than the lives of his men. And feeling bad about it, he realised, which was new. Cade hadn't been someone who felt guilt, or regretted things, in all the time he could remember.

Guilt was new.

Cade couldn't help wondering what Fuel-Air was up to.

There was no sense Cade could see in wasting any more time. He cracked open another bottle of water to wash up, making use of Frank's toothbrush and paste to get some of the taste out of his mouth while he was at it. He made a note of the area – he didn't know what the rest of

San Francisco looked like right now, and he'd probably want to come back here, or to another place like it nearby. So far, this looked to be a little oasis, untouched by any of the various factions he'd seen or any other looters who might have happened along – people like him, in other words.

Of course, he'd not met the hippies yet. Could be they just weren't too hung up on personal possessions, or maybe they had their own water supply fixed up and didn't feel the need to go looking for more. He might be deep in their territory and not know it – so far, he'd only met up with groups that'd been too far into their own craziness to sort out the basics of living, but it could be that they were the exceptions instead of the rule. After all, he didn't exactly know what big city life was like these days. It was something Cade would have to check for himself.

Cade figured the best thing to do right now would be to get onto Haight Street, by way of Divisadero. Then he'd just keep heading west. By the time he got to Haight-Ashbury, he'd have run into the hippies or they'd have run into him. Simple.

Nothing's simple in this world, dog. Just ask the Lieutenant.

Cade cursed under his breath. Fuel-Air was really starting to get on his last nerve now.

Fuck you, dog. I'm a motherfuckin' calming influence on your raging ass. Last time I left you alone for two minutes you took over a fuckin' cannibal cult and sent them to eat a man of God.

Cade gave him a stare and then stalked out of the front door of the coffee place and onto the street. The sun was already up – looked like another beautiful day.

Still, Fuel-Air had a point. He'd have to see how the situation with the Pastor and the cannibals had gone once he was all done with the hippies. It was starting to nag at him. What he was hoping was that the Pastor would deal with the cannibals and lose a lot of his own strength in the process – but if he was really lucky they'd have gotten themselves into a siege situation, something to wear both sides down a little and keep them occupied while he did what he needed to. He'd probably got as much as he could expect to get out of it just by staying alive, but a man could hope.

Of course, a worst case scenario would be the cannibals wiping the Pastor's people out. Eating the children. Tearing the babies from the wombs of their mothers and ripping them open, eating up the tiny organs like popcorn. And that all being Cade's fault.

That would be the worst case scenario.

He wondered why he cared all of a sudden. Still, it was a matter for another day.

Today was hippies.

Cade checked the time – about ten. He kept his eyes open crossing the street and heading down Divisadero, looking for anything that might smack of company. He'd heard a hell of a lot about the hippies, and while he doubted any of it was true, he didn't exactly want them to get the drop on him either.

He was crossing the intersection with Haight Street when he heard the engine.

It was a low growl in the distance – rumbling, chugging along. A van, by the sound, probably pretty old, coming from the east – from cannibal country. Cade ducked behind a bus shelter on the corner and drew his knife. Then he waited.

Eventually, the van trundled into view. It was a VW van – Cade was a little surprised it was still running, but it proved a lot of things. For one thing, the hippies had it together enough to drive, which expanded their territory some, and meant they had enough mechanical skill to keep cars in repair, or at least hot-wire them as needed. Still, that didn't mean much. You could say the same about him, and he was just one man.

What was interesting was how the van was painted. It was a bright, livid blue with a wide green stripe, dotted with pink and yellow flowers. Scrawled on one side in self-consciously 'psychedelic' writing were the words CONUNDRUM CAR.

Cade watched the van crawl past him, then stop in the middle of the intersection.

Looks like they're looking for you, dog.

Cade nodded. Fuel-Air was sitting cross-legged on top of the bus shelter, wearing a caftan, love beads and long hair. He still had half his face missing, though.

Fuel-Air was a hell of a comedian now he was dead.

Cade waited, and watched. He could hear voices from inside the van – young voices, not more than twenty years old – and then the back door opened and a couple of them got out.

Cade noticed the kid in the green oversized t-shirt first. Brown hair, scruffy up top, not too long, with a barely-grown goatee hanging off his chin. No muscles to speak of – Cade thought he had a kind of malnourished look to him. Half-starved, lean as a greyhound. He flopped about as he moved, like his arms and legs didn't have the co-ordination to propel him along.

Along with him, there was a brunette girl, short and dumpy, in an orange pullover that looked too big for her, and a pair of granny glasses with thick lenses. Cade wondered if she'd had a better pair before, but they'd gotten broken and she'd needed to scavenge for new ones. It was possible.

Neither of the kids looked like any kind of threat. Cade didn't peg them for Satanists, or killers, or the kind of people who'd burn a city to the ground. They just looked like the kind of hipster kids Cade had always seen on any trips he'd made to San Francisco, only a little thinner, a little dirtier, maybe a little bit more thrift-store than they had been. There was something else about them, too.

A kind of glassy-eyed look.

Right then, Cade was focussed on the dog. The dog was going to be the problem.

A Great Dane – a big one, big and brown, maybe half the height of the skinny kid. There wasn't much flab on the dog either, but what there was was muscle. Cade had a feeling that dog could probably cause him some trouble if they told it to attack. It could probably cause him some trouble if they didn't – it was already sniffing the air, catching his scent.

Cade listened, his knife tight in his grip, working out what his next move was.

"Are you sure you saw somebody here, Scruffy? I don't see anybody out here now!" The girl rubbed her chin, looking around the intersection.

"M-m-maybe he was a g-g-*ghost!*" mewled the boy. He had a voice like a surfer – probably spent most of his time down on the beach before the bad times.

"Well. Jeepers, this certainly is a way-out mystery!" chirped the girl, scratching the back of her head with a serious look on her face. "I mean, there sure weren't any cannibals over on the east side at all! It's like they've just vanished into thin air!"

Cade's eyes narrowed. He glanced up at Fuel-Air, who raised his remaining eyebrow.

Seriously, dog. 'Jeepers?' 'Way out?' What the fuck, man?

"It's, like, a spooky happening, Thelma! Like, what if they came this way? Or what if they got scared by a really big monster that's, like, waiting for us right now?" The skinny kid's voice trembled as he said it, and then he went into a bizarre pantomime of fear, clattering his teeth together and knocking his knees before finishing up with a theatrical gulp. Cade had never seen anything quite like it – he figured maybe it was some kind of drug paranoia. The kid seemed to be afraid of just about everything, looking at the buildings as though they were about to come to life and start coming for him. Cade figured that was probably why he had the dog.

If that was why he had the dog, then the dog was going to be trained to kill. Admittedly, the dog didn't look like much – if anything, he looked kind of goofy – but Cade knew better than to judge a book by its cover.

He just needed to let it get a little closer, and then he could take care of it. He took another look at the van, narrowing his eyes. The van was starting to rock – shifting to and fro in a regular rhythm. That was a little weird.

Maybe they had some kind of generator ticking over in there.

Cade shook his head, and concentrated on the two hippies and their dog. That was the important thing.

The dog looked in his direction, and sniffed the air again.

Cade held his breath.

"Like, what do you think, Doob?" said the skinny kid in that stupid-scared surfer voice of his. Cade's eyes narrowed as the dog reared up on his haunches and waggled its paws, giving a kind of shrug, lips pulling back from the jaws in a weird parody of a smile, before it barked twice – *rruhhuhh rro* – and fell back on all fours.

Dude, did that fuckin' dog just answer the question?

Cade doubted it. But that dog was definitely trained to perform a couple of tricks, and if the skinny kid had taught it to get up and do a little dance when it got asked a question, it was probably trained to disarm or disable an opponent. If they were regularly checking on the cannibals, the dog would need to be able to defend them. That was just common sense.

The dog sniffed the air again, then started padding in his direction.

"Well, it looks like Doobie's got the scent of something!" said the short girl. The dog was sniffing and walking in Cade's direction. He gripped the knife tight.

"Yeah, like, he's got the munchies, right, Doob? Maybe somebody, like, made a sandwich nearby!" The boy licked his lips, leading with his face, throat exposed. Cade let them get a little closer.

The girl wagged a finger at them. "Well, don't get too far off, you two! There have been some spooky goings-on around here and –"

Cade moved. The dog had to go first – that was obvious. He rolled out of cover and grabbed the mutt in a headlock, bringing the blade of the knife down near the base of the skull, between the second and third vertebrae, neatly severing the spine as it buried in the dog's neck. The dog gave a strangled bark and went limp as the skinny kid jerked back.

"It's a g-g-ghost! Like, run, Doob!" He jumped up like a jack in the box, turning pale, then turned and ran towards the van, hurling himself underneath it. The brunette didn't seem to blink.

"Don't be silly, Scruffy! That's no ghost – it must be the owner of the Ben & Jerry's! I'll bet he just dressed up as a ghost to warn people away from some buried treasure, that's all!" she smiled, still with the same wide, glassy eyes.

Cade looked at her for a second, then let the dog drop to the ground, sheathing the knife in his belt. He had a feeling maybe he'd read the situation wrong somewhere. He walked forward slowly, keeping an eye on them. As an afterthought, he hooked a hand through the dog's collar and dragged it behind him.

"You've got to excuse Scruffy, Mister! He sees ghosts just about everywhere ever since... well, ever since 'you-know-what'!" She did finger-quotes. "Don't worry, though, it's never actually ghosts. It's just people in masks. Scary masks. That's all." She grew thoughtful, looking at the dog's twitching corpse. "See, there's no such thing as ghosts. When you see things that couldn't possibly exist, it's most likely to be a man with a hidden movie projector or someone dressed up to scare people away from hidden treasure. Or a smuggling operation!" She beamed up at him, then looked at him suspiciously. "Is that your real face, or a mask?"

Cade blinked, then tried to get the conversation back on track. "Doc Clearly?"

The brunette smiled. "He's kind of the king around here. He's the one who gives us mysteries to solve! Well, more little tasks to take care of. Errands that need running, like checking on whether the cannibals are spreading into our territory." She pointed at the dead dog. "That's pretty realistic. Are you doing that with a hidden camera?"

"Sure," said Cade. He figured it was probably easier to go along with that for the second – at least until he met Doc Clearly. Besides, he kind of regretted killing the dog now – it was pretty clear these kids could barely train themselves to function, never mind a dog. Still, better safe than sorry. He cleared his throat.

"Got some questions. Hoping Doc Clearly could answer them. I'd be obliged."

The brunette brightened up. "Oh, Doc Clearly can answer all sorts of questions! You know, I'll bet he'll clear up an awful lot of things for you!" She smiled, brightly, and then opened up the back door of the van.

Cade blinked.

There were two more kids in the back – a big blond fella and a red-haired girl. The blond fella had a red neckerchief on, the redhead was wearing a purple hairband. Neither of them were wearing anything else. The girl was bent over, doggy-style, and the fella was slamming into her like there wasn't a complete stranger looking at the pair of them. The brunette smiled brightly.

"Company, guys! Mister... hey, what's your name?"

"Cade." said Cade.

"Mister Cade was wanting a ride to see Doctor Clearly! I thought he could come back with us!" the brunette didn't seem to mind what was happening in front of her. Cade didn't feel right pointing it out.

"Pleasure – *nnf* – to meet you, Sir!" said the blond kid with a sunny smile. The girl panted and nodded. Cade was glad they didn't offer to shake hands. He got gingerly into the back of the van as the brunette went around to the driving seat.

The girl lifted her head. "Ahhh... hey, what happened to Doobie-Doo?"

Cade swallowed. Didn't seem much point in denying it. "Killed him. Sorry."

Fuckin' heartfelt apology there, man. Shit, you'll kill just about anything, won't you? Kids, pets – you really are a brutal son of a bitch and you don't give a fuck who knows it, know what I'm saying? You feel me?

"Sorry," Cade muttered again. He didn't know where the hell to look.

"Don't apologise. I'm sure you..." – the blond fella inhaled sharply – "had your reasons..." He grimaced, freezing in place, then brought his hand down on the girl's backside with a hard *smack*. In turn, she closed her eyes and bucked her hips hard, squealing out through clenched teeth. Cade still didn't really know where to look. He wasn't used to being invited into these situations and he didn't want to offend anybody.

Then again, he had just killed their dog for pretty much no reason. If they were okay about that, he figured they were fine with him getting an eyeful.

The brunette buckled her seatbelt and put the van into gear, then stepped onto the accelerator. There was a strangled scream from underneath, cut off by a loud *crack*, then a crunch, as the back wheels of the van bucked upwards.

"Oh gosh! I forgot Scruffy was underneath the Conundrum Car! Jeepers! I killed him! Oh, Doc Clearly's going to be so cross!" The brunette put her hand to her mouth, continuing to drive the van as the blond kid shook his head with a lopsided grin.

Cade leant back against the wall of the van. Opposite him, Fuel-Air was shaking his head, blame in his one remaining eye.

It was going to be a long trip.

CHAPTER SIXTEEN

THE DOC

"SEE, WHAT I'M trying to say is that the motivating force in the universe is Love. It's that simple. Everything is defined by its capability to feel Love, and it follows that Love is the highest emotion because it's the thing that defines us as a species. And it follows from that that it's our duty, *as* a species, to rise *to* that highest definition and become a species motivated by Love. So we should be judged on how much we Love one another. It's like Doc Clearly says – within each of us lies the potential to become the balance of the universe. You get what I mean, Mister Cade?" The blond kid paused, sucking on the reefer he'd lit a minute ago.

Cade nodded, then looked at Fuel-Air. Fuel-Air grinned and shook his head slowly. He was back in his utilities, holding a reefer like the blond kid – Ted, Cade thought he was called. Cade raised an eyebrow, wondering what Fuel-Air made of all this talk. He'd been a similar age to these kids when he'd died. Maybe he'd talked like that once.

Shit, dog, I'd have said anything if there was a blowjob involved.

The redhead lifted her head – Cade had to wonder if it was a reaction to what Fuel-Air had said – cradling Ted absently while she spoke. "It's not just a sexual thing either, although I do resent the implication made by the previous society that sex for mutual pleasure has to be somehow inferior to sex that's been labelled as something 'deeper'" – Ted's balls flopped down in their sac as she made the finger quotes – "anyway, what we've achieved is Love shared by an entire community, and offered to anyone who comes to us, as well as the natural world around us that was neglected so badly by the previous society." Having made her point, she went back to what she'd been doing before, taking Ted in her mouth and bobbing her head slowly up and down, her fingers squeezing lightly. Cade looked back at Fuel-Air for want of anywhere else to look. He still hadn't quite figured out what the etiquette was for this, and while they'd forgiven him for killing the dog – and by extension the skinny kid – he didn't want to ruffle any feathers. He still felt a little guilty, which was odd for Cade.

Fuel-Air just grinned.

The brunette – Thelma, was it? – chimed in from the driver's seat. "We even Love the cannibals and that weird religious sect up to the north, although obviously we have to Love them from a distance, seeing as they're, um... well, they don't exactly Love us, if you see what I mean. But any who come by, we welcome with open arms. We've had a couple from the north, and once they saw how nice things were for us, they stuck around. I think they were maybe a little repressed. The cannibals, though – Jeepers! They're the opposite!"

"The cannibals are the ultimate 'me-first-and-screw-the-other-guy' society. They have no inhibitions, but they also have no sense of anything beyond themselves. It's like Doctor Clearly says – you need a balance between yourself and the world. See, the cannibals just don't care about other people. You can't be part of their culture and have any kind of relationship with another human being. It's no wonder they're dying off." With that, Ted closed his eyes, taking a drag on the reefer, idly putting a hand into the redhead's hair. Daisy, that was her name.

"And Scruffy?" Cade said, despite himself. Now wasn't the time to start an argument, but there was something about the way they'd just driven over the fella that didn't strike Cade as being right.

Didn't you drive right over someone a while back? You want to get judgemental, dog, you best take a look in the mirror.

Cade frowned and shot Fuel-Air a look. That was different.

Daisy raised her head. "That was an accident. Thelma – well, she's, uh..." She looked up, then raised her eyebrows, mouthing the words *not right.*

Thelma hissed. "There's nothing wrong with me! When we find the Pastor and take his mask off – well, you'll see! It'll all turn out to be a smuggling operation! You know he's going to get away with it, too, if we don't do something! Besides, Scruffy probably isn't dead. He's just hiding in a vase. What we felt was probably just projected by a movie camera..." She lapsed into silence. The van was moving a lot slower than it had been – Cade figured they were moving through a crowd. The kids were probably taking him directly to Clearly. That was fine – he wasn't in a hurry to end the conversation just yet.

Ted blew out a cloud of marijuana smoke. "I'm sorry about what happened to Doobie and Scruffy, but it's like Doc Clearly says... their individual egos are merged with the universe now. There's no point feeling bad about it. Sooner or later, we're going to make that trip too. I mean, even today... people still die all the time – even voluntarily, sometimes. If the end of your life comes from a decision that's been made, we have to respect that decision. I can understand that. It's hard to function sometimes. At least since 'you-know-what.'" Finger quotes again.

Cade wondered if Doc Clearly did finger quotes too, or talked in such a roundabout way about a man killing himself. Most likely.

Still, this answered a couple of questions. Cade figured the hippies were dealing with the bad times pretty much the same way as the Pastor's were – putting their faith in an afterlife and following the nearest authority figure. Clearly was going to have a hell of a long way to go to be worse than the Pastor, but Cade wasn't convinced yet. Ted and Daisy seemed relatively normal, despite the fact that they hadn't stopped screwing since Cade had met them, but Thelma shouldn't have been driving that damned van. Cade was slightly surprised they hadn't killed anybody else on the way.

There was something else, too. Cade wasn't a prude by any means, but at first he'd instinctively avoided looking at Ted and Daisy – the etiquette thing – but now he was getting a close look at them, he'd noticed something weird.

There were a lot of bruises on both of them. Some fresh, some old. And scratch marks as well – again, a couple fresh, most of them old. Like these kids got into a lot of fights.

Might be coincidence, though. Cade figured there was a lot of hard work involved in the hippie way of life, and if you were doing errands and lugging crap around the whole day there were ways to get a little banged up.

Fuel-Air snorted. *Face it, bitch, you're only cutting these weird-ass motherfuckers some slack because you don't want to have to kill another bajillion people. Sex Monkey and his girlfriend are fucked up, and the crazy freak-girl with the Choose Your Own Adventure fixation is super-duper-ultra fucked up and you fuckin'* know *it, bitch. I give you until midnight before you break some poor motherfucker's neck over this shit.*

Cade checked the clock on the dashboard. It was only about a quarter to twelve. Twelve hours without killing someone. Cade figured it could be done. "You're on."

"On what?" said Ted – then he stiffened, letting out a strangled grunt, at the same moment Thelma stopped the van.

"We're here, Mister Cade. Just open the door and hop out. Daisy, do you want to park the van when you're done? Then I can take Mister Cade to see the Doc."

"Mmm-hmmm," nodded Daisy. Cade turned away and opened up the back door without wishing them goodbye.

The smell of dope hit him the second he stepped out of the van. They'd gone past the Haight-Ashbury and the van had pulled up outside the entrance to Golden Gate Park – and the park was full of people.

Cade hadn't seen that many people in one place since the bad times – it made the Pastor's couple of hundred seem like a small group. Cade could see at least five hundred people here – stretched out on rugs, kissing underneath trees, sitting cross-legged and meditating, playing guitars and shaking tambourines, most just walking and talking. A couple of them were naked – Cade noticed a livid bruise on one girl's thigh – some were decorated with body and face paint or home-made jewellery. The rest dressed in simple, comfortable clothing that covered the arms and legs.

There was a paper sign thumbtacked to a tree, reading 'Softball game at Kezar Stadium today 2pm All welcome' in brightly-coloured marker. Cade wandered up to it, running his fingers over the letters. He wondered if the game was still going on.

Shit, bitch, you gonna cry?

Fuel-Air was sitting with a couple on a tartan rug, smoking the same joint he'd had in the van. The couple were eating a picnic of some kind - the man had a fresh tomato, the woman was eating some canned spam with a fork. Tomato plants at least – probably other produce. There was a botanical garden near here that'd be perfect for that. And a food distribution system that worked.

Shit, you are gonna cry. You motherfuckin' pussy.

Cade shook his head. "Been a while. That's all."

A thought struck him. Why did he have to take the insulin back to the trailer park? Why couldn't he just bring the Duchess here? If the population was as big as Cade figured it was, they'd have diabetics, and they could care for them. The Duchess and Woody could both move here – if Woody could drag himself away from his mother's. The cannibals were going to be a problem, but they'd do what he told them – and even if they didn't, by now they'd worn themselves down against the Pastor's people. As for the Pastor – hell, Cade could deal with him easy enough. There were ways and means.

His eyes went to the man sitting on the rug. He was wearing a white polo-neck, and Cade could see the edge of a fresh cut on his neck, that the polo-neck was hiding. He turned, smiling at Cade, and Cade noticed he had one black eye.

The people here certainly did seem accident prone, all right.

Fuel-Air was laughing. Cade looked at him, and almost flinched. Sitting next to the young couple was Fuel-Air as he was now – a rotting, decomposing skeleton, covered in writhing maggots. And laughing.

Listen to yourself, you dumb motherfucker. Shit, you're so fuckin' stupid I'm gonna let you find out for yourself, you fuckin' empty-headed shit. You motherfuckin' hippie-ass Alice B Toklas fuckin' bitch...

Cade looked away, back at the sign on the tree. He kept his eyes on the sign until he couldn't hear Fuel-Air laughing any more.

"Mister Cade?"

Cade turned – it was Thelma. She was smiling nervously. Behind her, there was a man of about fifty, with grey-brown curly hair and a drooping moustache, dressed in a light brown suit and a pink shirt. He smoked a pipe. He had a trustworthy air about him, like a college professor, which Cade figured was probably because he was one.

"You Clearly?" Cade's voice sounded wary in his own ears. He was waiting for the other shoe. Waiting for Fuel-Air to be proven right.

Thelma smiled, and then went back to the van, which still hadn't moved. Clearly stuck out his hand. Despite himself, Cade took it. Clearly smiled, taking the pipe from his mouth. "You must be Cade. Is that a first name or a last name?"

Cade narrowed his eyes. "You in charge of this place?"

Clearly chuckled. "Not one for small talk. All right. Yes, I am the head of the community, I suppose, if you want to make that kind of distinction. But I do a lot of delegation. We're run according to principles I set out, but a lot of the actual work – agriculture, food distribution, manufacture and supply of the essentials for living, entertainment and so forth – I leave to other hands. I just sort of keep an eye on the whole shebang, so to speak." He smiled, genially, his eyes dropping to the knife at Cade's belt, and the bloodstain on the white t-shirt. "Thelma told me how you, ah, met the gang."

Cade swallowed, feeling like a damned fool. "Sorry about the dog. And the boy. I should've said something when we got in the van without him."

Clearly shook his head. "Well, we'll talk about the dog. But..." He sighed. "Scruffy... he can't be laid at your door. I've been sending the gang on errands, mostly checking on the cannibals and the religious fanatics up north – trying to instil a sense of responsibility into them. But those are troubled kids – more than most who survived the plague. I'm of the opinion that they had serious problems even before they lost everyone they knew and loved. As I'm sure you've noticed, Thelma and Scruffy live – well, lived – in a fantasy world, and Ted and Daisy...

well, they have fun all the live-long day, I suppose you could say. Not that a lot of the people here aren't the same. In fact, being the, ah, spiritual guru around here doesn't preclude me from enjoying myself occasionally." He chuckled, paternally, as he looked over at a group of nudists passing a ball to one another. Cade saw a red bite mark on a man's shoulder, and one of the women had a deep scratch down her side. "Responsibly, of course. We're not short of birth control, or any other drugs we might need. Recreational or, uh, or otherwise." He looked off into the distance for a moment, as if debating whether or not he should continue the sentence.

Cade missed the cue. He had other things on his mind.

"Insulin?" he asked, scanning the man's eyes. He didn't seem like a liar. But you never could tell. There was definitely something not quite right about this whole set-up, though Cade couldn't put his finger on what that was exactly.

On the edge of his hearing, Fuel-Air was still laughing.

"Oh, we have a stockpile of that, as well as other... well, anyway. We've got a number of diabetics among us – a legacy of the days when we ate processed sugar instead of growing our own food – and there's enough to last them a good few years. Also..." he smiled, almost bashfully. After his slight stumble earlier, his confidence was coming back in force. "I am, as you may have heard, a noted drug pusher. Which brings us, in a roundabout way, back to the dog. You're a violent man, Cade, a lot more violent than we're used to around here. Did you come from the Pastor's camp?"

Cade nodded. "Passed through it."

"But you didn't start off there."

"No."

The Doctor nodded, taking a long draw on his pipe. "Hmm. Judging from the state of your palms, I knew you'd fallen afoul of the Pastor at some point." Cade reflectively clenched and unclenched his fists, feeling the wave of agony sweep up his arms. He'd almost forgotten about the constant throbbing of his palms since he'd cleaned out the cuts with whisky, but that didn't mean he shouldn't get them looked at properly sometime soon. Maybe now.

Clearly noted the gesture, nodded slowly, and then continued. "I would say... and feel free to correct me if I'm wrong... that you came into the city from the north and found yourself in the Pastor's territory, and you – being a man with a violent nature – presumably made some trouble for him. Well, that or your sexuality didn't meet his approval."

Cade nodded. "Along those lines."

Clearly smiled. "I can't help noticing you've got a lot of scratch-marks and bites on you too. You wouldn't have been given any, ah... black and white..." He paused, rethinking the sentence. "I mean, is there anything I should know about, ah, concerning that?"

"Had a run-in with the cannibals." Clearly was sharp, but Cade didn't see the need to tell him any more than he had to. Doc Clearly nodded, and smiled wide, sucking on his pipe. Cade was taking a liking to the man, but there was still something there that made Cade uneasy.

He could still hear Fuel-Air laughing at him.

The Doctor nodded. "Okay. So let's recap. Your first reaction when you came across the gang was to kill their dog. There's no two ways around that, Cade. You're a man to whom violence is second nature, and from the moment you came here – to San Francisco, I mean – you've been immersed in constant violence, which seems to have made you... well, jumpy." He shook his head. "But I don't think a reaction like that is healthy, Cade, and I doubt you do either. So I want to ask you, man to man – is that the normal way you'd react in that situation? To just kill without thinking? Without a second of hesitation?"

Cade looked into the Doc's eyes. He was serious. Cade had an inkling that if he got this question wrong, he'd be shown the door. Clearly probably wouldn't get violent about it – it'd be very polite – but it'd leave him without any answers to speak of, not to mention without any insulin either.

Cade needed to mingle with these folks a bit. Find out what their deal was. He figured he'd better tell Clearly what he wanted to hear.

"No. No, it ain't." lied Cade.

He could hear Fuel-Air laughing.

Doc Clearly breathed a sigh of relief. "Well, that's good. That's excellent, Cade. You see, I don't think violence should be unending. I think there should be a balance between a man's baser instincts, and the baser instincts of a society, and their higher selves. I believe that you can acknowledge all the awful things that have happened, and still build a community despite them. That's what I'm trying to do here. I'm trying to build a community, and... well, Cade, I think it'd be in your best interests to be a part of it."

Cade's eyebrow twitched.

Clearly smiled reassuringly, shaking his head. "Trust me, this isn't leading where you think it is. I know you've probably been given a recruitment speech a lot like that by the Pastor, most likely before he nailed you up, and I'm not going to head down that route and tell you to join me or else. It's your decision. If you don't think we've got anything here you want, you can leave right now." His face grew serious, and he put a hand on Cade's shoulder. "What I'm offering you, though, is a chance to breathe. A chance to live – a chance to... to work through the violence that's become your life, and... well, come out the other side.

Stay for the night, Cade. You might find you belong here. I won't deny we can use a man who's handy with a weapon – so long as he can put it down occasionally." He smiled, patting Cade's shoulder gently. Cade could see his thumb joint was badly bruised, as if it had been wrenched recently. He didn't pay much heed to it.

Accidents happened.

"Give us a try. See what you think." The Doc smiled.

Cade almost smiled back. "A test drive?"

Clearly chuckled – a warm, fatherly sound. "Sure, why not. Give us a test drive, Cade. I'll let you wander around, rather than give you a tour – let you take it all in without my input – but you can ask me any questions that come to mind, and I'll send someone to find you if there's something I want you to see, or experience, or... well." He grew contemplative for a moment. "What I'm trying to say is... I really don't want you to join our community unless you want to. If you feel like it, you can walk out of here tomorrow – right now – and head back where you came from or keep moving south, find somewhere that fits you. But what I do want you to do, at least for the time you're here, is try to be happy. Because I really don't think you're a happy man. Am I wrong?"

Cade didn't say anything. Cade was a lot of things, but happy wasn't one of them. In fact, even content would be pushing it.

Clearly waited for a response, then smiled, gently lifting his hand off Cade's shoulder. "Well, I'm rambling. But... do you think you can do that, Cade? I'd consider it a personal favour. Just... let yourself be happy for a little while."

Cade looked at Clearly for a long time. Then he nodded.

"I can do that."

And out of the corner of his eye, Cade saw Fuel-Air, laughing fit to burst as the maggots crawled over his shrivelled skin and in and out of empty eye-sockets. Laughing like he knew the biggest joke in the world. And maybe he did at that.

Fuel-Air knew it was Cade's second lie of the day.

CHAPTER SEVENTEEN

THE RITUAL

CADE ENDED UP going to the ballgame.

Kezar Stadium wasn't one of the bigger stadiums in the state, but for all that, it was a pretty impressive place to have a softball game. The stands could have held a good eight or nine thousand, even with the wear and tear of the bad times, but they were all but empty. Most people watching the game sat around or even inside the diamond itself, laughing as the foam ball sailed over their heads, cheering and catcalling as a grinning, joking Castro Street refugee, all muscle and tan and chewing gum, pitched a lazy, easy shot to an older woman in granny glasses and tight jeans and bad co-ordination, who swung her bat gamely but missed the ball all the same, face flushed with laughter. There was no competition to it – just folks having fun on a sunny day. The clowning kid had already struck a couple of batters out, and Cade guessed he was feeling bad about it – shooting that cocky grin one more time, he tossed the ball to someone in the crowd, flashed peace signs and sauntered off to hit on one of the batters. He was replaced by a burly type, a biker, all frayed denim and unwashed hair, who high-fived him on the way to the pitcher's mound to the cheers of the crowd. There weren't really teams as such as far as Cade could see – just people wanting to play.

Then again, Cade guessed that they hadn't really put a baseball league together just yet. That was the kind of thing Cade would term a luxury. He sat back and watched the game, shaking his head slightly. By now the biker was pitching some harder balls – hard as a foam ball could travel, anyway – and the laughing woman in glasses swung her plastic bat, full breasts bouncing in time with the swing, almost toppling over. The ball sailed past the bat – strike two.

Cade felt light-headed, like he was dreaming. It was surreal. It was like he'd fallen asleep in that van and everything since he'd stepped out of it had been an illusion. It was like the Wonderful Land of Oz. Like being in Technicolor.

The woman in the tight jeans struck out for the third time, and Cade felt his eye drawn to her ass as she bounced off the diamond to the good-natured claps and wolf-whistles of the crowd. She laughed and shook a finger at one of the crowd. Cade wondered how easy it'd be to get hold of her for a drink later. If they drank here at all.

Fuck, dog, how come everybody here's a hottie? What's up with that?

Cade sighed. He didn't look round.

I'm serious, dog. Nobody older than mid-forties, mostly young folks but no kids to get in the way, no fatties, even... Shit, this is fuckapalooza right here, bitch. It's fuckin' poon paradise. Come on, don't tell me you weren't thinking of bouncing a quarter off that ass. I'd bounce my life fuckin' savings off that.

Cade shook his head, watching a man in taped glasses with close-cropped hair and a t-shirt reading I BRAKE FOR CHRIST pick up the bat and stride out purposefully to the plate. One of the Pastor's people, maybe. One of the converts to Doc Clearly's way of thinking.

Shit, what's up with you? This is valuable information here, bitch. Valuable motherfuckin' information about the amount of poon-tang you could get, dog. Pay fuckin' attention.

"Ain't in the mood," said Cade. He wasn't. He felt tired, suddenly, a tiredness that crept through his muscles and sat in his bones and refused to go away. All of a sudden he didn't know what the hell he'd been doing. He could have come straight here at the beginning of it, right after the bad times, taken the Duchess and Woody and set up here where they all belonged, with people who smiled and laughed and played softball and ate good and all the rest. He wasn't fool enough to ever think he could be a part of this, not the way he was. But he could find a place on the outskirts, like he had in Muir Beach. Things could be like they were before the bad times.

Fuckin' pussy. You want a white picket fence too? That the reward for a dog-killer these days?

Cade lowered his head. There was a part of him that was right there with Fuel-Air, part of him that knew right in his tired bones that things wouldn't ever be like they had been again and maybe he didn't deserve them to be, and there wasn't any sense wishing otherwise. Part of him that felt sick to his bones.

Cade hadn't been a man who felt things like that before Fuel-Air had shown up.

Damn, but he was tired.

"Is this seat taken?"

Cade looked to his left, half-expecting to see Fuel-Air, maggots and all. Instead there was a blonde girl of about seventeen wearing a contrite smile and some kind of poncho – it was hand-woven, with a poorly-rendered caricature of Deputy Dawg. Cade figured she'd made it herself. She was looking down at his shirt, and Cade was suddenly glad he'd taken the time to pick a fresh one up – there'd been a box of them, free to all comers, and he'd grabbed one at random.

It was white, with the words HUG ME – I HAD A HARD DAY and some kind of cabbage patch kid staring winsomely out from the region of his right nipple.

Cade wasn't a man troubled overmuch by fashion.

"Sorry. Bad joke." She smiled, looking down at the ground. "You looked kind of, um, lonely. Well, I guess you would because you're sitting up here on your own, but, um – I mean you looked kind of down as well. I thought I'd say hi. See if you needed anything." She blushed. "Doc Clearly said you might need something, not that he sent me to..." She shook her head, giggling. "I'm making a real mess of this, aren't I?"

"It's okay. Just figuring things," said Cade, half-shrugging. He didn't much want to talk about it, but he didn't much want to make her feel bad either. She was already worried he was thinking she'd been pimped out to him by the Doc, by the sound of it. Wasn't any mileage in making her feel any more embarrassed.

"Um, my name's Cassie, by the way. Short of Cassiopeia – like the star? My dad was kind of into astronomy and Mom figured it'd be a good name. Sorry. Don't know why I'm telling you that." She laughed, a little bashful.

"Cade," said Cade. He didn't figure there was much he needed to add on top of that. There wasn't any sense in making small talk – asking where her folks were now or if she had any other family. If she had any other family, they were dead. Where her folks were now was in the ground pushing up tomato plants, or laying on some street corner, or in the belly of a cannibal. Wasn't any getting around that.

Small talk wasn't Cade's thing anyway.

She smiled, and looked at his palms, starting at the wounds. "Oh, gosh. Are your hands okay? God, nobody here did that, did they?"

Cade looked at her, wondering if she'd been told about the Pastor. He guessed there was no reason why she would've been – it wasn't going to make anyone sleep any better.

Every time someone mentioned the wounds in his hands, he was reminded of them – he was trying not to think too hard about them, himself. They were itching like crazy still – a constant, painful throb that was never far from the back of his mind. He shook his head, opening and closing them slowly, feeling the brutal rush of fire crackling through his nerves to the base of his skull.

She blinked. "Wow, you're kind of intense. You know what? You should definitely come to the thing later. After the TV show, I mean. The Doc was totally right. It'd really help you." She smiled, looking out at the softball game, and Cade noticed she had a livid scratch running down the back of one hand.

The batting team had stolen a couple of bases while they'd been talking – Cade noted without real surprise that the Castro refugee from before was now running from second to third base. He wondered how they even knew if any team had won or lost. Maybe there was no winning and losing here. Maybe Doc Clearly didn't believe in it.

Cade felt that dreamlike, light-headed feeling again. There wasn't a cloud in the sky. He turned to look at the girl, wondering if he'd heard right before. "TV show?" Maybe they'd rigged up a generator with some old DVDs.

"Well, it's not real TV," she said, looking down, embarrassed. "I mean, we've got electricity, but it's kind of precious. We need it for important stuff, like the hydroponics and the Doc's lab. But we kind of get together and, uh..." She shrugged, suddenly embarrassed, and clammed up.

Cade wasn't a man who felt much sympathy for people or for beasts, but he did feel a twinge of something for this girl. She was reaching out, as best she could, trying to bring him into the community. Probably out of a request from Doc Clearly, but still. He figured he should do better than he was doing.

Plus maybe then you can nail her, right, dog? Shit, fuck her for my sake, man. I ain't getting none lookin' like this.

Cade winced, but didn't acknowledge Fuel-Air – didn't even look at him. Instead, he looked over at the girl and nodded. "I'm listening."

She smiled sheepishly. "We get together and act out the old shows. Mostly comedy shows. Last week was *Frasier*." She giggled. "Oh wow! 'I'm listening.' You'd make a really wild Frasier, you know? You'd be like the most intense Frasier ever." She had the giggles now, and it took her a minute to calm them down. "'I'm listening.' I can totally see it! You should talk to Rob and see if he's got a part for you."

Cade blinked. He didn't have much to say to that, either. Amateur dramatics weren't really his line.

Over their heads, the sun shone down, warm and kind. Down on the baseball diamond, the kid from Castro street had stolen home and into the arms of the guy he'd been hitting on. The woman in the tight jeans was sharing a flask of coffee or tea with a bearded man roughly her age, flirting and joking. Cade remembered the kids in the van, talking about Love. A love shared by a whole community.

Cade was a fool to think there would be teams. He glanced over at the girl, who was looking shyly at him, evaluating him. He hoped she was just being friendly. It wasn't like he'd made the Duchess any promises – Cade wasn't the promising type – but she was too young for his tastes by a good twenty years.

Fuckin' MILF hunter. Shit, you got no taste at all, motherfucker.

Almost as if she'd heard Fuel-Air speak, she flushed, and her eyes darted away from Cade's to the softball game. She didn't speak for a few long seconds, and Cade could see her turning her thoughts over. "You know, I think it's better that way. The TV shows. Doing them like a play, I mean, with us. I think if we hooked up a, a..." – she groped for the word – "DVD player. I don't think I could take that. Seeing how it used to be, I mean."

Cade didn't speak.

"But when people are acting it out... it's different. Like an escape. Does that make sense?" She smiled, blushing again, and looking down at her bare feet, twisting them together and rubbing one on top of the other. Her big toenail was bruised black. "You don't talk much, do you?"

Cade shook his head, and the girl laughed. "I can't work out if you like me or not. Are you coming tonight? It's at the old movie house on Haight Street – everybody's going to go."

Cade twitched an eyebrow. "Everybody?"

The girl nodded. "All of us. Everybody crams in. There's even people on the street outside, so make sure you get there early if you want a seat. I mean, I'll save you a seat. If you want." She blushed again, fidgeted, then stood. "You'll be there?"

Hell with it, thought Cade, and nodded. The girl beamed, and walked off, turning and waving at him.

Cade turned and looked at the seat on the other side. Fuel-Air was there, rotting and flyblown, grinning his skeleton grin. *Didn't know you had it in you, dog.*

Cade shook his head and shrugged. Below, the ball game was starting to drift apart, with only a few die-hards still playing until they, too, gave up on it. There'd been no whistle, no signal, but everyone had decided that it was time to stop. Eventually, only the Castro boy and his new friend were left, kissing lazily under the stands.

Cade stood up. That feeling of unreality was stronger, now that the initial shock of seeing people even halfway normal had worn off. It was starting to occur to him that he didn't know the rules around here. These people had found their own rhythm, and their own system, and it didn't include him. Not yet. Maybe it never would.

Cade made his way down from the stands, figuring he'd slip out without disturbing the two kids. Castro Street broke off long enough to shout to him. "Hey, man! You going to the show later? It's *Rules of Engagement* tonight!"

Cade turned. On the one hand, he needed to get to know these people. On the other hand, it was *Rules of Engagement* that night. He thought about it.

"Might be busy."

The young kid laughed, disbelieving. He had a shallow cut on his forehead that Cade hadn't seen from up in the stands. "Busy doing *what?* The whole com-*mun*-ity's gonna be there. You've *gotta* be there. Nobody's *not* going to be there. What, you want to miss your treats?" He snickered.

Cade narrowed his eyes. The batter spoke up. "He's right, bud. Gotta be there. You new?"

Cade nodded, and the batter gave a dry chuckle. "Seriously, you never been before? Aw, man, no spoilers, but you need to be at this thing. Trust me, man. You will *love* it." he grinned, showing a gap where two of his front teeth had once been, then went back to frenching the Castro Street kid. Cade stared for a second, then went on his way.

He figured he could sit through an episode of *Rules of Engagement* if he had to.

"Too bad. It must be, uh, really hard," said the girl on the stage, lowering her eyes as if willing herself to remember the lines.

It was a girl of about twenty-three, with dark hair, and she looked quite a lot like the original actress – Cade figured that must have been why she got the part. But the delivery was stilted and wooden, even by the standards of a crappy sitcom, and Cade got the feeling that most of the audience were laughing from sympathy. Cade had never watched more than about ten minutes of this show – he didn't have much time for the tube at the best of times, and by all accounts this'd been a failure even by the low standards of the idiot box. Cade wondered why they'd decided to bring it back this way. Maybe there was something about it that people related to, even after the bad times. Or maybe anything better would just remind folks about what they'd lost.

"That's what she would've said," sighed a man of about forty, the one actor in the bunch, although he looked nothing like David Spade had – he had short hair, glasses and a heavy paunch. Nevertheless, Cassie started giggling on Cade's left and wouldn't stop, and the whole of the movie house erupted into a long burst of applause.

Easily pleased, Cade figured.

The place was packed – in a lot of the seats, people were sitting on each other's laps. The aisles were filled with people sitting cross-legged – even the sides of the stage had people sitting on them, occasionally getting in the way of the actors as they made their way on and off. Cade suddenly wondered if it was true, if everybody in the whole damned community liked old sitcoms so much that they'd come in here.

He scanned the crowd. There was nobody there Cade could have called *old* – the oldest person he'd met in the town was Clearly himself, and he wasn't yet fifty. And no kids. Not a single one.

He'd seen about a dozen in the Pastor's territory. The law of averages said he should be seeing the same here. It nagged him.

"Wasn't that *awesome?*"

Cade turned to look at Cassie and shrugged. There wasn't much more to say. He made a move to get up from his seat and she put a hand on his shoulder, gently. "Don't get up yet, silly. It's time for Doctor Clearly to hand out the treats."

Cade's eyes narrowed. The kid from Castro street had mentioned *treats*.

People were passing plastic bags filled with pills along the aisles – black pills and white pills. Everybody took two, one of each colour, then passed the bag along. Cassie took her two, smiling brightly, then passed the bag expectantly along to Cade. Cade met her eyes for a second, then gingerly reached out. To his right, a rail-thin man in a cheap suit and tie growled, "Don't bogart 'em, Mac, pass 'em down the line."

Cade hesitated, then took a black pill and a white pill, palming them. Slowly, the rustling plastic bags made their way through the audience, then vanished back into whatever storage they'd emerged from.

As Doc Clearly took the stage, there was muted applause – people could only clap so hard without dropping the precious pills.

"Everyone got a black pill and a white pill?" he smiled, holding up his own. Cade looked at him, eyes narrowed. He hadn't mentioned this during their brief talk. Cade wondered if that was just absent-mindedness. "Remember, take them both together – otherwise they don't work." He smiled. "I hope everyone's got something to say to God tonight." There was a ripple of laughter in the audience.

Cade straightened in his chair. He hadn't signed up for a suicide cult and he figured it was probably time to get out of there – either quietly or by force. Cassie noticed his sudden shift of posture and smiled, placing her hand on his shoulder again. "It's okay," she whispered. "We do this every night. The pills help us to see God, you know? We get to meet him."

Cade turned to the man on his right. "Yeah?"

The man played with his pills, almost nervously. "Sure. We see God, all right. You should try it."

"He's wonderful – a kindly old guy with a beard and big sad eyes. And he created us all." She sighed, her hand squeezing Cade's shoulder in a way that made him vaguely uncomfortable. She didn't give him the impression of someone totally in control of herself. Cade wasn't a man who got nervous exactly, but the way she'd attached herself to him in the past few hours made him a mite uneasy – restless, even. He didn't see it ending well. Not to mention all this God talk.

He'd had enough of that from the Pastor.

"I love God!" Cassie breathed, looking out into the middle distance, then downing her pills suddenly, almost furtively. Immediately she slumped in her seat, eyes rolling back.

The man on Cade's right grinned. "Comes on quick. Hey, y'know what God told me once? He made us, but he didn't make the world, or the bad times. That was someone else – Simon or Simeon or some shit. Satan figure, I guess. He said he was sorry, but there was nothing he could do." The man chuckled, light glinting off his oily skin. "Isn't that wild? Sorry. Don't that beat all?" He chuckled again, then swallowed the two pills and slumped down.

Cade looked around at the rest of the audience – without a word, they were all slumping, one by one, as the pills hit their systems, keeling over where they sat, heading into dreamland. Cade looked at the stage, and his eyes met Doc Clearly's – those kind, wise, infinitely patient eyes.

"Mister Cade. I guess I should have told you. Kept you informed. This is probably quite a shock to you." The Doc smiled, taking a seat in a prop chair, fiddling with the pills in his hand.

"Sure." said Cade, head cocked a little to the side, sizing the man up, Deciding if he was going to need to kill him.

He still seemed trustworthy.

"Our little... well, *ritual* seems strong. Our communal trip, put it that way." He smiled, genially. "It's one of the things we keep the generators for – running my laboratory. It's where I synthesise this stuff. My compound. It really does make you see God, you know. I think that's important these days – something people need. Faith, but without the evils of religion. Faith in pill form." He shrugged, then looked about him. "Does wonders for these people. A nightly escape from the horrors of the world... the terrible losses... every night, we can visit our Creator and get some answers, or shout at him, or hit him, or tell him about our day. God confesses to you, or you confess to God." He chuckled. "It's kind of theraputic. Even for me."

"You see God?" Cade raised an eyrbrow, leaning back in his seat. He was still evaluating. Wondering if he was going to need to do any killing.

Wondering if he should take the pills.

The Doc shrugged. "Or it's a drug trip. So sue me. The point is, this is what keeps these people sane. You can join in, or not. It's up to you. You sound like you've made your peace with the world as it is. You probably don't strictly need to take it. But I recommend you do. It really is something." He smiled, popping the pills into his mouth. "Try it, if only the once. I'll see you on the other side, Cade." He swallowed, and settled back, closing his eyes.

Cade was alone. All around him, he could hear the heavy breathing of the sleepers, lost in their drug dreams.

He looked at the pills in his hand, one black, one white. They felt heavy.

It was too damned risky, he figured. He wasn't about to take a drug – hell, two drugs, drugs he didn't know the first damned thing about – on the say-so of somebody he'd only just met, even if they did have a perfect community, even if everybody there was happier than anyone he'd met since the bad times, or before. It was too big a risk to swallow his damned pills even if God was at the other end of them.

Cade wondered what God would have to say.

It was a good sell, that Doc Clearly gave.

Cade made up his mind. Slowly, he put the pills in his mouth. They tasted metallic on his tongue, and he found that the black one was sour, like aniseed. He felt his head get light.

He could still spit them out, he knew that. Instead, he swallowed, slowly.

And closed his eyes.

CHAPTER EIGHTEEN

I AM AS I AM

Drrr-rrrr-rrrrrrrr goes the alarm. It's not really an alarm, but it's the alarm function on a cheap mobile phone and it does the job well enough. It vibrates against the makeshift bedside table that I put together out of boxes of old CDs, waiting against the day I go to IKEA and get a proper one. I still haven't gotten around to that. Eventually I will.

The phone chirps sadistically while it vibrates and for a moment I don't know where I am. I try to open my eyes and there's a stabbing pain in my eyeballs, and I keep them shut and rub at them for a minute, involuntary tears coursing down my cheeks. Clearly I didn't get enough sleep.

The phone's still chirping away, practically dancing about on the cardboard lid of the CD box. *Drrrrr. Drrrrrr. Drrrrrrr.* I need to find a more soothing way to wake up.

Drrrrrrrr-drrr-drrrrr, right through my head until I reach out blindly, fumbling for the thing, fingers poking at my glasses and an empty can of something from the night before, finally knocking the phone off the boxes and down the side of the bed, reaching and gripping and finally managing to get the damned thing to shut up.

Then I set it to go off an hour later, put it back and go back to sleep. What's the point in getting up?

Eventually I have to. There's work to be done and it's already after ten. I always hope that the morning will magically give me the will to carry on, and then once the morning finishes I hope for some renewed vigour in the afternoon. It never comes.

After the glasses go on, I rummage through drawers and pull on the first clothes I see. Nothing special – a drab maroon pullover/sweatshirt thing, black trousers, my jacket to keep out the cold. I don't need to make much of an effort today. I'm not seeing anybody, the flat's empty, everyone's gone. I've got the place to myself. Nobody's going to care how I dress, least of all me.

The face in the bathroom mirror is tired, eyes baggy, beard scraggy, face set in a dispirited scowl. I drag a flannel over it for the sake of habit, brush my teeth, look at the dark patches under the bloodshot, bleary eyes. I feel as bad as I look. I wasn't even drinking last night – I just didn't sleep. Too much news. Too depressed to sleep.

There's some leftover pizza that'll work well enough as breakfast. There are anchovies on it, and anchovies are the secret to eating cold pizza. An anchovy doesn't care if its hot or cold, it'll taste just the same and overpower anything else into the bargain. I highly recommend anchovies.

Of course, now I have to get myself into a world where there aren't any anchovies, and there isn't any pizza – not delivered, anyway, and certainly not the way we're used to, ordered online and perfectly customised for the ultimate leisure experience. This perfect community of Doc Clearly's probably makes pizza, but the old-fashioned way, like they used to in old Italy. I wonder what that is – I should look it up. I suppose the way things are going we'll all be finding out soon.

I made the mistake yesterday of looking at the financial news and the environmental news – I couldn't work for an hour after that, just listlessly trawled for some sign of hope, but there wasn't one. We're long past the stage where the naysayers can make me feel any better, and the doomers seem more and more credible all the time. It's no wonder everything's tanking – money's just a shared illusion, and the scales are methodically falling from our eyes as things get worse and worse. We're not going to need a pandemic.

I remember the last time I had to write a post-apocalyptic world. In the first draft I never bothered to explain how things got to be post-apocalyptic – the apocalypse was inevitable. Just extrapolate from now.

If anything, the world of *Afterblight* is too optimistic.

This line of thinking isn't going to help me write. I crack open the laptop and set things into motion, listening to the grind of the processors as they turn over.

The laptop's new, or relatively new – an HP monstrosity that gets very hot very quickly, probably a sign it's using too much power. I'm worried it'll burn out faster than another computer might, start acting up, developing minor glitches that turn into larger and larger problems until finally I'm trying hopelessly to get five hundred words out of the thing between grinding, shuddering crashes. The day is coming. Everything degrades. Everything falls apart.

I got a Samsung TV last year, and it didn't last the week. Neither did the replacement. The second replacement lasted quite a while but recently fell over and died in exactly the same way. According to the web, they use cheap components that have a problem with power surges in certain areas. That warranty's paying off, I'll tell you that much. It's the way the world is these days – things built to perform, but not necessarily to last. Not much thought about the future.

The word processor opens and I'm looking at a blank page.

And the blank page looks back at me.

I push the 'hibernate' button and the screen goes black. I've just remembered I've got a contract from some script work that needs to be sent out if I'm going to get paid, and I need to get stamps and envelopes.

Best get that done now, before I start writing anything.

I'm not procrastinating, you understand. This is very practical behaviour.

I pull on socks, shoes and a coat – it's midwinter and the air's bitter – then quickly check the mirror. A scruffy, bearded man looks back at me, scowling with tired eyes. It'll have to do.

I'm not likely to be making any first impressions on people, with any luck. I'm just going to get stamps. It's not like I'm going to the pub or anything.

Just a quick errand and then back to work.

THE ENVELOPE RACK in the post office is right next to the magazine rack, and while I'm there I pick up a copy of a games magazine on impulse. I don't play that many computer games these days, but I've got a soft spot for a few of them and there are some coming out this year I'm really looking forward to.

It won't do any harm to stop off for a sandwich somewhere while I read this. Maybe a lunchtime pint, too.

Just to get the juices flowing. I'm not going to have more than one.

There's work waiting at home, after all.

York isn't so much a city as a town with pretensions. It's got walls separating the city centre from the suburban sprawl, and a cathedral to cement its city status, but at the end of the day you can walk across it in fifteen minutes without breathing hard. Inside that fifteen-minute radius there are several dozen different pubs, maybe as many as a hundred. The city as a whole – apparently – has a pub for every single day of the year.

With so many pubs, there's something for every kind of drinker and every kind of drink. If you're a real ale snob, visit the Three-Legged Mare. If you fancy a fight, the Lowther on a Saturday night is a good place to make an enemy, although you probably won't be able to start anything until you're down the street. If you want to feel cramped, try the Maltings. Personally, I like nooks – quiet spots where I can either read a book or talk without shouting. The Golden Slipper's good for that.

They're not serving food, so I just get a pint of Worthy's and some peanuts. I've still got plenty of that pizza in my belly.

Besides, a drink might help.

I'm definitely not going to have more than one.

The magazine's full of news about the new *Sims* game. You'll have heard of that – little computer people you can play around with, control their lives. This one's promising to make the little computer people even more human with even more human personalities. You can tailor the personalities and then turn them loose on each other and watch the soap opera unfold, or dive in and tweak it in the directions you want to go.

A virtual world of self-creating stories, set in motion by a godlike player. I like games like that.

There's an upcoming superhero MMORPG where you can create your hero and an arch-nemesis and set them out in a virtual world to be admired. I'm definitely getting that.

The irony hasn't escaped me. Even when I'm avoiding work, I'm still working. I'm just not getting paid.

About halfway through the pint, the door opens and he walks in. I don't see him at first – the little nook I'm reading my magazine in is blocked off from the door – but I hear the conversation in the room stop.

I only notice him when he's looming over my table. The shadow falls across the magazine and I find myself looking up, right into his grey eyes.

He's six feet tall, shorter than me, but he looks so much taller. He's standing and I'm sitting, of course. I'm sure that's what it is.

He's got the face Mark gave him on the cover, and the clothes – the black tank top and chains – but instead of the close-cut mohican he's got a shock of black hair, like Bluto in Popeye. Mountain man hair. Just like I pictured him, in fact.

It could be a coincidence, just someone who looks the same.

But it's not.

It's him.

He doesn't speak. He just looks at me, eyes heavy-lidded, no expression on that face. Staring. Maybe he's got nothing to say.

When you think about it, there isn't much that can be said.

He breathes in, bunching one hand into a fist, then breathes out. The hand opens. The puncture wound running right through the palm bleeds a little. I still can't read the look in his eyes.

I'm very conscious of my own sweat. It's hard to swallow, but I manage it anyway.

He had a pair of railroad spikes knocked through his hands. I'm not sure why I did that – there was some symbolic value, and I wanted to show the hero enduring in a hopeless situation. To an extent, I thought myself into that situation, at least in his place and with the inhuman power to survive I'd given him. But I wasn't in that situation, of course.

He was.

Because of me.

I look up at his eyes, opening my mouth to say something, and think better of it. My mouth is bone dry, but I don't dare lift my pint.

I still can't read the look in his eyes.

Is he angry?

I wasn't the one who killed his world. It was like that when I got there. Someone else built the whole thing and started the dominos toppling, I just came along after the fact and used it as a handy backdrop.

He clenches his fist again.

That isn't quite true. I might not have thought up the setting, but I killed off his town, his friends – no, I made it so he couldn't have friends. I killed everyone he knew. I described the end of the world for him in loving detail. I made everything as horrific as it could possibly get, and then for good measure I made sure his past was horrific as well.

I stripped most of his human feelings from him, only allowing him the occasional hint, because I thought that'd make for a better protagonist.

And now this person – this damaged psychopath – is standing in front of me, flexing his ruined hands.

Idly, I wonder what the barmaid thinks of all this. I look over at her – she's looking suspiciously over at me, muttering something to the landlord. I look back at his eyes, grey and unreadable, to see if he's registered it.

Suddenly, his head drops slightly. He looks at the games magazine, at the half-finished pint. Then he looks back in my eyes.

He doesn't look angry. He never did.

He looks sad.

"I'm sorry," I mutter, cheeks flushing. He doesn't respond.

There isn't anything to say.

After a second, he walks out. I feel guilty, and angry at him for making me feel guilty. I listlessly finish the pint in a couple of swift gulps, then walk out, the accusing eyes of the barmaid following me. I won't be able to go back there for a while, I suppose.

I stop off at the Mason's Arms for another and get some food with it, and finish the rest of the magazine. I'm really interested in this game. You can actually reach into the game world and move their things about, even enlarge or shrink their houses while they're walking around in them. Change and edit their lives between moments.

I wonder if they notice?

I HAVE ANOTHER pint – coke, this time – over some sausage and mash, which takes me into the afternoon. The day's a write-off, frankly, but it's not too late for me to get a couple of thousand words down – I ask the barman if he'll let me have a can of Red Bull without opening it. He doesn't have a problem.

By the time I get back into the flat, it's become obvious that the bloke in the pub was just some random nutter. He looked a bit like... well, like *him*, but he was probably just some goth or a local Hell's Angel or something. I probably just took his chair while he was out having a fag in the street and he wanted to stare me out of it.

Or something. I don't know.

The laptop is still sitting open, screen black. I crack open the can and sip it, letting it wake me up a little and counteract the booze. The stuff makes me jittery, but it helps with the writing, especially on a deadline. It's past time I got some work done.

I'd left him in the theatre, and now I want to jump forward in time a little to that big orgy, and what happens after that... yes, with Cassie.

Right.

The machine judders back into life and I'm confronted by a loading screen and then the stark whiteness of the blank page. This time it doesn't seem so intimidating. My fingers find the keys.

'CHAPTER NINETEEN,' I type.

'Cade opened his eyes, and the sky was a livid red'... no. Bloody red.

No, not that either.

'Cade opened his eyes, and the sky was on fire, burning orange, with streaks of blood red that ran from horizon to horizon. He could feel Cassie...' No. No. Doesn't work.

'He could feel someone's fingers brushing through the hair on his chest.'

Better.

Fingers tap and words appear. I smile, happy to be back in the zone, back writing. The envelopes and the stamps are sitting forgotten in the bedroom, and I know I won't get around to posting off the contract until tomorrow, maybe not until the day after, but that doesn't matter. It took me a while to get into it today, but I'm there now.

I reach out and take another sip of the Red Bull, and then settle down to making Cade's life worse.

CHAPTER NINETEEN

THE HELTER SKELTER

CADE OPENED HIS eyes, and the sky was on fire, burning orange, with streaks of blood red that ran from horizon to horizon. He could feel someone's fingers brushing through the hair on his chest.

It took him a second or two to realise he was naked.

The fingers played over the fresh scabs on his chest, the cross that was cut there, then reached down to play slowly over his belly, and then Cassie's face filled his vision and before he knew what was going on, her lips were on his and her tongue was diving and darting against his own.

Cade figured he should be shocked at that, or at least surprised, but it felt like the most natural damned thing in all the world. He realised his hands were on her bottom, squeezing, fingertips rolling up the small of her back and into her hair, but he couldn't quite remember telling them to do that.

It didn't much matter, he figured.

Nothing much mattered.

In the back of his mind, he was finding it a mite strange, through – Cade wasn't a man to let his guard down lightly and Cassie, though she was sweet and pert and all the rest of it, wasn't Cade's type at all. Cade liked women with a good twenty or thirty years on them, and like as not a few years on him into the bargain. That was how come he got on so well with the Duchess.

Cade blinked, feeling her young, slim fingers taking a hold of him and half-stroking, half-tugging, in an inexpert sort of a way that was exactly the reason why he usually fooled around with older women. This time he didn't mind – as a matter of fact, it felt pretty damned good. Cade let his head drop onto the grass, and he felt each cool blade brush softly against his fingertips, and the muscles in his face twitched into something that anybody who'd known him long wouldn't recognise.

Cade smiled.

He was out in the park, then – Golden Gate park – and in the arms of a girl of no more than eighteen, maybe seventeen, which at any other time might raise a moral complication, but not now. Not during the zero hour.

Cade blinked, wondering where the hell that had come from, and then Cassie's lips were on his again and she was clambering onto him, and then he was in her. All around him, he could hear people together, in twos and sometimes threes and fours, laughing and sighing, tumbling over each other and intertwining like coiling snakes, some quiet as a whisper, some shouting out with every stroke. Cade lay back and let it all wash over him.

He turned his head to the left, and he saw the woman in the well-fitting jeans from the ball game – only now she was in nothing but an unbuttoned shirt, nuzzling with another girl about the same age and the actor from the TV show, or stage play or whatever the hell it was. The three of them were writhing and rubbing, not doing anything in particular but enjoying the contact of skin on skin. Cade guessed there was an element of polymorphous perversity to it. Then again, the same could be said of him.

He pulled Cassie close, breathing in the scent of her neck, and gave it some thought. That in itself was a feat for Cade – the thoughts in his head seemed like quicksilver, slippery and impossible to get any kind of a hold of. He'd been drugged, he knew that – or rather, he'd taken the damn drug himself. He'd forgotten why he'd ever been tempted to, although in the back of his mind he could remember meeting a fat, depressed-looking fella... the thought left him as soon as he latched on it, and was gone. They were all under the influence of whatever this was, and it was pretty good at that. Cade hadn't felt quite so free in a while.

Still, there was something wrong, he knew that.

Something in the way the shadows were lengthening across the park, spreading out like a black pool of contaminating liquid.

The sun was going down.

Cassie leaned in again, breathing him, her giggle filling his ear. He could hear something over that, and the sighs and the laughter.

He could hear screaming

It was the kind of screaming animals did, enraged, snarling beasts, and it was coming from the shadows – from those parts of the park where the shadows fell. Cade turned his head, and saw that the shadows were starting to fall over the park. Only natural.

The sun was going down.

He blinked, wondering why he didn't care, and then remembered the drugs. He'd taken a white pill and a black pill, and they were working together on him. He had an idea that it was the white pill that was making him so mellow and easily pleased, so ready to let Cassie do what she wanted and to do what he felt in return. He wondered, idly, what it was the black pill did.

The screaming was louder now.

And the sun was going down.

The shadows slowly crept towards him, flowing over the actor and the woman who filled her jeans so well, while she wore them, and the other girl between them, and they changed. It was such a sudden change that Cade almost couldn't see it – it was as though it was just one more kind of lovemaking. But their faces were twisted now, masks of rage and hate and pure menace, the actor flexing his arms and smashing out, backhanding the unknown girl across the face and sending her tumbling, while the woman reached out fingernails like long talons for his face, laughing cruelly as they raked down his cheeks and drew blood.

"Helter skelter!" she screamed, or maybe it was him, it was hard to say. Their mingled voices rose up as she clawed at him, and he struck out wildly at her, the girl out cold beside them, her nose bloody. Naked people clawing at each other and shrieking, maddened: "Helter skelter! Helter skelter! *Helter skelter!*"

And the whole park seemed to be shrieking it as the shadows lengthened and caught more people in their grip. Cade felt cold, suddenly, but didn't feel anything else but good, even though that wave of violence was spreading closer to him and Cassie.

She was in his arms, and her lips were on his neck, and somehow that was all that mattered. His hands slid up her back, taking hold of her shoulders, and he turned his head to kiss her, deep and long.

And then the shadow hit him.

At first, it was like nothing had changed, and it took him a second to work out what had. Only the sun had gone, after all.

Cade was now in a world with no sun.

It seemed as if there had always been an inferno at the front of his skull, burning and crisping his frontal lobes, sending white-hot needles of pure agony scorching down his spine and back up again, setting his blood alight and pumping it around his body. It seemed like he'd always been angry.

There'd never been a time he hadn't wanted to kill anything that moved.

Above him, the girl thing screeched and clawed, raking her nails over his chest, opening up the wounds. The pain hit him, but became lost in the red roaring flames that burnt and scorched his mind. It seemed that that heat – that burning, hateful rage and pain – had always been there and always would be. The girl-thing was screaming at him – "Helter skelter! Helter skelter!" over and over. He realised, without being surprised, that he was bellowing it as well.

Hell with it. It was how he felt, he might as well say it.

Helter skelter. Helter skelter.

Over and over.

The air was full of screams and snarls as fights and scuffles broke out all around – here and there Cade could see people scratching and clawing at themselves, unable to reach anyone else to hurt but needing to hurt *something.* Once people were unconscious, they were ignored – Cade realised he had to force himself to see them, as if now that they didn't pose him any threat his brain felt free to just pass over them and move on to something else.

Cade was rationalising, and he knew it – fighting the drug. That was no damn good. That just made it hurt more. What he needed was to take that hurt out on somebody. The girl-thing brought her fist down at his lip, splitting it, and all his attention was suddenly on her. She'd do as well as anybody.

His fist snapped up, slamming into her jaw and cracking it, skinning a knuckle in the process. That familiar blast of agony rolled down from his mutilated hand, but it was a weak thing now, compared to the fire in his brain and he paid it no heed.

He couldn't remember her name.

All he knew was that she was moving around, rolling on the grass, hissing and clutching at her face, and every time she moved it caused another wave of flaming pain in his mind. He needed to do something about that.

Through the fire and the fog in his mind, it came to him that everyone was lashing out almost randomly – they must be feeling the same pain that he was, the same rage and hate, but they weren't focussing. Cade guessed they'd never learned how to focus past pain, or maybe they just weren't of his mind. Maybe they just didn't feel as strongly about it as he did. They damn sure weren't going to do much in the way of damage in that state, although Cade figured he knew where all those little injuries he'd seen had come from now.

But Cade could damage them. Cade could damage them a hell of a lot.

And he would.

He reached down and grabbed the girl-thing by the throat, closing his screaming hands and twisting. Her spine went with a sickening crack of sound, but he kept squeezing, not realising that his teeth were gritted and his eyes were bulging right along with hers until after she'd gone still. Only then did his fingers relax, and once she'd flopped onto the ground, cold and heavy and without life, he simply forgot she'd ever been there.

The actor was swinging out wildly, not doing much more than bruising the woman he was fighting. Cade went for him next. He wished he had his knife, or his knuckledusters, or anything at all – maybe he left them in the movie theatre. He'd go there soon and find what he needed, but in the meantime he had work to do. The fire in his head wasn't going away.

It was all rational for Cade. It was the most natural, rational thing in the world to grab the actor's head in his hands and twist it round with one motion until it sat backwards on the neck, the flesh twisted and the vertebrae snapped apart, the man's bladder and bowels voiding on the grass. Cade kept kicking him as he shuddered and convulsed, the nerve endings sending their last signals to the dying body. Finally he went still, and vanished from Cade's head.

Cade moved on to the next one.

And the next.

And the next.

It was a long night, and there were a lot of people in that park, maybe fifty in all, maybe more – Cade went through them one by one, breaking necks for the most part, but occasionally getting in something closer to a real fight, trading brutal punches again and again until they crashed to the floor with nothing but a red smear where their face had been – whoever they were.

The only thing in Cade's head was pain, but he kept moving, cracking spines and snapping necks, choking and killing, while all the folks around him just fell to the dirt and hollered and shrieked, repeating their nonsense phrase over and over. Somehow, he managed to draw a kind of calm from it – a balm in his blazing, burning brain. He was a man reduced to one function, and that function was death,

And death had no mercy.

* * *

Eventually, there was nobody left to kill, and Cade slowed, and stopped, falling to his knees, a clockwork man with a stopped key. He would have broke his own neck or carved himself open like a turkey on a farm, but somehow he couldn't raise his hands anymore, so there he knelt until the dawn.

By the time the rays of the sun started to wash over the park, and the blood and the corpses on the ground, the pain in Cade's mind was almost faded anyway. The drug had worn off after a few hours, and the first light of dawn washed it out entirely.

Cade felt washed out right along with it.

He lifted his head, and saw someone walking towards him from the gates of the park. A man wearing a good suit, looking at the carnage Cade had caused. He looked horrified, stumbling through the dawn like a man who'd released some terrible virus, some contagion upon the world, without considering what it might do.

Like a biochemist, maybe.

Cade nodded. "Doc." His voice sounded ragged in his ears. He cleared his throat and spat the taste from his mouth.

Doc Clearly looked back at him. His face was white as ash. "Cade."

He looked around at the piled corpses. He reached out with the toe of one immaculate shoe and prodded the thing that had once been Cassie, raising a buzzing cloud of flies from her stiffened body. He swallowed hard, shaking his head. Then he looked back at Cade.

"I think... I think we'd better talk."

CHAPTER TWENTY

THE CONFESSION

"It was all about balance, you see. Balance and release."

Doc Clearly sighed, scratching his head, before leaning down quickly to check the pulse of one of the more recent kills, then standing slowly, sighing and shaking his head. He was dead, of course – a young man in his early twenties. Cade couldn't remember seeing his face, but there was nobody else who could've twisted his head around like that.

Doc Clearly seemed to read his thoughts. "It's possible not all of these were you. We do have fatalities sometimes. It's... it's the nature of it." He pinched the bridge of his nose, as if warding off a developing headache. "I'm sorry, Cade. I expect you're wanting to know why."

Cade nodded. "I'd be obliged."

Clearly sighed. "Why I dose them with it... the compound. Why they keep taking it, night after night, despite... well, despite this." He shook his head. "I should have warned you. I should have given you some kind of indication what to expect, or... well, or told Cassiopeia not to bother bringing you." He looked up, angry. "Damn it, Cade, you told me you didn't have this in you!"

Cade stared back, not moving. The Doc looked at him for a moment, then the anger dropped out of him and he just looked depressed. "Sorry... Sorry." he sighed, rubbing his brow. "Cassiopeia was someone... well, I liked her a lot." He shook his head, slowly, and turned away from Cade. Cade got the impression Clearly didn't want to look at him. He couldn't blame him for that.

He could sure as hell blame him for slipping him something that turned him into a killing machine, though. "Why didn't you tell me?"

Clearly sighed. "You killed the dog because you thought it was a threat. I didn't know how you'd react to hearing about the compound, whether you'd... oh, I don't know. Whether you'd think we were just like what you'd been through up north. I thought it would be safer to just introduce you to it; let you see for yourself. Experience how good it could be." He sighed. "Not one of my better ideas."

They were at the gate of the park now, and Cade could see a few of the love children staggering through the streets, bruised and sore, covered with bites and scratches, looking for their clothes. They looked tired, but there was something healthy about them all the same, as if the watches of the long night had drained some boil. They were standing straight and proud, despite their nakedness. A couple of them waved to the Doc.

"The park's off limits for now, everyone. I'll need a work party in an hour or two – about twenty, and they'd best be prepared for some ugly work. Oh, and we'll need someone to take census. Spread it around." The waving people nodded and went back to what they were doing. Satisfied, the Doctor walked on grimly, heading back towards Haight Street and the movie theatre. Cade followed. He was more aware of his own nudity now – the way the other folk didn't seem to give a damn about theirs seemed to have that effect on him. He shook his head, waiting for the Doc to carry on.

Eventually, he did.

"Most people just pick up afterwards and carry on, as you saw. Like I said, we have fatalities sometimes, but generally it's just bites, scratches, the occasional black eye... things have calmed down a lot from how they were. Most people... they still hold back, you see. From doing anything permanent. Even in the grip of it, we hold back." He looked at Cade. "I really should have known when you killed the dog, Cade. You don't hold back. Do you?"

Cade shook his head. He wasn't a man to hold back much when it came to killing, it had to be said. He looked up at the Doc, eyes narrowed. "Got some questions."

Clearly scratched the back of his head again, his moustache seeming to droop further. "Of course you have. We all have. Why do we do this to ourselves? Why do we take this terrible substance and put ourselves through a night of hell? What do we gain?" He looked down, at a man lying on the sidewalk, the left side of his face beaten raw, one eyelid puffy and closed. He was smiling serenely, looking up through his good eye at the clouds overhead. "You okay, Ed?"

Ed grinned, revealing missing teeth. "Just fine, Doc. Just fine."

They carried on walking in silence for a moment before turning the corner onto Haight Street. They were starting to see some people wearing clothes now – long-sleeved shirts, polo-necks and ponchos were popular, pulled down over the arms to hide the bruises and scratches, shades hiding black eyes. They smiled, and waved, and one girl walked up and threw her arms around the Doc and hugged him, then leant in to kiss Cade's cheek. Then she moved on, leaving her gesture to do the talking.

"You won't be so popular when they find out what you've done. That many dead... it's hard for the community to absorb. I'll need to decide what to do about that – whether you'll be staying. Whether I can trust you with any more of the compound. Punishment... I don't know. I don't think I can let you have any more."

Cade blinked, looking at Clearly out of the corner of his eye. "More?" Once was enough, he figured. That damned drug had sent him halfway to hell and turned his hand to the murder of maybe fifty men and women. He didn't like to think about what might have happened if there'd been kids and old folks there.

What it implied that there weren't any.

Clearly turned to look at him as they approached the livid red façade of the old movie theatre. "People always want more, Cade. But we're back to the 'why' of it." He closed his eyes, shaking his head. Suddenly he looked tired to Cade, bending over as if there was an infinitely heavy weight pressing down on his back, one that he didn't admit he wore for the most part, but one that was there all the same. "Cade... can I ask you a personal question? Tell me, how did you *feel* when things fell apart? When people were dying?"

Cade fell silent. After a moment or two, he spoke slowly, like he was admitting to a crime or guessing the answer to a quiz question. His eyes were guarded.

"Didn't."

Doc Clearly raised one sad eyebrow. "You didn't feel anything?"

Cade felt guilty all of a sudden, looking away. "There were things needed doing. Not much time to sit around." He shrugged.

Clearly smiled humourlessly. "Huh. I've never met a sociopath before." Then he winced, catching himself. "I'm sorry. That's... quite a value judgement, considering the kind of things people have been up to here. Even me, with my special pills, mixing up horror every night...

God. I didn't set out to do things this way, Cade. Believe me." He sighed, leading the way inside the building.

"When you lose everything – everyone – in a matter of days... I know I'm asking a lot, but put yourself in that place. You have a wife and children, a family, or at the very least friends. And if not friends, then structures – institutions, social conventions, things that are fixed. Even the lowest of the low, the loneliest of the lonely, know that when they turn on the television someone will be there. When they leave their hovel, people will be walking the streets. Aeroplanes will fly in the sky. There is a world and they are a part of it, no matter how small a part they might be."

They walked through the foyer, passing a smiling couple. The man was buttoning his shirt, covering up a criss-cross of scratches, a forest of them, some days old. A girl huddled into him, nuzzling like a cat, looking perfectly content. There was still blood under her nails, and a bruise was developing on her cheek. Doc Clearly half-waved to them, then turned back to Cade.

"There is a world, and then it goes – and what you're left with is flyblown corpses and filth in the streets and the complete dissolution of any structure or system you relied on. You understand, Cade? You could adapt – you have, for better or worse, a unique outlook that makes you perfectly adapted to these times. I imagine you didn't function all that well in the old world, did you?"

Cade shook his head. He had to admit that he'd not exactly distinguished himself.

Doc Clearly smiled. "You picked a good time to arrive yesterday. People had picked themselves up from the night, so you wandered in when things were at their best. You saw how normal everything was – especially in contrast with your ride in with the Gang. Not like anywhere else you've been, is it? The Pastor and his religious fanatics, the cannibals..."

Cade frowned, then spat. "Bunch of folks following blind after authority. After a fella says he's got the answers."

It was a long speech, and Cade meant every word.

Clearly looked at the carpet for a moment. "Well, I deserve that, I guess. Come on, I think your clothes are in here."

He led the way into the theatre they'd been in, and Cade saw his clothes – the t-shirt with Hug Me on it, the blood-spattered jeans, his chains, his knives, even the knuckledusters – laying in a heap where he'd sat, along with a few other piles of clothing here and there. It looked like everyone had stripped there and then, probably once they'd come out of that vision or whatever the hell it was – something about a bar, Cade remembered. It looked as if most of the clothes had been picked up and put back on by now, though.

Cade pulled on the t-shirt first, then the jeans – he'd fallen into the habit of going commando – while the Doc carried on talking behind him.

"There's a price for that normality, Cade. Trauma like the death of a world full of people... nobody living has ever been through something like that, nobody in history. The Black Death, the Spanish Influenza – chickenfeed." He shook his head. "Nobody's normal after that. Nobody's sane. The hate and the anger and the terror, the trauma, it builds up in you. The compound... well, it's like draining pus from a wound. It's cleansing. People let out their demons. Usually... usually nobody gets hurt, not badly. I try and make sure they're kept in check..."

Cade nodded, lacing up his boots. "That's your drug. Being in charge. Spiritual guru." He breathed in, disliking the necessity of talk, but some things had to be said. His eyes were cold as steel. "You burn Sausalito?"

Doc Clearly opened his mouth, then closed it.

Cade looked him in the eye. "Helter Skelter. That you?"

The Doc opened his mouth again... then hung his head, turning and walking up to the back of the theatre, away from the people who were trickling in to reclaim their clothes and shoes. There he sat, and waited for Cade to join him.

Cade took his time, fastening the chains about himself, locking them to biceps and waist, then checking his knives. It was a damned good thing he'd followed everyone else in stripping down – if he'd had his knives with him, he'd have killed everybody in the city.

Maybe he still would.

Slowly, he walked up to the Doc, who sat like a man in a confession booth. Cade didn't bother making anything out of that. He just sat, and waited.

After a minute, Clearly spoke.

"I developed the compound two months before the end came. Simple to manufacture – all I needed was a large quantity of raw materials and I could cook it up on a camping stove." For a moment he seemed like he was going to laugh. "Almost like it was meant to be. The high... well, you experienced that. Meetings with the divine – all the firing of certain chemicals in the brain, of course, but the experience seems quite real for all that. Then the charging of the libido, the mind becoming lost in a sea of pleasure, love, togetherness... and all completely legal." He chuckled, unable to help himself. "All I had to do was get rid of the after-effect of the black pill. If the light receptors weren't kept stimulated at a certain level – if it got dark – the compound brought on the other symptoms. The blazing anger, the hatred, the neural pain, the violence – barely controllable. In your case it was totally unrestrained..."

Cade nodded. He figured he knew where this was going, but he had time. Might as well hear it.

"The end came, and... well, at first there was just chaos. We managed to get a community together, but those were nightmarish days. I don't know why I suggested using the drug – maybe I thought the end would come more easily if we were stupefied." He put his head in his hands, suddenly. "No, no, that isn't it at all, is it? I handed it out at night – at night, you see? I knew what it would do. I knew what it *needed* to do..."

He swallowed, and Cade could see the disgust at himself written on his face. "I said it was like draining pus from a wound. But the pus builds up, and the horror builds up, and there was so much of it in us then... you have to understand, they were *eating people.* Some capitalist TV personality had actually got citizens to eat each other. The Pastor and his men, they took torches to Castro Street, grabbed people and dragged them away, and they were never heard from again. God, I heard those poor kids were crucified – I heard the Pastor actually nailed them up." He was shaking his head, and his whole body was trembling with the effort of remembering. "We were caught between all that. Trapped. We were angry and we were scared. And... well, with my compound in us..."

He stared ahead, into the middle distance. "I remember my brain was alight, and there were hundreds of us – there were several thousand survivors at that stage, although that number dropped fast – and I'd made so much of the compound we could all have some. And we went on the hunt – it seemed to last days, that first time. The Pastor's territory was to the north of Golden Gate Park –"

Cade nodded. "The Presidio."

Doc Clearly shuddered. "He called it the Garden of Eden. We burnt it. We drove him out and we smashed everything we could lay our hands on, and we burnt the ruins. And we weren't done. We ran up the highway, screaming like banshees, and the light of day couldn't dim it then. There was too much pain to be vented, you see? We kept running and running, up Highway 1, smashing the cars, grabbing fuel cans, killing anyone we found on those roads..."

Cade nodded. "Then you hit Sausalito."

There was some satisfaction in solving that one at last.

"We burned Sausalito to the ground. We murdered anyone we found and burned everything we could. Marin City too. We'd have demolished every building and laid it all flat if we could. Dear God, I still remember..." He shook his head, and raised a knuckle to his eye, wiping away the tears that were forming.

Cade didn't speak.

Doc Clearly was silent for a minute or two, then spoke, low and soft. "Eventually, the madness faded, enough to come home at least. There were some scavengers on our territory – a few of the Pastor's people, the occasional cannibal, although by then they'd already found their home in the BART tunnels and established their pattern of hunting for people who strayed too far east." He shrugged. "We killed them. We made it clear that Haight Street was ours, and we went to work clearing the bodies and setting it up so we could live there. We'd exorcised our pain, you see? We were refreshed, purified, ready to work. And work we did."

He sighed. "Eventually, we fell into the pattern – we'd work through the day, then take the pills in the evening, meet God – all very theraputic – have sex, and then... when the sun went down, we'd march, laughing and screaming, to somewhere we didn't own, and we'd put it to the torch. If you go below Seventeenth Street... well, there is no below Seventeenth Street. There are a few spots still standing around Twenty-Fourth, since the cannibals were protecting it, but... we smashed and burned everything we could. It's no Sausalito, but there are very few places left in the south of the city to live in, which had the side effect of mobilising most of the survivors who were living down there to join either us, if we kidnapped them, or the Pastor if we beat them and left them to die."

Cade looked at him. Clearly looked back.

"I'm not proud of those times."

Cade didn't speak. Eventually, Clearly shook his head and continued speaking. "The pain grew less with every use of the drug, until finally we'd exhausted it. The pain, I mean. Not the compound. Never the compound... we were happy, is what I'm trying to say. Content. Where the Pastor's bunch are still shell-shocked from the end of the world, we have shrugged off the culture shock and rebuilt thanks to the power of chemistry. Yes, every night we kick, and we bite, and we pummel each other, and occasionally people still die, but... there wasn't another way to get through it. I'm convinced there wasn't." He bowed his head. "I'm not looking for absolution, Cade. I don't think there's any to be had, and... well, I should know, shouldn't I?" He laughed, another humourless little chuckle. "I met God."

Cade turned his head, curious. "What'd he say?"

Doc Clearly smiled, wryly. "He told me I'd turned out a better person than he'd created me to be. Nonsense, of course. My guilty conscience speaking."

Cade shrugged. "Must count for something." He thought about how the Pastor'd almost broke down that time, begging to be told he was right. He'd believed in something, at least, even if it was crazy as a rattlesnake. Clearly didn't seem to believe in anything except keeping his people going, even if that meant killing a whole bunch of other folks. Cade didn't know if that made him any better than the Pastor. Maybe it made him worse, on account of how the Pastor at least had crazy for an excuse.

Made him dangerous, though.

Too dangerous.

Cade turned, looking Clearly in the eye. "Got some questions. There insulin here?" His eyes narrowed. "Your folks didn't burn it?"

Clearly shook his head. "No. We looted what we could find. There were things we burned, but I don't think we'd destroy something we're so dependent on. I do have a supply of insulin like that, but... well, I can't let you take any." He swallowed, looking nervous for the first time. "I can't, Cade. People depend on it."

"You use it to make your pills?"

"No!" the Doc looked offended. "We use it to treat *diabetes!* Nothing goes into the pills that we'd need for basic survival, although it could be argued those pills *are* our survival. Maybe in five or ten years we can cope without them – not now." He looked away, flushing, angry with himself as much as Cade. "We're addicts, I suppose. But the pills keep us alive... anyway, I'm not letting you have the insulin. We need it."

Cade nodded. He figured there'd be another supply somewhere – buried in a wrecked depot, maybe. He could go find it, if he had to.

If he had to.

"Your folks don't burn things any longer?"

There was a pause. Doc Clearly seemed to be contemplating his shoes. Finally he spoke.

"They were working out their pain, Mister Cade. That's what the rampages were all about. The better life got in the community, the less pain there was to work through in those night rampages – although there's always some. Life is about pain, even if you do build a paradise. That's what I meant earlier, about balance."

He lifted his head, still not looking at Cade.

"You left fifty corpses in that park, Mister Cade. I don't know what's going to happen when people find them. They've probably found them already – my word's only good for so much, it's not a police barricade. These corpses..." He shook his head. "These *people* are lovers, friends, workmates. People who've come to replace lost loves and lost family, you understand? I imagine for you, death is just part of your day – sorry, that came out wrong..."

Cade shrugged. Didn't seem so wrong as far as he was concerned.

"I don't know what kind of impact this is going to have. They're going to want to lynch you, and they're going to feel hurt and betrayed, and then when they take the compound – and they will want and need the compound tonight, Mister Cade, I very much doubt we'll be going through the ritual of performing a pre-pill show when my community needs to mourn fifty dead – when they take the compound, all that will come out."

He shook his head.

"And it's my fault. My fault entirely. I can't believe I thought you'd just... fall in line. Not after the dog." He stared straight ahead for a moment. "Perhaps I saw the opportunity to break a stalemate. Maybe we'll go after the Pastor tonight. Or maybe... maybe we'll just rage. Maybe that was what I was looking for." He sighed, his voice bitter. "Maybe that's the sort of spiritual guru I want to be. A Manson."

He shook his head, his voice breaking as the tears flowed. "Or maybe I just made a mistake. Maybe there isn't any psychology to it. Maybe I'm just a stupid man who let things get out of hand. I'm sorry, Cade. I wish things could have worked out for you here." He put his head in his hands. "I wish they could have worked out for all of us. Get lost, Cade. Go away and don't come back. Please, for your own sake, don't come back here."

Cade stood, looking down at the weeping man.

"I won't."

It was the third lie he told to Doc Clearly.

And the last.

CHAPTER TWENTY-ONE

THE SEIGE

CADE LEFT THE theatre and took the first turning north, up to Oak Street. He figured he had a lot of ground to cover if he wanted to get back to the Pastor's compound by nightfall.

He didn't look at the people he was walking past, but he could see their faces out of the corner of his eye. Some of them looked drained, some looked disbelieving. Some were openly weeping, asking over and over again whether it was true, if it could really be true... Cade thought back to what Doc Clearly had said. Lovers, friends, co-workers.

Damn it to Hell.

Everybody was walking towards the park except him – he was walking against the tide. Running from the scene of the crime, in other words. A couple of folks were starting to put two and two together and they turned towards him, eyes narrowed and shooting daggers, lips curled to a scowl, the accusation boiling towards the surface even as Cade marched past them and away. Word spread fast in a small community, and it was starting to spread about the massacre in the park.

His massacre.

Fifty-odd people, dead from his own two hands. Cade spat. Hell with it, anyway. He wasn't to blame. If that goddamned fool hadn't decided to drug him without even –

Can't kid a kidder, dog.

Cade didn't break step, but he turned his head and saw Fuel-Air, as whole and hearty as he'd been in life, marching alongside him like it was a parade ground. Doc Clearly's moustache bristled above his upper lip, looking out of place on his young face. He was grinning.

You were the one who lied, man. If you'd told the truth, he'd have told it to you. Shit, don't get me wrong, these people are fucked up – I mean, this is some Wicker-Man*-meets-fuckin'-Age-of-Aquarius shit right here, dog – but they were getting their sadomasochistic freak on just fine right up until you showed up. They were the most fuckin' self-regulating motherfuckers in this fuckin' town, dude, and killed them like fuckin' cockroaches because you couldn't handle something they were taking every night. And now, what, you want to cry like a bitch because you were all fucked up on their shit? It ain't the drug, dog, and you know it. If it was, those assholes would've killed each other inside of a day. It's you, dog. All the Doc's super shit did was break out what was already there.*

Cade stared for a long moment. It wasn't nearly that simple, but that didn't help him. He wondered if that was what Fuel-Air was going to be doing from now on. Pulling him up short when he bullshitted himself.

Fuel-Air smirked. *Fuck yeah, murder boy. Better get used to seeing my dead ass around.*

Cade frowned, turning east on Oak, hurrying past the people staring and whispering. Right or wrong, he didn't have much time for Fuel-Air right now. He needed to get out of Clearly's territory before somebody decided to take him on. People were starting to call out to him, asking where the hell he thought he was going. He didn't want to end up getting into a fight.

Cade fought to kill. And he'd killed enough of these folks for his taste.

Yeah? You think? 'Cause I think it's never enough, motherfucker, not for you. I don't think there's a body count big enough for you in the world, the way you been handling shit. You could've had a pretty good life here, you know? But you fucked it up for just about everybody, and now these assholes are going to go 28 Days Later *on your ass and anybody else they come across. Here comes the motherfuckin' night, bitch. Hope you're willing to take some responsibility for that.*

"Shut up, Fuel-Air." Cade muttered the words as he turned up Masonic. He tried to remember the layout of the city – if he kept on this street, he'd run into the University. For all he knew, that was Clearly's manufacturing base – at the very least, it'd be a haven for students, intellectuals, Clearly's people, the people he wanted to avoid.

East on Grove, then. He figured by the time he got to Divisadero he'd be well out of Clearly's reach – that was the road the Pastor'd wanted him to take originally, if he recalled right. He could follow that one up all the way to Lombard.

Already the people were starting to thin out. The few still on the street looked at him a little funny, but Cade could tell they hadn't heard the news yet. They would soon, though. They were heading down towards the park, where their friends and neighbours were gathered to count and carry the dead and spend the day thinking over their revenge, and when they got there, they'd know all about it.

Night was on the way.

When it came – when they'd taken their pills and the sun was going down and they started to burn with rage and hate – then they'd remember he'd gone in this direction. They'd know where he was headed. They'd come for him, and they'd come for the Pastor, and after that... well, after that they wouldn't stop. Clearly had made that plain. He'd scarred them, and any battle with the Pastor's people would scar them more.

And they took their scars out on the world in blood.

They'd come for Muir Beach, eventually. They'd get revenge on anything he might have touched – torch the whole damned woods, most likely. Maybe if he hadn't been so damn curious, if he hadn't taken the drug, if he'd gone through the night sober – but no.

That was the hell of it. He knew himself, and the second they'd started coming at him he'd have killed them where they stood, even if they were holding back on him. It was the same as with the dog – he wouldn't have risked it. He'd have killed them in their dozens.

Cade guessed you couldn't kid a kidder at that.

Hell with it, anyway. Nothing he could do about it now. He kept walking, along the empty street.

Not a soul to be seen. Nobody to see him go. He'd about made it.

Yeah, dog. You got away with murder.

And the sound of a slow handclap from behind him.

Cade didn't turn to look. He ignored the voice and kept walking. He had a hell of a lot of ground to cover, and he was on the clock, no doubt about it. He didn't have much in the way of time, and he had a hell of a lot of things to get done.

The killing hadn't stopped for the day, he knew.

Far from it.

By the time he'd gotten most of the way down Lombard Street, it was not quite eleven o'clock and Cade was starting to notice things.

Bodies, for the most part.

There was a trail of four cannibals, hair matted, bodies filthy, flies buzzing, laying on the road, dead as hell. A couple of metres in front of them was a hunting rifle, and a pretty good one too, as far as Cade could see, laying broken on the ground. Cade glanced up quickly, and saw a man hanging half out of a window. Strips of meat had been torn from his head and body, and one arm was hanging by dangling line of gristle – the other one was plain gone. The man was a ruin. A charnel house of one.

Hell of a way to go.

Cade figured him for one of the Pastor's snipers – he must've seen the cannibals swarming up from the south, started shooting... either he was slow reloading or he plain ran out of bullets. Either way, they tore into his hole like a tidal wave and pulled him apart with their bare hands.

It wasn't a good omen for the Pastor's people, Cade figured.

Damn, dog, you're a fast-working motherfucker. Shit, I'll bet you managed to ruin two perfectly good little communities right about the same time. Regular man with no fuckin' name.

"Nothing good about this place," muttered Cade. Fuel-Air cantered up beside him – he was maggot-ridden again, eyeballs staring out of his festering skull, wearing Cassie's hand-woven poncho, with the addition of a cowboy hat and a lit cigar. It was the skeleton horse he was riding that pissed Cade off – that was overkill, pure and simple. "The Pastor set Hell up on these damn streets and you know it."

He shook his head. Wasn't a good idea to start making speeches to Fuel-Air. It wasn't like he was about to listen to a damn word.

Fuel-Air grinned his skeleton grin, the bare hooves of the horse clip-clopping on the roadway. *Bullshit, dude. Kids didn't have toys. Boo fuckin' hoo. They got to eat, they got a roof over their heads, they got to live. That's the bottom fuckin' line right there, bitch. Only suddenly you decide in your role as king of the fuckin' zombies that you're gonna set a wave of fuckin' face-eatin' cannibals up their ass. Smooth fuckin' move, bitch. Hope they saved some kid stew, because I'm a hungry motherfucker and so is my horse, dog...*

Cade shook his head and kept walking. Another three dead cannibals on his right, next to a smashed-in door. Wouldn't be a prize for guessing what he'd find if he went in. For a second he thought about heading in there, retrieving the rifle from the cold dead fingers of the man who'd been using it – then decided against it. There probably weren't bullets for it, and he didn't want to be stuck with something that jammed or misfired or ran dry when he was in a tight spot.

Cade didn't like guns. Never had.

There were a couple more cannibals laying in the road as he walked east, along with a couple of the Pastor's people – wrinkled, lardy bodies draped in approved extra-large t-shirts. There'd been a running battle, and these were the ones who'd fell behind. Cade was trying to piece it together – had the snipers passed the word before they'd died? Had the Pastor sent an exploratory party to see what the hell was going on, or were these just luckless citizens on litter duty, or taking water for their sniping brethren in the Lord? Cade shook his head – no sense in playing detective. Whatever had happened, he'd find out soon enough.

Fillmore Street was a nightmare.

There had to be a hundred and eighty, maybe a couple of hundred corpses in the street outside the Moscone Recreation Centre, the Pastor's place of crucifixion. Cade could still tell the cannibals from the regular folk, although there were some with clothes torn, coated head to foot in blood, that could be either; he wasn't about to pick them over one at a time and check. It wasn't a football game, and Cade didn't exactly need a score.

Although there were a hell of a lot more of the Pastor's flock dead than the cannibals. He could see that much.

The tarmac was sticky with blood, and in the heat of the morning sun Cade could breathe it in, taste the hot metal of it in his mouth. It almost made him dizzy, the slick abattoir smell of it washing through him like wet paint.

Cade wasn't a man to get upset at blood – hot, cold or running – but there was something unsettling about seeing all those dead, reading them like a tracker might read the spoor of some big animal passing that way. There'd been some kind of gathering at the Recreation Centre, he figured; maybe another crucifixion, maybe some of Clearly's scouts caught on the Pastor's territory. Cade hadn't seen the Conundrum Car anyplace, but it was possible Thelma and what was left of the Gang had been sent off on an errand that way. Probably not, though – more likely it was just some hobo wandering in from the north, or nobody at all. Could be they just wanted to smell the corpses awhile.

Whatever they'd been doing, the cannibals had caught up to them in the middle of it – no, first they'd have got the word something was happening on Lombard Street, sent a posse to check it out. The posse'd come back with the crowd of cannibals snapping at their heels, and the battle had started.

Cade took another look at the slumped, stiffening bodies in the street. No women, no children. Not enough bodies fallen to make up the whole of the Pastor's people, which meant the rest of them had fled, and the cannibals with them.

He heard a sound to his right, and turned.

There was a cannibal picking through the bodies, peeling at the skin and trying to rip the muscles out of one of them. Cade got a closer look now – it was one of the Pastor's bodyguards, the aluminium bar laying by his side. There was a fair amount of meat on him still.

The cannibal saw Cade, and straightened. Cade wondered if he was one of the ones who'd seen him, or if he'd just gotten the word and followed along behind the rest of them. It was hard to tell – all the cannibals looked about the same to Cade, skin so coated with grease and grime that individual features were hard to pick out, faces lost beneath a scrubland of beard and ratty long hair. This one seemed to recognise him. He grinned, revealing his rotting teeth.

Cade wondered when he'd lost the ability to speak.

The cannibal looked at Cade's knife, then tugged at the exposed muscle, snarling like an animal. It was pretty obvious what he wanted – some help cutting the meat off the bone. Absently, Cade drew the knife, and the cannibal grinned, making a kind of grunting noise halfways between a dog and a monkey and clapping his hands.

Cade wondered how much he'd made a year. He wondered if Strong had told him when he started eating meat that he'd end up braindead and rotting. If he'd cared.

The cannibal was still making that dog-monkey grunting sound when Cade drove the knife through his belly and tore upwards, spilling his offal out onto the ground before the sharp blade split his heart. The cannibal made one last sound, a kind of shrill whine, as his eyes bulged and rolled back in his skull.

Then he flopped down on top of the other bodies.

Cade wiped his hands on his t-shirt, adding to the fresh splash of blood that now covered Hug Me. Ruining perfectly good shirts was getting to be a habit with Cade.

It was one less loose end to take care of, anyhow.

The cannibals weren't capable of speech, so far as he knew, but on the other hand he didn't want to take a chance that one of them had brain enough still in his head to tell the Pastor what he'd been up to. Besides, Cade figured even one still alive might be dangerous later on, after he'd solved the problem of the Pastor and Clearly. Last thing he wanted was one leaping out at him on a dark night while he was trying to find insulin.

Better to take care of it now.

There were more bodies up Bay Street, and at the corner where it met Buchanan, the stink of sweet roasted pork and stinking gasoline made Cade's eyes water.

There was a gas station on the corner of Bay and Buchanan, *was* being the operative word. Someone had taken a torch to it during the battle and now it was a smoking, smouldering ruin, littered with charred, blackened bodies and body parts. Cade figured they'd drained most of the gasoline from it a long time before, but they'd left enough in to make a big bang if they had to, and from the look of it, they'd had to.

It was mostly cannibals in the ruins, although there were a couple of dead men in their Jesus shirts. A couple more of the Pastor's bodyguards. A lot of the bodies were too charred to be recognisable.

Judging by the ways the bodies had fallen, Cade figured the forecourt of the place had been soaked down with what gas was left, and then someone had struck a match when the cannibals were charging it. After that, the fire would've ignited whatever gas fumes were left in the pumps.

A trap, then.

Self-sacrifice.

Something they'd set up for the occasion, maybe? Something planned, or a lucky inspiration that they'd found time for while the battle was raging outside the Centre?

Cade shook his head. There was no way of telling. He figured there were maybe fifty or sixty charred cannibal corpses, and the Pastor's fallen were in the single figures, so whatever it was, it'd worked.

Only maybe it hadn't worked enough.

The trail of dead led north, up Buchanan. Cade wasn't surprised. That was where the supermarket was. The Pastor's place of safety – that was where they'd have made the final stand.

The cannibals must have still outnumbered the Pastor's faithful – otherwise they'd have stayed and fought. At least, that was the way Cade figured it. To tell the truth, he was a little surprised how many cannibals there were dead on those streets. More than a hundred. Maybe two hundred, even; hard to say.

He hadn't figured on the cannibal lifestyle being healthy enough to keep that number of people alive any length of time. He'd figured he was just sending two or three dozen crazies to give the Pastor a headache. Instead, he'd called down an Armageddon upon them – a wave of screaming, blood-soaked freaks from George Romero's worst goddamned nightmare that outnumbered the Pastor's flock. And they'd had the strength and ferocity of madness on their side.

Cade was starting to wonder if there'd be anyone left alive in the supermarket at all.

Don't feel too bad if there is, dog. You tried your best.

Then that caffeinated snicker Cade was really coming to hate.

Goddamn Fuel-Air.

Cade turned the corner and found another bloodbath waiting for him in the supermarket's parking lot. By this time, he was used to the stink of blood – not to mention the piss and shit from bladders and bowels that'd let go – but there was a quality to this one that was a little different.

He took a deep breath, listening to the buzzing of flies as they landed on the older corpses. There were a good two dozen faithful, scattered and bloody, but for the most part the dead were cannibals – filthy bodies twisted in the positions they'd fallen. Cade blinked, narrowing his eyes, and stared for a moment. That didn't seem right, somehow. Most of the Pastor's people had died in front of the Recreation Centre, apart from the ones who'd blown up the gas station. Hand to hand, the cannibals should've torn what few of the Pastor's people remained to pieces, just through sheer weight of numbers.

The Pastor and his flock just didn't have what it took in a straight fight. Cade knew that from experience. He took another look. Maybe fifty, maybe a hundred cannibals.

Then Cade saw what he was missing. The common factor that'd killed all the cannibals in the parking lot.

Gunshot wounds.

From automatic weapons, if Cade was any judge.

Some had been shot in the front, brains blown out as they'd charged, some mown down in retreat, shot in the back. A couple had been hit in the legs and had bled out while crawling, leaving a slick red trail the length of the lot. A few had died dragging their wounded brethren towards shelter – although whether that was out of some vestigial sense of right and wrong or because they didn't want to waste good food, Cade couldn't say. But they'd died, and died by gunfire, every damned one of them.

The Pastor had had a stash of guns and ammunition that Cade hadn't known about. Machine pistols, definitely. Mac-10s or Uzis. Hell, maybe even an M16 or two.

Cade could see some of the corpses were a little fresher than others – less maggots, less flies. So the cannibals hadn't died all at once – they'd made more than one attempt to break the siege. Was that out of revenge for the ones who'd already died? Or were they following Cade's orders to the last man?

Cade hoped they had.

That would mean they were another problem solved. They wouldn't be something for Cade to worry about any longer. He had to face facts – if they weren't all dead, if they hadn't followed his orders to the grave, he'd have to deal with those few that'd survived. As in eliminate them.

As in genocide.

Which was strong meat even for Cade. He'd rather someone else did it.

Also, if the Pastor had had a cache of ammunition, wiping out the cannibals would mean it was running seriously low by now – maybe all gone. Which would be two bits of good news in one.

One fucking strategic motherfucker. You shoulda been a general, dog. You're real fuckin' good at it.

Cade shook his head. There was movement out on the far side of the parking lot.

One of the cannibals, skin coated with filth, hair matted, looking shaky and feverish, huddling in the relative shelter of a parked car that'd been riddled with bullets. He had a bullet wound in the meat of his thigh; a ricochet, or it would've torn right through and taken most of the femoral artery with it. As it was, he'd managed to bandage it with a strip of cloth. He was about five feet eight inches, with a lean, wiry build. He looked young, under the dirt, and Cade wondered what he'd been – an intern at a big office, maybe, or even middle management, one eye on the prize and one eye on the door, a dog eating dogs in the world of suits and ties and fake smiles.

Cade looked in the cannibal kid's eyes, and it was pretty clear the boy didn't have a damned idea how he'd come to this. He stood, shakily, limping forward, wincing, tears rolling from his eyes at the pain, then pitched forward as his bum leg gave way, his fall broken by the flyblown body of one of the first to die. Looking straight at Cade, the boy opened his toothless, rotting mouth. Cade couldn't tell what he was trying to say.

Was the kid going to curse him?

Ask for more orders, *General, Sir?*

Or just take a bite?

There was a gunshot from one of the broken windows of the supermarket, and the boy's head jerked, the body lifting up as the force of the bullet pushed his brains out through the shattered skull, then lay still.

Cade figured that this would probably be a good time to feel something. Anything. Remorse, maybe. Guilt. Triumph.

Something.

But Cade was sick and tired of feeling things.

And at the end of the day, he didn't give a damn about the kid, just like he didn't give a damn about anybody else lying dead in that lot. They'd made the decision to be there, one way or another. All Cade had done was give them a push.

When he was in the mood for it, Cade could be a real stone cold son of a bitch.

He looked up at the sound of the supermarket door opening, the creak of old metal on metal. The Pastor walked out, a smoking revolver in one hand and a bible in the other, eyes hooded and scowling as he shuffled towards Cade, feet twitching and shifting on the concrete like a snake's tail. He was flanked on either side by his bodyguards in black tees. They weren't carrying baseball bats this time. This time, they had Uzis.

"Brother Cade," hissed the Pastor, and his eyes were like stones in black well-water, ice cold and unreadable.

"Welcome home."

CHAPTER TWENTY-TWO

THE PRODIGAL SON

The Pastor didn't say much for a while after that. He just stared, looking Cade up and down. He clicked his tongue once as his eyes lingered over Hug me – I had a hard day, but whether that was because of the seventies imagery or the fresh, wet bloodstain, Cade couldn't tell.

Cade didn't say much either. He was bone tired, and there wasn't much to be said.

The bodyguards didn't break the silence. They stared straight ahead, a pair of tin soldiers waiting for a little boy to pick them up and clash them together. Cade figured right off they weren't much on thinking – they'd wait for the Pastor to make the move, if there was a move to be made.

Cade figured he was waiting for that as well.

He didn't figure he could outdraw a pair of machine pistols with a bowie knife, but if that's the way the Pastor wanted to handle this, then Cade was damned if he wasn't going to give it a damn good try anyhow. The two had a lot of muscle on them, but there was fast muscle and slow muscle, muscle that was built to move like lightning in a jar and muscle that was built for showroom purposes, for looking the part of a badass.

The difference between them was obvious as the difference between a greyhound at a racetrack and one at a dog show with a ribbon in its tail.

Cade had the one, and these two had the other. He figured the Uzis made it just about even, assuming they had any bullets in them.

He kept his eyes on the Pastor and the Pastor kept his eyes on him in turn, those cold grey ice-chip eyes boring into him and ferreting out his secrets. Cade stared back like a block of stone in the place of a man. He figured there was a good chance the Pastor knew he'd brought the cannibals down on them, either because he was an intuitive little snake when he wanted to be or because one of them had remembered how to talk in words instead of growls. If he did, that'd make it tough for Cade to get any more use out of him. Might even lead to Cade getting a bullet in his back inside the next twelve hours.

Of course, he wouldn't know for sure until that bullet hit him.

The Pastor reared back, swaying in place like a cobra. His eyes were narrow slits, and his lip curled softly, the cracked lines of his face splintering up one side as he did. It was almost a sneer, but there was a look of appraisal there, too. A look of judgement.

"Praise be to thee, O Lord, O Lord..." hissed the Pastor, almost beneath his breath. "For thou, in Thy holy *wisdom*... have delivered Thy soldier *back* unto his flock. Praise be unto the Lord of Hosts!"

He let the words hang a moment. Then he smiled, a sinister little grin, teeth bared like a dog's.

Cade still didn't know what the hell the Pastor was thinking, but he knew better than to start something now. For all he knew, they had a dozen guns trained on him in there, and he needed to know just what they had and how many people they had left.

Cade didn't have much of a plan concerning the bigger picture at this point, but what little he had depended on the two remaining sides, the Pastor's and Clearly's, being pretty much evenly matched – enough to smash them together and whittle them down to something he could manage or control, or at least something that wouldn't bother Muir Beach in the future. It wasn't much of a plan, and Cade wasn't much of a planner, but it'd have to do. Trouble was, it looked like the Pastor'd taken a bigger hit than Cade had figured on. Unless a hell of a lot more of the flock were breathing than Cade figured, they'd be wiped out to the last man, woman or child before the night had passed, and Clearly's love children would barrel right on to Muir Beach without stopping for breath.

Which meant the best thing right now, near as he could figure it, was to throw his weight behind the Pastor, if the Pastor didn't decide to kill him. If he didn't, maybe they could take down Clearly's whole community of psychopaths.

You're a dead man, dog. Nice knowin' ya.

Cade didn't twitch a muscle, but he scowled. Damn Fuel-Air, anyway. He was going to have to do something about that boy if he didn't shut up.

The Pastor turned and began to shuffle towards the doors of the supermarket, and Cade followed, the guards behind him. He didn't need to turn his head to know that their hands were on their guns and those guns were probably pointed at his back.

Time to get a few things straight, Cade figured.

"What the hell happened here?" he said, although he knew damn well.

The Pastor chuckled, a laugh like jackboots wading through broken glass. "Cannibals, brother. Heathens and degenerates, lusters..." – he hissed the word like a python – "I say, *lusters* after the foul stink of Mammon, most wretched and vile of all Satan's demons. Their thirty pieces of silver has become a pound of flesh, brother. Their craven need for money has become a thirst for blood..." The Pastor turned his head, fixing Cade with a long stare. "I can't help but *wonder,* Brother *Cade,* why Washington Strong would be so... aggressive. Do *you* know why, Brother Cade? Did he happen to mention? Hmm?"

"Who?" Cade looked puzzled. He was a little surprised the Pastor was trying such a simple trap, and more surprised that he knew that Strong had been the one in charge of the cannibals before Cade had come along. Cade was coming to the conclusion that he'd walked into a regular damned soap opera, where all the players knew each other but him.

The Pastor fell silent.

They walked through the doors and into the supermarket - not much had changed, at least as far as Cade could see. There was still that near-silent atmosphere, that reverential quality. Everyone still looked distant, almost brain-damaged, and where the kids had been quiet before they seemed shell-shocked now.

Nice work, dog, said Fuel-Air. This time he was harder to take than before – morphed horrifically into a ten-year-old's body, scampering between the huddling children with a yo-yo and a Snoopy t-shirt, but the same rotting, maggot-ridden face, the same flashing gold tooth. Cade winced. Every time he saw Fuel-Air, he was looking worse, and this one really took the prize.

Nice fucking work. This ain't no way for a kid to grow up, says Big Bad Cade, the Social Worker That Time Forgot, I'm gonna be fuckin' Santa and make sure every little dickens has a toy. A regular Miracle on Fucked-Up Street, *fuckin' 'Yes, Virginia, there is a Cade, and he's gonna get any father figure you managed to pick up since the shit went down eaten by motherfuckin' cannibals and turn whatever fuckin' life you had left into a river of fuckin' shit'; why don't you fuckin'* LOOK AT ME, *you fuckin' asshole, look me square in my fuckin' empty eyes because I'm every damn crime you're ever gonna commit, you goddamned motherfuckin'...*

Cade shook his head and squeezed his eyes tight shut for a moment, trying to focus past that incessant caffeinated whisper. Hadn't Fuel-Air been on his side once? A helping hand, helping him see things he'd missed?

What did it say that he wasn't on Cade's side any more?

What did it say that the thing Fuel-Air wanted him to see was his own body count?

Hell with it. Cade wasn't one for metaphysics and he wasn't one for psychology either, least of all his own. Best to ignore that gibbering thing scampering down between the legs of the trembling, ashen-faced women, caught up in horror beyond anything they'd imagined, horror that he'd brought down on them like a damned...

Hell with it.

Fuel-Air was right about one thing, though. Cade's cannibal army had taken a hell of a toll.

He'd been right to think the Pastor's force was broken. There were a few left – twitching, huddling shells of men cowering in corners, injured men cradling broken arms and open wounds, and those few who could still hold a gun and walk – about six or seven, by Cade's count. Cade figured the women had probably helped out with the ammunition, and maybe even fired a couple of guns themselves if the Pastor had allowed it.

He checked what ordnance they had left – a couple more hunting rifles, slow loaders, three shotguns, a Glock and the two Uzis the guards had. Not to mention the police special the Pastor was holding. There were a few more police specials laying on the ground, among the shell casings.

Cade could put two and two together. If those guns were any use, they'd be in somebody's hand. That meant ammo was scarce, maybe gone altogether. If a gun was in somebody's hand, Cade had to assume there were bullets in it, and the fella with the hunting rifle could probably scavenge a little from his dead friends on Lombard if he had a mind to, but everything else had been pumped into the mountain of fresh corpses in the parking lot.

The Pastor had spent all his strength on that battle. Now he needed Cade's information – if Clearly attacked in force, with the kind of raging, blazing, burning anger that he'd apparently unleashed back in the day, the Pastor needed to move out or die. That was one theory, anyway.

Of course, if the Pastor thought that was the case, he'd have started packing up already, so Cade figured he had something in reserve. The plot thickened. Cade figured he'd try and nudge the Pastor into showing his cards.

"Looking short of ammo." He kicked a shotgun shell casing with the toe of his boot, and it skittered across the floor, banging into a couple of nine-millimetre casings as it went.

The Pastor looked at him out of the corner of one eye, the cracks on his face shifting as he searched for an expression. Finally he smiled again. "Tell me, Brother Cade, what *did* you see during your pilgrimage to the land of the Devil? Anything I should know about?" He let the question dangle without any of his usual flourishes.

Cade weighed it up. The Pastor could probably order him killed right there. Now, ordering a man like Cade killed and actually killing him were two different things, and Cade didn't doubt that if need be he could make sure a lot of folks died in his place, but even for him there was a danger in facing down a pair of Uzis and a loaded shotgun or two.

Might as well be honest.

"I killed about fifty of Clearly's people. They were on something; me too. They ain't happy. Probably saw where I was going." He shrugged. "Coming tonight." Cade hoped that'd satisfy the Pastor. He'd gone over every detail at some length.

The Pastor raised an eyebrow. "You bearded the Devil in his lair and killed his demons..." He stared for long moments into Cade's eyes. "*Is* it true, Brother Cade?"

Cade wasn't used to being called a liar. It pissed him off something fierce, and the Pastor seemed to take note of that. He smiled wider. "You impress me, Brother Cade, with your dedication to the service of our Lord... so *many* have gone to the Devil and not returned, *tempted* and *twisted* by his potions and his powers and the *lies* spilling from his forked and hissing *tongue!* Oh *yes,* Brother, you stepped into the mouth of the *dragon,* the many-headed *Beast* of *Revelations* and breathed his poison *breath...* and found it in you to come back! And *join* the worshippers of the mighty and glorious Lord once again!" He reached, gripping Cade's shoulders for a moment with withered hands. "Lord *bless* you, Brother Cade! Lord *keep* you!" He chuckled, shattered glass raining down on slate, while his gimlet eyes fixed Cade's.

Cade frowned. There wasn't any mileage in this sort of bullshit as far as he was concerned. "Got a plan?"

After a moment of loaded silence, the Pastor turned again, shuffling towards the back of the store. Cade followed, shooting a quick glance at the handful of armed men still facing out of the window – all that was left of the Pastor's army, unless you counted the broken, sobbing heaps trying to burrow into the floor-tiles like moles, or the ashen-faced women the Pastor'd stupefied and brainwashed, or the kids, shell-shocked and malnourished. And Cade didn't.

Clearly's people were going to be as bad as the cannibals – maybe worse, since the cannibals were brain-damaged savages. The love children were going to turn into hate-crazed savages the second the sun went down, but right up until then they were keeping fit, drinking fruit juices and fresh water, probably getting any guns or knives they had ready into the bargain. Cade could picture the Doc looking on with his sad eyes as his followers raided kitchen drawers and police precincts, finding anything they could to kill folks with while he stood back and told himself that it'd all be worth it to make them whole again.

Cade wasn't exactly on the Pastor's side, but the kids didn't deserve to be torn to pieces by a bunch of feral junkies and he sure as hell wasn't going to let Muir Beach fall that way. Cade was hoping the Pastor had something to even up the score a little bit.

He wasn't disappointed.

The Pastor removed a bunch of jangling keys from his pocket, swinging them around on a bony finger, and then shuffled towards one of the double doors at the back of the store that led through to the storage area. Cade had figured this was where he'd kept his weapons cache up until now.

The turning of the key in the lock made a sound like a skeleton rattling undead bones in a cellar in the dead of night. Cade felt a sudden stab of instinct deep in his gut, and looked around for a sign of Fuel-Air. He'd vanished back to wherever he came from.

That made Cade uneasy, somehow.

Then the doors swung open, and Cade saw it.

It was squat and black, a huge ebon egg sitting on a wooden trestle. The metallic casing of the thing reflected the lights above it in a dull sheen, and towards the back of it there were fins and an opened container that had once held a parachute, now cannibalised for cloth. Bolted to the side was some kind of improvised detonator system, an electronic hotch-potch that had replaced the original detonator. Somebody had done a lot of work to make sure this could be delivered by land instead of by air, but the purpose was still the same. Cade didn't have to read the word THERMOBARIC, stencilled with military precision on the old, scratched casing, to know what it was.

He didn't have to look too closely at the face on the front of the bomb either. The grotesque warping of metal into flesh that only he could see, grinning a grin with a diamond in it.

He knew exactly what it was.

It was a Fuel-Air Bomb.

Howdy, Fuel-Air said, and winked one black metal eye. *How you like me now, bitch?*

Cade took a deep breath. Under the circumstances, there was one question that needed to be asked first.

"Everybody else see that?"

The Pastor looked at him quizzically, eyes narrowing. "A thermobaric explosive, Brother Cade. Doubtless the noble men of the FBI would have swooped down with all their fury on the terrorist cell who were planning to detonate it, had they not died of the Lord's displeasure, and the terrorists too. Leaving only their weapon behind, to be found by one who will put it to more righteous use."

Al-Qaeda, dog. The bomb pouted, mock-stern. *You stop fightin' those fuckers over there, they come over here, like Rush said all along. Chain of command, bitch. Shoulda listened, you fuckin' socialist.*

"Al-Qaeda?" said Cade. That sense of surreality was washing over him again.

The Pastor shook his head. "Domestic terrorists." He grinned, pointing to a blood-red slogan painted on the side of the bomb: SIC SEMPER TYRANNIS. WE SURROUND YOU. "Of my faith, in fact, which explains how they were taken to the glory of the Lord all the sooner. Or perhaps He thought their way was too merciful for the liberals and the deviants, compared with mine." He chuckled, a chain mail fist crushing a wineglass.

Damn. My bad. Guess I'm just politically incorrect or some shit. Fuck it, dude, let's go bombing. The bomb winked again and grinned, waggling its tailfins. Cade turned his back on it, looking the Pastor dead in the eye.

"You didn't use it earlier?"

The Pastor's smile faded. "He turned many of my flock with his lies. If such a device was driven into Clearly's territory and the chosen faithful failed to set it off... if they were *corrupted*... then *Satan* would hold this power. I... I could not risk even the most *pure* of my brethren..." He turned away, looking into the distance, as though trying to grasp some awful theological dilemma that had plagued him for years.

In other words, he was too much of a fuckin' pussy to do it himself. Jesus motherfuckin' Christ, can't a weapon of fuckin' giant-ass destruction get some respect around here?

Cade ignored the voice behind him. Fuel-Air's voice was grating and metallic now, and interspersed with little electronic blips and whines. Cade wasn't a man who got the creeps as such, but that voice was definitely driving him close. Not to mention pissing him off.

"So why now?"

The Pastor's head snapped towards Cade's, fixing him with those eyes again. They burned, and the face beneath them snarled like a cornered rat, or maybe – hell, why not – a rattlesnake, swaying in place the instant before it struck.

"Because now is the endgame, Cade. Now is where the battle between good and evil, between the Lord and the Devil, comes to it's final end... O my brother, I tell you *now*, I give you the *word* that before the dawn rises, either I or the demon Doctor Clearly will be *dead*..."

His eyes narrowed, and the words hissed from cracked lips like steam. *"And San Francisco, that Satan City, will die alongside us!"*

CHAPTER TWENTY-THREE

THE CONSCIENCE

Not much to say to a thing like that.

Cade just stared for a second, then looked back at the bomb. Fuel-Air looked pretty confused as well. Cade grunted, then turned back to the Pastor.

"This won't do that."

A bomb that size wasn't going to destroy San Francisco – a nuke might, but not this.

Cade didn't know what the hell the Pastor was getting at.

The Pastor looked at the floor for a second. "It's... it's enough to destroy Clearly's territory. Golden Gate Park." He muttered the words, suddenly looking smaller, like a boy caught out in a lie. Then he looked back up at Cade, defiant, his old self again. "With that Devil, that *Satan* gone, San Francisco, the city of sin, of filth, of *pre*-version, well, *that* city will no longer exist. You see?" He smiled, but his eyes twitched left and right. It wasn't a lie he'd been caught in, exactly – it was a vision. A vision of the apocalypse, an apocalypse he could bring on at his whim.

Now he was having to face up to the reality, which was that after his damned bomb went off, he was going to have to pick up the pieces and carry on, most likely.

"I... haven't decided on a new name for this city, but it *will* be one that reflects the glory of the Lord..." the Pastor tailed off, shuffling in place for a moment, then turned to the silent guards. "Brother Josiah, Brother Ezekiel, you go on and help Brother Cade load the bomb onto the truck. I... I will be praying..." He shuffled away, looking lost.

Cade wondered what kind of chink he'd just seen in the man's armour. The Pastor was on the verge of winning the war he'd set himself, or losing it decisively and for good, and in the face of that he seemed to have lost some of his fire. It left Cade wondering just how much of the Pastor was tied up in Clearly and his supposed evils, how much the Pastor needed an enemy, a Satan to battle. If he lived through what was coming, who'd he pick next?

Cade figured he knew the answer. Once his enemies to the south were all dead, the Pastor would start looking north.

To Muir Beach.

Unless the Pastor happened to be sitting on top of the bomb when it went off, mind. Cade filed that thought away for later.

Right now, he needed to be practical. He needed what was left of the Pastor's forces if he wanted to put a stop to what Clearly's love children were going to do to San Francisco and all points north. And he needed that bomb. No doubt about that.

Something occurred to him as he put his hands on the wheeled trestle and began to push it slowly and gently towards the doors. The Pastor had mentioned a truck. "My truck?"

Ezekiel – or it might have been Josiah – nodded, almost grunting through lips that barely parted. "Ayuh. Red pickup. S'yours." He snorted and then spat mucus on the floor, as if the effort required to speak had clogged his sinuses. Cade frowned. On the one hand, it was nice to meet a fella who had the same attitude to talking as he did. On the other hand...

Damn, dog. Woody's going to be fucking pissed if you blow up his momma's pickup. Better get an excuse ready.

For a bomb, Fuel-Air had a point. Woody wasn't going to take this one too kindly.

The children watched the bomb rolling past them with wide eyes, faces lost in a kind of religious awe – *man, this is some Ark of the Fuckin' Covenant* Indiana Jones *shit,* said the bomb – while the womenfolk busied themselves clearing the old urine-soaked mattresses and other detritus out of the way of its path, fearfully, as if any sudden bump in the bomb's way might wake it to destructive life. Cade wondered how much jostling the bomb would be able to take. The last thing he wanted was for the damned thing to go off right there, or in the truck on the way over, although at least he wouldn't know too much about it if it did.

I'll make it quick, dog. Promise.

"Shut up, Fuel-Air," muttered Cade. One of the children gave him a strange look.

The truck was waiting for them outside. A couple of the men had gone to fetch it from where the Pastor had hidden it, and now they stood next to it, waiting to help load the bomb onto the back and lash it down with straps and duct tape. It was a slow operation, and a delicate one, but it was done by the time one o'clock rolled around.

Cade wasn't too happy about that. Things were moving a mite too fast. If what he had in mind was going to work, the Pastor and his men needed to get a little less efficient.

He slowed things down some by making a couple of unworkable suggestions – for about a half hour they tried to fit six men onto the back of the truck, clambering gingerly over the damn bomb like it was the world's most dangerous climbing frame – but eventually the Pastor took matters into his own hands and suggested Josiah and Ezekiel ride on the truck and the other men follow on behind.

That suited Cade fine. It'd keep them at a walking pace.

By two, they were ready to set out. The sun was still high in the sky, a little too high for Cade's liking, and he thought a little on what he could do about that as he gunned the engine and peeled out, driving the truck out of the parking lot and turning down Laguna.

In the passenger seat, the Pastor clicked his tongue once, then rolled his lips back from his teeth. "Brother Cade..." He almost spat the words, like the bitter peel of some poison fruit. "Brother Cade..."

He was silent for a moment, as if weighing his words. Cade didn't speak. The truck rolled down Laguna, the few men left in the Pastor's force tramping behind, armed and ready.

Slowly, the Pastor ran his tongue over dry, cracked lips, his head slowly turning to face Cade as the scenery trundled lazily past them. "Brother *Cade...* I do not *lightly* treat what the Lord provides with *suspicion,* for my God is a God who provides *much;* and *mysterious,* oh yes, mysterious and *terrible* are his ways... *but.*" The sentence was cut off with clicking teeth, and there was a long pregnant pause before the soft, hissing voice resumed. "I know you hate me, Brother Cade. I know it, you need not hide the fact. You despise me and all I stand for, all of my works. All of my... *judgements.*" His slim fingers crept towards his revolver.

Cade watched out of the corner of one eye.

The truck rolled on.

"You need not hide it and you *don't,* Brother Cade, it flows out of you in waves of *disdain...* and *bile...*" He chuckled, his fingers stroking the butt of the gun. "And you could no more *hide* your true nature from the Lord above, no, nor his *servant,* than you could hide a crow amongst pure white doves..." He chuckled. Ice chips cascading onto a steel coffin-lid. "As I said, I do not *question* what the Lord provides, even when He brings me a wild beast such as *you.* For His wisdom is infinite and ineffable, yes it *is,* and *not* to be questioned by fallible men. But... curiosity *compels* me." He licked his lips again, before they dragged back in that awful cracked-paper smile. "*Why* join with us, Brother Cade? Why lend your strength in the service of the Lord when your *hate* for His *glor*-ious presence is writ in you so *very* deep?"

Hell of a question.

Cade figured honesty was his best policy, or something near enough to it. Didn't change the fact he was going to have to make yet another damned speech. Cade figured he'd said more since coming into this city than in his whole life before, and it was starting to wear on him some. He was looking forward to some peace and quiet, even if it was in a grave.

"Clearly's dangerous. You ain't." He shrugged, then figured he'd best elaborate. "You ain't gonna hurt me and mine." He looked down at the Pastor's revolver, then into the Pastor's eyes, then back on the road. "Clearly will. Needs fixing."

Cade's speeches were getting a little more to the point.

The Pastor chuckled, glass knives rattling on a surgeon's tray. "A practical man. A worldly man too, O Lord. Forgive him his great hubris." He looked over at Cade again, fingers brushing slowly over the police special, as if savouring it. "What makes you think I'll allow you to *leave,* Brother Cade?"

Cade frowned, then shrugged. "Don't try it. You've still got men living."

The Pastor stared at Cade for a moment, then nodded, bringing his fingers up to tap against one another. "But not many. The cannibals saw to that. I saw men *burn,* Brother Cade... burn for the Lord's glory, set themselves *ablaze* that we might *show* those heathens, those seekers of wealth and blood and worldly treasure and the *flesh* of men, that we might show them the *power* and the *strength* of *faith...* yes, O brother, of faith in the *Lord above,* the sweet Lord whose guidance and grace are *upon* us now..." He was working himself up again – he shook like a leaf on a tree, his whole body trembling for a long moment, before he flopped back in the seat and shook his head slowly, as if bringing himself out of some fugue. "Strange they should attack in force like that. They never did before." He smiled, and there was no humour in it. "Coincidence, Brother Cade?"

Cade shot the Pastor another look. He was getting sick of this.

"Try. Or don't. Your call."

The Pastor raised an eyebrow, then smiled that humourless smile of his. "Why, Brother Cade, are we not *allies* in the service of the Lord?" He lapsed into silence, idly fingering the butt of the gun for a moment before crossing his arms and staring out of the window at the moving scenery.

Cade let it rest there. No sense forcing a confrontation – he was still going to need the Pastor's men, or at least need them not to start shooting just at present.

He checked his watch. Almost three, and they were just passing Post Street. Sun wouldn't be going down for another four hours, maybe five. And if they went much further they'd be in Clearly's territory, and then the shooting would start.

Hell with it.

He slammed on the brakes of the truck and turned off the engine, letting it sputter and die. The Pastor sat up straight in his seat, his hand stealing for the pistol. "Brother *Cade...*"

"Guard the truck," muttered Cade, opening the driver's side door and swinging himself out. "No cannibals left, but look out for a blue-green van. Clearly's people." He started walking, heading down to the corner where Laguna met Geary Boulevard. He turned, calling back over his shoulder at the blinking Pastor. "Gonna scout. Dangerous here. I'll fix any surprises."

The Pastor looked back suspiciously at Cade. "Be sure you do, Brother Cade." He licked his lips again, eyes flicking to the side of the road, then back. "You wouldn't be thinking of *warning* the Devil of our approach, *Brother* Cade?"

Cade shook his head, not looking back. "They'd kill me." He felt those icy eyes on his back, and wondered whether the Pastor was going to try anything. But no bullet came. He turned the corner, out of the Pastor's sight, heading down Geary.

Cade was telling the truth. Warning Clearly wouldn't do any good anyway – they'd only shoot the messenger. The love children were primed to kill him, and they'd do their damnedest to, drugs or no. What Cade needed to do right now was stall for time a little, give the sun some time to crawl across the sky. He kept one eye out for somewhere to hole up for a while, like a coffee place. His attention was nearly caught by something on the other side of the street – HALLOWEEN STORE – but then he noticed there was a coffee place a little way down, and in he went. Cade figured he'd stick with what he knew.

The front window of the place was shattered, and it'd been picked clean a long time ago, but there was a clock on the wall, still keeping time. Battery powered, Cade figured. That was important – he wouldn't be able to keep an eye on the sun's position without being out in the open, and he wanted to be off the street in case the Pastor decided to send some goon to check up on him.

Wouldn't do to be caught sitting around.

Lazy-ass motherfucker.

Cade looked up, and there was Fuel-Air, dressed up in his utilities, flashing his gold tooth. His skin was black and metallic now, gleaming like a bomb-casing. Every time Cade saw him, he was looking more malevolent, and now it was like he'd absorbed all the black metal evil of the bomb. Almost like everything bad Cade stuck his hand into was retched back up at him by Fuel-Air; grinning, chuckling, swearing, shouting Fuel-Air.

Cade wasn't a man who worried about his actions too much – at least not before he came to San Francisco. What was done was done, and there wasn't any mileage in fretting over it. But more and more, Fuel-Air was acting like...

Cade searched for the word.

...like a conscience.

Cade sure as hell didn't need one of those.

Escpecially considering what he was about to do.

Damn right you don't, asswipe. You need to be one cold, calculating motherfucker for what you got planned. You need to be the motherfuckin' Terminator. Shit, don't let all those fuckin' innocent people you're gonna wipe out...

"Not innocent," muttered Cade. And they weren't. Clearly's people took a drug every night that cut them off from any kind of moral reality, and it wasn't a coincidence that there weren't any children or old men there. They'd killed the children and the elderly and burned everything they could find to the ground, no matter how peaceful they'd been since. Their crimes were still there, waiting to come out again, and tonight they were going to walk the night like monsters. No, Clearly's people weren't innocent. No such thing as innocent in San Francisco.

Wasn't any point getting into a debate with Fuel-Air, he knew. The son of a bitch knew everything he was thinking already. But he had to say something. "They're on drugs..."

Fuckin' Nancy Reagan! 'Just say no,' motherfuckers! Shit, you ever think not everybody in this world is fucked up the way you are? You caused this shit, dog. You walked in on a fuckin' stalemate that your new buddy, Pastor Nail-You-To-A-Fuckin'-Piece-Of-Wood, was happy to let carry on forever and a day, 'cause he didn't have fuck all else to do with himself! Shit, this place was a regular fuckin' ecosystem until you came to fuck things up...

Cade shook his head. "Wasn't like that."

Fuck it wasn't. You make things worse, dog. That's what you do.

You come into a situation and make it as bloody and fiery as it's gonna get. You're a fuckin' catalyst for all the shit-fire in the fuckin' world, and you like it that way, 'cause it means you get to kill folks and call it necessity when all it is is your own fuckin' disease taking root. And you been that way ever since the day you were fuckin' born. He grinned, and belched fuel and flames from his bomb-mouth. *Shit, don't tell me you don't remember your first kill?*

Cade's mouth twitched, nearly smiling. "Sure. Bastard needed it."

Fuel-Air sneered. *You don't remember shit, dog. That wasn't your first kill, you stupid son of a bitch.*

Cade stiffened. He saw what Fuel-Air was getting at, and he didn't like it much.

Fuel-Air grinned, teeth gleaming like wires, black metal eyes narrowed.

Told you you didn't remember. He laughed, a high whine that sounded like something falling from an aeroplane.

What kind of asshole don't even remember his own mother?

CHAPTER TWENTY-FOUR

THE FIRST KILL

CADE'S MOTHER DIED in childbirth, of course.

She was a slight woman, thin and frail, anaemic-looking, sickly and washed out. It was a difficult birth, and though the doctors did everything they possibly could, Cade's mother passed away shortly after delivering the boy.

Cade's father was never the same after that. His name was Tobias and he worked in construction, and by all accounts he was a man possessed of both uncommon strength and uncommon gentleness, who smiled readily and often. This Cade only found out at his funeral, as Tobias had never displayed such qualities during Cade's life.

When his wife died, something broke inside Tobias, some essential part of the mechanism that ran him. Some inner gear slipped and snapped, the jagged metal teeth tearing at the workings of his soul, damaging them beyond any repair. He began to drink, where he never had before – beer by the case at first, and when that failed to quiet his demons, rotgut whisky. To begin with, his sister cared for the boy while Tobias went on his benders, and she was one of the few who could calm the man when he came crashing through the door, howling and yelling, hitting out with fists as strong as brick at anyone unlucky enough to get within ten feet of him.

Cade was thus spared more than an occasional beating from his father, although perhaps it was a blow to the head, delivered at full strength, landing him a month's stay in a hospital – and this before his first birthday – that accounted for what he became later in life. More likely, he simply absorbed the atmosphere of that first home, a trailer on the edge of a small town near El Paso.

He grew up quiet – so quiet that most thought him retarded – and serious, a little boy who said nothing but observed much.

After he'd turned six, his father's sister died. There were some, mostly those few friends she'd kept after moving in with her brother, who said Tobias had worried her into her grave with his drinking and his rages and with the strain of looking after his boy, who surely suffered from autism if not worse – although most treated it as an unavoidable tragedy. Tobias laid the blame elsewhere. On returning from the funeral, tears rolling down his cheeks and a bottle of rotgut in his hand, he had told the boy that he'd murdered twice now, that he was born a killer and a killer he'd remain. Then he beat his hide black and blue with a leather belt.

Despite this, Tobias remained popular with the construction crew. His drinking was limited to after hours, and he gave little hint of any problems at home, making sure his boy wore long sleeves and hid the bruises when he came around to the site after school. His job was never in danger – in fact, before much time had passed, he found himself promoted to foreman. Success in his career didn't limit his drinking – in fact, it only made him drink more, because there was more to spend on it. Somehow, he always managed to drag himself to work every morning and put in a full day.

It was as if the time spent beating his only child gave him strength.

The boy was hospitalised four times over the next two years, but nothing was said. If a doctor did suspect that the broken bones and contusions were caused by something other than a fall down the stairs – despite the fact that there were no stairs in the trailer – he either kept his own counsel on the matter or was unable to break through the twin walls of Tobias's denial and Cade's deep silence to find the truth.

It was clear, in other words, that this was a problem Cade would have to solve himself, despite being all of eight years old.

Time passed, and every day after school Cade would wander down to the site to watch his father work, waiting for Tobias to finish working so they could go home, where the drink and the belt waited. Sometimes he skipped school, so as to watch his father and the construction crew work through the whole day. There was no punishment for playing truant beyond what his father already did to him.

The men enjoyed the strange, silent boy's company – they ruffled his hair and joked amongst themselves about how the boy was touched. His father joked with them, keeping his anger for later.

Cade just watched.

He especially liked to watch when they got the big tarmac spreader, and spread the hot black tarmac over the foundations to make a parking lot or a driveway, and then rolled the big steamroller over it to make it flat. He watched that very carefully. He had very good eyes, for an eight-year-old.

Then, one by one, the men would leave, and only his father would be left, checking through paperwork and time cards and locking the site up for the day. He'd either take Cade with him to the bar, where the drunks and the rummies would ruffle his hair and say how the boy was touched while his father drank himself stupid on rye, or he'd just drag the boy back to the trailer and beat the shit out of him before going to the bar.

Either way, Cade could count on at least a few cracks of the leather belt, and probably a kicking with a steel-toed work boot into the bargain.

This he tolerated until one day at the end of November.

The construction crew were building a new supermarket on the edge of the town, with a parking lot out front and another behind. They poured the tarmac for the first lot, and rolled it flat with the steamroller, and then it was clocking-off time and the men filed out. Marty Callaghan, who drove the steamroller, ruffled Cade's hair. "Poor fella's touched," he said, whereupon Cade hugged him tight – a gesture he'd not made before, and one that caused no end of laughter among the men. "I ain't your daddy, son," said Marty, chuckling. "Your daddy's over there." And he pointed to Tobias, who was standing in front of the steamroller, a blueprint in his hand, making a careful check of the equipment and what there was still to be done before he clocked off.

Cade knew where his daddy was, all right.

Marty Callaghan wasn't just the man who drove the steamroller. He was also, in his youth, what the papers had called a juvenile delinquent, and one of his souvenirs of that wild time was a switchblade knife with a skull carved on the handle in ivory, still as sharp as ever. Marty occasionally liked to show it off, flicking out the deadly blade for the appreciation of his co-workers.

Cade liked to watch him do that.

Soon, all the crew were gone, and Cade looked around himself for a moment, then picked up a loose chuck of brick and wandered down to the fresh-laid tarmac to say hello to his father.

"Dad?" he said. It was the first time he'd said a single word in about seven months.

Tobias hadn't kept count.

"Not now, boy," he said, not looking up from his blueprint. "Not now, you little –"

That was when Marty's switchblade, which Cade had carefully lifted from his pocket, severed Tobias's left Achilles tendon, and he went down like a ton of bricks, screaming at the top of his lungs. Cade swung the chunk of brick in his other hand and hit his father in the side of the temple with a hard *clunk*. Enough to put him out.

Then he turned his attention to the steamroller.

He'd lifted Marty's keys from his pocket along with the knife, and he'd watched closely enough over the past months to have a good understanding of how the steamroller was operated. He managed to get it going without too much fuss.

Then he set it rolling.

The big roller moved slowly, rumbling across the ground, and Tobias actually had time to wake up out of his daze, although by that time the great steel roller was less than three feet away from him. There was no way he could crawl or roll out of the way in time.

"Jesus!" he screamed. *"Jesus Christ, what the holy fuck are you doing? I'm your father, goddammit! Your father! Your –"*

He didn't say anything else after that. Just screamed.

The roller crunched over his feet first, rupturing the flesh and splintering the bone to fragments, and then slowly squashed the rest of him. Tobias was still alive when his belly burst open and his guts went flying, and he may even have been conscious when the hideous weight crushed his ribcage to powder and his heart with it, although that seems unlikely.

Cade waited until the roller had rumbled right over him, and then switched it off, and left the keys in it, and wandered home to the trailer that was now his alone.

He kept the knife.

YOU KILLED YOUR Mom and then you ran your Pops over with a steamroller, after you'd driven your Auntie to an early grave. Heartwarming fuckin' story, dog.

Cade nodded. Things had gotten a lot better after that. The orphanage was a pretty decent place if you were willing to get your knuckles a little dirty, and Cade had been more than willing. After they kicked him out, it was a pretty average story – gangs, robbery with violence, a murder here and there. Eventually, the marines had offered him something close to a reason for living, or he'd felt that way at the time.

Bullshit. They just offered you a way to kill a shitload of people without any comeback, that's all. Don't kid yourself you were there for the reasons any other motherfucker was, bitch.

Cade blinked, and looked at the clock. Getting on for half six. The Pastor'd be stewing, and the sun would be getting ready to go down. Probably they were all screwing in the Park by now.

Best to get a move on.

But there was something he had to get done first.

"Won't be needing you for this next bit, Fuel-Air."

Fuel-Air sneered, the metal skin glinting as he leaned forward. *Sure you don't. Want to commit your fuckin' atrocity in peace, right? Fuck you, dog. You're stuck with me, motherfucker, and I'm going to be on your fuckin' back until the day you die, about every goddamn fuck-up you –*

Cade took the gun out of his belt.

It was a Magnum .44, big and mean. Cade wasn't a fan of guns, but he'd figured he'd need one that'd do the job.

Fuel-Air stared at it, stunned. *Where the fuck did you get that?*

Cade shrugged. "Does it matter?"

Fuel-Air snarled, and suddenly his face was a writhing, suppurating mass of maggots, crawling and slithering over one another, a boiling, oozing sea of putrefaction that seemed to burn into Cade's vision.

You called me up, motherfucker, don't you get it? You brought me out. I'm part of you, you stupid-ass son of a bitch, and I'm never fucking letting you be, not ever again – shit, dog, you honestly think you can put a bullet in me? A fuckin' bullet*? You can't do shit. Let me draw you a picture, bitch – you snapped on that fuckin' road you were nailed to, you broke like fuckin' glass. Shit, it ain't no surprise, you know what I'm saying? You had to go a little crazy or a lot crazy, and I'm the crazy you went. I'm your fucking delusion, dog, your bloody conscience, the part of you that doesn't let you get away with this kind of fucking bullshit...*

Cade nodded, and shrugged. Wasn't anything he hadn't figured out.

So what are you going to do with that fuckin' piece of yours, bitch? Shoot me? I'm a figment of your motherfucking imagination!

"Yeah." Cade shrugged again. Then his eyes narrowed. "So's the gun."

The roar of the Magnum filled the room, and Fuel-Air flew backwards as the bullet hit him right between the eyes. For a moment he didn't look like Fuel-Air. He looked like Sergeant A, or maybe the Captain, or maybe Duke, or maybe his father, or maybe all of them at once. Then his head burst like an over-ripe melon and his body slumped down the wall in a trail of old corpse-blood.

Cade put the gun down on the table, then leant back for a moment and closed his eyes.

When he opened them, there was no body. There was no gun. There was just Cade, sitting in a coffee shop, watching a clock on the wall.

Okay, then.

On the way out, he caught a glimpse of something just across the street. HALLOWEEN STORE. This time he paid a little closer attention.

The glass was smashed, but there was plenty still in the front window of the store, waiting to be taken. Cade guessed there wasn't much call for anything a Halloween store might sell. The whole damn world was Halloween now.

He wondered what it was that kept drawing his eye, and then he saw it, sitting on a polystyrene head, dead centre. The whole plan fell into his head right there. It was crazy – maybe the craziest thing Cade had considered in his whole time in San Francisco, and that was saying somethin'.

Still, he figured it couldn't be that crazy.

After all, Cade wasn't crazy anymore.

WHEN CADE GOT back to the pickup, the bomb was just a bomb.

The Pastor didn't like being kept waiting. His face was dark as a thunderstorm and his fingers drummed the dashboard in a slow, deliberate pattern while he read through a pocket Bible. His men were slouched around the pickup, cocking and uncocking whatever guns they had like a bunch of kids playing cops and robbers. Cade wondered if they'd done anything sensible with the guns, like cleaning them or sharing out ammo, or if they'd just played and posed with them a while, trying to psyche themselves up for what was ahead, feel a little badass.

He wondered what the rate of misfires was going to be. If he knew anything at all about guns, those ones were going to jam after the first shot.

Hell with it. He'd find out soon enough.

"Brother *Cade*," hissed the Pastor, curling his lip back from his teeth in a cold, mocking sneer, "You've returned to us. I will *confess*, Brother, for a moment I took it in my mind to *doubt* you, even to wonder if you had de-*sert*-ed the true path of –"

Cade got behind the wheel and gunned the engine. "No time. Tell your men to run. Not got long. Sunset came quicker than I figured." That was a lie, of course. Cade had timed it damn near perfect.

The Pastor looked at him a moment, as if he didn't quite comprehend, and Cade wondered how much he'd found out about Clearly's people and their nightly cycle of free love and free hate. Cade didn't figure there was much point in explaining it. The point wasn't for them to live through this, after all.

"They're vulnerable. Let's go." Cade put her in gear and drove the truck forward at a clip, heading down Laguna, keeping just fast enough that the men behind had to run to keep up, but not fast enough to lose them. Not yet.

Cade looked to the passenger seat, and saw that the Pastor had the detonator clutched in his hand, his thumb caressing the button that would blow the both of them sky-high with one press. Not the best situation to work with.

Hell with it. It was what he had.

This was the endgame. This was where everything came to a head, for better or for worse.

If he was lucky, he was about to murder the city of San Francisco once and for all. The thought didn't bother him overmuch. In fact, he was starting to feel a hell of a lot more like his old self.

His palms didn't even itch any more. The corners of his mouth twitched slightly, almost, but not quite, a smile.

Then he gunned the engine, and turned right, heading down Haight Street towards the Golden Gate Park, and the not-quite-human things that were waiting there for him.

CHAPTER TWENTY-FIVE

THE ENDGAME

Haight Street in twilight.

In the end, it was all about the timing. If Cade hadn't killed a few hours in that coffee shop, they'd have hit Haight in the middle of the afternoon, breezing right into Clearly's territory just when it was busiest. That would've started a firefight – the Pastor's men would've held their own right up until they ran out of bullets, and then the mob would've torn them apart, or maybe the Pastor would've pressed his button and gone out in a blaze of glory first. Either way, most of Clearly's people would've made it out – only they'd have been even more ready to burn anything they saw.

If he'd left it any longer than now, the drugged-out mob of love children would've been long gone, most likely slipping right past them on the way to burn the Pastor's territory to the ground along with anybody left in it. Then they'd march on Muir Woods, most likely. Even if they didn't decide to head straight for Muir Beach, they'd most likely start the worst damned forest fire California had ever seen. It's a wonder they hadn't done that before, and Cade didn't want to take the risk twice.

No, the time to get onto Haight Street was now, with the sun just starting to dip down, and the shadows starting to lengthen. The streets were deserted, but Cade knew the love children were there, all around them, naked, without a thought in their heads but making love... but waiting, deep down, for the shadows to lengthen, for that switch inside their heads to flip.

Any time now.

He kept the pickup truck moving, watching the men running behind in the rear view mirror, noticing they were starting to sweat, panting a little, falling behind. These weren't the Pastor's best physical specimens – just what was left after the war with the cannibals. They weren't soldiers, and they damn sure weren't used to marching double-time.

To the west, the sun was beginning to lower itself below the buildings. The shadows were starting to fall.

The Pastor snapped to attention, his finger hovering over the button on the detonator. "What was that noise?"

His eyes swivelled, staring, while his head turned this way and that. Cade might have smiled, if Cade was a smiling man.

As it was, the corners of his mouth twitched again.

Just once.

"I thought I heard someone... *say* something." He muttered it, almost under his breath, looking to and fro, sweat beading. "Lord, Lord, be my shield in this time of danger..." His finger shook above the button. Cade reached out and gently gripped his wrist, shaking his head slowly.

"Not yet."

The Pastor looked at him for a long moment, then nodded and swallowed. He was scared, Cade could tell; terrified, in fact. Cade figured he was starting to flash back to the last time he was in enemy territory. That had ended with him being tortured for years in a bamboo cage. This might end worse – after all, as far as the Pastor was concerned, each and every man and woman in this part of town was a devil in human form, one of Satan's own, capable of any act of evil.

Cade frowned. He might be right at that. Cade hadn't exactly given the flower children any reason to be peaceful.

"Someone *did* say something! I heard it!" the Pastor hissed, eyes bright. Behind the truck, his men slowed, looking all around them, slick fingers holding wobbling guns that waved in all directions, trying to cover everywhere at once. The Pastor's face was glistening with cold, slippery sweat. "What are they *saying?*"

It was getting darker. Cade could hear it himself, now.

The chant.

"Helter skelter," he whispered, and felt the Pastor's wrist jerk in his grip. "Don't touch it. Not yet."

The Pastor pulled his hand away, lips curling into a snarl –

– and then they attacked.

It was like a swarm. A good two dozen of them, naked as the day they were born, crashing through doorways, snaking from around corners, a couple even hurling furniture through shop windows and launching themselves through the broken panes, cutting their feet on the glass as they landed. Two dozen men and women with foaming, twisted mouths, veins throbbing, faces red and contorted. Some held knives, improvised cudgels – most just had their fists.

The Pastor was white. "*Satan's children* –" he hissed, his finger jabbing down towards the detonator. Cade reached out and grabbed his wrist just in time, twisting it around hard. He heard the bones in the wrist snap first, then a tearing sound as the elbow joint popped. The Pastor screamed, and Cade took the opportunity to wrest the detonator out of his other hand and slam it in the glove box. Hopefully it wouldn't rattle too much. He shot the Pastor a look.

"Told you not to."

Some fools never took a telling.

He slammed on the gas.

The pickup truck roared forward, the front bumper crashing into a red-headed girl and sending her tumbling off to the side, bones broken. Any other of the love children in the way had the sense to get out, although some poor bastard tried to grab hold of the passenger side mirror and got a face full of road rash for his trouble.

In the mirror, Cade could see the small band of the Pastor's men, out of breath and left behind, firing wildly into the crowd, dropping two, three, four – then disappearing under the rest. They weren't soldiers and they didn't know how to carry a gun or keep it from getting taken away, and they sure as hell didn't know how to deal with an army of psychopaths who didn't give a damn whether they got shot or not. They'd dealt with the cannibals, but the love children were a hell of a lot worse than them – at least the cannibals had some self-preservation to them. Not to mention brain damage. The love children had that perfect mix of madness and intelligence, and that was what made them so damned dangerous.

Cade watched as the melee dwindled in the rear view mirror, a severed head arcing lazily out from the centre of the pack. Tough break for somebody. He turned his attention to the road ahead.

So much for the Pastor's army. Still left the two goons with the machine pistols up top – Cade could hear the low, growling *bra-a-aap* of the weapons being fired. The two bodyguards were shooting back at the crowd behind them, for all the good that'd do now. Hell, Zeke and Josiah were probably blowing their own people apart as much as they were Clearly's. They'd be better off firing ahead – Cade was veering through a slalom of love children, all bursting out of the surrounding buildings, screaming their battle-cry.

"Helter skelter!"

"Helter skelter!"

"*Helter skelter!*"

Cade kept ploughing into the sons of bitches, and every time one of them went under the truck the whole damn thing shook and he could hear that detonator rattling around in the glove box. Those assholes needed to be shooting in front, clearing a path. As it stood, all they were was extra weight, throwing off his driving.

Cade took a second to chew over whether he actually needed those guns or not. Most likely they hadn't been cleaned or treated right in months, so they were going to jam any second, and besides, there was the problem of getting them off the idiot twins up top. Hell with it. Cade figured he was better off without them.

This plan, such as it was, had come nearly full-formed into Cade's head when he'd seen what he'd seen in the window of the Halloween Store, but it was still about half actual planning and half improvisation, and this was one of the improvisation parts. Every time he heard that glove box rattle, he was about a split-second away from getting blown sky high.

In the seat next to him, the Pastor was clutching at the side of the seat with his good hand, while the other dangled uselessly at his side, twitching occasionally. His eyes were squeezed tight shut, and his lips were moving in what looked like a prayer. Cade figured he needed it.

This was likely to be tight.

He spun the wheel, sending the truck into a skid, the tyres already slippery with blood – jackknifing the whole rig and spinning it like a top. Zeke and Josiah hadn't had any warning, and, unlike the bomb, they weren't secured. They went down like a couple of ninepins, tumbling off the flatbed of the truck, skidding across the road, the Uzis slipping out of their hands as the roadway tore swathes of skin off them. Cade fought the wheel, prolonging the skid, inhaling burning rubber and blood, feeling the shock run through the steering column as something burst under his back wheel and the whole truck lurched sideways – he had a glimpse of Zeke in one of the mirrors, head pulped flat – and then he was pulling out of it, getting back control, gunning the truck up Broderick. Behind him, in the rear view mirror, he could see one of the love children screaming their mantra, the Uzi in her hand blazing like a string of firecrackers as it pumped bullets into Josiah's chest. The gun misfired just before he swung the truck left, the tyres screeching again as he drifted onto Oak Street, heading for Golden Gate Park.

When he had a mind to, Cade could drive one hell of a mean truck.

The streets were swarming with the love children now, and Cade figured they were primed to go after outsiders. He hoped so, anyhow. Still, it seemed like a fair guess. The second they saw the pickup, they stopped clawing and punching at each other and ran in his direction, lips curled into bloody clown grins, howling at the top of their lungs. "Helter skelter! *Helter skelter!*" Cade had to fight the wheel to keep from crashing into them and wrecking the truck right there. He didn't know how many more full-on impacts it could stand, and the bastards seemed to have a habit of bouncing off the bonnet. It was already dented all to hell. Cade hoped he could explain it to Woody.

The Pastor was crying now, scrabbling at the gun in the holster at his side. Cade didn't know whether the Pastor wanted to shoot him or shoot himself, but either way he wasn't going to let that happen. He reached over, quick as a snake, and grabbed the gun from the Pastor's trembling hand, tossing it out of the window.

"Fetch!" he yelled, and a couple of the love children did just that, hurling themselves after the gun like dogs. They weren't too far gone to know what could kill.

"Satan," sobbed the Pastor, fat tears rolling down his face. Cade almost felt a pang of sympathy for the man. This was the battle he'd spent two years waiting for, the final confrontation against the Devil he'd built up in his mind, and in one hot second Cade had taken it for himself, like a director stealing the leading man's part on the first night of the play. "Oh, Satan, why do you *torment* me?" The words were whined between hitching breaths.

"Be over soon," muttered Cade, keeping one hand on the wheel as he skidded the speeding truck between the Clearlyites, keeping one eye on the crowd building in the rear-view mirror. Word spread fast, and they were running like a stampede of rats, like the casts of three horror movies at once, just waiting for the truck to spin out or flip over so they could tear it open like a turtle's shell and rip out the meat. His other hand reached into his pocket for what he'd got from the Halloween store. For half a second, he was almost sorry he'd had to kill Fuel-Air the second time. He might've gotten the reference.

They're selling hippie wigs in Woolworth's, man.

Keeping the truck steady, Cade pulled on the shaggy blond wig – a cross between a seventies rock star and some kind of show dog – and then covered his own beard with a larger, shaggier one the same blond. It wasn't about to fool anyone, even in the twilight, but he was counting on the Pastor to help him out with that.

Cade was a brutal man. He was a man who'd kill at the drop of a hat, without even breathing hard. He was a man who'd shot his own conscience in the face so he could murder easier when it came time to. But that didn't mean he couldn't be smart.

And it sure as hell didn't mean he couldn't be sneaky.

He unlocked the glove box and grabbed the detonator.

Ahead of him, he could make out the gates of Golden Gate Park, and just inside them, another massive crowd, easily as big as the one running to catch him up. He could make out Clearly, standing at the front, facing the crowd with his back turned to the truck, yelling about something. Some reason to set them moving. Cade figured he'd taken a dose of his own drug – from this distance, he looked like a fire-and-brimstone preacher, not so different from the Pastor at that. Cade had figured they'd turn out to be the same in the end.

Cade knew what Clearly was saying, even without hearing the words. He was giving them a direction to follow, a target to burn, the way he had when the bad times had come the first time around. He was being the ruler, the man in charge, the Daddy, letting his children play outside to keep them from wrecking the furniture. Oh, it was all for the good of the people. It was all excellent therapy. They needed it. It was the only way the community could survive. There were a hundred excuses you could make, but at the end they were all just more bullshit from Doctor Len Clearly, PhD.

Hell with that.

"There he is, Pastor," growled Cade. "This is it."

The Pastor blinked, sniffling, then straightened in his seat. Some of the old fire seemed to creep back into him, the serpentine bastard who'd nailed Cade to the street and killed anyone he didn't agree with.

Cade figured a man should die as he lived. "Go on," he muttered. "Let him know."

The Pastor breathed in hard, a snuffling, snot-filled breath, then screamed as Cade gunned the engine, his eyes almost popping from their sockets, face red, mucus flying from his throat with the force of the shout.

"Saaataaaaaaan!"

Cade hit the accelerator hard, slamming his foot to the floor, hurling the truck forward at maximum speed, heading right for the Doctor.

The truck hit Clearly first, snapping his legs like twigs and cracking his pelvis with a sound like a gunshot, sending him flying over the bonnet until his head smashed through the windscreen, almost landing in the Pastor's lap.

The truck ploughed into the crowd, crashing into three dozen bodies with the force of a sledgehammer smashing into a box of breadsticks.

'Carnage' wasn't the word.

"Satan!" screamed the Pastor, howling at the top of his lungs as Clearly blinked up at him, blood beginning to seep from his open mouth,

somehow still conscious. *"Satan! I know you! Devil! Spawn of the goat! I know you! I know your works! Your time is come and into hellfire will you be delivered! Satan, the time is come! The time is NOW!"*

The love children had a habit of turning on outsiders, and Cade figured you couldn't get much further outside than that. He popped his seatbelt and checked his wig was straight, then started yelling at the top of his lungs.

"HELTER SKELTER! HELTER SKELTER! HELTER SKELTER!"

In the movies, there's often a part of a plan that involves something being done 'in the confusion.' Cade had never actually been in a confusion before, but he'd been in a clusterfuck, and he understood them pretty well.

He rolled out of the truck, and then started kicking and punching at it, driving his fist through the side window, shrieking like a madman. "HELTER SKELTER! HELTER SKELTER! *HELTER SKELTER!*"

Cade figured pretty much everybody in this crowd hated his guts about as much as they hated the Pastor's. If the Pastor was sitting in the truck that'd just mown half their people down, screaming his Jesus talk at the top of his lungs, Cade figured they'd pay less attention to the blond dude who looked a bit like some other dude they hated. Especially if they were fucked up on Clearly's compound. Cade had been on it and he hadn't even recognised himself, never mind anyone else.

Oh, if Cade had tried a stunt like that on his own, they'd have torn him into pieces, no doubt about it. They'd have hung his guts from the railings and played softball with his skull.

But the Pastor made a pretty damn good distraction. He had his good hand locked around Clearly's throat now, trying to strangle him before he died of his internal injuries. He looked like he might do it, too.

"Satan! Oh horned goat! Oh corruptor! Oh scavenger of men's souls! I know you! I know your stench and your rot and I will END you –"

Clearly's eyes bulged, looking right into the Pastor's, and the Pastor was the only one to see the look Clearly wore as he went to his grave. Confused, maybe. Sad. Apologetic. Raging with the fury of his own drug. Any of those might have done.

Clearly's shattered legs weaved and twitched on the bonnet like a spastic doll.

Hell of an undignified way to go, Cade figured.

The crowd seemed to agree. They rushed at the truck, pushing each other back to get at it, tearing at the doors and windows, reaching in like zombies in a motion picture, trying to claw Clearly free and tear the Pastor apart. Cade let himself be muscled back, shoved out of the way by the love children. He kept on yelling, trying to get the timbre right, to keep that cracked edge of madness in his voice. "Helter skelter! Helter skelter!"

Then he just dropped back, heading towards the west side of the park, making as good a pace as he could without drawing attention. He figured pretty much all of the love children would be swarming around the truck soon enough, trampling each other for the chance to take vengeance on the Pastor, never mind that he'd not even been driving.

He could still hear the Pastor screaming in his maddened voice, yelling about danger and terror and lust, howling like a banshee. There was pain in those cries, now – Cade figured they'd got their hands on him and they were tearing him out of that truck piece by piece.

He figured he'd got about eighty metres away from the truck now, but with a Fuel-Air Bomb that was definitely danger close. And then some.

"O Lord! Oh spare me the torments of Hell! Didn't your servant do right, O Lord, O God...? Dei! Dei! Deiiiii!*"*

The voice drifting over the screaming roar of the crowd was an agonised shriek, bubbling up out of a throat full of blood. The Pastor had about run out of time.

So had Cade.

As soon as the Pastor's body was cold, they'd look around them and go for the next outsider, and hippie wig or not, that was him. Hell, even if they didn't, they'd scatter in all directions, and then next night they'd probably do it all over again.

He thought about what they'd likely do with Woody and the Duchess.

A hundred metres.

Still danger close.

Cade saw the Pastor's head shoot up into the air, ripped off of his body, a length of spine flapping out of the neck. They were playing football with it.

Hell with it, thought Cade, I guess *danger close* really is coward talk after all.

He pressed the button.

CHAPTER TWENTY-SIX

AND THEN

THE SKY BURST OPEN
AND A HAND OF SOLID FIRE
SMACKED HIM TO THE GROUND.

CHAPTER TWENTY-SEVEN

THE AFTERMATH

He came to three days later.

Or it may have been four.

He'd got third degree burns over a fair amount of his body, probably more than a man should have and still be walking, or even breathing. His skin was cracked and leaking something that looked like pus. He was blind in his right eye, which was a shapeless blob of jelly oozing from the socket, and there was a constant ringing in his ears that, in the end, took a full three weeks to go away. He'd lost two fingers on his left hand. His eyebrows, and most of his beard and hair, had been singed clean off.

He was halfway down Nineteenth Avenue, and everything on all sides was a blackened ruin. He had no idea how he'd gotten there or what he was doing there.

He stood, swaying, blinking with his one good eye, and ran a dry, sandpaper tongue over cracked lips.

After a couple of minutes, he remembered what his name was.

Cade.

Then the blackness rushed up to claim him all over again.

* * *

He wasn't sure how much time passed, but when he opened his eyes he could have sworn the Duchess was standing over him, soaking a cool sponge loaded with ice water over his skin, and he was seeing her with two eyes.

Then he blinked, and realised that everything was flat and a little blurred and his skin was in agony. The pain came in waves, washing over him like chips of broken glass rubbing into his flesh. Hadn't there been a fella with a laugh like broken glass at one time? A laugh like broken glass and a walk like a snake. Cade maybe killed him, or somebody else did. Probably Cade.

Cade winced. His head was like crazy paving, one thought running into another. It came to him that he was in a coffee shop somewhere, which made sense. He seemed to pass a lot of time in coffee shops. He realised he was laying on his side, on a leather bench that was sticking to his suppurating, pus-coated skin. That didn't make as much sense, on account of every time he moved, the leather tugged at him. Moving hurt so much that he figured he should just pass out again. Pass out and maybe not wake up this time.

He tried for a while, but he couldn't.

Hell with it.

Somehow, Cade got himself onto his feet and wandered into a back room. He didn't see any corpses around, and that meant something, but he wasn't sure exactly what right at the moment.

On a table in the back room, there were bandages and antiseptic, and some kind of shiny hinged blades that Cade couldn't remember the name of. Handle-blades. Finger-blades. Dammit. Skin-blades. Skin-saws. Scythe-saws. Something close.

Scissors. That was it.

He looked at them for almost a minute.

Then he blacked out again.

The first couple of weeks were like that.

It was kind of a wonder that Cade didn't lie down and die at any point during this, but Cade wasn't the lying down and dying type, even in as much pain as he was in. Gradually, agonisingly, his body started to put itself back together, and his mind followed suit.

Somehow, he managed to keep his burns from killing him and do what he needed to do to bandage and treat them. To begin with, he did this using the contents of medicine cabinets and whatever drugs he could scrounge from other places, but after a while he was spending whatever time he could stand on his feet scavenging around Haight Street and the surrounding blocks, looking for any storehouses of medical supplies Clearly might have had. The Park was a ruin, of course, and big sections of Stanyan Street, Oak Street, Fell Street... it was a big blast, and it'd damaged a hell of a lot of the area. Cade still wasn't sure how he'd survived it.

Hand of a generous God, he figured.

He knew there were a couple of the love children left – he hadn't got all of them with the Pastor's bomb – but whenever he saw them they were wandering the streets like broken dolls whose clockwork had yet to come to a halt. It took him a day or two to realise that anyone who knew where Clearly's compound was stockpiled had taken their knowledge into the grave with them.

After a while, he didn't see the love children anymore. They just wandered away, whether to start again somewhere new or just to die away from the memories of their strange, good/evil community, Cade didn't know.

He didn't much care, either.

The last love child he saw on the streets was Thelma. He came across her suddenly – just a matter of turning the corner and seeing her at the other end of the street. She was looking broken – she'd lost an eye too, and it looked like she had a broken arm – but instead of running, or cursing him, like the other flower children did, she'd smiled, and raised something up in her hand.

The burnt remains of a blond wig.

"I told you!" she yelled at him, laughing. *"Disguises! I told you!"*

Then she ran around the corner, laughing giddily, as if the world had just begun to make sense.

He never saw any of the love children again.

It was another week before he found Clearly's medical stores, in a warehouse just outside the blast radius on Frederick street, complete with an eighteen-wheeler sitting outside. The Doc had been right – there was enough insulin there for hundreds of people, maybe thousands.

Enough to keep the Duchess going until she died of old age, Cade figured, and he'd still have enough space left in the trailer for some other bits and pieces that'd come in handy.

Of course, he couldn't load it as quickly as he'd have liked to, not in his condition. Time was, it'd have taken him less than a day to fill the damn thing top to bottom, but now it was a full week of agonising labour as every inch of his body screamed at him, every damn box of insulin like hefting blazing lava against his burned flesh. Loading that damned eighteen-wheeler up was like a punishment from the depths of Hell, and Cade was still messed up enough in his mind to wonder if he hadn't ended up there, if the Pastor hadn't been right. If he hadn't damned himself by standing against the snake-legged little bastard. Cade had never in his whole damned life been in so much pain.

Cade being Cade, he loaded the damned thing anyway.

And then he spent a couple of days sleeping, drinking any whisky he could find and getting ready to find the gasoline.

Another week, or near as. Five and a half days of trudging from gas station to gas station, all over San Francisco, trying to find ones that hadn't burned to the ground, ones that still had gas in pumps or in cans, and the right kind of gas for an eighteen-wheeler at that. And on those rare occasions he found it, Cade had to drag it back to Frederick Street in the hot sun, with every muscle screaming at him.

Hell with it. Cade figured he could rest when he got back to Muir Beach.

In the end, he got most of the gas he needed from the Pastor's people, or what was left of them. It was just women and children now, as well as a couple of shaky-looking fellas, the people who'd cracked during the battle with the cannibals. When Cade limped back into the supermarket parking lot, he was greeted like some kind of returning royalty, and they pretty much let him take what he wanted. Things were changing a little – they had clean mattresses now, and he saw one kid with a colouring book, and another with a GI Joe figure. A woman named Emily was the head of the community, and she was talking a lot about planting seeds and raising some kind of crop. And about Jesus, too. Cade figured it was better than nothing at all.

AFTER HE'D FUELED up the rig, and checked the engine over, and loaded the trailer, and gotten a couple days rest to make sure he wasn't going to pass out on the way back to Muir Beach, Cade figured it was about time to go. He'd seen enough of San Francisco, and he had a strong feeling San Francisco had seen enough of him, given that he'd killed about ninety-eight per cent of it with his own two hands.

He threw the eighteen-wheeler into gear, coaxing the engine into life and feeling the vibration of it rush through the leather seats of the cab and into his body. It was painful, sure – pretty much anything was going to be painful for at least the next year – but it felt pretty damned good, all the same. Gave Cade the feeling of a job well done. The roar of that engine was as good a note as any to end on, at least the way Cade figured it.

Still, there was an itch in him – something that went deeper than the crawling feeling of his burned skin as the hot leather hummed underneath him.

It wasn't like he'd had fun, exactly. He'd been carved up, staked out, damn near fed to a bear, blown up, drugged and had his shoulder cried on a couple times, which he wasn't used to.

But.

Cade thought about the routine of life in Muir Beach. Whittling down wood. Screwing the Duchess every day. Playing solitaire. A beer with Woody once a week.

It could be a lot worse, Cade figured. That wasn't a bad routine at all for a man to have.

Cade sighed.

No killing, though.

He'd have to get used to that.

HALFWAY ACROSS THE Golden Gate Bridge, Cade realised he owed Woody a new pickup truck and he was going to have to go get one from somewhere.

He figured San Diego.

THE END

AL EWING's written a mess of stuff over the years. He wrote a couple of novels before – *El Sombra* and *I, Zombie,* they were called. Mainly, though, he writes for comic books. He's one of the fellas who write that *Judge Dredd* – never much cared for it myself, though I did see the film once. He's not much of a man, or much of a God, come to think of it. But he tries, and I guess when all's said and done that's the important thing.

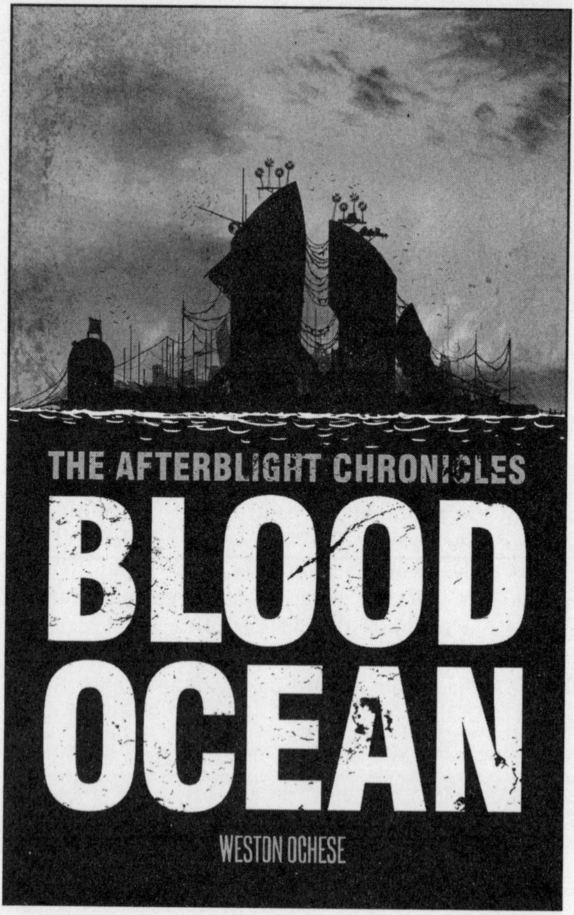